THE SCRIBNER
ANTHOLOGY OF
CONTEMPORARY
SHORT FICTION

50 NORTH AMERICAN SHORT STORIES SINCE 1970

Edited by Lex Williford and Michael Martone

A Touchstone Book
Published by Simon & Schuster
New York   London   Toronto   Sydney

Touchstone
A Division of Simon & Schuster, Inc.
1230 Avenue of the Americas
New York, NY 10020

This Touchstone trade paperback edition December 2007

TOUCHSTONE and colophon are registered trademarks of Simon & Schuster, Inc.

For information about special discounts for bulk purchases,
please contact Simon & Schuster Special Sales at
1-800-456-6798 or business@simonandschuster.com.

Designed by Mary Austin Speaker

Manufactured in the United States of America

20 19 18 17

Library of Congress Cataloging-in-Publication Data
The Scribner anthology of contemporary short fiction : 50 North American short stories
since 1970 / edited by Lex Williford and Michael Martone.—2nd ed.
    p. cm.
  "A Touchstone book."
  1. Short stories, American. 2. Short stories, Canadian. 3. American fiction—
20th century. 4. Canadian fiction—20th century. 5. American fiction—21st century.
6. Canadian fiction—21st century. 7. United States—Social life and customs—
Fiction. 8. Canada—Social life and customs—Fiction. I. Williford, Lex, 1954–
II. Martone, Michael.
  PS648.S5S425 2007
  813'.0108054—dc22   2007036319

ISBN-13: 978-1-4165-3227-9
ISBN-10:   1-4165-3227-7

Please see page 649 for continuation of copyright page.

ACKNOWLEDGMENTS

The editors would like to thank editors Cherise Davis and Meghan Stevenson for their hard work and advocacy for this second edition. Putting the anthology together took much longer than any of us expected—problems with crashed computers, software, authors' permissions, and the like—and we appreciate their patience in the face of fast-approaching production deadlines. We would also like to thank Jeff Wilson, executive director of contracts at Simon & Schuster, for his calm and generous support with permissions and contracts. This anthology would not have been possible without the technical expertise of Amit Ghosh's terrific BorderSenses Technology team (http://bstelpaso.com)—Javier Sanchez, Ernesto Flores, and Edevaldo Orozco—who designed the Web site and the survey's complex databases, administered the surveys, and then compiled all the data for simple-minded literary types who can barely add up a column of numbers.

Once again, we'd also like to thank Rosellen Brown for her lovely new introduction for the second edition and the many teaching writers who took time out of their busy summers—the only time many of them could write—to take our survey: Robert Abel, Elisa Albert, Laurie Alberts, Marcia Aldrich, Sherman Alexie, Dorothy Allison, Carol Anshaw, Rilla Askew, Thomas Averill, Christopher Bakken, Kim Barnes, Jim Barnes, Mary Baron, Steven Bauer, Geoffrey Becker, Leslie Becker, William Boast, David Borofka, Marshall Boswell, Rus Bradburd, John Gregory Brown, Rosellen Brown, Janet Burroway, Kevin Canty, H. G. Carrillo, Dan Chaon, Kim Chinquee, Laurie Chinquee, Eric Chock, Steven Church, Jane Ciabattari, Jan Clausen, Lawrence Coates, Alicia Conroy, Kenneth Cook, Elizabeth Cook-Lynn, Jameson Currier, John Dalton, Tracy Daugherty, Rob Davidson, Alan Davis, Burke Davis, Cathy Day, Robb Dew, Debra Di Biasi, Anthony Doerr, Tony Earley, Julie Edelson, Edward Falco, Mark Farrington, Monica Ferrell, Ernesto Flores, Abby Frucht, Gloria Frym, Mary Gaitskill, Louis Gallo, Mark George, Carole Glickfeld, Tod Goldberg, Elizabeth Graver, Daniel Green, Geoffrey Green, Mary Grimm, Lauren Grodstein, Marian Haddad, Alyson Hagy, J. C. Hallman, Jane Eaton Hamilton, Stephanie Harrison, Ehud Havazelet, Chris Haven, Reed Hearne, Alan Heathcock, Robert Hellenga, Susan Henderson, Michelle Herman, David Huddle, Marjorie Hudson, Juli Huss, Susan Ito, Honoree Jeffers, Laura Kasischke, N. M. Kelby, Barry Kitterman, Michael Knight, Alex Kuo, David

Leavitt, Sara Levine, Paul Lisicky, Robert Long, George Looney, Elizabeth Macklin, Adrianne Marcus, Lee Martin, Nancy McCabe, Richard McCann, Thomas McConnell, Yona McDonough, Margaret McMullan, Eric Melbye, Corey Mesler, Judith Claire Mitchell, Nicholas Montemarano, Faye Moskowitz, Manuel Muñoz, Richard Newman, Phong Nguyen, Tom Noyes, Nathan Oates, Sondra Spatt Olsen, Daniel Orozco, Susan Perabo, Michael Pettit, Leslie Pietrzyk, James Reed, Ibby Reilly, Nancy Reisman, Luis Rodriguez, Jim Ruland, Josh Russell, Edward Schwarzschild, Daryl Scroggins, Robbie Clipper Sethi, Enid Shomer, Robert Anthony Siegel, Joan Silber, Nea Simone, Jane St. Clair, Mary Helen Stefaniak, Cynthia Thayer, Melanie Rae Thon, Jessica Treadway, Jessica Treat, Sergio Troncoso, Mary Troy, Donna Trussell, Marianne Villanueva, Charlotte Walker, Ronald Wallace, Sharon Oard Warner, Kellie Wells, Allen Wier, Robert Wilder, Judy Wilson, Dick Wimmer, and Richard Yañez.

For interested fiction writers who have also published at least three stories in nationally distributed literary magazines, please e-mail lex@utep.edu, and we'll add your name to our database so you may participate in surveys for any future edition.

CONTENTS

Acknowledgments   *v*

Foreword   *ix*

Introduction by Rosellen Brown   *xiii*

RUSSELL BANKS Sarah Cole: A Type of Love Story   1

DONALD BARTHELME The School   19

RICK BASS The Hermit's Story   22

RICHARD BAUSCH The Fireman's Wife   33

CHARLES BAXTER The Disappeared   52

AMY BLOOM Silver Water   72

T. C. BOYLE Caviar   80

KEVIN BROCKMEIER The Ceiling   93

ROBERT OLEN BUTLER Jealous Husband Returns in Form of Parrot 103

SANDRA CISNEROS Never Marry a Mexican   109

PETER HO DAVIES Relief   120

JANET DESAULNIERS After Rosa Parks   129

JUNOT DÍAZ, Nilda   144

ANTHONY DOERR The Caretaker   152

STUART DYBEK We Didn't   181

DEBORAH EISENBERG Twilight of the Superheroes   190

RICHARD FORD Communist   214

MARY GAITSKILL Tiny, Smiling Daddy   228

DAGOBERTO GILB Winners on the Pass Line   239

RON HANSEN Wickedness   253

A. M. HOMES A Real Doll   266

MARY HOOD How Far She Went   281

DENIS JOHNSON Car Crash While Hitchhiking   288

EDWARD P. JONES Marie   293

THOM JONES The Pugilist at Rest   304

JAMAICA KINCAID Girl   319

JHUMPA LAHIRI A Temporary Matter   321

DAVID LEAVITT Territory   335

KELLY LINK Stone Animals   351

REGINALD MCKNIGHT The Kind of Light That Shines on Texas   386

DAVID MEANS The Secret Goldfish   397

SUSAN MINOT Lust   405

RICK MOODY Boys   413

BHARATI MUKHERJEE The Management of Grief   417

ANTONYA NELSON Female Trouble   431

JOYCE CAROL OATES The Translation   452

TIM O'BRIEN The Things They Carried   469

DANIEL OROZCO Orientation   484

JULIE ORRINGER Pilgrims   489

ZZ PACKER Brownies   503

E. ANNIE PROULX The Half-Skinned Steer   520

STACEY RICHTER The Cavemen in the Hedges   533

GEORGE SAUNDERS Sea Oak   547

JOAN SILBER My Shape   567

LESLIE MARMON SILKO Tony's Story   579

SUSAN SONTAG The Way We Live Now   585

AMY TAN Two Kinds   599

MELANIE RAE THON Xmas, Jamaica Plain   609

ALICE WALKER Nineteen Fifty-five   616

STEVE YARBROUGH The Rest of Her Life   628

Permissions   649

FOREWORD

Rarely has the world changed so much from the first edition of an anthology to the second, one published at the end of a millennium and the next beginning the new. In 1999, when the first edition of *The Scribner Anthology of Contemporary Short Fiction* was published, no one had ever heard of Osama bin Laden or *Brokeback Mountain*. Almost a decade later, both inhabit the everyday vernacular. The idea that two Wyoming cowboys could fall in love or that two great towers could fall seemed impossible then, but what began as a somewhat obscure story in *The New Yorker*, published in the first edition of the *Scribner Anthology*, and later written for the film by Larry McMurtry and Diana Ossana, has won three Academy Awards, and people in line to fly across the country think nothing at all of x-raying their shoes.

Like democracy, when it works, the most compelling fiction often responds to the deeper implications of world events slowly, sometimes taking years to articulate the incomprehensible, the unsaid—perhaps even the un*say*able at any given moment in history—until writers with distinctive voices and stories find a way to bring to consciousness what people were thinking about all along but were too afraid to say aloud. For this reason, it would be an exaggeration to say that this, the second edition of *The Scribner Anthology of Contemporary Short Fiction*, has changed as much as the world it comes into. But it has changed significantly.

This anthology contains more than a dozen contemporary stories from the original first edition, stories that continue to haunt us and our students long after we've been teaching them for years, stories that hold up to many readings, stories that refuse to offer easy answers and still seem to ask all the right questions. And it contains many new voices and stories that have just begun to articulate the new questions arising from the first decade of this new millennium.

Though the methods of story selection have changed somewhat because of advances in technology—moving from mailed paper surveys in 1997 to a sophisticated online survey in 2006—our original goals for the first edition remain the same: to democratize as much as possible the evolving contemporary canon; to survey the most qualified people: freelance fiction writers and fiction writers who teach in creative writing programs all across the United States and Canada; to keep alive and thriving the most compelling North American short stories written since 1970; to recognize new and emerging voices; and to create the highest quality, least expensive anthology we could, affordable to everyone, especially students who have found that the cost of text-books has risen beyond all reasonable means.

THE ONLINE SURVEYS

For the entire month of July 2006, we conducted two separate online surveys of freelance and teaching writers for the second edition of *The Scribner Anthology of Contemporary Short Fiction* and the new *Touchstone Anthology of Contemporary Nonfiction*. After a long, arduous search using many sources including Google, the *Poets & Writers Directory of Writers,* and many university and writers' Web sites, we obtained the names and e-mail addresses of more than two thousand poets, fiction and nonfiction writers, those with well-established reputations as well as those at the beginning, we hope, of distinguished careers.

From this larger pool of writers from many genres, we sent out thirteen hundred e-mails to fiction writers only, and we received survey responses from 148 writers, with responses that startled us with their insights.* Without the technical expertise of those we hired to conduct this sophisticated online survey and the literary expertise of the writers who responded so intelligently and passionately, this anthology would not have been possible. We've included their names in our acknowledgments, with our thanks.

The *Scribner Anthology* survey itself was composed of two parts, the first to help us determine which stories to retain from the original first edition, the second to rank other stories based upon the following questions:

- What contemporary short stories published since 1970 would you most like to see in an anthology for your Studies in Contemporary Short Fiction, Form, and Theory of Short Fiction and undergraduate and graduate fiction writing workshops? (In other words, what stories do you most often photocopy and bring to your classes to discuss?)
- Why do you teach these stories? What specific technical or thematic concerns do they best illustrate?

The stories with the highest rankings we retained from the first edition were, in this order: Jamaica Kincaid's "Girl," Russell Banks's "Sarah Cole: A Type of Love Story," Reginald McKnight's "The Kind of Light That Shines on Texas,"

---

* We tried as much as possible to respect the privacy of writers, often solitary and protective of their time, and gave all the writers we surveyed the option of having their names removed from our e-mail list, and we did so, if they wished, immediately. We also asked authors to nominate *only* stories by *other* writers, and when a few of them couldn't resist the temptation to nominate their own, we eliminated those nominations, also immediately.

Bharati Mukherjee's "The Management of Grief," Amy Bloom's "Silver Water," Tim O'Brien's "The Things They Carried," Amy Tan's "Two Kinds," David Leavitt's "Territory," Alice Walker's "Nineteen Fifty-five," Edward P. Jones's "Marie," Donald Barthelme's "The School," and Susan Sontag's "The Way We Live Now."

Several nominations ranking high among these but not listed above also received comments from those surveyed who wished to see different stories by the same authors rather than the stories from the first edition, and we chose the following stories, based upon those rankings, in this order: Robert Olen Butler's "Jealous Husband Returns in Form of Parrot," Ron Hansen's "Wickedness," Denis Johnson's "Car Crash While Hitchhiking," Rick Bass's "The Hermit's Story," and Stuart Dybek's "We Didn't."

We also received many nominations for stories not included in the first edition, some of which had not yet even been written or published at the time the first edition was published. The highest rankings among these were, in this order: Deborah Eisenberg's "Twilight of the Superheroes," George Saunders's "Sea Oak," Kevin Brockmeier's "The Ceiling," and ZZ Packer's "Brownies," all with a minimum of four nominations each. And among these were many other highly ranked stories left for us to research, find, and then read and consider closely.

Readers of this anthology will also find a few of their favorite stories missing from this edition, partly because it's difficult to please everyone and partly because we simply couldn't afford permissions for some highly nominated stories. Our most difficult obstacle was obtaining affordable permissions for an anthology that would sell at just over $15. It was a huge disappointment at first, but we believe the anthology is actually stronger now because we moved on to select many diverse and exciting new voices for this edition.

Democracy is messy—the worst form of government except for all the rest, according to that twentieth-century pugilist Winston Churchill—and trying to represent these diverse and divergent nominations with a sense of balance was as difficult as it was both a privilege and a joy.

Michael Martone and I originally came together as editors of the first edition primarily because we saw our own diverse and divergent voices and aesthetics—one arising from the contemporary realistic tradition, the other from more experimental impulses—as complementary, not as weaknesses but as strengths, and we hold to that conviction. While some may argue over our choices and some may mourn the loss of a favorite, most "teachable" story, we believe we've chosen others equal to those, and we can only hope these stories will bring about as many complex and interesting discussions of theme, form, and craft as the previously published stories.

We offer this anthology not so much as a compromise but as a celebration of many voices, many of them like the voices one might hear in a New York marketplace or along the Mexican or Canadian borders or along the East or West coasts or any small town in the wide expanse of the Midwest, all of them compelling and important.

—LEX WILLIFORD

INTRODUCTION

I don't like to think of myself as doctrinaire about anything but certain ethical matters and perhaps the superiority of dark to milk chocolate. But I realize that I do have one unalterable rule that I wish I could also demand of others: When I teach a writing workshop, we must read published work on the grounds that, no matter how accomplished we may think ourselves to be, we need better writers in the room than even the best of us.

This anthology and the previous edition (only a few of whose stories are repeated here—it's well worth having as a companion volume) present perfect examples of occasions for teaching and learning. Of course this collection will gratify even the casual reader, one who, like most moviegoers or opera aficionados, appreciates exceptional accomplishment without particularly caring how its effects are achieved. It is not a textbook. But its genesis as a response to the question put to hundreds of writers/teachers who also instruct by enthusiasm and example—*Which stories do you assign, return to, find especially effective as models, stimuli, provocations?*—makes it unusually useful for students in search of both inspiration and on-the-ground technical instruction.

After all, as I insist to my students, they will not always have teachers to guide them in that long future that awaits them after they've paid off their loans. Yes, assuming they continue to write, their work will be read, appreciated, and criticized by friends and—let's hope—by editors and a world of readers. But before that, when they sit down to evaluate their own fiction, they need to be able, themselves, to interrogate and probe and poke and be skeptical, and so—back a step, before *that*—in the generative and then the writing stage, it would be hugely useful to be able to do the same to a body of the most celebrated work being published today. And not just to read critically: to read practically. To assemble a tool kit, or amass a set of skeleton keys that will open just about any door.

One of the more successful of the low-residency graduate writing programs even demands of its students that they make what are called "annotations" as they move through their studies; that is, they must choose a technical question they'd like to pursue and search in their reading for a variety of possible solutions. I still find myself doing exactly that, and I can't imagine I'll ever stop: Quite consciously, I'll anatomize some aspect of a story or a novel, not to imitate it (although that's a fine way to imbibe a given piece's style and structure) but, admiring and curious, to see if I can figure out how an effect was achieved. I am talking about taking stories apart like watches, studying the kinds and sizes of the parts they contain, and the way those parts move and affect one another.

So, to mix metaphors (sample question: Can one do that?), what are the kinds of things an attentive reader might ask, either to follow a road or to break away from it and pave a new one? (All right: too many metaphors. Find your own.)

Everyone agrees that any story can be told in dozens of ways, though each makes it a different story. But for many student writers, first thought is assumed to be best thought. It usually isn't. I begin again and again and again because my first thoughts are usually banal and verbally slack. What can we learn, then, by studying opening paragraphs word by word? The reader starts with no more of a preconception of what's to come than the title might provide. If we think of ourselves as sleuths amassing clues—not yet about the large thematic questions, at the macro level, but, rather, at the micro level, where we are being led—we can learn what we need to by parsing who is speaking, and when, at what distance in time and space, in what kind of language and in what tone, on what occasion or for what reason at this particular time, before the significant action or after it . . . on and on and on. Often it turns out that the important dynamics of the story are all there already. So much is evident before a single page is turned that I have sometimes filled whole classroom hours talking, more fruitfully than one might guess, about the first hundred or so words. It takes patience to squeeze out of every syllable the effect it is intended to have on the innocent reader, but it is not an idle exercise. Try it (and also ask what would be different if the opening were constructed otherwise):

"We didn't in the light; we didn't in darkness. We didn't in the fresh-cut summer grass or in the mounds of autumn leaves or on the snow where moonlight threw down our shadows."

"At six Mr. Frendt comes on the P.A. and shouts 'Welcome to Joysticks!'"

"Those are the offices and these are the cubicles. That's my cubicle there, and this is your cubicle."

These opening sentences are fraught with overtones and undertones; they are not doors to be sped through but, implicitly, plans for the entire building.

And the questions proliferate: What can we learn by studying the pace at which a story unfolds? How fast does it move? Is the speed of its deployment of detail consistent or does it contract and expand, rush forward, slow down, opening up from time to time like a climber coming to a level place and resting? How does the language hurry us along or slow us down? Does the plot seem to be taking place before our eyes or in retrospect, or in unreal—purely literary—

time? What creates its intensity (if indeed it is intense)? The jam of words? ["Boys enter the house, boys enter the house. Boys, and with them the ideas of boys (ideas leaden, reductive, inflexible), enter the house."] The elision of connectives? (Ditto.) The absence of detail or explication? ("At first he was just losing weight, he felt only a little ill, Max said to Ellen, and he didn't call for an appointment with his doctor, according to Greg, because he was managing to keep on working at more or less the same rhythm, but he did stop smoking . . .") a single sentence that ends far down the page, and while you're there, consider the generality of the title.

A measured, deliberate opening can yield to great passion and mystery but so can an apparently casual one. ("Well, we had all these children out planting trees, see, because we figured that . . . that was part of their education" . . . and "Never marry a Mexican, my ma said once and always.") How does the transition to something far less offhand take place? In stories as mad as George Saunders's "Sea Oak" or Robert Olen Butler's "Jealous Husband Returns in Form of Parrot," how does the author fracture the conventional surface? Is there a refrain that returns and returns? (Melanie Rae Thon's "I'm your worst fear" or Jamaica Kincaid's "this is how . . . this is how . . . this is how . . .")

The questions, the contrasts—the possibilities—are almost infinite, but to read as a writer is to investigate them with an urgency different from that of the reader who might (or might not) take notice of an effect and move on. These are functional methods, available for us to pick up, turn over in our hands, weigh, and use.

And, finally, the bigger question and the most difficult: What makes almost every story here unique? What has all this technical expertise to do with the unreplicable intensity of stories—experiences—that are one of a kind? They are, after all, not clocks or watches, not simply cunningly calibrated machines. The only way I know how to say it is that, whatever they have chosen to be, they are *consummately that*. They are extreme. They proceed with the conviction that their means and ends are inseparable, and they take chances; they exaggerate, they make vivid their choices; they dominate us. To quote from my introduction to the first edition (yes, you can steal from yourself; I recommend it): "Where is the force of personality in (your story)? Do you convince us that this is the way it *must* be? You are an actor now: Inhabit your role. Fiction is not for the faint of heart."

—ROSELLEN BROWN

ROSELLEN BROWN, novelist, short story writer, and poet, teaches at the School of the Art Institute of Chicago.

Russell Banks

SARAH COLE: A TYPE OF LOVE STORY

RUSSELL BANKS (1940–), a member of the American Academy of Arts and Letters and president of the International Parliament of Writers, is the New York State Author. His work has been translated into twenty languages and has received numerous international prizes and awards. He lives in upstate New York with his wife, poet Chase Twichell.

I

To begin, then, here is a scene in which I am the man and my friend Sarah Cole is the woman. I don't mind describing it now, because I'm a decade older and don't look the same now as I did then, and Sarah is dead. That is to say, on hearing this story you might think me vain if I looked the same now as I did then, because I must tell you that I was extremely handsome then. And if Sarah were not dead, you'd think I was cruel, for I must tell you that Sarah was very homely. In fact, she was the homeliest woman I have ever known. Personally, I mean. I've *seen* a few women who were more unattractive than Sarah, but they were clearly freaks of nature or had been badly injured or had been victimized by some grotesque, disfiguring disease. Sarah, however, was quite normal, and I knew her well, because for three and a half months we were lovers.

Here is the scene. You can put it in the present, even though it took place ten years ago, because nothing that matters to the story depends on when it took place, and you can put it in Concord, New Hampshire, even though that is indeed where it took place, because it doesn't matter where it took place, so it might as well be Concord, New Hampshire, a place I happen to know well and can therefore describe with sufficient detail to make the story believable. Around six o'clock on a Wednesday evening in late May a man enters a bar. The place, a cocktail lounge at street level with a restaurant upstairs, is decorated with hanging plants and unfinished wood paneling, butcher-block tables and captain's chairs, with a half dozen darkened, thickly upholstered booths along one wall. Three or four men between the ages of twenty-five and thirty-five are drinking at the bar, and they, like the man who has just entered, wear three-piece suits and loosened neckties. They are probably lawyers, young, unmarried lawyers gossiping with their brethren over martinis so as to postpone arriving home alone at their whitewashed townhouse apartments, where they will fix their evening meals in Radaranges and, afterwards, while their TVs chuckle quietly in front of them, sit on their couches and do a little extra work for tomorrow. They are, for the most part, honorable, educated, hard-working, shallow, and moderately unhappy young men. Our man, call him Ronald, Ron, in most ways is like these men, except that he is unusually good-looking, and that makes him a little less unhappy than they. Ron is effortlessly attractive, a genetic wonder, tall, slender, symmetrical, and clean. His flaws, a small mole on the left corner of his square but not-too-prominent chin, a slight excess of blond hair on the tops of his tanned hands, and somewhat underdeveloped buttocks, insofar as they keep him from resembling too closely a men's store mannequin, only contribute to his beauty, for he is beautiful, the way we usually think of a woman as being beautiful. And he is nice, too, the consequence, perhaps, of his seeming not to know how beautiful he is, to men as well as women, to young people, even children, as well as old, to attractive people, who realize immediately that he is so much more attractive than they as not to be competitive with them, as well as unattractive people, who see him and gain thereby a comforting perspective on those they have heretofore envied for their good looks.

Ron takes a seat at the bar, unfolds the evening paper in front of him, and before he can start reading, the bartender asks to help him, calling him "Sir," even though Ron has come into this bar numerous times at this time of day, especially since his divorce last fall. Ron got divorced because, after three years of marriage, his wife had chosen to pursue the career that his had interrupted, that of a fashion designer, which meant that she had to live in New York City while he had to continue to live in New Hampshire, where his career had got its start. They agreed to live apart until he could continue his career near New York City, but after a few months, between conjugal visits, he started sleeping with other women, and she started sleeping with other men, and that was that. "No big deal," he explained to friends, who liked both Ron and his wife, even though he was slightly more beautiful than she. "We really were too young when we got married, college sweethearts. But we're still best friends," he assured them. They understood. Most of Ron's friends were divorced by then too.

Ron orders a scotch and soda, with a twist, and goes back to reading his paper. When his drink comes, before he takes a sip of it, he first carefully finishes reading an article about the recent re-appearance of coyotes in northern New Hampshire and Vermont. He lights a cigarette. He goes on reading. He takes a second sip of his drink. Everyone in the room, the three or four men scattered along the bar, the tall, thin bartender, and several people in the booths at the back, watches him do these ordinary things.

He has got to the classified section, is perhaps searching for someone willing to come in once a week and clean his apartment, when the woman who will turn out to be Sarah Cole leaves a booth in the back and approaches him. She comes up from the side and sits next to him. She's wearing heavy, tan cowboy boots and a dark brown, suede cowboy hat, lumpy jeans, and a yellow tee shirt that clings to her arms, breasts, and round belly like the skin of a sausage. Though he will later learn that she is thirty-eight years old, she looks older by about ten years, which makes her look about twenty years older than he actually is. (It's difficult to guess accurately how old Ron is; he looks anywhere from a mature twenty-five to a youthful forty, so his actual age doesn't seem to matter.)

"It's not bad here at the bar," she says, looking around. "More light, anyhow. Whatcha readin'?" she asks brightly, planting both elbows on the bar.

Ron looks up from his paper with a slight smile on his lips, sees the face of a woman homelier than any he has ever seen or imagined before, and goes on smiling lightly. He feels himself falling into her tiny, slightly crossed, dark brown eyes, pulls himself back, and studies for a few seconds her mottled, pocked complexion, bulbous nose, loose mouth, twisted and gapped teeth, and heavy but receding chin. He casts a glance over her thatch of dun-colored hair and along her neck and throat, where acne burns against gray skin, and returns to her eyes, and again feels himself falling into her.

"What did you say?" he asks.

She knocks a mentholated cigarette from her pack, and Ron swiftly lights it. Blowing smoke from her large, wing-shaped nostrils, she speaks again. Her voice is thick and nasal, a chocolate-colored voice. "I asked you whatcha readin', but I can see now." She belts out a single, loud laugh. "The paper!"

Ron laughs, too. "The paper! *The Concord Monitor!*" He is not hallucinating, he clearly sees what is before him and admits—no, he asserts—to himself that he is speaking to the most unattractive woman he has ever seen, a fact which fascinates him, as if instead he were speaking to the most beautiful woman he has ever seen or perhaps ever will see, so he treasures the moment, attempts to hold it as if it were a golden ball, a disproportionately heavy object which—if he doesn't hold it lightly yet with precision and firmness—will slip from his hand and roll across the lawn to the lip of the well and down, down to the bottom of the well, lost to him forever. It will be merely a memory, something to speak of wistfully and with wonder as over the years the image fades and comes in the end to exist only in the telling. His mind and body waken from their sleepy self-absorption, and all his attention focuses on the woman, Sarah Cole, her ugly face, like a warthog's, her thick, rapid voice, her dumpy, off-center wreck of a body, and to keep this moment here before him, he begins to ask questions of her, he buys her a drink, he smiles, until soon it seems, even to him, that he is taking her and her life, its vicissitudes and woe, quite seriously.

He learns her name, of course, and she volunteers the information that she spoke to him on a dare from one of the two women still sitting in the booth behind her. She turns on her stool and smiles brazenly, triumphantly, at her friends, two women, also homely (though nowhere as homely as she) and dressed, like her, in cowboy boots, hats, and jeans. One of the women, a blonde with an underslung jaw and wearing heavy eye makeup, flips a little wave at her, and as if embarrassed, she and the other woman at the booth turn back to their drinks and sip fiercely at straws.

Sarah returns to Ron and goes on telling him what he wants to know, about her job at the Rumford Press, about her divorced husband who was a bastard and stupid and "sick," she says, as if filling suddenly with sympathy for the man. She tells Ron about her three children, the youngest, a girl, in junior high school and boy-crazy, the other two, boys, in high school and almost never at home anymore. She speaks of her children with genuine tenderness and concern, and Ron is touched. He can see with what pleasure and pain she speaks of her children; he watches her tiny eyes light up and water over when he asks their names.

"You're a nice woman," he informs her.

She smiles, looks at her empty glass. "No. No, I'm not. But you're a nice man, to tell me that."

Ron, with a gesture, asks the bartender to refill Sarah's glass. She is drinking white Russians. Perhaps she has been drinking them for an hour or two, for she seems very relaxed, more relaxed than women usually do when they come up and without introduction or invitation speak to him.

She asks him about himself, his job, his divorce, how long he has lived in Concord, but he finds that he is not at all interested in telling her about himself. He wants to know about her, even though what she has to tell him about herself is predictable and ordinary and the way she tells it unadorned and clichéd. He wonders about her husband. What kind of man would fall in love with Sarah Cole?

II

That scene, at Osgood's Lounge in Concord, ended with Ron's departure, alone, after having bought Sarah's second drink, and Sarah's return to her friends in the booth. I don't know what she told them, but it's not hard to imagine. The three women were not close friends, merely fellow workers at Rumford Press, where they stood at the end of a long conveyor belt day after day packing *TV Guide*s into cartons. They all hated their jobs, and frequently after work, when they worked the day shift, they would put on their cowboy hats and boots, which they kept all day in their lockers, and stop for a drink or two on their way home. This had been their first visit to Osgood's, a place that, prior to this, they had avoided out of a sneering belief that no one went there but lawyers and insurance men. It had been Sarah who had asked the others why that should keep them away, and when they had no answer for her, the three had decided to stop at Osgood's. Ron was right, they had been there over an hour when he came in, and Sarah was a little drunk. "We'll hafta come in here again," she said to her friends, her voice rising slightly.

Which they did, that Friday, and once again Ron appeared with his evening newspaper. He put his briefcase down next to his stool and ordered a drink and proceeded to read the front page, slowly, deliberately, clearly a weary, unhurried, solitary man. He did not notice the three women in cowboy hats and boots in the booth in back, but they saw him, and after a few minutes Sarah was once again at his side.

"Hi."

He turned, saw her, and instantly regained the moment he had lost when, the previous night, once outside the bar, he had forgotten about the ugliest woman he had ever seen. She seemed even more grotesque to him now than before, which made the moment all the more precious to him, and so once again he held the moment as if in his hands and began to speak with her, to ask questions, to offer his opinions and solicit hers.

I said earlier that I am the man in this story and my friend Sarah Cole, now dead, is the woman. I think back to that night, the second time I had seen Sarah, and I tremble, not with fear but in shame. My concern then, when I was first becoming involved with Sarah, was merely with the moment, holding on to it, grasping it wholly as if its beginning did not grow out of some other prior moment in her life and my life separately and at the same time did not lead into future moments in our separate lives. She talked more easily than she had the night before, and I listened as eagerly and carefully as I had before, again, with the same motives, to keep her in front of me, to draw her forward from the context of her life and place her, as if she were an object, into the context of mine. I did not know how cruel this was. When you have never done a thing before and that thing is not simply and clearly right or wrong, you frequently do not know if it is a cruel thing, you just go ahead and do it, and maybe later you'll be able to determine whether you acted cruelly. That way you'll know if it was right or wrong of you to have done it in the first place.

While we drank, Sarah told me that she hated her ex-husband because of the way he treated the children. "It's not so much the money," she said, nervously wagging her booted feet from her perch on the high barstool. "I mean, I get by, barely, but I get them fed and clothed on my own okay. It's because he won't even write them a letter or anything. He won't call them on the phone, all he calls for is to bitch at me because I'm trying to get the state to take him to court so I can get some of the money he's s'posed to be paying for child support. And he won't even think to talk to the kids when he calls. Won't even ask about them."

"He sounds like a bastard," I said.

"He is, he is," she said. "I don't know why I married him. Or stayed married. Fourteen years, for Christ's sake. He put a spell over me or something, I don't know," she said with a note of wistfulness in her voice. "He wasn't what you'd call good-looking."

After her second drink, she decided she had to leave. Her children were at home, it was Friday night and she liked to make sure she ate supper with them and knew where they were going and who they were with when they went out on their dates. "No dates on school nights," she said to me. "I mean, you gotta have rules, you know."

I agreed, and we left together, everyone in the place following us with his or her gaze. I was aware of that, I knew what they were thinking, and I didn't care, because I was simply walking her to her car.

It was a cool evening, dusk settling onto the lot like a gray blanket. Her car, a huge, dark green Buick sedan at least ten years old, was battered, scratched, and almost beyond use. She reached for the door handle on the driver's side and yanked. Nothing. The door wouldn't open. She tried again. Then I tried. Still nothing.

Then I saw it, a V-shaped dent in the left front fender creasing the fender where the door joined it, binding the metal of the door against the metal of the fender in a large crimp that held the door fast. "Someone must've backed into you while you were inside," I said to her.

She came forward and studied the crimp for a few seconds, and when she looked back at me, she was weeping. "Jesus, Jesus, Jesus!" she wailed, her large, frog-like mouth wide open and wet with spit, her red tongue flopping loosely over gapped teeth. "I can't pay for this! I *can't!*" Her face was red, and even in the dusky light I could see it puff out with weeping, her tiny eyes seeming almost to disappear behind wet cheeks. Her shoulders slumped, and her hands fell limply to her sides.

Placing my briefcase on the ground, I reached out to her and put my arms around her body and held her close to me, while she cried wetly into my shoulder. After a few seconds, she started pulling herself back together and her weeping got reduced to sniffling. Her cowboy hat had been pushed back and now clung to her head at a precarious, absurdly jaunty angle. She took a step away from me and said, "I'll get in the other side."

"Okay," I said almost in a whisper. "That's fine."

Slowly, she walked around the front of the huge, ugly vehicle and opened the door on the passenger's side and slid awkwardly across the seat until she had positioned herself behind the steering wheel. Then she started the motor, which came to life with a roar. The muffler was shot. Without saying another word to me, or even waving, she dropped the car into reverse gear and backed it loudly out of the parking space and headed out the lot to the street.

I turned and started for my car, when I happened to glance toward the door of the bar, and there, staring after me, were the bartender, the two women who had come in with Sarah, and two of the men who had been sitting at the bar. They were lawyers, and I knew them slightly. They were grinning at me. I grinned back and got into my car, and then, without looking at them again, I left the place and drove straight to my apartment.

III

One night several weeks later, Ron meets Sarah at Osgood's, and after buying her three white Russians and drinking three scotches himself, he takes her back to his apartment in his car—a Datsun fastback coupe that she says she admires—for the sole purpose of making love to her.

I'm still the man in this story, and Sarah is still the woman, but I'm telling it this way because what I have to tell you now confuses me, embarrasses me, and makes me sad, and consequently, I'm likely to tell it falsely. I'm likely to cover the truth by making Sarah a better woman than she actually was, while making myself appear worse than I actually was or am; or else I'll do the opposite, make Sarah worse than she was and me better. The truth is, I was pretty, extremely so, and she was not, extremely so, and I knew it and she knew it. She walked out the door of Osgood's determined to make love to a man much prettier than any she had seen up close before, and I walked out determined to make love to a woman much homelier than any I had made love to before. We were, in a sense, equals.

No, that's not exactly true. (You see? This is why I have to tell the story the way I'm telling it.) I'm not at all sure she feels as Ron does. That is to say, perhaps she genuinely likes the man, in spite of his being the most physically attractive man she has ever known. Perhaps she is more aware of her homeliness than of his beauty, just as he is more aware of her homeliness than of his beauty, for Ron, despite what I may have implied, does not think of himself as especially beautiful. He merely knows that other people think of him that way. As I said before, he is a nice man.

Ron unlocks the door to his apartment, walks in ahead of her, and flicks on the lamp beside the couch. It's a small, single bedroom, modern apartment, one of thirty identical apartments in a large brick building on the heights just east of downtown Concord. Sarah stands nervously at the door, peering in.

"Come in, come in," he says.

She steps timidly in and closes the door behind her. She removes her cowboy hat, then quickly puts it back on, crosses the livingroom, and plops down in a blond easy chair, seeming to shrink in its hug out of sight to safety. Ron, behind her, at the entry to the kitchen, places one hand on her shoulder, and she stiffens. He removes his hand.

"Would you like a drink?"

"No ... I guess not," she says, staring straight ahead at the wall opposite where a large framed photograph of a bicyclist advertises in French the Tour de France. Around a corner, in an alcove off the living room, a silver-gray ten-speed bicycle leans casually against the wall, glistening and poised, slender as a thoroughbred racehorse.

"I don't know," she says. Ron is in the kitchen now, making himself a drink. "I don't know . . . I don't know."

"What? Change your mind? I can make a white Russian for you. Vodka, cream, Kahlúa, and ice, right?"

Sarah tries to cross her legs, but she is sitting too low in the chair and her legs are too thick at the thigh, so she ends, after a struggle, with one leg in the air and the other twisted on its side. She looks as if she has fallen from a great height.

Ron steps out from the kitchen, peers over the back of the chair, and watches her untangle herself, then ducks back into the kitchen. After a few seconds, he returns. "Seriously. Want me to fix you a white Russian?"

"No."

Ron, again from behind, places one hand on Sarah's shoulder, and this time she does not stiffen, though she does not exactly relax, either. She sits there, a block of wood, staring straight ahead.

"Are you scared?" he asks gently. Then he adds, "*I* am."

"Well, no, I'm not scared." She remains silent for a moment. "You're scared? Of what?" She turns to face him but avoids his eyes.

"Well . . . I don't do this all the time, you know. Bring home a woman I . . ." He trails off.

"Picked up in a bar."

"No. I mean, I like you, Sarah, I really do. And I didn't just pick you up in a bar, you know that. We've gotten to be friends, you and me."

"You want to sleep with me?" she asks, still not meeting his steady gaze.

"Yes." He seems to mean it. He does not take a gulp or even a sip from his drink. He just says, "Yes," straight out, and cleanly, not too quickly, either, and not after a hesitant delay. A simple statement of a simple fact. The man wants to make love to the woman. She asked him, and he told her. What could be simpler?

"Do you want to sleep with *me?*" he asks.

She turns around in the chair, faces the wall again, and says in a low voice, "Sure I do, but . . . it's hard to explain."

"What? But what?" Placing his glass down on the table between the chair and the sofa, he puts both hands on her shoulders and lightly kneads them. He knows he can be discouraged from pursuing this, but he is not sure how easily. Having got this far without bumping against obstacles (except the ones he has placed in his way himself), he is not sure what it will take to turn him back. He does not know, therefore, how assertive or how seductive he should be with her. He suspects that he can be stopped very easily, so he is reluctant to give her a chance to try. He goes on kneading her doughy shoulders.

"You and me . . . we're real different." She glances at the bicycle in the corner.

"A man . . . and a woman," he says.

"No, not that. I mean, different. That's all. Real different. More than you . . . you're nice, but you don't know what I mean, and that's one of the things that makes you so nice. But we're different. Listen," she says, "I gotta go. I gotta leave now."

The man removes his hands and retrieves his glass, takes a sip, and watches her over the rim of the glass, as, not without difficulty, she rises from the chair and moves swiftly toward the door. She stops at the door, squares her hat on her head, and glances back at him.

"We can be friends. Okay?"

"Okay. Friends."

"I'll see you again down at Osgood's, right?"

"Oh, yeah, sure."

"Good. See you," she says, opening the door.

The door closes. The man walks around the sofa, snaps on the television set, and sits down in front of it. He picks up a *TV Guide* from the coffee table and flips through it, stops, runs a finger down the listings, stops, puts down the magazine and changes the channel. He does not once connect the magazine in his hand to the woman who has just left his apartment, even though he knows she spends her days packing *TV Guide*s into cartons that get shipped to warehouses in distant parts of New England. He'll think of the connection some other night; but by then the connection will be merely sentimental. It'll be too late for him to understand what she meant by "different."

IV

But that's not the point of my story. Certainly it's an aspect of the story, the political aspect, if you want, but it's not the reason I'm trying to tell the story in the first place. I'm trying to tell the story so that I can understand what happened between me and Sarah Cole that summer and early autumn ten years ago. To say we were lovers says very little about what happened; to say we were friends says even less. No, if I'm to understand the whole thing, I have to say the whole thing, for, in the end, what I need to know is whether what happened between me and Sarah Cole was right or wrong. Character is fate, which suggests that if a man can know and then to some degree control his character, he can know and to that same degree control his fate.

But let me go on with my story. The next time Sarah and I were together we were at her apartment in the south end of Concord, a second-floor flat in a tenement building on Perley Street. I had stayed away from Osgood's for several weeks, deliberately trying to avoid running into Sarah there, though I never quite put it that way to myself. I found excuses and generated interests in and reasons for going elsewhere after work. Yet I was obsessed with Sarah by then, obsessed with the idea of making love to her, which, because it was not an actual *desire* to make love to her, was an unusually complex obsession. Passion without desire, if it gets expressed, may in fact be a kind of rape, and perhaps I sensed the danger that lay behind my obsession and for that reason went out of my way to avoid meeting Sarah again.

Yet I did meet her, inadvertently, of course. After picking up shirts at the cleaner's on South Main and Perley streets, I'd gone down Perley on my way to South State and the post office. It was a Saturday morning, and this trip on my bicycle was part of my regular Saturday routine. I did not remember that Sarah lived on Perley Street, although she had told me several times in a complaining way—it's a rough neighborhood, packed dirt yards, shabby apartment buildings, the carcasses of old, half-stripped cars on cinder blocks in the driveways, broken red and yellow plastic tricycles on the cracked sidewalks—but as soon as I saw her, I remembered. It was too late to avoid meeting her, I was riding my bike, wearing shorts and tee shirt, the package containing my folded and starched shirts hooked to the carrier behind me, and she was walking toward me along the sidewalk, lugging two large bags of groceries. She saw me, and I stopped. We talked, and I offered to carry her groceries for her. I took the bags while she led the bike, handling it carefully as if she were afraid she might break it.

At the stoop we came to a halt. The wooden steps were cluttered with half-opened garbage bags spilling eggshells, coffee grounds, and old food wrappers to the walkway. "I can't get the people downstairs to take care of their garbage," she explained. She leaned the bike against the banister and reached for her groceries.

"I'll carry them up for you," I said. I directed her to loop the chain lock from the bike to the banister rail and snap it shut and told her to bring my shirts up with her.

"Maybe you'd like a beer?" she said as she opened the door to the darkened hallway. Narrow stairs disappeared in front of me into heavy, damp darkness, and the air smelled like old newspapers.

"Sure," I said and followed her up.

"Sorry there's no light. I can't get them to fix it."

"No matter, I can see you and follow along," I said, and even in the dim light of the hall I could see the large, dark blue veins that cascaded thickly down the backs of her legs. She wore tight, white-duck bermuda shorts, rubber shower sandals, and a pink sleeveless sweater. I pictured her in the cashier's line at the supermarket. I would have been behind her, a stranger, and on seeing her, I would have turned away and studied the covers of the magazines, *TV Guide*, *People*, *The National Enquirer*, for there was nothing of interest in her appearance that in the hard light of day would not have slightly embarrassed me. Yet here I was inviting myself into her home, eagerly staring at the backs of her ravaged legs, her sad, tasteless clothing, her poverty. I was not detached, however, was not staring at her with scientific curiosity, and because of my passion, did not feel or believe that what I was doing was perverse. I felt warmed by her presence and was flirtatious and bold, a little pushy, even.

Picture this. The man, tanned, limber, wearing red jogging shorts, Italian leather sandals, a clinging net tee shirt of Scandinavian design and manufacture, enters the apartment behind the woman, whose dough-colored skin, thick, short body, and homely, uncomfortable face all try, but fail, to hide themselves. She waves him toward the table in the kitchen, where he sets down the bags and looks good-naturedly around the room. "What about the beer you bribed me with?" he asks. The apartment is dark and cluttered with old, oversized furniture, yard sale and second-hand stuff bought originally for a large house in the country or a spacious apartment on a boulevard forty or fifty years ago, passed down from antique dealer to used furniture store to yard sale to thrift shop, where it finally gets purchased by Sarah Cole and gets lugged over to Perley Street and shoved up the narrow stairs, she and her children grunting and sweating in the darkness of the hallway—overstuffed armchairs and couch, huge, ungainly dressers, upholstered rocking chairs, and in the kitchen, an old maple desk for a table, a half dozen heavy oak dining room chairs, a high, glass-fronted cabinet, all peeling, stained, chipped and squatting heavily on a dark green linoleum floor.

The place is neat and arranged in a more or less orderly way, however, and the man seems comfortable there. He strolls from the kitchen to the livingroom and peeks into the three small bedrooms that branch off a hallway behind the livingroom. "Nice place!" he calls to the woman. He is studying the framed pictures of her three children arranged like an altar atop the buffet. "Nice-looking kids!" he calls out. They are. Blond, round-faced, clean, and utterly ordinary-looking, their pleasant faces glance, as instructed, slightly off camera and down to the right, as if they are trying to remember the name of the capital of Montana.

When he returns to the kitchen, the woman is putting away her groceries, her back to him. "Where's that beer you bribed me with?" he asks again. He takes a position against the doorframe, his weight on one hip, like a dancer resting. "You sure are quiet today, Sarah," he says in a low voice. "Everything okay?"

Silently, she turns away from the grocery bags, crosses the room to the man, reaches up to him, and holding him by the head, kisses his mouth, rolls her torso against his, drops her hands to his hips and yanks him tightly to her, and goes on kissing him, eyes closed, working her face furiously against his. The man places his hands on her shoulders and pulls away, and they face each other, wide-eyed, as if amazed and frightened. The man drops his hands, and the woman lets go of his hips. Then, after a few seconds, the man silently turns, goes to the door, and leaves. The last thing he sees as he closes the door behind him is the woman standing in the kitchen doorframe, her face looking down and slightly to one side, wearing the same pleasant expression on her face as her children in their photographs, trying to remember the capital of Montana.

V

Sarah appeared at my apartment door the following morning, a Sunday, cool and rainy. She had brought me the package of freshly laundered shirts I'd left in her kitchen, and when I opened the door to her, she simply held the package out to me as if it were a penitent's gift. She wore a yellow rain slicker and cap and looked more like a disconsolate schoolgirl facing an angry teacher than a grown woman dropping a package off at a friend's apartment. After all, she had nothing to be ashamed of.

I invited her inside, and she accepted my invitation. I had been reading the Sunday *New York Times* on the couch and drinking coffee, lounging through the gray morning in bathrobe and pajamas. I told her to take off her wet raincoat and hat and hang them in the closet by the door and started for the kitchen to get her a cup of coffee, when I stopped, turned, and looked at her. She closed the closet door on her yellow raincoat and hat, turned around, and faced me.

What else can I do? I must describe it. I remember that moment of ten years ago as if it occurred ten minutes ago, the package of shirts on the table behind her, the newspapers scattered over the couch and floor, the sound of windblown rain washing the sides of the building outside, and the silence of the room, as we stood across from one another and watched, while we each simultaneously removed our own clothing, my robe, her blouse and skirt, my pajama top, her slip and bra, my pajama bottom, her underpants, until we were both standing naked in the harsh, gray light, two naked members of the same species, a male and a female, the male somewhat younger and less scarred than the female, the female somewhat less delicately constructed than the male, both individuals pale-skinned with dark thatches of hair in the area of their genitals, both individuals standing slackly, as if a great, protracted tension between them had at last been released.

VI

We made love that morning in my bed for long hours that drifted easily into afternoon. And we talked, as people usually do when they spend half a day or half a night in bed together. I told her of my past, named and described the people I had loved and had loved me, my ex-wife in New York, my brother in the Air Force, my father and mother in their condominium in Florida, and I told her of my ambitions and dreams and even confessed some of my fears. She listened patiently and intelligently throughout and talked much less than I. She had already told me many of these things about herself, and perhaps whatever she had to say to me now lay on the next inner circle of intimacy or else could not be spoken of at all.

During the next few weeks we met and made love often and always at my apartment. On arriving home from work, I would phone her, or if not, she would phone me, and after a few feints and dodges, one would suggest to the other that we get together tonight, and a half hour later she'd be at my door. Our lovemaking was passionate, skillful, kindly, and deeply satisfying. We didn't often speak of it to one another or brag about it, the way some couples do when they are surprised by the ease with which they have become contented lovers. We did occasionally joke and tease each other, however, playfully acknowledging that the only thing we did together was make love but that we did it so frequently there was no time for anything else.

Then one hot night, a Saturday in August, we were lying in bed atop the tangled sheets, smoking cigarettes and chatting idly, and Sarah suggested that we go out for a drink.

"Now?"

"Sure. It's early. What time is it?"

I scanned the digital clock next to the bed. "Nine forty-nine."

"There. See?"

"That's not so early. You usually go home by eleven, you know. It's almost ten."

"No, it's only a little after nine. Depends on how you look at things. Besides, Ron, it's Saturday night. Don't you want to go out and dance or something? Or is this the only thing you know how to do?" she teased and poked me in the ribs. "You know how to dance? You like to dance?"

"Yeah, sure . . . sure, but not tonight. It's too hot. And I'm tired."

But she persisted, happily pointing out that an air-conditioned bar would be cooler than my apartment, and we didn't have to go to a dance bar, we could go to Osgood's. "As a compromise," she said.

I suggested a place called the El Rancho, a restaurant with a large, dark cocktail lounge and dance bar located several miles from town on the old Portsmouth highway. Around nine the restaurant closed and the bar became something of a roadhouse, with a small country-western houseband and a clientele drawn from the four or five villages that adjoined Concord on the north and east. I had eaten at the restaurant once but had never gone to the bar, and I didn't know anyone who had.

Sarah was silent for a moment. Then she lit a cigarette and drew the sheet over her naked body. "You don't want anybody to know about us, do you? Do you?"

"That's not it . . . I just don't like gossip, and I work with a lot of people who show up sometimes at Osgood's. On a Saturday night especially."

"No," she said firmly. "You're ashamed of being seen with me. You'll sleep with me, but you won't go out in public with me."

"That's not true, Sarah."

She was silent again. Relieved, I reached across her to the bed table and got my cigarettes and lighter.

"You owe me, Ron," she said suddenly, as I passed over her. "You owe me."

"What?" I lay back, lit a cigarette, and covered my body with the sheet.

"I said, 'You owe me.'"

"I don't know what you're talking about, Sarah. I just don't like a lot of gossip going around, that's all. I like keeping my private life private, that's all. I don't *owe* you anything."

"Friendship you owe me. And respect. Friendship and respect. A person can't do what you've done with me without owing them friendship and respect."

"Sarah, I really don't know what you're talking about," I said. "I am your friend, you know that. And I respect you. I really do."

"You really think so, don't you?"

"Yes."

She said nothing for several long moments. Then she sighed and in a low, almost inaudible voice said, "Then you'll have to go out in public with me. I don't care about Osgood's or the people you work with, we don't have to go there or see any of them," she said. "But you're gonna have to go to places like the El Rancho with me, and a few other places I know, too, where there's people *I* work with, people *I* know, and maybe we'll even go to a couple of parties, because *I* get invited to parties sometimes, you know. I have friends, and I have some family, too, and you're gonna have to meet my family. My kids think I'm just going around bar-hopping when I'm over here with you, and I don't like that, so you're gonna have to meet them so I can tell them where I am when I'm not at home nights. And sometimes you're gonna come over and spend the evening at my place!" Her voice had risen as she heard her demands and felt their rightness, until now she was almost shouting at me. "You *owe* that to me. Or else you're a bad man. It's that simple."

It was.

VII

The handsome man is over-dressed. He is wearing a navy blue blazer, taupe shirt open at the throat, white slacks, white loafers. Everyone else, including the homely woman with the handsome man, is dressed appropriately, dressed, that is, like everyone else—jeans and cowboy boots, blouses or cowboy shirts or tee shirts with catchy sayings printed across the front, and many of the women are wearing cowboy hats pushed back and tied under their chins. The man doesn't know anyone at the bar or, if they're at a party, in the room, but the woman knows most of the people there, and she gladly introduces him. The men grin and shake his hand, slap him on his jacketed shoulder, ask him where he works, what's his line, after which they lapse into silence. The women flirt briefly with their faces, but they lapse into silence even before the men do. The woman with the man in the blazer does most of the talking for everyone. She talks for the man in the blazer, for the men standing around the refrigerator, or if they're at a bar, for the other men at the table, and for the other women, too. She chats and rambles aimlessly through loud monologues, laughs uproariously at trivial jokes, and drinks too much, until soon she is drunk, thick-tongued, clumsy, and the man has to say her goodbyes and ease her out the door to his car and drive her home to her apartment on Perley Street.

This happens twice in one week, and then three times the next—at the El Rancho, at the Ox Bow in Northwood, at Rita's and Jimmy's apartment on Thorndike Street, out in Warner at Betsy Beeler's new house, and, the last time, at a cottage on Lake Sunapee rented by some kids in shipping at Rumford Press. Ron no longer calls Sarah when he gets home from work; he waits for her call, and sometimes, when he knows it's she, he doesn't answer the phone. Usually, he lets it ring five or six times, and then he reaches down and picks up the receiver. He has taken his jacket and vest off and loosened his tie and is about to put supper, frozen manicotti, into the Radarange.

"Hello?"

"*Hi.*"

"How're you doing?"

"*Okay, I guess. A little tired.*"

"Still hung over?"

"*No. Not really. Just tired. I hate Mondays.*"

"You have fun last night?"

"*Well, yeah, sorta. It's nice out there, at the lake. Listen,*" she says, brightening. "*Whyn't you come over here tonight? The kids're all going out later, but if you come over before eight, you can meet them. They really want to meet you.*"

"You told them about me?"

"*Sure. Long time ago. I'm not supposed to tell my own kids?*"

Ron is silent.

"*You don't want to come over here tonight. You don't want to meet my kids. No, you don't want my kids to meet you, that's it.*"

"No, no, it's just . . . I've got a lot of work to do . . ."

"*We should talk,*" she announces in a flat voice.

"Yes," he says, "we should talk."

They agree that she will meet him at his apartment, and they'll talk, and they say goodbye and hang up.

While Ron is heating his supper and then eating alone at his kitchen table and Sarah is feeding her children, perhaps I should admit, since we are nearing the end of my story, that I don't actually know that Sarah Cole is dead. A few years ago I happened to run into one of her friends from the press, a blond woman with an underslung jaw. Her name, she reminded me, was Glenda; she had seen me at Osgood's a couple of times, and we had met at the El Rancho once when I had gone there with Sarah. I was amazed that she could remember me and a little embarrassed that I did not recognize her at all, and she laughed at that and said, "You haven't changed much, mister!" I pretended to recognize her, but I think she knew she was a stranger to me. We were standing outside the Sears store on South Main Street, where I had gone to buy paint. I had recently remarried, and my wife and I were redecorating my apartment.

"Whatever happened to Sarah?" I asked Glenda. "Is she still down at the press?"

"Jeez, no! She left a long time ago. Way back. I heard she went back with her ex-husband. I can't remember his name. Something Cole."

I asked her if she was sure of that, and she said no, she had only heard it around the bars and down at the press, but she had assumed it was true. People said Sarah had moved back with her ex-husband and was living in a trailer in a park near Hooksett, and the whole family had moved down to Florida that winter because he was out of work. He was a carpenter, she said.

"I thought he was mean to her. I thought he beat her up and everything. I thought she hated him," I said.

"Oh, well, yeah, he was a bastard, all right. I met him a couple of times, and I didn't like him. Short, ugly, and mean when he got drunk. But you know what they say."

"What do they say?"

"Oh, you know, about water seeking its own level."

"Sarah wasn't mean when she was drunk."

The woman laughed. "Naw, but she sure was short and ugly!"

I said nothing.

"Hey, don't get me wrong, I liked Sarah. But you and her . . . well, you sure made a funny-looking couple. She probably didn't feel so self-conscious and all with her husband," the woman said seriously. "I mean, with you . . . all tall and blond, and poor old Sarah . . . I mean, the way them kids in the press room used to kid her about her looks, it was embarrassing just to hear it."

"Well . . . I loved her," I said.

The woman raised her plucked eyebrows in disbelief. She smiled. "Sure, you did, honey," she said, and she patted me on the arm. "Sure, you did." Then she let the smile drift off her face, turned and walked away.

When someone you have loved dies, you accept the fact of his or her death, but then the person goes on living in your memory, dreams, and reveries. You have imaginary conversations with him or her, you see something striking and remind yourself to tell your loved one about it and then get brought up short by the knowledge of the fact of his or her death, and at night, in your sleep, the dead person visits you. With Sarah, none of that happened. When she was gone from my life, she was gone absolutely, as if she had never existed in the first place. It was only later, when I could think of her as dead and could come out and say it, my friend Sarah Cole is dead, that I was able to tell this story, for that is when she began to enter my memories, my dreams, and my reveries. In that way I learned that I truly did love her, and now I have begun to grieve over her death, to wish her alive again, so that I can say to her the things I could not know or say when she was alive, when I did not know that I loved her.

VIII

The woman arrives at Ron's apartment around eight. He hears her car, because of the broken muffler, blat and rumble into the parking lot below, and he crosses quickly from the kitchen and peers out the livingroom window and, as if through a telescope, watches her shove herself across the seat to the passenger's side to get out of the car, then walk slowly in the dusky light toward the apartment building. It's a warm evening, and she's wearing her white bermuda shorts, pink sleeveless sweater, and shower sandals. Ron hates those clothes. He hates the way the shorts cut into her flesh at the crotch and thigh, hates the large, dark caves below her arms that get exposed by the sweater, hates the flapping noise made by the sandals.

Shortly, there is a soft knock at his door. He opens it, turns away and crosses to the kitchen, where he turns back, lights a cigarette, and watches her. She closes the door. He offers her a drink, which she declines, and somewhat formally, he invites her to sit down. She sits carefully on the sofa, in the middle, with her feet close together on the floor, as if she were being interviewed for a job. Then he comes around and sits in the easy chair, relaxed, one leg slung over the other at the knee, as if he were interviewing her for the job.

"Well," he says, "you wanted to talk."

"Yes. But now you're mad at me. I can see that. I didn't do anything, Ron."

"I'm not mad at you."

They are silent for a moment. Ron goes on smoking his cigarette.

Finally, she sighs and says, "You don't want to see me anymore, do you?"

He waits a few seconds and answers, "Yes. That's right." Getting up from the chair, he walks to the silver-gray bicycle and stands before it, running a fingertip along the slender cross-bar from the saddle to the chrome-plated handlebars.

"You're a son of a bitch," she says in a low voice. "You're worse than my ex-husband." Then she smiles meanly, almost sneers, and soon he realizes that she is telling him that she won't leave. He's stuck with her, she informs him with cold precision. "You think I'm just so much meat, and all you got to do is call up the butcher shop and cancel your order. Well, now you're going to find out different. You *can't* cancel your order. I'm not meat, I'm not one of your pretty little girlfriends who come running when you want them and go away when you get tired of them. I'm *different*. I got nothing to lose, Ron. Nothing. You're stuck with me, Ron."

He continues stroking his bicycle. "No, I'm not."

She sits back in the couch and crosses her legs at the ankles. "I think I *will* have that drink you offered."

"Look, Sarah, it would be better if you go now."

"No," she says flatly. "You offered me a drink when I came in. Nothing's changed since I've been here. Not for me, and not for you. I'd like that drink you offered," she says haughtily.

Ron turns away from the bicycle and takes a step toward her. His face has stiffened into a mask. "Enough is enough," he says through clenched teeth. "I've given you enough."

"Fix me a drink, will you, honey?" she says with a phony smile.

Ron orders her to leave.

She refuses.

He grabs her by the arm and yanks her to her feet.

She starts crying lightly. She stands there and looks up into his face and weeps, but she does not move toward the door, so he pushes her. She regains her balance and goes on weeping.

He stands back and places his fists on his hips and looks at her. "Go on and leave, you ugly bitch," he says to her, and as he says the words, as one by one they leave his mouth, she's transformed into the most beautiful woman he has ever seen. He says the words again, almost tenderly. "Leave, you ugly bitch." Her hair is golden, her brown eyes deep and sad, her mouth full and affectionate, her tears the tears of love and loss, and her pleading, outstretched arms, her entire body, the arms and body of a devoted woman's cruelly rejected love. A third time he says the words. "Leave me, you disgusting, ugly bitch." She is wrapped in an envelope of golden light, a warm, dense haze that she seems to have stepped into, as into a carriage. And then she is gone, and he is alone again.

He looks around the room, as if searching for her. Sitting down in the easy chair, he places his face in his hands. It's not as if she has died; it's as if he has killed her.

Donald Barthelme

THE SCHOOL

DONALD BARTHELME (1931–1989) published twelve books, including two novels and a prizewinning children's book. A regular contributor to *The New Yorker,* he divided his time between New York and Houston, where he taught creative writing at the University of Houston. In his career, he won a Guggenheim Fellowship, a National Book Award, and a National Institute of Arts and Letters Award, among other honors. Mr. Barthelme died in July 1989.

Well, we had all these children out planting trees, see, because we figured that . . . that was part of their education, to see how, you know, the root systems . . . and also the sense of responsibility, taking care of things, being individually responsible. You know what I mean. And the trees all died. They were orange trees. I don't know why they died, they just died. Something wrong with the soil possibly or maybe the stuff we got from the nursery wasn't the best. We complained about it. So we've got thirty kids there, each kid had his or her own little tree to plant, and we've got these thirty dead trees. All these kids looking at these little brown sticks, it was depressing.

It wouldn't have been so bad except that just a couple of weeks before the thing with the trees, the snakes all died. But I think that the snakes—well, the reason that the snakes kicked off was that . . . you remember, the boiler was shut off for four days because of the strike, and that was explicable. It was something you could explain to the kids because of the strike. I mean, none of their parents would let them cross the picket line and they knew there was a strike going on and what it meant. So when things got started up again and we found the snakes they weren't too disturbed.

With the herb gardens it was probably a case of overwatering, and at least now they know not to overwater. The children were very conscientious with the herb gardens and some of them probably . . . you know, slipped them a little extra water when we weren't looking. Or maybe . . . well, I don't like to think about sabotage, although it did occur to us. I mean, it was something that crossed our minds. We were thinking that way probably because before that the gerbils had died, and the white mice had died, and the salamander . . . well, now they know not to carry them around in plastic bags.

Of course we *expected* the tropical fish to die, that was no surprise. Those numbers, you look at them crooked and they're belly-up on the surface. But the lesson plan called for a tropical-fish input at that point, there was nothing we could do, it happens every year, you just have to hurry past it.

We weren't even supposed to have a puppy.

We weren't even supposed to have one, it was just a puppy the Murdoch girl found under a Gristede's truck one day and she was afraid the truck would run over it when the driver had finished making his delivery, so she stuck it in her knapsack and brought it to school with her. So we had this puppy. As soon as I saw the puppy I thought, Oh Christ, I bet it will live for about two weeks and then ... And that's what it did. It wasn't supposed to be in the classroom at all, there's some kind of regulation about it, but you can't tell them they can't have a puppy when the puppy is already there, right in front of them, running around on the floor and yap yap yapping. They named it Edgar—that is, they named it after me. They had a lot of fun running after it and yelling, "Here, Edgar! Nice Edgar!" Then they'd laugh like hell. They enjoyed the ambiguity. I enjoyed it myself. I don't mind being kidded. They made a little house for it in the supply closet and all that. I don't know what it died of. Distemper, I guess. It probably hadn't had any shots. I got it out of there before the kids got to school. I checked the supply closet each morning, routinely, because I knew what was going to happen. I gave it to the custodian.

And then there was this Korean orphan that the class adopted through the Help the Children program, all the kids brought in a quarter a month, that was the idea. It was an unfortunate thing, the kid's name was Kim and maybe we adopted him too late or something. The cause of death was not stated in the letter we got, they suggested we adopt another child instead and sent us some interesting case histories, but we didn't have the heart. The class took it pretty hard, they began (I think; nobody ever said anything to me directly) to feel that maybe there was something wrong with the school. But I don't think there's anything wrong with the school, particularly, I've seen better and I've seen worse. It was just a run of bad luck. We had an extraordinary number of parents passing away, for instance. There were I think two heart attacks and two suicides, one drowning, and four killed together in a car accident. One stroke. And we had the usual heavy mortality rate among the grandparents, or maybe it was heavier this year, it seemed so. And finally the tragedy.

The tragedy occurred when Matthew Wein and Tony Mavrogordo were playing over where they're excavating for the new federal office building. There were all these big wooden beams stacked, you know, at the edge of the excavation. There's a court case coming out of that, the parents are claiming that the beams were poorly stacked. I don't know what's true and what's not. It's been a strange year.

I forgot to mention Billy Brandt's father, who was knifed fatally when he grappled with a masked intruder in his home.

One day, we had a discussion in class. They asked me, where did they go? The trees, the salamander, the tropical fish, Edgar, the poppas and mommas, Matthew and Tony, where did they go? And I said, I don't know, I don't know. And they said, who knows? and I said, nobody knows. And they said, is death that which gives meaning to life? and I said, no, life is that which gives meaning to life. Then they said, but isn't death, considered as a fundamental datum, the means by which the taken-for-granted mundanity of the everyday may be transcended in the direction of—

I said, yes, maybe.

They said, we don't like it.

I said, that's sound.

They said, it's a bloody shame!

I said, it is.

They said, will you make love now with Helen (our teaching assistant) so that we can see how it is done? We know you like Helen.

I do like Helen but I said that I would not.

We've heard so much about it, they said, but we've never seen it.

I said I would be fired and that it was never, or almost never, done as a demonstration. Helen looked out of the window.

They said, please, please make love with Helen, we require an assertion of value, we are frightened.

I said that they shouldn't be frightened (although I am often frightened) and that there was value everywhere. Helen came and embraced me. I kissed her a few times on the brow. We held each other. The children were excited. Then there was a knock on the door, I opened the door, and the new gerbil walked in. The children cheered wildly.

THE HERMIT'S STORY

RICK BASS (1958–) is the author of twenty-four books of fiction and nonfiction, including novels, short stories, and essays. He lives with his family in northwest Montana's Yaak Valley, where he has long been active in a campaign to protect as designated wilderness the last roadless lands in the Kootenai National Forest.

An ice storm, following seven days of snow; the vast fields and drifts of snow turning to sheets of glazed ice that shine and shimmer blue in the moonlight, as if the color is being fabricated not by the bending and absorption of light but by some chemical reaction within the glossy ice; as if the source of all blueness lies somewhere up here in the north—the core of it beneath one of those frozen fields; as if blue is a thing that emerges, in some parts of the world, from the soil itself, after the sun goes down.

Blue creeping up fissures and cracks from depths of several hundred feet; blue working its way up through the gleaming ribs of Ann's buried dogs; blue trailing like smoke from the dogs' empty eye sockets and nostrils—blue rising as if from deep-dug chimneys until it reaches the surface and spreads laterally and becomes entombed, or trapped—but still alive, and drifting—within those moonstruck fields of ice.

Blue like a scent trapped in the ice, waiting for some soft release, some thawing, so that it can continue spreading.

It's Thanksgiving. Susan and I are over at Ann and Roger's house for dinner. The storm has knocked out all the power down in town—it's a clear, cold, starry night, and if you were to climb one of the mountains on snowshoes and look forty miles south toward where town lies, instead of seeing the usual small scatterings of light—like fallen stars, stars sunken to the bottom of a lake, but still glowing—you would see nothing but darkness—a bowl of silence and darkness in balance for once with the mountains up here, rather than opposing or complementing our darkness, our peace.

As it is, we do not climb up on snowshoes to look down at the dark town—the power lines dragged down by the clutches of ice—but can tell instead just by the way there is no faint glow over the mountains to the south that the power is out: that this Thanksgiving, life for those in town is the same as it always is for us in the mountains, and it is a good feeling, a familial one, coming on the holiday as it does—though doubtless too the townspeople are feeling less snug and cozy about it than we are.

We've got our lanterns and candles burning. A fire's going in the stove, as it will all winter long and into the spring. Ann's dogs are asleep in their straw nests, breathing in that same blue light that is being exhaled from the skeletons of their ancestors just beneath and all around them. There is the faint smell of cold-storage meat—slabs and slabs of it—coming from down in the basement, and we have just finished off an entire chocolate pie and three bottles of wine. Roger, who does not know how to read, is examining the empty bottles, trying to read some of the words on the labels. He recognizes the words *the* and *in* and *USA*. It may be that he will never learn to read—that he will be unable to—but we are in no rush; he has all of his life to accomplish this. I for one believe that he will learn.

Ann has a story for us. It's about a fellow named Gray Owl, up in Canada, who owned half a dozen speckled German shorthaired pointers and who hired Ann to train them all at once. It was twenty years ago, she says—her last good job.

She worked the dogs all summer and into the autumn, and finally had them ready for field trials. She took them back up to Gray Owl—way up in Saskatchewan—driving all day and night in her old truck, which was old even then, with dogs piled up on top of one another, sleeping and snoring: dogs on her lap, dogs on the seat, dogs on the floorboard.

Ann was taking the dogs up there to show Gray Owl how to work them: how to take advantage of their newfound talents. She could be a sculptor or some other kind of artist, in that she speaks of her work as if the dogs are rough blocks of stone whose internal form exists already and is waiting only to be chiseled free and then released by her, beautiful, into the world.

Basically, in six months the dogs had been transformed from gangling, bouncing puppies into six wonderful hunters, and she needed to show their owner which characteristics to nurture, which ones to discourage. With all dogs, Ann said, there was a tendency, upon their leaving her tutelage, for a kind of chitinous encrustation to set in, a sort of oxidation, upon the dogs leaving her hands and being returned to someone less knowledgeable and passionate, less committed than she. It was as if there were a tendency for the dogs' greatness to disappear back into the stone.

So she went up there to give both the dogs and Gray Owl a checkout session. She drove with the heater on and the windows down; the cold Canadian air was invigorating, cleaner. She could smell the scent of the fir and spruce, and the damp alder and cottonwood leaves beneath the many feet of snow. We laughed at her when she said it, but she told us that up in Canada she could taste the fish in the water as she drove alongside creeks and rivers.

She got to Gray Owl's around midnight. He had a little guest cabin but had not heated it for her, uncertain as to the day of her arrival, so she and the six dogs slept together on a cold mattress beneath mounds of elk hides: their last night together. She had brought a box of quail with which to work the dogs, and she built a small fire in the stove and set the box of quail next to it.

The quail muttered and cheeped all night and the stove popped and hissed and Ann and the dogs slept for twelve hours straight, as if submerged in another time, or as if everyone else in the world were submerged in time—and as if she and the dogs were pioneers, or survivors of some kind: upright and exploring the present, alive in the world, free of that strange chitin.

She spent a week up there, showing Gray Owl how his dogs worked. She said he scarcely recognized them afield, and that it took a few days just for him to get over his amazement. They worked the dogs both individually and, as Gray Owl came to understand and appreciate what Ann had crafted, in groups. They traveled across snowy hills on snowshoes, the sky the color of snow, so that often it was like moving through a dream, and, except for the rasp of the snowshoes beneath them and the pull of gravity, they might have believed they had ascended into some sky-place where all the world was snow.

They worked into the wind—north—whenever they could. Ann would carry birds in a pouch over her shoulder and from time to time would fling a startled bird out into that dreary, icy snowscape. The quail would fly off with great haste, a dark feathered buzz bomb disappearing quickly into the teeth of cold, and then Gray Owl and Ann and the dog, or dogs, would go find it, following it by scent only, as always.

Snot icicles would be hanging from the dogs' nostrils. They would always find the bird. The dog, or dogs, would point it, Gray Owl or Ann would step forward and flush it, and the beleaguered bird would leap into the sky again, and once more they would push on after it, pursuing that bird toward the horizon as if driving it with a whip. Whenever the bird wheeled and flew downwind, they'd quarter away from it, then get a mile or so downwind from it and push it back north.

When the quail finally became too exhausted to fly, Ann would pick it up from beneath the dogs' noses as they held point staunchly, put the tired bird in her game bag, and replace it with a fresh one, and off they'd go again. They carried their lunch in Gray Owl's daypack, as well as emergency supplies—a tent and some dry clothes—in case they should become lost, and around noon each day (they could rarely see the sun, only an eternal ice-white haze, so that they relied instead only on their internal rhythms) they would stop and make a pot of tea on the sputtering little gas stove. Sometimes one or two of the quail would die from exposure, and they would cook that on the stove and eat it out there in the tundra, tossing the feathers up into the wind as if to launch one more flight, and feeding the head, guts, and feet to the dogs.

Seen from above, their tracks might have seemed aimless and wandering rather than with the purpose, the focus that was burning hot in both their and the dogs' hearts. Perhaps someone viewing the tracks could have discerned the pattern, or perhaps not, but it did not matter, for their tracks—the patterns, direction, and tracing of them—were obscured by the drifting snow, sometimes within minutes after they were laid down.

Toward the end of the week, Ann said, they were finally running all six dogs at once, like a herd of silent wild horses through all that snow, and as she would be going home the next day there was no need to conserve any of the birds she had brought, and she was turning them loose several at a time: birds flying in all directions; the dogs, as ever, tracking them to the ends of the earth.

It was almost a whiteout that last day, and it was hard to keep track of all the dogs. Ann was sweating from the exertion as well as the tension of trying to keep an eye on, and evaluate, each dog, and the sweat was freezing on her as if she were developing an ice skin. She jokingly told Gray Owl that next time she was going to try to find a client who lived in Arizona, or even South America. Gray Owl smiled and then told her that they were lost, but no matter, the storm would clear in a day or two.

They knew it was getting near dusk—there was a faint dulling to the sheer whiteness, a kind of increasing heaviness in the air, a new density to the faint light around them—and the dogs slipped in and out of sight, working just at the edges of their vision.

The temperature was dropping as the north wind increased—"No question about which way south is," Gray Owl said, "so we'll turn around and walk south for three hours, and if we don't find a road, we'll make camp"—and now the dogs were coming back with frozen quail held gingerly in their mouths, for once the birds were dead, the dogs were allowed to retrieve them, though the dogs must have been puzzled that there had been no shots. Ann said she fired a few rounds of the cap pistol into the air to make the dogs think she had hit those birds. Surely they believed she was a goddess.

They turned and headed south—Ann with a bag of frozen birds over her shoulder, and the dogs, knowing that the hunt was over now, once again like a team of horses in harness, though wild and prancy.

After an hour of increasing discomfort—Ann's and Gray Owl's hands and feet numb, and ice beginning to form on the dogs' paws, so that the dogs were having to high-step—they came in day's last light to the edge of a wide clearing: a terrain that was remarkable and soothing for its lack of hills. It was a frozen lake, which meant—said Gray Owl—they had drifted west (or perhaps east) by as much as ten miles.

Ann said that Gray Owl looked tired and old and guilty, as would any host who had caused his guest some unasked-for inconvenience. They knelt down and began massaging the dogs' paws and then lit the little stove and held each dog's foot, one at a time, over the tiny blue flame to help it thaw out.

Gray Owl walked out to the edge of the lake ice and kicked at it with his foot, hoping to find fresh water beneath for the dogs; if they ate too much snow, especially after working so hard, they'd get violent diarrhea and might then become too weak to continue home the next day, or the next, or whenever the storm quit.

Ann said that she had barely been able to see Gray Owl's outline through the swirling snow, even though he was less than twenty yards away. He kicked once at the sheet of ice, the vast plate of it, with his heel, then disappeared below the ice.

Ann wanted to believe that she had blinked and lost sight of him, or that a gust of snow had swept past and hidden him, but it had been too fast, too total: she knew that the lake had swallowed him. She was sorry for Gray Owl, she said, and worried for his dogs—afraid they would try to follow his scent down into the icy lake and be lost as well—but what she had been most upset about, she said—to be perfectly honest—was that Gray Owl had been wearing the little daypack with the tent and emergency rations. She had it in her mind to try to save Gray Owl, and to try to keep the dogs from going through the ice, but if he drowned, she was going to have to figure out how to try to get that daypack off the drowned man and set up the wet tent in the blizzard on the snowy prairie and then crawl inside and survive. She would have to go into the water naked, so that when she came back out—if she came back out—she would have dry clothes to put on.

The dogs came galloping up, seeming as large as deer or elk in that dim landscape against which there was nothing else to give the viewer a perspective, and Ann whoaed them right at the lake's edge, where they stopped immediately, as if they had suddenly been cast with a sheet of ice.

Ann knew the dogs would stay there forever, or until she released them, and it troubled her to think that if she drowned, they too would die—that they would stand there motionless, as she had commanded them, for as long as they could, until at some point—days later, perhaps—they would lie down, trembling with exhaustion—they might lick at some snow, for moisture—but that then the snows would cover them, and still they would remain there, chins resting on their front paws, staring straight ahead and unseeing into the storm, wondering where the scent of her had gone.

Ann eased out onto the ice. She followed the tracks until she came to the jagged hole in the ice through which Gray Owl had plunged. She was almost half again lighter than he, but she could feel the ice crackling beneath her own feet. It sounded different, too, in a way she could not place—it did not have the squeaky, percussive resonance of the lake-ice back home—and she wondered if Canadian ice froze differently or just sounded different.

She got down on all fours and crept closer to the hole. It was right at dusk. She peered down into the hole and dimly saw Gray Owl standing down there, waving his arms at her. He did not appear to be swimming. Slowly, she took one glove off and eased her bare hand down into the hole. She could find no water, and, tentatively, she reached deeper.

Gray Owl's hand found hers and he pulled her down in. Ice broke as she fell, but he caught her in his arms. She could smell the wood smoke in his jacket from the alder he burned in his cabin. There was no water at all, and it was warm beneath the ice.

"This happens a lot more than people realize," he said. "It's not really a phenomenon; it's just what happens. A cold snap comes in October, freezes a skin of ice over the lake—it's got to be a shallow one, almost a marsh. Then a snowfall comes, insulating the ice. The lake drains in fall and winter—percolates down through the soil"—he stamped the spongy ground beneath them—"but the ice up top remains. And nobody ever knows any different. People look out at the surface and think, *Aha, a frozen lake*." Gray Owl laughed.

"Did you know it would be like this?" Ann asked.

"No," he said. "I was looking for water. I just got lucky."

Ann walked back to shore beneath the ice to fetch her stove and to release the dogs from their whoa command. The dry lake was only about eight feet deep, but it grew shallow quickly closer to shore, so that Ann had to crouch to keep from bumping her head on the overhead ice, and then crawl; and then there was only space to wriggle, and to emerge she had to break the ice above her by bumping and then battering it with her head and elbows, struggling like some embryonic hatchling; and when she stood up, waist-deep amid sparkling shards of ice—it was nighttime now—the dogs barked ferociously at her, but they remained where she had ordered them. She was surprised at how far off course she was when she climbed out; she had traveled only twenty feet, but already the dogs were twice that far away from her. She knew humans had a poorly evolved, almost nonexistent sense of direction, but this error—over such a short distance—shocked her. It was as if there were in us a thing—an impulse, a catalyst—that denies our ever going straight to another thing. Like dogs working left and right into the wind, she thought, before converging on the scent.

Except that the dogs would not get lost, while she could easily imagine herself and Gray Owl getting lost beneath the lake, walking in circles forever, unable to find even the simplest of things: the shore.

She gathered the stove and dogs. She was tempted to try to go back in the way she had come out—it seemed so easy—but she considered the consequences of getting lost in the other direction, and instead followed her original tracks out to where Gray Owl had first dropped through the ice. It was true night now, and the blizzard was still blowing hard, plastering snow and ice around her face like a mask. The dogs did not want to go down into the hole, so she lowered them to Gray Owl and then climbed gratefully back down into the warmth herself.

The air was a thing of its own—recognizable as air, and breathable as such, but with a taste and odor, an essence, unlike any other air they'd ever breathed. It had a different density to it, so that smaller, shallower breaths were required; there was very much the feeling that if they breathed in too much of the strange, dense air, they would drown.

They wanted to explore the lake, and were thirsty, but it felt like a victory simply to be warm—or rather, not cold—and they were so exhausted that instead they made pallets out of the dead marsh grass that rustled around their ankles, and they slept curled up on the tiniest of hammocks, to keep from getting damp in the pockets and puddles of water that still lingered here and there.

All eight of them slept as if in a nest, heads and arms draped across other ribs and hips; and it was, said Ann, the best and deepest sleep she'd ever had—the sleep of hounds, the sleep of childhood. How long they slept, she never knew, for she wasn't sure, later, how much of their subsequent time they spent wandering beneath the lake, and then up on the prairie, homeward again, but when they awoke, it was still night, or night once more, and clearing, with bright stars visible through the porthole, their point of embarkation; and even from beneath the ice, in certain places where, for whatever reasons—temperature, oxygen content, wind scour—the ice was clear rather than glazed, they could see the spangling of stars, though more dimly; and strangely, rather than seeming to distance them from the stars, this phenomenon seemed to pull them closer, as if they were up in the stars, traveling the Milky Way, or as if the stars were embedded in the ice.

It was very cold outside—up above—and there was a steady stream, a current like a river, of the night's colder, heavier air plunging down though their porthole—as if trying to fill the empty lake with that frozen air—but there was also the hot muck of the earth's massive respirations breathing out warmth and being trapped and protected beneath that ice, so that there were warm currents doing battle with the lone cold current.

The result was that it was breezy down there, and the dogs' noses twitched in their sleep as the images brought by these scents painted themselves across their sleeping brains in the language we call dreams but which, for the dogs, was reality: the scent of an owl *real*, not a dream; the scent of bear, cattail, willow, loon, *real*, even though they were sleeping, and even though those things were not visible, only over the next horizon.

The ice was contracting, groaning and cracking and squeaking up tighter, shrinking beneath the great cold—a concussive, grinding sound, as if giants were walking across the ice above—and it was this sound that awakened them. They snuggled in warmer among the rattly dried yellowing grasses and listened to the tremendous clashings, as if they were safe beneath the sea and were watching waves of starlight sweeping across their hiding place; or as if they were in some place, some position, where they could watch mountains being born.

After a while the moon came up and washed out the stars. The light was blue and silver and seemed, Ann said, to be like a living thing. It filled the sheet of ice just above their heads with a shimmering cobalt light, which again rippled as if the ice were moving, rather than the earth itself, with the moon tracking it—and like deer drawn by gravity getting up in the night to feed for an hour or so before settling back in, Gray Owl and Ann and the dogs rose from their nests of straw and began to travel.

"You didn't—you know—*engage?*" Susan asks, a little mischievously.

Ann shakes her head. "It was too cold," she says.

"But you would have, if it hadn't been so cold, right?" Susan asks, and Ann shrugs.

"He was an old man—in his fifties—he seemed old to me then, and the dogs were around. But yeah, there was something about it that made me think of . . . those things," she says, careful and precise as ever.

They walked a long way, Ann continues, eager to change the subject. The air was damp down there, and whenever they'd get chilled, they'd stop and make a little fire out of a bundle of dry cattails. There were little pockets and puddles of swamp gas pooled in place, and sometimes a spark from the cattails would ignite one of those, and those little pockets of gas would light up like when you toss gas on a fire—explosions of brilliance, like flashbulbs, marsh pockets igniting like falling dominoes, or like children playing hopscotch—until a large enough flash-pocket was reached—sometimes thirty or forty yards away—that the puff of flame would blow a chimney-hole through the ice, venting the other pockets, and the fires would crackle out, the scent of grass smoke sweet in their lungs, and they could feel gusts of warmth from the little flickering fires, and currents of the colder, heavier air sliding down through the new vent-holes and pooling around their ankles. The moonlight would strafe down through those rents in the ice, and shards of moon-ice would be glittering and spinning like diamond-motes in those newly vented columns of moonlight; and they pushed on, still lost, but so alive.

The small explosions were fun, but they frightened the dogs, so Ann and Gray Owl lit twisted bundles of cattails and used them for torches to light their way, rather than building warming fires, though occasionally they would still pass through a pocket of methane and a stray ember would fall from their torches, and the whole chain of fire and light would begin again, culminating once more with a vent-hole being blown open and shards of glittering ice tumbling down into their lair ...

What would it have looked like, seen from above—the orange blurrings of their wandering trail beneath the ice; and what would the sheet of lake-ice itself have looked like that night—throbbing with ice-bound, subterranean blue and orange light of moon and fire? But again, there was no one to view the spectacle: only the travelers themselves, and they had no perspective, no vantage from which to view or judge themselves. They were simply pushing on from one fire to the next, carrying their tiny torches.

They knew they were getting near a shore—the southern shore, they hoped, as they followed the glazed moon's lure above—when the dogs began to encounter shore birds that had somehow found their way beneath the ice through small fissures and rifts and were taking refuge in the cattails. Small winter birds—juncos, nuthatches, chickadees—skittered away from the smoky approach of their torches; only a few late-migrating (or winter-trapped) snipe held tight and steadfast; and the dogs began to race ahead of Gray Owl and Ann, working these familiar scents—blue and silver ghost-shadows of dog muscle weaving ahead through slants of moonlight.

The dogs emitted the odor of adrenaline when they worked, Ann said—a scent like damp, fresh-cut green hay—and with nowhere to vent, the odor was dense and thick around them, so that Ann wondered if it too might be flammable, like the methane—if in the dogs' passions they might literally immolate themselves.

They followed the dogs closely with their torches. The ceiling was low—about eight feet—so that the tips of their torches' flames seared the ice above them, leaving a drip behind them and transforming the milky, almost opaque cobalt and orange ice behind them, wherever they passed, into wandering ribbons of clear ice, translucent to the sky—a script of flame, or buried flame, ice-bound flame—and they hurried to keep up with the dogs.

Now the dogs had the snipe surrounded, as Ann told it, and one by one the dogs went on point, each dog freezing as it pointed to the birds' hiding places, and Gray Owl moved in to flush the birds, which launched themselves with vigor against the roof of the ice above, fluttering like bats; but the snipe were too small, not powerful enough to break through those frozen four inches of water (though they could fly four thousand miles to South America each year and then back to Canada six months later—is freedom a lateral component, or a vertical one?), and as Gray Owl kicked at the clumps of frost-bent cattails where the snipe were hiding and they burst into flight, only to hit their heads on the ice above them, they came tumbling back down, raining limp and unconscious back to their soft grassy nests.

The dogs began retrieving them, carrying them gingerly, delicately—not caring for the taste of snipe, which ate only earthworms—and Ann and Gray

Owl gathered the tiny birds from the dogs, placed them in their pockets, and continued on to the shore, chasing that moon, the ceiling lowering to six feet, then four, then to a crawlspace, and after they had bashed their way out and stepped back out into the frigid air, they tucked the still-unconscious snipe into little crooks in branches, up against the trunks of trees and off the ground, out of harm's way, and passed on, south—as if late in their own migration—while the snipe rested, warm and terrified and heart-fluttering, but saved, for now, against the trunks of those trees.

Long after Ann and Gray Owl and the pack of dogs had passed through, the birds would awaken, their bright, dark eyes luminous in the moonlight, and the first sight they would see would be the frozen marsh before them, with its chain of still-steaming vent-holes stretching back across all the way to the other shore. Perhaps these were birds that had been unable to migrate owing to injuries, or some genetic absence. Perhaps they had tried to migrate in the past but had found either their winter habitat destroyed or the path so fragmented and fraught with danger that it made more sense—to these few birds—to ignore the tuggings of the stars and seasons and instead to try to carve out new lives, new ways of being, even in such a stark and severe landscape: or rather, in a stark and severe period—knowing that lushness and bounty were still retained with that landscape, that it was only a phase, that better days would come. That in fact (the snipe knowing these things with their blood, ten million years in the world) the austere times were the very thing, the very imbalance, that would summon the resurrection of that frozen richness within the soil—if indeed that richness, that magic, that hope, did still exist beneath the ice and snow. Spring would come like its own green fire, if only the injured ones could hold on.

And what would the snipe think or remember, upon reawakening and finding themselves still in that desolate position, desolate place and time, but still alive, and with hope?

Would it seem to them that a thing like grace had passed through, as they slept—that a slender winding river of it had passed through and rewarded them for their faith and endurance?

Believing, stubbornly, that that green land beneath them would blossom once more. Maybe not soon; but again.

If the snipe survived, they would be among the first to see it. Perhaps they believed that the pack of dogs, and Gray Owl's and Ann's advancing torches, had only been one of winter's dreams. Even with the proof—the scribings—of grace's passage before them—the vent-holes still steaming—perhaps they believed it was a dream.

Gray Owl, Ann, and the dogs headed south for half a day until they reached the snow-scoured road on which they'd parked. The road looked different, Ann said, buried beneath snowdrifts, and they didn't know whether to turn east or west. The dogs chose west, and Gray Owl and Ann followed them. Two hours later they were back at their truck, and that night they were back at Gray Owl's cabin; by the next night Ann was home again.

She says that even now she still sometimes has dreams about being beneath the ice—about living beneath the ice—and that it seems to her as if she was down there for much longer than a day and a night; that instead she might have been gone for years.

It was twenty years ago, when it happened. Gray Owl has since died, and all those dogs are dead now, too. She is the only one who still carries—in the flesh, at any rate—the memory of that passage.

Ann would never discuss such a thing, but I suspect that it, that one day and night, helped give her a model for what things were like for her dogs when they were hunting and when they went on point: how the world must have appeared to them when they were in that trance, that blue zone, where the odors of things wrote their images across the dogs' hot brainpans. A zone where sight, and the appearance of things—*surfaces*—disappeared, and where instead their essence—the heat molecules of scent—was revealed, illuminated, circumscribed, possessed.

I suspect that she holds that knowledge—the memory of that one day and night—especially since she is now the sole possessor—as tightly, and securely, as one might clench some bright small gem in one's fist: not a gem given to one by some favored or beloved individual but, even more valuable, some gem found while out on a walk—perhaps by happenstance, or perhaps by some unavoidable rhythm of fate—and hence containing great magic, great strength.

Such is the nature of the kinds of people living, scattered here and there, in this valley.

Richard Bausch

THE FIREMAN'S WIFE

RICHARD BAUSCH (1945–) is the author of ten novels and seven collections of stories, including the novels *Rebel Powers, Violence, The Last Good Time, In the Night Season, Hello to the Cannibals,* and the recently published *Thanksgiving Night;* and the collections *Rare & Endangered Species, Selected Stories* (Modern Library), *Someone to Watch Over Me, The Stories of Richard Bausch,* and *Wives & Lovers: 3 Short Novels.* His short fiction has appeared in *The Atlantic Monthly, Esquire, The New Yorker, GQ, Playboy, Harper's,* and other magazines, and is widely anthologized, notably in *Best American Short Stories, The O. Henry Prize Stories, New Stories from the South,* and *Pushcart Prize Stories.* Chancellor of the Fellowship of Southern Writers, he is the recipient of the 2004 PEN/Malamud Award for Excellence in short fiction, and he holds the Moss Chair of Excellence in the Writing Program at the University of Memphis.

Jane's husband, Martin, works for the fire department. He's on four days, off three; on three, off four. It's the kind of shift work that allows plenty of time for sustained recreation, and during the off times Martin likes to do a lot of socializing with his two shift mates, Wally Harmon and Teddy Lynch. The three of them are like brothers: they bicker and squabble and compete in a friendly way about everything, including their common hobby, which is the making and flying of model airplanes. Martin is fanatical about it—spends way too much money on the two planes he owns, which are on the worktable in the garage, and which seem to require as much maintenance as the real article. Among the arguments between Jane and her husband—about money, lack of time alone together, and housework—there have been some about the model planes, but Jane can't say or do much without sounding like a poor sport: Wally's wife, Milly, loves watching the boys, as she calls them, fly their planes, and Teddy Lynch's ex-wife, before they were divorced, had loved the model planes too. In a way, Jane is the outsider here: Milly Harmon has known Martin most of his life, and Teddy Lynch was once point guard to Martin's power forward on their high school basketball team. Jane is relatively new, having come to Illinois from Virginia only two years ago, when Martin brought her back with him from his reserve training there.

This evening, a hot September twilight, they're sitting on lawn chairs in the

33

dim light of the coals in Martin's portable grill, talking about games. Martin and Teddy want to play Risk, though they're already arguing about the rules. Teddy says that a European version of the game contains a wrinkle that makes it more interesting, and Martin is arguing that the game itself was derived from some French game.

"Well, go get it," Teddy says, "and I'll show you. I'll bet it's in the instructions."

"Don't get that out now," Jane says to Martin.

"It's too long," Wally Harmon says.

"What if we play cards," Martin says.

"Martin doesn't want to lose his bet," Teddy says.

"We don't have any bets, Teddy."

"Okay, so let's bet."

"Let's play cards," Martin says. "Wally's right. Risk takes too long."

"I feel like conquering the world," Teddy says.

"Oh, Teddy," Milly Harmon says. "Please shut up."

She's expecting. She sits with her legs out, holding her belly as though it were unattached, separate from her. The child will be her first, and she's excited and happy; she glows, as if she knows everyone's admiring her.

Jane thinks Milly is spreading it on a little thick at times: lately all she wants to talk about is her body and what it's doing.

"I had a dream last night," Milly says now. "I dreamed that I was pregnant. Big as a house. And I woke up and I was. What I want to know is, was that a nightmare?"

"How did you feel in the dream?" Teddy asks her.

"I said. Big as a house."

"Right, but was it bad or good?"

"How would you feel if you were big as a house?"

"Well, that would depend on what the situation was."

"The situation is, you're big as a house."

"Yeah, but what if somebody was chasing me? I'd want to be big, right?"

"Oh, Teddy, please shut up."

"I had a dream," Wally says. "A bad dream. I dreamed I died. I mean, you know, I was dead—and what was weird was that I was also the one who had to call Milly to tell her about it."

"Oh, God," Milly says. "Don't talk about this."

"It was weird. I got killed out at sea or something. Drowned, I guess. I remember I was standing on the deck of this ship talking to somebody about how it went down. And then I was calling Milly to tell her. And the thing is, I talked like a stranger would—you know, 'I'm sorry to inform you that your husband went down at sea.' It was weird."

"How did you feel when you woke up?" Martin says.

"I was scared. I didn't know who I was for a couple of seconds."

"Look," Milly says, "I don't want to talk about dreams."

"Let's talk about good dreams," Jane says. "I had a good dream. I was fishing with my father out at a creek—some creek that felt like a real place. Like if I ever really did go fishing with my father, this is where we would have fished when I was small."

"What?" Martin says after a pause, and everyone laughs.

"Well," Jane says, feeling the blood rise in her cheeks, "I never—my father died when I was just a baby."

"I dreamed I got shot once," Teddy says. "Guy shot me with a forty-five automatic as I was running downstairs. I fell and hit bottom, too. I could feel the cold concrete on the side of my face before I woke up."

Milly Harmon sits forward a little and says to Wally, "Honey, why did you have to tell about having a dream like that? Now *I'm* going to dream about it, I just know it."

"I think we all ought to call it a night," Jane says. "You guys have to get up at six o'clock in the morning."

"What're you talking about?" Martin says. "We're going to play cards, aren't we?"

"I thought we were going to play Risk," Teddy says.

"All right," Martin says, getting out of his chair. "Risk it is."

Milly groans, and Jane gets up and follows Martin into the house. "Honey," she says. "Not Risk. Come on. We'd need four hours at least."

He says over his shoulder, "So then we need four hours."

"Martin, I'm tired."

He's leaning up into the hall closet, where the games are stacked. He brings the Risk game down and turns, holding it in both hands like a tray. "Look, where do you get off, telling everybody to go home the way you did?"

She stands there staring at him.

"These people are our friends, Jane."

"I just said I thought we ought to call it a night."

"Well *don't* say—all right? It's embarrassing."

He goes around her and back out to the patio. The screen door slaps twice in the jamb. She waits a moment and then moves through the house to the bedroom. She brushes her hair, thinks about getting out of her clothes. Martin's uniforms are lying across the foot of the bed. She picks them up, walks into the living room with them and drapes them over the back of the easy chair.

"Jane," Martin calls from the patio. "Are you playing or not?"

"Come on, Jane," Milly says. "Don't leave me alone out here."

"What color armies do you want?" Martin asks.

She goes to the patio door and looks out at them. Martin has lighted the tiki lamps; everyone's sitting at the picnic table in the moving firelight. "Come on,"

Martin says, barely concealing his irritation. She can hear it, and she wants to react to it—wants to let him know that she is hurt. But they're all waiting for her, so she steps out and takes her place at the table. She chooses green for her armies, and she plays the game to lose, attacking in all directions until her forces are so badly depleted that when Wally begins to make his own move she's the first to lose all her armies. This takes more than an hour. When she's out of the game, she sits for a while, cheering Teddy on against Martin, who is clearly going to win; finally she excuses herself and goes back into the house. The glow from the tiki lamps makes weird patterns on the kitchen wall. She pours herself a glass of water and drinks it down; then she pours more and swallows some aspirin. Teddy sees this as he comes in for more beer, and he grasps her by the elbow and asks if she wants something a little better than aspirin for a head-ache.

"Like what?" she says, smiling at him. She's decided a smile is what one offers under such circumstances; one laughs things off, pretends not to notice the glazed look in the other person's eyes.

Teddy is staring at her, not quite smiling. Finally he puts his hands on her shoulders and says, "What's the matter, lady?"

"Nothing," she says. "I have a headache. I took some aspirin."

"I've got some stuff," he says. "It makes America beautiful. Want some?"

She says, "Teddy."

"No problem," he says. He holds both hands up and backs away from her. Then he turns and is gone. She hears him begin to tease Martin about the French rules of the game. Martin is winning. He wants Wally Harmon to keep playing, and Wally wants to quit. Milly and Teddy are talking about flying the model airplanes. They know about an air show in Danville on Saturday. They all keep playing and talking, and for a long time Jane watches them from the screen door. She smokes half a pack of cigarettes, and she paces a little. She drinks three glasses of orange juice, and finally she walks into the bedroom and lies down with her face in her hands. Her forehead feels hot. She's thinking about the next four days, when Martin will be gone and she can have the house to herself. She hasn't been married even two years, and she feels crowded; she's depressed and tired every day. She never has enough time to herself. And yet when she's alone, she feels weak and afraid. Now she hears someone in the hallway and she sits up, smooths her hair back from her face. Milly Harmon comes in with her hands cradling her belly.

"Ah," Milly says. "A bed." She sits down next to Jane and then leans back on her hands. "I'm beat," she says.

"I have a headache," Jane says.

Milly nods. Her expression seems to indicate how unimportant she finds this, as if Jane had told her she'd already got over a cold or something. "They're in the garage now," she says.

"Who?"

"Teddy, Wally, Martin. Martin conquered the world."

"What're they doing?" Jane asks. "It's almost midnight."

"Everybody's going to be miserable in the morning," Milly says.

Jane is quiet.

"Oh," Milly says, looking down at herself. "He kicked. Want to feel it?"

She takes Jane's hand and puts it on her belly. Jane feels movement under her fingers, something very slight, like one heartbeat.

"Wow," she says. She pulls her hand away.

"Listen," Milly says. "I know we can all be overbearing sometimes. Martin doesn't realize some of his responsibilities yet. Wally was the same way."

"I just have this headache," Jane says. She doesn't want to talk about it, doesn't want to get into it. Even when she talks to her mother on the phone and her mother asks how things are, she says it's all fine. She has nothing she wants to confide.

"You feel trapped, don't you," Milly says.

Jane looks at her.

"Don't you?"

"No."

"Okay—you just have a headache."

"I do," Jane says.

Milly sits forward a little, folds her hands over the roundness of her belly. "This baby's jumping all over the place."

Jane is silent.

"Do you believe my husband and that awful dream? I wish he hadn't told us about it—now I know I'm going to dream something like it. You know pregnant women and dreams. I begin to shake just thinking of it."

"Try not to think of it," Jane says.

Milly waits a moment and then clears her throat and says, "You know, for a while there after Wally and I were married, I thought maybe I'd made a mistake. I remember realizing that I didn't like the way he laughed. I mean, let's face it, Wally laughs like a hyena. And somehow that took on all kinds of importance—you know, I had to absolutely like everything about him or I couldn't like anything. Have you ever noticed the way he laughs?"

Jane has never really thought about it. But she says nothing now. She simply nods.

"But you know," Milly goes on, "all I had to do was wait. Just—you know, wait for love to come around and surprise me again."

"Milly, I have a headache. I mean, what do you think is wrong, anyway?"

"Okay," Milly says, rising.

Then Jane wonders whether the other woman has been put up to this conversation. "Hey," she says, "did Martin say something to you?"

"What would Martin say?"

"I don't know. I mean, I really don't know, Milly. Jesus Christ, can't a person have a simple headache?"

"Okay," Milly says. "Okay."

"I like the way everyone talks around me here, you know it?"

"Nobody's talking around you—"

"I think it's wonderful how close you all are."

"All right," Milly says, standing there with her hands folded under the bulge of her belly. "You just look so unhappy these days."

"Look," Jane says, "I have a headache, all right? I'm going to go to bed. I mean, the only way I can get rid of it is to lie down in the dark and be very quiet—okay?"

"Sure, honey," Milly says.

"So—goodnight, then."

"Right," Milly says. "Goodnight." She steps toward Jane and kisses her on the cheek. "I'll tell Martin to call it a night. I know Wally'll be miserable to-morrow."

"It's because they can take turns sleeping on shift," Jane says.

"I'll tell them," Milly says, going down the hall.

Jane steps out of her jeans, pulls her blouse over her head and crawls under the sheets, which are cool and fresh and crisp. She turns the light off and closes her eyes. She can't believe how bad it is. She hears them all saying goodnight, and she hears Martin shutting the doors and turning off the lights. In the dark she waits for him to get to her. She's very still, lying on her back with her hands at her sides. He goes into the bathroom at the end of the hall. She hears him cough, clear his throat. He's cleaning his teeth. Then he comes to the entrance of the bedroom and stands in the light of the hall.

"I know you're awake," he says.

She doesn't answer.

"Jane," he says.

She says, "What?"

"Are you mad at me?"

"No."

"Then what's wrong?"

"I have a headache."

"You always have a headache."

"I'm not going to argue now, Martin. So you can say what you want."

He moves toward her, is standing by the bed. He's looming above her in the dark. "Teddy had some dope."

She says, "I know. He offered me some."

"I'm flying," Martin says.

She says nothing.

"Let's make love."

"Martin," she says. Her heart is beating fast. He moves a little, staggers taking off his shirt. He's so big and quick and powerful; nothing fazes him. When he's like this, the feeling she has is that he might do anything. "Martin," she says.

"All right," he says. "I won't. Okay? You don't have to worry your little self about it."

"Look," she says.

But he's already headed into the hall.

"Martin," she says.

He's in the living room. He turns the television on loud. A rerun of *Kojak*. She hears Theo calling someone sweetheart. "Sweetheart," Martin says. When she goes to him, she finds that he's opened a beer and is sitting on the couch with his legs out. The beer is balanced on his stomach.

"Martin," she says. "You have to start your shift in less than five hours."

He holds the beer up. "Baby," he says.

In the morning he's sheepish, obviously in pain. He sits at the kitchen table with his hands up to his head while she makes coffee and hard-boiled eggs. She has to go to work, too, at a car dealership in town. All day she sits behind a window with a circular hole in the glass, where people line up to pay for whatever the dealer sells or provides, including mechanical work, parts, license plates, used cars, rental cars and, of course, new cars. Her day is long and exhausting, and she's already feeling as though she worked all night. The booth she has to sit in is right off the service bay area, and the smell of exhaust and grease is everywhere. Everything seems coated with a film of grime. She's standing at her sink, looking at the sun coming up past the trees beyond her street, and without thinking about it she puts the water on and washes her hands. The idea of the car dealership is like something clinging to her skin.

"Jesus," Martin says. He can't eat much.

She's drying her hands on a paper towel.

"Listen," he says, "I'm sorry, okay?"

"Sorry?" she says.

"Don't press it, all right? You know what I mean."

"Okay," she says, and when he gets up and comes over to put his arms around her, she feels his difference from her. She kisses him. They stand there.

"Four days," he says.

When Teddy and Wally pull up in Wally's new pickup, she stands in the kitchen door and waves at them. Martin walks down the driveway, carrying his tote bag of uniforms and books to read. He turns around and blows her a kiss. This morning is like so many other mornings. They drive off. She goes back into the bedroom and makes the bed, and puts his dirty uniforms in the wash.

She showers and chooses something to wear. It's quiet. She puts the radio on and then decides she'd rather have the silence. After she's dressed, she stands at the back door and looks out at the street. Children are walking to school in little groups of friends. She thinks about the four days ahead. What she needs is to get into the routine and stop thinking so much. She knows that problems in a marriage are worked out over time.

Before she leaves for work she goes out into the garage to look for signs of Teddy's dope. She doesn't want someone stumbling on incriminating evidence. On the worktable along the back wall are Martin's model planes. She walks over and stands staring at them. She stands very still, as if waiting for something to move.

At work her friend Eveline smokes one cigarette after another, apologizing for each one. During Martin's shifts Jane spends a lot of time with Eveline, who is twenty-nine and single and wants very much to be married. The problem is she can't find anyone. Last year, when Jane was first working at the dealership, she got Eveline a date with Teddy Lynch. Teddy took Eveline to Lum's for hot dogs and beer, and they had fun at first. But then Eveline got drunk and passed out—put her head down on her arms and went to sleep like a child asked to take a nap in school. Teddy put her in a cab for home and then called Martin to laugh about the whole thing. Eveline was so humiliated by the experience that she goes out of her way to avoid Teddy—doesn't want anything to do with him or with any of Martin's friends, or with Martin, for that matter. She will come over to the house only when she knows Martin is away at work. And when Martin calls the dealership and she answers the phone, she's very stiff and formal, and she hands the phone quickly to Jane.

Today things aren't very busy, and they work a crossword together, making sure to keep it out of sight of the salesmen, who occasionally wander in to waste time with them. Eveline plays her radio and hums along with some of the songs. It's a long, slow day, and when Martin calls Jane feels herself growing anxious—something is moving in the pit of her stomach.

"Are you still mad at me?" he says.

"No," she tells him.

"Say you love me."

"I love you."

"Everybody's asleep here," he says. "I wish you were with me."

She says, "Right."

"I do," he says.

"Okay."

"You don't believe me?"

"I said *okay*."

"Is it busy today?" he asks.

"Not too."

"You're bored, then."

"A little," she says.

"How's the headache?"

"Just the edge of one."

"I'm sorry," he says.

"It's not your fault."

"Sometimes I feel like it is."

"How's *your* head?" she says.

"Terrible."

"Poor boy."

"I wish something would happen around here," he says. "A lot of guys snoring."

"Martin," she says, "I've got to go."

"Okay."

"You want me to stop by tonight?" she asks.

"If you want to."

"Maybe I will."

"You don't have to."

She thinks about him where he is: she imagines him, comfortable, sitting on a couch in front of a television. Sometimes, when nothing's going on, he watches all the soaps. He was hooked on *General Hospital* for a while. That he's her husband seems strange, and she thinks of the nights she's lain in his arms, whispering his name over and over, putting her hands in his hair and rocking with him in the dark. She tells him she loves him, and hangs the phone up. Eveline makes a gesture of frustration and envy.

"Nuts," Eveline says. "Nuts to you and your lovey-dovey stuff."

Jane is sitting in a bath of cold inner light, trying to think of her husband as someone she recognizes.

"Let's do something tonight," Eveline says. "Maybe I'll get lucky."

"I'm not going with you if you're going to be giving strange men the eye," Jane says. She hasn't quite heard herself. She's surprised when Eveline reacts.

"How dare you say a nasty thing like that? I don't know if I want to go out with someone who doesn't think any more of me than *that*."

"I'm sorry," Jane says, patting the other woman's wrist. "I didn't mean anything by it, really. I was just teasing."

"Well, don't tease that way. It hurts my feelings."

"I'm sorry," Jane says again. "Please—really." She feels near crying.

"Well, okay," Eveline says. "Don't get upset. I'm half teasing myself."

Jane sniffles, wipes her eyes with the back of one hand.

"What's wrong, anyway?" Eveline says.

"Nothing," Jane says. "I hurt your feelings."

• • •

That evening they ride in Eveline's car over to Shakey's for a pizza, and then stroll down to the end of the block, to the new mini-mall on Lincoln Avenue. The night is breezy and warm. A storm is building over the town square. They window-shop for a while, and finally they stop at a new corner café, to sit in a booth by the windows, drinking beer. Across the street one of the movies has ended, and people are filing out, or waiting around. A few of them head this way.

"They don't look like they enjoyed the movie very much," Eveline says.

"Maybe they did, and they're just depressed to be back in the real world."

"Look, what is it?" Eveline asks suddenly.

Jane returns her gaze.

"What's wrong?"

"Nothing."

"Something's wrong," Eveline says.

Two boys from the high school come past, and one of them winks at Jane. She remembers how it was in high school—the games of flirtation and pursuit, of ignoring some people and noticing others. That seemed like such an unbearable time, and it's already years ago. She watches Eveline light yet another cigarette and feels very much older than her own memory of herself. She sees the person she is now, with Martin, somewhere years away, happy, with children, and with different worries. It's a vivid daydream. She sits there fabricating it, feeling it for what it is and feeling, too, that nothing will change: the Martin she sees in the daydream is nothing like the man she lives with. She thinks of Milly Harmon, pregnant and talking about waiting to be surprised by love.

"I think I'd like to have a baby," she says. She hadn't known she would say it.

Eveline says, "Yuck," blowing smoke.

"Yuck," Jane says. "That's great. Great response, Evie."

They're quiet awhile. Beyond the square the clouds break up into tatters, and lightning strikes out. They hear thunder, and the smell of rain is in the air. The trees in the little park across from the theater move in the wind, and leaves blow out of them.

"Wouldn't you like to have a family?" Jane says.

"Sure."

"Well, the last time I checked, that meant having babies."

"Yuck," Eveline says again.

"Oh, all right—you just mean because of the pain and all."

"I mean yuck."

"Well, what does 'yuck' mean, okay?"

"What *is* the matter with you?" Eveline says. "What difference does it make?"

"I'm trying to have a normal conversation," Jane says, "and I'm getting these weird one-word answers, that's all. I mean what's 'yuck,' anyway? What's it mean?"

"Let's say it means I don't want to talk about having babies."

"I wasn't talking about you."

Each is now a little annoyed with the other. Jane has noticed that whenever she talks about anything that might border on plans for the future, the other woman becomes irritatingly sardonic and closemouthed. Eveline sits there smoking her cigarette and watching the storm come. From beyond the square they hear sirens, which seem to multiply. The whole city seems to be mobilizing. Jane thinks of Martin out there where all those alarms are converging. How odd to know where your husband is by a sound everyone hears. She remembers lying awake nights early in the marriage, hearing sirens and worrying about what might happen. And now, through a slanting sheet of rain, as though something in these thoughts has produced her, Milly Harmon comes, holding an open magazine above her head. She sees Jane and Eveline in the window and waves at them. "Oh, God," Eveline says. "Isn't that Milly Harmon?"

Milly comes into the café and stands for a moment, shaking water from herself. Her hair is wet, as are her shoulders. She pushes her hair away from her forehead, and wipes the rain away with the back of one hand. Then she walks over and says, "Hi, honey," to Jane, bending down to kiss her on the side of the face. Jane manages to seem glad to see her. "You remember my friend Eveline from work," she says.

"I think I do, sure," Milly says.

"Maybe not," Eveline says.

"No, I think I do."

"I have one of those faces that remind you of somebody you never met," Eveline says.

Jane covers this with a laugh as Milly settles on her side of the booth.

Milly is breathless, all bustle and worry, arranging herself, getting comfortable. "Do you hear that?" she says about the sirens. "I swear, it must be a big one. I wish I didn't hear the sirens. It makes me so jumpy and scared. Wally would never forgive me if I did, but I wish I could get up the nerve to go see what it is."

"So," Eveline says, blowing smoke, "how's the baby coming along?"

Milly looks down at herself. "Sleeping now, I think."

"Wally—is it Wally?"

"Wally, yes."

"Wally doesn't let you chase ambulances?"

"I don't chase ambulances."

"Well, I mean—you aren't allowed to go see what's what when you hear sirens?"

"I don't want to see."

"I guess not."

"He's seen some terrible things. They all have. It must be terrible sometimes."

"Right," Eveline says. "It must be terrible."

Milly waves her hand in front of her face. "I wish you wouldn't smoke."

"I was smoking before you came," Eveline says. "I didn't know you were coming."

Milly looks confused for a second. Then she sits back a little and folds her hands on the table. She's chosen to ignore Eveline. She looks at Jane and says, "I had that dream last night."

Jane says, "What dream?"

"That Wally was gone."

Jane says nothing.

"But it wasn't the same, really. He'd left me, you know—the baby was born and he'd just gone off. I was so mad at him. And I had this crying little baby in my lap."

Eveline swallows the last of her beer and then gets up and goes out to stand near the line of wet pavement at the edge of the awninged sidewalk.

"What's the matter with her?" Milly asks.

"She's just unhappy."

"Did I say something wrong?"

"No—really. It's nothing," Jane says.

She pays for the beer. Milly talks to her for a while, but Jane has a hard time concentrating on much of anything now, with sirens going and Eveline standing out there at the edge of the sidewalk. Milly goes on, talking nervously about Wally's leaving her in her dream and how funny it is that she woke up mad at him, that she had to wait a few minutes and get her head clear before she could kiss him good morning.

"I've got to go," Jane says. "I came in Eveline's car."

"Oh, I'm sorry—sure. I just stepped in out of the rain myself."

They join Eveline outside, and Milly says she's got to go get her nephews before they knock down the ice-cream parlor. Jane and Eveline watch her walk away in the rain, and Eveline says, "Jesus."

"She's just scared," Jane says. "God, leave her alone."

"I don't mean anything by it," Eveline says. "A little malice, maybe."

Jane says nothing. They stand there watching the rain and lightning, and soon they're talking about people at work, the salesmen and the boys in the parts shop. They're relaxed now; the sirens have stopped and the tension between them has lifted. They laugh about one salesman who's apparently interested in Eveline. He's a married man—an overweight, balding, middle-aged Texan who wears snakeskin boots and a string tie, and who has an enormous fake-diamond ring on the little finger of his left hand. Eveline calls him Disco Bill. And yet Jane thinks her friend may be secretly attracted to him. She teases her about this, or begins to, and then a clap of thunder so frightens them both that they laugh about it, off and on, through the rest of the evening. They wind up visiting Eveline's parents, who live only a block from the café. Eveline's parents have been married almost thirty years, and, sitting in their living room, Jane looks at their things—the love seat and the antique chairs, the handsome grandfather clock in the hall, the paintings. The place has a lovely *tended* look about it. Everything seems to stand for the kind of life she wants for herself: an attentive, loving husband; children; and a quiet house with a clock that chimes. She knows this is all very dreamy and childish, and yet she looks at Eveline's parents, those people with their almost thirty years' love, and her heart aches. She drinks four glasses of white wine and realizes near the end of the visit that she's talking too much, laughing too loudly.

It's very late when she gets home. She lets herself in the side door of the house and walks through the rooms, turning on all the lights, as is her custom—she wants to be sure no one is hiding in any of the nooks and crannies. Tonight she looks at everything and feels demeaned by it. Martin's clean uniforms are lying across the back of the lounge chair in the living room. The TV and the TV trays are in one corner, next to the coffee table, which is a gift from Martin's parents, something they bought back in the fifties, before Martin was born. Martin's parents live on a farm ten miles outside town, and for the past year Jane has had to spend Sundays out there, sitting in that living room with its sparse, starved look, listening to Martin's father talk about the weather, or what he had to eat for lunch, or the wrestling matches he watches on TV. He's a kindly man but he has nothing whatever of interest to say, and he seems to know it—his own voice always seems to surprise him at first, as if some profound inner silence had been broken; he pauses, seems to gather himself, and then continues with the considered, slow cadences of oration. He's tall and lean and powerful looking; he wears coveralls, and he reminds Jane of those pictures of hungry, bewildered men in the Dust Bowl thirties—with their sad, straight, combed hair and their desperation. Yet he's a man who seems quite certain about things, quite calm and satisfied. His wife fusses around him, making sure of his comfort, and he speaks to her in exactly the same soft, sure tones he uses with Jane.

Now, sitting in her own living room, thinking about this man, her father-in-law, Jane realizes that she can't stand another Sunday afternoon listening to him talk. It comes to her like a bad premonition, and quite suddenly, with a kind of tidal shifting inside her, she feels the full weight of her unhappiness. For the first time it seems unbearable, something that might drive her out of her mind. She breathes, swallows, closes her eyes and opens them. She looks at her own reflection in one of the darkened windows of the kitchen, and then she finds herself in the bedroom, pulling her things out of the closet and throwing them on the bed. Something about this is a little frantic, as though each motion fed some impulse to go further, go through with it—use this night, make her way somewhere else. For a long time she works, getting the clothes out where she can see them. She's lost herself in the practical matter of getting packed. She can't decide what to take, and then she can't find a suitcase or an overnight bag. Finally she settles on one of Martin's travel bags, from when he was in the reserves. She's hurrying, stuffing everything into the bag, and when the bag is almost full she stops, feeling spent and out of breath. She sits down at her dressing table for a moment, and now she wonders if perhaps this is all the result of what she's had to drink. The alcohol is wearing off. She has the beginning of a headache. But she knows that whatever she decides to do should be done in the light of day, not now, at night. At last she gets up from the chair and lies down on the bed to think. She's dizzy. Her mind swims. She can't think, so she remains where she is, lying in the tangle of clothes she hasn't packed yet. Perhaps half an hour goes by. She wonders how long this will go on. And then she's asleep. She's nowhere, not even dreaming.

She wakes to the sound of voices. She sits up and tries to get her eyes to focus, tries to open them wide enough to see in the light. The imprint of the wrinkled clothes is in the skin of her face; she can feel it with her fingers. And then she's watching as two men bring Martin in through the front door and help him lie down on the couch. It's all framed in the perspective of the hallway and the open bedroom door, and she's not certain that it's actually happening.

"Martin?" she murmurs, getting up, moving toward them. She stands in the doorway of the living room, rubbing her eyes and trying to clear her head. The two men are standing over her husband, who says something in a pleading voice to one of them. He's lying on his side on the couch, both hands bandaged, a bruise on the side of his face as if something had spilled there.

"Martin," Jane says.

And the two men move, as if startled by her voice. She realizes she's never seen them before. One of them, the younger one, is already explaining. They're from another company. "We were headed back this way," he says, "and we thought it'd be better if you didn't hear anything over the phone." While he talks, the older one is leaning over Martin, going on about insurance. He's a big square-shouldered man with an extremely rubbery look to his face. Jane notices this, notices the masklike quality of it, and she begins to tremble. Everything is oddly exaggerated—something is being said, they're telling her that Martin burned his hands, and another voice is murmuring something. Both men go on talking, apologizing, getting ready to leave her there. She's not fully awake. The lights in the room hurt her eyes; she feels a little sick to her stomach. The two men go out on the porch and then look back through the screen. "You take it easy, now," the younger one says to Jane. She closes the door, understands that what she's been hearing under the flow of the past few moments is Martin's voice muttering her name, saying something. She walks over to him.

"Jesus," he says. "It's awful. I burned my hands and I didn't even know it. I didn't even feel it."

She says, "Tell me what happened."

"God," he says. "Wally Harmon's dead. God. I saw it happen."

"Milly—" she begins. She can't speak.

He's crying. She moves to the entrance of the kitchen and turns to look at him. "I saw Milly tonight." The room seems terribly small to her.

"The Van Pickel Lumberyard went up. The warehouse. Jesus."

She goes into the kitchen and runs water. Outside the window above the sink she sees the dim street, the shadows of houses without light. She drinks part of a glass of water and then pours the rest down the sink. Her throat is still very dry. When she goes back into the living room, she finds him lying on his side, facing the wall.

"Martin?" she says.

"What?"

But she can't find anything to tell him. She says, "God—poor Milly." Then she makes her way into the bedroom and begins putting away the clothes. She doesn't hear him get up, and she's startled to find him standing in the doorway, staring at her.

"What're you doing?" he asks.

She faces him, at a loss—and it's her hesitation that gives him his answer.

"Jane?" he says, looking at the travel bag.

"Look," she tells him, "I had a little too much to drink tonight."

He just stares at her.

"Oh, this," she manages. "I—I was just going through what I have to wear." But it's too late. "Jesus," he says, turning from her a little.

"Martin," she says.

"What."

"Does—did somebody tell Milly?"

He nods. "Teddy. Teddy stayed with her. She was crazy. Crazy."

He looks at his hands. It's as if he just remembered them. They're wrapped tight; they look like two white clubs. "Jesus, Jane, are you—" He stops, shakes his head. "Jesus."

"Don't," she says.

"Without even talking to me about it—"

"Martin, this is not the time to talk about anything."

He's quiet a moment, standing there in the doorway. "I keep seeing it," he says. "I keep seeing Wally's face. The—the way his foot jerked. His foot jerked like with electricity and he was—oh, Christ, he was already dead."

"Oh, don't," she says. "Please. Don't talk. Stop picturing it."

"They gave me something to make me sleep," he says. "And I won't sleep." He wanders back into the living room. A few minutes later she goes to him there and finds that whatever the doctors gave him has worked. He's lying on his back, and he looks smaller somehow, his bandaged hands on his chest, his face pinched with grief, with whatever he's dreaming. He twitches and mutters something and moans. She turns the light off and tiptoes back to the bedroom. She's the one who won't sleep. She gets into the bed and huddles there, leaving the light on. Outside the wind gets up—another storm rolls in off the plains. She listens as the rain begins, and hears the far-off drumming of thunder. The whole night seems deranged. She thinks of Wally Harmon, dead out in the blowing, rainy dark. And then she remembers Milly and her bad dreams, how she looked coming from the downpour, the wet street, with the magazine held over her head—her body so rounded, so weighted down with her baby, her love, the love she had waited for, that she said had surprised her. These events are too much to think about, too awful to imagine. The world seems cruelly immense now, and remorselessly itself. When Martin groans in the other room, she wishes he'd stop, and then she imagines that it's another time, that she's just awakened from a dream and is trying to sleep while they all sit in her living room and talk the hours of the night away.

In the morning she's awake first. She gets up and wraps herself in a robe and then shuffles into the kitchen and puts coffee on. For a minute it's like any other morning. She sits at the table to wait for the coffee water to boil. He comes in like someone entering a stranger's kitchen—his movements are tentative, almost shy. She's surprised to see that he's still in his uniform. He says, "I need you to help me go to the bathroom. I can't get my pants undone." He starts trying to work his belt loose.

"Wait," she says. "Here, hold on."

"I have to get out of these clothes, Jane. I think they smell like smoke."

"Let me do it," she says.

"Milly's in the hospital—they had to put her under sedation."

"Move your hands out of the way," Jane says to him.

She has to help with everything, and when the time comes for him to eat, she has to feed him. She spoons scrambled eggs into his mouth and holds the coffee cup to his lips, and when that's over with, she wipes his mouth and chin with a damp napkin. Then she starts bathwater running and helps him out of his underclothes. They work silently, and with a kind of embarrassment, until he's sitting down and the water is right. When she begins to run a soapy rag over his back, he utters a small sound of satisfaction and comfort. But then he's crying again. He wants to talk about Wally Harmon's death. He says he has to. He tells her that a piece of hot metal the size of an arrow dropped from the roof of the Van Pickel warehouse and hit poor Wally Harmon on the top of the back.

"It didn't kill him right away," he says, sniffling. "Oh, Jesus. He looked right at me and asked if I thought he'd be all right. We were talking about it, honey. He reached up—he—over his shoulder. He took ahold of it for a second. Then he—then he looked at me and said he could feel it down in his stomach."

"Don't think about it," Jane says.

"Oh, God." He's sobbing. "God."

"Martin, honey—"

"I've done the best I could," he says. "Haven't I?"

"Shhh," she says, bringing the warm rag over his shoulders and wringing it, so that the water runs down his back.

They're quiet again. Together they get him out of the tub, and then she dries him off, helps him into a pair of jeans.

"Thanks," he says, not looking at her. Then he says, "Jane."

She's holding his shirt out for him, waiting for him to turn and put his arms into the sleeves. She looks at him.

"Honey," he says.

"I'm calling in," she tells him. "I'll call Eveline. We'll go be with Milly."

"Last night," he says.

She looks straight at him.

He hesitates, glances down. "I—I'll try and do better." He seems about to cry again. For some reason this makes her feel abruptly very irritable and nervous. She turns from him, walks into the living room and begins putting the sofa back in order. When he comes to the doorway and says her name, she doesn't answer, and he walks through to the kitchen door.

"What're you doing?" she says to him.

"Can you give me some water?"

She moves into the kitchen and he follows her. She runs water, to get it cold, and he stands at her side. When the glass is filled, she holds it to his mouth. He swallows, and she takes the glass away. "If you want to talk about anything—" he says.

"Why don't you try to sleep awhile?" she says.

He says, "I know I've been talking about Wally—"

"Just please—go lie down or something."

"When I woke up this morning, I remembered everything, and I thought you might be gone."

"Well, I'm not gone."

"I knew we were having some trouble, Jane—"

"Just let's not talk about it now," she says. "All right? I have to go call Eveline." She walks into the bedroom, and when he comes in behind her she tells him very gently to please go get off his feet. He backs off, makes his way into the living room. "Can you turn on the television?" he calls to her.

She does so. "What channel do you want?"

"Can you just go through them a little?"

She's patient. She waits for him to get a good look at each channel. There isn't any news coverage; it's all commercials and cartoons and children's shows. Finally he settles on a rerun of *The Andy Griffith Show,* and she leaves him there. She fills the dishwasher and wipes off the kitchen table. Then she calls Eveline to tell her what's happened.

"You poor thing," Eveline says. "You must be so relieved. And I said all that bad stuff about Wally's wife."

Jane says, "You didn't mean it," and suddenly she's crying. She's got the handset held tight against her face, crying.

"You poor thing," Eveline says. "You want me to come over there?"

"No, it's all right—I'm all right."

"Poor Martin. Is he hurt bad?"

"It's his hands."

"Is it very painful?"

"Yes," Jane says.

Later, while he sleeps on the sofa, she wanders outside and walks down to the end of the driveway. The day is sunny and cool, with little cottony clouds—the kind of clear day that comes after a storm. She looks up and down the street. Nothing is moving. A few houses away someone has put up a flag, and it flutters in a stray breeze. This is the way it was, she remembers, when she first lived here—when she first stood on this sidewalk and marveled at how flat the land was, how far it stretched in all directions. Now she turns and makes her way back to the house, and then she finds herself in the garage. It's almost as if she's saying good-bye to everything, and as this thought occurs to her, she feels a little stir of sadness. Here on the worktable, side by side under the light from the one window, are Martin's model airplanes. He won't be able to work on them again for weeks. The light reveals the miniature details, the crevices and curves on which he lavished such care, gluing and sanding and painting. The little engines are lying on a paper towel at one end of the table; they smell just like real engines, and they're shiny with lubrication. She picks one of them up and turns it in the light, trying to understand what he might see in it that could require such time and attention. She wants to understand him. She remembers that when they dated, he liked to tell her about flying these planes, and his eyes would widen with excitement. She remembers that she liked him best when he was glad that way. She puts the little engine down, thinking how people change. She knows she's going to leave him, but just for this moment, standing among these things, she feels almost peaceful about it. There's no need to hurry.

As she steps out on the lawn, she realizes she can take the time to think clearly about when and where; she can even change her mind. But she doesn't think she will.

He's up. He's in the hallway—he had apparently wakened and found her gone. "Jesus," he says. "I woke up and you weren't here."

"I didn't go anywhere," she says, and she smiles at him.

"I'm sorry," he says, starting to cry. "God, Janey, I'm so sorry. I'm all messed up here. I've got to go to the bathroom again."

She helps him. The two of them stand over the bowl. He's stopped crying now, though he says his hands hurt something awful. When he's finished he thanks her, and then tries a bawdy joke. "You don't have to let go so soon."

She ignores this, and when she has him tucked safely away, he says quietly, "I guess I better just go to bed and sleep some more if I can."

She's trying to hold on to the feeling of peace and certainty she had in the garage. It's not even noon, and she's exhausted. She's very tired of thinking about everything. He's talking about his parents; later she'll have to call them. But then he says he wants his mother to hear his voice first, to know he's all right. He goes on—something about Milly and her unborn baby, and Teddy Lynch—but Jane can't quite hear him: he's a little unsteady on his feet, and they have trouble negotiating the hallway together.

In their bedroom she helps him out of his jeans and shirt, and she actually tucks him into the bed. Again he thanks her. She kisses his forehead, feels a sudden, sick-swooning sense of having wronged him somehow. It makes her stand straighter, makes her stiffen slightly.

"Jane?" he says.

She breathes. "Try to rest some more. You just need to rest now." He closes his eyes and she waits a little. He's not asleep. She sits at the foot of the bed and watches him. Perhaps ten minutes go by. Then he opens his eyes.

"Janey?"

"Shhh," she says.

He closes them again. It's as if he were her child. She thinks of him as he was when she first saw him, tall and sure of himself in his uniform, and the image makes her throat constrict.

At last he's asleep. When she's certain of this, she lifts herself from the bed and carefully, quietly withdraws. As she closes the door, something in the flow of her own mind appalls her, and she stops, stands in the dim hallway, frozen in a kind of wonder: she had been thinking in an abstract way, almost idly, as though it had nothing at all to do with her, about how people will go to such lengths leaving a room—wishing not to disturb, not to awaken, a loved one.

Charles Baxter

THE DISAPPEARED

CHARLES BAXTER (1947–) is the author of four novels, four collections of stories, two books of literary essays, and a collection of poetry. He has also edited or coedited several books, including *A William Maxwell Portrait* and *The Business of Memory*. His novel *The Feast of Love* was a finalist for the National Book Award and has been adapted for film. He has been the recipient of the Award in Literature from the American Academy of Arts and Letters. Graywolf Press will publish his book *The Art of Subtext: Beyond Plot* in 2007. He lives in Minneapolis and is the Edelstein-Keller Professor of Creative Writing at the University of Minnesota.

What he first noticed about Detroit and therefore America was the smell. Almost as soon as he walked off the plane, he caught it: an acrid odor of wood ash. The smell seemed to go through his nostrils and take up residence in his head. In Sweden, his own country, he associated this smell with autumn, and the first family fires of winter, the smoke chuffing out of chimneys and settling familiarly over the neighborhood. But here it was midsummer, and he couldn't see anything burning.

On the way in from the airport, with the windows of the cab open and hot stony summer air blowing over his face, he asked the driver about it.

"You're smelling Detroit," the driver said.

Anders, who spoke very precise school English, thought that perhaps he hadn't made himself understood. "No," he said. "I am sorry. I mean the burning smell. What is it?"

The cab driver glanced in the rearview mirror. He was wearing a knitted beret, and his dreadlocks flapped in the breeze. "Where you from?"

"Sweden."

The driver nodded to himself. "Explains why," he said. The cab took a sharp right turn on the freeway and entered the Detroit city limits. The driver gestured with his left hand toward an electronic signboard, a small windowless factory at its base, and a clustered group of cramped clapboard houses nearby. When he gestured, the cab wobbled on the freeway. "Fires here most all the time," he said. "Day in and day out. You get so you don't notice. Or maybe you get so you do notice and you like it."

"I don't see any fires," Anders said.

"That's right."

Feeling that he was missing the point somehow, Anders decided to change the subject. "I see a saxophone and a baseball bat next to you," he said, in his best English. "Do you like to play baseball?"

"Not in this cab, I don't," the driver said quietly. "It's no game then, you understand?"

The young man sat back, feeling that he had been defeated by the American idiom in his first native encounter with it. An engineer, he was in Detroit to discuss his work in metal alloys that resist oxidation. The company that had invited him had suggested that he might agree to become a consultant on an exclusive contract, for what seemed to him an enormous, American-sized fee. But the money meant little to him. It was America he was curious about, attracted by, especially its colorful disorderliness.

Disorder, of which there was very little in Sweden, seemed sexy to him: the disorder of a disheveled woman who has rushed down two flights of stairs to offer a last long kiss. Anders was single, and before he left the country he hoped to sleep with an American woman in an American bed. It was his ambition. He wondered if the experience would have any distinction. He had an idea that he might be able to go home and tell one or two friends about it.

At the hotel, he was met by a representative of the automobile company, a gray-haired man with thick glasses who, to Anders's surprise, spoke rather good Swedish. Later that afternoon, and for the next two days, he was taken down silent carpeted hallways and shown into plush windowless rooms with recessed lighting. He showed them his slides and metal samples, cited chemical formulas, and made cost projections; he looked at the faces looking back at him. They were interested, friendly, but oddly blank, like faces he had seen in the military. He saw corridor after corridor. The building seemed more expressive than the people in it. The lighting was both bright and diffuse, and a low-frequency hum of power and secrecy seemed to flow out from the ventilators. Everyone complimented him on his English. A tall woman in a tailored suit, flashing him a secretive smile, asked him if he intended to stay in this country for long. Anders smiled, said that his plans on that particular point were open, and managed to work the name of his hotel into his conversation.

At the end of the third day, the division head once again shook Anders's hand in the foyer of the hotel lobby and said they'd be getting in touch with him very soon. Finally free, Anders stepped outside the hotel and sniffed the air. All the rooms he had been in since he had arrived had had no windows, or windows so blocked by drapes or blinds that he couldn't see out.

He felt restless and excited, with three days free for sightseeing in a wide-open American city, not quite in the Wild West but close enough to it to suit him. He returned to his room and changed into a pair of jeans, a light cotton shirt, and a pair of running shoes. In the mirror, he thought he looked relaxed and handsome. His vanity amused him, but he felt lucky to look the way he did. Back out on the sidewalk, he asked the doorman which direction he would recommend for a walk.

The doorman, who had curly gray hair and sagging pouches under his eyes, removed his cap and rubbed his forehead. He did not look back at Anders. "You want my recommendation? Don't walk anywhere. I would not recommend a walk. Sit in the bar and watch the soaps." The doorman stared at a fire hydrant as he spoke.

"What about running?"

The doorman suddenly glanced at Anders, sizing him up. "It's a chance. You might be okay. But to be safe, stay inside. There's movies on the cable, you want them."

"Is there a park here?"

"Sure, there's parks. There's always parks. There's Belle Isle. You could go there. People do. I don't recommend it. Still and all you might enjoy it if you run fast enough. What're you planning to do?"

Anders shrugged. "Relax. See your city."

"You're seeing it," the doorman said. "Ain't nobody relaxed, seeing this place. Buy some postcards, you want sights. This place ain't built for tourists and amateurs."

Anders thought that perhaps he had misunderstood again and took a cab out to Belle Isle; as soon as he had entered the park, he saw a large municipal fountain and asked the cabbie to drop him off in front of it. On its rim, children were shouting and dangling their legs in the water. The ornamentation of the stone lions was both solemn and whimsical and reminded him of forced humor of Danish public sculpture. Behind the fountain he saw families grouped in evening picnics on the grass, and many citizens, of various apparent ethnic types, running, bicycling, and walking. Anders liked the way Americans walked, a sort of busyness in their step, as if, having no particular goal, they still had an unconscious urgency to get somewhere, to seem purposeful.

He began to jog, and found himself passing a yacht club of some sort, and then a small zoo, and more landscaped areas where solitaries and couples sat on the grass listening to the evening baseball game on their radios. Other couples were stretched out by themselves, self-absorbed. The light had a bluish-gold quality. It looked like almost any city park to him, placid and decorative, a bit hushed.

He found his way to an old building with a concession stand inside. After admiring the building's fake Corinthian architecture, he bought a hot dog and a cola. Thinking himself disguised as a native—America was full of foreigners anyway—he walked to the west windows of the dining area to check on the unattached women. He wanted to praise, to an American, this evening, and this park.

There were several couples on this side of the room, and what seemed to be several unattached men and women standing near the open window and listening to their various earphones. One of these women, with her hair partially pinned up, was sipping a lemonade. She had just the right faraway look. Anders thought he recognized this look. It meant that she was in a kind of suspension, between engagements.

He put himself in her line of sight and said, in his heaviest accent, "A nice evening!"

"What?" She removed the earphones and looked at him. "What did you say?"

"I said the evening was beautiful." He tried to sound as foreign as he could, the way Germans in Sweden did. "I am a visitor here," he added quickly, "and not familiar with any of this." He motioned his arm to indicate the park.

"Not familiar?" she asked. "Not familiar with what?"

"Well, with this park. With the sky here. The people."

"Parks are the same everywhere," the woman said, leaning her hip against the wall. She looked at him with a vague interest. "The sky is the same. Only the people are different."

"Yes? How?"

"Where are you from?"

He explained, and she looked out the window toward the Canadian side of the Detroit River, at the city of Windsor. "That's Canada, you know," she said, pointing a finger at the river. "They make Canadian whiskey right over there." She pointed at some high buildings and what seemed to be a grain elevator. "I've never drunk the whiskey. They say it tastes of acid rain. I've never been to Canada. I mean, I've seen it, but I've never been there. If I can see it from here, why should I go there?"

"To be in Canada," Anders suggested. "Another country."

"But I'm *here*," she said suddenly, turning to him and looking at him directly. Her eyes were so dark they were almost colorless. "Why should I be anywhere else? Why are *you* here?"

"I came to Detroit for business," he said. "Now I'm sightseeing."

"Sightseeing?" She laughed out loud, and Anders saw her arch her back. Her breasts seemed to flare in front of him. Her body had distinct athletic lines. "No one sightsees here. Didn't anyone tell you?"

"Yes. The doorman at the hotel. He told me not to come."

"But you did. How did you get here?"

"I came by taxi."

"You're joking," she said. Then she reached out and put her hand momentarily on his shoulder. "You took a taxi to this park? How do you expect to get back to your hotel?"

"I suppose," he shrugged, "I will get another taxi."

"Oh no you won't," she said, and Anders felt himself pleased that things were working out so well. He noticed again her pinned-up hair and its intense black. Her skin was deeply tanned or naturally dark, and he thought that she herself might be black or Hispanic, he didn't know which, being unpracticed in making such distinctions. Outside he saw fireflies. No one had ever mentioned fireflies in Detroit. Night was coming on. He gazed up at the sky. Same stars, same moon.

"You're here *alone?*" she asked. "In America? And in this city?"

"Yes," he said. "Why not?"

"People shouldn't be left alone in this country," she said, leaning toward him with a kind of vehemence. "They shouldn't have left you here. It can get kind of weird, what happens to people. Didn't they tell you?"

He smiled and said that they hadn't told him anything to that effect.

"Well, they should have." She dropped her cup into a trash can, and he thought he saw the beginning of a scar, a white line, traveling up the underside of her arm toward her shoulder.

"Who do you mean?" he asked. "You said 'they.' Who is 'they'?"

"Any they at all," she said. "Your guardians." She sighed. "All right. Come on. Follow me." She went outside and broke into a run. For a moment he thought that she was running away from him, then realized that he was expected to run *with* her; it was what people did now, instead of holding hands, to get acquainted. He sprinted up next to her, and as she ran, she asked him, "Who are you?"

Being careful not to tire—she wouldn't like it if his endurance was poor—he told her his name, his professional interests, and he patched together a narrative about his mother, father, two sisters, and his aunt Ingrid. Running past a slower couple, he told her that his aunt was eccentric and broke china by throwing it on the floor on Fridays, which she called "the devil's day."

"Years ago, they would have branded her a witch," Anders said. "But she isn't a witch. She's just moody."

He watched her reactions and noticed that she didn't seem at all interested in his family, or any sort of background. "Do you run a lot?" she asked. "You look as if you're in pretty good shape."

He admitted that, yes, he ran, but that people in Sweden didn't do this as much as they did in America.

"You look a little like that tennis star, that Swede," she said. "By the way, I'm Lauren." Still running, she held out her hand, and, still running, he shook it. "Which god do you believe in?"

"Excuse me?"

"Which god?" she asked. "Which god do you think is in control?"

"I had not thought about it."

"You'd better," she said. "Because one of them is." She stopped suddenly and put her hands on her hips and walked in a small circle. She put her hand to her neck and took her pulse, timing it on her wristwatch. Then she placed her fingers on Ander's neck and took his pulse. "One hundred fourteen," she said. "Pretty good." Again she walked away from him and again he found himself following her. In the growing darkness he noticed other men, standing in the parking lot, watching her, this American with pinned-up hair, dressed in a running outfit. He thought she was pretty, but maybe Americans had other standards so that here, in fact, she wasn't pretty, and it was some kind of optical illusion.

When he caught up with her, she was unlocking the door of a blue Chevrolet rusting near the hubcaps. He gazed down at the rust with professional interest—it had the characteristic blister pattern of rust caused by salt. She slipped inside the car and reached across to unlock the passenger side, and when he got in—he hadn't been invited to get in, but he thought it was all right—he sat down on several small plastic tape cassette cases. He picked them out from underneath him and tried to read their labels. She was taking off her shoes. Debussy, Bach, 10,000 Maniacs, Screamin' Jay Hawkins.

"Where are we going?" he asked. He glanced down at her bare foot on the accelerator. She put the car into reverse. "Wait a minute," he said. "Stop this car." She put on the brake and turned off the ignition. "I just want to look at you," he said.

"Okay, look." She turned on the interior light and kept her face turned so that he was looking at her in profile. Something about her suggested a lovely disorder, a ragged brightness toward the back of her face.

"Are we going to do things?" he asked, touching her on the arm.

"Of course," she said. "Strangers should always do things."

She said that she would drop him off at his hotel, that he must change clothes. This was important. She would then pick him up. On the way over, he saw almost no one downtown. For some reason, it was quite empty of shoppers, strollers, or pedestrians of any kind. "I'm going to tell you some things you should know," she said. He settled back. He was used to this kind of talk on dates: everyone, everywhere, liked to reveal intimate details. It was an international convention.

They were slowing for a red light. "God is love," she said, downshifting, her bare left foot on the clutch. "At least I think so. It's my hope. In the world we have left, only love matters. Do you understand? I'm one of the Last Ones. Maybe you've heard of us."

"No, I have not. What do you do?"

"We do what everyone else does. We work and we go home and have dinner and go to bed. There is only one thing we do that is special."

"What is that?" he asked.

"We don't make plans," she said. "No big plans at all."

"That is not so unusual," he said, trying to normalize what she was saying. "Many people don't like to make—"

"It's not liking," she said. "It doesn't have anything to do with liking or not liking. It's a faith. Look at those buildings." She pointed toward several abandoned multistoried buildings with broken or vacant windows. "What face is moving behind all that? Something is. I live and work here. I'm not blind. *Anyone* can see what's taking place here. You're not blind either. Our church is over on the east side, off Van Dyke Avenue. It's not a good part of town but we want to be near where the face is doing its work."

"Your church?"

"The Church of the Millennium," she said. "Where they preach the Gospel of Last Things." They were now on the freeway, heading up toward the General Motors Building and his hotel. "Do you understand me?"

"Of course," he said. He had heard of American cult religions but thought they were all in California. He didn't mind her talk of religion. It was like talk of the sunset or childhood; it kept things going. "Of course I have been listening."

"Because I won't sleep with you unless you listen to me," she said. "It's the one thing I care about, that people listen. It's so damn rare, listening I mean, that you might as well care about it. I don't sleep with strangers too often. Almost never." She turned to look at him. "Anders," she said, "what do you pray to?"

He laughed. "I don't."

"Okay, then, what do you plan for?"

"A few things," he said.

"Like what?"

"My dinner every night. My job. My friends."

"You don't let accidents happen? You should. Things reveal themselves in accidents."

"Are there many people like you?" he asked.

"What do you think?" He looked again at her face, taken over by the darkness in the car but dimly lit by the dashboard lights and the oncoming flare of traffic. "Do you think there are many people like me?"

"Not very many," he said. "But maybe more than there used to be."

"Any of us in Sweden?"

"I don't think so. It's not a religion over there. People don't . . . They didn't tell us in Sweden about American girls who listen to Debussy and 10,000 Maniacs in their automobiles and who believe in gods and accidents."

"They don't say 'girls' here," she told him. "They say 'women.'"

• • •

She dropped him off at the hotel and said that she would pick him up in forty-five minutes. In his room, as he chose a clean shirt and a sport coat and a pair of trousers, he found himself laughing happily. He felt giddy. It was all happening so fast; he could hardly believe his luck. I am a very lucky man, he thought.

He looked out his hotel window at the streetlights. They had an amber glow, the color of gemstones. This city, this American city, was unlike any he had ever seen. A downtown area emptied of people; a river with huge ships going by silently; a park with girls who believe in the millennium. No, not girls: women. He had learned his lesson.

He wanted to open the hotel window to smell the air, but the casement frames were welded shut.

After walking down the stairs to the lobby, he stood out in front of the hotel doorway. He felt a warm breeze against his face. He told the doorman, Luis, that he had met a woman on Belle Isle who was going to pick him up in a few minutes. She was going to take him dancing. The doorman nodded, rubbing his chin with his hand. Anders said that she was friendly and wanted to show him, a foreigner, things. The doorman shook his head. "Yes, I agree," Luis said. "Dancing. Make sure that this is what you do."

"What?"

"Dancing," Luis said, "yes. Go dancing. You know this woman?"

"I just met her."

"Ah," Luis said, and stepped back to observe Anders, as if to remember his face. "Dangerous fun." When her car appeared in front of the hotel, she was wearing a light summer dress, and when she smiled, she looked like the melancholy baby he had heard about in an American song. As they pulled away from the hotel, he looked back at Luis, who was watching them closely, and then Anders realized that Luis was reading the numbers on Lauren's license plate. To break the mood, he leaned over to kiss her on the cheek. She smelled of cigarettes and something else—soap or cut flowers.

She took him uptown to a club where a trio played soft rock and some jazz. Some of this music was slow enough to dance to, in the slow way he wanted to dance. Her hand in his felt bony and muscular; physically, she was direct and immediate. He wondered, now, looking at her face, whether she might be an American Indian, and again he was frustrated because he couldn't tell one race in this country from another. He knew it was improper to ask. When he sat at the table, holding hands with her and sipping from his drink, he began to feel as if he had known her for a long time and was related to her in some obscure way.

Suddenly he asked her, "Why are you so interested in me?"

"Interested?" She laughed, and her long black hair, no longer pinned up, shook in quick thick waves. "Well, all right. I have an interest. I like it that you're so foreign that you take cabs to the park. I like the way you look. You're kind of cute. And the other thing is, your soul is so raw and new, Anders, it's like an oyster."

"What?" He looked at her near him at the table. Their drinks were half finished. "My soul?"

"Yeah, your soul. I can almost see it."

"Where is it?"

She leaned forward, friendly and sexual and now slightly elegant. "You want me to show you?"

"Yes," Anders said. "Sure."

"It's in two places," she said. "One part is up here." She released his hand and put her thumb on his forehead. "And the other part is down here." She touched him in the middle of his stomach. "Right there. And they're connected."

"What are they like?" he asked, playing along.

"Yours? Raw and shiny, just like I said."

"And what about your soul?" he asked.

She looked at him. "My soul is radioactive," she said. "It's like plutonium. Don't say you weren't warned."

He thought that this was another American idiom he hadn't heard before, and he decided not to spoil things by asking her about it. In Sweden, people didn't talk much about the soul, at least not in conjunction with oysters or plutonium. It was probably some local metaphor he had never heard in Sweden.

In the dark he couldn't make out much about her building, except that it was several floors high and at least fifty years old. Her living-room window looked out distantly at the river—once upstairs, he could see the lights of another passing freighter—and through the left side of the window he could see an electrical billboard. The name of the product was made out of hundreds of small incandescent bulbs, which went on and off from left to right. One of the letters was missing.

It's today's CHEVR LET!

All around her living-room walls were brightly framed watercolors, almost celebratory and Matisse-like, but in vague shapes. She went down the hallway, tapped on one of the doors, and said, "I'm home." Then she returned to the living room and kicked off her shoes. "My grandmother," she said. "She has her own room."

"Are these your pictures?" he asked. "Did you draw them?"

"Yes."

"I can't tell what they are. What are they?"

"They're abstract. You use wet paper to get that effect. They're abstract because God has gotten abstract. God used to have a form but now He's dissolving into pure light. That's what you see in those pictures. They're pictures of the trails that God leaves behind."

"Like the vapor trails," he smiled, "behind jets."

"Yes," she said. "Like that."

He went over to her in the dark and drew her to him and kissed her. Her breath was layered with smoke, apparently from cigarettes. Immediately he felt an unusual physical sensation inside his skin, like something heating up on a frypan.

She drew back. He heard another siren go by on the street outside. He wondered whether they should talk some more in the living room—share a few more verbal intimacies—to be really civilized about this and decided, no, it was not necessary, not when strangers make love, as they do, sometimes, in strange cities, away from home. They went into her bedroom and undressed each other. Her body, by the light of a dim bedside lamp, was as beautiful and as exotic as he hoped it would be, darker than his own skin in the dark room, native somehow to this continent. She had the flared shoulders and hips of a dancer. She bent down and snapped off the bedside light, and as he approached her, she was lit from behind by the billboard. Her skin felt vaguely electrical to him.

They stood in the middle of her bedroom, arms around each other, swaying, and he knew, in his arousal, that something odd was about to occur: he had no words for it in either his own language or in English.

They moved over and under each other, changing positions to stay in the breeze created by the window fan. They were both lively and attentive, and at first he thought it would be just the usual fun, this time with an almost anonymous American woman. He looked at her in the bed and saw her dark leg alongside his own, and he saw that same scar line running up her arm to her shoulder, where it disappeared.

"Where did you get that?" he asked.

"That?" She looked at it. "That was an accident that was done to me."

Half an hour later, resting with her, his hands on her back, he felt a wave of happiness; he felt it was a wave of color traveling through his body, surging from his forehead down to his stomach. It took him over again, and then a third time, with such force that he almost sat up.

"What is it?" she asked.

"I don't know. It is like . . . I felt a color moving through my body."

"Oh, that?" She smiled at him in the dark. "It's your soul, Anders. That's all. That's all it is. Never felt it before, huh?"

"I must be very drunk," he said.

She put her hand up into his hair. "Call it anything you want to. Didn't you feel it before? Our souls were curled together."

"You're crazy," he said. "You are a crazy woman."

"Oh yeah?" she whispered. "Is that what you think? Watch. Watch what happens now. You think this is all physical. Guess what. You're the crazy one. Watch. Watch."

She went to work on him, and at first it was pleasurable, but as she moved over him it became a succession of waves that had specific colorations, even when he turned her and thought he was taking charge. Soon he felt some substance, some glossy blue possession entangled in the air above him.

"I bet you're going to say that you're imagining all this," she said, her hand skidding across him.

"Who are you?" he said. "Who in the world are you?"

"I warned you," she whispered, her mouth directly over his ear. "I warned you. You people with your things, your rusty things, you suffer so bad when you come into where *we* live. Did they tell you we were all soulless here? Did they say that?"

He put his hands on her. "This is not love, but it—"

"Of course not," she said. "It's something else. Do you know the word? Do you know the word for something that opens your soul at once? Like that?" She snapped her fingers on the pillow. Her tongue was touching his ear. "Do you?" The words were almost inaudible.

"No."

"Addiction." She waited. "Do you understand?"

"Yes."

In the middle of the night he rose up and went to the window. He felt like a stump, amputated from the physical body of the woman. At the window he looked down, to the right of the billboard, and saw another apartment building with heavy decorations with human forms near the roof's edge, and on the third floor he saw a man at the window, as naked as he himself was but almost completely in shadow, gazing out at the street. There were so far away from each other that being unclothed didn't matter. It was vague and small and impersonal.

"Do you always stand at the window without clothes on?" she asked, from the bed.

"Not in Sweden," he said. He turned around. "This is odd," he said. "At night no one walks out on the streets. But there, over on that block, there's a man like me, at the window, and he is looking out, too. Do people stand everywhere at the windows here?"

"Come to bed."

"When I was in the army, the Swedish army," he said, still looking out, "they taught us to think that we could *decide* to do anything. They talked about the will. Your word 'willpower.' All Sweden believes this—choice, will, willpower. Maybe not so much now. I wonder if they talk about it here."

"You're funny," she said. She had moved up from behind him and embraced him.

In the morning he watched her as she dressed. His eyes hurt from sleeplessness. "I have to go," she said. "I'm already late." She was putting on a light blue skirt. As she did, she smiled. "You're a lovely lover," she said. "I like your body very much."

"What are we going to do?" he asked.

"We? There is no 'we,' Anders. There's you and then there's me. We're not a couple. I'm going to work. You're going back to your country soon. What are you planning to do?"

"May I stay here?"

"For an hour," she said, "and then you should go back to your hotel. I don't think you should stay. You don't live here."

"May I take you to dinner tonight?" he asked, trying not to watch her as he watched her. "What can we do tonight?"

"There's that 'we' again. Well, maybe. You can teach me a few words of Swedish. Why don't you hang around at your hotel and maybe I'll come by around six and get you, but don't call me if I don't come by, because if I don't, I don't."

"I can't call you," he said. "I don't know your last name."

"Oh, that's right," she said. "Well, listen. I'll probably come at six." She looked at him lying in the bed. "I don't believe this," she said.

"What?"

"You think you're in love, don't you?"

"No," he said. "Not exactly." He waited. "Oh, I don't know."

"I get the point," she said. "Well, you'd better get used to it. Welcome to our town. We're not always good at love but we are good at that." She bent to kiss him and then was gone. Happiness and agony simultaneously reached down and pressed against his chest. They, too, were like colors, but when you mixed the two together, you got something greenish-pink, excruciating.

He stood up, put on his trousers, and began looking into her dresser drawers. He expected to find trinkets and whatnot, but all she had were folded clothes, and, in the corner of the top drawer, a small turquoise heart for a charm bracelet. He put it into his pocket.

In the bathroom, he examined the labels on her medicines and facial creams before washing his face. He wanted evidence but didn't know for what. He looked, to himself, like a slightly different version of what he had once been. In the mirror his face had a puffy look and a passive expression, as if he had been assaulted during the night.

After he had dressed and entered the living room, he saw Lauren's grandmother sitting at a small dining-room table. She was eating a piece of toast and looking out of the window toward the river. The apartment, in daylight, had an aggressively scrubbed and mopped look. On the kitchen counter a small black-and-white television was blaring, but the old woman wasn't watching it. Her black hair was streaked with gray, and she wore a ragged pink bathrobe decorated with pictures of orchids. She was very frail. Her skin was as dark as her granddaughter's. Looking at her, Anders was once again unable to guess what race she was. She might be Arabic, or a Native American, or Hispanic, or black. Because he couldn't tell, he didn't care.

Without even looking at him, she motioned at him to sit down.

"Want anything?" she asked. She had a high, distant voice, as if it had come into the room over wires. "There are bananas over there." She made no gesture. "And grapefruit, I think, in the refrigerator."

"That's all right." He sat down on the other side of the table and folded his hands together, studying his fingers. The sound of traffic came up from the street outside.

"You're from somewhere," she said. "Scandinavia?"

"Yes," he said. "How can you tell?" Talking had become a terrible effort.

"Vowels," she said. "You sound like one of those Finns up north of here. When will you go back? To your country?"

"I don't know," he said. "Perhaps a few days. Perhaps not. My name is Anders." He held out his hand.

"Nice to meet you." She touched but did not shake his hand. "Why don't you know when you're going back?" She turned to look at him at last. It was a face on which curiosity still registered. She observed him as if he were an example of a certain kind of human being in whom she still had an interest.

"I don't know . . . I am not sure. Last night, I . . ."

"You don't finish your sentences," the old woman said.

"I am trying to. I don't want to leave your granddaughter," he said. "She is"—he tried to think of the right adjective—"amazing to me."

"Yes, she is." The old woman peered at him. "You don't think you're in love, do you?"

"I don't know."

"Well, don't be. She won't ever be married, so there's no point in being in love with her. There's no point in being married *here*. I see them, you know."

"Who?"

"All the young men. Well, there aren't many. A few. Every so often. They come and sleep here with her and then in the morning they come out for breakfast with me and then they go away. We sit and talk. They're usually very pleasant. Men are, in the morning. They should be. She's a beautiful girl."

"Yes, she is."

"But there's no future in her, you know," the old woman said. "Sure you don't want a grapefruit? You should eat something."

"No, thank you. What do you mean, 'no future'?"

"Well, the young men usually understand that." The old woman looked at the television set, scowled, and shifted her eyes to the window. She rubbed her hands together. "You can't invest in her. You can't do that at all. She won't let you. I know. I know how she thinks."

"We have women like that in my country," Anders said. "They are—"

"Oh no you don't," the old woman said. "Sooner or later they want to get married, don't they?"

"I suppose most of them."

She glanced out the window toward the Detroit River and the city of Windsor on the opposite shore. Just when he thought that she had forgotten all about him, he felt her hand, dry as a winter leaf, taking hold of his own. Another siren went by outside. He felt a weight descending in his stomach. The touch of the old woman's hand made him feel worse than before, and he stood up quickly, looking around the room as if there were some object nearby he had to pick up and take away immediately. Her hand dropped away from his.

"No plans," she said. "Didn't she tell you?" the old woman asked. "It's what she believes." She shrugged. "It makes her happy."

"I am not sure I understand."

The old woman lifted her right hand and made a dismissive wave in his direction. She pursed her mouth; he knew she had stopped speaking to him. He called a cab, and in half an hour he was back in his hotel room. In the shower he realized that he had forgotten to write down her address or phone number.

He felt itchy: he went out running, returned to his room, and took another shower. He did thirty push-ups and jogged in place. He groaned and shouted, knowing that no one would hear. How would he explain this to anyone? He was feeling passionate puzzlement. He went down to the hotel's dining room for lunch and ordered Dover sole and white wine but found himself unable to eat much of anything. He stared at his plate and at the other men and women consuming their meals calmly, and he was suddenly filled with wonder at ordinary life.

He couldn't stand to be by himself, and after lunch he had the doorman hail a cab. He gave the cabdriver a fifty and asked him to drive him around the city until all the money was used up.

"You want to see the nice parts?" the cabbie asked.

"No."

"What is it you want to see, then?"

"The city."

"You tryin' to score, man? That it?"

Anders didn't know what he meant. He was certain that no sport was intended. He decided to play it safe. "No," he said.

The cabdriver shook his head and whistled. They drove east and then south;

Anders watched the water-ball compass stuck to the front window. Along Jefferson Avenue they went past the shells of apartment buildings, and then, heading north, they passed block after block of vacated or boarded-up properties. One old building with Doric columns was draped with a banner.

PROGRESS! THE OLD MUST MAKE WAY
FOR THE NEW
Acme Wrecking Company

The banner was worn and tattered. Anders noticed broken beer bottles, sharp brown glass, on sidewalks and vacant lots, and the glass, in the sun, seemed perversely beautiful. Men were sleeping on sidewalks and in front of stairwells; one man, wearing a hat, urinated against the corner of a burned-out building. He saw other men—there were very few women out here in the light of day—in groups gazing at him with cold slow deadly expressions. In his state of mind, he understood it all; he identified with it. All of it, the ruins and the remnants, made perfect sense.

At six o'clock she picked him up and took him to a Greek restaurant. All the way over, he watched her. He examined her with the puzzled curiosity of someone who wants to know how another person who looks rather attractive but also rather ordinary could have such power. Her physical features didn't explain anything.

"Did you miss me today?" she asked, half-jokingly.

"Yes," he said. He started to say more but didn't know how to begin. "It was hard to breathe," he said at last.

"I know," she said. "It's the air."

"No, it isn't. Not the air."

"Well, what then?"

He looked at her.

"Oh, come on, Anders. We're just two blind people who staggered into each other and we're about to stagger off in different directions. That's all."

Sentences struggled in his mind, then vanished before he could say them. He watched the pavement pass underneath the car.

In the restaurant, a crowded and lively place smelling of beer and roasted meat and cigars, they sat in a booth and ordered an antipasto plate. He leaned over and took her hands. "Tell me, please, who and what you are."

She seemed surprised that he had asked. "I've explained," she said. She waited, then started up again. "When I was younger I had an idea that I wanted to be a dancer. I had to give that up. My timing was off." She smiled. "Onstage, I looked like a memory of what had already happened. The other girls would do something and then *I'd* do it. I come in late on a lot of things. That's good for me. I've told you where I work. I live with my grandmother. I go with her into the parks in the fall and we watch for birds. And you know what else I believe." He gazed at the gold hoops of her earrings. "What else do you want to know?"

"I feel happy and terrible," he said. "Is it you? Did you do this?"

"I guess I did," she said, smiling faintly. "Tell me some words in Swedish."

"Which ones?"

"House."

"Hus."

"Pain."

"Smärta."

She leaned back. "Face."

"Ansikte."

"Light."

"Ljus."

"Never."

"Aldrig."

"I don't like it," she said. "I don't like the sound of those words at all. They're too cold. They're cold-weather words."

"Cold? Try another one."

"Soul."

"Själ."

"No, I don't like it." She raised her hand to the top of his head, grabbed a bit of his hair, and laughed. "Too bad."

"Do you do this to everyone?" he asked. "I feel such confusion."

He saw her stiffen. "You want to know too much. You're too messed up. Too messed up with plans. You and your rust. All that isn't important. Not here. We don't do all that explaining. I've told you *everything* about me. We're just supposed to be enjoying ourselves. Nobody has to explain. That's freedom, Anders. Never telling why." She leaned over toward him so that her shoulders touched his, and with a sense of shock and desperation, he felt himself becoming aroused. She kissed him, and her lips tasted slightly of garlic. "Just say hi to the New World," she said.

"You feel like a drug to me," he said. "You feel experimental."

"We don't use that word that way," she said. Then she said, "Oh," as if she had understood something, or remembered another engagement. "Okay. I'll explain all this in a minute. Excuse me." She rose and disappeared behind a corner of the restaurant, and Anders looked out the window at a Catholic church the color of sandstone, on whose front steps a group of boys sat, eating popsicles. One of the boys got up and began to ask passersby for money; this went on until a policeman came and sent the boys away. Anders looked at his watch. Ten minutes had gone by since she had left. He looked up. He knew without thinking about it that she wasn't coming back.

He put a ten-dollar bill on the table and left the restaurant, jogging into the parking structure where she had left the car. Although he wasn't particularly surprised to see that it wasn't there, he sat down on the concrete and felt the floor of the structure shaking. He ran his hands through his hair, where she had grabbed at it. He waited as long as he could stand to do so, then returned to the hotel.

Luis was back on duty. Anders told him what had happened.

"Ah," Luis said. "She is disappeared."

"Yes. Do you think I should call the police?"

"No," Luis said. "I do not think so. They have too many disappeared already."

"Too many disappeared?"

"Yes. All over this city. Many many disappeared. For how many times do you take this lady out?"

"Once. No, twice."

"And this time is the time she leave you?"

Anders nodded.

"I have done that," Luis said. "When I get sick of a woman, I too have disappeared. Maybe," he said suddenly, "she will reappear. Sometimes they do."

"I don't think she will." He sat down on the sidewalk in front of the hotel and cupped his chin in his hands.

"No, no," Luis said. "You cannot do that in front of the hotel. This looks very bad. Please stand up." He felt Luis reaching around his shoulders and pulling him to his feet. "What you are acting is impossible after one night," Luis said. "Be like everyone else. Have another night." He took off his doorman's cap and combed his hair with precision. "Many men and women also disappear from each other. It is one thing to do. You had a good time?"

Anders nodded.

"Have another good time," Luis suggested, "with someone else. Beer, pizza, go to bed. Women who have not disappeared will talk to you, I am sure."

"I think I'll call the police," Anders said.

"Myself, no, I would not do that."

He dialed a number he found in the telephone book for a local precinct station. As soon as the station officer understood what Anders was saying to him, he became angry, said it wasn't a police matter, and hung up on him. Anders sat for a moment in the phone booth, then looked up the Church of the Millennium in the directory. He wrote down its address. Someone there would know about her, and explain.

The cab let him out in front. It was like no other church he had ever seen before. Even the smallest places of worship in his own country had vaulted roofs, steeples, and stained glass. This building seemed to be someone's remodeled house. On either side of it, two lots down, were two skeletal homes, one of which had been burned and which now stood with charcoal windows and a charcoal portal where the front door had once been. The other house was boarded up; in the evening wind, sheets of newspaper were stuck to its south wall. Across the street was an almost deserted playground. The saddles had been removed from the swing set, and the chains hung down from the upper bar and moved slightly in the wind. Four men stood together under a basketball hoop, talking together. One of the men bounced a basketball occasionally.

A signboard had been planted into the ground in front of the church, but so many letters had been removed from it that Anders couldn't make out what it was supposed to say.

Ch r ch of e Mill n i m
Rev. H r old T. oodst   th, Pas or
Everyo e elco e!
"Love on   other, lest ye f ll to d t le for r le m!"

On the steps leading up to the front door, he turned around and saw, to the south, the lights of the office buildings of downtown Detroit suspended like enlarged stars in the darkness. After hearing what he thought was some sound in the bushes, he opened the front doors of the church and went inside.

Over a bare wood floor, folding chairs were lined up in five straight rows, facing toward a front chest intended as an altar, and everywhere there was a smell of incense, of ashy pine. Above the chest, and nailed to the far wall where a crucifix might be located in a Protestant church, was a polished brass circle with a nimbus of rays projecting out from its top. The rays were extended along the wall for a distance of four feet. One spotlight from a corner behind him lit up the brass circle, which in the gloom looked either like a deity-sun or some kind of explosion. The bare walls had been painted with flames: buildings of the city, some he had already seen, painted in flames, the earth in flames. There was an open Bible on the chest, and in one of the folding chairs a deck of playing cards. Otherwise, the room was completely empty. Glancing at a side door, he decided that he had never seen a church so small, or one that filled him with a greater sense of desolation. Behind him, near the door, was a bench. He had the feeling that the bench was filled with the disappeared. He sat down on it, and as he looked at the folding chairs it occurred to him that the disappeared were in fact here now, in front of him, sitting or standing or kneeling.

He composed himself and went back out onto the street, thinking that perhaps a cab would go by, but he saw neither cabs nor cars, not even pedestrians. After deciding that he had better begin walking toward the downtown area, he made his way down two blocks, past a boarded-up grocery store and a vacated apartment building, when he heard what he thought was the sound of footsteps behind him.

He felt the blow at the back of his head; it came to him not as a sensation of pain but as an instant crashing explosion of light in his brain, a bursting circle with a shooting aura irradiating from it. As he turned to fall, he felt hands touching his chest and his trousers; they moved with speed and almost with tenderness, until they found what they were looking for and took it away from him.

He lay on the sidewalk in a state somewhere between consciousness and unconsciousness, hearing the wind through the trees overhead and feeling some blood trickling out of the back of his scalp, until he felt the hands again, perhaps the same hands, lifting him up, putting him into something, taking him somewhere. Inside the darkness he now inhabited, he found that at some level he could still think: *Someone hit me and I've been robbed.* At another, later, point, he understood that he could open his eyes; he had that kind of permission. He was sitting in a wheelchair in what was clearly a hospital emergency room. It felt as though someone were pushing him toward a planetary corridor. They asked him questions, which he answered in Swedish. "Det gör ont," he said, puzzled that they didn't understand him. "Var är jag?" he asked. They didn't know. English was what they wanted. He tried to give them some.

They X-rayed him and examined his cut; he would need four stitches, they said. He found that he could walk. They told him he was lucky, that he had not been badly hurt. A doctor, and then a nurse, and then another nurse, told him that he might have been killed—shot or knifed—and that victims of this type, strangers who wandered into the wrong parts of the city, were not unknown. He mentioned the disappeared. They were polite, but said that there was no such phrase in English. When he mentioned the name of his hotel, they said, once again, that he was lucky: it was only a few blocks away, walking distance. They smiled. You're a lucky man, they said, grinning oddly. They knew something but weren't saying it.

As the smaller debris of consciousness returned to him, he found himself sitting in a brightly lit room, like a waiting room, near the entryway for emergency medicine. From where he sat, he could see, through his fluent tidal headache, the patients arriving, directed to the Triage Desk, where their condition was judged.

They brought in a man on a gurney, who was hoarsely shouting. They rushed him through. He was bleeding, and they were holding him down as his feet kicked sideways.

They brought in someone else, a girl, who was stumbling, held up on both sides by friends. Anders heard something that sounded like Odie. Who was Odie? Her boyfriend? Odie, she screamed. Get me Odie.

Anders stood up, unable to watch any more. He shuffled through two doorways and found himself standing near an elevator. From a side window, he saw light from the sun rising. He hadn't realized that it was day. The sun made the inside of his head shriek. To escape the light, he stepped on the elevator and pressed the button for the fifth floor.

As the elevator rose, he felt his knees weakening. In order to clear his head, he began to count the other people on the elevator: seven. They seemed normal to him. The signs of this were coats and ties on the men, white frocks and a stethoscope on one of the women, and blouses and jeans on the other women. None of them looked like her. From now on, none of them ever would.

He felt that he must get home to Sweden quickly, before he became a very different person, unrecognizable even to himself.

At the fifth floor the doors opened and he stepped out. Close to the elevators was a nurses' station, and beyond it a long hallway leading to an alcove. He walked down this hallway, turned the corner, and heard small squalling sounds ahead. At the same time, he saw the windows in the hallway and understood that he had wandered onto the maternity floor. He made his way to the viewer's window and looked inside. He counted twenty-five newborns, each one in its own clear plastic crib. He stared down at the babies, hearing, through the glass, the cries of those who were awake.

He was about to turn around and go back to his hotel when one of the nurses saw him. She raised her eyebrows quizzically and spread her hands over the children. He shook his head to indicate no. Still she persisted. She pointed to a baby with white skin and a head of already-blond hair. He shook his head no once again. He would need to get back to the hotel, call his bank in Sweden, get money for the return trip. He touched his pants pocket and found that the wallet was still there. What had they taken? The nurse, smiling, nodded as if she understood, and motioned toward the newborns with darker skin, the Hispanics and light-skinned blacks and all the others, babies of a kind he never saw in Sweden.

Well, he thought, why not? Now that they had done this to him.

He felt himself nodding. Sure. That American word. His right arm rose. He pointed at a baby whose skin was the color of clay, the color of polished bronze, or flames. Now the nurse was wheeling the baby he had pointed to closer to the window. When it was directly in front of him, she left it there, returning to the back of the nursery. Standing on the other side of the glass, staring down at the sleeping infant, he tapped on the panel twice and waved, as he thought fathers should. The baby did not awaken. Anders put his hand in his pocket and touched the little turquoise heart, then pressed his forehead against the glass of the window and recovered himself. He stood for what seemed to him a long time, before taking the elevator down to the ground floor and stepping out onto the front sidewalk, and to the air, which smelled as it always had, of powerful combustible materials and their traces, fire and ash.

Amy Bloom

SILVER WATER

AMY BLOOM (1953–) is the author of two novels and two collections of short stories; she is also a nominee for both the National Book Award and the National Book Critics Circle Award. Her stories have appeared in *Best American Short Stories*, *The O. Henry Prize Stories*, and numerous anthologies in the United States and abroad. She has written for *The New Yorker*, *The New York Times Magazine*, *The Atlantic Monthly*, *Vogue*, *Slate*, and *Salon*, among many other publications, and has won a National Magazine Award. Her first book of nonfiction, *Normal: Transsexual CEOs, Crossdressing Cops, and Hermaphrodites with Attitude*, is an exploration of the varieties of gender. A practicing psychotherapist, she lives in Connecticut and teaches at Yale University.

My sister's voice was like mountain water in a silver pitcher; the clear, blue beauty of it cools you and lifts you up beyond your heat, beyond your body. After we went to see *La Traviata*, when she was fourteen and I was twelve, she elbowed me in the parking lot and said, "Check this out." And she opened her mouth unnaturally wide and her voice came out, so crystalline and bright, that all the departing operagoers stood frozen by their cars, unable to take out their keys or open their doors until she had finished and then they cheered like hell.

That's what I like to remember and that's the story I told to all of her therapists. I wanted them to know her, to know that who they saw was not all there was to see. That before the constant tinkling of commercials and fast-food jingles, there had been Puccini and Mozart and hymns so sweet and mighty, you expected Jesus to come down off his cross and clap. That before there was a mountain of Thorazined fat, swaying down the halls in nylon maternity tops and sweatpants, there had been the prettiest girl in Arrandale Elementary School, the belle of Landmark Junior High. Maybe there were other pretty girls, but I didn't see them. To me, Rose, my beautiful blond defender, my guide to Tampax and my mother's moods, was perfect.

She had her first psychotic break when she was fifteen. She had been coming home moody and tearful, then quietly beaming, then she stopped coming home. She would go out into the woods behind our house and not come in until my mother would go out at dusk, and step gently into the briars and saplings and pull her out, blank-faced, her pale blue pullover covered with crumbled leaves, her white jeans smeared with dirt. After three weeks of this, my mother, who is a musician and widely regarded as eccentric, said to my father, who is a psychiatrist and a kind, sad man, "She's going off."

"What is that, your professional opinion?" He picked up the newspaper and put it down again, sighing. "I'm sorry, I didn't mean to snap at you. I know something's bothering her. Have you talked to her?"

"What's there to say? David, she's going crazy, she doesn't need a heart-to-heart talk with Mom, she needs a hospital."

They went back and forth and my father sat down with Rose for a few hours and she sat there, licking the hairs on her forearm, first one way, then the other. My mother stood in the hallway, dry-eyed and pale, watching the two of them. She had already packed Rose's bag and when three of my father's friends dropped by to offer free consultations and recommendations, my mother and Rose's suitcase were already in the car. My mother hugged me and told me that they would be back that night, but not with Rose. She also said, divining my worst fear, "It won't happen to you, honey. Some people go crazy and some people never do. You never will." She smiled and stroked my hair. "Not even when you want to."

Rose was in hospitals, great and small, for the next ten years. She had lots of terrible therapists and a few good ones. One place had no pictures on the walls, no windows, and the patients all wore slippers with the hospital crest on them. My mother didn't even bother to go to Admissions. She turned Rose around and the two of them marched out, my father, trailing behind them, apologizing to his colleagues. My mother ignored the psychiatrists, the social workers and the nurses and she played Handel and Bessie Smith for the patients on whatever piano was available. At some places, she had a Steinway donated by a grateful, or optimistic, family; at others, she banged out "Gimme a Pigfoot" on an old, scarred box that hadn't been tuned since there'd been English-speaking physicians on the grounds. My father talked in serious, appreciative voices to the administrators and unit chiefs and tried to be friendly with whoever was managing Rose's case. We all hated the family therapists.

The worst family therapist we ever had sat in a pale green room with us, visibly taking stock of my mother's ethereal beauty and her faded blue T-shirt and girl-sized jeans, my father's rumpled suit and stained tie and my own unreadable, sixteen-year-old fashion statement. Rose was beyond fashion that year, in one of her dancing-teddy-bear smocks and extra-extra-large Celtics sweatpants. Mr. Walker read Rose's file in front of us and then watched, in alarm, as Rose began crooning, beautifully, and slowly massaging her breasts. My mother and I started to laugh and even my father started to smile. This was Rose's usual opening salvo for new therapists.

Mr. Walker said, "I wonder why it is that everyone is so entertained by Rose behaving inappropriately."

Rose burped and then we all laughed. This was the seventh family therapist we had seen and none of them had lasted very long. Mr. Walker, unfortunately, was determined to do right by us.

"What do you think of Rose's behavior, Violet?" They did this sometimes. In their manual, it must say, if you think the parents are too weird, try talking to the sister.

"I don't know. Maybe she's trying to get you to stop talking about her in the third person."

"Nicely put," my father said.

"Indeed," my mother said.

"Fuckin' A," Rose said.

"Well, this is something that the whole family agrees upon," Mr. Walker said, trying to act as if he understood, or even liked us.

"That was not a successful intervention, Ferret Face." Rose tended to function better when she was angry. He did look like a blond ferret and we all laughed again. Even my father, who tried to give these people a chance out of some sense of collegiality, had given it up.

Mr. Walker decided, after fourteen minutes, that our time was up and walked out, leaving us grinning at each other. Rose was still nuts, but at least we'd all had a little fun.

Our best family therapist started out almost as badly. We scared off a resident and then scared off her supervisor, who sent us Dr. Thorne. Three hundred pounds of Texas chili, cornbread and Lone Star beer, finished off with big black cowboy boots and a little string tie around the area of his neck.

"Oh, frabjous day, it's Big Nut." Rose was in heaven and stopped massaging her breasts immediately.

"Hey, Little Nut." You have to understand how big a man would have to be to call my sister "little." He christened us all, right away. "And it's the good Doctor Nut, and Madame Hickory Nut, 'cause they are the hardest damn nuts to crack, and over here in the overalls and not much else, is No One's Nut"—a name which summed up both my sanity and my loneliness. We all relaxed.

Dr. Thorne was good for us. Rose moved into a halfway house, whose director loved Big Nut so much she kept Rose even when Rose went through a period of having sex with everyone who passed her door. She was in a fever for a while, trying to still the voices by fucking her brains out.

Big Nut said, "Darlin', I can't. I cannot make love to every beautiful woman I meet and, furthermore, I can't do that and be your therapist, too. It's a great shame, but I think you might be able to find a really nice guy, someone who treats you just as sweet and kind as I would, if I were lucky enough to be your beau. I don't want you to settle for less." And she stopped propositioning the crack addicts and the alcoholics and the guys at the shelter. We loved Dr. Thorne.

My father cut back on seeing rich neurotics and helped out one day a week at Dr. Thorne's walk-in clinic. My mother finished a record of Mozart concerti and played at fund-raisers for Rose's halfway house. I went back to college and found a wonderful linebacker from Texas to sleep with. In the dark, I would make him call me "darlin'." Rose took her meds, lost about fifty pounds and began singing at the A.M.E. Zion Church, down the street from the halfway house.

At first, they didn't know what to do with this big, blond lady, dressed funny and hovering wistfully in the doorway during their rehearsals, but she gave them a few bars of "Precious Lord" and the choir director felt God's hand and saw that, with the help of His sweet child, Rose, the Prospect Street Choir was going all the way to the Gospel Olympics.

Amidst a sea of beige, umber, cinnamon and espresso faces, there was Rose, bigger, blonder and pinker than any two white women could be. And Rose and the choir's contralto, Addie Robicheaux, laid out their gold and silver voices and wove them together in strands as fine as silk, as strong as steel. And we wept as Rose and Addie, in their billowing garnet robes, swayed together, clasping hands until the last perfect note floated up to God and then they smiled down at us.

Rose would still go off from time to time and the voices would tell her to do bad things, but Dr. Thorne or Addie or my mother could usually bring her back. After five good years, Big Nut died. Stuffing his face with a chili dog, sitting in his un-air-conditioned office in the middle of July, he had one big, Texas-sized aneurism and died.

Rose held on tight for seven days; she took her meds, went to choir practice and rearranged her room about a hundred times. His funeral was a Lourdes for the mentally ill. If you were psychotic, borderline, bad-off neurotic, or just very hard to get along with, you were there. People shaking so bad from years of heavy meds that they fell out of the pews. People holding hands, crying, moaning, talking to themselves; the crazy and the not-so-crazy were all huddled together, like puppies at the pound.

Rose stopped taking her meds and the halfway house wouldn't keep her after she pitched another patient down the stairs. My father called the insurance company and found out that Rose's new, improved psychiatric coverage wouldn't begin for forty-five days. I put all of her stuff in a garbage bag and we walked out of the halfway house, Rose winking at the poor, drooling boy on the couch.

"This is going to be difficult—not all bad, but difficult—for the whole family and I thought we should discuss everybody's expectations. I know I have some concerns." My father had convened a family meeting as soon as Rose had finished putting each one of her thirty stuffed bears in its own special place.

"No meds," Rose said, her eyes lowered, her stubby fingers, those fingers that had braided my hair and painted tulips on my cheeks, pulling hard on the hem of her dirty smock.

My father looked in despair at my mother.

"Rosie, do you want to drive the new car?" my mother asked.

Rose's face lit up. "I'd love to drive that car. I'd drive to California, I'd go see the bears at the San Diego Zoo. I would take you, Violet, but you always hated the zoo. Remember how she cried at the Bronx Zoo when she found out that the animals didn't get to go home at closing?" Rose put her damp hand on mine and squeezed it, sympathetically. "Poor Vi."

"If you take your medication, after a while you'll be able to drive the car. That's the deal. Meds, car." My mother sounded accommodating but unenthusiastic, careful not to heat up Rose's paranoia.

"You got yourself a deal, darlin'."

I was living about an hour away then, teaching English during the day, writing poetry at night. I went home every few days, for dinner. I called every night.

My father said, quietly, "It's very hard. We're doing all right, I think. Rose has been walking in the mornings with your mother and she watches a lot of TV. She won't go to the day hospital and she won't go back to the choir. Her friend, Mrs. Robicheaux, came by a couple of times. What a sweet woman. Rose wouldn't even talk to her; she just sat there, staring at the wall and humming. We're not doing all that well, actually, but I guess we're getting by. I'm sorry, sweetheart, I don't mean to depress you."

My mother said, emphatically, "We're doing fine. We've got our routine and we stick to it and we're fine. You don't need to come home so often, you know. Wait till Sunday, just come for the day. Lead your life, Vi. She's leading hers."

I stayed away until Sunday, afraid to pick up my phone, grateful to my mother for her harsh calm and her reticence, the qualities that had enraged me throughout my childhood.

I came on a Sunday, in the early afternoon, to help my father garden, something we had always enjoyed together. We weeded and staked tomatoes and killed aphids while my mother and Rose were down at the lake. I didn't even get into the house until four, when I needed a glass of water.

Someone had broken the piano bench into five neatly stacked pieces and placed them where the piano bench usually was.

"We were having such a nice time, I couldn't bear to bring it up," my father said, standing in the doorway, carefully keeping his gardening boots out of the kitchen.

"What did Mommy say?"

"She said, 'Better the bench than the piano.' And your sister lay down on the floor and just wept. Then, your mother took her down to the lake. This can't go on, Vi. We have twenty-seven days left, your mother gets no sleep because Rose doesn't sleep and if I could just pay twenty-seven thousand dollars to keep her in the hospital until the insurance takes over, I'd do it."

"All right. Do it. Pay the money and take her back to Hartley-Rees. It was the prettiest place and she liked the art therapy there."

"I would if I could. The policy states that she must be symptom-free for at least forty-five days before her coverage begins. Symptom-free means no hospitalization."

"Jesus, Daddy, how could you get that kind of policy? She hasn't been symptom-free for forty-five minutes."

"It's the only one I could get for long-term psychiatric." He put his hand over his mouth to block whatever he was about to say and went back out to the garden. I couldn't see if he was crying.

He stayed outside and I stayed inside, until Rose and my mother came home from the lake. Rose's soggy sweatpants were rolled up to her knees and she had a bucketful of shells and gray stones, which my mother persuaded her to leave on the back porch. My mother kissed me lightly and told Rose to go up to her room and change out of her wet pants.

Rose's eyes grew very wide. "Never. I will never . . ." She began banging her head with rhythmic intensity, against the kitchen floor, throwing all of her weight behind each attack. My mother put her arms around Rose's waist and tried to hold her back. Rose shook her off, not even looking around to see what was slowing her down. My mother crumpled next to the refrigerator.

"Violet, please . . ."

I threw myself onto the kitchen floor, becoming the spot that Rose was smacking her head against. She stopped a fraction of an inch short of my stomach.

"Oh, Vi, Mommy, I'm sorry. I'm sorry, don't hate me." She staggered to her feet and ran, wailing, to her room.

My mother got up and washed her face, brusquely, rubbing it dry with a dishcloth. My father heard the wailing and came running in, slipping his long bare feet out of his rubber boots.

"Galen, Galen, let me see." He held her head and looked closely for bruises on her pale, small face. "What happened?" My mother looked at me. "Violet, what happened? Where's Rose?"

"Rose got upset and when she went running upstairs, she pushed Mommy out of the way." I've only told three lies in my life and that was my second.

"She must feel terrible, pushing you, of all people. It would have to be you, but I know she didn't want it to be." He made my mother a cup of tea and all the love he had for her, despite her silent rages and her vague stares, came pouring through the teapot, warming her cup, filling her small, long-fingered hands. He stood by her and she rested her head against his hip. I looked away.

"Let's make dinner, then I'll call her. Or you call her, David, maybe she'd rather see your face first."

Dinner was filled with all of our starts and stops and Rose's desperate efforts to control herself. She could barely eat and hummed the McDonald's theme song over and over again, pausing only to spill her juice down the front of her smock and begin weeping. My father looked at my mother and handed Rose his napkin. She dabbed at herself, listlessly, but the tears stopped.

"I want to go to bed. I want to go to bed and be in my head. I want to go to bed and be in my bed and in my head and just wear red. For red is the color that my baby wore and once more, it's true, yes, it is, it's true. Please don't wear red tonight, ohh, ohh, please don't wear red tonight, for red is the color—"

"Okay, okay, Rose. It's okay. I'll go upstairs with you and you can get ready for bed. Then, Mommy will come up and say good night, too. It's okay, Rose." My father reached out his hand and Rose grasped it and they walked out of the dining room together, his long arm around her middle.

My mother sat at the table for a moment, her face in her hands, and then she began clearing the table. We cleared without talking, my mother humming Schubert's "Schlummerlied," a lullaby about the woods and the river calling to the child to go to sleep. She sang it to us every night, when we were small.

My father came back into the kitchen and signaled to my mother. She went upstairs and they came back down together, a few minutes later.

"She's asleep," they said and we went to sit on the porch and listen to the crickets. I don't remember the rest of the evening, but I remember it as quietly sad and I remember the rare sight of my parents holding hands, sitting on the picnic table, watching the sunset.

I woke up at three o'clock in the morning, feeling the cool night air through my sheet. I went down the hall for another blanket and looked into Rose's room, for no reason. She wasn't there. I put on my jeans and a sweater and went downstairs. I could feel her absence. I went outside and saw her wide, draggy footprints darkening the wet grass, into the woods.

"Rosie," I called, too softly, not wanting to wake my parents, not wanting to startle Rose. "Rosie, it's me. Are you here? Are you all right?"

I almost fell over her. Huge and white in the moonlight, her flowered smock bleached in the light and shadow, her sweatpants now completely wet. Her head was flung back, her white, white neck exposed like a lost Greek column.

"Rosie, Rosie—" Her breathing was very slow and her lips were not as pink as they usually were. Her eyelids fluttered.

"Closing time," she whispered. I believe that's what she said.

I sat with her, uncovering the bottle of white pills by her hand, and watched the stars fade.

When the stars were invisible and the sun was warming the air, I went back to the house. My mother was standing on the porch, wrapped in a blanket, watching me. Every step I took overwhelmed me; I could picture my mother slapping me, shooting me for letting her favorite die.

"Warrior queens," she said, wrapping her thin strong arms around me. "I raised warrior queens." She kissed me fiercely and went into the woods by herself.

A little later, she woke my father, who could not go into the woods, and still later she called the police and the funeral parlor. She hung up the phone, lay down, and didn't get back out of bed until the day of the funeral. My father fed us both and called the people who needed to be called and picked out Rose's coffin by himself.

My mother played the piano and Addie sang her pure gold notes and I closed my eyes and saw my sister, fourteen years old, lion's mane thrown back and her eyes tightly closed against the glare of the parking lot lights. That sweet sound held us tight, flowing around us, eddying through our hearts, rising, still rising.

T. C. Boyle

CAVIAR

T. C. BOYLE (1948–) is the author of nineteen books of fiction, including *Talk Talk*, *Tooth and Claw*, and *The Tortilla Curtain*.

I ought to tell you right off I didn't go to college. I was on the wrong rung of the socioeconomic ladder, if you know what I mean. My father was a commercial fisherman on the Hudson, till the PCBs got to him, my mother did typing and filing down at the lumberyard, and my grandmother crocheted doilies and comforters for sale to rich people. Me, I took over my father's trade. I inherited the shack at the end of the pier, the leaky fourteen-foot runabout with the thirty-five-horse Evinrude motor and the seine that's been in the family for three generations. Also, I got to move into the old man's house when he passed on, and he left me his stamp collection and the keys to his '62 Rambler, rusted through till it looked like a gill net hung out to dry.

Anyway, it's a living. Almost. And if I didn't go to college I do read a lot, magazines mostly, but books on ecology and science too. Maybe it was the science part that did me in. You see, I'm the first one around here—I mean, me and Marie are the first ones—to have a baby this new way, where you can't have it on your own. Dr. Ziss said not to worry about it, a little experiment, think of it as a gift from heaven.

Some gift.

But don't get me wrong, I'm not complaining. What happens happens, and I'm as guilty as anybody, I admit it. It's just that when the guys at the Flounder Inn are sniggering in their beer and Marie starts looking at me like I'm a toad or something, you've got to put things in perspective, you've got to realize that it was her all along, she's the one that started it.

"I want a baby," was how she put it.

It was April, raw and wet. Crocuses and dead man's fingers were poking through the dirt along the walk, and the stripers were running. I'd just stepped in the door, beat, chilled to the teeth, when she made her announcement. I went straight for the coffeepot. "Can't afford it," I said.

She didn't plead or try to reason with me. All she did was repeat herself in a matter-of-fact tone, as if she were telling me about some new drapes or a yard

80

sale, and then she marched through the kitchen and out the back door. I sipped at my coffee and watched her through the window. She had a shovel. She was burying something. Deep. When she came back in, her nose was running a bit and her eyes were crosshatched with tiny red lines.

"What were you doing out there?" I asked.

Her chin was crumpled, her hair was wild. "Burying something."

I waited while she fussed with the teapot, my eyebrows arched like question marks. Ten seconds ticked by. "Well, what?"

"My diaphragm."

I've known Marie since high school. We were engaged for five years while she worked for *Reader's Digest* and we'd been married for three and a half when she decided she wanted some offspring. At first I wasn't too keen on the idea, but then I had to admit she was right: the time had come. Our lovemaking had always been lusty and joyful, but after she buried the diaphragm it became tender, intense, purposeful. We tried. For months we tried. I'd come in off the river, reeking of the creamy milt and silver roe that floated two inches deep in the bottom of the boat while fifty- and sixty-pound stripers gasped their last, come in like a wild bull or something, and Marie would be waiting for me upstairs in her nightie and we'd do it before dinner, and then again after. Nothing happened.

Somewhere around July or August, the sweet blueclaw crabs crawling up the riverbed like an army on maneuvers and the humid heat lying over the valley like a cupped hand, Marie went to Sister Eleazar of the Coptic Brotherhood of Ethiop. Sister Eleazar was a black woman, six feet tall at least, in a professor's gown and a fez with a red tassel. Leroy Lent's wife swore by her. Six years Leroy and his wife had been going at it, and then they went to Sister Eleazar and had a pair of twins. Marie thought it was worth a try, so I drove her down there.

The Coptic Brotherhood of Ethiop occupied a lime-green building the size of a two-car garage with a steeple and cross pinned to the roof. Sister Eleazar answered our knock scowling, a little crescent of egg yolk on her chin. "What you want?" she said.

Standing there in the street, a runny-eyed Chihuahua sniffing at my heels, I listened to Marie explain our problem and watched the crescent of egg on Sister Eleazar's face fracture with her smile. "Ohhh," she said, "well, why didn't you say so? Come own in, come own in."

There was one big room inside, poorly lit. Old bottom-burnished pews stretched along three of the four walls and there was a big shiny green table in the center of the floor. The table was heaped with religious paraphernalia—silver salvers and chalices and tinted miniatures of a black man with a crown dwarfing his head. A cot and an icebox huddled against the back wall, which was decorated with magazine clippings of Africa. "Right here, sugar," Sister Eleazar said, leading Marie up to the table. "Now, you take off your coat and your dress, and less ex-amine them wombs."

Marie handed me her coat, and then her tight blue dress with the little white clocks on it, while Sister Eleazar cleared the chalices and whatnot off the table. The Chihuahua had followed us in, and now it sprang up onto the cot with a sigh and buried its nose in its paws. The room stank of dog.

"All right," Sister Eleazar said, turning back to Marie, "you climb up own the table now and stretch yourself out so Sister 'Leazar can listen to your insides and say a prayer over them barren wombs." Marie complied with a nervous smile, and the black woman leaned forward to press an ear to her abdomen. I watched the tassel of Sister Eleazar's fez splay out over Marie's rib cage and I began to get excited: the place dark and exotic, Marie in brassiere and panties, laid out on the table like a sacrificial virgin. Then the sister was mumbling something—a prayer, I guess—in a language I'd never heard before. Marie looked embarrassed. "Don't you worry about nothin'," Sister Eleazar said, looking up at me and winking. "I got just the thing."

She fumbled around underneath the cot for a minute, then came back to the table with a piece of blue chalk—the same as they use in geography class to draw rivers and lakes on the blackboard—and a big yellow can of Colman's dry mustard. She bent over Marie like a heart surgeon, and then, after a few seconds of deliberation, made a blue X on Marie's lower abdomen and said, "Okay, honey, you can get up now."

I watched Marie shrug into her dress, thinking the whole thing was just a lot of superstitious mumbo jumbo and pisantry, when I felt Sister Eleazar's fingers on my arm; she dipped her head and led me out the front door. The sky was overcast. I could smell rain in the air. "Listen," the black woman whispered, handing me the can of mustard, "the problem ain't with her, it's with you. Must be you ain't penetratin' deep enough." I looked into her eyes, trying to keep my face expressionless. Her voice dropped. "What you do is this: make a plaster of this here mustard and rub it on your parts before you go into her, and it'll force out that 'jaculation like a torpedo coming out a submarine—know what I mean?" Then she winked. Marie was at the door. A man with a hoe was digging at his garden in the next yard over. "Oh yeah," the sister said, holding out her hand, "you want to make a donation to the Brotherhood, that'll be eleven dollars and fifty cent."

I never told Marie about the mustard—it was too crazy. All I said was that the sister had told me to give her a mustard plaster on the stomach an hour after we had intercourse—to help the seeds take. It didn't work, of course. Nothing worked. But the years at *Reader's Digest* had made Marie a superstitious woman, and I was willing to go along with just about anything as long as it made her feel better. One night I came to bed and she was perched naked on the edge of the footstool, wound round three times with a string of garlic. "I thought that was for vampires?" I said. She just parted her lips and held out her arms.

In the next few weeks she must have tried every quack remedy in the book. She kept a toad in a clay pot under the bed, ate soup composed of fish eyes and roe, drank goat's milk and cod-liver oil, and filled the medicine chest with elixirs made from nimble weed and rhinoceros horn. Once I caught her down in the basement, dancing in the nude round a live rooster. I was eating meat three meals a day to keep my strength up. Then one night I came across an article about test-tube babies in *Science Digest*. I studied the pictures for a long while, especially the one at the end of the article that showed this English couple, him with a bald dome and her fat as a sow, with their little test-tube son. Then I called Marie.

Dr. Ziss took us right away. He sympathized with our plight, he said, and would do all he could to help us. First he would have to run some tests to see just what the problem was and whether it could be corrected surgically. He led us into the examining room and looked into our eyes and ears, tapped our knees, measured our blood pressure. He drew blood, squinted at my sperm under a microscope, took X rays, did a complete pelvic exam on Marie. His nurse was Irene Goddard, lived up the street from us. She was a sour, square-headed woman in her fifties with little vertical lines etched around her lips. She prodded and poked and pricked us and then had us fill out twenty or thirty pages of forms that asked about everything from bowel movements to whether my grandmother had any facial hair. Two weeks later I got a phone call. The doctor wanted to see us.

We'd hardly got our jackets off when Mrs. Goddard, with a look on her face like she was about to pull the switch at Sing Sing, showed us into the doctor's office. I should tell you that Dr. Ziss is a young man—about my age, I guess—with narrow shoulders, a little clipped mustache, and a woman's head of hair that he keeps brushing back with his hand. Anyway, he was sitting behind his desk sifting through a pile of charts and lab reports when we walked in. "Sit down," he said. "I'm afraid I have some bad news for you." Marie went pale, like she did the time the state troopers called about her mother's accident; her ankles swayed over her high heels and she fell back into the chair as if she'd been shoved. I thought she was going to cry, but the doctor forestalled her. He smiled, showing off all those flossed and fluoridated teeth: "I've got some good news too."

The bad news was that Marie's ovaries were shot. She was suffering from the Stein-Leventhal syndrome, he said, and was unable to produce viable ova. He put it to us straight: "She's infertile, and there's nothing we can do about it. Even if we had the facilities and the know-how, test-tube reproduction would be out of the question."

Marie was stunned. I stared down at the linoleum for a second and listened to her sniffling, then took her hand.

Dr. Ziss leaned across the desk and pushed back a stray lock of hair. "But there is an alternative."

We both looked at him.

"Have you considered a surrogate mother? A young woman who'd be willing to impregnate herself artificially with the husband's semen—for a fee, of course—and then deliver the baby to the wife at the end of the term." He was smoothing his mustache. "It's being done all over the country. And if Mrs. Trimpie pads herself during her 'pregnancy' and 'delivers' in the city, none of your neighbors need ever know that the child isn't wholly and naturally yours."

My mind was racing. I was bombarded with selfish and acquisitive thoughts, seething with scorn for Marie—*she* was the one, *she* was defective, not me—bursting to exercise my God-given right to a child and heir. It's true, it really is—you never want something so much as when somebody tells you you can't have it. I found myself thinking aloud: "So it would really be half ours, and . . . and half—"

"That's right, Mr. Trimpie. And I have already contacted a young woman on your behalf, should you be interested."

I looked at Marie. Her eyes were watering. She gave me a weak smile and pressed my hand.

"She's Caucasian, of course, attractive, fit, very bright: a first-year medical student in need of funds to continue her education."

"Um, uh," I fumbled for the words, "how much; I mean, if we decide to go along with it, how much would it cost?"

The doctor was ready for this one. "Ten thousand dollars," he said without hesitation, "plus hospital costs."

Two days later there was a knock at the door. A girl in peacoat and blue jeans stood there, flanked by a pair of scuffed aquamarine suitcases held shut with masking tape. She looked to be about sixteen, stunted and bony and pale, cheap mother-of-pearl stars for earrings, her red hair short and spiky, as if she were letting a crew cut grow out. I couldn't help thinking of those World War II movies where they shave the actresses' heads for consorting with the Germans; I couldn't help thinking of waifs and wanderers and runaway teenagers. Dr. Ziss's gunmetal Mercedes sat at the curb, clouds of exhaust tugging at the tailpipe in the chill morning air; he waved, and then ground away with a crunch of gravel. "Hi," the girl said, extending her hand, "I'm Wendy."

It had all been arranged. Dr. Ziss thought it would be a good idea if the mother-to-be came to stay with us two weeks or so before the "procedure," to give us a chance to get to know one another, and then maybe stay on with us through the first couple of months so we could experience the pregnancy first-hand; when she began to show she'd move into an apartment on the other side of town, so as not to arouse any suspicion among the neighbors. He was delicate about the question of money, figuring a commercial fisherman and a part-time secretary, with no college and driving a beat-up Rambler, might not exactly be rolling in surplus capital. But the money wasn't a problem really. There was the insurance payoff from Marie's mother—she'd been blindsided by a semi coming off the ramp on the thruway—and the thirty-five hundred I'd got for delivering spawning stripers to Con Ed so they could hatch fish to replace the ones sucked into the screens at the nuclear plant. It was sitting in the County Trust, collecting five and a quarter percent, against the day some emergency came up. Well, this was it. I closed out the account.

The doctor took his fee and explained that the girl would get five thousand dollars on confirmation of pregnancy, and the balance when she delivered. Hospital costs would run about fifteen hundred dollars, barring complications. We shook hands on it, and Marie and I signed a form. I figured I could work nights at the bottling plant if I was strapped.

Now, with the girl standing there before me, I couldn't help feeling a stab of disappointment—she was pretty enough, I guess, but I'd expected something a little more, well, substantial. And red hair. It was a letdown. Deep down I'd been hoping for a blonde, one of those Scandinavian types you see in the cigarette ads. Anyway, I told her I was glad to meet her, and then showed her up to the spare room, which I'd cleaned up and outfitted with a chest of drawers, a bed and a Salvation Army desk, and some cheery knickknacks. I asked her if I could get her a bite to eat, Marie being at work and me waiting around for the tide to go out. She was sitting on the bed, looking tired; she hadn't even bothered to glance out the window at the view of Croton Bay. "Oh yeah," she said after a minute, as if she'd been asleep or daydreaming. "Yeah, that would be nice." Her eyes were gray, the color of drift ice on the river. She called me Nathaniel, soft and formal, like a breathless young schoolteacher taking attendance. Marie never called me anything but Nat, and the guys at the marina settled for Ace. "Have you got a sandwich, maybe? And a cup of hot Nestlé's? I'd really like that, Nathaniel."

I went down and fixed her a BLT, her soft syllables tingling in my ears like a kiss. Dr. Ziss had called her an "oh pear" girl, which I guess referred to her shape. When she'd slipped out of her coat I saw that there was more to her than I'd thought—not much across the top, maybe, but sturdy in the hips and thighs. I couldn't help thinking it was a good sign, but then I had to check myself: I was looking at her like a horse breeder or something.

She was asleep when I stepped in with the sandwich and hot chocolate. I shook her gently and she started up with a gasp, her eyes darting round the room as if she'd forgotten where she was. "Oh yes, yes, thanks," she said, in that maddening, out-of-breath, little girl's voice. I sat on the edge of the desk and watched her eat, gratified to see that her teeth were strong and even, and her nose just about right. "So you're a medical student, Dr. Ziss tells me."

"Hm-hmm," she murmured, chewing. "First-year. I'm going to take the spring semester off, I mean for the baby and all—"

This was the first mention of our contract, and it fell over the conversation like a lead balloon. She hesitated, and I turned red. Here I was, alone in the house with a stranger, a pretty girl, and she was going to have my baby.

She went on, skirting the embarrassment, trying to brighten her voice. "I mean, I love it and all—med school—but it's a grind already and I really don't see how I can afford the tuition, without, without"—she looked up at me—"without your help."

I didn't know what to say. I stared into her eyes for a minute and felt strangely excited, powerful, like a pasha interviewing a new candidate for the harem. Then I picked up the china sturgeon on the desk and turned it over in my hands. "I didn't go to college," I said. And then, as if I were apologizing, "I'm a fisherman."

A cold rain was falling the day the three of us drove down to Dr. Ziss's for the "procedure." The maples were turning, the streets splashed with red and gold, slick, glistening, the whole world a cathedral. I felt humbled somehow, respectful in the face of life and the progress of the generations of man: *My seed is going to take hold*, I kept thinking. *In half an hour I'll be a father*. Marie and Wendy, on the other hand, seemed oblivious to the whole thing, chattering away like a sewing circle, talking about shoes and needlepoint and some actor's divorce. They'd hit it off pretty well, the two of them, sitting in the kitchen over coffee at night, going to movies and thrift shops together, trading gossip, looking up at me and giggling when I stepped into the room. Though Wendy didn't do much around the house—didn't do much more than lie in bed and stare at textbooks—I don't think Marie really minded. She was glad for the company, and there was something more too, of course: Wendy was making a big sacrifice for us. Both of us were deeply grateful.

Dr. Ziss was all smiles that afternoon, pumping my hand, kissing the girls, ushering us into his office like an impresario on opening night. Mrs. Goddard was more restrained. She shot me an icy look, as if I was conspiring to overthrow the Pope or corrupt Girl Scouts or something. Meanwhile, the doctor leaned toward Marie and Wendy and said something I didn't quite catch, and suddenly they were all three of them laughing like Canada geese. Were they laughing at me, I wondered, all at once feeling self-conscious and vulnerable, the odd man out. Dr. Ziss, I noticed, had his arm around Wendy's waist.

If I felt left out, I didn't have time to brood over it. Because Mrs. Goddard had me by the elbow and she was marching me down the hallway to the men's room, where she handed me a condom sealed in tinfoil and a couple of tattered girlie magazines. I didn't need the magazines. Just the thought of what was going to happen in the next room—Marie had asked the doctor if she could do the insemination herself—gave me an erection like a tire iron. I pictured Wendy leaning back on the examining table in a little white smock, nothing underneath, and Marie, my big loving wife, with this syringelike thing . . . that's all it took. I was out of the bathroom in sixty seconds, the wet condom tucked safely away in a sterilized jar.

Afterward, we shared a bottle of pink champagne and a lasagna dinner at Mama's Pasta House. My treat.

One morning, about a month later, I was lying in bed next to Marie and I heard Wendy pad down the hallway to the bathroom. The house was still, and a soft gray light clung to the window sill like a blanket. I was thinking of nothing, or maybe I was thinking of striped bass, sleek and silver, how they ride up out of the deep like pieces of a dream. Next thing I heard was the sound of gagging. Morning sickness, I thought, picking up on a phrase from one of the countless baby books scattered round the house, and suddenly, inexplicably, I was doubled over myself. "Aaaaargh," Wendy gasped, the sound echoing through the house, "aaaargh," and it felt like somebody was pulling my stomach inside out.

At breakfast, she was pale and haggard, her hair greasy and her eyes puffed out. She tried to eat a piece of dry toast, but wound up spitting it into her hand. I couldn't eat, either. Same thing the next day, and the next: she was sick, I was sick. I'd pull the cord on the outboard and the first whiff of exhaust would turn my stomach and I'd have to lean over and puke in the river. Or I'd haul the gill nets up off the bottom and the exertion would nearly kill me. I called the doctor.

"Sympathetic pregnancy," he said, his voice cracking at the far end of a bad connection. "Perfectly normal. The husband identifies with the wife's symptoms."

"But I'm not her husband."

"Husband, father: what difference does it make. You're it."

I thought about that. Thought about it when Wendy and I began to eat like the New York Jets at the training table, thought about it nights at the bottling plant, thought about it when Wendy came into the living room in her underwear one evening and showed us the hard white bulge that was already beginning to open her navel up like a flower. Marie was watching some soppy hospital show on TV; I was reading about the dead water between Manhattan and Staten Island—nothing living there, not even eels. "Look," Wendy said, an angels-in-heaven smile on her face, "it's starting to show." Marie got up and embraced her. I grinned like an idiot, thrilled at the way the panties grabbed her thighs—white nylon with dancing pink flowers—and how her little pointed breasts were beginning to strain at the brassiere. I wanted to put my tongue in her navel.

Next day, while Marie was at work, I tapped on Wendy's door. "Come on in," she said. She was wearing a housecoat, Japanese-y, with dragons and pagodas on it, propped up against the pillows reading an anatomy text. I told her I didn't feel like going down to the river and wondered if she wanted anything. She put the book down and looked at me like a pat of butter sinking into a halibut steak. "Yes," she said, stretching it to two syllables, "as a matter of fact I do." Then she unbuttoned the robe. Later she smiled at me and said: "So what did we need the doctor for, anyway?"

If Marie suspected anything, she didn't show it. I think she was too caught up in the whole thing to have an evil thought about either one of us. I mean, she doted on Wendy, hung on her every word, came home from work each night and shut herself up in Wendy's room for an hour or more. I could hear them giggling. When I asked her what the deal was, Marie just shrugged. "You know," she said, "the usual—girls' talk and such." The shared experience had made them close, closer than sisters, and sometimes I would think of us as one big happy family. But I stopped short of telling Marie what was going on when she was out of the house. Once, years ago, I'd had a fling with a girl we'd known in high school—an arrow-faced little fox with starched hair and raccoon eyes. It had been brief and strictly biological, and then the girl had moved to Ohio. Marie never forgot it. Just the mention of Ohio—even so small a thing as the TV weatherman describing a storm over the Midwest—would set her off.

I'd like to say I was torn, but I wasn't. I didn't want to hurt Marie—she was my wife, my best friend, I loved and respected her—and yet there was Wendy, with her breathy voice and gray eyes, bearing my child. The thought of it, of my son floating around in his own little sea just behind the sweet bulge of her belly ... well, it inflamed me, got me mad with lust and passion and spiritual love too. Wasn't Wendy as much my wife as Marie? Wasn't marriage, at bottom, simply a tool for procreating the species? Hadn't Sarah told Abraham to go in unto Hagar? Looking back on it, I guess Wendy let me make love to her because maybe she was bored and a little horny, lying around in a negligee day and night and studying all that anatomy. She sure didn't feel the way I did—if I know anything, I know that now. But at the time I didn't think of it that way, I didn't think at all. Surrogate mother, surrogate wife. I couldn't get enough of her.

Everything changed when Marie taped a feather bolster around her waist and our "boarder" had to move over to Depew Street. ("Don't know what happened," I told the guys down at the Flounder, "she just up and moved out. Low on bucks, I guess." Nobody so much as looked up from their beer until one of the guys mentioned the Knicks game and Alex DeFazio turned to me and said, "So you got a bun in the oven, is what I hear.") I was at a loss. What with Marie working full-time now, I found myself stuck in the house, alone, with nothing much to do except wear a path in the carpet and eat my heart out. I could walk down to the river, but it was February and nothing was happening, so I'd wind up at the Flounder Inn with my elbows on the bar, watching the mollies and swordtails bump into the sides of the aquarium, hoping somebody would give me a lift across town. Of course Marie and I would drive over to Wendy's after dinner every couple of days or so, and I could talk to her on the telephone till my throat went dry—but it wasn't the same. Even the few times I did get over there in the day, I could feel it. We'd make love, but she seemed shy and reluctant, as if she were performing a duty or something. "What's wrong?" I asked her. "Nothing," she said. It was as if someone had cut a neat little hole in the center of my life.

One time, a stiff windy day in early March, I couldn't stand the sight of four walls any more and I walked the six miles across town and all the way out Depew Street. It was an ugly day. Clouds like steel wool, a dirty crust of ice underfoot, dog turds preserved like icons in the receding snowbanks. The whole way over there I kept thinking up various scenarios: Wendy and I would take the bus for California, then write Marie to come join us; we'd fly to the Virgin Islands and raise the kid on the beach; Marie would have an accident. When I got there, Dr. Ziss's Mercedes was parked out front. I thought that was pretty funny, him being there in the middle of the day, but then I told myself he was her doctor after all. I turned around and walked home.

Nathaniel Jr. was born in New York City at the end of June, nine pounds, one ounce, with a fluff of orange hair and milky gray eyes. Wendy never looked so beautiful. The hospital bed was cranked up, her hair, grown out now, was fresh-washed and brushed, she was wearing the turquoise earrings I'd given her. Marie, meanwhile, was experiencing the raptures of the saints. She gave me a look of pride and fulfillment, rocking the baby in her arms, cooing and beaming. I stole a glance at Wendy. There were two wet circles where her nipples touched the front of her gown. When she put Nathaniel to her breast I thought I was going to faint from the beauty of it, and from something else too: jealousy. I wanted her, then and there.

Dr. Ziss was on the scene, of course, all smiles, as if he'd been responsible for the whole thing. He pecked Marie's cheek, patted the baby's head, shook my hand, and bent low to kiss Wendy on the lips. I handed him a cigar. Three days later Wendy had her five thousand dollars, the doctor and the hospital had been paid off, and Marie and I were back in Westchester with our son. Wendy had been dressed in a loose summer gown and sandals when I gave her the check. I remember she was sitting there on a lacquered bench, cradling the baby, the hospital corridor lit up like a clerestory with sunbeams. There were tears— mainly Marie's—and promises to keep in touch. She handed over Nathaniel as if he was a piece of meat or a sack of potatoes, no regrets. She and Marie embraced, she rubbed her cheek against mine and made a perfunctory little kissing noise, and then she was gone.

I held out for a week. Changing diapers, heating formula, snuggling up with Marie and little Nathaniel, trying to feel whole again. But I couldn't. Every time I looked at my son I saw Wendy, the curl of the lips, the hair, the eyes, the pout—in my distraction, I even thought I heard something of her voice in his gasping howls. Marie was asleep, the baby in her arms. I backed the car out and headed for Depew Street.

The first thing I saw when I rounded the corner onto Depew was the doctor's Mercedes, unmistakable, gunmetal gray, gleaming at the curb like a slap in the face. I was so startled to see it there I almost ran into it. What was this, some kind of postpartum emergency or something? It was 10:00 a.m. Wendy's curtains were drawn. As I stamped across the lawn my fingers began to tremble like they do when I'm tugging at the net and I can feel something tugging back.

The door was open. Ziss was sitting there in T-shirt and jeans, watching cartoons on TV and sipping at a glass of milk. He pushed the hair back from his brow and gave me a sheepish grin. "David?" Wendy called from the back room. "David? Are you going out?" I must have looked like the big loser on a quiz show or something, because Ziss, for once, didn't have anything to say. He just shrugged his shoulders. Wendy's voice, breathy as a flute, came at us again: "Because if you are, get me some sweetcakes and yogurt, and maybe a couple of corn muffins, okay? I'm hungry as a bear."

Ziss got up and walked to the bedroom door, mumbled something I couldn't hear, strode past me without a glance and went on out the back door. I watched him bend for a basketball, dribble around in the dirt, and then cock his arm for a shot at an imaginary basket. On the TV, Sylvester the cat reached into a trash can and pulled out a fish stripped to the bones. Wendy was standing in the doorway. She had nothing to say.

"Look, Wendy," I began. I felt betrayed, cheated, felt as if I was the brunt of a joke between this girl in the housecoat and the curly-headed hotshot fooling around on the lawn. What was his angle, I wondered, heart pounding at my chest, what was hers? "I suppose you two had a good laugh over me, huh?"

She was pouting, the spoiled child. "I fulfilled my part of the bargain."

She had. I got what I'd paid for. But all that had changed, couldn't she see that? I didn't want a son, I didn't want Marie; I wanted her. I told her so. She said nothing. "You've got something going with Ziss, right?" I said, my voice rising. "All along, right?"

She looked tired, looked as if she'd been up for a hundred nights running. I watched her shuffle across the room into the kitchenette, glance into the refrigerator, and come up with a jar of jam. She made herself a sandwich, licking the goo from her fingers, and then she told me I stank of fish. She said she couldn't have a lasting relationship with me because of Marie.

"That's a lot of crap, and you know it." I was shouting. Ziss, fifty feet away, turned to look through the open door.

"All right. It's because we're—" She put the sandwich down, wiped a smear of jelly from her lip. "Because we move in different circles."

"You mean because I'm not some fancy-ass doctor, because I didn't go to college."

She nodded. Slow and deliberate, no room for argument, she held my eyes and nodded.

I couldn't help it. Something just came loose in my head, and the next second I was out the door, knocking Ziss into the dirt. He kicked and scratched, tried to bite me on the wrist, but I just took hold of his hair and laid into his face while Wendy ran around in her Japanese housecoat, screeching like a cat in heat. By the time the police got there I'd pretty well closed up both his eyes and rearranged his dental work. Wendy was bending over him with a bottle of rubbing alcohol when they put the cuffs on me.

Next morning there was a story in the paper. Marie sent Alex DeFazio down with the bail money, and then she wouldn't let me in the house. I banged on the door halfheartedly, then tried one of the windows, only to find she'd nailed it shut. When I saw that, I was just about ready to explode, but then I figured what the hell and fired up the Rambler in a cloud of blue smoke. Cops, dogs, kids, and pedestrians be damned, I ran it like a stock car eight blocks down to the dock and left it steaming in the parking lot. Five minutes later I was planing across the river, a wide brown furrow fanning out behind me.

This was my element, sun, wind, water, life pared down to the basics. Gulls hung in the air like puppets on a wire, spray flew up in my face, the shore sank back into my wake until docks and pleasure boats and clapboard houses were swallowed up and I was alone on the broad gray back of the river. After a while I eased up on the throttle and began scanning the surface for the buoys that marked my gill nets, working by rote, the tight-wound spool in my chest finally beginning to pay out. Then I spotted them, white and red, jogged by the waves. I cut the engine, coasted in and caught hold of the nearest float.

Wendy, I thought, as I hauled at the ropes, ten years, twenty-five, a lifetime: every time I look at my son I'll see your face. Hand over hand, Wendy, Wendy, Wendy, the net heaving up out of the swirling brown depths with its pounds of flesh. But then I wasn't thinking about Wendy any more, or Marie or Nathaniel Jr.—I was thinking about the bottom of the river, I was thinking about fins and scales and cold lidless eyes. The instant I touched the lead rope I knew I was on to something. This time of year it would be sturgeon, big as logs, long-nosed and barbeled, coasting up the riverbed out of some dim watery past, anadromous, preprogrammed, homing in on their spawning grounds like guided missiles. Just then I felt a pulsing in the soles of my sneakers and turned to glance up at the Day Liner, steaming by on its way to Bear Mountain, hundreds of people with picnic baskets and coolers, waving. I jerked at the net like a penitent.

There was a single sturgeon in the net, tangled up like a ball of string. It was dead. I strained to haul the thing aboard, six feet long, two hundred pounds. Cold from the depths, still supple, it hadn't been dead more than an hour— while I banged at my own front door, locked out, it had been thrashing in the dark, locked in. The gulls swooped low, mocking me. I had to cut it out of the net.

Back at the dock I got one of the beer drinkers to give me a hand and we dragged the fish over to the skinning pole. With sturgeon, we hang them by the gills from the top of a ten-foot pole, and then we peel back the scutes like you'd peel a banana. Four or five of the guys stood there watching me, nobody saying anything. I cut all the way round the skin just below the big stiff gill plates and then made five vertical slits the length of the fish. Flies settled on the blade of the knife. The sun beat at the back of my head. I remember there was a guy standing there, somebody I'd never seen before, a guy in a white shirt with a kid about eight or so. The kid was holding a fishing pole. They stepped back, both of them, when I tore the first strip of skin from the fish.

Sturgeon peels back with a raspy, nails-on-the-blackboard sort of sound, reminds me of tearing up sheets or ripping bark from a tree. I tossed the curling strips of leather in a pile, flies sawing away at the air, the big glistening pink carcass hanging there like a skinned deer, blood and flesh. Somebody handed me a beer: it stuck to my hand and I drained it in a gulp. Then I turned to gut the fish, me a doctor, the knife a scalpel, and suddenly I was digging into the vent like Jack the Ripper, slitting it all the way up to the gills in a single violent motion.

"How do you like that?" the man in the white shirt said. "She's got eggs in her."

I glanced down. There they were, wet, beaded, and gray, millions of them, the big clusters tearing free and dropping to the ground like ripe fruit. I cupped my hands and held the trembling mass of it there against the gashed belly, fifty or sixty pounds of the stuff, slippery roe running through my fingers like the silver coins from a slot machine, like a jackpot.

Kevin Brockmeier

THE CEILING

KEVIN BROCKMEIER (1974–) is the author of the novels *The Brief History of the Dead* and *The Truth About Celia*, the story collection *Things That Fall from the Sky*, and the children's novels *City of Names* and *Grooves: A Kind of Mystery*. He has published stories in *The New Yorker, The Georgia Review, McSweeney's, The Oxford American, Best American Short Stories, The Year's Best Fantasy and Horror*, and *The O. Henry Prize Stories* anthology. He has received the *Chicago Tribune*'s Nelson Algren Award, an Italo Calvino Short Fiction Award, a James Michener–Paul Engle Fellowship, three O. Henry Awards (one, a first prize), and an NEA grant. He lives in Little Rock, Arkansas.

There was a sky that day, sun-rich and open and blue. A raft of silver clouds was floating along the horizon, and robins and sparrows were calling from the trees. It was my son Joshua's seventh birthday and we were celebrating in our backyard. He and the children were playing on the swing set, and Melissa and I were sitting on the deck with the parents.

Earlier that afternoon, a balloon and gondola had risen from the field at the end of our block, sailing past us with an exhalation of fire. Joshua told his friends that he knew the pilot. "His name is Mister Clifton," he said, as they tilted their heads back and slowly revolved in place. "I met him at the park last year. He took me into the air with him and let me drop a soccer ball into a swimming pool. We almost hit a helicopter. He told me he'd come by on my birthday." Joshua shielded his eyes against the sun. "Did you see him wave?" he asked. "He just waved at me."

This was a story.

The balloon drifted lazily away, turning to expose each delta and crease of its fabric, and we listened to the children resuming their play. Mitch Nauman slipped his sunglasses into his shirt pocket. "Ever notice how kids their age will handle a toy?" he said. Mitch was our next-door neighbor.

He was the single father of Bobby Nauman, Joshua's strange best friend.

His other best friend, Chris Boschetti, came from a family of cosmetics executives. My wife had taken to calling them "Rich and Strange."

Mitch pinched the front of his shirt between his fingers and fanned himself with it. "The actual function of the toy is like some sort of obstacle," he said. "They'll dream up a new use for everything in the world."

I looked across the yard at the swing set: Joshua was trying to shinny up one of the Apoles; Taylor Tugwell and Sam Yoo were standing on the teeter swing; Adam Smithee was tossing fistfuls of pebbles onto the slide and watching them rattle to the ground.

My wife tipped one of her sandals onto the grass with the ball of her foot. "Playing as you should isn't Fun," she said: "it's Design." She parted her toes around the front leg of Mitch's lawn chair. He leaned back into the sunlight, and her calf muscles tautened.

My son was something of a disciple of flying things. On his bedroom wall were posters of fighter planes and wild birds. A model of a helicopter was chandeliered to his ceiling. His birthday cake, which sat before me on the picnic table, was decorated with a picture of a rocket ship—a silver-white missile with discharging thrusters. I had been hoping that the baker would place a few stars in the frosting as well (the cake in the catalog was dotted with yellow candy sequins), but when I opened the box I found that they were missing. So this is what I did: as Joshua stood beneath the swing set, fishing for something in his pocket, I planted his birthday candles deep in the cake. I pushed them in until each wick was surrounded by only a shallow bracelet of wax. Then I called the children over from the swing set. They came tearing up divots in the grass.

We sang happy birthday as I held a match to the candles.

Joshua closed his eyes.

"Blow out the stars," I said, and his cheeks rounded with air.

That night, after the last of the children had gone home, my wife and I sat outside drinking, each of us wrapped in a separate silence. The city lights were burning, and Joshua was sleeping in his room. A nightjar gave one long trill after another from somewhere above us.

Melissa added an ice cube to her glass, shaking it against the others until it whistled and cracked. I watched a strand of cloud break apart in the sky. The moon that night was bright and full, but after a while it began to seem damaged to me, marked by some small inaccuracy. It took me a moment to realize why this was: against its blank white surface was a square of perfect darkness. The square was without blemish or flaw, no larger than a child's tooth, and I could not tell whether it rested on the moon itself or hovered above it like a cloud. It looked as if a window had been opened clean through the floor of the rock, presenting to view a stretch of empty space. I had never seen such a thing before.

"What is that?" I said.

Melissa made a sudden noise, a deep, defeated little oh.

"My life is a mess," she said.

Within a week, the object in the night sky had grown perceptibly larger. It would appear at sunset, when the air was dimming to purple, as a faint granular blur, a certain filminess at the high point of the sky, and would remain there through the night. It blotted out the light of passing stars and seemed to travel across the face of the moon, but it did not move. The people of my town were uncertain as to whether the object was spreading or approaching—we could see only that it was getting bigger—and this matter gave rise to much speculation. Gleason the butcher insisted that it wasn't there at all, that it was only an illusion. "It all has to do with the satellites," he said. "They're bending the light from that place like a lens. It just looks like something's there." But though his manner was relaxed and he spoke with conviction, he would not look up from his cutting board.

The object was not yet visible during the day, but we could feel it above us as we woke to the sunlight each morning: there was a tension and strain to the air, a shift in its customary balance. When we stepped from our houses to go to work, it was as if we were walking through a new sort of gravity, harder and stronger, not so yielding.

As for Melissa, she spent several weeks pacing the house from room to room. I watched her fall into a deep abstraction. She had cried into her pillow the night of Joshua's birthday, shrinking away from me beneath the blankets. "I just need to sleep," she said, as I sat above her and rested my hand on her side. "Please. Lie down. Stop hovering." I soaked a washcloth for her in the cold water of the bathroom sink, folding it into quarters and leaving it on her nightstand in a porcelain bowl.

The next morning, when I found her in the kitchen, she was gathering a coffee filter into a little wet sachet. "Are you feeling better?" I asked.

"I'm fine." She pressed the foot lever of the trash can, and its lid popped open with a rustle of plastic.

"Is it Joshua?"

Melissa stopped short, holding the pouch of coffee in her outstretched hand. "What's wrong with Joshua?" she said. There was a note of concern in her voice.

"He's seven now," I told her. When she didn't respond, I continued with, "You don't look a day older than when we met, honey. You know that, don't you?"

She gave a puff of air through her nose—this was a laugh, but I couldn't tell what she meant to express by it, bitterness or judgment or some kind of easy cheer. "It's not Joshua," she said, and dumped the coffee into the trash can. "But thanks all the same."

It was the beginning of July before she began to ease back into the life of our family. By this time, the object in the sky was large enough to eclipse the full moon. Our friends insisted that they had never been able to see any change in my wife at all, that she had the same style of speaking, the same habits and twists and eccentricities as ever. This was, in a certain sense, true. I noticed the difference chiefly when we were alone together.

After we had put Joshua to bed, we would sit with one another in the living room, and when I asked her a question, or when the telephone rang, there was always a certain brittleness to her, a hesitancy of manner that suggested she was hearing the world from across a divide. It was clear to me at such times that she had taken herself elsewhere, that she had constructed a shelter from the wood and clay and stone of her most intimate thoughts and stepped inside, shutting the door. The only question was whether the person I saw tinkering at the window was opening the latches or sealing the cracks.

One Saturday morning, Joshua asked me to take him to the library for a story reading. It was almost noon, and the sun was just beginning to darken at its zenith. Each day, the shadows of our bodies would shrink toward us from the west, vanish briefly in the midday soot, and stretch away into the east, falling off the edge of the world. I wondered sometimes if I would ever see my reflection pooled at my feet again. "Can Bobby come, too?" Joshua asked as I tightened my shoes.

I nodded, pulling the laces up in a series of butterfly loops. "Why don't you run over and get him," I said, and he sprinted off down the hallway.

Melissa was sitting on the front porch steps, and I knelt down beside her as I left. "I'm taking the boys into town," I said. I kissed her cheek and rubbed the base of her neck, felt the cirrus curls of hair there moving back and forth through my fingers.

"Shh." She held a hand out to silence me. "Listen."

The insects had begun to sing, the birds to fall quiet. The air gradually became filled with a peaceful chirring noise.

"What are we listening for?" I whispered.

Melissa bowed her head for a moment, as if she were trying to keep count of something. Then she looked up at me. In answer, and with a sort of weariness about her, she spread her arms open to the world.

Before I stood to leave, she asked me a question: "We're not all that much alike, are we?" she said.

The plaza outside the library was paved with red brick. Dogwood trees were planted in hollows along the perimeter, and benches of distressed metal stood here and there on concrete pads. A member of a local guerrilla theater troupe was delivering a recitation from beneath a streetlamp; she sat behind a wooden desk, her hands folded one atop the other, and spoke as if into a camera. "Where did this object come from?" she said. "What is it, and when will it stop its descent? How did we find ourselves in this place? Where do we go from here? Scientists are baffled. In an interview with this station, Dr. Stephen Mandruzzato, head of the prestigious Horton Institute of Astronomical Studies, had this to say: 'We don't know. We don't know. We just don't know.' " I led Joshua and Bobby Nauman through the heavy dark glass doors of the library, and we took our seats in the Children's Reading Room. The tables were set low to the ground so that my legs pressed flat against the underside, and the air carried that peculiar, sweetened-milk smell of public libraries and elementary schools. Bobby Nauman began to play the Where Am I? game with Joshua. "Where am I?" he would ask, and then he'd warm-and-cold Joshua around the room until Joshua had found him. First he was in a potted plant, then on my shirt collar, then beneath the baffles of an air vent. After a time, the man who was to read to us moved into place. He said hello to the children, coughed his throat clear, and opened his book to the title page: "Chicken Little," he began.

As he read, the sky grew bright with afternoon. The sun came through the windows in a sheet of fire.

Joshua started the second grade in September. His new teacher mailed us a list of necessary school supplies, which we purchased the week before classes began—pencils and a utility box, glue and facial tissues, a ruler and a notebook and a tray of watercolor paints. On his first day, Melissa shot a photograph of Joshua waving to her from the front door, his backpack wreathed over his shoulder and a lunch sack in his right hand. He stood in the flash of hard white light, then kissed her good-bye and joined Rich and Strange in the car pool.

Autumn passed in its slow, sheltering way, and toward the end of November, Joshua's teacher asked the class to write a short essay describing a community of local animals. The paragraph Joshua wrote was captioned "What Happened to the Birds." We fastened it to the refrigerator with magnets.

There were many birds here before, but now they're gone. Nobody knows where they went. I used to see them in the trees. I fed one at the zoo when I was little. It was big. The birds went away when no one was looking. The trees are quiet now. They do not move.

All of this was true. As the object in the sky became visible during the daylight—and as, in the tide of several months, it descended over our town—the birds and migrating insects disappeared. I did not notice they were gone, though, nor the muteness with which the sun rose in the morning, nor the stillness of the grass and trees, until I read Joshua's essay.

The world at this time was full of confusion and misgiving and unforeseen changes of heart. One incident that I recall clearly took place in the Main Street Barber Shop on a cold winter Tuesday. I was sitting in a pneumatic chair while Wesson the barber trimmed my hair. A nylon gown was draped over my body to catch the cuttings, and I could smell the peppermint of Wesson's chewing gum. "So how 'bout this weather?" he chuckled, working away at my crown.

Weather gags had been circulating through our offices and barrooms ever since the object—which was as smooth and reflective as obsidian glass, and which the newspapers had designated "the ceiling"—had descended to the level of the cloud base. I gave my usual response, "A little overcast today, wouldn't you say?" and Wesson barked an appreciative laugh.

Wesson was one of those men who had passed his days waiting for the rest of his life to come about. He busied himself with his work, never marrying, and doted on the children of his customers. "Something's bound to happen soon," he would often say at the end of a conversation, and there was a quickness to his eyes that demonstrated his implicit faith in the proposition. When his mother died, this faith seemed to abandon him. He went home each evening to the small house that they had shared, shuffling cards or paging through a magazine until he fell asleep. Though he never failed to laugh when a customer was at hand, the eyes he wore became empty and white, as if some essential fire in them had been spent.

His enthusiasm began to seem like desperation. It was only a matter of time.

"How's the pretty lady?" he asked me.

I was watching him in the mirror, which was both parallel to and coextensive with a mirror on the opposite wall. "She hasn't been feeling too well," I said. "But I think she's coming out of it."

"Glad to hear it. Glad to hear it," he said. "And business at the hardware store?"

I told him that business was fine. I was on my lunch break.

The bell on the door handle gave a tink, and a current of cold air sent a little eddy of cuttings across the floor. A man we had never seen before leaned into the room. "Have you seen my umbrella?" he said. "I can't find my umbrella, have you seen it?" His voice was too loud—high and sharp, fluttery with worry—and his hands shook with a distinct tremor.

"Can't say that I have," said Wesson. He smiled emptily, showing his teeth, and his fingers tensed around the back of my chair.

There was a sudden feeling of weightlessness to the room.

"You wouldn't tell me anyway, would you?" said the man. "Jesus," he said. "You people."

Then he took up the ashtray stand and slammed it against the window.

A cloud of gray cinders shot out around him, but the window merely shuddered in its frame. He let the stand fall to the floor and it rolled into a magazine rack. Ash drizzled to the ground. The man brushed a cigarette butt from his jacket. "You people," he said again, and he left through the open glass door.

As I walked home later that afternoon, the scent of barbershop talcum blew from my skin in the winter wind. The plane of the ceiling was stretched across the firmament, covering my town from end to end, and I could see the lights of a thousand streetlamps caught like constellations in its smooth black polish. It occurred to me that if nothing were to change, if the ceiling were simply to hover where it was forever, we might come to forget that it was even there, charting for ourselves a new map of the night sky.

Mitch Nauman was leaving my house when I arrived. We passed on the lawn, and he held up Bobby's knapsack. "He leaves this thing everywhere," he said. "Buses. Your house. The schoolroom. Sometimes I think I should tie it to his belt." Then he cleared his throat. "New haircut? I like it."

"Yeah, it was getting a bit shaggy."

He nodded and made a clicking noise with his tongue. "See you next time," he said, and he vanished through his front door, calling to Bobby to climb down from something.

By the time the object had fallen as low as the tree spires, we had noticed the acceleration in the wind. In the thin strip of space between the ceiling and the pavement, it narrowed and kindled and collected speed. We could hear it buffeting the walls of our houses at night, and it produced a constant low sigh in the darkness of movie halls. People emerging from their doorways could be seen to brace themselves against the charge and pressure of it. It was as if our entire town were an alley between tall buildings.

I decided one Sunday morning to visit my parents' gravesite: the cemetery in which they were buried would spread with knotgrass every spring, and it was necessary to tend their plot before the weeds grew too thick. The house was still peaceful as I showered and dressed, and I stepped as quietly as I could across the bath mat and the tile floor. I watched the water in the toilet bowl rise and fall as gusts of wind channeled their way through the pipes. Joshua and Melissa were asleep, and the morning sun flashed at the horizon and disappeared.

At the graveyard, a small boy was tossing a tennis ball into the air as his mother swept the dirt from a memorial tablet. He was trying to touch the ceiling with it, and with each successive throw he drew a bit closer, until, at the height of its climb, the ball jarred to one side before it dropped. The cemetery was otherwise empty, its monuments and trees the only material presence.

My parents' graves were clean and spare. With such scarce sunlight, the knotgrass had failed to blossom, and there was little tending for me to do.

I combed the plot for leaves and stones and pulled the rose stems from the flower wells. I knelt at the headstone they shared and unfastened a zipper of moss from it. Sitting there, I imagined for a moment that my parents were living together atop the ceiling: they were walking through a field of high yellow grass, beneath the sun and the sky and the tousled white clouds, and she was bending in her dress to examine a flower, and he was bending beside her, his hand on her waist, and they were unaware that the world beneath them was settling to the ground.

When I got home, Joshua was watching television on the living room sofa, eating a plump yellow doughnut from a paper towel. A dollop of jelly had fallen onto the back of his hand. "Mom left to run an errand," he said.

The television picture fluttered and curved for a moment, sending spits of rain across the screen, then it recrystallized. An aerial transmission tower had collapsed earlier that week—the first of many such fallings in our town—and the quality of our reception had been diminishing ever since.

"I had a dream last night," Joshua said. "I dreamed that I dropped my bear through one of the grates on the sidewalk." He owned a worn-down cotton teddy bear, its seams looped with clear plastic stitches, that he had been given as a toddler. "I tried to catch him, but I missed. Then I lay down on the ground and stretched out my arm for him. I was reaching through the grate, and when I looked beneath the sidewalk, I could see another part of the city. There were people moving around down there.

"There were cars and streets and bushes and lights. The sidewalk was some sort of bridge, and in my dream I thought, 'Oh yeah. Now why didn't I remember that?' Then I tried to climb through to get my bear, but I couldn't lift the grate up."

The morning weather forecaster was weeping on the television.

"Do you remember where this place was?" I asked.

"Yeah."

"Maybe down by the bakery?" I had noticed Melissa's car parked there a few times, and I remembered a kid tossing pebbles into the grate.

"That's probably it."

"Want to see if we can find it?"

Joshua pulled at the lobe of his ear for a second, staring into the middle distance. Then he shrugged his shoulders. "Okay," he decided.

I don't know what we expected to discover there. Perhaps I was simply seized by a whim—the desire to be spoken to, the wish to be instructed by a dream. When I was Joshua's age, I dreamed one night that I found a new door in my house, one that opened from my cellar onto the bright, aseptic aisles of a drugstore: I walked through it, and saw a flash of light, and found myself sitting up in bed. For several days after, I felt a quickening of possibility, like the touch of some other geography, whenever I passed by the cellar door. It was as if I'd opened my eyes to the true inward map of the world, projected according to our own beliefs and understandings.

On our way through the town center, Joshua and I waded past a cluster of people squinting into the horizon. There was a place between the post office and the library where the view to the west was occluded by neither hills nor buildings, and crowds often gathered there to watch the distant blue belt of the sky. We shouldered our way through and continued into town.

Joshua stopped outside the Kornblum Bakery, beside a trash basket and a newspaper carrel, where the light from two streetlamps lensed together on the ground. "This is it," he said, and made a gesture indicating the iron grate at our feet. Beneath it we could see the shallow basin of a drainage culvert. It was even and dry, and a few brittle leaves rested inside it.

"Well," I said. There was nothing there. "That's disappointing."

"Life's disappointing," said Joshua.

He was borrowing a phrase of his mother's, one that she had taken to using these last few months. Then, as if on cue, he glanced up and a light came into his eyes. "Hey," he said. "There's Mom."

Melissa was sitting behind the plate glass window of a restaurant on the opposite side of the street. I could see Mitch Nauman talking to her from across the table, his face soft and casual. Their hands were cupped together beside the pepper crib, and his shoes stood empty on the carpet. He was stroking her left leg with his right foot, its pad and arch curved around her calf. The image was as clear and exact as a melody.

I took Joshua by the shoulders. "What I want you to do," I said, "is knock on Mom's window. When she looks up, I want you to wave."

And he did exactly that—trotting across the asphalt, tapping a few times on the glass, and waving when Melissa started in her chair. Mitch Nauman let his foot fall to the carpet. Melissa found Joshua through the window. She crooked her head and gave him a tentative little flutter of her fingers. Then she met my eyes. Her hand stilled in the air. Her face seemed to fill suddenly with movement, then just as suddenly to empty—it reminded me of nothing so much as a flock of birds scattering from a lawn. I felt a kick of pain in my chest and called to Joshua from across the street. "Come on, sport," I said. "Let's go home."

It was not long after—early the next morning, before we awoke—that the town water tower collapsed, blasting a river of fresh water down our empty streets. Hankins the grocer, who had witnessed the event, gathered an audience that day to his lunch booth in the coffee shop: "I was driving past the tower when it happened," he said. "Heading in early to work. First I heard a creaking noise, and then I saw the leg posts buckling. Wham!"—he smacked the table with his palms—"So much water! It surged into the side of my car, and I lost control of the wheel. The stream carried me right down the road. I felt like a tiny paper boat." He smiled and held up a finger, then pressed it to the side of a half-empty soda can, tipping it gingerly onto its side. Coca-Cola washed across the table with a hiss of carbonation. We hopped from our seats to avoid the spill.

The rest of the town seemed to follow in a matter of days, falling to the ground beneath the weight of the ceiling. Billboards and streetlamps, chimneys and statues. Church steeples, derricks, and telephone poles. Klaxon rods and restaurant signs. Apartment buildings and energy pylons. Trees released a steady sprinkle of leaves and pinecones, then came timbering to the earth—those that were broad and healthy cleaving straight down the heartwood, those that were thin and pliant bending until they cracked. Maintenance workers installed panels of light along the sidewalk, routing the electricity through underground cables. The ceiling itself proved unassailable. It bruised fists and knuckles. It stripped the teeth from power saws. It broke drill bits. It extinguished flames. One afternoon the television antenna tumbled from my rooftop, landing on the hedges in a zigzag of wire. A chunk of plaster fell across the kitchen table as I was eating dinner that night. I heard a board split in the living room wall the next morning, and then another in the hallway, and then another in the bedroom. It sounded like gunshots detonating in a closed room. Melissa and Joshua were already waiting on the front lawn when I got there. A boy was standing on a heap of rubble across the street playing Atlas, his up-raked shoulders supporting the world. A man on a stepladder was pasting a sign to the ceiling: SHOP AT CARSON'S. Melissa pulled her jacket tighter. Joshua took my sleeve. A trough spread open beneath the shingles of our roof, and we watched our house collapse into a mass of brick and mortar.

I was lying on the ground, a tree root pressing into the small of my back, and I shifted slightly to the side. Melissa was lying beside me, and Mitch Nauman beside her. Joshua and Bobby, who had spent much of the day crawling aimlessly about the yard, were asleep now at our feet. The ceiling was no higher than a coffee table, and I could see each pore of my skin reflected in its surface. Above the keening of the wind there was a tiny edge of sound—the hum of the sidewalk lights, steady, electric, and warm.

"Do you ever get the feeling that you're supposed to be someplace else?" said Melissa. She paused for a moment, perfectly still. "It's a kind of sudden dread," she said.

Her voice seemed to hover in the air for a moment.

I had been observing my breath for the last few hours on the polished undersurface of the ceiling: every time I exhaled, a mushroom-shaped fog would cover my reflection, and I found that I could control the size of this fog by adjusting the force and the speed of my breathing. When Melissa asked her question, the first I had heard from her in many days, I gave a sudden puff of air through my nose and two icicle-shaped blossoms appeared. Mitch Nauman whispered something into her ear, but his voice was no more than a murmur, and I could not make out the words. In a surge of emotion that I barely recognized, some strange combination of rivalry and adoration, I took her hand in my own and squeezed it. When nothing happened, I squeezed it again. I brought it to my chest, and I brought it to my mouth, and I kissed it and kneaded it and held it tight.

I was waiting to feel her return my touch, and I felt at that moment, felt with all my heart, that I could wait the whole life of the world for such a thing, until the earth and the sky met and locked and the distance between them closed forever.

JEALOUS HUSBAND RETURNS
IN FORM OF PARROT

ROBERT OLEN BUTLER (1945–) has published ten novels—*The Alleys of Eden, Sun Dogs, Countrymen of Bones, On Distant Ground, Wabash, The Deuce, They Whisper, The Deep Green Sea, Mr. Spaceman,* and *Fair Warning*—and five volumes of short fiction—*Tabloid Dreams, Had a Good Time, Severance, Weegee Stories,* and *A Good Scent from a Strange Mountain,* which won the 1993 Pulitzer Prize for Fiction. Butler has also published a volume of his lectures on the creative process, *From Where You Dream,* edited and with an introduction by Janet Burroway. Among his numerous other awards are a Guggenheim Fellowship in Fiction, the Richard and Hinda Rosenthal Foundation Award from the American Academy of Arts and Letters, and two National Magazine Awards in Fiction. His stories have appeared widely in such publications as *The New Yorker, Esquire, Harper's, The Atlantic Monthly, Zoetrope,* and *The Paris Review* and have been frequently anthologized. He is the Francis Eppes Distinguished Professor holding the Michael Shaara Chair in Creative Writing at Florida State University in Tallahassee, Florida.

I never can quite say as much as I know. I look at other parrots and I wonder if it's the same for them, if somebody is trapped in each of them paying some kind of price for living their life in a certain way. For instance, "Hello" I say, and I'm sitting on a perch in a pet store in Houston and what I'm really thinking is "Holy shit. It's you." And what's happened is I'm looking at my wife.

"Hello," she says, and she comes over to me and I can't believe how beautiful she is. Those great brown eyes, almost as dark as the center of mine. And her nose—I don't remember her for her nose but its beauty is clear to me now. Her nose is a little too long, but it's redeemed by the faint hook to it.

She scratches the back of my neck.

Her touch makes my tail flare. I feel the stretch and rustle of me back there. I bend my head to her and she whispers, "Pretty bird."

For a moment I think she knows it's me. But she doesn't, of course. I say "Hello" again and I will eventually pick up "pretty bird." I can tell that as soon as she says it, but for now I can only give her another hello. Her fingertips move through my feathers and she seems to know about birds. She knows that to pet a bird you don't smooth his feathers down, you ruffle them.

But of course she did that in my human life, as well. It's all the same for her. Not that I was complaining, even to myself, at that moment in the pet shop when she found me like I presume she was supposed to. She said it again, "Pretty bird," and this brain that works like it does now could feel that tiny little voice of mine ready to shape itself around these sounds. But before I could get them out of my beak there was this guy at my wife's shoulder and all my feathers went slick flat like to make me small enough not to be seen and I backed away. The pupils of my eyes pinned and dilated and pinned again.

He circled around her. A guy that looked like a meat packer, big in the chest and thick with hair, the kind of guy that I always sensed her eyes moving to when I was alive. I had a bare chest and I'd look for little black hairs on the sheets when I'd come home on a day with the whiff of somebody else in the air. She was still in the same goddamn rut.

A hello wouldn't do and I'd recently learned good night but it was the wrong suggestion altogether, so I said nothing and the guy circled her and he was looking at me with a smug little smile and I fluffed up all my feathers, made myself about twice as big, so big he'd see he couldn't mess with me. I waited for him to draw close enough to take off the tip of his finger.

But she intervened. Those pine-nut brown eyes were before me and she said, "I want him."

And that's how I ended up in my own house once again. She bought me a large black wrought-iron cage, very large, convinced by some young guy who clerked in the bird department and who took her aside and made his voice go much too soft when he was doing the selling job. The meat packer didn't like it. I didn't either. I'd missed a lot of chances to take a bite out of this clerk in my stay at the shop and I regretted that suddenly.

But I got my giant cage and I guess I'm happy enough about that. I can pace as much as I want. I can hang upside down. It's full of bird toys. That dangling thing over there with knots and strips of rawhide and a bell at the bottom needs a good thrashing a couple of times a day and I'm the bird to do it. I look at the very dangle of it and the thing is rough, the rawhide and the knotted rope, and I get this restlessness back in my tail, a burning thrashing feeling, and it's like all the times when I was sure there was a man naked with my wife. Then I go to this thing that feels so familiar and I bite and bite and it's very good.

I could have used the thing the last day I went out of this house as a man. I'd found the address of the new guy at my wife's office. He'd been there a month in the shipping department and three times she'd mentioned him. She didn't even have to work with him and three times I heard about him, just dropped into the conversation. "Oh," she'd say when a car commercial came on the television, "that car there is like the one the new man in shipping owns. Just like it."

Hey, I'm not stupid. She said another thing about him and then another and right after the third one I locked myself in the bathroom because I couldn't rage about this anymore. I felt like a damn fool whenever I actually said anything about this kind of feeling and she looked at me like she could start hating me real easy and so I was working on saying nothing, even if it meant locking myself up. My goal was to hold my tongue about half the time. That would be a good start.

But this guy from shipping. I found out his name and his address and it was one of her typical Saturday afternoons of vague shopping. So I went to his house, and his car that was just like the commercial was outside. Nobody was around in the neighborhood and there was this big tree in the back of the house going up to a second-floor window that was making funny little sounds. I went up. The shade was drawn but not quite all the way. I was holding on to a limb with arms and legs wrapped around it like it was her in those times when I could forget the others for a little while. But the crack in the shade was just out of view and I crawled on along till there was no limb left and I fell on my head. Thinking about that now, my wings flap and I feel myself lift up and it all seems so avoidable. Though I know I'm different now. I'm a bird.

Except I'm not. That's what's confusing. It's like those times when she would tell me she loved me and I actually believed her and maybe it was true and we clung to each other in bed and at times like that I was different. I was the man in her life. I was whole with her. Except even at that moment, holding her sweetly, there was this other creature inside me who knew a lot more about it and couldn't quite put all the evidence together to speak.

My cage sits in the den. My pool table is gone and the cage is sitting in that space and I come all the way down to one end of my perch. I can see through the door and down the back hallway to the master bedroom. When she keeps the bedroom door open I can see the space at the foot of the bed but not the bed itself. That I can sense to the left, just out of sight. I watch the men go in and I hear the sounds but I can't quite see. And they drive me crazy.

I flap my wings and I squawk and I fluff up and I slick down and I throw seed and I attack that dangly toy as if it was the guy's balls, but it does no good. It never did any good in the other life either, the thrashing around I did by myself. In that other life I'd have given anything to be standing in this den with her doing this thing with some other guy just down the hall and all I had to do was walk down there and turn the corner and she couldn't deny it anymore.

But now all I can do is try to let it go. I sidestep down to the opposite end of the cage and I look out the big sliding glass doors to the backyard. It's a pretty yard. There are great placid live oak trees with good places to roost. There's a blue sky that plucks at the feathers on my chest. There are clouds. Other birds. Fly away. I could just fly away.

I tried once and I learned a lesson. She forgot and left the door to my cage open and I climbed beak and foot, beak and foot, along the bars and curled around to stretch sideways out the door and the vast scene of peace was there at the other end of the room. I flew.

And a pain flared through my head and I fell straight down and the room whirled around and the only good thing was she held me. She put her hands under my wings and lifted me and clutched me to her breast and I wish there hadn't been bees in my head at the time so I could have enjoyed that, but she put me back in the cage and wept awhile. That touched me, her tears. And I looked back to the wall of sky and trees. There was something invisible there between me and that dream of peace. I remembered, eventually, about glass, and I knew I'd been lucky, I knew that for the little hollow-boned skull I was doing all this thinking in, it meant death.

She wept that day but by the night she had another man. A guy with a thick Georgia truck-stop accent and pale white skin and an Adam's apple big as my seed ball. This guy has been around for a few weeks and he makes a whooping sound down the hallway, just out of my sight. At times like that I want to fly against the bars of the cage, but I don't. I have to remember how the world has changed.

She's single now, of course. Her husband, the man that I was, is dead to her. She does not understand all that is behind my "hello." I know many words, for a parrot. I am a yellow-nape Amazon, a handsome bird, I think, green with a splash of yellow at the back of my neck. I talk pretty well, but none of my words are adequate. I can't make her understand. And what would I say if I could?

I was jealous in life. I admit it. I would admit it to her. But it was because of my connection to her. I would explain that. When we held each other, I had no past at all, no present but her body, no future but to lie there and not let her go. I was an egg hatched beneath her crouching body, I entered as a chick into her wet sky of a body, and all that I wished was to sit on her shoulder and fluff my feathers and lay my head against her cheek, my neck exposed to her hand. And so the glances that I could see in her, the movement of her eyes in public to other men, the laughs sent across a room, the tracking of her mind behind her blank eyes, pursuing images of others, her distraction even in our bed, the ghosts that were there of men who'd touched her, perhaps even that very day. I was not part of all those other men who were part of her. I didn't want to connect to all that. It was only her that I would fluff for but these others were there also and I couldn't put them aside. I sensed them inside her and so they were inside me. If I had the words, these are the things I would say.

But half an hour ago there was a moment that thrilled me. A word, a word we all knew in the pet shop, was just the right word after all. This guy with his cowboy belt buckle and rattlesnake boots and his pasty face and his twanging words of love trailed after my wife through the den, past my cage, and I said,

"Cracker." He even flipped his head back a little at this in surprise. He'd been called that before to his face, I realized. I said it again, "Cracker." But to him I was a bird and he let it pass. "Cracker," I said. "Hello, cracker." That was even better. They were out of sight through the hall doorway and I hustled along the perch and I caught a glimpse of them before they made the turn to the bed and I said, "Hello, cracker," and he shot me one last glance.

It made me hopeful. I eased away from that end of the cage, moved toward the scene of peace beyond the far wall. The sky is chalky blue today, blue like the brow of the blue-front Amazon who was on the perch next to me for about a week at the store. She was very sweet and I watched her carefully for a day or two when she first came in and it wasn't long before she ruffled herself for a Mexican redhead named Cosmo and I knew she'd break my heart. But her color now in the sky is sweet, really. I left all those feelings behind me when my wife showed up. I am a faithful man, for all my suspicions of women. Too faithful, maybe. I am ready to give too much and maybe that's the problem.

The whooping began down the hall and I focused on a tree out there. A crow flapped down, his mouth open, his throat throbbing, though I could not hear his sound. I was feeling very odd. At least I'd made my point to the guy in the other room. "Pretty bird," I said, referring to myself. She called me pretty bird and I believed her and I told myself again, "Pretty bird."

But then something new happened, something very difficult for me. She appeared in the den naked. I have not seen her naked since I fell from the tree and had no wings to fly. She always had a certain tidiness in things. She was naked in the bedroom, clothed in the den. But now she appears from the hallway and I look at her and she is still slim and she is beautiful, I think, at least I clearly remember that as her husband I found her beautiful in this state. Now, though, she seems *too* naked. Plucked. I find that a sad thing. I am sorry for her and she goes by me and she disappears into the kitchen. I want to pluck some of my own feathers, the feathers from my chest, and give them to her. I love her more in that moment, seeing her terrible nakedness, than I ever have before.

And since I've had success in the last few minutes with words, when she comes back I am moved to speak. "Hello," I say, meaning, You are still connected to me, I still want only you. "Hello," I say again. Please listen to this tiny heart that beats fast at all times for you.

And she does indeed stop and she comes to me and bends to me. "Pretty bird," I say, and I am saying you are beautiful, my wife, and your beauty cries out for protection. "Pretty." I want to cover you with my own nakedness. "Bad bird," I say. If there are others in your life, even in your mind, then there is nothing I can do. "Bad." Your nakedness is touched from inside by the others. "Open," I say. How can we be whole together if you are not empty in the place that I am to fill?

She smiles at this and she opens the door to my cage. "Up," I say, meaning, Is there no place for me in this world where I can be free of this terrible sense of others?

She reaches in now and offers her hand and I climb onto it and I tremble and she says, "Poor baby."

"Poor baby," I say. You have yearned for wholeness too and somehow I failed you. I was not enough. "Bad bird," I say. I'm sorry.

And then the cracker comes around the corner. He wears only his rattlesnake boots. I take one look at his miserable, featherless body and shake my head. We keep our sexual parts hidden, we parrots, and this man is a pitiful sight. "Peanut," I say. I presume that my wife simply has not noticed. But that's foolish, of course. This is, in fact, what she wants. Not me. And she scrapes me off her hand onto the open cage door and she turns her naked back to me and embraces this man and they laugh and stagger in their embrace around the corner.

For a moment I still think I've been eloquent. What I've said only needs repeating for it to have its transforming effect. "Hello," I say. "Hello. Pretty bird. Pretty. Bad bird. Bad. Open. Up. Poor baby. Bad bird." And I am beginning to hear myself as I really sound to her. "Peanut." I can never say what is in my heart to her. Never.

I stand on my cage door now and my wings stir. I look at the corner to the hallway and down at the end the whooping has begun again. I can fly there and think of things to do about all this.

But I do not. I turn instead and I look at the trees moving just beyond the other end of the room. I look at the sky the color of the brow of a blue-front Amazon. A shadow of birds spanks across the lawn. And I spread my wings. I will fly now. Even though I know there is something between me and that place where I can be free of all these feelings, I will fly. I will throw myself again and again there. Pretty bird. Bad bird. Good night.

Sandra Cisneros

NEVER MARRY A MEXICAN

SANDRA CISNEROS (1954–) is a novelist, poet, short story writer, and essayist. Her novel, *The House on Mango Street,* won the Before Columbus Foundation's American Book Award in 1985. *Woman Hollering Creek and Other Stories* won the PEN Center USA West Award for Best Fiction of 1991, the Quality Paperback Book Club New Voices Award, the Anisfield-Wolf Book Award, the Lannan Foundation Literary Award, and was selected as a noteworthy book of the year by *The New York Times* and the *American Library Journal.* It was also nominated for Best Book of Fiction for 1991 by the *Los Angeles Times.* Cisneros has written three volumes of poetry—*Bad Boys, My Wicked Wicked Ways,* and *Loose Woman*—the children's book *Hairs/Pelitos,* and the novel *Caramelo,* and she was awarded the MacArthur Foundation Fellowship and other literary honors, including two fellowships, for fiction and poetry, from the NEA. Her work has appeared in *The New York Times,* the *Los Angeles Times, The New Yorker, Glamour, Elle, Ms., Story, Grand Street,* and *The Village Voice.* Cisneros received her BA from Loyola University and her MFA from the University of Iowa. She shares a home in San Antonio, Texas, with several cats, dogs, parrots, and guest writers.

Never marry a Mexican, my ma said once and always. She said this because of my father. She said this though she was Mexican too. But she was born here in the U.S., and he was born there, and it's *not* the same, you know.

I'll *never* marry. Not any man. I've known men too intimately. I've witnessed their infidelities, and I've helped them to it. Unzipped and unhooked and agreed to clandestine maneuvers. I've been accomplice, committed premeditated crimes. I'm guilty of having caused deliberate pain to other women. I'm vindictive and cruel, and I'm capable of anything.

I admit, there was a time when all I wanted was to belong to a man. To wear that gold band on my left hand and be worn on his arm like an expensive jewel brilliant in the light of day. Not the sneaking around I did in different bars that all looked the same, red carpets with a black grillwork design, flocked wallpaper, wooden wagon-wheel light fixtures with hurricane lampshades a sick amber color like the drinking glasses you get for free at gas stations.

Dark bars, dark restaurants then. And if not—my apartment, with his toothbrush firmly planted in the toothbrush holder like a flag on the North Pole. The bed so big because he never stayed the whole night. Of course not.

Borrowed. That's how I've had my men. Just the cream skimmed off the top. Just the sweetest part of the fruit, without the bitter skin that daily living with a spouse can rend. They've come to me when they wanted the sweet meat then.

So, no. I've never married and never will. Not because I couldn't, but because I'm too romantic for marriage. Marriage has failed me, you could say. Not a man exists who hasn't disappointed me, whom I could trust to love the way I've loved. It's because I believe too much in marriage that I don't. Better to not marry than live a lie.

Mexican men, forget it. For a long time the men clearing off the tables or chopping meat behind the butcher counter or driving the bus I rode to school every day, those weren't men. Not men I considered as potential lovers. Mexican, Puerto Rican, Cuban, Chilean, Colombian, Panamanian, Salvadorean, Bolivian, Honduran, Argentine, Dominican, Venezuelan, Guatemalan, Ecuadorean, Nicaraguan, Peruvian, Costa Rican, Paraguayan, Uruguayan, I don't care. I never saw them. My mother did this to me.

I guess she did it to spare me and Ximena the pain she went through. Having married a Mexican man at seventeen. Having had to put up with all the grief a Mexican family can put on a girl because she was from *el otro lado*, the other side, and my father had married down by marrying her. If he had married a white woman from *el otro lado*, that would've been different. That would've been marrying up, even if the white girl was poor. But what could be more ridiculous than a Mexican girl who couldn't even speak Spanish, who didn't know enough to set a separate plate for each course at dinner, nor how to fold cloth napkins, nor how to set the silverware.

In my ma's house the plates were always stacked in the center of the table, the knives and forks and spoons standing in a jar, help yourself. All the dishes chipped or cracked and nothing matched. And no tablecloth, ever. And newspapers set on the table whenever my grandpa sliced watermelons, and how embarrassed she would be when her boyfriend, my father, would come over and there were newspapers all over the kitchen floor and table. And my grandpa, big hardworking Mexican man, saying Come, come and eat, and slicing a big wedge of those dark green watermelons, a big slice, he wasn't stingy with food. Never, even during the Depression. Come, come and eat, to whoever came knocking on the back door. Hobos sitting at the dinner table and the children staring and staring. Because my grandfather always made sure they never went without. Flour and rice, by the barrel and by the sack. Potatoes. Big bags of pinto beans. And watermelons, bought three or four at a time, rolled under his bed and brought out when you least expected. My grandpa had survived three wars, one Mexican, two American, and he knew what living without meant. He knew.

My father, on the other hand, did not. True, when he first came to this country he had worked shelling clams, washing dishes, planting hedges, sat on the back of the bus in Little Rock and had the bus driver shout, You—sit up here, and my father had shrugged sheepishly and said, No speak English.

But he was no economic refugee, no immigrant fleeing a war. My father ran away from home because he was afraid of facing his father after his first-year grades at the university proved he'd spent more time fooling around than studying. He left behind a house in Mexico City that was neither poor nor rich, but thought itself better than both. A boy who would get off a bus when he saw a girl he knew board if he didn't have the money to pay her fare. That was the world my father left behind.

I imagine my father in his *fanfarrón* clothes, because that's what he was, a *fanfarrón*. That's what my mother thought the moment she turned around to the voice that was asking her to dance. A big show-off, she'd say years later. Nothing but a big show-off. But she never said why she married him. My father in his shark-blue suits with the starched handkerchief in the breast pocket, his felt fedora, his tweed topcoat with the big shoulders, and heavy British wing tips with the pin-hole design on the heel and toe. Clothes that cost a lot. Expensive. That's what my father's things said. *Calidad.* Quality.

My father must've found the U.S. Mexicans very strange, so foreign from what he knew at home in Mexico City where the servant served watermelon on a plate with silverware and a cloth napkin, or mangos with their own special prongs. Not like this, eating with your legs wide open in the yard, or in the kitchen hunkered over newspapers. *Come, come and eat.* No, never like this.

How I make my living depends. Sometimes I work as a translator. Sometimes I get paid by the word and sometimes by the hour, depending on the job. I do this in the day, and at night I paint. I'd do anything in the day just so I can keep on painting.

I work as a substitute teacher, too, for the San Antonio Independent School District. And that's worse than translating those travel brochures with their tiny print, believe me. I can't stand kids. Not any age. But it pays the rent.

Any way you look at it, what I do to make a living is a form of prostitution. People say, "A painter? How nice," and want to invite me to their parties, have me decorate the lawn like an exotic orchid for hire. But do they buy art?

I'm amphibious. I'm a person who doesn't belong to any class. The rich like to have me around because they envy my creativity; they know they can't buy *that.* The poor don't mind if I live in their neighborhood because they know I'm poor like they are, even if my education and the way I dress keeps us worlds apart. I don't belong to any class. Not to the poor, whose neighborhood I share. Not to the rich, who come to my exhibitions and buy my work. Not to the middle class from which my sister Ximena and I fled.

When I was young, when I first left home and rented that apartment with my sister and her kids right after her husband left, I thought it would be glamorous to be an artist. I wanted to be like Frida or Tina. I was ready to suffer with my camera and my paint brushes in that awful apartment we rented for $150 each because it had high ceilings and those wonderful glass skylights that convinced us we had to have it. Never mind there was no sink in the bathroom, and a tub that looked like a sarcophagus, and floorboards that didn't meet, and a hallway to scare away the dead. But fourteen-foot ceilings was enough for us to write a check for the deposit right then and there. We thought it all romantic. You know the place, the one on Zarzamora on top of the barber shop with the Casasola prints of the Mexican Revolution. Neon BIRRIA TEPATITLÁN sign round the corner, two goats knocking their heads together, and all those Mexican bakeries, Las Brisas for *huevos rancheros* and *carnitas* and *barbacoa* on Sundays, and fresh fruit milk shakes, and mango *paletas*, and more signs in Spanish than in English. We thought it was great, great. The barrio looked cute in the daytime, like Sesame Street. Kids hopscotching on the sidewalk, blessed little boogers. And hardware stores that still sold ostrich-feather dusters, and whole families marching out of Our Lady of Guadalupe Church on Sundays, girls in their swirly-whirly dresses and patent-leather shoes, boys in their dress Stacys and shiny shirts.

But nights, that was nothing like what we knew up on the north side. Pistols going off like the Wild, Wild West, and me and Ximena and the kids huddled in one bed with the lights off listening to it all, saying, Go to sleep, babies, it's just firecrackers. But we knew better. Ximena would say, Clemencia, maybe we should go home. And I'd say, Shit! Because she knew as well as I did there was no home to go home to. Not with our mother. Not with that man she married. After Daddy died, it was like we didn't matter. Like Ma was so busy feeling sorry for herself, I don't know. I'm not like Ximena. I still haven't worked it out after all this time, even though our mother's dead now. My half brothers living in that house that should've been ours, me and Ximena's. But that's—how do you say it?—water under the dam? I can't ever get the sayings right even though I was born in this country. We didn't say shit like that in our house.

Once Daddy was gone, it was like my ma didn't exist, like if she died, too. I used to have a little finch, twisted one of its tiny red legs between the bars of the cage once, who knows how. The leg just dried up and fell off. My bird lived a long time without it, just a little red stump of a leg. He was fine, really. My mother's memory is like that, like if something already dead dried up and fell off, and I stopped missing where she used to be. Like if I never had a mother. And I'm not ashamed to say it either. When she married that white man, and he and his boys moved into my father's house, it was as if she stopped being my mother. Like I never even had one.

Ma always sick and too busy worrying about her own life, she would've sold us to the Devil if she could. "Because I married so young, *mi'ja*," she'd say. "Because your father, he was so much older than me, and I never had a chance to be young. Honey, try to understand . . ." Then I'd stop listening.

That man she met at work, Owen Lambert, the foreman at the photofinishing plant, who she was seeing even while my father was sick. Even then. That's what I can't forgive.

When my father was coughing up blood and phlegm in the hospital, half his face frozen, and his tongue so fat he couldn't talk, he looked so small with all those tubes and plastic sacks dangling around him. But what I remember most is the smell, like death was already sitting on his chest. And I remember the doctor scraping the phlegm out of my father's mouth with a white washcloth, and my daddy gagging and I wanted to yell, Stop, you stop that, he's my daddy. Goddamn you. Make him live. Daddy, don't. Not yet, not yet, not yet. And how I couldn't hold myself up, I couldn't hold myself up. Like if they'd beaten me, or pulled my insides out through my nostrils, like if they'd stuffed me with cinnamon and cloves, and I just stood there dry-eyed next to Ximena and my mother, Ximena between us because I wouldn't let her stand next to me. Everyone repeating over and over the Ave Marías and Padre Nuestros. The priest sprinkling holy water, *mundo sin fin, amén.*

Drew, remember when you used to call me your Malinalli? It was a joke, a private game between us, because you looked like a Cortez with that beard of yours. My skin dark against yours. Beautiful, you said. You said I was beautiful, and when you said it, Drew, I was.

My Malinalli, Malinche, my courtesan, you said, and yanked my head back by the braid. Calling me that name in between little gulps of breath and the raw kisses you gave, laughing from that black beard of yours.

Before daybreak, you'd be gone, same as always, before I even knew it. And it was as if I'd imagined you, only the teeth marks on my belly and nipples proving me wrong.

Your skin pale, but your hair blacker than a pirate's. Malinalli, you called me, remember? *Mi doradita.* I liked when you spoke to me in my language. I could love myself and think myself worth loving.

Your son. Does he know how much I had to do with his birth? I was the one who convinced you to let him be born. Did you tell him, while his mother lay on her back laboring his birth, I lay in his mother's bed making love to you?

You're nothing without me. I created you from spit and red dust. And I can snuff you between my finger and thumb if I want to. Blow you to kingdom come. You're just a smudge of paint I chose to birth on canvas. And when I made you over, you were no longer a part of her, you were all mine. The landscape of your body taut as a drum. The heart beneath that hide thrumming and thrumming. Not an inch did I give back.

I paint and repaint you the way I see fit, even now. After all these years. Did you know that? Little fool. You think I went hobbling along with my life, whimpering and whining like some twangy country-and-western when you went back to her. But I've been waiting. Making the world look at you from my eyes. And if that's not power, what is?

Nights I light all the candles in the house, the ones to La Virgen de Guadalupe, the ones to El Niño Fidencio, Don Pedrito Jaramillo, Santo Niño de Atocha, Nuestra Señora de San Juan de los Lagos, and, especially, Santa Lucía, with her beautiful eyes on a plate.

Your eyes are beautiful, you said. You said they were the darkest eyes you'd ever seen and kissed each one as if they were capable of miracles. And after you left, I wanted to scoop them out with a spoon, place them on a plate under these blue blue skies, food for the blackbirds.

The boy, your son. The one with the face of that redheaded woman who is your wife. The boy red-freckled like fish food floating on the skin of water. That boy.

I've been waiting patient as a spider all these years, since I was nineteen and he was just an idea hovering in his mother's head, and I'm the one that gave him permission and made it happen, see.

Because your father wanted to leave your mother and live with me. Your mother whining for a child, at least *that*. And he kept saying, Later, we'll see, later. But all along it was me he wanted to be with, it was me, he said.

I want to tell you this evenings when you come to see me. When you're full of talk about what kind of clothes you're going to buy, and what you used to be like when you started high school and what you're like now that you're almost finished. And how everyone knows you as a rocker, and your band, and your new red guitar that you just got because your mother gave you a choice, a guitar or a car, but you don't need a car, do you, because I drive you everywhere. You could be my son if you weren't so light-skinned.

This happened. A long time ago. Before you were born. When you were a moth inside your mother's heart, I was your father's student, yes, just like you're mine now. And your father painted and painted me, because he said I was his *doradita*, all golden and sun-baked, and that's the kind of woman he likes best, the ones brown as river sand, yes. And he took me under his wing and in his bed, this man, this teacher, your father. I was honored that he'd done me the favor. I was that young.

All I know is I was sleeping with your father the night you were born. In the same bed where you were conceived. I was sleeping with your father and didn't give a damn about that woman, your mother. If she was a brown woman like me, I might've had a harder time living with myself, but since she's not, I don't care. I was there first, always. I've always been there, in the mirror, under his skin, in the blood, before you were born. And he's been here in my heart before

I even knew him. Understand? He's always been here. Always. Dissolving like a hibiscus flower, exploding like a rope into dust. I don't care what's right anymore. I don't care about his wife. She's not *my* sister.

And it's not the last time I've slept with a man the night his wife is birthing a baby. Why do I do that, I wonder? Sleep with a man when his wife is giving life, being suckled by a thing with its eyes still shut. Why do that? It's always given me a bit of crazy joy to be able to kill those women like that, without their knowing it. To know I've had their husbands when they were anchored in blue hospital rooms, their guts yanked inside out, the baby sucking their breasts while their husband sucked mine. All this while their ass stitches were still hurting.

Once, drunk on margaritas, I telephoned your father at four in the morning, woke the bitch up. Hello, she chirped. I want to talk to Drew. Just a moment, she said in her most polite drawing-room English. Just a moment. I laughed about that for weeks. What a stupid ass to pass the phone over to the lug asleep beside her. Excuse me, honey, it's for you. When Drew mumbled hello I was laughing so hard I could hardly talk. Drew? That dumb bitch of a wife of yours, I said, and that's all I could manage. That stupid stupid stupid. No Mexican woman would react like that. Excuse me, honey. It cracked me up.

He's got the same kind of skin, the boy. All the blue veins pale and clear just like his mama. Skin like roses in December. Pretty boy. Little clone. Little cells split into you and you and you. Tell me, baby, which part of you is your mother. I try to imagine her lips, her jaw, her long long legs that wrapped themselves around this father who took me to his bed.

This happened. I'm asleep. Or pretend to be. You're watching me, Drew. I feel your weight when you sit on the corner of the bed, dressed and ready to go, but now you're just watching me sleep. Nothing. Not a word. Not a kiss. Just sitting. You're taking me in, under inspection. What do you think already?

I haven't stopped dreaming you. Did you know that? Do you think it's strange? I never tell, though. I keep it to myself like I do all the thoughts I think of you.

After all these years.

I don't want you looking at me. I don't want you taking me in while I'm asleep. I'll open my eyes and frighten you away.

There. What did I tell you? *Drew? What is it?* Nothing. I'd knew you'd say that.

Let's not talk. We're no good at it. With you I'm useless with words. As if somehow I had to learn to speak all over again, as if the words I needed haven't been invented yet. We're cowards. Come back to bed. At least there I feel I have you for a little. For a moment. For a catch of the breath. You let go. You ache and tug. You rip my skin.

You're almost not a man without your clothes. How do I explain it? You're so much a child in my bed. Nothing but a big boy who needs to be held. I won't let anyone hurt you. My pirate. My slender boy of a man.

After all these years.

I didn't imagine it, did I? A Ganges, an eye of the storm. For a little. When we forgot ourselves, you tugged me, I leapt inside you and split you like an apple. Opened for the other to look and not give back. Something wrenched itself loose. Your body doesn't lie. It's not silent like you.

You're nude as a pearl. You've lost your train of smoke. You're tender as rain. If I'd put you in my mouth you'd dissolve like snow.

You were ashamed to be so naked. Pulled back. But I saw you for what you are, when you opened yourself for me. When you were careless and let yourself through. I caught that catch of the breath. I'm not crazy.

When you slept, you tugged me toward you. You sought me in the dark. I didn't sleep. Every cell, every follicle, every nerve, alert. Watching you sigh and roll and turn and hug me closer to you. I didn't sleep. I was taking *you* in that time.

Your mother? Only once. Years after your father and I stopped seeing each other. At an art exhibition. A show on the photographs of Eugène Atget. Those images, I could look at them for hours. I'd taken a group of students with me.

It was your father I saw first. And in that instant I felt as if everyone in the room, all the sepia-toned photographs, my students, the men in business suits, the high-heeled women, the security guards, everyone, could see me for what I was. I had to scurry out, lead my kids to another gallery, but some things destiny has cut out for you.

He caught up with us in the coat-check area, arm in arm with a redheaded Barbie doll in a fur coat. One of those scary Dallas types, hair yanked into a ponytail, big shiny face like the women behind the cosmetic counters at Neiman's. That's what I remember. She must've been with him all along, only I swear I never saw her until that second.

You could tell from a slight hesitancy, only slight because he's too suave to hesitate, that he was nervous. Then he's walking toward me, and I didn't know what to do, just stood there dazed like those animals crossing the road at night when the headlights stun them.

And I don't know why, but all of a sudden I looked at my shoes and felt ashamed at how old they looked. And he comes up to me, my love, your father, in that way of his with that grin that makes me want to beat him, makes me want to make love to him, and he says in the most sincere voice you ever heard,

"Ah, Clemencia! *This* is Megan." No introduction could've been meaner. *This* is Megan. Just like that.

I grinned like an idiot and held out my paw—"Hello, Megan"—and smiled too much the way you do when you can't stand someone. Then I got the hell out of there, chattering like a monkey all the ride back with my kids. When I got home I had to lie down with a cold washcloth on my forehead and the TV on. All I could hear throbbing under the washcloth in that deep part behind my eyes: *This* is Megan.

And that's how I fell asleep, with the TV on and every light in the house burning. When I woke up it was something like three in the morning. I shut the lights and TV and went to get some aspirin, and the cats, who'd been asleep with me on the couch, got up too and followed me into the bathroom as if they knew what's what. And then they followed me into bed, where they aren't allowed, but this time I just let them, fleas and all.

This happened, too. I swear I'm not making this up. It's all true. It was the last time I was going to be with your father. We had agreed. All for the best. Surely I could see that, couldn't I? My own good. A good sport. A young girl like me. Hadn't I understood ... responsibilities. Besides, he could *never* marry *me*. You didn't think ...? *Never marry a Mexican. Never marry a Mexican* ... No, of course not. I see. I see.

We had the house to ourselves for a few days, who knows how. You and your mother had gone somewhere. Was it Christmas? I don't remember.

I remember the leaded-glass lamp with the milk glass above the dining-room table. I made a mental inventory of everything. The Egyptian lotus design on the hinges of the doors. The narrow, dark hall where your father and I had made love once. The four-clawed tub where he had washed my hair and rinsed it with a tin bowl. This window. That counter. The bedroom with its light in the morning, incredibly soft, like the light from a polished dime.

The house was immaculate, as always, not a stray hair anywhere, not a flake of dandruff or a crumpled towel. Even the roses on the dining-room table held their breath. A kind of airless cleanliness that always made me want to sneeze.

Why was I so curious about this woman he lived with? Every time I went to the bathroom, I found myself opening the medicine cabinet, looking at all the things that were hers. Her Estée Lauder lipsticks. Corals and pinks, of course. Her nail polishes—mauve was as brave as she could wear. Her cotton balls and blond hairpins. A pair of bone-colored sheepskin slippers, as clean as the day she'd bought them. On the door hook—a white robe with a MADE IN ITALY label, and a silky nightshirt with pearl buttons. I touched the fabrics. *Calidad.* Quality.

I don't know how to explain what I did next. While your father was busy in the kitchen, I went over to where I'd left my backpack, and took out a bag of gummy bears I'd bought. And while he was banging pots, I went around the house and left a trail of them in places I was sure *she* would find them. One in her lucite makeup organizer. One stuffed inside each bottle of nail polish. I untwisted the expensive lipsticks to their full length and smushed a bear on the top before recapping them. I even put a gummy bear in her diaphragm case in the very center of that luminescent rubber moon.

Why bother? Drew could take the blame. Or he could say it was the cleaning woman's Mexican voodoo. I knew that, too. It didn't matter. I got a strange satisfaction wandering about the house leaving them in places only she would look.

And just as Drew was shouting, "Dinner!" I saw it on the desk. One of those wooden babushka dolls Drew had brought her from his trip to Russia. I know. He'd bought one just like it for me.

I just did what I did, uncapped the doll inside a doll inside a doll, until I got to the very center, the tiniest baby inside all the others, and this I replaced with a gummy bear. And then I put the dolls back, just like I'd found them, one inside the other, inside the other. Except for the baby, which I put inside my pocket. All through dinner I kept reaching in the pocket of my jean jacket. When I touched it, it made me feel good.

On the way home, on the bridge over the *arroyo* on Guadalupe Street, I stopped the car, switched on the emergency blinkers, got out, and dropped the wooden toy into that muddy creek where winos piss and rats swim. The Barbie doll's toy stewing there in that muck. It gave me a feeling like nothing before and since.

Then I drove home and slept like the dead.

These mornings, I fix coffee for me, milk for the boy. I think of that woman, and I can't see a trace of my lover in this boy, as if she conceived him by immaculate conception.

I sleep with this boy, their son. To make the boy love me the way I love his father. To make him want me, hunger, twist in his sleep, as if he'd swallowed glass. I put him in my mouth. Here, little piece of my *corazón*. Boy with hard thighs and just a bit of down and a small hard downy ass like his father's, and that back like a valentine. Come here, *mi cariñito*. Come to *mamita*. Here's a bit of toast.

I can tell from the way he looks at me, I have him in my power. Come, sparrow. I have the patience of eternity. Come to *mamita*. My stupid little bird. I don't move. I don't startle him. I let him nibble. All, all for you. Rub his belly. Stroke him. Before I snap my teeth.

. . .

What is it inside me that makes me so crazy at 2 A.M.? I can't blame it on alcohol in my blood when there isn't any. It's something worse. Something that poisons the blood and tips me when the night swells and I feel as if the whole sky were leaning against my brain.

And if I killed someone on a night like this? And if it was *me* I killed instead, I'd be guilty of getting in the line of crossfire, innocent bystander, isn't it a shame. I'd be walking with my head full of images and my back to the guilty. Suicide? I couldn't say. I didn't see it.

Except it's not me who I want to kill. When the gravity of the planets is just right, it all tilts and upsets the visible balance. And that's when it wants to out from my eyes. That's when I get on the telephone, dangerous as a terrorist. There's nothing to do but let it come.

So. What do you think? Are you convinced now I'm as crazy as a tulip or a taxi? As vagrant as a cloud?

Sometimes the sky is so big and I feel so little at night. That's the problem with being cloud. The sky is so terribly big. Why is it worse at night, when I have such an urge to communicate and no language with which to form the words? Only colors. Pictures. And you know what I have to say isn't always pleasant.

Oh, love, there. I've gone and done it. What good is it? Good or bad, I've done what I had to do and needed to. And you've answered the phone, and startled me away like a bird. And now you're probably swearing under your breath and going back to sleep, with that wife beside you, warm, radiating her own heat, alive under the flannel and down and smelling a bit like milk and hand cream, and that smell familiar and dear to you, oh.

Human beings pass me on the street, and I want to reach out and strum them as if they were guitars. Sometimes all humanity strikes me as lovely. I just want to reach out and stroke someone, and say There, there, it's all right, honey. There, there, there.

Peter Ho Davies

RELIEF

PETER HO DAVIES (1966–) was born in Coventry to Welsh and Chinese parents. He studied physics at Manchester University and English at Cambridge. The author of two short story collections, *The Ugliest House in the World* (winner of the John Llewellyn Rhys and PEN/Macmillan Prizes in the UK) and *Equal Love* (a finalist for the *Los Angeles Times* Book Prize), Davies currently directs the graduate program in creative writing at the University of Michigan.

Sometime between the cheese and the fruit, while the port was still being passed, Lieutenant Wilby allowed a sweet but rather too boisterous fart to slip between his buttocks. The company around the mess table was talking quietly, listening to the sound of the liquor filling the glasses, holding it up in the lamplight to relish its color against the white canvas of the tent. It was, Lieutenant Bromhead had just explained, a bottle from General Chelmsford's own stock, and not the regulation port issued to officers. A hush of appreciation had fallen over the table.

Of course, Wilby had known the fart was coming, but it was much louder and more prolonged than he had anticipated, and the look of surprise on his face would have given him away even if Major Black, to his left, the port already extended, had not said, "Wilby!" in a sharp, shocked bellow.

"Sorry, sir," Wilby said. His face burned as if he'd been sitting in front of the hearth at home, reading by the firelight. He risked one quick glance up and around the table. "Sorry, sirs." Chaplain Pierce was looking down into his lap, exactly as he did when saying grace, and Captain Ferguson's mustache was jumping slightly at the corners, like the whiskers of a cat that had just scented a bowl of cream. Lieutenant Chard, however, sat just as he appeared in his photographs, his huge pale face tipped back like a great slab rising above his thick dark beard.

As for Bromhead, he looked only slightly puzzled. "What?" he said. "What is it?"

Wilby, staring down at the crumbs of Stilton on his plate, groaned inwardly. Bromhead's famed deafness was going to be the end of him.

He looked up under his brow as Bromhead's batman, who had just placed the fruit on the table, leaned forward and whispered all too audibly in his ear, "The lieutenant farted, sir."

"Chard?" Bromhead asked. Behind his beard, the older lieutenant turned the color of claret. Bromhead himself wore only a thin mustache and sideburns, and Wilby thought he saw a flicker of a smile cross his face.

The batman leaned in to him again. "Wilby," he whispered.

"Ah," Bromhead said sadly. He stared at his glass. An uncomfortable silence fell over the mess table. Wilby's mortification was complete. And, perhaps because he wished himself dead, a small portion of his recent life flashed before his eyes.

The lieutenant had been suffering from terrible flatulence all the way from Helpmakaar. At first he had thought it was something to do with his last meal (a deer shot, several times, by Major Black, which he could hardly have refused in any case), but as the column approached Rourke's Drift, his bowels seemed in as great an uproar as ever. Fortunately, the ride had been made at a canter and he'd been able to clench his mount between his legs and smother the worst farts against his saddle—although the horse had tossed her head at some of the more drawn-out ones—but as they came in sight of the mission station, the major spurred them into a trot and then a gallop so that their pennant snapped overhead like a whip. Legs braced in the stirrups, knees bent, his body canted forward over his mount's neck, the lieutenant had had no choice but to release a crackling stream of utterance.

At first there was some undeniable relief in this, but as each dip and rise and tussock jarred loose further bursts, he was obliged to cry "Ya" and "Ho," as if encouraging his horse, to mask the worst outbreaks. He was grateful that over the drumming of hooves and the blare of the bugler who had hastily run out to welcome them to camp, no one seemed to notice, but the severity of the attack made him doubt that he had not soiled his breeches, and at the first opportunity he sought out the latrine to reassure himself.

Having put his mind at rest, seen to his tentage, and placed his horse in the care of the groom he shared with the other junior officers, Wilby had taken himself off to the perimeter of the camp. Despite the newly built walls and the freshly dug graves—they were overgrown already, but their silhouettes clearly visible in the long pale grass—it was all familiar to him from the articles in the *Army Gazette*, and in his mind he traced the events of the famous defense that had been fought there not three months before.

Fewer than a hundred able-bodied men, a single company plus those left behind at the mission hospital, had fought off a force of some five thousand Zulus—part of the same *impi* that had wiped out fifteen hundred men at Isandhlwana the previous day. They had held out for upwards of ten hours of continuous close fighting and inflicted almost five hundred casualties on the enemy. It was a glorious tale, and Wilby didn't need to look at the page from the *Gazette* that he kept in his tunic pocket to recall all the details. He had read and reread it so often on the ride out from Durban that it felt as fragile as an illuminated manuscript. "You'd think it was a love letter," the major had scoffed.

He should be rejoicing to be here, standing on the ground of the most famous battle in the world, and yet he felt only the churning of his wretched stomach. Tomorrow they would ride out, the first patrol to visit the site of Isandhlwana since the massacre.

He stared off in the direction they would take in the morning. The ferry across the drift was moored about two hundred yards away, and on the far bank the track ran beside the river for a half mile or so and then cut away over a low rise and out of sight. Wilby found himself thinking of the Derbyshire countryside near his home . . . and fishing—up to his thighs in the dark cool water, feeling the pull of the current but dry inside his thick leather waders. He supposed the sight of the river must have brought it to mind.

It was Ferguson who found him out there. He saw the captain running toward him, his red tunic among the waving grass, shouting his news.

"Wils, we are invited to dine with Bromhead and Chard. You, myself, the major, and Pierce."

"Truly?" Wilby caught his friend's arm, and Ferguson stooped for a moment to catch his breath. Then he shook himself free and took a step back, squared his shoulders and held up his hand as if reading from a card.

"Lieutenants Bromhead and Chard request the pleasure of Major Black and his staff's company for dinner in their mess at eight o'clock."

Of course, it was a little unusual for two lieutenants to invite a major to dinner, but by then Bromhead and Chard were expected to be made majors themselves—not to mention the Victoria Crosses everyone was predicting—and the breach of etiquette seemed altogether forgivable to Wilby. A dinner with Gonville Bromhead and Merrior Chard was simply the most sought-after invitation in the whole of Natal in the spring of 1889.

"Good Lord, Fergie," he said. "Why, I must change."

He had spent the next hour in his suspenders and undershirt, polishing the buttons of his tunic, slipping a small brass plate behind them to protect the fabric and then working the polish into the raised regimental crests and burnishing them to a glow. Next he worked on his boots, smearing long streaks of bootblack up and down, working them into the hide with a swift circular motion and then bringing the leather to a shine with a stiff brush. He thought hard about the thin beard and mustache he had begun to grow three weeks before and with a sigh pulled out his razor. Ferguson, waxing his own mustache, paused and watched him in silence, but Wilby refused to meet his eye. His mustache would never be as good as the captain's anyway. Fergie's handlebar was justly famous in the regiment, said to be wide enough for troopers riding behind him to see both ends. Wilby knew that wasn't quite true. The captain had made him check, with Wilby standing behind him trying to make out both waxed tips. In the end they had had to call in the chaplain, and standing shoulder to shoulder, about five feet behind Ferguson, Wilby and Pierce had each been able to see a tip of mustache on either side.

Wilby lathered the soap in his shaving mug and applied it with the badger-hair brush his father had given him before he'd come out on campaign. The razor was dull and he had to pause to strop it, but he managed to shave without drawing blood.

Finally, he extracted his second set of epaulets and his best collar from the tissue paper he kept them in and had Ferguson fix them in place. The fragrant smell of hair oil filled their tent as they each in turn vigorously applied a brush to the other's tunic. Without a decent mirror, they paused and scrutinized each other carefully, then bowed deeply—Wilby from the waist, Ferguson taking a step back and dropping his arm in a flourish.

The meal had gone well at first. The major had introduced him to first Chard and then Bromhead and he'd looked them both in the eyes (Chard's gray, Bromhead's brown) and shaken hands firmly. In between, he had made to clasp his hands behind his back and been sure to rub them on his tunic to ensure they were dry. "How do you do, sir?" he had said to each in turn.

"Very well," Chard had said in his gruff way.

"Splendid," Bromhead had told him a little too loudly. The story of Bromhead's deafness—that he would almost certainly have been pensioned off if his older brother had not been on Chelmsford's staff—was well known among the junior officers. It was said that he had only been given B company of the 2nd/24th because it was composed almost entirely of Welshmen and it was thought that his deafness wouldn't be so noticeable or important to men who spoke English with such an impenetrable accent. There was even a joke that Bromhead's company had only received its posting at Rourke's Drift because the lieutenant thought the general had been offering him more *pork rib* at the mess table. "Rather," he was reputed to have said. "Very tasty."

Some of the officers still made fun of Bromhead, but Wilby put it down to simple jealousy. For his own part, he thought it more, not less, heroic that Bromhead had overcome his disability. He had a theory that amid all the noise of battle a deaf man might have an advantage, might come to win the respect of men hoarse from shouting and deafened by the report of their arms.

At dinner, Wilby had waited until the major and Ferguson had each made some remark or other, nodded at each response, and echoed the chaplain's compliments on the food. Only then, as the batman passed the gravy boat among them, did he ask a question of his own.

"How does it feel?" he said. "I mean, how does it feel to be heroes?"

Bromhead looked at him closely for a moment, but it was Chard who answered.

"Well," he began. He stroked his beard, and it made an audible rasping sound. "I would have to say, principally, the sensation is one of relief. Relief to be alive after all—not like the poor devils you'll see tomorrow—but also relief to have learned some truth about myself. To have found I am possessed of—for want of a better word—courage."

"I say," murmured Ferguson. He grinned at Wilby.

What a blowhard, Bromhead thought. It pained him that Chard's name and his own should be so inextricably linked. Bromhead and Chard. Chard and Bromhead. He felt like a blasted vaudevillian.

"It's an ambition fulfilled," Chard went on, ignoring the interruption. "Since I was a little chap I remember wondering—as who has not?—if I were a brave fellow. Cowardice, funk—more than any imagined beast or goblin, that was my great terror. And now I have my answer." He paused and looked around the table slowly, and this time it was harder for Wilby to hold his gaze. "If the chaplain will be so good as to forgive me, I rather fancy it is as if I have stood before Saint Peter himself, not knowing if I were a bally sinner or no, and dashed me if he hasn't found my name there among the elect."

The chaplain smiled and bobbed his head complacently. Wilby and Ferguson glanced at each other again, their eyes bright but not quite meeting in their excitement.

"Heavens!" said Bromhead, clearing his throat. "For my part, being a hero is nothing so like how I fancy a beautiful young debutante must feel." There was a puzzled round of laughter, but Wilby saw Chard press his lips together—a white line behind his dark beard—and kept his own features still. "You've seen them at balls, gentlemen, there are one or two each season, those girls who aren't quite sure but then discover all of a sudden quite how delightful they are. Oh, I don't know. Perhaps their mamas had told them so, but they'd not believed them. After all, that's what mamas are for. They'd not known whether to listen to their doting fathers and all those old loyal servants, surely too ugly to know what was beautiful or not anymore. And then, in one evening, confound it, they know. And all around them, suddenly, why who but our own good selves, gentlemen—suitors all."

Wilby could see Ferguson smile, and he knew he was thinking of Ethel, his betrothed. He had seen such women as Bromhead described, but his own smile was more rueful. (He remembered one long conversation with a certain Miss Fanshaw, who had cheerfully told him that she had sent no less than five white feathers to men she knew at the time of the Crimea—"And you know," she had told him earnestly, "not one of them returned home alive.") The major he knew would be thinking of his wife, home in Bath, and the chaplain, he supposed, of God. He saw Chard, bored, study his reflection in the silverware.

"Anyway," the major said. "Put us out of our misery. Let's hear the details of this famous defense of yours, eh? Give us the story from the horse's mouth, so to speak."

"Oh, well." Bromhead opened his hands. "It was fairly fierce, I suppose. The outcome was in doubt for some hours." He faltered, and Wilby, who had been leaning forward eagerly, sat back and saw the others look disappointed. This was, after all, what they had come for.

Chard, however, stepped in. He was an officer of engineers and he believed in telling a tale correctly.

He told them about the hours of hand-to-hand combat, of the bayonets that the men called lungers, and of the assegais of the Zulus. How the men's guns had become so hot from firing that they cooked off rounds as soon as they were loaded, causing the men to miss; so hot that the soft brass shell casings melted in the breeches and had to be dug out with a knife before the whole futile process could begin again. He told them about men climbing up on the wall they'd built of biscuit boxes and mealie bags and lunging down into the darkness; of the black hands reaching up to grab the barrels and the shrieks of pain when they touched the hot glowing metal—shrieks that were oddly louder than the soft grunts men gave as a bayonet or assegai found its mark. He told them about the sound of bullets clattering into the biscuit boxes at the base of the wall and rustling in the mealie bags nearer the top, so that you knew the Zulus were getting their range. He described men overpowered, dragged from the walls, surrounded by warriors. How the Zulus knocked them down and ripped open their tunics, and the popping sound of buttons flying loose. "That would be the last sound a lot of our chaps heard," he said. With their tunics open, the Zulus would disembowel them, opening men from balls to breastbone with one swift strike.

"I swear I'll never be able to see another button pop loose from a shirt without thinking of it," Chard said. He took a sip of wine. "Of course, you'll see a good deal of that handiwork tomorrow, I'll warrant."

That was when Wilby began to feel his flatulence return, and his discomfort grew even when Bromhead broke in and explained that the Zulus believed that opening a man's chest was the only way to set his spirit free from his dead body.

"Really, it's an act of mercy as they see it," he said. "I hope so, at least. There was one poor chap of mine, a Private Williams. Bit of a no-account, but a decent sort. I saw him get fairly dragged over the wall before I caught hold his leg. This was quite in the thick of it. There were so many Zulus trying to rush us from all sides, they were like water swirling round a rock in a stream. Quite a ghastly tug of war I had for him with them. Every time they had him to their side he'd give one of those little grunts Chard was talking about, but then I'd pull like mad, and when I had him more to me he'd look up and say in a cheery way, 'Much obliged, sir.' In the end, they began to swarm over the walls all about us and I had to let him go to draw my pistol. I told him I was sorry—I fancied he'd be in a bad panic, you know—but he just said, 'Not at all, sir,' and 'Thank you kindly, sir.'"

Bromhead paused.

"I was going to write to his people. Say how sorry I was I couldn't save him. But dashed if he didn't join up under a false name. A lot of the Welshmen do, it seems. For a long time I thought they were all just called Evans and Williams and Jones and what-have-you, but it turns out that those are just the most obvious false names for them to choose. His blamed leg—you know, I can't get it out of my mind, how remarkably warm it was."

He sat back, and the batman took the opportunity to step forward with the port. Bromhead watched in silence as the glasses filled with redness.

Wilby had managed a few quiet expulsions, but then came the surprising and ruinous fart.

The silence around the table seemed to go on for hours—Wilby could hear the pickets calling out their challenge to the final patrols of the evening. Finally Bromhead looked over and said genially, "Preserved potatoes." He shook his head. "Make you fart like a confounded horse."

He waved his man forward with the cigars, and as they passed around he leaned in toward the table and looked around at them all.

"Reminds me of a story," he said, cutting the end of his cigar. "I haven't thought of it in years, mind you—about a bally Latin class, of all things." He ran the end of the cigar around his tongue and raised his chin for the batman to light him. "Hardly the story you expected to hear, but I'll beg your indulgence." He took a mighty puff and began.

"Well, we had this old tyrant of a master—Marlow, his name was—of the habit of making us work at our books in silence every other afternoon. Any noise and he would beat you with a steel ruler that he carried from his days in the navy. Now that was fear. I swear it was rumored among us—a rumor spread no doubt by older lads to put a fright on us—that boys had lost fingers, chopped clean off at the knuckle by that ruler.

"I must have been upwards of twelve or so. I can't recall quite the circumstances, but I'd bent over from my desk to retrieve a pen I'd dropped—or more likely some blighter had thrown—on the floor. We were always trying to get some other poor bugger to make a sound and bring down the tyrant's wrath upon his head, but anyhow, as I say, I'd bent over to pick up my pen—I was in the middle of translating 'Horatio on the Bridge' or some such rot—and what do you know but I farted. Quite surprised myself. Quite taken aback, I was. Not that it was an especially, you know, loud one. More of a pop really. Or a squeak. Hang me if that's not it either. Let's just say somewhere between a pop and a squeak. Hardly a decent fart at all—if the truth be told, it's rather astonishing I can remember it so well. No matter. Whatever the precise sound of the expulsion, in that room with everyone trying to be still it was like a bally pistol shot, like the crack of a whip.

"Well, the fellows behind me, of course, went off into absolute fits and gales. Up jumps the tyrant, brandishing his ruler, and I fancy I'm for the high jump now. The whole room falls silent as the grave as the old man stalks up the aisle between our desks, looking hard all about him.

" 'John Beddows,' he says to one of the chaps behind me, and his voice is veritable steel, 'would you mind telling me what is the source of this hilarity?'

" 'Nothing, sir,' says John—a decent enough sort, loafer that he was—and I begin to think I might be spared, but dash me if the old man doesn't persist.

" 'Nothing,' he says. 'You had to be laughing at something, boy. Only idiots laugh at nothing. Are you an idiot, Mister Beddows?' And he bent that ruler in his hands.

" 'No, sir,' says John, pulling a long face. 'Please, sir. Gonville Bromhead farted, sir.'"

Wilby glanced around the table and saw that Ferguson was grinning broadly, his teeth showing around his cigar. The chaplain, too, was struggling to keep a straight face, and even Major Black had a curious look in his eye. Only Chard showed no glimmer of humor. He had stubbed out his cigar and taken an apple, which he was chewing steadily.

"Of course," Bromhead went on, "you can imagine the pandemonium. You'd have thought there was a murder in progress, and to be honest I could have cheerfully strangled Beddows. I let out a swear or two under my breath, but the tyrant himself was at a loss for a moment. All I could do was snatch my hands up from where they'd been lying on the desk and press them into my pockets.

" 'Silence!' the tyrant finally bellowed, and then, with me cringing, 'That's quite enough drollery, gentlemen. Back to work. All of you.'

"Of course, it was only a reprieve of sorts. The worst was still to come. By and by we came out for our break and the other chaps started up a game of tag. I was too angry or ashamed to join them. I took myself off to a corner of the yard and watched. One person would be on, his tie would be undone, and he'd tag another, who'd also pull his tie open, and they'd keep tagging until they all had their ties hanging loose. Only when some of them ran closer to me did I catch the name of the game. 'Funky Farters.'" Bromhead looked around him, his face a mask of tragedy.

"That dashed game became the craze at school for months, although I can tell you I never played it. I had dreams, nightmares really, of boys going home at the holidays and teaching it to their friends and in this way the detestable game—and my disgrace—spreading to every durned school in England. Can you imagine? I couldn't shake the notion. I thought with certitude that affair would be the only thing I'd be known for in my whole life. I thought, *I'll die and my only lasting contribution to this life will be a fart in a confounded Latin class.*"

The table was roaring with laughter by now, the chaplain dabbing at his eyes with his napkin, Ferguson clutching his sides, and the major positively braying. Ash from the almost extinguished cigar in his hand peppered the table as he shook. Wilby found himself laughing too, uncontrollably relieved. He caught Bromhead's eye and the older lieutenant nodded.

The meal broke up shortly after—the major's patrol would have to leave camp at first light—and the men went out into the night to find their own tents. Bromhead leaned back in his chair and watched the major sidle up to Wilby and Ferguson and say, "I remember once letting loose a mighty one on parade in India," and the two young officers staggered with laughter. The chaplain was the last to leave. He smiled at Bromhead and shook his head. "An edifying tale." Then he hurried after the other three, and Bromhead saw him put an arm around Wilby's shoulder.

Only Chard stalked off alone, his back straight and his chin held high. "Now that man," Bromhead said to his batman, "mark my words, has never farted in his life. It'd break his back to let rip now." He lit another cigar and smoked it thoughtfully while the batman cleared the plates from the table.

"It's a terrible thing being afraid, Watkins, do you not think?"

The batman said he thought it was.

"Join me," Bromhead said, and he poured out two glasses of the celebrated port and they sat and drank in silence for a moment.

"Bloody rum thing. Zulus thinking to find a fellow's soul in his entrails, eh?"

The batman nodded. The port tasted like syrup to him, and later he would need a swig of his squareface—the army-issue gin in its square bottle—to take the taste away.

It was late, and the light breeze through the tent felt cold to Bromhead. He always took more of a chill when he'd been drinking. He pulled a blanket off the cot behind him and draped it around his shoulders. "Like an old woman," he said. He wrapped his arms around himself under the blanket, clutching his shoulders, and thought again how really remarkably *warm* Private Williams's leg had felt.

"Wake me," he said to the batman, "before the major's patrol leaves in the morning. I think I should like to see them off."

AFTER ROSA PARKS

JANET DESAULNIERS (1954–) is an Associate Professor in the MFA in Writing Program at the School of the Art Institute of Chicago. Her collection of stories, *What You've Been Missing*, won the 2004 John Simmons Award. Her short fiction has been awarded prizes from *Glimmer Train* and *Ploughshares* magazines; included in the *Pushcart Prize* anthology; published in *The New Yorker, Other Voices, TriQuarterly*, and elsewhere. She has received grants and fellowships from the National Endowment for the Arts, the Illinois Arts Council, the Millay Colony, and the Michener/Copernicus Society.

Ellie found her son in the school nurse's office, laid out on a leatherette fainting couch like some child gothic, his shoes off, his arms crossed over his chest, his face turned to the wall.

"What's the deal, Kid Cody?"

When he heard her voice, he turned only his head toward her, slowly, as if he were beyond surprise. "I have a stomachache," he said.

"Yeah?" Ellie sat down beside him and stroked his bare arm. "That's the message I got."

"It's a nervous stomachache, Mom. It's right in the middle." He pointed to his belt buckle, a nicked metal casting of a race car. "It's right where Mrs. Schumacher said my nerves are."

Cody was in kindergarten, and he did not like school. He told anyone who would listen that he did not like school. Yesterday, from just inside their back door, Ellie overheard him telling their next-door neighbor Mrs. Schumacher that school gave him a bad feeling behind his stomach, "the kind of feeling," he said, "that you get before something happens." Ellie stood still in the doorway and watched as Mrs. Schumacher looked up from grooming one of her half dozen cats. Mrs. Schumacher was a stringy wild-haired widow—dirt poor, bone thin and half-crazy with loneliness and neglect.

Sometimes when Cody and Ellie would haul trash back to the cans in the alley, she'd wave and call out her kitchen window to Ellie, "You pull those shoulders back, girl. Divorce is no sin." Yesterday she picked cat hair out of a long metal comb and told Cody, "There are two kinds of stomachaches, you know. Now a sick one just swirls through your gut like a bad wind, but a nervous one sits real still." She pressed one gnarled hand to Cody's belly. "Almost like you've swallowed a baseball," she said. "And it glows."

"That's the one I get at school," Cody told her. "That's the one." After he said it, Ellie pressed her head against the cool storm door and felt sorry for herself, sorry she lived in the only run-down pocket of this suburb on probably the only street for miles where a woman could put her hands on her child and tell him such things. The school nurse, a young red-haired woman strangely overdressed in a carnation-pink suit, came from behind her desk to the couch.

Ellie leaned back as the nurse ran her hand over Cody's forehead. "He doesn't have a fever as far as I can tell. But he won't take the thermometer in his mouth. He says he wants it under the arm."

"Axillary," Ellie said. "That's how we do it at home."

Cody lay still under the nurse's hand. "I told her that," he said.

"Well, at school we do it by mouth," the nurse said. "You need to try doing it that way at home so it won't be new at school." Cody and Ellie both looked at the nurse, then Cody looked back at the ceiling.

"It's a nervous stomachache, Mom," he said softly. "I can tell."

"Let's sit up, Cody," Ellie said. "You look sicker than you are like that, and lying down is not what you need. A break is what you need. Put your shoes on now."

Ellie stood up and took the nurse's elbow, led her to a window that looked out over an empty play yard. "He gets nervous," she said quietly. "It seems to happen most often when too many people treat him like a child." The nurse looked at her. "I mean when too many people try to tell him what to do," Ellie said. "See, he's an only child, and he lives half his time with his dad in their house and half his time with me in ours. So he's accustomed to partnership, you know, to being a partner in his own management. I mean, you live alone with a child, and there's none of that usual 'us versus him' kind of thing. You live alone with a child, and he's part of the us."

"Oh," the nurse said. She took a step back. People often did that when they learned how Cody lived. A social worker, new to their city from California, had concocted the scheme during the divorce. To Ellie and her ex-husband it had sounded humane, but Ellie and her ex-husband did not live in California. They lived in an old and mostly refined Midwestern suburb, a place where tall trees and wide driveways led back behind big houses to double and triple garages. "I'm wondering," the nurse said, "if I have the correct home phone number for you. A man took the message when I called." She looked Ellie in the eye, insinuating now. "I think I woke him up."

"That's my brother. He's been staying with us to help out." Disappointed in herself for revealing more of their life than was necessary to this woman, Ellie added, "I'm sure you did wake him up. He's ill today."

Cody looked up from struggling with his shoelaces. "Uncle Frank is a night person," he said. "When I'm asleep, he's awake. He does life the opposite." Ellie smiled at him and looked back at the nurse. "Frank works nights, is what he means." The nurse's face said that even this fact made her suspicious.

"Look, I think Cody just needs extra time is all," Ellie said. "This is his first year of school. He didn't go the play group and preschool route. His father and I kept him home so he could get wise to both of us still being there for him, even though it was in different houses. He's fine about that, but he's no wise guy when it comes to school. Are you, Cody?"

Cody stood up and smiled. "I get stomachaches," he said. Both his shoes tied, he was ready to go now. Ellie saw that he believed the hard part of this day was behind him. Next to her, the nurse narrowed her eyes at his sudden good humor, and Ellie felt her hesitate, weighing for a moment whether Cody was a liar or only a new and distinct form of damaged child. Then she looked at Ellie, and Ellie saw that what the nurse had decided was that Cody was an odd child, that he was an ill-equipped child—a child with a strange and probably damaged life—and probably, Ellie understood the nurse was thinking, probably it was Ellie's fault. They stared at each other a moment. Then Ellie went to Cody and took his hand.

"I'll just take him now. We'll just be on our way. We'll try school again tomorrow, right, Cody?"

"Okay," he said.

"You have to sign him out." The nurse pointed to a binder on her desk. "For our records."

"Right," Ellie said. "No problem." They drove away slowly from the school. Cody rolled the window down and rested his head on the door frame so that the wind lifted his hair off his forehead. Ellie didn't know if he was pensive or only relieved. Maybe he had sensed what the nurse thought of her. Or of him. She turned the radio on low.

"Do you want to drive by the lake?" she said. "It's warm today. We could climb down the rocks to the beach." The beach was where Cody told Ellie things, where he confided in her. The wide expanse of sand and water loosened something in him. It was there, digging a hole one day last spring with a new miniature folding spade, that he had looked up and said, "Do you want to hear something secret?"

"Sure," Ellie told him, and then he recited, nearly word for word, an ugly desperate argument she and her ex-husband had had just before they gave it all up. He recited it so precisely that the night came back to Ellie. She'd made a formal dinner in the middle of the week—cornish hens stuffed with herbs and rice. A friendly Greek man at the liquor store had helped her choose a nice wine which she served in their wedding crystal. She'd left the bottle on the table, tucked in a hammered silver ice bucket, while she and her ex-husband said horrible, hurtful things they'd never said before or since.

On the beach that day, Cody recited it all. He paused in his digging and looked up at her. "I was under the table," he said. "You just didn't see me there." For a moment, Ellie believed him. Then she remembered another moment, carrying their salad plates to the kitchen, when she'd been so ashamed she'd gone back to Cody's room to check on him. He lay sideways in his youth bed, one foot wedged between the bars. From the doorway she listened to his breathing before she went to his bed and straightened him, sliding his foot from the bars, folding his quilt up over his shoulders. On the beach, she felt the same relief she'd felt at his door. He'd been asleep. He'd slept through it. She watched him dig the hole, throwing sand over his shoulder, hunkering down to his work, and suddenly she was shaken again.

"Daddy didn't tell you those things, did he? Did Daddy tell you those things?"

"No." He looked up from his digging, a little wary of her.

"Oh."

"Daddy says I probably dreamed it."

They were both quiet then. He finished his hole and sat back on his heels to admire it. It was deep, the deepest he'd dug, and he fingered his new shovel lightly. Then he crawled into the hole, tucking his legs up to his chest and folding his arms around them. "Cover me up, Mom," he said, smiling then. She slid the warm sand over him as he watched her. When the sand covered the tops of his knees, she smoothed it around his chest. He looked up at her. "I did see it," he said.

She took her hands away from him and sat back. "I know," she said. "I know you did." Now, in the car, she looked at him. "How about it?" she asked.

"No, thanks. I don't feel like the beach."

"We could try the library."

"No," he said. "Thanks."

"Well, I need a milk shake. I'm going to pull into that hot dog stand under the train tracks and have a chocolate shake." He didn't answer, but Ellie pulled in anyway and settled him outside under a striped umbrella, where she brought his milk shake out to him. He drank it quickly, tipping his head back, while Ellie looked up at the train platform where a few late commuters stood next to their briefcases. She was glad now she and Cody were not going anywhere, glad she had taken the rest of the day off when she got the call at the office, glad they could sit here half the morning and then stop at the park if they felt like it. The gift of her child was that in his presence life lengthened and uncoiled. Though it was nearly eleven o'clock, this day spread out before them as sweetly as at dawn.

"I like ice cream in the morning," Cody said. "This is the first time I've had ice cream this early."

"It's a quiet pleasure," Ellie said. "That and the weather. This is the warmest January we've ever had, I think."

"I remembered it was your day," Cody said. "So I told her to call you and not Dad."

Ellie touched his wrist. "You were right. Exactly right. You're getting very good at this. You're becoming a big boy."

Cody looked out over the parking lot. The umbrellas rippled in the breeze like sails, and above them late commuters swayed lightly like distant buoys. "I would kick a bad guy in the stomach if he came near our table."

"That would do it," Ellie said.

"I'd karate kick him in the stomach and then in the knee."

"He'd go limping off to the other side of the world," Ellie said. This was something new for them that had started with school—this imagined violence, her child's sense of himself as a warrior and her quiet affirmation. School had forced Ellie to see how divorce had changed her—that she had become a cautious person, a person who lived as if she were allowed only one mistake in life and had already made it—and school had forced her to see that she was sending her son off into the world with the rigid moral sense of a saint.

He'd see a child steal another child's hat in the play yard, and he'd suffer it all day. When he came home, he'd tell her the story of the theft and then lie on the rug, exhausted, looking up at her to say, "That was a terrible thing, don't you think, Mom? Don't you think that was an awful thing to do?"—as if he'd witnessed a murder. So now she let Cody talk this way, imagining his own power, and lately she had begun to surprise him with figures from a set of fierce dinosaurs and cavemen as a way of making up for all the early years she'd encouraged a pristine sensibility.

"Cody, did anything happen today, I mean before you went to the nurse with a stomachache?"

"No."

"Nothing?"

"Well, the playground lady made me take a time-out."

"Why was that?"

"I was swinging on my belly."

"Uh-huh."

"And that's all." He rolled the edge of his cup around one finger. "There's a rule against swinging on your belly."

"I didn't know that."

"I didn't know that either, but the lady said that now I would know and now I would remember."

"Oh. Well, I guess she's the boss."

"She is."

Ellie ran her hand along the rough close-cropped hair at the nape of his neck. He looked away from her when she did it. "So then what happened?"

"I had to sit on the ground by her feet for a while and then I had to say I was sorry."

"Did you?"

"Yes."

"And then what?"

"Then she called me Cory and told me I could go."

"She called you by the wrong name."

"Uh-huh. Yes."

"Did you tell her?"

"No." He leaned against her then and tilted his head back to look into her face. "I didn't want her to know me by my right name, Mom."

She put one arm lightly around his shoulders and rested her chin on the top of his head. "What should we do now?" she said softly.

"Go home."

At home, Frank was on the couch, an afghan pulled over his legs, watching the noon news.

"You're awake early," Cody said.

Frank looked up. "You're home early."

Cody quieted when he said it. He dropped his knapsack under the hat rack, pulled out his box of dinosaurs and cavemen and began to arrange them delicately, as though he were being watched. Frank raised his eyebrows at Ellie. She shook her head.

"I guess I'll make soup or something," she said.

A few minutes later, Frank joined her in the kitchen. He moved stiffly to the sink, leaned there a moment, then drew a glass of water from the tap and sat down at the table.

"It's vegetable soup." Ellie turned from the pot on the stove. "Can you tolerate it?"

"Not today." He raised his glass. "Today I'm drinking water." Frank suffered from colitis—at least that's what he said it was. He'd been a medic in the army and learned just enough about medicine to believe he could treat himself. Last week, though, he'd been so sick that Ellie had convinced him to let her drive him to the VA hospital for some tests. Nudged into a pocket of darkness between two high-rise office buildings, the hospital was a spooky place—cavernous and forbidding and full of old and middle-aged men shuffling the hallways in paper slippers.

"This is awful," Ellie whispered to Frank as they stood in some line. "Why don't you get real health insurance?"

"Forget it," Frank said. "I spent three years of my life defending the Golden Gate Bridge to earn this." She noticed as he walked away from her that day, and again this morning as he came into the kitchen, that he had begun to look like those men at the VA. He'd begun to look like a damaged man. Though he was tall and thick with muscle, he carried himself lightly, his arms held away from his body, as though he were hollow. Today his rumpled hair stood up from his head. Under each eye was a white translucent spot of pain.

"You look pale, Frank."

"I feel pale."

"Did you call on your test results?"

"They said they'd call me."

"You should check."

"They said they would call, Ellie."

She turned back to the stove and then called, "Soup in twenty minutes, Cody."

"And biscuits, please," he called back.

"Okay, and biscuits." She peered into the refrigerator, looking for the plastic container of dough.

"That is not a sick child," Frank said.

"He was nervous. Something happened on the playground."

Ellie went about her work quietly, spreading flour on the countertop, rolling out the dough, but she felt like Cody had looked a moment ago in the other room. She felt like she was being watched. Frank sat at the table, the glass of water between his broad hands. Her brother was an odd man. There was such power to him, in his hands and legs and the set of his jaw, but around other people—even Ellie and Cody—he was always quiet and watchful, slightly ill at ease. Ellie believed that life—real life, life in society, whatever it was she was living—was a confusion to Frank. She couldn't settle on why. Sometimes she blamed the army. Frank had been one of the last men drafted into Vietnam. Though the war ended not long after he finished basic, the army changed him—perhaps in ways worse than a year fighting in the jungle might have changed him. She didn't know. She wasn't even sure exactly what he'd done during those years or what had been done to him. Occasionally, he'd written to Ellie of demotions, restrictions, extra duty, a few short stays in the brig. She had tried to imagine what circumstances could have landed her brother in a military jail, in a cage. As a boy he had been cocksure and strong-willed, and sometimes he'd had a smart mouth, but all boys had seemed like that to Ellie back then.

When the war ended Frank wrote to say that he was glad, but for an odd reason. If he'd gone to war, he'd written, his resistance might have become inflated even in his own mind into some kind of grand refusal. He might have gone the rest of his life thinking that what he had learned was that he could not kill anyone or that a big country should keep its nose out of a little country's affairs. Then he would have missed what he said was the only real lesson of the army, which was that people who tell you what to do—no matter what reasons they claim—are performing an act of aggression. You're in their way, is what Frank had written to her; they'd just as soon you die.

When he was discharged, he roamed the world—Ellie imagined he roamed it with that credo—crewing sailboats to New Zealand, working illegal shrimp boats out of Key West, leading tourists across the Yucatán Peninsula. For fifteen years he lived like that, never settling long enough for anyone or anything to impose itself upon him. That he came when she needed him had surprised her—though both their parents had died and there was no one else to help her. Frank spotted her first at the airport, and when she recognized him it was by the easy certain smile she remembered. When she came close, though, he stepped lightly away from her. He shook her hand first and then he shook Cody's. The nature of his support was also a surprise. He said very little, never entered into the acrimony of her divorce, never said more to her son than a benevolent stranger might say. He simply sat nearby while she found a job, a place to live, a car, while she went about the business of solving her life, and each Saturday morning, on the hall stand outside her bedroom door, he left two one-hundred-dollar bills folded under an old candy dish of their mother's.

Only once, just after he arrived, while they sat next to each other on a commuter train bringing them back from the courtroom where she had been ordered to sell her home, had he spoken up.

"You're getting screwed," he told her.

"I know."

"You're just standing there letting it happen."

"It's worse if you make a fuss. I tried that once and even my own attorney yelled at me. You're just supposed to stand there and take it. It's all a glorified trip to the principal's office." She looked out the window when she said it.

"You're nuts. You're only seeing what's in front of you." When she didn't turn around, he leaned closer to her and lowered his voice. "For what you'll end up paying that lawyer we could buy a little guest camp I once stayed at in Bali. It's real popular with the Australians, but far enough away that you'd never be found. Cody could grow up knowing how to catch his own dinner."

Still looking out the window, she considered it. She could take a few books, a bag of mementos, and her son, and disappear into a tropical life of light, loose clothing, modest shelter, balmy breezes. She turned to Frank. Perhaps this was how he had solved his life—not so much by running away from danger as by following closely the slender path of peace.

"It's against the law," she said.

He shook his head. "If you're not careful, that's the law you're going to leave your kid. You have a choice, you know." Ellie looked out the window again. Maybe she had never known she had a choice. She was a woman, a divorced mother of a young child. For a long time, her life had been one of necessity and ultimatum, not choice. But Frank was different, and she realized that his time in the army most likely marked the beginning of a deal he'd struck with himself, because since those years ended she could not name one thing he had done that he had not chosen to do. She turned to face him again.

"I can't do it, Frank."

He looked at her then with the same expression she had seen flash over him in the courtroom earlier that day. His face became quizzical as an aborigine's. As he settled back into his seat and looked past her at the city dimming into twilight she saw something else, too. She saw his resignation. Never would they live together in a tropical guest camp. She had slipped, somehow, away from him. She felt that loss carve out a hole next to the loss of her marriage, her home, the life she had believed would be hers and her son's, and she felt the nature of Frank's love for her, and of hers for him, change from hope to regret. Moved suddenly at this memory, she sat down with him at the kitchen table. She felt tears behind her eyes and pressed the palms of her hands against them.

"What?" Frank said.

"Nothing. I don't know. Maybe I should talk with his dad. We could put him in a different school, I guess."

"All schools are the same." Frank placed his thick hands flat on the table and looked at them. "They're the same man in a different hat."

"Maybe he'll get used to it. Maybe it just takes time."

Frank took a small sip of water and then glanced to the pot of soup, which was boiling too fast on the stove. "Look," he said, "why don't you go back to work? I'll watch him. You can work late and make up the hours. He and I'll walk up to the chicken place for dinner and then I'll get him to bed."

She looked at him, suddenly tired, but acquiescent, too.

"Go on," he said.

She worked until past nine that night, leaving for home when lightning from a sudden thunderstorm flickered the lamp at her desk. On the drive home, the rain turned to a fraudulent snow—huge wet flakes out of a sentimental movie. She could still hear thunder out over the lake, though, rumbling distantly like doom, and she leaned over the steering wheel, anxious to be home. More and more lately, the thought came to her that in all the world, she had only two blood relatives. In the company of that fact she felt skittish and threatened, as if two blood relatives might be too slender a tie to bind her to the world.

The front of the house was dark except for the flicker of the TV in the living room. Frank was asleep on the couch, his breathing ragged and shallow. She stopped to turn off the TV and then saw the slant of light from Cody's doorway down the hall.

"Hey," she said.

He was sitting up in bed with a big book open in his lap. "Uncle Frank felt sick so I'm reading my own night story."

She came to sit beside him. "That was good of you. But it's late. Lights out."

"We went to Chicken in a Basket and I got a Coke. A large. That's why I'm so awake."

"Still." She closed his book and slid him down so that his head settled on his pillow.

"I saw the snow. Is that why you're late?"

"I worked extra so I could take you to story hour at the library tomorrow."

"Oh," he said, already drifting off. Then he opened his eyes. "After dinner, we watched the freak feature on TV. It was about giant ants that hide in the sewer. Have you seen that one?"

"I think so. It's a scary one. Don't tell about it now. You'll have bad dreams. Tell me about it in the morning."

He closed his eyes again and rolled on his side to sleep. She stroked his hair off his forehead, and he took her hand and tucked it under his chin. Without opening his eyes, he said, "I'm going to tell Daddy, too, when I see him, and I'm going to find out if they have that giant ant movie at the movie store so he can watch it, too."

"You're full of plans," she said, leaning down to kiss him. Before she had sat up again, he was asleep, and he had let go of her hand. In the kitchen she gathered their paper cups and the boxes of chicken bones. At the trash can she stopped, holding the lid open with one hand, and stared at four empty beer cans. Drinking was something Frank had chosen not to do in her home. He never used the word *alcoholism*, but he had asked her when he moved in not to keep liquor in the house. "It distracts me," he told her. For the first month or so of his time with them, he drank a lot of everything else—water, soft drinks, iced tea—and he slept a lot.

Occasionally, too, he took long hushed phone calls from men Ellie believed must belong to AA or some support group—extremely polite, low-voiced men, men she thought of as veterans of another kind. She closed the lid of the trash can and moved to stand by the sink, still holding the chicken boxes and paper cups.

Frank came in then from the living room. "What's up?" he said when he saw her face. "Is Cody okay?"

She set the trash back on the kitchen table. "You drank."

"I know."

"Well, why? I mean, what am I supposed to do now, Frank? Am I supposed to kick you out?"

"You're not supposed to kick me out. Jesus, Ellie. You're supposed to drive me downtown to detox or something." She sat down at the table, the vision of those men in paper slippers at the VA clanging around in her head. Frank filled a tall glass with water from the tap and sat down across from her. When she looked at him, he straightened his spine and set his shoulders, but his eyes drifted unsteadily. He lowered his head.

"What's going on?" she asked.

"The VA called."

"What is it? Is it colitis?"

"A long time ago it was probably colitis." He looked at her. "Now it's cancer, Ellie." She put her hand on his. He leaned back in his chair and she felt his privacy, his strict isolation. His hand was still on the table beneath hers. It did not seem fair that he be forced to suffer more isolation. "I'm sorry," she said, and took her hand away.

He shook his head. "It gets worse," he said, smiling lightly. "They went ahead and scheduled me for more tests and then this clerk called back and told me I don't qualify for treatment. 'This is not a service-related ailment,' he told me. 'The VA treats only the indigent and service-related ailments.'"

"You didn't know that?" she said softly.

He rubbed his temples with both hands and pushed his hair roughly away from his face. "No."

"So what this means," she began slowly.

"What this means is I have cancer and no health insurance."

She sat back in her chair, stunned by the precision of this cruelty. Her brother had stepped off a plane just over a year ago tanned and strong, his only weakness that he would not keep track of rules. He had balked even when she suggested he get a driver's license. She closed her eyes at the memory. She was the reason he'd come back to this place where his weakness could turn on him so cruelly.

"We'll figure it out, Frank. We'll figure something out."

"No. No. I've already done that. I just hate to leave you in a bind. I've got a little money I was saving to go back to Negril this spring. I'll leave you some of it and still make out pretty well there myself."

"What are you saying?"

"I'm saying I'm going to Negril." He looked sad for her when he said it, as if he believed she were the one with the greater loss. "I'll leave in a couple days."

"Frank, my God. You have to take care of this. You can't just walk away from it."

"I'm not walking away, Ellie. There are doctors in Negril. I'm not saying I won't take care of it. I'm just saying I can't take care of it here." He was lying, she thought. He had decided somehow that to die whole on ground he understood would be better than struggling here. She sat rigidly across from him, her mind wildly in search of hope, of a kindly Jamaican doctor down there who would take Frank in and cure him for no more reward than the satisfaction of having preserved such a man. But she had never met a doctor like that. She wasn't sure the world was a large and varied enough place to hold even one doctor like that.

"How can I stop you," she said, "from doing this?"

"You can't." He pushed back his chair and stood up. "I'm tired, Ellie. I'm going to go to bed now." He didn't go to bed. For hours she heard his silence as he moved through rooms. She wondered if perhaps he was saying good-bye to the house, to its small comforts, but then she understood that he no longer saw her home as a safe place. She was frightened for herself, knowing that. He stood in the kitchen a long time, the house so quiet around him she felt she could hear his resolve building. Then he went into Cody's room. She sat up in bed and put one foot on the floor, listening until he came out again. When she opened her eyes next, Cody stood at her bedside.

"Is it morning?" he asked.

She looked to the window. Outside the snow was gone and the sun shone brightly.

"Yes."

"I had a bad dream. I had a dream someone got into our house."

"Uncle Frank was up late last night. You probably heard Uncle Frank."

"I dreamed it was someone else."

"It wasn't," she said. "It was Uncle Frank."

They washed and dressed hurriedly, though it was still early. Ellie let Cody watch cartoons as he ate, grateful for the noise and distraction. As they were leaving, she lingered in the quiet front room, looking down the hallway to Frank's closed door. Cody stood in his coat and hat, watching her.

"Let's go now." She took his hand. "Time to go."

They were early to Cody's school, and his teacher looked up surprised from a table in the back of the room, but she came to greet them in the hallway.

"A new day and a new start," she said merrily.

Cody reached up to hold on to a corner of Ellie's jacket.

"Today the Green Star group is going to spend the morning at the sand table," his teacher said to him. "Why don't you hang up your coat and get started?" She looked to Ellie. "Cody is in the Green Star group."

Ellie nodded.

"I have to tell my mom something," Cody said.

"Well, hurry along. We don't want to make Mom late for work or whatever."

"Okay," Cody said, and then stood mute next to Ellie, still clutching her jacket. His teacher watched him for a moment and then went back into the classroom.

"Hurry along," she called. "I'll take the top off the sand table."

Cody stiffened and began to cry as Ellie slipped his coat off his shoulders. She took his hands, warm with the moist heat of emotion and fear.

"What is it you want to tell me, Cody?"

He shook his head, his eyes a little desperate and lost.

"You don't know what it is?"

He shook his head again.

She nodded and pulled him close. "I love you, child," she said into his ear. Then she drew him away from her. "I think you can do this. I think it's important that you do this." He wouldn't look at her when she said it.

Pulling up to the school that afternoon, she saw his face at the door, a bobbing pale moon in the glass that drew an ache up from her own stomach, but he ran down the slope to her car like the other children, trailing his knapsack behind him.

"Did it go okay?"

"Yeah." He closed his door, locked it, and drew the seat belt around him. "At the bad parts, I just pretended I was somewhere else. I pretended it wasn't really happening."

They were early to story hour and Cody hovered near the librarian at her desk, telling her the story of the giant ant movie he had seen. She was a kind older woman, wise in the ways of children, and she listened raptly to Cody's story, then led him off to a far corner of the children's room. Ellie sat with their coats in a small low chair and watched the other mothers and children arrive. A few minutes later, Cody came running back carrying some books the librarian had found for him. They were junior novelizations of old monster movies: *The Mummy, Frankenstein* and *King Kong.*

"Oh, these are too scary for you, Cody. These things even give me the willies."

"Mom," he said. "She gave them to me. I was going to show them to Uncle Frank."

"Oh. Well, let me see." She flipped the pages while he leaned against her shoulder. Mainly they were just a collection of black-and-white stills from the old movies.

"Maybe they give you the willies because the monsters are always after a lady." Cody pointed to a picture of the Mummy carrying a woman into a dark wood.

"Maybe," she said, closing the book. "I don't know."

"Could I show them to Uncle Frank? They won't scare him, I bet."

"Sure," she said. "I guess."

He crawled into her lap then, and Ellie watched the preparations for story hour while Cody paged through his books.

"I read the sign," Ellie said. "Today is a special puppet show for Martin Luther King's birthday."

"Our teacher told us about him in school."

"I'm glad. He was a good brave man."

"Once nothing was fair for brown-skinned people."

"Martin Luther King changed some of that, though."

Cody turned around and looked at her. "He got killed," he said.

"I know. I was a girl. It was very sad."

Cody leaned back against her then and fingered his monster books. His body grew slack against hers, and she thought he must be tired, but then she felt heat move out of him, the same heat she had felt in his hands that morning. She turned him around in her lap.

"What's wrong, Cody?" He shook his head and she remembered this morning, how he had wanted to tell her something he didn't know.

"What is it?"

"Don't tell Daddy," he said.

He had never spoken those words to her before. Perhaps because of the way he lived or perhaps because of his own good nature, Cody had always been unstintingly fair in his attachments to each of his parents.

"I don't know," Ellie said. "Why not Daddy?"

"It's not a man's secret."

"It's a woman's secret?"

"Uh-huh. I think so."

"What is it?"

"I'm afraid about dying. Do you just fall down one day and then it hurts forever?" After he said it, she pulled him close. Children did this, she had read somewhere, picked up the unspoken cues and terror in their homes.

"It doesn't hurt," she told him. "It stops all the hurt."

She drew her hand across his forehead.

"It feels like this," she said.

She knew when she said it that something was terribly wrong with her. To portray death to her own child as more dignified and easeful than life was some sort of abomination larger than she could fathom. But she did not take it back. She rocked Cody gently as the librarian rang a small bell and called for the children to gather around the puppet theater. She sat blankly, Cody curled against her, as the show began with a cardboard cut-out of a strictly segregated bus—a cluster of white circles at the front, a cluster of black circles at the back. *Before Rosa Parks,* the caption under the bus read. Then the librarian explained to the children that Rosa Parks was tired and believed she had as much right to sit down and rest as anyone else.

It's a woman's secret, Ellie thought. This was what her son believed. How he must have wondered to find a woman's secret in his own mind, to understand that to the teeming power and circumstance of the world he would lose many things—one day even his life. Cody's head lolled against her shoulder. She realized he was asleep in her arms. The monster books slid out of his hands and she held them a moment, looking into the shy pain on King Kong's face. She shook Cody lightly.

"We have to go," she said. "We have to hurry."

At home, Frank was on the couch in front of the news. He smiled briefly when they came in, then looked back at the television. Cody ran to him with the monster books. He wanted Frank to read them to him.

"In one minute," Frank said. "When the news is over, I'll read all three."

While Ellie hung up their coats, Cody eased himself onto the couch next to Frank and sat stiffly next to him, thumping his feet against the cushion. Frank lay one hand on his knee to quiet him. An old newsreel of Martin Luther King's last speech was playing on the TV.

"I saw him at the library," Cody said. "A picture of him. It's his birthday."

"Monday," Frank said.

"My friend Bennie's dad is off work Monday, and Bennie doesn't have school, but I do."

"How come you have school? I thought everyone was off," Frank said. "It's a holiday." Cody was quiet then, and Ellie saw that he was a little teary, blinking and looking away from Frank to the TV.

"I don't know," he said. "I just do."

Frank shook Cody's knee gently. "Well, that stinks," he said, smiling. "That's not fair." He shook his knee more roughly until Cody began to smile, too, and then he leaned close to him.

"Just don't go," Frank said. "Stay home."

Cody looked at him. Ellie could see that Cody had not considered that an option before, that he had never completely understood he had an option, and next she knew he was going to look to her. She turned away quickly to the front window, afraid to watch the idea of freedom dawn in her son's face, but outside in the evening sky growing up at the end of her block, she saw it anyway—the sudden knowledge loose in his mind, spreading like the shadows that spilled from under stoops, crawled across lawns and bloomed up from the dark center of even her own scraggly hedgerow. Her son was free. Behind her, music signaled the end of the news. It was late. She knew she should turn around, start dinner, but she stood a moment longer, staring out at the dark, and felt rising in her own mind the strangest and most fearsome comfort.

Junot Díaz

NILDA

JUNOT DÍAZ (1968–) is the author of the story collection *Drown*, and has had stories published in *Story*, *The New Yorker*, *The Paris Review*, *Best American Short Stories*, and *African Voices*. His novel, *The Brief Wondrous Life of Oscar Wao*, was published in September 2007 by Riverhead Books. Díaz was born in Santo Domingo, Dominican Republic, and now teaches fiction writing at MIT.

Nilda was my brother's girlfriend.

This is how all these stories begin.

She was Dominican from here and had super-long hair, like those Pentecostal girls, and a chest you wouldn't believe—I'm talking world-class. Rafa would sneak her down into our basement bedroom after our mother went to bed and do her to whatever was on the radio right then. The two of them had to let me stay, because if my mother heard me upstairs on the couch everybody's ass would have been fried. And since I wasn't about to spend my night out in the bushes this is how it was.

Rafa didn't make no noise, just a low something that resembled breathing. Nilda was the one. She seemed to be trying to hold back from crying the whole time. It was crazy hearing her like that. The Nilda I'd grown up with was one of the quietest girls you'd ever meet. She let her hair wall away her face and read *The New Mutants*, and the only time she looked straight at anything was when she looked out a window.

But that was before she'd gotten that chest, before that slash of black hair had gone from something to pull on the bus to something to stroke in the dark. The new Nilda wore stretch pants and Iron Maiden shirts; she had already run away from her mother's and ended up at a group home; she'd already slept with Toño and Nestor and Little Anthony from Parkwood, older guys. She crashed over at our apartment a lot because she hated her moms, who was the neighborhood borracha. In the morning she slipped out before my mother woke up and found her. Waited for heads at the bus stop, fronted like she'd come from her own place, same clothes as the day before and greasy hair so everybody thought her a skank. Waited for my brother and didn't talk to anybody and nobody talked to her, because she'd always been one of those quiet, semi-retarded girls who you couldn't talk to without being dragged into a whirlpool of dumb

144

stories. If Rafa decided that he wasn't going to school, then she'd wait near our apartment until my mother left for work. Sometimes Rafa let her in right away. Sometimes he slept late and she'd wait across the street, building letters out of pebbles until she saw him crossing the living room.

She had big stupid lips and a sad moonface and the driest skin. Always rubbing lotion on it and cursing the moreno father who'd given it to her.

It seemed like she was always waiting for my brother. Nights she'd knock and I'd let her in and we'd sit on the couch while Rafa was off at his job at the carpet factory or working out at the gym. I'd show her my newest comics and she'd read them real close, but as soon as Rafa showed up she'd throw them in my lap and jump into his arms. I missed you, she'd say in a little-girl voice, and Rafa would laugh. You should have seen him in those days: he had the face bones of a saint. Then Mami's door would open and Rafa would detach himself and cowboy-saunter over to Mami and say, You got something for me to eat, vieja? Claro que sí, Mami'd say, trying to put her glasses on.

He had us all, the way only a pretty nigger can.

Once when Rafa was late from the job and we were alone in the apartment a long time, I asked her about the group home. It was three weeks before the end of the school year and everybody had entered the Do-Nothing Stage. I was fourteen and reading *Dhalgren* for the second time; I had an IQ that would have broken you in two but I would have traded it in for a halfway decent face in a second.

It was pretty cool up there, she said. She was pulling on the front of her halter top, trying to air her chest out. The food was *bad* but there were a lot of cute guys in the house with me. They *all* wanted me.

She started chewing on a nail. Even the guys who worked there were calling me after I left, she said.

The only reason Rafa went after her was because his last full-time girlfriend had gone back to Guyana—she was this dougla girl with a single eyebrow and skin to die for—and because Nilda had pushed up to him. She'd only been back from the group home a couple of months, but by then she'd already gotten a rep as a cuero. A lot of the Dominican girls in town were on some serious lockdown—we saw them on the bus and at school and maybe at the Pathmark, but since most families knew exactly what kind of tigueres were roaming the neighborhood these girls weren't allowed to hang out. Nilda was different. She was brown trash. Her moms was a mean-ass drunk and always running around South Amboy with her white boyfriends—which is a long way of saying Nilda could hang and, man, did she ever. Always out in the world, always cars stopping where she was smoking cigarettes. Before I even knew she was back from the group home she got scooped up by this older nigger from the back apartments. He kept her on his dick for almost four months, and I used to see them driving around in his fucked-up rust-eaten Sunbird while I delivered my papers. Motherfucker was like three hundred years old, but because he had a car and a record collection and foto albums from his Vietnam days and because he bought her clothes to replace the old shit she was wearing, Nilda was all lost on him.

I hated this nigger with a passion, but when it came to guys there was no talking to Nilda. I used to ask her, What's up with Wrinkle Dick? And she would get so mad she wouldn't speak to me for days, and then I'd get this note, *I want you to respect my man. Whatever,* I'd write back. Then the old cat bounced, no one knew where, the usual scenario in my neighborhood, and for a couple of months she got tossed by those cats from Parkwood. On Thursdays, which was comic-book day, she'd drop in to see what I'd picked up and she'd talk to me about how unhappy she was. We'd sit together until it got dark and then her beeper would fire up and she'd peer into its display and say, I have to go. Sometimes I could grab her and pull her back on the couch, and we'd stay there a long time, me waiting for her to fall in love with me, her waiting for whatever, but other times she'd be serious. I have to go see my man, she'd say.

One of those comic-book days she saw my brother coming back from his five-mile run. Rafa was still boxing then and he was cut up like crazy, the muscles on his chest and abdomen so striated they looked like something out of a Frazetta drawing. He noticed her because she was wearing these ridiculous shorts and this tank that couldn't have blocked a sneeze and a thin roll of stomach was poking from between the fabrics and he smiled at her and she got real serious and uncomfortable and he told her to fix him some iced tea and she told him to fix it himself. You a guest here, he said. You should be earning your fucking keep. He went into the shower and as soon as he did she was in the kitchen stirring and I told her to leave it, but she said, I might as well. We drank all of it.

I wanted to warn her, tell her he was a monster, but she was already headed for him at the speed of light.

The next day Rafa's car turned up broken—what a coincidence—so he took the bus to school and when he was walking past our seat he took her hand and pulled her to her feet and she said, Get off me. Her eyes were pointed straight at the floor. I just want to show you something, he said. She was pulling with her arm but the rest of her was ready to go. Come on, Rafa said, and finally she went. Save my seat, she said over her shoulder, and I was like, Don't worry about it. Before we even swung onto 516 Nilda was in my brother's lap and he had his hand so far up her skirt it looked like he was performing a surgical procedure. When we were getting off the bus Rafa pulled me aside and held his hand in front of my nose. Smell this, he said. This, he said, is what's wrong with women.

You couldn't get anywhere near Nilda for the rest of the day. She had her hair pulled back and was glorious with victory. Even the white girls knew about my overmuscled about-to-be-a-senior brother and were impressed. And while Nilda sat at the end of our lunch table and whispered to some girls me and my boys ate our crap sandwiches and talked about the X-Men—this was back when the X-Men still made some kind of sense—and even if we didn't want to admit it the truth was now patent and awful: all the real dope girls were headed up to the high school, like moths to a light, and there was nothing any of us younger cats could do about it. My man José Negrón—a.k.a. Joe Black—took Nilda's defection the hardest, since he'd actually imagined he had a chance with her. Right after she got back from the group home he'd held her hand on the bus, and even though she'd gone off with other guys, he'd never forgotten it.

I was in the basement three nights later when they did it. That first time neither of them made a sound.

They went out that whole summer. I don't remember anyone doing anything big. Me and my pathetic little crew hiked over to Morgan Creek and swam around in water stinking of leachate from the landfill; we were just getting serious about the licks that year and Joe Black was stealing bottles out of his father's stash and we were drinking them down to the corners on the swings behind the apartments. Because of the heat and because of what I felt inside my chest a lot, I often just sat in the crib with my brother and Nilda. Rafa was tired all the time and pale: this had happened in a matter of days. I used to say, Look at you, white boy, and he used to say, Look at you, you black ugly nigger. He didn't feel like doing much, and besides his car had finally broken down for real, so we would all sit in the air-conditioned apartment and watch TV. Rafa had decided he wasn't going back to school for his senior year, and even though my moms was heartbroken and trying to guilt him into it five times a day, this was all he talked about. School had never been his gig, and after my pops left us for his twenty-five-year-old he didn't feel he needed to pretend any longer. I'd like to take a long fucking trip, he told us. See California before it slides into the ocean. California, I said. California, he said. A nigger could make a showing out there. I'd like to go there, too, Nilda said, but Rafa didn't answer her. He had closed his eyes and you could see he was in pain.

We never talked about our father. I'd asked Rafa once, right at the beginning of the Last Great Absence, where he thought he was, and Rafa said, Like I fucking care.

End of conversation. World without end.

On days niggers were really out of their minds with boredom we trooped down to the pool and got in for free because Rafa was boys with one of the lifeguards. I swam, Nilda went on missions around the pool just so she could show off how tight she looked in her bikini, and Rafa sprawled under the awning and took it all in. Sometimes he called me over and we'd sit together for a while and he'd close his eyes and I'd watch the water dry on my ashy legs and then he'd tell me to go back to the pool. When Nilda finished promenading and came back to where Rafa was chilling she kneeled at his side and he would kiss her real long, his hands playing up and down the length of her back. Ain't nothing like a fifteen-year-old with a banging body, those hands seemed to be saying, at least to me.

Joe Black was always watching them. Man, he muttered, she's so fine I'd lick her asshole *and* tell you niggers about it.

Maybe I would have thought they were cute if I hadn't known Rafa. He might have seemed enamora'o with Nilda but he also had mad girls in orbit. Like this one piece of white trash from Sayreville, and this morena from Amsterdam Village who also slept over and sounded like a freight train when they did it. I don't remember her name, but I do remember how her perm shone in the glow of our night-light.

In August Rafa quit his job at the carpet factory—I'm too fucking tired, he complained, and some mornings his leg bones hurt so much he couldn't get out of bed right away. The Romans used to shatter these with iron clubs, I told him while I massaged his shins. The pain would kill you instantly. Great, he said. Cheer me up some more, you fucking bastard. One day Mami took him to the hospital for a checkup and afterward I found them sitting on the couch, both of them dressed up, watching TV like nothing had happened. They were holding hands and Mami appeared tiny next to him.

Well?

Rafa shrugged. The doc thinks I'm anemic.

Anemic ain't bad.

Yeah, Rafa said, laughing bitterly. God bless Medicaid.

In the light of the TV, he looked terrible.

That was the summer when everything we would become was hovering just over our heads. Girls were starting to take notice of me; I wasn't good-looking but I listened and was sincere and had boxing muscles in my arms. In another universe I probably came out O.K., ended up with mad novias and jobs and a sea of love in which to swim, but in this world I had a brother who was dying of cancer and a long dark patch of life like a mile of black ice waiting for me up ahead.

One night, a couple of weeks before school started—they must have thought I was asleep—Nilda started telling Rafa about her plans for the future. I think even she knew what was about to happen. Listening to her imagining herself was about the saddest thing you ever heard. How she wanted to get away from her moms and open up a group home for runaway kids. But this one would be real cool, she said. It would be for normal kids who just got problems. She must have loved him because she went on and on. Plenty of people talk about having a flow, but that night I really heard one, something that was unbroken, that fought itself and worked together all at once. Rafa didn't say nothing. Maybe he had his hands in her hair or maybe he was just like, Fuck you. When she finished he didn't even say wow. I wanted to kill myself with embarrassment. About a half hour later she got up and dressed. She couldn't see me or she would have known that I thought she was beautiful. She stepped into her pants and pulled them up in one motion, sucked in her stomach while she buttoned them. I'll see you later, she said.

Yeah, he said.

After she walked out he put on the radio and started on the speed bag. I stopped pretending I was asleep; I sat up and watched him.

Did you guys have a fight or something?

No, he said.

Why'd she leave?

He sat down on my bed. His chest was sweating. She had to go.

But where's she gonna stay?

I don't know. He put his hand on my face, gently. Why ain't you minding your business?

A week later he was seeing some other girl. She was from Trinidad, a coco pañyol, and she had this phony-as-hell English accent. It was the way we all were back then. None of us wanted to be niggers. Not for nothing.

I guess two years passed. My brother was gone by then, and I was on my way to becoming a nut. I was out of school most of the time and had no friends and I sat inside and watched Univisión or walked down to the dump and smoked the mota I should have been selling until I couldn't see. Nilda didn't fare so well, either. A lot of the things that happened to her, though, had nothing to do with me or my brother. She fell in love a couple more times, really bad with this one moreno truck driver who took her to Manalapan and then abandoned her at the end of the summer. I had to drive over to get her, and the house was one of those tiny box jobs with a fifty-cent lawn and no kind of charm; she was acting like she was some Italian chick and offered me a joint in the car, but I put my hand on hers and told her to stop it. Back home she fell in with more stupid niggers, relocated kids from the City, and they came at her with drama and some of their girls beat her up, a Brick City beat-down, and she lost her bottom front teeth. She was in and out of school and for a while they put her on home instruction, and that was when she finally dropped.

My junior year she started delivering papers so she could make money, and since I was spending a lot of time outside I saw her every now and then. Broke my heart. She wasn't at her lowest yet but she was aiming there and when we passed each other she always smiled and said hi. She was starting to put on weight and she'd cut her hair down to nothing and her moonface was heavy and alone. I always said Wassup and when I had cigarettes I gave them to her. She'd gone to the funeral, along with a couple of his other girls, and what a skirt she'd worn, like maybe she could still convince him of something, and she'd kissed my mother but the vieja hadn't known who she was. I had to tell Mami on the ride home and all she could remember about her was that she was the one who smelled good. It wasn't until Mami said it that I realized it was true.

It was only one summer and she was nobody special, so what's the point of all this? He's gone, he's gone, he's gone. I'm twenty-three and I'm washing my clothes up at the minimall on Ernston Road. She's here with me—she's folding her shit and smiling and showing me her missing teeth and saying, It's been a long time, hasn't it, Yunior?

Years, I say, loading my whites. Outside the sky is clear of gulls, and down at the apartment my moms is waiting for me with dinner. Six months earlier we were sitting in front of the TV and my mother said, Well, I think I'm finally over this place.

Nilda asks, Did you move or something?

I shake my head. Just been working.

God, it's been a long, long time. She's on her clothes like magic, making everything neat, making everything fit. There are four other people at the counters, broke-ass-looking niggers with knee socks and croupier's hats and scars snaking up their arms, and they all seem like sleepwalkers compared with her. She shakes her head, grinning. Your brother, she says.

Rafa.

She points her finger at me like my brother always did.

I miss him sometimes.

She nods. Me, too. He was a good guy to me.

I must have disbelief on my face because she finishes shaking out her towels and then stares straight through me. He treated me the best.

Nilda.

He used to sleep with my hair over his face. He used to say it made him feel safe.

What else can we say? She finishes her stacking, I hold the door open for her. The locals watch us leave. We walk back through the old neighborhood, slowed down by the bulk of our clothes. London Terrace has changed now that the landfill has shut down. Kicked-up rents and mad South Asian people and white folks living in the apartments, but it's our kids you see in the streets and hanging from the porches.

Nilda is watching the ground as though she's afraid she might fall. My heart is beating and I think, We could do anything. We could marry. We could drive off to the West Coast. We could start over. It's all possible but neither of us speaks for a long time and the moment closes and we're back in the world we've always known.

Remember the day we met? she asks.

I nod.

You wanted to play baseball.

It was summer, I say. You were wearing a tank top.

You made me put on a shirt before you'd let me be on your team. Do you remember?

I remember, I say.

We never spoke again. A couple of years later I went away to college and I don't know where the fuck she went.

Anthony Doerr

THE CARETAKER

ANTHONY DOERR (1973–) is the author of a story collection, *The Shell Collector;* a novel, *About Grace;* and a recent book of nonfiction, *Four Seasons in Rome: On Twins, Insomnia, and the Biggest Funeral in the History of the World.* Named one of *Granta*'s 20 Best Young American Novelists, he has had fiction published in seven languages and has won awards including the Rome Prize from the American Academy of Arts and Letters, the New York Public Library's Young Lions Award, Barnes & Noble's Discover Prize, two O. Henry Prizes, two Ohioana Book Awards, and the Hodder Fellowship from Princeton University. He has lived in Africa, New Zealand, Italy, and Ohio. He currently lives with his wife and twin sons in Boise, Idaho.

For his first thirty-five years, Joseph Saleeby's mother makes his bed and each of his meals; each morning she makes him read a column of the English dictionary, selected at random, before he is allowed to set foot outside. They live in a small collapsing house in the hills outside Monrovia in Liberia, West Africa. Joseph is tall and quiet and often sick; beneath the lenses of his oversized eyeglasses, the whites of his eyes are a pale yellow. His mother is tiny and vigorous; twice a week she stacks two baskets of vegetables on her head and hikes six miles to sell them in her stall at the market in Mazien Town. When the neighbors come to compliment her garden, she smiles and offers them Coca-Cola. "Joseph is resting," she tells them, and they sip their Cokes, and gaze over her shoulder at the dark shuttered windows of the house, behind which, they imagine, the boy lies sweating and delirious on his cot.

Joseph clerks for the Liberian National Cement Company, transcribing invoices and purchase orders into a thick leatherbound ledger. Every few months he pays one more invoice than he should, and writes the check to himself. He tells his mother the extra money is part of his salary, a lie he grows comfortable making. She stops by the office every noon to bring him rice—the cayenne she heaps onto it will keep illness at bay, she reminds him, and watches him eat at his desk. "You're doing so well," she says. "You're helping make Liberia strong."

In 1989 Liberia descends into a civil war that will last seven years. The cement plant is sabotaged, then transformed into a guerilla armory, and Joseph finds himself out of a job. He begins to traffic in goods—sneakers, radios, calculators, calendars—stolen from downtown businesses. It is harmless, he tells himself, everybody is looting. We need the money. He keeps it in the cellar, tells his mother he's storing boxes for a friend. While his mother is at the market, a truck comes and carries the merchandise away. At nights he pays a pair of boys to roam the townships, bending window bars, unhinging doors, depositing what they steal in the yard behind Joseph's house.

He spends most of his time squatting on the front step watching his mother tend her garden. Her fingers pry weeds from the soil or cull spent vines or harvest snap beans, the beans plunking regularly into a metal bowl, and he listens to her diatribes on the hardships of war, the importance of maintaining a structured lifestyle. "We cannot stop living because of conflict, Joseph," she says. "We must persevere."

Spurts of gunfire flash on the hills; airplanes roar over the roof of the house. The neighbors stop coming by; the hills are bombed, and bombed again. Trees burn in the night like warnings of worse evil to come. Policemen splash past the house in stolen vans, the barrels of their guns resting on the sills, their eyes hidden behind mirrored sunglasses. Come and get me, Joseph wants to yell at them, at their tinted windows and chrome tailpipes. Just you try. But he does not; he keeps his head down and pretends to busy himself among the rosebushes.

In October of 1994 Joseph's mother goes to the market in the morning with three baskets of sweet potatoes and does not return. He paces the rows of her garden, listening to the far-off thump-thump of artillery, the keening of sirens, the interminable silences between. When finally the last hem of light drops behind the hills, he goes to the neighbors. They peer at him through the rape gate across the doorway to their bedroom and issue warnings: "The police have been killed. Taylor's guerillas will be here any minute."

"My mother . . ."

"Save yourself," they say and slam the door. Joseph hears chains clatter, a bolt slide home. He leaves their house and stands in the dusty street. At the horizon columns of smoke rise into a red sky. After a moment he walks to the end of the paved road and turns up a muddy track, the way to Mazien Town, the way his mother traveled that morning. At the market he sees what he expected: fires, a smoldering truck, crates hacked open, teenagers plundering stalls. On a cart he finds three corpses; none is his mother's, none is familiar.

No one he sees will speak to him. When he collars a girl running past, cassettes spill from her pockets; she looks away and will not answer his questions. Where his mother's stall stood there is only a pile of charred plywood, neatly stacked, as if someone had already begun to rebuild. It is light before he returns home.

The next night—his mother does not return—he goes out again. He sifts through remains of market stalls; he shouts his mother's name down the abandoned aisles. In a place where the market sign once hung between two iron posts, a man has been suspended upside-down. His insides, torn out of him, swing beneath his arms like black infernal ropes, marionette strings cut free.

In the days to come Joseph wanders farther. He sees men leading girls by chains; he stands aside so a dumptruck heaped with corpses can pass. Twenty times he is stopped and harassed; at makeshift checkpoints soldiers press the muzzles of rifles into his chest and ask if he is Liberian, if he is a Krahn, why he is not helping them fight the Krahns. Before they let him go they spit on his shirt. He hears that a band of guerillas wearing Donald Duck masks has begun eating the organs of its enemies; he hears about terrorists in football cleats trampling the bellies of pregnant women.

Nowhere does anyone claim to know his mother's whereabouts. From the front step he watches the neighbors raid the garden. The boys he paid to loot stores no longer come by. On the radio a soldier named Charles Taylor brags of killing fifty Nigerian peacekeepers with forty-two bullets. "They die so easily," he boasts. "It is like sprinkling salt onto the backs of slugs."

After a month, with no more information about his mother than he had the night she disappeared, Joseph takes her dictionary under his arm, stuffs his shirt, pants and shoes with money, locks the cellar—stocked with stolen note-pads, cold medicine, boom boxes, an air compressor—and leaves the house for good. He travels awhile with four Christians fleeing to the Ivory Coast; he falls in with a band of machete-toting kids roving from village to village. The things he sees—decapitated children, drugged boys tearing open a pregnant girl, a man hung over a balcony with his severed hands in his mouth—do not bear elaboration. He sees enough in three weeks to provide ten lifetimes of night-mares. In Liberia, in that war, everything is left unburied, and anything once buried is now dredged up: corpses lie in stacks in pit latrines, wailing children drag the bodies of their parents through the streets. Krahns kill Manos; Gios kills Mandingoes; half the travelers on the highway are armed; half the cross-roads smell of death.

Joseph sleeps where he can: in leaves, under bushes, on the floorboards of abandoned houses. A pain blooms inside his skull. Every seventy-two hours he is rocked with fever—he burns, then freezes. On the days when he is not fever-ish, it hurts to breathe; it takes all his energy to continue walking.

Eventually he comes to a checkpoint where a pair of jaundiced soldiers will not let him pass. He recites his story as well as he can—the disappearance of his mother, his attempts to gather information about her whereabouts. He is not a Krahn or a Mandingo, he tells them; he shows them the dictionary, which they confiscate. His head throbs steadily; he wonders if they plan to kill him. "I have money," he says. He unbuttons his collar, shows them the bills in his shirt.

One of the soldiers talks on a radio for a few minutes, then returns. He orders Joseph into the back of a Toyota and takes him up a long, gated drive.

Rubber trees run out in seemingly endless rows beneath a plantation house with a tiled roof. The soldier leads him behind the house and through a gate onto a tennis court. On it are a dozen boys, perhaps sixteen years old, lounging on lawn furniture with assault rifles in their laps. White sunlight reflects off the concrete. They sit, and Joseph stands, and the sun bears down upon them. No one speaks.

After several minutes, a sweating captain hauls a man from the back door of the house, down the breezeway to the tennis court, and throws him onto the center line. The man wears a blue beret; his hands are tied behind his back. When they turn him over, Joseph sees his cheekbones have been broken; the face sags inward. "This parasite," the captain says, toeing the man's ribs, "piloted an airplane which bombed towns east of Monrovia for a month."

The man tries to sit up. His eyes drift obscenely in their sockets. "I am a cook," he says. "I am traveling from Yekepa. They tell me to go by road to Monrovia. So I try to go. But then I am arrested. Please. I cook steaks. I have bombed nobody."

The boys in the lawn furniture groan. The captain takes the beret from the man's head and flings it over the fence. The pain in Joseph's head sharpens; he wants to crumple; he wants to be down in the shade and go to sleep.

"You are a killer," the captain says to the prisoner. "Why not come clean? Why not own up to what you have done? There are dead mothers, dead girls, in those towns. You think you had no hand in their deaths?"

"Please! I am a cook! I grill steaks in the Stillwater Restaurant in Yekepa! I have been traveling to see my fiancée!"

"You have been bombing the countryside."

The man tries to say more but the captain presses his sneaker over his mouth. There is a faraway grinding sound, like pebbles knocking together inside a rag "You," the captain says, pointing at Joseph. "You are the one whose mother has been killed?"

Joseph blinks. "She sold vegetables in the market at Mazien Town," he says. "I have not seen her for three months."

The captain takes the gun from the holster on his hip and holds it out to Joseph. "This parasite has killed probably one thousand people," the captain says. "Mothers and daughters. It makes me sick to look at him." The captain's hands are on Joseph's hips: he draws Joseph forward as if they are dancing. The light reflecting off the tennis court is dazzling. The boys in the chairs watch, whisper. The soldier who brought Joseph leans against the fence and lights a cigarette.

The captain's lips are in Joseph's ear. "You do your mother a favor," he murmurs. "You do the whole country a favor."

The gun is in Joseph's hand—its handle is warm and slick with sweat. The pain in his head quickens. Everything before him—the dusty and still rows of trees, the captain breathing in his ear, the man on the asphalt, crawling now, feebly, like a sick child—stretches and blurs; it is as though the lenses of his glasses have liquefied. He thinks of his mother making that final walk to the market, the sun and shadow of the long trail, the wind muscling through the leaves. He should have been with her; he should have gone in her stead. He should be the one who felt the ground open beneath him, the one who disappeared. They bombed her into vapor, Joseph thinks. They bombed her into smoke. Because she thought we needed the money.

"He is not worth the blood in his body," the captain whispers. "He is not worth the air in his lungs."

Joseph lifts the pistol and shoots the prisoner through the head. The sound of the shot is quickly swallowed, dissipated by the thick air, the heavy trees. Joseph slumps to his knees; glittering rockets of light detonate behind his eyes. Everything reels in white. He collapses onto his chest, and faints.

He wakes on the floor inside the plantation house. The ceiling is bare and cracked and a fly buzzes against it. He stumbles from the room and finds himself in a hallway with no doors at either end and columns of rubber trees below stretching our nearly to the horizon. His clothes are damp; his money—even the bills beneath the soles of his boots—is gone.

At the doorway two boys loll in lounge chairs. Behind them, through the fence of the tennis court, Joseph can see the body of the man he has killed, unburied, slumped on the asphalt. He descends through the long rows of trees. None of the soldiers he sees pays him any mind. After an hour or so of walking he reaches a road; he waves to the first car that passes and they give him water to drink and a ride to the port city of Buchanan.

Buchanan is at peace—no tribes of gun-toting boys patrol the streets; no planes roar overhead. He sits by the sea and watches the dirty water wash back and forth along the pilings. There is a new kind of pain in his head, dull and trembling, no longer sharp; it is the pain of absence. He wants to cry; he wants to throw himself into the bay and drown himself. It would be impossible, he thinks, to get far enough away from Liberia.

He boards a chemical tanker and begs work washing pans in the galley. He scrubs the pans carefully enough, the hot spray washing over him as the tanker bucks its way across the Atlantic, into the Gulf of Mexico and through the Panama Canal. In the bunkroom he studies his shipmates and wonders if they can tell he is a murderer, if he wears it like a mark on his forehead. At night he leans over the bow rail and watches the hull as it cleaves the darkness. Everything feels empty and ragged; he feels as if he has left behind a thousand unfinished tasks, a thousand miscalculated ledgers. The waves continue on their anonymous journeys. The tanker churns north up the Pacific Coast.

• • •

He disembarks in Astoria, Oregon; the immigration police tell him he is a refugee of war and issue him a visa. Some days later, in the hostel where he stays, he is shown an ad in a newspaper: *Handy person needed for winter season to tend Ocean Meadows, a ninety-acre estate, orchard and home. We're desperate!*

Joseph washes his clothes in the bathroom sink and studies himself in a mirror—his beard is long and knotted; through the lenses of his glasses, his eyes look warped and yellow. He remembers the definition from his mother's dictionary: *Desperate: beyond hope of recovery, at one's last extreme.*

He takes a bus to Bandon, then thirty miles down 101, and walks the last two miles down an unmarked dirt road. Ocean Meadows: a bankrupted cranberry farm turned summer playground, the original house demolished to make way for a three-story mansion. He picks his way past the shrapnel of broken wine bottles on the porch.

"I am Joseph Saleeby, from Liberia," he tells the owner, a stout man in cowboy boots called Mr. Twyman. "I am thirty-six years old, my country is at war. I seek only peace. I can fix your shingles, your deck. Anything." His hands shake as he says this. Twyman and his wife retreat, shout at each other behind the kitchen doors. Their gaunt and taciturn daughter drags a bowl of cereal to the dining table, eats quietly, leaves. The clock on the wall chimes once, twice.

Eventually Twyman returns and hires him. They have advertised for two months, he says, and Joseph is the only applicant. "Your lucky day," he says, and eyes Joseph's boots warily.

They give him a pair of old coveralls and the apartment above the garage. During his first month the estate bulges with guests: children, babies, young men on the deck shouting into cell phones, a parade of smiling women. They are millionaires from something to do with computers; when they get out of their cars they inspect the doors for scratches; if they find one they lick their thumbs and try to buff it out. Half-finished vodka tonics on the railings, guitar music from loudspeakers dragged onto the porch, the whine of yellow jackets around half-cleaned plates, plump trash bags piling up in the shed: these are their leavings, these are Joseph's chores. He fixes a burner on the stove, sweeps sand out of the hallways, scrubs salmon off the walls after a food fight. When he isn't working he sits on the edge of the tub in his apartment and stares at his hands.

In September Twyman comes to him with a list of winter duties: install storm windows, aerate the lawns, clear ice from the roof and walkways, make sure no one comes to rob the house. "Can you handle that?" Twyman asks. He leaves keys to the caretaker's pickup and a phone number. The next morning everybody is gone. Silence floods the place. The trees swing in the wind as if shaking off a spell. Three white geese crawl out from under the shed and amble across the lawn. Joseph wanders the main house, the living room with its massive stone fireplace, the glass atrium, the huge closets. He lugs a television halfway down the stairs but cannot summon the will to steal it. Where would he take it? What would he do with it?

Each morning the day ranges before him, vast and empty. He walks the beach, fingering up stones and scanning them for uniqueness—an embedded fossil, the imprint of a shell, a glittering vein of mineral. It is rare that he doesn't pocket the stone; they are all unique, all beautiful. He brings them to his apartment and sets them on the sills—a room lined with rows of pebbles like small, unfinished battlements, fortifications against tiny invaders.

For two months he speaks to no one, sees no one. There is only the slow, steady tracking of headlights along 101, two miles away, or the contrails of a jet as its hurtles overhead, the sound of it lost somewhere in the space between sky and earth.

Rape, murder, an infant kicked against a wall, a boy with a clutch of dried ears suspended from his neck: in nightmares Joseph replays the worst things men do to each other. He sweats through his blankets and wakes throttling his pillow. His mother, his money, his neat, ordered life: all are gone—not finished, but vanished, as if some madman kidnapped each element of his life and dragged it to the bottom of a dungeon. He wants terribly to do something good with himself; he wants to do something right.

In November five sperm whales strand on the beach a half mile from the estate. The largest—slumped on the sand a few hundred yards north of the others—is over fifty feet long and is half the size of the garage where Joseph lives. Joseph is not the first to discover them: already a dozen Jeeps are parked in the dunes; men run back and forth between the animals, lugging buckets of seawater, brandishing needles.

Several women in neon anoraks have lashed a rope around the flukes of the smallest whale and are trying to tow it off the sand with a motorized skiff. The skiff churns and skates over the breaking waves; the rope tightens, slips and bites into the whale's fluke; the flesh parts and shows white. Blood wells up. The whale does not budge.

Joseph approaches a circle of onlookers: a man with a fishing pole, three girls with plastic baskets half full of clams. A woman in a blood-smeared lab coat is explaining that there is little hope of rescuing the whales: already they are over-heating, hemorrhaging, organs pulping, vital tubes conceding to the weight. Even if the whales could be towed off the beach, she says, they would probably turn and swim back onto shore. She has seen this happen before. "But," she adds, "it is a great opportunity to learn. Everything must be handled carefully."

The whales are written over with scars; their backs are mottled with pocks and craters and plates of barnacles. Joseph presses his palm to the side of one and the skin around the scar trembles beneath his touch. Another whale slaps its flukes against the beach and emits clicks that seem to originate from the center of it. Its brown bloodshot eye rolls forward, then back.

For Joseph it is as if some portal from his nightmares has opened and the horrors crouched there, breathing at the door, have come galloping through. On the half-mile trail back to Ocean Meadows, he falters in his step and has to kneel, his body quaking, the ragged clouds coursing overhead. Tears pour from his eyes. His flight has been futile; everything remains unburied, floating just at the surface, a breeze away from being dredged back up. And why? Save yourself, the neighbors had told him. Save yourself. Joseph wonders if he is beyond saving, if the only kind of man who can be saved is the man who never needed saving in the first place.

He lies in the trail until it is dark. Pain rolls behind his forehead. He watches the stars blazing in their lightless tracts, their twisting and writhing, their relentless burning, and wonders what the woman meant, what he should be learning from this.

By morning four of the five whales have died. From the dunes they look like a flotilla of black submarines run aground. Yellow tape has been strung around them on stakes and the crowds have swelled further: there are new, more civilian spectators—a dozen Girls Scouts, a mail carrier, a man in wing tips posing for a photo.

The bodies of the whales have distended with gas; their sides sag like the skin of withered balloons. In death the white cross-hatchings of scars on their backs look like ghastly lightning strokes, nets the whales have snared themselves in. Already the first and largest of them—the cow that stranded several hundred yards north of the others—has been beheaded, its jaw turned up at the sky, bits of beach sand stuck to the fist-sized teeth. Using chainsaws and long-handled knives, men in lab coats strip blubber from its flanks. Joseph watches them haul out steaming purple sacs that must be organs. Onlookers mill around; some, he sees, have taken souvenirs, peeling off thin membranes of skin and rolling them up in their fists like gray parchment.

The researchers in lab coats labor between the ribs of the largest whale, finally manage to extract what must be the heart—a massive lump of striated muscle, bunched with valves at one end. It takes four of them to roll it onto the sand. Joseph cannot believe the size of it; maybe this whale had a large heart or maybe all whales have hearts this big, but the heart is the size of a riding mower. The tubes running into it are large enough to stick his head into. One of the researchers jabs it with a needle, draws some tissue and deposits it in a jar. His colleagues are already back in the whale; there is the sound of a saw starting up. The researcher with the needle joins the others. The heart steams lightly in the sand.

Joseph finds a forest service cop eating a sandwich in the dunes.

"Is that the heart?" he asks. "That they've left there?"

She nods. "They're after the lungs, I think. To see if they're diseased."

"What will they do with the hearts?"

"Burn them, I'd guess. They'll burn everything. Because of the smell."

All day he digs. He chooses a plot on a hill, concealed by the forest, overlooking the western edge of the main house and a slice of lawn. Through the trunks behind him he can just see the ocean shimmer between the treetops. He digs until well after dusk, setting out a lantern and digging in its white circle of light. The earth is wet and sandy, rife with stones and roots, and the going is rough. His chest feels like it has cracks running through it. When he sets down the shovel, his fingers refuse to straighten. Soon the hole is deeper than Joseph is tall; he throws dirt over the rim.

Hours after midnight he has a tarp, a shovel, a tree saw and an alloy-cased hand winch in the bed of the estate's truck, the load rattling softly as he eases over the back lawn of the house and down the narrow lane to the beach. Tribes of white birch stand bunched and storm-broken in the headlights like bundles of shattered bones; their branches scrape the sides of the truck.

Twin campfires smolder by the four whales to the south but nobody is near the cow to the north, and he has no trouble driving past the hanks of kelp at tideline to the dark, beheaded hulk lying at the foot of the dunes like the caved-in hull of a wrecked ship.

Viscera and blubber is everywhere. Intestines lie unfurled across the beach like parade streamers. He holds a flashlight in his teeth and, through the giant slats of its ribs, studies the interior of the whale: everything is wet and shadowed and run-together. A few yards away the heart sits in the sand like a boulder. Crabs tear plugs from its sides; gulls squabble in the shadows.

He lays the tarp over the beach, anchors the hand winch to a crossbar at the head of the bed of the truck and hooks the bowshackle through the grommets on the corners of the tarp. With great difficulty he rolls the heart onto the plastic; then it is merely a matter of winching the entire gory bundle into the bed. He turns the crank, the gears ratcheting loudly; the winch tackle growls; the corners of the tarp come up. The heart inches toward him, plowing through the sand, and soon the truck takes its weight.

The first pale streaks of light show in the sky as he parks the pickup beside the hole he has made above the property. He lowers the tailgate and lays the tarp flat. The heart, stuck all over with sand, lies in the bed like a slain beast. Joseph wedges his body between it and the cab, and pushes. It rolls out easily enough, sliding heavily over the slick tarp, and bounces into the hole with a wet, heavy thump.

He kicks out the extra pieces of flesh and muscle and gore still in the flatbed and drives slowly, in a daze, down the hill and back onto the beach where the other four whales lie in various stages of decomposition.

Three men stand over the dregs of a campfire, soaked in gore, drinking coffee from Styrofoam cups. The heads of two of the whales are missing; all the teeth from the remaining heads have been taken away. Sand fleas jump from the carcasses. There is a sixth whale lying in the sand, Joseph sees, a near-term fetus hauled from the body of its mother. He gets out, steps over the yellow tape and walks to them.

"I'll take the hearts," he says. "If you're done with them."

They stare. He takes the tree saw from the back of the truck bed and goes to the first whale, lifting the flap of skin and stepping inside the great tree of its ribs.

A man seizes Joseph's arm. "We're supposed to burn them. Save what we can and burn the rest."

"I'll bury the hearts." He does not look at the man but keeps his eyes away, on the horizon. "It will be less work for you."

"You can't . . ." But he has released Joseph, who is already back in the whale, sawing at tissue. With the tree saw as his flensing knife he hacks through three ribs, then a thick, dense tube that could be an artery. Blood spurts onto his hands: congealed and black and slightly warm. The cavern inside the whale smells, already, like rot, and twice Joseph has to step back and breathe deeply, the saw hanging from his fist, his forearms matted with blood, the front of his coveralls soaked from mucus and blubber and seawater.

He had told himself it would be like cleaning a fish, but it is completely different—it's more like eviscerating a giant. The plumbing of the whale is on a massive scale; housecats could gallop through its veins. He parts a final layer of blubber and lays a hand on what he decides must be the heart. It is still a bit damp, and warm, and very dark. He thinks: I did not make the hole large enough for five of these.

It takes ten minutes to saw through three remaining veins; when he does the heart comes loose easily enough, sliding toward him and settling muscularly against his ankles and knees. He has to tug his feet free. A man appears, thrusts a syringe into the heart and draws up some matter. "Okay," the man says. "Take it."

Joseph tows it into the truck. He does this all morning and all afternoon, hacking out the hearts and depositing them in the hole on the hill. None of the hearts were as big as the first whale's but they are huge, the size of the range in Twyman's kitchen or the engine in the truck. Even the fetus's heart is extraordinary; as big as a man's torso, and as heavy. He cannot hold it in his arms.

By the time Joseph is pushing the last heart into the hole on the hill, his body has begun to fail him. Purple halos spin at the fringes of his vision; his back and arms are rigid and he has to walk slightly bent over. He fills the hole, and as he leaves it, a mound of earth and muscle, stark amid a thicket of salmonberry with the trunks of spruce falling back all around it, high above the property in the late evening, he feels removed from himself, as though his body were a clumsy tool needed only a little longer. He parks in the yard and falls into bed, gore-soaked and unwashed, the door to the apartment open, the hearts of all six whales wrapped in earth, slowly cooling. He thinks: I have never been so tired. He thinks: At least I have buried something.

During the following days he does not have the energy or will to climb out of bed. He tortures himself with questions: Why doesn't he feel any better, any more healed? What is revenge? Redemption? The hearts are still there, sitting just beneath the earth, waiting. What good does burying something really do? In nightmares it always manages to dig itself out. Here was a word from his mother's dictionary: *Inconsolable: not to be consoled, spiritless, hopeless, brokenhearted.*

An ocean between himself and Liberia and still he will not be saved. The wind brings curtains of yellow-black smoke over the trees and past his windows. It smells of oil, like bad meat frying. He buries his face in the pillow to avoid inhaling it.

Winter. Sleet sings through the branches. The ground freezes, thaws, freezes again into something like sludge, immovably thick. Joseph has never seen snow; he turns his face to the sky and lets it fall on his glasses. He watches the flakes melt, their spiked struts and delicate vaulting, the crystals softening to water like a thousand microscopic lights blinking out.

He forgets his job. From the window he notices he has left the mower in the yard but the will to return it to the garage does not come. He knows he ought to flush the pipes in the main house, sweep the deck, install storm windows, switch on the cables to melt ice from the shingles. But he does not do any of it. He tells himself he is exhausted from burying the whale hearts and not from a greater fatigue, from the weight of memory all around him.

Some mornings, when the air feels warmer, he determines to go out; he throws off the covers and pulls on his trousers. Walking the muddy lane down from the main house, cresting the dunes, the sea laid out under the sky like molten silver, the low forested islands and gulls wheeling above them, a cold rain slashing through the trees, the sight of the world—the utter terror of being out in it—is too much for him, and he feels something splitting apart, a wedge falling through the center of him. He clenches his temples and turns, and has to go sit in the toolshed, among the axes and shovels, in the dark, trying to find his breath, waiting for the fear to pass.

Twyman had said the coast didn't get much snow but now the snow comes heavily. It falls for ten days straight and because Joseph does not switch on the de-icing cables, the weight of it collapses a section of the roof. In the master bedroom warped sheets of plywood and insulation sag onto the bed like ramps to the heavens. Joseph splays on the floor and watches the big clusters of flakes fall through the gap and gather on his body. The snow melts, runs down his sides, freezes again on the floor in smooth, clear sheets.

He finds jars of preserves in the basement and eats them with his fingers at the huge dining room table. He cuts a hole in a wool blanket, pulls it over his head and wears it like a cloak. Fevers come and go like wildfires; they force him to his knees and he must wait, wrapped in the blanket, until the shivers pass.

In a sprawling marble bathroom he studies his reflection. His body has thinned considerably; tendons stand out along his forearms; the slats of his ribs make drastic arcs across his sides. A yellow like the color of chicken broth floats in his eyes. He runs his hand over his hair, feels the hard surface of skull just beneath the scalp. Somewhere, he thinks, there is a piece of ground waiting for me.

He sleeps, and sleeps, and dreams of whales inside the earth, swimming through soil like they would through water, the tremors of their passage quaking the leaves. They breach up through the grass, turning over in a spray of roots and pebbles, then fall back, disappearing through the ground which stitches itself over them, whole again.

Warblers in the fog, ladybugs traversing the windows, fiddleheads nosing their way up through the forest floor—spring. He crosses the yard with the blanket over his shoulders and examines the first pale sleeves of crocuses rising from the lawn. Swatches of dirty slush lie melting in the shade. A memory rises unbidden: every April in his home, in the hills outside Monrovia, a wind blew down from the Sahara and piled red dust inches deep against the walls of the house. Dust in his ears, dust on his tongue. His mother fought back with brooms and whisks, enlisted him in the defense. Why? he would ask. Why sweep the steps when tomorrow they'll be covered again? She would look at him, fierce and disappointed, and say nothing.

He thinks of the dust, blowing now through the gaps in the shutters, piling up against the walls. It hurts him to imagine it: their house, empty, soundless, dust on the chairs and tables, the garden plundered and grown over. Stolen goods still stacked in the cellar. He hopes someone has crammed the place with explosives and bombed it into splinters; he hopes the dust will close over the roof and bury the house forever.

Soon—who is to say how many days had passed?—there is the sound of a truck grinding up the drive. It is Twyman; Joseph is discovered. He retreats to the apartment, crouches behind the windowsill and his neatly stacked rows of pebbles. He takes one, rolls it in his palm. There is shouting in the main house. He watches Twyman stride across the lawn.

Cowboy boots thud upon the stairs. Already Twyman is bellowing.

"The roof! The floors are flooded! The walls are buckling! The mower's rusted to hell!"

Joseph wipes his glasses with his fingers. "I know," he says. "It is not good."

"Not good?! Damn! Damn! Damn! Damn!" Twyman's throat is turning red; the words clog on their way out. "My God!" he manages to spit. "You fucker!"

"It is okay. I understand."

Twyman turns, studies the pebbles along the sills. "Fucker! Fucker!"

Twyman's wife drives him north in a sleek, silent truck, the wipers slipping smoothly over the windshield. She keeps one hand in her purse, clenched around what Joseph guesses to be Mace or perhaps a gun. She thinks I am an idiot, thinks Joseph. To her I am a barbarian from Africa who knows nothing about work, nothing about caretaking. I am disrespectful, I am a nigger.

They stop at a red light in Bandon and Joseph says, "I will get out here."

"Here?" Mrs. Twyman glances around as if seeing the town for the first time. Joseph climbs out. She keeps her hand in the purse. "*Duty*," she says. "It's an issue of duty." Her voice tremors; inside, he can see, she is raging. "I told him not to hire you. I told him what good is it hiring someone who runs from his country at the first sign of trouble? He won't know duty, responsibility. He won't be able to understand it. And now look."

Joseph stands, his hand on the door. "I never want to see you again," she says. "Close the fucking door."

For three days he lies on a bench in a Laundromat. He studies cracks in the ceiling tiles; he watches colors drift across the undersides of his eyelids. Clothes turn loops behind portholes in the dryers. *Duty: behavior required by moral obligation.* Twyman's wife was right; what does he understand about that? He thinks of the hearts lumped into the earth, ground bacteria chewing microscopic labyrinths through their centers. Hadn't burying those hearts been the right thing, the decent thing to do? Save yourself, they said. Save yourself. There were things he had been learning at Ocean Meadows, things yet unfinished.

Hungry but not conscious of his hunger, he walks south down the road, loping through the sogged, muddy grass on the shoulder. All around him the trees stir. When he hears a car or truck approaching, tires hissing over the wet pavement, he retreats into the woods, draws his blanket around him and waits for it to pass.

Before dawn he is back on Twyman's property, high above the main house, hiking through dense growth. The rain has stopped, and the sky has brightened, and Joseph's limbs feel light. He climbs to the small clearing between the trunks where he buried the whale hearts and lays down armfuls of dead spruce boughs for a bed and lies among them on top of the buried hearts, half buried himself, and watches the stars wheel overhead.

I will become invisible, he thinks. I will work only at night. I will be so careful they will never suspect me; I will be like the swallows on their gutter, the insects in their lawn, concealed, a scavenger, part of the scenery. When the trees shift in the wind, so I will shift, and when rain falls I will fall too. It will be a kind of disappearing.

This is my home now, he thinks, looking around him. This is what things have come to.

In the morning he parts the brambles and peers down at the house where two vans are on the lawn, ladders propped against the siding, the small figure of a man kneeling on the roof. Other men cart boxes or planking into the house. There is the industrious sound of banging.

On the shady hillside below his plot of ground Joseph finds mushrooms standing among the leaves. They taste like silt and make his stomach hurt but he swallows them all, forcing them down.

He waits until dusk, squatting, watching a slow fog collect in the trees. When it is finally night he goes down the hill to the toolshed beside the garage and takes a hoe from the wall and fumbles in the shadows around the seed box. In a paper pouch he can feel seeds—this he tucks into the pocket of his trousers and retreats, back through the clubfoot and fern, onto the wet, needled floor of the forest, to the ring of trunks and his small plot. In the dim, silvery light he opens the packet. There are maybe two palmfuls of seeds, some thin and black like thistle, some wide and white, some fat and tan. He stows them in his pocket. Then he stands, lifts the hoe, and drives it into the earth. A smell comes up: sweet, wealthy.

All through the smallest hours he turns earth. There is no sign of whale hearts; the soil is black and airy. Earthworms come up flailing, shining in the night. By dawn he is asleep again. Mosquitoes whine around his neck. He does not dream.

The next night he uses his index finger to make rows of tiny holes, and drops one seed like a tiny bomb into each hole. He is so weak from hunger that he must stop often to rest; if he stands quickly his vision floods away and the sky rushes into the horizon, and for a moment it feels like he will dissolve. He eats several of the seeds and imagines them sprouting in his gut, vines pushing up his throat, roots twisting from the soles of his shoes. Blood drips from one of his nostrils; it tastes like copper.

In the ruins of a cranberry press he finds a rusted five-gallon drum. There is a small, vigorous brook that threads between boulders by the beach and he fills the drum with the water and carts it, sloshing and spilling, up the hill to his garden.

He eats kelp, salmonberries, hazelnuts, ghost shrimp, a dead sculpin washed up by the tide. He tears mussels from rocks and boils them in the salvaged drum. One midnight he creeps down to the lawn and gathers dandelions. They taste bitter; his stomach cramps.

The workmen finish rebuilding the roof. The tide of people builds. Mrs. Twyman arrives one afternoon with a flourish of activity; she whirls across the deck in a business suit, a young man at her heels taking notes in a pad. Her daughter takes long, lonesome hikes across the dunes. The evening parties begin, paper lanterns hung from the eaves, a swing band blowing horns in the gazebo, laughter drifting on the wind.

With the hoe and several hours of persistence Joseph manages to knock a chickadee from a low bough and kill it. In the dead of night he roasts it over a tiny fire; he cannot believe how little meat there is on it; it is all bone and feather. It tastes of nothing. Now, he thinks, I really am a savage, killing tiny birds and tearing the tendons from their bones with my teeth. If Mrs. Twyman saw me she would not be surprised.

Besides daily carting water up the hill and splashing it over the rows of seeds, there is little to do but sit. The scents of the forest run like rivers between the trunks: growing, rotting. Questions come in bevies: Is the soil warm enough? Didn't his mother start plants in small pots before setting them in the ground? How much sun do seeds need? And how much water? What if these seeds were wrapped in paper because they were sterile, or old? He worries the rust from his watering drum will foul the garden; he scrapes it as clean as he can with a wedge of slate.

Memories, too, volunteer themselves up: three charred corpses in the smoking wreck of a Mercedes, a black beetle crossing the back of a broken hand. The head of a boy kicked open and lying in red dust, Joseph's own mother pushing a barrow of compost, the muscles in her legs straining as she crosses the yard. For thirty-five years Joseph had envisioned a quiet, safe thread running through his life—a thread made for him, incontrovertible, assured. Trips to the market, trips to work, rice with cayenne for lunch, trim columns of numbers in his ledger: these were life, as regular and probable as the sun's rising. But in the end that thread turned out to be illusion—there was no rope, no guide, no truth to bind Joseph's life. He was a criminal; his mother was a gardener. Both of them turned out to be as mortal as anything else, the roses in her garden, whales in the sea.

Now, finally, he is remaking an order, a structure to his hours. It feels good, tending the soil, hauling water. It feels healthy.

● ● ●

In June the first green noses of his seedlings begin to show above the soil. When he wakes in the evening and sees them in the paling light, he feels his heart might burst. Within days the entire plot of ground, an unbroken black a week ago, is populated with small dashes of green. It is the greatest of miracles. He becomes convinced that some of the shoots—a dozen or so proud thumbs pointed at the sky—are zucchini plants. On his hands and knees he examines them through the scratched lenses of his glasses: the stalks are already separating into distinct blades, tiny platters of leaves poised to unfold. Are there zucchinis in there? Big shining vegetables carried somehow in the shoots? It doesn't seem possible.

He agonizes over what to do next. Should he water more, or less? Should he prune, mulch, heel in, make cuttings? Should he limb the surrounding trees, clear some of the bramble away to provide more light? He tries to remember what his mother had done, the mechanics of her gardening, but can only recall the way she stood, a fistful of weeds trailing from her fist, looking down at her plants as if they were children, gathered at her feet.

He finds a nest of fishing tackle washed up on the rocks, untangles the monofilament and coils it around a block of driftwood. Around the dull and rusty hook he sheaths an earthworm; he weights the line and lowers it into the sea from a ledge. Some nights he manages to hook a salmon, grab it around the tail and knock its head against a rock. In the moonlight he lays it on a flat stone and eviscerates it with a piece of oyster shell. The meat he roasts over a tiny fire and eats thoughtlessly, chewing as he scuttles back up the rocks, into the woods. He does not think of taste; he goes about eating in the same manner he might go about digging a hole: it is a job, vaguely troubling, hardly satisfying.

The mansion, like the garden, swings into life. Every night there are the sounds of parties: music, the clink of silver against china, laughter. He can smell their cigarettes, their fried potatoes, the gasoline of landscapers' weedeaters and tractors. Cars rotate through the driveway. One afternoon Twyman appears on the deck and begins firing a shotgun into the trees. He is dressed in shorts and dark socks and stumbles across the planks of the deck. He reloads the gun, shoulders it, fires. Joseph crouches against a trunk. Does he know? Has Twyman seen him out there? The shot tears through the leaves.

By mid-June the stems of his plants are inches high. When he sticks his face close he can see that several of the buds have separated into delicate flowers; what looked like a solid green shoot was actually a tightly folded blossom. He feels like shouting with joy. Because of their pale, toothed leaflets, he decides some of the seedlings might be tomatoes, so he tries to construct small trellises with sticks and vine, as his mother used to do with wire and string, upon which the plants might climb. When he finishes he picks his way down the hillside to the sea and kicks a depression in the dunes and sleeps.

An hour later he wakes to see a sneaker shuffle past, hardly ten yards away. Adrenaline rockets to the tips of his fingers. His heart riots inside his chest. The sneaker is small, clean, white. Its mate moves past him, dragging through the sand, moving toward the sea.

He could run. Or he could ambush the person, claw him to death or drown him or fill his throat with sand. He could rise screaming and improvise from there. But there is no time for anything—on his stomach he flattens himself as much as possible and hopes his shape in the darkness resembles driftwood, or a tangled mess of kelp.

But the sneakers do not slow. Their owner labors down the front of the dunes, stooped and straining, lugging in the basket of its arms what looks to Joseph like a pair of cinder blocks. When it crosses the tideline Joseph raises his head and makes out features: curly, unbound hair, small shoulders, thin ankles. A girl. There is something wrong with the way she carries her head, the way it lolls on her neck, the way her shoulders ride so low—she looks defeated, overcome. She stops often to rest; her legs strain beneath her as she muscles her load forward. Joseph lowers his eyes, feels the cool sand against his chin, and tries to calm his heartbeat. Above him the clouds have blown away, and the spray of stars sends a frail light onto the sea.

When he looks again the girl is a hundred feet away. In the surf she squats with what looks like a bight of rope and runs it through the holes in a cinder block—she seems to be lashing her wrist to it. As he watches she fastens one wrist to one block, the other to the other. Then she struggles to her feet, dragging the blocks and staggering into the water. Waves clap against her chest. The blocks drop into the water with heavy splashes. She goes to her knees, then to her back, and floats, arms pulled behind and under her, still affixed to the cinder blocks. The flux of water bears her up, then closes over her chin and she is gone.

Joseph understands: the cinder blocks will hold her down and she will drown.

He lets his forehead back down against the sand. There is only the sound of waves collapsing against the shore and that starlight, faint and clean, reflecting off the mica in the sand. It is the same all over the world, Joseph thinks, in the smallest hours of the night. He wonders what would have happened if he had decided to sleep elsewhere, if he had spent one more hour framing trellises in the garden, if his seedlings had failed to shoot. If he had never seen an ad in a newspaper. If his mother had not gone to market that day. Order, chance, fate: it does not matter what brought him here. The stars burn in their constellations. Beneath the surface of the ocean countless lives are being lived out every minute.

He runs down the dunes and dives into the water. She floats just below the waves, her eyes closed; her hair washed out in a fan. Her shoelaces, untied, drift in the current. Her arms disappear beneath her into the murk.

She is, Joseph realizes, Twyman's daughter.

He dives under and lifts one of the cinder blocks from the sand and frees her wrist. With his arms beneath her body, dragging the other block, he hauls her onto the sand. "Everything is okay," he tries to say, but his voice is unused and it cracks and the words do not come. For a long moment nothing happens. Goose pimples stand up on her throat and arms. Then she coughs and her eyes fly open. She scrambles up, one arm still tied to its anchor, and flails her feet. "Wait," Joseph says. "Wait." He reaches down and lifts the block and frees her wrist. She pulls back, terrified. Her lips tremble; her arms shake. He can see how young she is—maybe fifteen years old, small pearls in her earlobes, big eyes above pink, unmarked cheeks. Water pours from her jeans. Her shoelaces trail in the sand.

"Please," he says. "Don't." But she is already gone, running hard and fast over the slope of the dunes, in the direction of the house.

Joseph shivers; the ragged blanket he still wears over his shoulders drips. If she tells someone, he considers, there will be searches. Twyman will comb the woods with his shotgun; his guests will make a game of capturing the trespasser in the woods. He must not let them find the garden. He must find a new place to sleep, acres away from the house, a damp depression in a thicket or—better still—a hole in the ground. And he will stop making fires; he will eat only those things he is willing to eat cold. He will visit the garden only every third night, only in the darkest, deepest hours, carrying water to his plants, being careful to cover his tracks. . . .

Out on the sea the reflected stars quiver and shake. The crest of each wave is limned with light, a thousand white rivers running together—it is beautiful. It is, he thinks, the most beautiful thing he has ever seen. He watches, shivering, until the sun begins to color the sky behind him, then trots down the beach, into the forest.

Four nights later: jazz, a woman on the porch making slow turns in the twilight, her skirt flaring out. Softly he creeps into his garden to weed, to yank out intruders. The music washes through the trees, piano, a saxophone. He strains to see the shoots standing up from the dirt. Blight—tiny bull's-eyes of rot—stains many of the leaves. A slug is chewing another shoot and a few of the plants have been cropped off at the ground. Over half the seedlings are dead or dying. He knows he should fence off the garden, spray the plants with something to protect them. He ought to construct a blind and stake out whatever is grazing the garden, scare it off or bludgeon it with the hoe. But he cannot—he can hardly afford the luxury of weed pulling. Everything must be done softly, must be made to look untended.

No longer does he go down to the shore or cross the lawns of the estate—they make him feel exposed, naked. He prefers the cover of the woods, the towering firs, the patches of giant clover and groves of maples; here is just one of many, here he is small.

With a flashlight she begins searching the woods at night. He knows it is she because he has hidden in a hollowed nurse log and waited for her to pass; first the light swinging frantically through the ferns, then her pinched, scared face, eyes unblinking. She moves noisily, snapping twigs, breathing hard on the hills. But she is determined; her light prowls the woods, ranges over the dunes, hurries across the lawn. Every night for a week he watches the light drifting across the property like a displaced star.

Once, in a moment of courage, he calls hello, but she doesn't hear. She continues on, stepping down through the dark shapes of the trees, the noise of her passage and the beam of the light growing fainter until they finally disappear.

On a stump not a hundred yards from his garden she begins leaving food: a tuna sandwich, a bag of carrots, a napkin full of chips. He eats them but feels slightly guilty about it, as if he's cheating, as if it's unfair that she's making it easier for him.

After another week of midnights, watching her blunder through the forest, he cannot stand it anymore and places himself in the field of her light. She stops. Her eyes, already wide, widen. She switches off her flashlight and sets it in the leaves. A pale fog hovers in the branches. They have a sort of standoff. The girl does not seem threatened although she keeps her hands just off her hips like a gunfighter.

Then she begins to move her arms in a short, intricate dance, striking the palm of one hand with the edge of the other, circling her fingers through the air, touching her right ear, finally pointing both index fingers at Joseph.

He does not know what to make of it. Her fingers repeat the dance: her hands draw a circle; the palms turn up; the fingers lock. Her lips move but no sound comes out. There is a large silver watch on her wrist which rides up and down her forearm as she gesticulates.

"I don't understand." His voice cracks from disuse. He waves toward the house. "Go away. I'm sorry. You must not come through here anymore. Someone will come looking for you." But the girl is running through the routine a third time, rolling her hand, tapping her chest, moving her lips in silence.

And then Joseph sees; he places his hands over his ears. The girl nods.

"You cannot hear?" She shakes her head. "But you know what I say? You understand?" She nods again. She points to her lips, then opens her hands like a book: lip-reading.

She pulls a notebook from her shirt and opens it. With a pencil hung around her neck, she scribbles. She holds the page out. In the dimness he reads: *How do you live?*

"I eat what I can. I sleep in the leaves. I have all I need. Please go home, miss. Go to bed."

I won't tell, she writes.

When she leaves he watches the light bob and sweep until it becomes just a spark, a firefly spiraling through the gloom. He is surprised when he realizes it makes him lonely, watching the light fade, as if, although he told her to go, he had hoped she would stay.

Two nights later, full moon, her light is back, wobbling through the forest. He knows he should leave; he should start walking north and not stop until he is a hundred miles into Canada. Instead he paces through the leaves, finally goes to her. She is wearing jeans, a hooded sweatshirt, a knapsack over her shoulders. She switches off the light as before. Moonlight spills over the boughs, sends a patchwork of shadows shifting over their shoulders. He leads her through the bramble, past the verbena, to a ledge overlooking the sea. At the horizon a lone freighter blinks its tiny light.

"I almost did it too," he says. "The thing you tried to do." She holds her hands before her like two thin and pale birds. "I was leaning over the bow of a tanker, looking down at the waves a hundred feet below. We were in the middle of the ocean. All I needed to do was push with my feet and I would have gone over."

She writes in her pad. *I thought you were an angel. I thought you had come to take me to heaven.*

"No," Joseph says. "No."

She looks at him, looks away. *Why did you come back?* she writes. *After you got fired?*

The light of the ship begins to fade. "Because it's beautiful here," he says. "Because I had nowhere else to go."

A night later they again face each other in the dimness. Her hands flutter in front of her, rolling in loops, rising to her neck, her eyes. She touches an elbow, points at him.

"I'm going for water," he says. "You can come if you like."

She follows him down through the forest until they reach the stream. He leans over a lichened rock, finds his rusty drum, and fills it. They climb back through the ferns and moss and deadfall to the top of the hill. He pulls aside some cut boughs of spruce.

"This is my garden," he says, and steps in among the plants, tendrils clinging greenly to their trellises, creepers running out over the bare soil. In the air there is the fragrance of earth and leaf and sea. "This is why I came back. I needed to do this. It's why I stay."

• • •

In the nights to come she visits the garden and they crouch among the plants. She brings him a blanket and a baguette he reluctantly chews. She brings him a book of sign language—several thousand cartoon drawings of hands, each with a word beneath. There are hands above *tree*, hands above *bicycle*, hands above *house*. He studies the pages, wonders how anyone could ever learn all the signs. Her name is Belle, he learns: he practices making it in the air with his long, clumsy fingers.

He teaches her to find pests—slugs, iridescent beetles, aphids, tiny red spider mites—and crush them between her fingers. Some of the vines have grown knee high; they range across the soil; rain pops against the leaves. "What is it like?" he asks her. "Is it very quiet? Is it silent?" She doesn't see him speak or else chooses not to answer. She sits and stares down at the house.

She brings a plant food that they mix with creek water and pour over the rows. Each time she leaves he finds himself watching her go, her body moving down through the trees, finally appearing down on the lawn, a dim silhouette slipping back into the house.

Some nights, sitting among ferns far from the garden, watching headlights creep down 101 in the distance, he clamps his palms over his ears and tries to imagine what it must be like. He shuts his eyes, tries to quiet himself. For a moment he thinks he has it; a kind of void, a nothingness, an oblivion. But it doesn't—it cannot—last; there is always noise, the flux and murmur of his body's machinery, a hum in his head. His heart beats and flexes in its cage. His body, in those moments, sounds to him like an orchestra, a rock band, an entire prison of inmates crowded into one cell. What must it be like to not hear that? To never know even the whisper of your own pulse?

The garden explodes into life; Joseph gets the impression it would grow even if the world was plunged into permanent darkness. Each night there are changes; clusters of green spheres materialize and swell on the tomato sterns; yellow flowers emerge from the vines like burning lamps. He begins to wonder if the large, bushy creepers are zucchini after all—maybe they are squash, some kind of gourds.

But they are melons. Days later he and Belle find six pale spheres sitting in the soil under the broad leaves. Each night they seem to grow larger, drawing more mass from the earth. They nearly glow in the midnight. He cakes their flanks with mud, patting them down, hiding them. He coats the tomatoes, too—it seems to him that their pale yellows and reds must shine like beacons, easily visible from the lawns of the estate, too outrageous to miss.

She is in the garden, sitting and staring down at the house, and he leaves the cover of the forest to join her. He taps her shoulder and makes the sign for night, and the sign for *how are you.* Her face brightens; her fingers flash a response.

"Slow down, slow down," laughs Joseph. "*Good night* was as far as I got."

She smiles, stands, brushes off her knees. She's written something on her pad: *Something to show you.* From her knapsack she takes a map and unfolds it over the dirt. It is worn along its creases and very soft. When he takes the whole thing in, he can see that it is a map of the entire Pacific Coast of the Americas, beginning with Alaska and ending at Tierra del Fuego.

Belle points at herself, then the map. She draws her finger down a series of highways, all north-south, that she has highlighted in color. Then she places her hands on an imaginary steering wheel and mimes driving a car.

"You want to drive this? You are going to drive this far?"

Yes, she nods. Yes. She leans forward and with her pencil, writes, *When I turn sixteen I get a Volkswagen. From my father.*

"Can you even drive?"

She shakes her head, holds up ten fingers, then six. *When I'm sixteen.*

He studies the map awhile. "Why? I don't get it."

She looks away. She makes a series of signs he does not know. On the paper she writes, *I want to leave,* and underlines it furiously. The tip of the pencil breaks.

"Belle," Joseph says. "No one could drive that far. There probably aren't even roads the whole way." She is looking at him; her mouth hangs open.

"You are, what, fifteen years old? You cannot drive to South America. You would be kidnapped. You would run out of petrol." He laughs, then, and puts his hand over his mouth. After a moment he begins to work, his fingers prying a leaf miner from the underside of a melon. Belle studies her map in the paling light.

When he looks up she is gone, her light moving quickly down the hillside, disappearing. He watches the thin shape of her hurry across the lawn.

She stops coming into the woods. As far as he can tell, she stops going outside altogether. Maybe she uses the front door, he thinks. He wonders how long she'd harbored that strange dream—to drive from Oregon to Tierra del Fuego, alone, a deaf girl.

A week passes and Joseph finds himself crouching beside the trail to the beach, sleeping on the fringes of the dunes, waking several times in the afternoon and wandering in a circle, his heart quick-beating. After dawn he studies the sign language book, working his fingers into knots, his hands aching, admiring in his memory the precision of Belle's signing, the abrupt dips, the way her hands pour together like liquid, then stop, then worry and gnash like the teeth of gears grinding. He never imagined the body could be so eloquent.

But he is learning. It is as if he is learning all over again how to put the world into words. A tree is an open hand shaken twice by your right ear; whale is three fingers dipped through a sea made by the opposite forearm. The sky is two hands touched above the head, then swept apart, as though a rift has formed in the clouds and you are swimming through them, into heaven.

Thunder over the ocean, ravens screaming in the high branches. A little longer, Joseph thinks. The tomatoes will be ready. It begins to rain—cold, earnest drops fly through the boughs. He has not seen Belle in two weeks when he finds her in the garden, wearing a blue raincoat, stooped among the rows of plants, yanking weeds from the ground and hurling them into the brambles. The drops pop off her shoulders. He watches for a moment. Lightning strobes the sky. Rain runs off the end of her nose.

He steps in among the plants, the tomatoes weighing dreamily on their stems, the melons a pale green against the gray mud on their flanks. He pulls a thin weed and shakes the mud from its roots. "Last year," he says, "whales died here. On the beach. Six of them. Whales have their own language, clicks and creaks and clinking like bottles being smashed together. On the beach they talked to each other as they died. Like old ladies."

She shakes her head. Her eyes are red. I'm sorry, he signs. Please. He says, "I was stupid. Your idea is not any more strange than probably every idea I have ever had."

After a moment he adds, "I buried the hearts from the whales in the forest." He makes the sign for heart over his chest.

She looks at him, canting her head. Her face softens. *What?* she signs.

"I buried them here." He wants to say more, wants to tell her the whales' story. But does he even know it? Does he even know why they came ashore, what they do when they don't come ashore? What happens to the bodies of whales which do not strand—do they wash up, rolling in the surf one day, rotten and bloated? Do they sink? Are their bodies mulled over at the bottom of the oceans where some strange, deepwater garden can grow up through their bones?

She studies him, her hands spread in the dirt. It's her attention, he thinks. The way she fixes me with her eyes. The way I feel like she's listening all the time, enwombed in that impenetrable silence. Her pale fingers browse among the stems, a raindrop slips down the curve of a green tomato, he has a sudden need to tell her everything. All his petty crimes, the way his mother left for the market in the morning while he *slept*—a hundred confessions surge through him. He has been waiting too long; the words have been building behind a dyke and now the dyke is breached and the river is slipping its banks. He wants to tell her what he has learned about the miracles of light, the way a day's light fluxes in tides: pale and gleaming at dawn, the glare of noon, the gold of evening, the promise of twilight—every second of every day has its own magic. He wants to tell her that when things vanish they become something else, in death we rise again in the blades of grass, the splitting bodies of seeds. But his past is flooding out: the dictionary, the ledger, his mother, the horrors he has seen.

"I had a mother," he says. "She disappeared." He cannot tell if Belle is reading his lips; she is looking away, lifting a tomato and scraping some mud from its underside, letting it back down. Joseph squats in front of her. The storm stirs the trees.

"She had a garden. Like this but nicer. More ... orderly."

He realizes he does not know how to talk about his mother; he has no words for it. "For years I stole money," he says. He is not sure she understands. Rain pours over his glasses. "And I killed a man." She looks over the top of his head and makes no sign.

"I did not even know who he was or if he was the man they said he was. But I killed him."

Now Belle looks at him with her forehead creased as if in fear and Joseph cannot bear the look but he cannot stop either. There are so many things to give words to: how beached whales smother themselves with the black cannons of their own bodies, the songs of the forest, starlight limning the crests of waves, the way his mother bent in furrows to scatter seeds. He wants to use hand signs that will remake them; he wants her to see his poor, sordid histories reassembled out of the darkness. Every corpse he passed and left unburied; the body of the man slumped on the tennis court; the stolen junk locked even now in the cellar of his mother's house.

Instead he speaks of the whales. "One of the whales," he says, "lived longer than the others. People were tearing skin and fat from the dead one beside it. It watched them do it with its big brown eye and in the end it beat the beach with its flippers, slapping the sand. I was as far away as the house is from us right now and I could feel the ground shaking."

Belle is looking at him, a dirty tomato in her palm. Joseph is on his knees. Tears are flooding his eyes.

A ripening: one last warm day, a half dozen tanagers poised on a branch like golden flowers, a leaning of tomatoes to the sun. The silk of the melon flowers seem infused with light; any moment they could burst into flame. Joseph watches Belle fight on the lawn with her mother—they are returning from the beach. Belle slashes the air with her hands. Her mother flings down her beach chair, signs something back. Does the girl, Joseph wonders, carry her secrets deep within her? Or do they sit on the edges of her fingertips, ready to fly into language, ready to sign to her mother? *The African you fired lives in the woods. He embezzled money and killed a man.* Do secrets boil inside her like steam in a kettle? Or do they settle like seeds, waiting to open until the time is right? No, Joseph thinks, Belle understands. She has kept her secrets far better than I've kept mine.

He smells the sweet fruit of a tomato, pink now with a swatch of yellow on one side, and the aroma is almost too much to bear.

But in the morning he is discovered. It is just dawn and he is tearing mussels from the rocks and placing them in his rusted drum when a figure appears atop the dunes. Bars of light break through the trees and then—as if the sun conspired to give him away—a single ray fixes him against the water. Behind the figure appear several others; they tumble down the dunes, wading in the loose sand, laughing toward him.

They are carrying drinks and their voices sound drunken and he considers dumping his drum and turning and swimming out to sea to be swept away in some current and dashed forever against the rocks of a faraway place. When they get close to him they stop. Twyman's wife is with them and she walks right to him—her face flushed and twitching—and throws her drink against his chest and screams.

He does not think to get rid of the book of hand signs and when they see it tucked inside the waistband of his trousers things become more serious. Mrs. Twyman turns the book over in her hands and shakes her head and seems unable to speak. "Where did he get that?" the others say. Two men move to flank him, their faces quivering, their fists clenched.

They take him over the dunes, up the trail and across the lawn, past the garage where he lived, the shed he raided for his hoe and seeds. There is no sign of Belle. Mr. Twyman charges out of the house shirtless, hitching up his sweatpants. The words tangle inside him. "The nerve," he spits. "The *nerve*."

There is the sound of sirens, far off. From the lawn Joseph tries to make out the spot atop the hill where the garden is, a small break in a bulwark of spruce, but there is only a smear of green, and soon they are pushing him forward into the house and there is nothing at all to see, only the massive dining table strewn with dishes and half-empty drinks and the faces all around him, spitting questions.

They drive him, handcuffed, to Bandon and place him in an office with antique sirens and plastic softball trophies along the shelves. Two policemen sit on the edge of a desk and take turns repeating questions. They ask what he did with the girl, why, where they went. Twyman rages somewhere in the building: Joseph cannot hear the words but only the cracking of Twyman's voice as it reaches its limits. The policemen on the desk are blank-faced, leaning in.

"What did you eat? Did you eat anything? You don't look like you've eaten at all." "How much time did you spend with the girl? Where did you take her?" "Why don't you speak to us? We can make it easier for you." They ask for the fiftieth time how he got the book of sign language. I'm a gardener, he wants to tell them. Leave me be. But he says nothing.

They lock him in a cell where the texture has been painted off of every-thing—the cinder block walls, the floor, the frame of the cot, the bars in the window, all rounded over with coats of paint. Only the sink and toilet are unpainted, the curling design of a thousand scrubbings worked into the steel. The window looks onto a brick wall fifteen or so feet away. A naked bulb hangs from the ceiling, too high to reach. Even at night it burns, a tiny, unnatu-ral sun.

He sits on the floor and imagines weeds overwhelming the garden, their blades hauling down the tomato plants, their interloping roots curling through whatever is left of the whales' hearts. He imagines the tomatoes blooming into full ripeness, drooping from the vines, black spots opening like burns on their sides, finally falling, eaten hollow by flies. The melons turning over and crum-pling. Platoons of ants tunneling through rinds, bearing off shining chunks of fruit. In a year the garden will be nothing but salmonberry and nettle, no differ-ent than anywhere else, nothing to tell its story.

He wonders where Belle is. He hopes she is far away and tries to picture her behind the wheel of a Volkswagen, a forearm on the sill, some southern high-way unrolling before her, the wide fields of the sea coming into view as she rounds a bend.

He does not eat the peanut butter sandwiches they slide under the bars. After two days the marshal stands at the bars and asks if he wants something else. Joseph shakes his head.

"A body has to eat," the marshal declares. He slides a pack of crackers through. "Eat these. You'll feel better."

Joseph does not. It is not protest or sickness, as the policemen seem to think. It is merely the idea of eating that makes him queasy, the idea of mashing food in his teeth and forcing lumps of it down his throat. He sets the crackers beside the sandwiches, on the rim of the sink.

The marshal watches him a full minute before turning to go. "You know," he says, "I'll put you in the hospital and you can die there."

A lawyer tries to coerce a story out of him. "What did you do in Liberia? These people think you're dangerous—they're saying you're retarded. Are you? Why won't you speak?" There is no fight in Joseph, no anger, no outrage at injustice. He is not guilty of their crimes but he is guilty of so many others. There has never been a man guilty of so much, he thinks, a man more deserving of penalty. "Guilty!" he wants to scream. "I have been guilty all my life." But he has no energy. He shifts and feels his bones settling against the floor. The lawyer, exas-perated, departs.

There are no more gates within him, no more divisions. It is as if everything he has done in his life has pooled together inside him and slops dully against his edges. His mother, the man he has killed, the languishing garden—he will never be able to live it down, never live through it, never live enough to compensate for all the things he has stolen.

Two more days without food and he is taken to a hospital—they carry him like his skin is a bag inside which his bones knock together. He can remember only the dull pain of knuckles on his sternum. He wakes in a room, propped on a bed, with tubes plugged into his arms.

In half-dreams he sees terrible visions: the limbless bodies of men materialized on the bureau or the corner chair; the floor lined with corpses in the unnatural poses of death, flies on their eyes, dried blood in their ears. Sometimes when he wakes he sees the man he has killed kneeling on the foot of the bed, his blue beret in his lap, his arms still tied behind his back. The wound in his forehead is fresh, a drill hole rimmed in black, his eyes open. "I have never even *been* in an airplane," he says. Any minute now a nurse will come into the room and see the dead man kneeling on the foot of the bed and that will be it. Finally, Joseph thinks, I must pay for it.

There are other visitors: Mrs. Twyman in the corner chair, her thin arms crossed over her chest. Her eyes are on his; purple stains like bruises throb beneath her eye sockets. "What?" she screams. "What?" And Belle comes, or what might have been Belle—Joseph wakes and remembers her sliding open the window, pointing at gulls on the Dumpsters. But he does not know if he dreamed it, if she is on her way to Argentina, if she even thinks of him. His window is closed, the curtains drawn. When the nurse opens it he can see there are no Dumpsters, just lawn, a parking lot.

Another week or so and a lawyer comes, a clean-shaven pink man with acne around his collar. He reads to Joseph from a newspaper article that says Liberia has held democratic elections; Charles Taylor is the new president, the war is over, refugees are flooding back. "You are to be deported, Mr. Saleeby," he says. "It's very very good for you. The tools you stole and the trespassing—the court will drop these things. Negligence and the accusations of abuse are dropped too. You're absolved, Mr. Saleeby. Free."

Joseph leans back in his bed and realizes that he does not care.

A nurse announces a visitor. She has to help him from the bed and when he stands black spots fill his vision. She folds him into a wheelchair and carts him down the hall and out a side door into a small fenced courtyard.

It is so bright Joseph feels as if his head might crack open. She wheels him to a picnic table in the center of the lawn, fringed by a fence, with cars parked in a lot behind it, and returns the way she came. Joseph strains his eyes toward the sky; it is dazzling, a seething bowl of clouds. A bank of trees beyond the lot tosses in the wind—half the leaves are down and the branches swing together.

It is autumn, he realizes. He imagines the blackened, withered roots of his garden, the shriveled tomatoes and wrinkled leaves, a frost paralyzing everything. He wonders if this is where they'll leave him, finally, to die. The nurse will return in a few days, empty him from the chair and bury what's left, the leather of his skin pulling back, the black seed of his heart giving way, the bones settling into the earth.

A door opens into the courtyard and from the doorway steps Belle. She has her knapsack over her shoulders and she walks toward Joseph with a shy smile and seats herself at the picnic table. Beneath the collar of her windbreaker he can see the strap of her shirt, a pale collarbone, a trio of freckles above it. The wind lifts strands of her hair and sets them back down.

He holds his head in his hands and studies her and she studies him. She makes the sign for *how are you* and Joseph tries to make it back. They smile and sit. Sun winks off the cars in the lot. "Is this real?" Joseph asks. Belle cocks her head. "Are you real? Am I awake?" She squints and nods as if to say, *Of course.* She points over her shoulder, at the parking lot. I drove here, she signs. Joseph says nothing but smiles and props his head in his hands because his neck will not hold it up.

Then she seems to remember why she has come and takes the knapsack from her shoulder and produces two melons, which she sets on the table between them. Joseph looks at her with his eyes wide. "Are those . . . ?" he asks. She nods. He takes one of the melons in his hands. It is heavy and cool; he raps his knuckles against it.

Belle takes a penknife from the pocket of her windbreaker and stabs the other melon, cutting in an arc across its diameter, and when, with a tiny sound of yielding, the melon splits into two hemispheres, a sweet smell washes up. In the wet, stringy cup within are dozens of seeds.

Joseph scoops them out and spreads them over the wood of the table, each white and marbled with pulp and perfect. They shine in the sun. The girl saws a wedge from one of the halves. The flesh is wet and shining and Joseph cannot believe the color—it is as if the melon carried light within it. They each lift a chunk of it to their lips and eat. It seems to him that he can taste the forest, the trees, the storms of the winter and the size of the whales, the stars and the wind. A tiny gob of melon slides down Belle's chin. Her eyes are closed. When they open she sees him and her mouth splits into a smile.

They eat and eat and Joseph feels the wet pulp of the melon slipping down his throat. His hands and lips are sticky. Joy mounts in his chest; any moment his whole body could dissolve into light.

They eat the second melon too, again taking the seeds from the core and spreading them over the table to dry. When they are done they divide the seeds and the girl wraps each half in a piece of notebook paper and they put the damp packets of seeds in their pockets.

Joseph sits and feels the sun come down on his skin. His head feels weightless, as though it would float away if not for his neck. He thinks: If I had to do it over again, I'd bury the whole whales. I'd sow the ground with bucketfuls of seeds—not just tomatoes and melons, but pumpkins and beans and potatoes and broccoli and maize. I'd fill the beds of a hundred dumptrucks with seeds. Huge gardens would come up. I'd make a garden so huge and colorful everyone would see it; I'd let the weeds grow and the ivy, everything would grow, everything would get its chance.

Belle is crying. He takes her hands and holds her thin, articulate fingers against his own. He wonders if the dust has piled up against the walls of the house in the hills outside Monrovia. He wonders if hummingbirds still flit between the cups of the flowers, if by some miracle his mother could be there, kneeling in the soil, if they could work together cleaning away the dust, sweeping, brooming it up, carrying it out the door and pitching it into the yard, watching it unfurl in great rust-colored clouds, to be taken up by the wind and scattered somewhere else.

"Thank you," he says, but cannot be sure if he says it aloud. The clouds split and the sky brims over with light—it pours onto them, glazing the surface of the picnic table, the backs of their hands, the wet, carved bowls of the melon rinds. Everything feels very tenuous, just then, and terribly beautiful, as if he is straddling two worlds, the one he came from and the one he is going to. He wonders if this is what it was like for his mother, in the moments before she died, if she saw the same kind of light, if she felt like anything was possible.

Belle has reclaimed her hands and is pointing somewhere far off, somewhere over the horizon. Home, she signs. You are going home.

Stuart Dybek

WE DIDN'T

STUART DYBEK (1942–) is the author of three books of fiction—*I Sailed with Magellan, The Coast of Chicago,* and *Childhood and Other Neighborhoods*—and two collections of poetry—*Streets in Their Own Ink* and *Brass Knuckles.* His fiction, poetry, and nonfiction have appeared in *The New Yorker, Harper's, The Atlantic Monthly, Poetry, Tin House,* and many other magazines, and have been widely anthologized, including work in both *Best American Fiction* and *Best American Poetry.* His awards include a PEN/Malamud Prize, a Lannan Award, a Whiting Writers' Award, an Award in Fiction from the Academy of Arts and Letters, several O. Henry Prizes, and fellowships from the NEA and the Guggenheim Foundation.

> We did it in front of the mirror
> And in the light. We did it in darkness,
> In water, and in the high grass.
> —Yehuda Amichai, "We Did It"

We didn't in the light; we didn't in darkness. We didn't in the fresh-cut summer grass or in the mounds of autumn leaves or on the snow where moonlight threw down our shadows. We didn't in your room on the canopy bed you slept in, the bed you'd slept in as a child, or in the backseat of my father's rusted Rambler, which smelled of the smoked chubs and kielbasa he delivered on weekends from my uncle Vincent's meat market. We didn't in your mother's Buick Eight, where a rosary twined the rearview mirror like a beaded, black snake with silver, cruciform fangs.

At the dead end of our lovers' lane—a side street of abandoned factories— where I perfected the pinch that springs open a bra; behind the lilac bushes in Marquette Park, where you first touched me through my jeans and your nipples, swollen against transparent cotton, seemed the shade of lilacs; in the balcony of the now defunct Clark Theater, where I wiped popcorn salt from my palms and slid them up your thighs and you whispered, "I feel like Doris Day is watching us," we didn't.

How adept we were at fumbling, how perfectly mistimed our timing, how utterly we confused energy with ecstasy.

181

Remember that night becalmed by heat, and the two of us, fused by sweat, trembling as if a wind from outer space that only we could feel was gusting across Oak Street Beach? Entwined in your faded Navajo blanket, we lay soul-kissing until you wept with wanting.

We'd been kissing all day—all summer—kisses tasting of different shades of lip gloss and too many Cokes. The lake had turned hot pink, rose rapture, pearl amethyst with dusk, then washed in night black with a ruff of silver foam. Beyond a momentary horizon, silent bolts of heat lightning throbbed, perhaps setting barns on fire somewhere in Indiana. The beach that had been so crowded was deserted as if there was a curfew. Only the bodies of lovers remained, visible in lightning flashes, scattered like the fallen on a battlefield, a few of them moaning, waiting for the gulls to pick them clean.

On my fingers your slick scent mixed with the coconut musk of the suntan lotion we'd repeatedly smeared over each other's bodies. When your bikini top fell away, my hands caught your breasts, memorizing their delicate weight, my palms cupped as if bringing water to parched lips.

Along the Gold Coast, high-rises began to glow, window added to window, against the dark. In every lighted bedroom, couples home from work were strip-ping off their business suits, falling to the bed, and doing it. They did it before mirrors and pressed against the glass in streaming shower stalls; they did it against walls and on the furniture in ways that required previously unimagined gymnastics, which they invented on the spot. They did it in honor of man and woman, in honor of beast, in honor of God. They did it because they'd been released, because they were home free, alive, and private, because they couldn't wait any longer, couldn't wait for the appointed hour, for the right time or tem-perature, couldn't wait for the future, for Messiahs, for peace on earth and jus-tice for all. They did it because of the Bomb, because of pollution, because of the Four Horsemen of the Apocalypse, because extinction might be just a blink away. They did it because it was Friday night. It was Friday night and some-where delirious music was playing—flutter-tongued flutes, muted trumpets meowing like cats in heat, feverish plucking and twanging, tom-toms, congas, and gongs all pounding the same pulsebeat.

I stripped your bikini bottom down the skinny rails of your legs, and you tugged my swimsuit past my tan. Swimsuits at our ankles, we kicked like swim-mers to free our legs, almost expecting a tide to wash over us the way the tide rushes in on Burt Lancaster and Deborah Kerr in *From Here to Eternity*—a love scene so famous that although neither of us had seen the movie, our bodies as-sumed the exact position of movie stars on the sand and you whispered to me softly, "I'm afraid of getting pregnant," and I whispered back, "Don't worry, I have protection," then, still kissing you, felt for my discarded cutoffs and the wallet in which for the last several months I had carried a Trojan as if it was a talisman. Still kissing, I tore its flattened, dried-out wrapper, and it sprang through my fingers like a spring from a clock and dropped to the sand between our legs. My hands were shaking. In a panic, I groped for it, found it, tried to dust it off, tried as Burt Lancaster never had to, to slip it on without breaking the mood, felt the grains of sand inside it, a throb of lightning, and the Great Lake behind us became, for all practical purposes, the Pacific, and your skin tasted of salt and to the insistent question that my hips were asking your body answered yes, your thighs opened like wings from my waist as we surfaced panting from a kiss that left you pleading *Oh, Christ yes,* a *yes* gasped sharply as a cry of pain so that for a moment I thought that we *were* already doing it and that somehow I had missed the instant when I entered you, entered you in the bloodless way in which a young man discards his own virginity, entered you as if passing through a gateway into the rest of my life, into a life as I wanted it to be lived *yes* but Oh then I realized that we were still floundering unconnected in the slick between us and there was sand in the Trojan as we slammed together still feeling for that perfect fit, still in the *Here* groping for an *Eternity* that was only a fine adjustment away, just a millimeter to the left or a fraction of an inch farther south though with all the adjusting the sandy Trojan was slipping off and then it was gone but *yes* you kept repeating although your head was shaking *no-not-quite-almost* and our hearts were going like mad and you said, *Yes. Yes wait . . . Stop!*

"What?" I asked, still futilely thrusting as if I hadn't quite heard you.

"Oh. God!" You gasped, pushing yourself up. "What's coming?"

"Gin, what's the matter?" I asked, confused, and then the beam of a spotlight swept over us and I glanced into its blinding eye.

All around us lights were coming, speeding across the sand. Blinking blindness away, I rolled from your body to my knees, feeling utterly defenseless in the way that only nakedness can leave one feeling. Headlights bounded toward us, spotlights crisscrossing, blue dome lights revolving as squad cars converged. I could see other lovers, caught in the beams, fleeing bare-assed through the litter of garbage that daytime hordes had left behind and that night had deceptively concealed. You were crying, clutching the Navajo blanket to your breasts with one hand and clawing for your bikini with the other, and I was trying to calm your terror with reassuring phrases such as "Holy shit! I don't fucking believe this!"

Swerving and fishtailing in the sand, police calls pouring from their radios, the squad cars were on us, and then they were by us while we struggled to pull on our clothes.

They braked at the water's edge, and cops slammed out, brandishing huge flashlights, their beams deflecting over the dark water. Beyond the darting of those beams, the far-off throbs of lightning seemed faint by comparison.

"Over there, goddamn it!" one of them hollered, and two cops sloshed out into the shallow water without even pausing to kick off their shoes, huffing aloud for breath, their leather cartridge belts creaking against their bellies.

"Grab the sonofabitch! It ain't gonna bite!" one of them yelled, then they came sloshing back to shore with a body slung between them.

It was a woman—young, naked, her body limp and bluish beneath the play of flashlight beams. They set her on the sand just past the ring of drying, washed-up alewives. Her face was almost totally concealed by her hair. Her hair was brown and tangled in a way that even wind or sleep can't tangle hair, tangled as if it had absorbed the ripples of water—thick strands, slimy looking like dead seaweed.

"She's been in there awhile, that's for sure," a cop with a beer belly said to a younger, crew-cut cop, who had knelt beside the body and removed his hat as if he might be considering the kiss of life.

The crew-cut officer brushed the hair away from her face, and the flashlight beams settled there. Her eyes were closed. A bruise or a birthmark stained the side of one eye. Her features appeared swollen, her lower lip protruding as if she was pouting.

An ambulance siren echoed across the sand, its revolving red light rapidly approaching.

"Might as well take their sweet-ass time," the beer-bellied cop said.

We had joined the circle of police surrounding the drowned woman almost without realizing that we had. You were back in your bikini, robed in the Navajo blanket, and I had slipped on my cutoffs, my underwear dangling out of a back pocket.

Their flashlight beams explored her body, causing its whiteness to gleam. Her breasts were floppy; her nipples looked shriveled. Her belly appeared inflated by gallons of water. For a moment, a beam focused on her mound of pubic hair, which was overlapped by the swell of her belly, and then moved almost shyly away down her legs, and the cops all glanced at us—at you, especially—above their lights, and you hugged your blanket closer as if they might confiscate it as evidence or to use as a shroud.

When the ambulance pulled up, one of the black attendants immediately put a stethoscope to the drowned woman's swollen belly and announced, "Drowned the baby, too."

Without saying anything, we turned from the group, as unconsciously as we'd joined them, and walked off across the sand, stopping only long enough at the spot where we had lain together like lovers, in order to stuff the rest of our gear into a beach bag, to gather our shoes, and for me to find my wallet and kick sand over the forlorn, deflated Trojan that you pretended not to notice. I was grateful for that.

Behind us, the police were snapping photos, flashbulbs throbbing like lightning flashes, and the lightning itself, still distant but moving in closer, rumbling
audibly now, driving a lake wind before it so that gusts of sand tingled against
the metal sides of the ambulance.

Squinting, we walked toward the lighted windows of the Gold Coast, while
the shadows of gapers attracted by the whirling emergency lights hurried past
us toward the shore.

"What happened? What's going on?" they asked without waiting for an answer, and we didn't offer one, just continued walking silently in the dark.

It was only later that we talked about it, and once we began talking about the
drowned woman it seemed we couldn't stop.

"She was pregnant," you said. "I mean, I don't want to sound morbid, but
I can't help thinking how the whole time we were, we almost—you know—
there was this poor, dead woman and her unborn child washing in and out behind us."

"It's not like we could have done anything for her even if we had known she
was there."

"But what if we *had* found her? What if after we had—you know," you said,
your eyes glancing away from mine and your voice tailing into a whisper, "what
if after we did it, we went for a night swim and found her in the water?"

"But, Gin, we didn't," I tried to reason, though it was no more a matter of
reason than anything else between us had ever been.

It began to seem as if each time we went somewhere to make out—on the
back porch of your half-deaf, whiskery Italian grandmother, who sat in the
front of the apartment cackling at *I Love Lucy* reruns; or in your girlfriend
Tina's basement rec room when her parents were away on bowling league nights
and Tina was upstairs with her current crush, Brad; or way off in the burbs, at
the Giant Twin Drive-In during the weekend they called Elvis Fest—the
drowned woman was with us.

We would kiss, your mouth would open, and when your tongue flicked repeatedly after mine, I would unbutton the first button of your blouse, revealing
the beauty spot at the base of your throat, which matched a smaller spot I loved
above a corner of your lips, and then the second button, which opened on a
delicate gold cross—which I had always tried to regard as merely a fashion
statement—dangling above the cleft of your breasts. The third button exposed
the lacy swell of your bra, and I would slide my hand over the patterned mesh,
feeling for the firmness of your nipple rising to my fingertip, but you would pull
slightly away, and behind your rapid breath your kiss would grow distant, and I
would kiss harder, trying to lure you back from wherever you had gone, and finally, holding you as if only consoling a friend, I'd ask, "What are you thinking?"
although of course I knew.

"I don't want to think about her but I can't help it. I mean, it seems like some kind of weird omen or something, you know?"

"No, I don't know," I said. "It was just a coincidence."

"Maybe if she'd been farther away down the beach, but she was so close to us. A good wave could have washed her up right beside us."

"Great, then we could have had a ménage à trois."

"Gross! I don't believe you just said that! Just because you said it in French doesn't make it less disgusting."

"You're driving me to it. Come on, Gin, I'm sorry," I said. "I was just making a dumb joke to get a little different perspective on things."

"What's so goddamn funny about a woman who drowned herself and her baby?"

"We don't even know for sure she did."

"Yeah, right, it was just an accident. Like she just happened to be going for a walk pregnant and naked, and she fell in."

"She could have been on a sailboat or something. Accidents happen; so do murders."

"Oh, like murder makes it less horrible? Don't think that hasn't occurred to me. Maybe the bastard who knocked her up killed her, huh?"

"How should I know? You're the one who says you don't want to talk about it and then gets obsessed with all kinds of theories and scenarios. Why are we arguing about a woman we don't even know, who doesn't have the slightest thing to do with us?"

"I *do* know about her," you said. "I dream about her."

"You dream about her?" I repeated, surprised. "Dreams you remember?"

"Sometimes they wake me up. In one I'm at my *nonna*'s cottage in Michigan, swimming for a raft that keeps drifting farther away, until I'm too tired to turn back. Then I notice there's a naked person sunning on the raft and start yelling, 'Help!' and she looks up and offers me a hand, but I'm too afraid to take it even though I'm drowning because it's her."

"God! Gin, that's creepy."

"I dreamed you and I are at the beach and you bring us a couple hot dogs but forget the mustard, so you have to go all the way back to the stand for it."

"Hot dogs, no mustard—a little too Freudian, isn't it?"

"Honest to God, I dreamed it. You go back for mustard and I'm wondering why you're gone so long, then a woman screams that a kid has drowned and everyone stampedes for the water. I'm swept in by the mob and forced under, and I think, This is it, I'm going to drown, but I'm able to hold my breath longer than could ever be possible. It feels like a flying dream—flying under water— and then I see this baby down there flying, too, and realize it's the kid everyone thinks has drowned, but he's no more drowned than I am. He looks like Cupid or one of those baby angels that cluster around the face of God."

"Pretty weird. What do you think all the symbols mean?—hot dogs, water, drowning ..."

"It means the baby who drowned inside her that night was a love child—a boy—and his soul was released there to wander through the water."

"You don't really believe that?"

We argued about the interpretation of dreams, about whether dreams are symbolic or psychic, prophetic or just plain nonsense, until you said, "Look, Dr. Freud, you can believe what you want about your dreams, but keep your nose out of mine, okay?"

We argued about the drowned woman, about whether her death was a suicide or a murder, about whether her appearance that night was an omen or a coincidence which, you argued, is what an omen is anyway: a coincidence that means something. By the end of summer, even if we were no longer arguing about the woman, we had acquired the habit of arguing about everything else. What was better: dogs or cats, rock or jazz, Cubs or Sox, tacos or egg rolls, right or left, night or day?—we could argue about anything.

It no longer required arguing or necking to summon the drowned woman; everywhere we went she surfaced by her own volition: at Rocky's Italian Beef, at Lindo Mexico, at the House of Dong, our favorite Chinese restaurant, a place we still frequented because when we'd first started seeing each other they had let us sit and talk until late over tiny cups of jasmine tea and broken fortune cookies. We would always kid about going there. "Are you in the mood for Dong tonight?" I'd whisper conspiratorially. It was a dopey joke, meant for you to roll your eyes at its repeated dopiness. Back then, in winter, if one of us ordered the garlic shrimp we would both be sure to eat them so that later our mouths tasted the same when we kissed.

Even when she wasn't mentioned, she was there with her drowned body—so dumpy next to yours—and her sad breasts, with their wrinkled nipples and sour milk—so saggy beside yours, which were still budding—with her swollen belly and her pubic bush colorless in the glare of electric light, with her tangled, slimy hair and her pouting, placid face—so lifeless beside yours—and her skin a pallid white, lightning-flash white, flash-bulb white, a whiteness that couldn't be duplicated in daylight—how I'd come to hate that pallor, so cold beside the flush of your skin.

There wasn't a particular night when we finally broke up, just as there wasn't a particular night when we began going together, but it was a night in fall when I guessed that it was over. We were parked in the Rambler at the dead end of the street of factories that had been our lovers' lane, listening to a drizzle of rain and dry leaves sprinkle the hood. As always, rain revitalized the smells of smoked fish and kielbasa in the upholstery. The radio was on too low to hear, the windshield wipers swished at intervals as if we were driving, and the windows were steamed as if we'd been making out. But we'd been arguing, as usual, this time about a woman poet who had committed suicide, whose work you were reading. We were sitting, no longer talking or touching, and I remember thinking that I didn't want to argue with you anymore. I didn't want to sit like this in hurt silence; I wanted to talk excitedly all night as we once had. I wanted to find some way that wasn't corny sounding to tell you how much fun I'd had in your company, how much knowing you had meant to me, and how I had suddenly realized that I'd been so intent on becoming lovers that I'd overlooked how close we'd been as friends. I wanted you to know that. I wanted you to like me again.

"It's sad," I started to say, meaning that I was sorry we had reached the point of silence, but before I could continue you challenged the statement.

"What makes you so sure it's sad?"

"What do you mean, what makes me so sure?" I asked, confused by your question.

You looked at me as if what was sad was that I would never understand. "For all either one of us knows," you said, "death could have been her triumph!"

Maybe when it really ended was the night I felt we had just reached the beginning, that one time on the beach in the summer when our bodies rammed so desperately together that for a moment I thought we did it, and maybe in our hearts we did, although for me, then, doing it in one's heart didn't quite count. If it did, I supposed we'd all be Casanovas.

We rode home together on the El train that night, and I felt sick and defeated in a way I was embarrassed to mention. Our mute reflections emerged like negative exposures on the dark, greasy window of the train. Lightning branched over the city, and when the train entered the subway tunnel, the lights inside flickered as if the power was disrupted, though the train continued rocketing beneath the Loop.

When the train emerged again we were on the South Side of the city and it was pouring, a deluge as if the sky had opened to drown the innocent and guilty alike. We hurried from the El station to your house, holding the Navajo blanket over our heads until, soaked, it collapsed. In the dripping doorway of your apartment building, we said good night. You were shivering. Your bikini top showed through the thin blouse plastered to your skin. I swept the wet hair away from your face and kissed you lightly on the lips, then you turned and went inside. I stepped into the rain, and you came back out, calling after me.

"What?" I asked, feeling a surge of gladness to be summoned back into the doorway with you.

"Want an umbrella?"

I didn't. The downpour was letting up. It felt better to walk back to the station feeling the rain rinse the sand out of my hair, off my legs, until the only places where I could still feel its grit were in the crotch of my cutoffs and each squish of my shoes. A block down the street, I passed a pair of jockey shorts lying in a puddle and realized they were mine, dropped from my back pocket as we ran to your house. I left them behind, wondering if you'd see them and recognize them the next day.

By the time I had climbed the stairs back to the El platform, the rain had stopped. Your scent still hadn't washed from my fingers. The station—the entire city it seemed—dripped and steamed. The summer sound of crickets and nighthawks echoed from the drenched neighborhood. Alone, I could admit how sick I felt. For you, it was a night that would haunt your dreams. For me, it was another night when I waited, swollen and aching, for what I had secretly nicknamed the Blue Ball Express.

Literally lovesick, groaning inwardly with each lurch of the train and worried that I was damaged for good, I peered out at the passing yellow-lit stations, where lonely men stood posted before giant advertisements, pictures of glamorous models defaced by graffiti—the same old scrawled insults and pleas: fuck you, eat me. At this late hour the world seemed given over to men without women, men waiting in abject patience for something indeterminate, the way I waited for our next times. I avoided their eyes so that they wouldn't see the pity in mine, pity for them because I'd just been with you, your scent was still on my hands, and there seemed to be so much future ahead.

For me it was another night like that, and by the time I reached my stop I knew I would be feeling better, recovered enough to walk the dark street home making up poems of longing that I never wrote down. I was the D. H. Lawrence of not doing it, the voice of all the would-be lovers who ached and squirmed. From our contortions in doorways, on stairwells, and in the bucket seats of cars we could have composed a Kama Sutra of interrupted bliss. It must have been that night when I recalled all the other times of walking home after seeing you, so that it seemed as if I was falling into step behind a parade of my former selves—myself walking home on the night we first kissed, myself on the night when I unbuttoned your blouse and kissed your breasts, myself on the night when I lifted your skirt above your thighs and dropped to my knees—each succeeding self another step closer to that irrevocable moment for which our lives seemed poised.

But we didn't, not in the moonlight, or by the phosphorescent lanterns of lightning bugs in your backyard, not beneath the constellations we couldn't see, let alone decipher, or in the dark glow that replaced the real darkness of night, a darkness already stolen from us, not with the skyline rising behind us while a city gradually decayed, not in the heat of summer while a Cold War raged, despite the freedom of youth and the license of first love—because of fate, karma, luck, what does it matter?—we made not doing it a wonder, and yet we didn't, we didn't, we never did.

Deborah Eisenberg

TWILIGHT OF THE SUPERHEROES

DEBORAH EISENBERG (1945–) is the author of the short story collections *Transactions in a Foreign Currency, Under the 82nd Airborne, All Around Atlantis,* and *Twilight of the Superheroes.* She has been awarded numerous awards and fellowships including the American Academy of Arts and Letters Award in Literature, a Whiting Writers' Award, and a Guggenheim Fellowship.

NATHANIEL RECALLS THE MIRACLE

The grandchildren approach.

Nathaniel can make them out dimly in the shadows. When it's time, he'll tell them about the miracle.

It was the dawn of the new millennium, he'll say. *I was living in the Midwest back then, but my friends from college persuaded me to come to New York.*

I arrived a few days ahead of the amazing occasion, and all over the city there was an atmosphere of feverish anticipation. The year two thousand! The new millennium! Some people thought it was sure to be the end of the world. Others thought we were at the threshold of something completely new and better. The tabloids carried wild predictions from celebrity clairvoyants, and even people who scoffed and said that the date was an arbitrary and meaningless one were secretly agitated. In short, we were suddenly aware of ourselves standing there, staring at the future blindfolded.

I suppose, looking back on it, that all the commotion seems comical and ridiculous. And perhaps you're thinking that we churned it up to entertain ourselves because we were bored or because our lives felt too easy—trivial and mundane. But consider: ceremonial occasions, even purely personal ones like birthdays or anniversaries, remind us that the world is full of terrifying surprises and no one knows what even the very next second will bring!

Well, shortly before the momentous day, a strange news item appeared: experts were saying that a little mistake had been made—just one tiny mistake, a little detail in the way computers everywhere had been programmed. But the consequences of this detail, the experts said, were potentially disastrous; tiny as it was, the detail might affect everybody, and in a very big way!

You see, if history has anything to teach us, it's that—despite all our efforts, despite our best (or worst) intentions, despite our touchingly indestructible faith in our own foresight—we poor humans cannot actually think ahead; there are just too many variables. And so, when it comes down to it, it always turns out that no one is in charge of the things that really matter.

It must be hard for you to imagine—it's even hard for me to remember—but people hadn't been using computers for very long. As far as I know, my mother (your great-grandmother) never even touched one! And no one had thought to inform the computers that one day the universe would pass from the years of the one thousands into the years of the two thousands. So the machines, as these experts suddenly realized, were not equipped to understand that at the conclusion of 1999 time would not start over from 1900, time would keep going.

People all over America—all over the world!—began to speak of "a crisis of major proportions" (which was a phrase we used to use back then). Because, all the routine operations that we'd so blithely delegated to computers, the operations we all took for granted and depended on—how would they proceed?

Might one be fatally trapped in an elevator? Would we have to huddle together for warmth and scrabble frantically through our pockets for a pack of fancy restaurant matches so we could set our stacks of old New York Reviews *ablaze? Would all the food rot in heaps out there on the highways, leaving us to pounce on fat old street rats and grill them over the flames? What was going to happen to our bank accounts— would they vaporize? And what about air traffic control? On December 31 when the second hand moved from 11:59:59 to midnight, would all the airplanes in the sky collide?*

Everyone was thinking of more and more alarming possibilities. Some people committed their last night on this earth to partying, and others rushed around buying freeze-dried provisions and cases of water and flashlights and radios and heavy blankets in the event that the disastrous problem might somehow eventually be solved.

And then, as the clock ticked its way through the enormous gatherings in celebration of the era that was due to begin in a matter of hours, then minutes, then seconds, we waited to learn the terrible consequences of the tiny oversight. Khartoum, Budapest, Paris—we watched on television, our hearts fluttering, as midnight, first just a tiny speck in the east, unfurled gently, darkening the sky and moving toward us over the globe.

But the amazing thing, Nathaniel will tell his grandchildren, *was that nothing happened! We held our breath . . . And there was nothing! It was a miracle. Over the face of the earth, from east to west and back again, nothing catastrophic happened at all.*

Oh, well. Frankly, by the time he or any of his friends get around to producing a grandchild (or even a child, come to think of it) they might well have to explain what computers had been. And freeze-dried food. And celebrity clairvoyants and airplanes and New York and America and even cities, and heaven only knows what.

FROGBOIL

Lucien watches absently as his assistant, Sharmila, prepares to close up the gallery for the evening; something keeps tugging at his attention . . .

Oh, yes. It's the phrase Yoshi Matsumoto used this morning when he called from Tokyo. *Back to normal . . . Back to normal . . .*

What's that famous, revolting, sadistic experiment? Something like, you drop the frog into a pot of boiling water and it jumps out. But if you drop it into a pot of cold water and slowly bring the water to a boil, the frog stays put and gets boiled.

Itami Systems is reopening its New York branch, was what Matsumoto called to tell Lucien; he'll be returning to the city soon. Lucien pictured his old friend's mournful, ironic expression as he added, "They tell me they're 'exploring additional avenues of development now that New York is back to normal.'"

Lucien had made an inadvertent squawklike sound. He shook his head, then he shook his head again.

"Hello?" Matsumoto said.

"I'm here," Lucien said. "Well, it'll be good to see you again. But steel yourself for a wait at customs; they're fingerprinting."

VIEW

Mr. Matsumoto's loft is a jungle of big rubbery trees, under which crouch sleek items of chrome and leather. Spindly electronic devices blink or warble amid the foliage, and here and there one comes upon an immense flat-screen TV—the first of their kind that Nathaniel ever handled.

Nathaniel and his friends have been subletting—thanks, obviously, to Uncle Lucien—for a ridiculously minimal rent and on Mr. Matsumoto's highly tolerable conditions of catsitting and general upkeep. Nathaniel and Lyle and Amity and Madison each have something like an actual bedroom, and there are three whole bathrooms, one equipped with a Jacuzzi. The kitchen, stone and steel, has cupboards bigger than most of their friends' apartments. Art—important, soon to be important, or very recently important, most of which was acquired from Uncle Lucien—hangs on the walls.

And the terrace! One has only to open the magic sliding panel to find oneself halfway to heaven. On the evening, over three years ago, when Uncle Lucien completed the arrangements for Nathaniel to sublet and showed him the place, Nathaniel stepped out onto the terrace and tears shot right up into his eyes.

There was that unearthly palace, the Chrysler Building! There was the Empire State Building, like a brilliant violet hologram! There were the vast, twinkling prairies of Brooklyn and New Jersey! And best of all, Nathaniel could make out the Statue of Liberty holding her torch aloft, as she had held it for each of his parents when they arrived as children from across the ocean—terrified, filthy, and hungry—to safety.

Stars glimmered nearby; towers and spires, glowing emerald, topaz, ruby, sapphire, soared below. The avenues and bridges slung a trembling net of light across the rivers, over the buildings. Everything was spangled and dancing; the little boats glittered. The lights floated up and up like bubbles.

Back when Nathaniel moved into Mr. Matsumoto's loft, shortly after his millennial arrival in New York, sitting out on the terrace had been like looking down over the rim into a gigantic glass of champagne.

UNCLE LUCIEN'S WORDS OF REASSURANCE

So, Matsumoto is returning. And Lucien has called Nathaniel, the nephew of his adored late wife, Charlie, to break the news.

Well, of course it's hardly a catastrophe for the boy. Matsumoto's place was only a sublet in any case, and Nathaniel and his friends will all find other apartments.

But it's such an ordeal in this city. And all four of the young people, however different they might be, strike Lucien as being in some kind of holding pattern—as if they're temporizing, or muffled by unspoken reservations. Of course, he doesn't really know them. Maybe it's just the eternal, poignant weariness of youth.

The strangest thing about getting old (or one of the many strangest things) is that young people sometimes appear to Lucien—as, in fact, Sharmila does at this very moment—in a nimbus of tender light. It's as if her unrealized future were projecting outward like ectoplasm.

"Doing anything entertaining this evening?" he asks her.

She sighs. "Time will tell," she says.

She's a nice young woman; he'd like to give her a few words of advice, or reassurance.

But what could they possibly be? "Don't—" he begins.

Don't worry? HAHAHAHAHA! Don't feel *sad*? "Don't bother about the phones," is what he settles down on. A new show goes up tomorrow, and it's become Lucien's custom on such evenings to linger in the stripped gallery and have a glass of wine. "I'll take care of them."

But how has he *gotten* so old?

SUSPENSION

So, there was the famous, strangely blank New Year's Eve, the nothing at all that happened, neither the apocalypse nor the failure of the planet's computers, nor, evidently, the dawning of a better age. Nathaniel had gone to parties with his old friends from school and was asleep before dawn; the next afternoon he awoke with only a mild hangover and an uneasy impression of something left undone.

Next thing you knew, along came that slump, as it was called—the general economic blight that withered the New York branch of Mr. Matsumoto's firm and clusters of jobs all over the city. There appeared to be no jobs at all, in fact, but then—somehow—Uncle Lucien unearthed one for Nathaniel in the architectural division of the subway system. It was virtually impossible to afford an apartment, but Uncle Lucien arranged for Nathaniel to sublet Mr. Matsumoto's loft.

Then Madison and his girlfriend broke up, so Madison moved into Mr. Matsumoto's, too. Not long afterward, the brokerage house where Amity was working collapsed resoundingly, and she'd joined them. Then Lyle's landlord jacked up his rent, so Lyle started living at Mr. Matsumoto's as well.

As the return of Mr. Matsumoto to New York was contingent upon the return of a reasonable business climate, one way or another it had sort of slipped their minds that Mr. Matsumoto was real. And for over three years there they've been, hanging in temporary splendor thirty-one floors above the pavement.

They're all out on the terrace this evening. Madison has brought in champagne so that they can salute with an adequate flourish the end of their tenure in Mr. Matsumoto's place. And except for Amity, who takes a principled stand against thoughtful moods, and Amity's new friend or possibly suitor, Russell, who has no history here, they're kind of quiet.

REUNION

Now that Sharmila has gone, Lucien's stunning, cutting-edge gallery space blurs a bit and recedes. The room, in fact, seems almost like an old snapshot from that bizarre, quaintly futuristic century, the twentieth. Lucien takes a bottle of white wine from the little fridge in the office, pours himself a glass, and from behind a door in that century emerges Charlie.

Charlie—Oh, how long it's been, how unbearably long! Lucien luxuriates in the little pulse of warmth just under his skin that indicates her presence. He strains for traces of her voice, but her words degrade like the words in a dream, as if they're being rubbed through a sieve.

Yes, yes, Lucien assures her. He'll put his mind to finding another apartment for her nephew. And when her poor, exasperating sister and brother-in-law call frantically about Nathaniel, as they're bound to do, he'll do his best to calm them down.

But what a nuisance it all is! The boy is as opaque to his parents as a turnip. He was the child of their old age and he's also, obviously, the repository of all of their baroque hopes and fears. By their own account, they throw up their hands and wring them, lecture Nathaniel about frugality, then press spending money upon him and fret when he doesn't use it.

Between Charlie's death and Nathaniel's arrival in New York, Lucien heard from Rose and Isaac only at what they considered moments of emergency: Nathaniel's grades were erratic! His friends were bizarre! Nathaniel had expressed an interest in architecture, an unreliable future! He drew, and Lucien had better sit down, *comics*!

The lamentations would pour through the phone, and then, the instant Lucien hung up, evaporate. But if he had given the matter one moment's thought, he realizes, he would have understood from very early on that it was only a matter of time until the boy found his way to the city.

It was about four years ago now that Rose and Isaac put in an especially urgent call. Lucien held the receiver at arm's length and gritted his teeth. "You're an important man," Rose was shouting. "We understand that, we understand how busy you are, you know we'd never do this, but it's an emergency. The boy's in New York, and he sounds terrible. He doesn't have a job, lord only knows what he eats—I don't know what to think, Lucien, he *drifts*, he's just *drifting*. Call him, promise me, that's all I'm asking."

"Fine, certainly, good," Lucien said, already gabbling; he would have agreed to anything if Rose would only hang up.

"But whatever you do," she added, "please, please, under no circumstances should you let him know that we asked you to call."

Lucien looked at the receiver incredulously. "But how else would I have known he was in New York?" he said. "How else would I have gotten his number?"

There was a silence, and then a brief, amazed laugh from Isaac on another extension. "Well, I don't know what you'll tell him," Isaac said admiringly. "But you're the brains of the family, you'll think of something."

INNOCENCE

And actually, Russell (who seems to be not only Amity's friend and possible suitor but also her agent) has obtained for Amity a whopping big advance from some outfit that Madison refers to as Cheeseball Editions, so whatever else they might all be drinking to (or drinking about) naturally Amity's celebrating a bit. And Russell, recently arrived from L.A., cannot suppress his ecstasy about how *ur* New York, as he puts it, Mr. Matsumoto's loft is, tactless as he apparently recognizes this untimely ecstasy to be.

"It's *fantastic*," he says. "Who did it, do you know?"

Nathaniel nods. "Matthias Lehmann."

"That's what I thought, I thought so," Russell says. "It *looks* like Lehmann. Oh, wow, I can't believe you guys have to move out—I mean, it's just so totally amazing!"

Nathaniel and Madison nod and Lyle sniffs peevishly. Lyle is stretched out on a yoga mat that Nathaniel once bought in preparation for a romance (as yet manqué) with a prettily tattooed yoga teacher he runs into in the bodega on the corner. Lyle's skin has a waxy, bluish cast; there are dark patches beneath his eyes. He looks like a child too precociously worried to sleep. His boyfriend, Jahan, has more or less relocated to London, and Lyle has been missing him frantically. Lying there so still on the yoga mat with his eyes closed, he appears to be a tomb sculpture from an as yet nonexistent civilization.

"And the view!" Russell says. "This is probably the most incredible view on the *planet*."

The others consider the sight of Russell's eager face. And then Amity says, "More champagne, anyone?"

Well, sure, who knows where Russell had been? Who knows where he would have been on that shining, calm, perfectly blue September morning when the rest of them were here having coffee on the terrace and looked up at the annoying racket of a low-flying plane? Why should they expect Russell—now, nearly three years later—to imagine that moment out on the terrace when Lyle spilled his coffee and said, "Oh, shit," and something flashed and something tore, and the cloudless sky ignited.

HOME

Rose and Isaac have elbowed their way in behind Charlie, and no matter how forcefully Lucien tries to boot them out, they're making themselves at home, airing their dreary history.

Both sailed as tiny, traumatized children with their separate families and on separate voyages right into the Statue of Liberty's open arms. Rose was almost eleven when her little sister, Charlie, came into being, along with a stainless American birth certificate.

Neither Rose and Charlie's parents nor Isaac's ever recovered from their journey to the New World, to say nothing of what had preceded it. The two sets of old folks spoke, between them, Yiddish, Polish, Russian, German, Croatian, Slovenian, Ukrainian, Ruthenian, Rumanian, Latvian, Czech, and Hungarian, Charlie had once told Lucien, but not one of the four ever managed to learn more English than was needed to procure a quarter pound of smoked sturgeon from the deli. They worked impossible hours, they drank a little schnapps, and then, in due course, they died.

Isaac did fairly well manufacturing vacuum cleaners. He and Rose were solid members of their temple and the community, but, according to Charlie, no matter how uneventful their lives in the United States continued to be, filling out an unfamiliar form would cause Isaac's hands to sweat and send jets of acid through his innards. When he or Rose encountered someone in uniform—a train conductor, a meter maid, a crossing guard—their hearts would leap into their throats and they would think: *passport*!

Their three elder sons, Nathaniel's brothers, fulfilled Rose and Isaac's deepest hopes by turning out to be blindingly inconspicuous. The boys were so reliable and had so few characteristics it was hard to imagine what anyone could think up to kill them for. They were Jewish, of course, but even Rose and Isaac understood that this particular criterion was inoperative in the United States—at least for the time being.

The Old World, danger, and poverty were far in the past. Nevertheless, the family lived in their tidy, midwestern house with its two-car garage as if secret police were permanently hiding under the matching plastic-covered sofas, as if Brown-shirts and Cossacks were permanently rampaging through the suburban streets.

Lucien knew precious little about vacuum cleaners and nothing at all about childhood infections or lawn fertilizers. And yet, as soon as Charlie introduced him, Isaac and Rose set about soliciting his views as if he were an authority on everything that existed on their shared continent.

His demurrals, disclaimers, and protestations of ignorance were completely ineffective. Whatever guess he was finally strong-armed into hazarding was received as oracular. Oracular!

Fervent gratitude was expressed: Thank God Charlie had brought Lucien into the family! How brilliant he was, how knowledgeable and subtle! And then Rose and Isaac would proceed to pick over his poor little opinion as if they were the most ruthless and highly trained lawyers, and on the opposing side.

After Charlie was diagnosed, Lucien had just enough time to understand perfectly what that was to mean. When he was exhausted enough to sleep, he slept as though under heavy anesthetic during an amputation. The pain was not alleviated, but it had been made inscrutable. A frightful thing seemed to lie on top of him, heavy and cold. All night long he would struggle to throw it off, but when dawn delivered him to consciousness, he understood what it was, and that it would never go away.

During his waking hours, the food on his plate would abruptly lose its taste, the painting he was studying would bleach off the canvas, the friend he was talking to would turn into a stranger. And then, one day, he was living in a world all made out of paper, where the sun was a wad of old newspapers and the only sounds were the sounds of tearing paper.

He spoke with Rose and Isaac frequently during Charlie's illness, and they came to New York for her memorial service, where they sat self-consciously and miserably among Lucien and Charlie's attractive friends. He took them to the airport for their return to the Midwest, embraced them warmly, and as they shuffled toward the departure door with the other passengers, turning once to wave, he breathed a sigh of relief all that, at least, was over, too.

As his senses began to revive, he felt a brief pang—he would miss, in a minor way, the heartrending buffoonery of Charlie's sister and brother-in-law. After all, it had been part of his life with Charlie, even if it had been the only annoying part.

But Charlie's death, instead of setting him utterly, blessedly adrift in his grief, had left him anchored permanently offshore of her family like an island. After a long silence, the infuriating calls started up again. The feudal relationship was apparently inalterable.

CONTEXT

When they'd moved in, it probably *was* the best view on the planet. Then, one morning, out of a clear blue sky, it became, for a while, probably the worst.

For a long time now they've been able to hang out here on the terrace without anyone running inside to be sick or bursting into tears or diving under something at a loud noise or even just making macabre jokes or wondering what sort of debris is settling into their drinks. These days they rarely see—as for a time they invariably did—the sky igniting, the stinking smoke bursting out of it like lava, the tiny figures raining down from the shattered tower as Lyle faints.

But now it's unclear what they are, in fact, looking at.

INFORMATION

What would Charlie say about the show that's about to go up? It's work by a youngish Belgian painter who arrived, splashily, on the scene sometime after Charlie's departure.

It's good work, but these days Lucien can't get terribly excited about any of the shows. The vibrancy of his brain arranging itself in response to something of someone else's making, the heart's little leap—his gift, reliable for so many years, is gone. Or mostly gone; it's flattened out into something banal and tepid. It's as if he's got some part that's simply worn out and needs replacing. Let's hope it's still available, he thinks.

How *did* he get so old? The usual stupid question. One had snickered all one's life as the plaintive old geezers doddered about baffled, as if looking for a misplaced sock, tugging one's sleeve, asking sheepishly: *How did I get so old?*

The mere sight of one's patiently blank expression turned them vicious. *It will happen to you,* they'd raged.

Well, all right, it would. But not in the ridiculous way it had happened to *them*. And yet, here he is, he and his friends, falling like so much landfill into the dump of old age. Or at least struggling desperately to balance on the brink. Yet one second ago, running so swiftly toward it, they hadn't even seen it.

And what had happened to his youth? Unlike a misplaced sock, it isn't any-where; it had dissolved in the making of him.

Surprising that after Charlie's death he did not take the irreversible step. He'd had no appetite to live. But the body has its own appetite, apparently—that pitiless need to continue with its living, which has so many disguises and so many rationales.

A deep embarrassment has been stalking him. Every time he lets his guard down these days, there it is. Because it's become clear: he and even the most dissolute among his friends have glided through their lives on the assumption that the sheer fact of their existence has in some way made the world a better place. As deranged as it sounds now, a better place. Not a leafy bower, maybe, but still, a somewhat better place—more tolerant, more amenable to the won-derful adventures of the human mind and the human body, more capable of outrage against injustice ...

For shame! One has been shocked, all one's life, to learn of the blind eye turned to children covered with bruises and welts, the blind eye turned to the men who came at night for the neighbors. And yet ... And yet one has clung to the belief that the sun shining inside one's head is evidence of sunshine else-where.

Not everywhere, of course. Obviously, at every moment something terrible is being done to someone somewhere—one can't really know about each instance of it!

Then again, how far away does something have to be before you have the right to not really know about it?

Sometime after Charlie's death, Lucien resumed throwing his parties. He and his friends continued to buy art and make art, to drink and reflect. They voted responsibly, they gave to charity, they read the paper assiduously. And while they were basking in their exclusive sunshine, what had happened to the planet? Lucien gazes at his glass of wine, his eyes stinging.

HOMESICK

Nathaniel was eight or nine when his aunt and uncle had come out to the Mid-west to visit the family, lustrous and clever and comfortable and humorous and affectionate with one another, in their soft, stylish clothing. They'd brought books with them to read. When they talked to each other—and they habitually did—not only did they take turns, but also, what *one* said followed on what the *other* said. What world could they have come from? What was the world in which beings like his aunt and uncle could exist?

A world utterly unlike his parents', that was for sure—a world of freedom and lightness and beauty and the ardent exchange of ideas and ... and ... *fun*.

A great longing rose up in Nathaniel like a flower with a lovely, haunting fragrance. When he was ready, he'd thought—when he was able, when he was worthy, he'd get to the world from which his magic aunt and uncle had once briefly appeared.

The evidence, though, kept piling up that he was not worthy. Because even when he finished school, he simply didn't budge. How unfair it was—his friends had flown off so easily, as if going to New York were nothing at all.

Immediately after graduation, Madison found himself a job at a fancy New York PR firm. And it seemed that there was a place out there on the trading floor of the Stock Exchange for Amity. And Lyle had suddenly exhibited an astonishing talent for sound design and engineering, so where else would he sensibly live, either?

Yes, the fact was that only Nathaniel seemed slated to remain behind in their college town. Well, he told himself, his parents were getting on; he would worry, so far away. And he was actually employed as a part-time assistant with an actual architectural firm, whereas in New York the competition, for even the lowliest of such jobs, would be ferocious. And also, he had plenty of time, living where he did, to work on *Passivityman*.

And that's what he told Amity, too, when she'd called one night, four years ago, urging him to take the plunge.

"It's time for you to try, Nathaniel," she said. "It's time to commit. This oddball, slacker stance is getting kind of old, don't you think, kind of stale. You cannot let your life be ruled by fear any longer."

"Fear?" He flinched. "By what fear, exactly, do you happen to believe my life is ruled?"

"Well, I mean, fear of failure, obviously. Fear of mediocrity."

For an instant he thought he might be sick.

"Right," he said. "And why should I fear failure and mediocrity? Failure and mediocrity have such august traditions! Anyhow, what's up with you, Amity?"

She'd been easily distracted, and they chatted on for a while, but when they hung up, he felt very, very strange, as if his apartment had slightly changed shape. Amity was right, he'd thought; it was fear that stood between him and the life he'd meant to be leading.

That was probably the coldest night of the whole, difficult millennium. The timid midwestern sun had basically gone down at the beginning of September; it wouldn't be around much again till May. Black ice glared on the street outside like the cloak of an extra-cruel witch. The sink faucet was dripping into a cracked and stained teacup: *Tick tock tick tock . . .*

What was he *doing*? Once he'd dreamed of designing tranquil and ennobling dwellings, buildings that urged benign relationships, rich inner harmonies; he'd dreamed of meeting fascinating strangers. True, he'd managed to avoid certain pitfalls of middle-class adulthood—he wasn't a white-collar criminal, for example; he wasn't (at least as far as he knew) a total blowhard. But what was he *actually doing?* His most exciting social contact was the radio. He spent his salaried hours in a cinder-block office building, poring over catalogues of plumbing fixtures. The rest of the day—and the whole evening, too—he sat at the little desk his parents had bought for him when he was in junior high, slaving over *Passivityman*, a comic strip that ran in free papers all over parts of the Midwest, a comic strip that was doted on by whole dozens, the fact was, of stoned undergrads.

He was twenty-four years old! Soon he'd be twenty-eight. In a few more minutes he'd be thirty-five, then fifty. Five zero. How had that happened? He was eighty! He could feel his vascular system and brain clogging with paste, he was drooling . . .

And if history had anything to teach, it was that he'd be broke when he was eighty, too, and that his personal life would still be a disaster.

But wait. Long ago, panic had sent his grandparents and parents scurrying from murderous Europe, with its death camps and pogroms, to the safe harbor of New York. Panic had kept them going as far as the Midwest, where grueling labor enabled them and eventually their children to lead blessedly ordinary lives. And sooner or later, Nathaniel's pounding heart was telling him, that same sure-footed guide, panic, would help him retrace his family's steps all the way back to Manhattan.

OPPORTUNISM

Blip! Charlie scatters again as Lucien's attention wavers from her, and the empty space belonging to her is seized by Miss Mueller.

Huh, but what do you know—death *suits* Miss Mueller! In life she was drab, but now she absolutely throbs with ghoulishness. *You there, Lucien*—the shriek echoes around the gallery—*What are the world's three great religions?*

Zen Buddhism, Jainism, and Sufism, he responds sulkily.

Naughty boy! She cackles flirtatiously. *Bang bang, you're dead!*

THE HALF-LIFE OF PASSIVITY

Passivityman is taking a snooze, his standard response to stress, when the alarm rings. "I'll check it out later, boss," he murmurs.

"You'll check it out *now*, please," his girlfriend and superior, the beautiful Princess Prudence, tells him. "Just put on those grubby corduroys and get out there."

"Aw, is it really *urgent?*" he asks.

"Don't you get it?" she says. "I've been warning you. Episode after episode! And now, from his appliance-rich house on the Moon, Captain Corporation has tightened his Net of Evil around the planet Earth, and he's dragging it out of orbit! The U.S. Congress is selected by pharmaceutical companies, the state of Israel is run by Christian fundamentalists, the folks that haul toxic sludge manufacture cattle feed and process burgers, your sources of news and information are edited by a giant mouse, New York City and Christian fundamentalism are holdings of a family in Kuwait—*and all of it's owned by Captain Corporation!*"

Passivityman rubs his eyes and yawns. "Well gosh, Pru, sure—but, like, what am I supposed to do about it?"

"*I* don't know," Princess Prudence says. "It's hardly my job to figure that out, is it? I mean, *you're* the superhero. Just—just—just go out and do something conspicuously lacking in monetary value! Invent some stinky, profit-proof gloop to pour on stuff. Or, I don't know, whatever. But you'd better do *something*, before it's too late."

"Sounds like it's totally too late already," says Passivityman, reaching for a cigarette.

It was quite a while ago now that Passivityman seemed to throw in the towel. Nathaniel's friends looked at the strip with him and scratched their heads.

"Hm, *I* don't know, Nathaniel," Amity said. "This episode is awfully complicated. I mean, Passivityman's seeming kind of passive-*aggressive*, actually."

"Can Passivityman not be bothered any longer to protect the abject with his greed-repelling Shield of Sloth?" Lyle asked.

"It's not going to be revealed that Passivityman is a double agent, is it?" Madison said. "I mean, what about his undying struggle against corporate-model efficiency?"

"The truth is, I don't really know what's going on with him," Nathaniel said. "I was thinking that maybe, unbeknownst to himself, he's come under the thrall of his morally neutral, transgendering twin, Ambiguityperson."

"Yeah," Madison said. "But I mean, the problem here is that he's just not dealing with the paradox of his own being—he seems kind of *intellectually* passive . . ."

Oh, dear. Poor Passivityman. He was a *tired* old crime fighter. Nathaniel sighed; it was hard to live the way his superhero lived—constantly vigilant against the premature conclusion, scrupulously rejecting the vulgar ambition, rigorously deferring judgment and action . . . and all for the greater good.

"Huh, well, I guess he's sort of losing his superpowers," Nathaniel said.

The others looked away uncomfortably.

"Oh, it's probably just one of those slumps," Amity said. "I'm sure he'll be back to normal, soon."

But by now, Nathaniel realizes, he's all but stopped trying to work on *Passivityman.*

ALL THIS

Thanks for pointing that out, Miss Mueller. Yes, humanity seems to have reverted by a millennium or so. Goon squads, purporting to represent each of the *world's three great religions*—as they used to be called to fifth-graders, and perhaps still so misleadingly are—have deployed themselves all over the map, apparently in hopes of annihilating not only each other, but absolutely everyone, themselves excepted.

Just a few weeks earlier, Lucien was on a plane heading home from Los Angeles, and over the loudspeaker, the pilot requested that all Christians on board raise their hands. The next sickening instants provided more than enough time for conjecture as to who, exactly, was about to be killed—Christians or non-Christians. And then the pilot went on to ask those who had raised their hands to talk about their "faith" with the others.

Well, better him than Rose and Isaac; that would have been two sure heart attacks, right there. And anyhow, why should he be so snooty about religious fanaticism? Stalin managed to kill off over thirty million people in the name of no god at all, and not so very long ago.

At the moment when *all this*—as Lucien thinks of it—began, the moment when a few ordinary-looking men carrying box cutters sped past the limits of international negotiation and the frontiers of technology, turning his miraculous city into a nightmare and hurling the future into a void, Lucien was having his croissant and coffee.

The television was saying something. Lucien wheeled around and stared at it, then turned to look out the window; downtown, black smoke was already beginning to pollute the perfect, silken September morning. On the screen, the ruptured, flaming colossus was shedding veils of tiny black specks.

All circuits were busy, of course; the phone might as well have been a toy. Lucien was trembling as he shut the door of the apartment behind him. His face was wet. Outside, he saw that the sky in the north was still insanely blue.

THE AGE OF DROSS

Well, superpowers are probably a feature of youth, like Wendy's ability to fly around with that creepy Peter Pan. Or maybe they belonged to a loftier period of history. It seems that Captain Corporation, his swaggering lieutenants and massed armies have actually neutralized Passivityman's superpower. Passivityman's astonishing reserves of resistance have vanished in the quicksand of Captain Corporation's invisible account books. His rallying cry, No way, which once rang out over the land, demobilizing millions, has been altered by Captain Corporation's co-optophone into, Whatever. And the superpowers of Nathaniel's friends have been seriously challenged, too. Challenged, or . . . outgrown.

Amity's superpower, her gift for exploiting systemic weaknesses, had taken a terrible beating several years ago when the gold she spun out on the trading floor turned—just like everyone else's—into straw. And subsequently, she plummeted from job to job, through layers of prestige, ending up behind a counter in a fancy department store where she sold overpriced skin-care products.

Now, of course, the sale of *Inner Beauty Secrets*—her humorous, lightly fictionalized account of her experiences there with her clients—indicates that perhaps her powers are regenerating. But time will tell.

Madison's superpower, an obtuse, patrician equanimity in the face of damning fact, was violently and irremediably terminated one day when a girl arrived at the door asking for him.

"I'm your sister," she told him. "Sorry," Madison said, "I've never seen you before in my life." "Hang on," the girl said. "I'm just getting to that."

For months afterward, Madison kept everyone awake late into the night repudiating all his former beliefs, his beautiful blue eyes whirling around and his hair standing on end as if he'd stuck his hand into a socket. He quit his lucrative PR job and denounced the firm's practices in open letters to media watchdog groups (copies to his former boss). The many women who'd been running after him did a fast about-face.

Amity called him a "bitter skeptic"; he called Amity a "dupe." The heated quarrel that followed has tapered off into an uneasy truce, at best.

Lyle's superpower back in school was his spectacular level of aggrievedness and his ability to get anyone at all to feel sorry for him. But later, doing sound with a Paris-based dance group, Lyle met Jahan, who was doing the troupe's lighting.

Jahan is (a) as handsome as a prince, (b) as charming, as intelligent, as noble in his thoughts, feelings, and actions as a prince, and (c) a prince, at least of some attenuated sort. So no one feels sorry for Lyle at all any longer, and Lyle has apparently left the pleasures of even *self*-pity behind him without a second thought.

A while ago, though, Jahan was mistakenly arrested in some sort of sweep near Times Square, and when he was finally released from custody, he moved to London, and Lyle does nothing but pine, when he can't be in London himself.

"Well, look on the bright side," Nathaniel said. "At least you might get your superpower back."

"You know, Nathaniel . . ." Lyle said. He looked at Nathaniel for a moment, and then an unfamiliar kindness modified his expression. He patted Nathaniel on the shoulder and went on his way.

Yikes. So much for Lyle's superpower, obviously.

• • •

"It's great that you got to live here for so long, though," Russell is saying.

Nathaniel has the sudden sensation of his whole four years in New York twisting themselves into an arrow speeding through the air and twanging into the dead center of this evening. All so hard to believe. "This is not happening," he says.

"I think it might really *be* happening, though," Lyle says.

"Fifty percent of respondents say that the event taking place is not occurring," Madison says. "The other fifty percent remain undecided. Clearly, the truth lies somewhere in between."

Soon it might be as if he and Lyle and Madison and Amity had never even lived here. Because this moment is joined to all the other moments they've spent together here, and all of those moments are Right Now. But soon this moment and all the others will be cut off—in the past, not part of Right Now at all. Yeah, he and his three friends might all be going their separate ways, come to think of it, once they move out.

CONTINUITY

While the sirens screamed, Lucien had walked against the tide of dazed, smoke-smeared people, down into the fuming cauldron, and when he finally reached the police cordon, his feet aching, he wandered along it for hours, searching for Charlie's nephew, among all the other people who were searching for family, friends, lovers.

Oh, that day! One kept waiting—as if a morning would arrive from before that day to take them all along a different track. One kept waiting for that shattering day to unhappen, so that the real—the intended—future, the one that had been implied by the past, could unfold. Hour after hour, month after month, waiting for that day to not have happened. But it had happened. And now it was always going to have happened.

Most likely on the very mornings that first Rose and then Isaac had disembarked at Ellis Island, each clutching some remnant of the world they were never to see again, Lucien was being wheeled in his pram through the genteel world, a few miles uptown, of brownstones.

The city, more than his body, contained his life. His life! The schools he had gone to as a child, the market where his mother had bought the groceries, the park where he had played with his classmates, the restaurants where he had courted Charlie, the various apartments they'd lived in, the apartments of their friends, the gallery, the newsstand on the corner, the dry cleaner's . . . The things he did in the course of the day, year after year, the people he encountered.

• • •

A sticky layer of crematorium ash settled over the whole of Matsumoto's neighborhood, even inside, behind closed windows, as thick in places as turf, and water was unavailable for a time. Nathaniel and his friends all stayed elsewhere, of course, for a few weeks. When it became possible, Lucien sent crews down to Matsumoto's loft to scour the place and restore the art.

FAREWELL

A memorandum hangs in Mr. Matsumoto's lobby, that appeared several months ago when freakish blackouts were rolling over the city.

Emergency Tips from the Management urges residents to assemble a Go Bag, in the event of an evacuation, as well as an In-Home Survival Kit. Among items to include: a large amount of cash in small denominations, water and nonperishable foods such as granola bars, a wind-up radio, warm clothing and sturdy walking shoes, unscented bleach and an eyedropper for purifying water, plastic sheeting and duct tape, a whistle, a box cutter.

Also recommended is a Household Disaster Plan and the practicing of emergency drills.

A hand-lettered sign next to the elevator says THINK TWICE.

Twenty-eight years old, no superhero, a job that just *might* lead down to a career in underground architecture, a vanishing apartment, a menacing elevator . . . Maybe he should view Mr. Matsumoto's return as an opportunity, and regroup. Maybe he should *do* something—take matters in hand. Maybe he should go try to find Delphine, for example.

But how? He hasn't heard from her, and she could be anywhere now; she'd mentioned Bucharest, she'd mentioned Havana, she'd mentioned Shanghai, she'd mentioned Istanbul . . .

He'd met her at one his uncle's parties. There was the usual huge roomful of people wearing strangely pleated black clothes, like the garments of a somber devotional sect, and there she was in electric-blue taffeta, amazingly tall and narrow, lazy and nervous, like an electric bluebell.

She favored men nearly twice Nathaniel's age and millions of times richer, but for a while she let Nathaniel come over to her apartment and play her his favorite CDs. They drank perfumey infusions from chipped porcelain cups, or vodka. Delphine could become thrillingly drunk, and she smoked, letting long columns of ash form on her tarry, unfiltered cigarettes. One night, when he lost his keys, she let him come over and sleep in her bed while she went out, and when the sky fell, she actually let him sleep on her floor for a week.

Her apartment was filled with puffy, silky little sofas, and old, damaged mirrors and tarnished candlesticks, and tall vases filled with slightly wilting flowers. It smelled like powder and tea and cigarettes and her Abyssinian cats, which prowled the savannas of the white, long-haired rugs or posed on the marble mantelpiece.

Delphine's father was Armenian and he lived in Paris, which according to Delphine was a bore. Her mother was Chilean. Delphine's English had been acquired at a boarding school in Kent for dull-witted rich girls and castaways, like herself, from everywhere.

She spoke many languages, she was self-possessed and beautiful and fascinating. She could have gone to live anywhere. And she had come, like Nathaniel, to New York.

"But look at it now," she'd raged. Washington was dropping bombs on Afghanistan and then Iraq, and every few weeks there was a flurry of alerts in kindergarten colors indicating the likelihood of terrorist attacks: yellow, orange, red, *duck!*

"Do you know how I get the news here?" Delphine said. "From your newspapers? Please! From your newspapers I learn what restaurant has opened. News I learn in taxis, from the drivers. And how do they get it? From their friends and relatives back home, in Pakistan or Uzbekistan or Somalia. The drivers sit around at the airport, swapping information, and they can tell you *anything*. But do you ask? Or sometimes I talk to my friends in Europe. Do you know what they're saying about you over there?"

"Please don't say 'you,' Delphine," he had said faintly.

"Oh, yes, here it's not like stuffy old Europe, where everything is stifled by tradition and trauma. Here you're able to speak freely, within reason, of course, and isn't it wonderful that you all happen to want to say exactly what they want you to say? Do you know how many people you're killing over there? No, how would you? Good, just keep your eyes closed, panic, don't ask any questions, and you can speak freely about whatever you like. And if you have any suspicious-looking neighbors, be sure to tell the police. You had everything here, everything, and you threw it all away in one second."

She was so beautiful; he'd gazed at her as if he were already remembering her. "Please don't say 'you,'" he murmured again.

"Poor Nathaniel," she said. "This place is nothing now but a small-minded, mean-spirited provincial town."

THE AGE OF DIGITAL REASONING

One/two. On/off. The plane crashes/doesn't crash.

The plane he took from L.A. didn't crash. It wasn't used as a missile to blow anything up, and not even one passenger was shot or stabbed. Nothing happened. So, what's the problem? What's the difference between having been on that flight and having been on any other flight in his life?

Oh, what's the point of thinking about death all the time! Think about it or not, you die. Besides—and here's something that sure hasn't changed—you don't have to do it more than once. And as you don't have to do it *less* than once, either, you might as well do it on the plane. Maybe there's no special problem these days. Maybe the problem is just that he's old.

Or maybe his nephew's is the last generation that will remember what it had once felt like to blithely assume there would be a future—at least a future like the one that had been implied by the past they'd all been familiar with.

But the future actually ahead of them, it's now obvious, had itself been implied by a past; and the terrible day that pointed them toward that future had been prepared for a long, long time, though it had been prepared behind a curtain.

It was as if there had been a curtain, a curtain painted with the map of the earth, its oceans and continents, with Lucien's delightful city. The planes struck, tearing through the curtain of that blue September morning, exposing the dark world that lay right behind it, of populations ruthlessly exploited, inflamed with hatred, and tired of waiting for change to happen by.

The stump of the ruined tower continued to smolder far into the fall, and an unseasonable heat persisted. When the smoke lifted, all kinds of other events, which had been prepared behind a curtain, too, were revealed. Flags waved in the brisk air of fear, files were demanded from libraries and hospitals, droning helicopters hung over the city, and heavily armed policemen patrolled the parks. Meanwhile, one read that executives had pocketed the savings of their investors and the pensions of their employees.

The wars in the East were hidden behind a thicket of language: *patriotism, democracy, loyalty, freedom*—the words bounced around, changing purpose, as if they were made out of some funny plastic. What did they actually refer to? It seemed that they all might refer to money.

Were the sudden power outages and spiking level of unemployment related? And what was causing them? The newspapers seemed for the most part to agree that the cause of both was terrorism. But lots of people said they were both the consequence of corporate theft. It was certainly all beyond Lucien! Things that had formerly appeared to be distinct, or even at odds, now seemed to have been smoothly blended, to mutual advantage. Provocation and retribution, arms manufacture and statehood, oil and war, commerce and dogma, and the spinning planet seemed to be boiling them all together at the center of the earth into a poison syrup. Enemies had soared toward each other from out of the past to unite in a joyous fireball; planes had sheared through the heavy, painted curtain and from the severed towers an inexhaustible geyser had erupted.

• • •

Styles of pets revolved rapidly, as if the city's residents were searching for a type of animal that would express a stance appropriate to the horrifying assault, which for all anyone knew was only the first of many.

For a couple of months everyone was walking cute, perky things. Then Lucien saw snarling hounds everywhere and the occasional boa constrictor draped around its owner's shoulders. After that, it was tiny, trembling dogs that traveled in purses and pockets.

New York had once been the threshold of an impregnable haven, then the city had become in an instant the country's open wound, and now it was the occasion—the pretext!—for killing and theft and legislative horrors all over the world. The air stank from particulate matter—chemicals and asbestos and blood and scorched bone. People developed coughs and strange rashes.

What should be done, and to whom? Almost any word, even between friends, could ignite a sheet of flame. What were the bombings for? First one imperative was cited and then another; the rationales shifted hastily to cover successive gaps in credibility. Bills were passed containing buried provisions, and loopholes were triumphantly discovered—alarming elasticities or rigidities in this law or that. One was sick of trying to get a solid handle on the stream of pronouncements—it was like endlessly trying to sort little bits of paper into stacks when a powerful fan was on.

Friends in Europe and Asia sent him clippings about his own country. *What's all this,* they asked—secret arrests and detentions, his president capering about in military uniform, crazy talk of preemptive nuclear strikes? Why were they releasing a big science fiction horror movie over there, about the emperor of everything everywhere, for which the whole world was required to buy tickets? What on earth was going on with them all, why were they all so silent? Why did they all seem so confused?

How was he to know, Lucien thought. If his foreign friends had such great newspapers, why didn't *they* tell *him*!

No more smiles from strangers on the street! Well, it was reasonable to be frightened; everyone had seen what those few men were able do with the odds and ends in their pockets. The heat lifted, and then there was unremitting cold. No one lingered to joke and converse in the course of their errands, but instead hurried irritably along, like people with bad consciences.

And always in front of you now was the sight that had been hidden by the curtain, of all those irrepressibly, murderously angry people.

Private life shrank to nothing. All one's feelings had been absorbed by an arid wasteland—policy, strategy, goals. One's past, one's future, one's ordinary daily pleasures were like dusty little curios on a shelf.

Lucien continued defiantly throwing his parties, but as the murky wars dragged on, he stopped. It was impossible to have fun or to want to have fun. It was one thing to have fun if the sun was shining generally, quite another thing to have fun if it was raining blood everywhere but on your party. What did he and his friends really have in common, anyway? Maybe nothing more than their level of privilege.

In restaurants and cafés all over the city, people seemed to have changed. The good-hearted, casually wasteful festival was over. In some places the diners were sullen and dogged, as if they felt accused of getting away with something.

In other places, the gaiety was cranked up to the level of completely unconvincing hysteria. For a long miserable while, in fact, the city looked like a school play about war profiteering. The bars were overflowing with very young people from heaven only knew where, in hideous, ludicrously showy clothing, spending massive amounts of money on green, pink, and orange cocktails, and laughing at the top of their lungs, as if at filthy jokes.

No, not like a school play—like a movie, though the performances and the direction were crude. The loud, ostensibly carefree young people appeared to be extras recruited from the suburbs, and yet sometime in the distant future, people seeing such a movie might think oh, yes, that was a New York that existed once, say, at the end of the millennium.

It was Lucien's city, Lucien's times, and yet what he appeared to be living in wasn't the actual present—it was an inaccurate representation of the *past*. True, it looked something like the New York that existed before *all this* began, but Lucien remembered, and he could see: the costumes were not quite right, the hairstyles were not quite right, the gestures and the dialogue were not quite right.

Oh. Yes. Of course none of it was quite right—the movie was a *propaganda* movie. And now it seems that the propaganda movie has done its job: things, in a grotesque sense, are back to normal.

Money is flowing a bit again, most of the flags have folded up, those nerve-wracking terror alerts have all but stopped, the kids in the restaurants have calmed down, no more rolling blackouts, and the dogs on the street encode no particular messages. Once again, people are concerned with getting on with their lives. Once again, the curtain has dropped.

Except that people seem a little bit nervous, a little uncomfortable, a little wary. Because you can't help sort of knowing that what you're seeing is only the curtain. And you can't help guessing what might be going on behind it.

THE FURTHER IN THE PAST THINGS ARE, THE BIGGER THEY BECOME

Nathaniel remembers more and more rather than less and less vividly the visit of his uncle and aunt to the Midwest during his childhood.

He'd thought his aunt Charlie was the most beautiful woman he'd ever seen. And for all he knows, she really was. He never saw her after that one visit; by the time he came to New York and reconnected with Uncle Lucien she had been dead for a long time. She would still have been under fifty when she died—crushed, his mother had once, in a mood, implied, by the weight of her own pretensions.

His poor mother! She had cooked, cleaned, and fretted for . . . months, it had seemed, in preparation for that visit of Uncle Lucien and Aunt Charlie. And observing in his memory the four grown-ups, Nathaniel can see an awful lot of white knuckles.

He remembers his mother picking up a book Aunt Charlie had left lying on the kitchen table, glancing at it and putting it back down with a tiny shrug and a lifted eyebrow. "You don't approve?" Aunt Charlie said, and Nathaniel is shocked to see, in his memory, that she is tense.

His mother, having gained the advantage, makes another bitter little shrug. "I'm sure it's over my head," she says.

When the term of the visit came to an end, they dropped Uncle Lucien and Aunt Charlie at the airport. His brother was driving, too fast. Nathaniel can hear himself announcing in his child's piercing voice, *"I want to live in New York like Uncle Lucien and Aunt Charlie!"* His exile's heart was brimming, but it was clear from his mother's profile that she was braced for an execution.

"Slow *down*, Bernie!" his mother said, but Bernie hadn't. "Big shot," she muttered, though it was unclear at whom this was directed—whether at his brother or himself or his father, or his Uncle Lucien, or at Aunt Charlie herself.

BACK TO NORMAL

Do dogs have to fight sadness as tirelessly as humans do? They seem less involved with retrospect, less involved in dread and anticipation. Animals other than humans appear to be having a more profound experience of the present. But who's to say? Clearly their feelings are intense, and maybe grief and anxiety darken all their days. Maybe that's why they've acquired their stripes and polka dots and fluffiness—to cheer themselves up.

Poor old Earth, an old sponge, a honeycomb of empty mine shafts and dried wells. While he and his friends were wittering on, the planet underfoot had been looted. The waterways glint with weapons-grade plutonium, sneaked on barges between one wrathful nation and another, the polar ice caps melt, Venice sinks.

In the horrible old days in Europe when Rose and Isaac were hunted children, it must have been pretty clear to them how to behave, minute by minute. Men in jackboots? Up to the attic!

But even during that time when it was so dangerous to speak out, to act courageously, heroes emerged. Most of them died fruitlessly, of course, and unheralded. But now there are even monuments to some of them, and information about such people is always coming to light.

Maybe there really is no problem, maybe everything really is back to normal and maybe the whole period will sink peacefully away, to be remembered only by scholars. But if it should end, instead, in dire catastrophe, whom will the monuments of the future commemorate?

Today, all day long, Lucien has seen the president's vacant, stricken expression staring from the ubiquitous television screens. He seemed to be talking about positioning weapons in space, colonizing the moon.

Open your books to page 167, class, Miss Mueller shrieks. *What do you see?*

Lucien sighs.

The pages are thin and sort of shiny. The illustrations are mostly black and white.

This one's a photograph of a statue, an emperor, apparently, wearing his stone toga and his stone wreath. The real people, the living people, mill about just beyond the picture's confines, but Lucien knows more or less what they look like—he's seen illustrations of them, too. He knows what a viaduct is and that the ancient Romans went to plays and banquets and that they had a code of law from which his country's own is derived. Are the people hidden by the picture frightened? Do they hear the stones working themselves loose, the temples and houses and courts beginning to crumble?

Out the window, the sun is just a tiny, tiny bit higher today than it was at this exact instant yesterday. After school, he and Robbie Stern will go play soccer in the park. In another month it will be bright and warm.

PARADISE

So, Mr. Matsumoto will be coming back, and things seem pretty much as they did when he left. The apartment is clean, the cats are healthy, the art is undamaged, and the view from the terrace is exactly the same, except there's that weird, blank spot where the towers used to stand.

"Open the next?" Madison says, holding up a bottle of champagne. "Strongly agree, agree, undecided, disagree, strongly disagree."

"Strongly agree," Lyle says.

"Thanks," Amity says.

"Okay," Russell says. "I'm in."

Nathaniel shrugs and holds out his glass.

Madison pours. "Polls indicate that 100 percent of the American public approves heavy drinking," he says.

"Oh, god, Madison," Amity says. "Can't we ever just *drop* it? Can't we ever just have a nice time?"

Madison looks at her for a long moment. "Drop what?" he says, evenly.

But no one wants to get into *that*.

When Nathaniel was in his last year at college, his father began to suffer from heart trouble. It was easy enough for Nathaniel to come home on the weekends, and he'd sit with his father, gazing out the window as the autumnal light gilded the dry grass and the fallen leaves glowed.

His father talked about his own time at school, working night and day, the pride his parents had taken in him, the first college student in their family.

Over the years Nathaniel's mother and father had grown gentler with one another and with him. Sometimes after dinner and the dishes, they'd all go out for a treat. Nathaniel would wait, an acid pity weakening his bones, while his parents debated worriedly over their choices, as if nobody ever had before or would ever have again the opportunity to eat ice cream.

Just last night, he dreamed about Delphine, a delicious champagne-style dream, full of love and beauty—a weird, high-quality love, a feeling he doesn't remember ever having had in his waking life—a pure, wholehearted, shining love.

It hangs around him still, floating through the air out on the terrace—fragrant, shimmering, fading.

WAITING

The bell is about to ring. Closing his book Lucien hears the thrilling crash as the bloated empire tumbles down.

Gold star, Lucien! Miss Mueller cackles deafeningly, and then she's gone.

Charlie's leaving, too. Lucien lifts his glass; she glances back across the thin, inflexible divide.

From farther than the moon she sees the children of some distant planet study pictures in their text: there's Rose and Isaac at their kitchen table, Nathaniel out on Mr. Matsumoto's terrace, Lucien alone in the dim gallery—and then the children turn the page.

COMMUNIST

RICHARD FORD (1944–) was born in Jackson, Mississippi, the only child of a traveling salesman for a starch company, and was raised in Mississippi and in Arkansas. He went to college at Michigan State University, where he met Kristina Hensley, to whom he has been married since 1968. Ford attended law school briefly before entering the University of California at Irvine, where he received his MFA in fiction writing in 1970. His novels are *A Piece of My Heart, The Ultimate Good Luck, The Sportswriter, Wildlife,* and, most recently, *The Lay of the Land, Women with Men,* and *Independence Day,* the only novel to win both the Pulitzer Prize and the PEN/Faulkner Award for Fiction. Ford has taught writing and literature at the University of Michigan at Ann Arbor, Princeton University, and Williams College. Ford, who lived for a while in New Orleans, has moved to Jamestown, Rhode Island.

My mother once had a boyfriend named Glen Baxter. This was in 1961. We—my mother and I—were living in the little house my father had left her up the Sun River, near Victory, Montana, west of Great Falls. My mother was thirty-two at the time. I was sixteen. Glen Baxter was somewhere in the middle, between us, though I cannot be exact about it.

We were living then off the proceeds of my father's life insurance policies, with my mother doing some part-time waitressing work up in Great Falls and going to the bars in the evenings, which I know is where she met Glen Baxter. Sometimes he would come back with her and stay in her room at night, or she would call up from town and explain that she was staying with him in his little place on Lewis Street by the GN yards. She gave me his number every time, but I never called it. I think she probably thought that what she was doing was terrible, but simply couldn't help herself. I thought it was all right, though. Regular life it seemed, and still does. She was young, and I knew that even then.

Glen Baxter was a Communist and liked hunting, which he talked about a lot. Pheasants. Ducks. Deer. He killed all of them, he said. He had been to Vietnam as far back as then, and when he was in our house he often talked about shooting the animals over there—monkeys and beautiful parrots—using military guns just for sport. We did not know what Vietnam was then, and

Glen, when he talked about that, referred to it only as "the Far East." I think now he must've been in the CIA and been disillusioned by something he saw or found out about and been thrown out, but that kind of thing did not matter to us. He was a tall, dark-eyed man with short black hair, and was usually in a good humor. He had gone halfway through college in Peoria, Illinois, he said, where he grew up. But when he was around our life he worked wheat farms as a ditcher, and stayed out of work winters and in the bars drinking with women like my mother, who had work and some money. It is not an uncommon life to lead in Montana.

What I want to explain happened in November. We had not been seeing Glen Baxter for some time. Two months had gone by. My mother knew other men, but she came home most days from work and stayed inside watching television in her bedroom and drinking beers. I asked about Glen once, and she said only that she didn't know where he was, and I assumed they had had a fight and that he was gone off on a flyer back to Illinois or Massachusetts, where he said he had relatives. I'll admit that I liked him. He had something on his mind always. He was a labor man as well as a Communist, and liked to say that the country was poisoned by the rich, and strong men would need to bring it to life again, and I liked that because my father had been a labor man, which was why we had a house to live in and money coming through. It was also true that I'd had a few boxing bouts by then—just with town boys and one with an Indian from Choteau—and there were some girlfriends I knew from that. I did not like my mother being around the house so much at night, and I wished Glen Baxter would come back, or that another man would come along and entertain her somewhere else.

At two o'clock on a Saturday, Glen drove up into our yard in a car. He had had a big brown Harley-Davidson that he rode most of the year, in his black-and-red irrigators and a baseball cap turned backwards. But this time he had a car, a blue Nash Ambassador. My mother and I went out on the porch when he stopped inside the olive trees my father had planted as a shelter belt, and my mother had a look on her face of not much pleasure. It was starting to be cold in earnest by then. Snow was down already onto the Fairfield Bench, though on this day a chinook was blowing, and it could as easily have been spring, though the sky above the Divide was turning over in silver and blue clouds of winter.

"We haven't seen you in a long time, I guess," my mother said coldly.

"My little retarded sister died," Glen said, standing at the door of his old car. He was wearing his orange VFW jacket and canvas shoes we called wino shoes, something I had never seen him wear before. He seemed to be in a good humor. "We buried her in Florida near the home."

"That's a good place," my mother said in a voice that meant she was a wronged party in something.

"I want to take this boy hunting today, Aileen," Glen said. "There're snow geese down now. But we have to go right away, or they'll be gone to Idaho by tomorrow."

"He doesn't care to go," my mother said.

"Yes I do," I said, and looked at her.

My mother frowned at me. "Why do you?"

"Why does he need a reason?" Glen Baxter said and grinned.

"I want him to have one, that's why." She looked at me oddly. "I think Glen's drunk, Les."

"No, I'm not drinking," Glen said, which was hardly ever true. He looked at both of us, and my mother bit down on the side of her lower lip and stared at me in a way to make you think she thought something was being put over on her and she didn't like you for it. She was very pretty, though when she was mad her features were sharpened and less pretty by a long way. "All right, then I don't care," she said to no one in particular. "Hunt, kill, maim. Your father did that too." She turned to go back inside.

"Why don't you come with us, Aileen?" Glen was smiling still, pleased.

"To do what?" my mother said. She stopped and pulled a package of cigarettes out of her dress pocket and put one in her mouth.

"It's worth seeing."

"See dead animals?" my mother said.

"These geese are from Siberia, Aileen," Glen said. "They're not like a lot of geese. Maybe I'll buy us dinner later. What do you say?"

"Buy what with?" my mother said. To tell the truth, I didn't know why she was so mad at him. I would've thought she'd be glad to see him. But she just suddenly seemed to hate everything about him.

"I've got some money," Glen said. "Let me spend it on a pretty girl tonight."

"Find one of those and you're lucky," my mother said, turning away toward the front door.

"I already found one," Glen Baxter said. But the door slammed behind her, and he looked at me then with a look I think now was helplessness, though I could not see a way to change anything.

My mother sat in the backseat of Glen's Nash and looked out the window while we drove. My double gun was in the seat between us beside Glen's Belgian pump, which he kept loaded with five shells in case, he said, he saw something beside the road he wanted to shoot. I had hunted rabbits before, and had ground-sluiced pheasants and other birds, but I had never been on an actual hunt before, one where you drove out to some special place and did it formally. And I was excited. I had a feeling that something important was about to happen to me, and that this would be a day I would always remember.

My mother did not say anything for a long time, and neither did I. We drove up through Great Falls and out the other side toward Fort Benton, which was on the benchland where wheat was grown.

"Geese mate for life," my mother said, just out of the blue, as we were driving. "I hope you know that. They're special birds."

"I know that," Glen said in the front seat. "I have every respect for them."

"So where were you for three months?" she said. "I'm only curious."

"I was in the Big Hole for a while," Glen said, "and after that I went over to Douglas, Wyoming."

"What were you planning to do there?" my mother asked.

"I wanted to find a job, but it didn't work out."

"I'm going to college," she said suddenly, and this was something I had never heard about before. I turned to look at her, but she was staring out her window and wouldn't see me.

"I knew French once," Glen said. "*Rosé*'s pink. *Rouge*'s red." He glanced at me and smiled. "I think that's a wise idea, Aileen. When are you going to start?"

"I don't want Les to think he was raised by crazy people all his life," my mother said.

"Les ought to go himself," Glen said.

"After I go, he will."

"What do you say about that, Les?" Glen said, grinning.

"He says it's just fine," my mother said.

"It's just fine," I said.

Where Glen Baxter took us was out onto the high flat prairie that was disked for wheat and had high, high mountains out to the east, with lower heartbreak hills in between. It was, I remember, a day for blues in the sky, and down in the distance we could see the small town of Floweree, and the state highway running past it toward Fort Benton and the Hi-line. We drove out on top of the prairie on a muddy dirt road fenced on both sides, until we had gone about three miles, which is where Glen stopped.

"All right," he said, looking up in the rearview mirror at my mother. "You wouldn't think there was anything here, would you?"

"*We're* here," my mother said. "You brought us here."

"You'll be glad though," Glen said, and seemed confident to me. I had looked around myself but could not see anything. No water or trees, nothing that seemed like a good place to hunt anything. Just wasted land. "There's a big lake out there, Les," Glen said. "You can't see it now from here because it's low. But the geese are there. You'll see."

"It's like the moon out here, I recognize that," my mother said, "only it's worse." She was staring out at the flat wheatland as if she could actually see something in particular, and wanted to know more about it. "How'd you find this place?"

"I came once on the wheat push," Glen said.

"And I'm sure the owner told you just to come back and hunt anytime you like and bring anybody you wanted. Come one, come all. Is that it?"

"People shouldn't own land anyway," Glen said. "Anybody should be able to use it."

"Les, Glen's going to poach here," my mother said. "I just want you to know that, because that's a crime and the law will get you for it. If you're a man now, you're going to have to face the consequences."

"That's not true," Glen Baxter said, and looked gloomily out over the steering wheel down the muddy road toward the mountains. Though for myself I believed it was true, and didn't care. I didn't care about anything at that moment except seeing geese fly over me and shooting them down.

"Well, I'm certainly not going out there," my mother said. "I like towns better, and I already have enough trouble."

"That's okay," Glen said. "When the geese lift up you'll get to see them. That's all I wanted. Les and me'll go shoot them, won't we, Les?"

"Yes," I said, and I put my hand on my shotgun, which had been my father's and was heavy as rocks.

"Then we should go on," Glen said, "or we'll waste our light."

We got out of the car with our guns. Glen took off his canvas shoes and put on his pair of black irrigators out of the trunk. Then we crossed the barbed wire fence, and walked out into the high, tilled field toward nothing. I looked back at my mother when we were still not so far away, but I could only see the small, dark top of her head, low in the backseat of the Nash, staring out and thinking what I could not then begin to say.

On the walk toward the lake, Glen began talking to me. I had never been alone with him, and knew little about him except what my mother said—that he drank too much, or other times that he was the nicest man she had ever known in the world and that someday a woman would marry him, though she didn't think it would be her. Glen told me as we walked that he wished he had finished college, but that it was too late now, that his mind was too old. He said he had liked the Far East very much, and that people there knew how to treat each other, and that he would go back some day but couldn't go now. He said also that he would like to live in Russia for a while and mentioned the names of people who had gone there, names I didn't know. He said it would be hard at first, because it was so different, but that pretty soon anyone would learn to like it and wouldn't want to live anywhere else, and that Russians treated Americans who came to live there like kings. There were Communists everywhere now, he said. You didn't know them, but they were there. Montana had a large number, and he was in touch with all of them. He said that Communists were always in danger and that he had to protect himself all the time. And when he said that he pulled back his VFW jacket and showed me the butt of a pistol he had stuck under his shirt against his bare skin. "There are people who want to kill me right now," he said, "and I would kill a man myself if I thought I had to." And we kept walking. Though in a while he said, "I don't think I know much about you, Les. But I'd like to. What do you like to do?"

"I like to box," I said. "My father did it. It's a good thing to know."

"I suppose you have to protect yourself too," Glen said.

"I know how to," I said.

"Do you like to watch TV," Glen asked, and smiled.

"Not much."

"I love to," Glen said. "I could watch it instead of eating if I had one."

I looked out straight ahead over the green tops of sage that grew to the edge of the disked field, hoping to see the lake Glen said was there. There was an airishness and a sweet smell that I thought might be the place we were going, but I couldn't see it. "How will we hunt these geese?" I said.

"It won't be hard," Glen said. "Most hunting isn't even hunting. It's only shooting. And that's what this will be. In Illinois you would dig holes in the ground and hide and set out your decoys. Then the geese come to you, over and over again. But we don't have time for that here." He glanced at me. "You have to be sure the first time here."

"How do you know they're here now," I asked. And I looked toward the Highwood Mountains twenty miles away, half in snow and half dark blue at the bottom. I could see the little town of Floweree then, looking shabby and dimly lighted in the distance. A red bar sign shone. A car moved slowly away from the scattered buildings.

"They always come November first," Glen said.

"Are we going to poach them?"

"Does it make any difference to you," Glen asked.

"No, it doesn't."

"Well then, we aren't," he said.

We walked then for a while without talking. I looked back once to see the Nash far and small in the flat distance. I couldn't see my mother, and I thought that she must've turned on the radio and gone to sleep, which she always did, letting it play all night in her bedroom. Behind the car the sun was nearing the rounded mountains southwest of us, and I knew that when the sun was gone it would be cold. I wished my mother had decided to come along with us, and I thought for a moment of how little I really knew her at all.

Glen walked with me another quarter-mile, crossed another barbed-wire fence where sage was growing, then went a hundred yards through wheatgrass and spurge until the ground went up and formed a kind of long hillock bunker built by a farmer against the wind. And I realized the lake was just beyond us. I could hear the sound of a car horn blowing and a dog barking all the way down in the town, then the wind seemed to move and all I could hear then and after then were geese. So many geese, from the sound of them, though I still could not see even one. I stood and listened to the high-pitched shouting sound, a sound I had never heard so close, a sound with size to it—though it was not loud. A sound that meant great numbers and that made your chest rise and your shoulders tighten with expectancy. It was a sound to make you feel separate from it and everything else, as if you were of no importance in the grand scheme of things.

"Do you hear them singing," Glen asked. He held his hand up to make me stand still. And we both listened. "How many do you think, Les, just hearing?"

"A hundred," I said. "More than a hundred."

"Five thousand," Glen said. "More than you can believe when you see them. Go see."

I put down my gun and on my hands and knees crawled up the earthwork through the wheatgrass and thistle, until I could see down to the lake and see the geese. And they were there, like a white bandage laid on the water, wide and long and continuous, a white expanse of snow geese, seventy yards from me, on the bank, but stretching far onto the lake, which was large itself—a half-mile across, with thick rules on the far side and wild plums farther and the blue mountain behind them.

"Do you see the big raft?" Glen said from below me, in a whisper.

"I see it," I said, still looking. It was such a thing to see, a view I had never seen and have not since.

"Are any on the land?" he said.

"Some are in the wheatgrass," I said, "but most are swimming."

"Good," Glen said. "They'll have to fly. But we can't wait for that now."

And I crawled backwards down the heel of land to where Glen was, and my gun. We were losing our light, and the air was purplish and cooling. I looked toward the car but couldn't see it, and I was no longer sure where it was below the lighted sky.

"Where do they fly to?" I said in a whisper, since I did not want anything to be ruined because of what I did or said. It was important to Glen to shoot the geese, and it was important to me.

"To the wheat," he said. "Or else they leave for good. I wish your mother had come, Les. Now she'll be sorry."

I could hear the geese quarreling and shouting on the lake surface. And I wondered if they knew we were here now. "She might be," I said with my heart pounding, but I didn't think she would be much.

It was a simple plan he had. I would stay behind the bunker, and he would crawl on his belly with his gun through the wheatgrass as near to the geese as he could. Then he would simply stand up and shoot all the ones he could close up, both in the air and on the ground. And when all the others flew up, with luck some would turn toward me as they came into the wind, and then I could shoot them and turn them back to him, and he would shoot them again. He could kill ten, he said, if he was lucky, and I might kill four. It didn't seem hard.

"Don't show them your face," Glen said. "Wait till you think you can touch them, then stand up and shoot. To hesitate is lost in this."

"All right," I said. "I'll try it."

"Shoot one in the head, and then shoot another one," Glen said. "It won't be hard." He patted me on the arm and smiled. Then he took off his VFW jacket and put it on the ground, climbed up the side of the bunker, cradling his shotgun in his arms, and slid on his belly into the dry stalks of yellow grass out of my sight.

Then, for the first time in that entire day, I was alone. And I didn't mind it. I sat squat down in the grass, loaded my double gun and took my other two shells out of my pocket to hold. I pushed the safety off and on to see that it was right. The wind rose a little, scuffed the grass and made me shiver. It was not the warm chinook now, but a wind out of the north, the one geese flew away from if they could.

Then I thought about my mother, in the car alone, and how much longer I would stay with her, and what it might mean to her for me to leave. And I wondered when Glen Baxter would die and if someone would kill him, or whether my mother would marry him and how I would feel about it. And though I didn't know why, it occurred to me that Glen Baxter and I would not be friends when all was said and done, since I didn't care if he ever married my mother or didn't.

Then I thought about boxing and what my father had taught me about it. To tighten your fists hard. To strike out straight from the shoulder and never punch backing up. How to cut a punch by snapping your fist inwards, how to carry your chin low, and to step toward a man when he is falling so you can hit him again. And most important, to keep your eyes open when you are hitting in the face and causing damage, because you need to see what you're doing to encourage yourself, and because it is when you close your eyes that you stop hitting and get hurt badly. "Fly all over your man, Les," my father said. "When you see your chance, fly on him and hit him till he falls." That, I thought, would always be my attitude in things.

And then I heard the geese again, their voices in unison, louder and shouting, as if the wind had changed again and put all new sounds in the cold air. And then a *boom*. And I knew Glen was in among them and had stood up to shoot. The noise of geese rose and grew worse, and my fingers burned where I held my gun too tight to the metal, and I put it down and opened my fist to make the burning stop so I could feel the trigger when the moment came. *Boom*, Glen shot again, and I heard him shuck a shell, and all the sounds out beyond the bunker seemed to be rising—the geese, the shots, the air itself going up. *Boom*, Glen shot another time, and I knew he was taking his careful time to make his shots good. And I held my gun and started to crawl up the bunker so as not to be surprised when the geese came over me and I could shoot.

From the top I saw Glen Baxter alone in the wheatgrass field, shooting at a white goose with black tips of wings that was on the ground not far from him, but trying to run and pull into the air. He shot it once more, and it fell over dead with its wings flapping.

Glen looked back at me and his face was distorted and strange. The air around him was full of white rising geese and he seemed to want them all. "Behind you, Les," he yelled at me and pointed. "They're all behind you now." I looked behind me, and there were geese in the air as far as I could see, more than I knew how many, moving so slowly, their wings wide out and working calmly and filling the air with noise, though their voices were not as loud or as shrill as I had thought they would be. And they were so close! Forty feet, some of them. The air around me vibrated and I could feel the wind from their wings and it seemed to me I could kill as many as the times I could shoot—a hundred or a thousand—and I raised my gun, put the muzzle on the head of a white goose, and fired. It shuddered in the air, its wide feet sank below its belly, its wings cradled out to hold back air, and it fell straight down and landed with an awful sound, a noise a human would make, a thick, soft, *hump* noise. I looked up again and shot another goose, could hear the pellets hit its chest, but it didn't fall or even break its pattern for flying. *Boom*, Glen shot again. And then again. "Hey," I heard him shout. "Hey, hey." And there were geese flying over me, flying in line after line. I broke my gun and reloaded, and thought to myself as I did: I need confidence here, I need to be sure with this. I pointed at another goose and shot it in the head, and it fell the way the first one had, wings out, its belly down, and with the same thick noise of hitting. Then I sat down in the grass on the bunker and let geese fly over me.

By now the whole raft was in the air, all of it moving in a slow swirl above me and the lake and everywhere, finding the wind and heading out south in long wavering lines that caught the last sun and turned to silver as they gained a distance. It was a thing to see, I will tell you now. Five thousand white geese all in the air around you, making a noise like you have never heard before. And I thought to myself then: this is something I will never see again. I will never forget this. And I was right.

Glen Baxter shot twice more. One he missed, but with the other he hit a goose flying away from him, and knocked it half falling and flying into the empty lake not far from shore, where it began to swim as though it was fine and make its noise.

Glen stood in the stubby grass, looking out at the goose, his gun lowered. "I didn't need to shoot that one, did I, Les?"

"I don't know," I said, sitting on the little knoll of land, looking at the goose swimming in the water.

"I don't know why I shoot 'em. They're so beautiful." He looked at me.

"I don't know either," I said.

"Maybe there's nothing else to do with them." Glen stared at the goose again and shook his head. "Maybe this is exactly what they're put on earth for."

I did not know what to say because I did not know what he could mean by that, though what I felt was embarrassment at the great numbers of geese there were, and a dulled feeling like a hunger because the shooting had stopped and it was over for me now.

Glen began to pick up his geese, and I walked down to my two that had fallen close together and were dead. One had hit with such an impact that its stomach had split and some of its inward parts were knocked out. Though the other looked unhurt, its soft white belly turned up like a pillow, its head and jagged bill-teeth, its tiny black eyes looking as they would if they were alive.

"What's happened to the hunters out here?" I heard a voice speak. It was my mother, standing in her pink dress on the knoll above us, hugging her arms. She was smiling though she was cold. And I realized that I had lost all thought of her in the shooting. "Who did all this shooting? Is this your work, Les?"

"No," I said.

"Les is a hunter, though, Aileen," Glen said. "He takes his time." He was holding two white geese by their necks, one in each hand, and he was smiling. He and my mother seemed pleased.

"I see you didn't miss too many," my mother said and smiled. I could tell she admired Glen for his geese, and that she had done some thinking in the car alone. "It *was* wonderful, Glen," she said. "I've never seen anything like that. They were like snow."

"It's worth seeing once, isn't it?" Glen said. "I should've killed more, but I got excited."

My mother looked at me then. "Where's yours, Les?"

"Here," I said and pointed to my two geese on the ground beside me.

My mother nodded in a nice way, and I think she liked everything then and wanted the day to turn out right and for all of us to be happy. "Six, then. You've got six in all."

"One's still out there," I said, and motioned where the one goose was swimming in circles on the water.

"Okay," my mother said and put her hand over her eyes to look. "Where is it?"

Glen Baxter looked at me then with a strange smile, a smile that said he wished I had never mentioned anything about the other goose. And I wished I hadn't either. I looked up in the sky and could see the lines of geese by the thousands shining silver in the light, and I wished we could just leave and go home.

"That one's my mistake there," Glen Baxter said and grinned. "I shouldn't have shot that one, Aileen. I got too excited."

My mother looked out on the lake for a minute, then looked at Glen and back again. "Poor goose." She shook her head. "How will you get it, Glen?"

"I can't get that one now," Glen said.

My mother looked at him. "What do you mean?"

"I'm going to leave that one," Glen said.

"Well, no. You can't leave one," my mother said. "You shot it. You have to get it. Isn't that a rule?"

"No," Glen said.

And my mother looked from Glen to me. "Wade out and get it, Glen," she said in a sweet way, and my mother looked young then, like a young girl, in her flimsy short-sleeved waitress dress and her skinny, bare legs in the wheatgrass.

"No." Glen Baxter looked down at his gun and shook his head. And I didn't know why he wouldn't go, because it would've been easy. The lake was shallow. And you could tell that anyone could've walked out a long way before it got deep, and Glen had on his boots.

My mother looked at the white goose, which was not more than thirty yards from the shore, its head up, moving in slow circles, its wings settled and relaxed so you could see the black tips. "Wade out and get it, Glenny, won't you, please?" she said. "They're special things."

"You don't understand the world, Aileen," Glen said. "This can happen. It doesn't matter."

"But that's so cruel, Glen," she said, and a sweet smile came on her lips.

"Raise up your own arms, 'Leeny," Glen said. "I can't see any angel's wings, can you, Les?" He looked at me, but I looked away.

"Then you go on and get it, Les," my mother said. "You weren't raised by crazy people." I started to go, but Glen Baxter suddenly grabbed me by my shoulder and pulled me back hard, so hard his fingers made bruises in my skin that I saw later.

"Nobody's going," he said. "This is over with now."

And my mother gave Glen a cold look then. "You don't have a heart, Glen," she said. "There's nothing to love in you. You're just a son of a bitch, that's all."

And Glen Baxter nodded at my mother, then, as if he understood something he had not understood before, but something that he was willing to know. "Fine," he said, "that's fine." And he took his big pistol out from against his belly, the big blue revolver I had only seen part of before and that he said protected him, and he pointed it out at the goose on the water, his arm straight away from him, and shot and missed. And then he shot and missed again. The goose made its noise once. And then he hit it dead, because there was no splash.

And then he shot it three times more until the gun was empty and the goose's head was down and it was floating toward the middle of the lake where it was empty and dark blue. "Now who has a heart?" Glen said. But my mother was not there when he turned around. She had already started back to the car and was almost lost from sight in the darkness. And Glen smiled at me then and his face had a wild look on it. "Okay, Les?" he said.

"Okay," I said.

"There're limits to everything, right?"

"I guess so," I said.

"Your mother's a beautiful woman, but she's not the only beautiful woman in Montana." And I did not say anything. And Glen Baxter suddenly said, "Here," and he held the pistol out at me. "Don't you want this? Don't you want to shoot me? Nobody thinks they'll die. But I'm ready for it right now." And I did not know what to do then. Though it is true that what I wanted to do was to hit him, hit him as hard in the face as I could, and see him on the ground bleeding and crying and pleading for me to stop. Only at that moment he looked scared to me, and I had never seen a grown man scared before—though I have seen one since—and I felt sorry for him, as though he was already a dead man. And I did not end up hitting him at all.

A light can go out in the heart. All of this happened years ago, but I still can feel now how sad and remote the world was to me. Glen Baxter, I think now, was not a bad man, only a man scared of something he'd never seen before—something soft in himself—his life going a way he didn't like. A woman with a son. Who could blame him there? I don't know what makes people do what they do, or call themselves what they call themselves, only that you have to live someone's life to be the expert.

My mother had tried to see the good side of things, tried to be hopeful in the situation she was handed, tried to look out for us both, and it hadn't worked. It was a strange time in her life then and after that, a time when she had to adjust to being an adult just when she was on the thin edge of things. Too much awareness too early in life was her problem, I think.

And what I felt was only that I had somehow been pushed out into the world, into the real life then, the one I hadn't lived yet. In a year I was gone to hard-rock mining and no-paycheck jobs and not to college. And I have thought more than once about my mother saying that I had not been raised by crazy people, and I don't know what that could mean or what difference it could make, unless it means that love is a reliable commodity, and even that is not always true, as I have found out.

Late on the night that all this took place I was in bed when I heard my mother say, "Come outside, Les. Come and hear this." And I went out onto the front porch barefoot and in my underwear, where it was warm like spring, and there was a spring mist in the air. I could see the lights of the Fairfield Coach in the distance, on its way up to Great Falls.

And I could hear geese, white birds in the sky, flying. They made their high-pitched sound like angry yells, and though I couldn't see them high up, it seemed to me they were everywhere. And my mother looked up and said, "Hear them?" I could smell her hair wet from the shower. "They leave with the moon," she said. "It's still half wild out here."

And I said, "I hear them," and I felt a chill come over my bare chest, and the hair stood up on my arms the way it does before a storm. And for a while we listened.

"When I first married your father, you know, we lived on a street called Blue-bird Canyon, in California. And I thought that was the prettiest street and the prettiest name. I suppose no one brings you up like your first love. You don't mind if I say that, do you?" She looked at me hopefully.

"No," I said.

"We have to keep civilization alive somehow." And she pulled her little housecoat together because there was a cold vein in the air, a part of the cold that would be on us the next day. "I don't feel part of things tonight, I guess."

"It's all right," I said.

"Do you know where I'd like to go?"

"No," I said. And I suppose I knew she was angry then, angry with life, but did not want to show me that.

"To the Straits of Juan de Fuca. Wouldn't that be something? Would you like that?"

"I'd like it," I said. And my mother looked off for a minute, as if she could see the Straits of Juan de Fuca out against the line of mountains, see the lights of things alive and a whole new world.

"I know you liked him," she said after a moment. "You and I both suffer fools too well."

"I didn't like him too much," I said. "I didn't really care."

"He'll fall on his face. I'm sure of that," she said. And I didn't say anything because I didn't care about Glen Baxter anymore, and was happy not to talk about him. "Would you tell me something if I asked you? Would you tell me the truth?"

"Yes," I said.

And my mother did not look at me. "Just tell the truth," she said.

"All right," I said.

"Do you think I'm still very feminine? I'm thirty-two years old now. You don't know what that means. But do you think I am?"

And I stood at the edge of the porch, with the olive trees before me, looking straight up into the mist where I could not see geese but could still hear them flying, could almost feel the air move below their white wings. And I felt the way you feel when you are on a trestle all alone and the train is coming, and you know you have to decide. And I said, "Yes, I do." Because that was the truth. And I tried to think of something else then and did not hear what my mother said after that.

And how old was I then? Sixteen. Sixteen is young, but it can also be a grown man. I am forty-one years old now, and I think about that time without regret, though my mother and I never talked in that way again, and I have not heard her voice now in a long, long time.

Mary Gaitskill

TINY, SMILING DADDY

MARY GAITSKILL (1954–) is the author of the collection *Because They Wanted To*, nominated for the PEN/Faulkner Award, and the novels *Bad Behavior; Two Girls, Fat and Thin;* and *Veronica.* Her stories and essays have appeared in *The New Yorker, Harper's, Esquire, Best American Short Stories,* and *The O. Henry Prize Stories.* Her story "Secretary" was the basis for the film of the same name. A Guggenheim Fellowship recipient, she teaches creative writing at Syracuse University and lives in New York.

He lay in his reclining chair, barely awake enough to feel the dream moving just under his thoughts. It felt like one of those pure, beautiful dreams in which he was young again, and filled with the realization that the friends who had died, or gone away, or decided that they didn't like him anymore, had really been there all along, loving him. A piece of the dream flickered, and he made out the lips and cheekbones of a tender woman, smiling as she leaned toward him. The phone rang, and the sound rippled through his pliant wakefulness, into the pending dream. But his wife had turned the answering machine up too loud again, and it attacked him with a garbled, furred roar that turned into the voice of his friend Norm.

Resentful at being waked and grateful that for once somebody had called him, he got up to answer. He picked up the phone, and the answering machine screeched at him through the receiver. He cursed as he fooled with it, hating his stiff fingers. Irritably, he exchanged greetings with his friend, and then Norm, his voice oddly weighted, said, "I saw the issue of *Self* with Kitty in it."

He waited for an explanation. None came, so he said, "What? Issue of *Self* ? What's *Self* ?"

"Good grief, Stew, I thought for sure you'd of seen it. Now I feel funny."

The dream pulsed forward and receded again. "Funny about what?"

"My daughter's got a subscription to this magazine, *Self.* And they printed an article that Kitty wrote about fathers and daughters talking to each other, and she, well, she wrote about you. Laurel showed it to me."

"My God."

"It's ridiculous that I'm the one to tell you. I just thought—"

"It was bad?"

228

"No, she didn't say anything bad. I just didn't understand the whole idea of it. And I wondered what you thought."

He got off the phone and walked back into the living room, now fully awake. His daughter, Kitty, was living in South Carolina, working in a used-record store and making animal statuettes, which she sold on commission. She had never written anything that he knew of, yet she'd apparently published an article in a national magazine about him. He lifted his arms and put them on the windowsill; the air from the open window cooled his underarms. Outside, the Starlings' tiny dog marched officiously up and down the pavement, looking for someone to bark at. Maybe she had written an article about how wonderful he was, and she was too shy to show him right away. This was doubtful. Kitty was quiet, but she wasn't shy. She was untactful and she could be aggressive. Uncertainty only made her doubly aggressive.

He turned the edge of one nostril over with his thumb and nervously stroked his nose hairs with one finger. He knew it was a nasty habit, but it soothed him. When Kitty was a little girl he would do it to make her laugh. "Well," he'd say, "do you think it's time we played with the hairs in our nose?" And she would giggle, holding her hands against her face, eyes sparkling over her knuckles.

Then she was fourteen, and as scornful and rejecting as any girl he had ever thrown a spitball at when he was that age. They didn't get along so well anymore. Once, they were sitting in the rec room watching TV, he on the couch, she on the footstool. There was a Charlie Chan movie on, but he was mostly watching her back and her long, thick brown hair, which she had just washed and was brushing. She dropped her head forward from the neck to let the hair fall between her spread legs and began slowly stroking it with a pink nylon brush.

"Say, don't you think it's time we played with the hairs in our nose?"

No reaction from bent back and hair.

"Who wants to play with the hairs in their nose?"

Nothing.

"Hairs in the nose, hairs in the nose," he sang.

She bolted violently up from the stool. "You are so gross you disgust me!" She stormed from the room, shoulders in a tailored jacket of indignation.

Sometimes he said it just to see her exasperation, to feel the adorable, futile outrage of her violated girl delicacy.

He wished that his wife would come home with the car, so that he could drive to the store and buy a copy of *Self*. His car was being repaired, and he could not walk to the little cluster of stores and parking lots that constituted "town" in this heat. It would take a good twenty minutes, and he would be completely worn out when he got there. He would find the magazine and stand there in the drugstore and read it, and if it was something bad, he might not have the strength to walk back.

He went into the kitchen, opened a beer, and brought it into the living room. His wife had been gone for over an hour, and God knew how much longer she would be. She could spend literally all day driving around the county, doing nothing but buying a jar of honey or a bag of apples. Of course, he could call Kitty, but he'd probably just get her answering machine, and besides, he didn't want to talk to her before he understood the situation. He felt helplessness move through his body the way a swimmer feels a large sea creature pass beneath him. How could she have done this to him? She knew how he dreaded exposure of any kind, she knew the way he guarded himself against strangers, the way he carefully drew all the curtains when twilight approached so that no one could see them walking through the house. She knew how ashamed he had been when, at sixteen, she announced that she was lesbian.

The Starling dog was now across the street, yapping at the heels of a bow-legged old lady in a blue dress who was trying to walk down the sidewalk. "Dammit," he said. He left the window and got the afternoon opera station on the radio. They were in the final act of *La Bohème*.

He did not remember precisely when it had happened, but Kitty, his beautiful, happy little girl, turned into a glum, weird teenager that other kids picked on. She got skinny and ugly. Her blue eyes, which had been so sensitive and bright, turned filmy, as if the real Kitty had retreated so far from the surface that her eyes existed to shield rather than reflect her. It was as if she deliberately held her beauty away from them, only showing glimpses of it during unavoidable lapses, like the time she sat before the TV, daydreaming and lazily brushing her hair. At moments like this, her dormant charm broke his heart. It also annoyed him. What did she have to retreat from? They had both loved her. When she was little and she couldn't sleep at night, Marsha would sit with her in bed for hours. She praised her stories and her drawings as if she were a genius. When Kitty was seven, she and her mother had special times, during which they went off together and talked about whatever Kitty wanted to talk about.

He tried to compare the sullen, morbid Kitty of sixteen with the slender, self-possessed twenty-eight-year-old lesbian who wrote articles for *Self*. He pictured himself in court, waving a copy of *Self* before a shocked jury. The case would be taken up by the press. He saw the headlines: Dad Sues Mag—Dyke Daughter Reveals . . . reveals what? What had Kitty found to say about him that was of interest to the entire country, that she didn't want him to know about?

Anger overrode his helplessness. Kitty could be vicious. He hadn't seen her vicious side in years, but he knew it was there. He remembered the time he'd stood behind the half-open front door when fifteen-year-old Kitty sat hunched on the front steps with one of her few friends, a homely blonde who wore white lipstick and a white leather jacket. He had come to the door to view the weather and say something to the girls, but they were muttering so intently that curiosity got the better of him, and he hung back a moment to listen. "Well, at least your mom's smart," said Kitty. "My mom's not only a bitch, she's stupid."

This after the lullabies and special times! It wasn't just an isolated incident, either; every time he'd come home from work, his wife had something bad to say about Kitty. She hadn't set the table until she had been asked four times. She'd gone to Lois's house instead of coming straight home like she'd been told to do. She'd worn a dress to school that was short enough to show the tops of her panty hose.

By the time Kitty came to dinner, looking as if she'd been doing slave labor all day, he would be mad at her. He couldn't help it. Here was his wife doing her damnedest to raise a family and cook dinner, and here was this awful kid looking ugly, acting mean, and not setting the table. It seemed unreasonable that she should turn out so badly after taking up so much of their time. Her afflicted expression made him angry too. What had anybody ever done to her?

He sat forward and gently gnawed the insides of his mouth as he listened to the dying girl in *La Bohème*. He saw his wife's car pull into the driveway. He walked to the back door, almost wringing his hands, and waited for her to come through the door. When she did, he snatched the grocery bag from her arms and said, "Give me the keys." She stood openmouthed in the stairwell, looking at him with idiotic consternation. "Give me the keys!"

"What is it, Stew? What's happened?"

"I'll tell you when I get back."

He got in the car and became part of it, this panting mobile case propelling him through the incredibly complex and fast-moving world of other people, their houses, their children, their dogs, their lives. He wasn't usually so aware of this unpleasant sense of disconnection between him and everyone else, but he had the feeling that it had been there all along, underneath what he thought about most of the time. It was ironic that it should rear up so visibly at a time when there was in fact a mundane yet invasive and horribly real connection between him and everyone else in Wayne County: the hundreds of copies of *Self* magazine sitting in countless drugstores, bookstores, groceries, and libraries. It was as if there were a tentacle plugged into the side of the car, linking him with the random humans who picked up the magazine, possibly his very neighbors. He stopped at a crowded intersection, feeling like an ant in an enemy swarm.

Kitty had projected herself out of the house and into this swarm very early, ostensibly because life with him and Marsha had been so awful. Well, it had been awful, but because of Kitty, not them. As if it weren't enough to be sullen and dull, she turned into a lesbian. Kids followed her down the street, jeering at her. Somebody dropped her books in a toilet. She got into a fistfight. Their neighbors gave them looks. This reaction seemed only to steel Kitty's grip on her new identity; it made her romanticize herself, like the kid she was. She wrote poems about heroic women warriors, she brought home strange books and magazines, which, among other things, seemed to glorify prostitutes. Marsha looked for them and threw them away. Kitty screamed at her, the tendons leaping out on her slender neck. He punched Kitty and knocked her down. Marsha tried to stop him, and he yelled at her. Kitty jumped up and leapt between them, as if to defend her mother. He grabbed her and shook her, but he could not shake the conviction off her face.

Most of the time, though, they continued as always, eating dinner together, watching TV, making jokes. That was the worst thing; he would look at Kitty and see his daughter, now familiar in her withdrawn sullenness, and feel comfort and affection. Then he would remember that she was a lesbian, and a morass of complication and wrongness would come down between them, making it impossible for him to see her. Then she would just be Kitty again. He hated it.

She ran away at sixteen, and the police found her in the apartment of an eighteen-year-old bodybuilder named Dolores, who had a naked woman tattooed on her sinister bicep. Marsha made them put her in a mental hospital so psychiatrists could observe her, but he hated the psychiatrists—mean, supercilious sons of bitches who delighted in the trick question—so he took her out. She finished school, and they told her if she wanted to leave it was all right with them. She didn't waste any time getting out of the house.

She moved into an apartment near Detroit with a girl named George and took a job at a home for retarded kids. She would appear for visits with a huge bag of laundry every few weeks. She was thin and neurotically muscular, her body having the look of a fighting dog on a leash. She cut her hair like a boy's and wore black sunglasses, black leather half-gloves, and leather belts. The only remnant of her beauty was her erect, martial carriage and her efficient movements; she walked through a room like the commander of a guerrilla force. She would sit at the dining room table with Marsha, drinking tea and having a laconic verbal conversation, her body speaking its precise martial language while the washing machine droned from the utility room, and he wandered in and out, trying to make sense of what she said. Sometimes she would stay into the evening, to eat dinner and watch *All in the Family*. Then Marsha would send her home with a jar of homemade tapioca pudding or a bag of apples and oranges.

One day, instead of a visit they got a letter postmarked San Francisco. She had left George, she said. She listed strange details about her current environment and was vague about how she was supporting herself. He had nightmares about Kitty, with her brave, proudly muscular little body, lost among big fleshy women who danced naked in go-go bars and took drugs with needles, terrible women whom his confused, romantic daughter invested with oppressed heroism and intensely female glamour. He got up at night and stumbled into the bathroom for stomach medicine, the familiar darkness of the house heavy with menacing images that pressed about him, images he saw reflected in his own expression when he turned on the bathroom light over the mirror.

Then one year she came home for Christmas. She came into the house with her luggage and a shopping bag of gifts for them, and he saw that she was beautiful again. It was a beauty that both offended and titillated his senses. Her short, spiky hair was streaked with purple, her dainty mouth was lipsticked, her nose and ears were pierced with amethyst and dangling silver. Her face had opened in thousands of petals. Her eyes shone with quick perception as she put down her bag, and he knew that she had seen him see her beauty. She moved toward him with fluid hips; she embraced him for the first time in years. He felt her live, lithe body against his, and his heart pulsed a message of blood and love. "Merry Christmas, Daddy," she said.

Her voice was husky and coarse; it reeked of knowledge and confidence. Her T-shirt said "Chicks With Balls." She was twenty-two years old.

She stayed for a week, discharging her strange jangling beauty into the house and changing the molecules of its air. She talked about the girls she shared an apartment with, her job at a coffee shop, how Californians were different from Michiganders. She talked about her friends: Lorraine, who was so pretty men fell off their bicycles as they twisted their bodies for a better look at her; Judy, a martial arts expert; and Meredith, who was raising a child with her husband, Angela. She talked of poetry readings, ceramics classes, workshops on piercing.

He realized, as he watched her, that she was now doing things that were as bad as or worse than the things that had made him angry at her five years before, yet they didn't quarrel. It seemed that a large white space existed between him and her, and that it was impossible to enter this space or to argue across it. Besides, she might never come back if he yelled at her.

Instead, he watched her, puzzling at the metamorphosis she had undergone. First she had been a beautiful, happy child turned homely, snotty, miserable adolescent. From there she had become a martinet girl with the eyes of a stifled pervert. Now she was a vibrant imp, living, it seemed, in a world constructed of topsy-turvy junk pasted with rhinestones. Where had these three different people come from? Not even Marsha, who had spent so much time with her as a child, could trace the genesis of the new Kitty from the old one. Sometimes he bitterly reflected that he and Marsha weren't even real parents anymore but bereft old people rattling around in a house, connected not to a real child who was going to college, or who at least had some kind of understandable life, but to a changeling who was the product of only their most obscure quirks, a being who came from recesses that neither of them suspected they'd had.

• • •

There were only a few cars in the parking lot. He wheeled through it with pointless deliberation before parking near the drugstore. He spent irritating seconds searching for *Self*, until he realized that its air-brushed cover girl was grinning right at him. He stormed the table of contents, then headed for the back of the magazine. "Speak Easy" was written sideways across the top of the page in round turquoise letters. At the bottom was his daughter's name in a little box. "Kitty Thorne is a ceramic artist living in South Carolina." His hands were trembling.

It was hard for him to rationally ingest the beginning paragraphs, which seemed, incredibly, to be about a phone conversation they'd had some time ago about the emptiness and selfishness of people who have sex but don't get married and have children. A few phrases stood out clearly: ". . . my father may love me but he doesn't love the way I live." ". . . even more complicated because I'm gay." ". . . because it still hurts me."

For reasons he didn't understand, he felt a nervous smile tremble under his skin. He suppressed it.

"This hurt has its roots deep in our relationship, starting, I think, when I was a teenager."

He was horribly aware of being in public, so he paid for the thing and took it out to the car. He drove slowly to another spot in the lot, as far away from the drugstore as possible, picked up the magazine, and began again. She described the "terrible difficulties" between him and her. She recounted, briefly and with hieroglyphic politeness, the fighting, the running away, the return, the tacit reconciliation.

"There is an emotional distance that we have both accepted and chosen to work around, hoping the occasional contact—love, anger, something—will get through."

He put the magazine down and looked out the window. It was near dusk; most of the stores in the little mall were closed. There were only two other cars in the parking lot, and a big, slow, frowning woman with two grocery bags was getting ready to drive one away. He was parked before a weedy piece of land at the edge of the lot. In it were rough, picky weeds spread out like big green tarantulas, young yellow dandelions, frail old dandelions, and bunches of tough blue chickweed. Even in his distress he vaguely appreciated the beauty of the blue weeds against the cool white-and-gray sky. For a moment the sound of insects comforted him. Images of Kitty passed through his memory with terrible speed: her nine-year-old forehead bent over her dish of ice cream, her tiny nightgowned form ran up the stairs, her ringed hand brushed her face, the keys on her belt jiggled as she walked her slow blue-jeaned walk away from the house. Gone, all gone.

The article went on to describe how Kitty hung up the phone feeling frustrated and then listed all the things she could've said to him to let him know how hurt she was, paving the way for "real communication"; it was all in ghastly talk-show language. He was unable to put these words together with the Kitty he had last seen lounging around the house. She was twenty-eight now, and she no longer dyed her hair or wore jewels in her nose. Her demeanor was serious, bookish, almost old-maidish. Once, he'd overheard her saying to Marsha, "So then this Italian girl gives me the once-over and says to Joanne, 'You 'ang around with too many Wasp.' And I said, 'I'm not a Wasp, I'm white trash.'"

"Speak for yourself," he'd said.

"If the worst occurred and my father was unable to respond to me in kind, I still would have done a good thing. I would have acknowledged my own needs and created the possibility to connect with what therapists call 'the good parent' in myself."

Well, if that was the kind of thing she was going to say to him, he was relieved she hadn't said it. But if she hadn't said it to him, why was she saying it to the rest of the country?

He turned on the radio. It sang: "Try to remember, and if you remember, then follow, follow." He turned it off. The interrupted dream echoed faintly. He closed his eyes. When he was nine or ten, an uncle of his had told him, "Everybody makes his own world. You see what you want to see and hear what you want to hear. You can do it right now. If you blink ten times and then close your eyes real tight, you can see anything you want to see in front of you." He'd tried it, rather halfheartedly, and hadn't seen anything but the vague suggestion of a yellowish-white ball moving creepily through the dark. At the time, he'd thought it was perhaps because he hadn't tried hard enough.

He had told Kitty to do the same thing, or something like it, when she was eight or nine. They were sitting on the back porch in striped lawn chairs, holding hands and watching the fireflies turn on and off.

She closed her eyes for a long time. Then very seriously, she said, "I see big balls of color, like shaggy flowers. They're pink and red and turquoise. I see an island with palm trees and pink rocks. There's dolphins and mermaids swimming in the water around it." He'd been almost awed by her belief in this impossible vision. Then he was sad, because she would never see what she wanted to see. Then he thought she was sort of stupid, even for a kid.

His memory flashed back to his boyhood. He was walking down the middle of the street at dusk, sweating lightly after a basketball game. There were crickets and the muted barks of dogs and the low, affirming mumble of people on their front porches. Securely held by the warm night and its sounds, he felt an exquisite blend of happiness and sorrow that life could contain this perfect moment, and a sadness that he would soon arrive home, walk into bright light, and be on his way into the next day, with its loud noise and alarming possibility. He resolved to hold this evening walk in his mind forever, to imprint in a permanent place all the sensations that occurred to him as he walked by the Oat-landers' house, so that he could always take them out and look at them. He dimly recalled feeling that if he could successfully do that, he could stop time and hold it.

He knew he had to go home soon. He didn't want to talk about the article with Marsha, but the idea of sitting in the house with her and not talking about it was hard to bear. He imagined the conversation grinding into being, a future conversation with Kitty gestating within it. The conversation was a vast, complex machine like those that occasionally appeared in his dreams; if he could only pull the switch, everything would be all right, but he felt too stupefied by the weight and complexity of the thing to do so. Besides, in this case, everything might not be all right. He put the magazine under his seat and started the car.

Marsha was in her armchair, reading. She looked up, and the expression on her face seemed like the result of internal conflict as complicated and strong as his own, but cross-pulled in different directions, uncomprehending of him and what he knew. In his mind, he withdrew from her so quickly that for a moment the familiar room was fraught with the inexplicable horror of a banal nightmare. Then the ordinariness of the scene threw the extraordinary event of the day into relief, and he felt so angry and bewildered he could've howled.

"Everything all right, Stew?" asked Marsha.

"No, nothing is all right. I'm a tired old man in a shitty world I don't want to be in. I go out there, it's like walking on knives. Everything is an attack—the ugliness, the cheapness, the rudeness, everything." He sensed her withdrawing from him into her own world of disgruntlement, her lips drawn together in that look of exasperated perseverance she'd gotten from her mother. Like Kitty, like everyone else, she was leaving him. "I don't have a real daughter, and I don't have a real wife who's here with me, because she's too busy running around on some—"

"We've been through this before. We agreed I could—"

"That was different! That was when we had two cars!" His voice tore through his throat in a jagged whiplash and came out a cracked half scream. "I don't have a car, remember? That means I'm stranded, all alone for hours, and Norm Pisarro can call me up and casually tell me that my lesbian daughter has just betrayed me in a national magazine and what do I think about that?" He wanted to punch the wall until his hand was bloody. He wanted Kitty to see the blood. Marsha's expression broke into soft, openmouthed consternation. The helplessness of it made his anger seem huge and terrible, then impotent and helpless itself. He sat down on the couch and, instead of anger, felt pain.

"What did Kitty do? What happened? What does Norm have—"

"She wrote an article in *Self* magazine about being a lesbian and her problems and something to do with me. I don't know; I could barely read the crap."

Marsha looked down at her nails.

He looked at her and saw the aged beauty of her ivory skin, sagging under the weight of her years and her cockeyed bifocals, the emotional receptivity of her face, the dark down on her upper lip, the childish pearl buttons of her sweater, only the top button done.

"I'm surprised at Norm, that he would call you like that."

"Oh, who the hell knows what he thought." His heart was soothed and slowed by her words, even if they didn't address its real unhappiness.

"Here," she said. "Let me rub your shoulders."

He allowed her to approach him, and they sat sideways on the couch, his weight balanced on the edge by his awkwardly planted legs, she sitting primly on one hip with her legs tightly crossed. The discomfort of the position negated the practical value of the massage, but he welcomed her touch. Marsha had strong, intelligent hands that spoke to his muscles of deep safety and love and the delight of physical life. In her effort, she leaned close, and her sweatered breast touched him, releasing his tension almost against his will. Through half-closed eyes he observed her sneakers on the floor—he could not quite get over this phenomenon of adult women wearing what had been boys' shoes—in the dim light, one toe atop the other as though cuddling, their laces in pretty disorganization.

Poor Kitty. It hadn't really been so bad that she hadn't set the table on time. He couldn't remember why he and Marsha had been so angry over the table. Unless it was Kitty's coldness, her always turning away, her sarcastic voice. But she was a teenager, and that's what teenagers did. Well, it was too bad, but it couldn't be helped now.

He thought of his father. That was too bad too, and nobody was writing articles about that. There had been a distance between them, so great and so absolute that the word "distance" seemed inadequate to describe it. But that was probably because he had known his father only when he was a very young child; if his father had lived longer, perhaps they would've become closer. He could recall his father's face clearly only at the breakfast table, where it appeared silent and still except for lip and jaw motions, comforting in its constancy. His father ate his oatmeal with one hand working the spoon, one elbow on the table, eyes down, sometimes his other hand holding a cold rag to his head, which always hurt with what seemed to be a noble pain, willingly taken on with his duties as a husband and father. He had loved to stare at the big face with its deep lines and long earlobes, its thin lips and loose, loopily chewing jaws. Its almost god-like stillness and expressionlessness filled him with admiration and reassurance, until one day his father slowly looked up from his cereal, met his eyes, and said, "Stop staring at me, you little shit."

In the other memories, his father was a large, heavy body with a vague oblong face. He saw him sleeping in the armchair in the living room, his large, hairy-knuckled hands grazing the floor. He saw him walking up the front walk with the quick, clipped steps that he always used coming home from work, the straight-backed choppy gait that gave the big body an awesome mechanical-ness. His shirt was wet under the arms, his head was down, the eyes were abstracted but alert, as though keeping careful watch on the outside world in case something nasty came at him while he attended to the more important business inside.

"The good parent in yourself."

What did the well-meaning idiots who thought of these phrases mean by them? When a father dies, he is gone; there is no tiny, smiling daddy who appears, waving happily, in a secret pocket in your chest. Some kinds of loss are absolute. And no amount of self-realization or self-expression will change that.

As if she had heard him, Marsha urgently pressed her weight into her hands and applied all her strength to relaxing his muscles. Her sweat and scented deodorant filtered through her sweater, which added its muted wooliness to her smell. "All righty!" She rubbed his shoulders and briskly patted him. He reached back and touched her hand in thanks.

Across from where they sat had once been a red chair, and in it had once sat Kitty, looking away from him, her fist hiding her face.

"You're a lesbian? Fine," he said. "You mean nothing to me. You walk out that door, it doesn't matter. And if you come back in, I'm going to spit in your face. I don't care if I'm on my deathbed, I'll still have the energy to spit in your face."

She did not move when he said that. Tears ran over her fist and down her arm, but she didn't look at him.

Marsha's hands lingered on him for a moment. Then she moved and sat away from him on the couch.

Dagoberto Gilb

WINNERS ON THE PASS LINE

DAGOBERTO GILB (1950–) was born in Los Angeles and spent many years in El Paso. His most recent novel is *The Flowers*. His previous works are *Gritos*, an essay collection and a finalist for the National Book Critics Circle Award; *Woodcuts of Women; The Last Known Residence of Mickey Acuña;* and *The Magic of Blood*, which won the 1994 PEN/Hemingway Award and was a PEN/ Faulkner finalist. His fiction and nonfiction are anthologized widely and have appeared in a range of magazines including *The New Yorker, The Threepenny Review, Harper's, Latina,* and *The Texas Observer*. Gilb spent most of his adult years as a construction worker and a journeyman high-rise carpenter with the United Brotherhood of Carpenters. He lives in Austin, Texas.

In an office swivel chair, Ray Muñoz faced his jobsite and a pane of fixed glass. He'd missed a few days of work without explanation and the field superintendent was due anytime. He would be expected to say something. Only one of the foremen had even brought up his absence this morning, asking with an uncomfortable laugh whether Ray had tied one on or what.

The majority of the men were huddled in pairs and small groups near the coffee truck next to the gate, holding styrofoam cups and sandwiches and burritos, the steam from which quickly became indistinguishable from the overcast sky. Ray could hear a couple of them near his window talking about the leftovers they still had from Thanksgiving, about Christmas, about the sex in the movie last night and about what they were probably going to do today at the job. They were sitting on a stack of large but not full sheets of plywood waiting for the foreman to start them to work. When the time came, Ray rocked in his swivel chair and watched the wobbly manlift roll up the cable line to the eighteenth and the nineteenth floors where most of the men unloaded, and then to the roof where the lift clicked off to let two laborers load several empty oxygen and acetylene bottles. He saw the operator pull the cage door together when they were finished and the counterweight rise as the manlift coasted down where stragglers were waiting for the next trip up.

Ray thought about how only a few years ago he believed he'd be wearing leather bags into retirement. Never did he imagine a chair and a secretary. He worked construction with callused hands that made the tools feel like they had grips, hands that held so many nails and hammers for so many hours they stayed clenched like fists in his off hours. But they earned him a living, not a rich one, but enough not to be ashamed. He remembered how his wife changed his thinking about that. She told him he should stop thinking like he'd just crossed the border and couldn't do better and to remember the where of his birth, to think about the miracle of possibilities on this side. He knew she was right about miracles because he could touch her with his palms and fingers, always cut and smashed and lumpy with splinters, always dry because of cement and rust, and they could still record the sensation of such a contrary texture. That she fell in love with him should have sent him back faithfully to Mass every Sunday. There was no other explanation: she'd been to college and still married him and lived his life of wages and alcohol, rented apartments and, when children came, rented houses which would never have been homes otherwise. Houston was her idea. He never would have left El Paso. But she was convinced there were opportunities and she was the smart one. And soon there was a new truck, then a new house, and finally, when he got this job, a savings account he planned to surprise her with someday.

His secretary peeked through a crack in the door. "You're here," she said as though he never was. "Sorry I'm late. I'm making some coffee right now." He didn't say anything to her. He'd fired his last secretary six months ago for not typing well enough and being on the phone too much, but the real reason was that she'd been coming on to him and that was too disruptive to his life. He'd already had his youth, was what he'd decided, and this new world, Houston, had offered him winning dice: while his childhood friends were still struggling near the border, he'd become a superintendent in a major construction company. He was on a roll and he didn't want to complicate the betting.

He should have known better. Looking back, it was easy to see. Just as his wife had started teasing him about that secretary, she'd been telling him about all the women she worked with at her job in the federal building, about all the fantasies and even affairs that began at their more than an hour lunch breaks with lawyers and government administrators and sometimes diplomats. She even told him about the one she met who spoke—besides Spanish—French, German, and even some Russian. He just never suspected, probably because he was so preoccupied with his new status. He just never suspected that she'd moved with the times too.

Before the phone call, Sylvia Molina had been methodically packing their luggage, neatly folding all the clothes that she and her husband and their youngest son might need. She'd been thinking about the things she had learned growing up, because this certainly was not one of them. Vacations were a time when her father got to sleep in and nap in the afternoon and talk about it happily if it was a gift from the job, or worriedly if it was because he was unemployed. She could only remember taking a trip once, to Durango, when her grandmother on her mother's side died. Her father's parents were from this side and lived with them.

"Are you just about done?" her husband asked.

"Uh-huh."

"And Jimmy . . ."

"Is already over at Peter's." She said that strongly and it even surprised her.

"Is everything okay?"

She could hear the department store's Christmas music in the background. A voiceless Noel. "I'm a little nervous. I don't know why."

"We'll have a good time. Look, I'll be home in an hour, maybe two. I gotta go."

Sylvia hung up the phone guiltily. Everything mental told her that the trip was going to go well. A weekend in Las Vegas before her husband got bogged down with the holidays and then inventory. They'd catch a show, gamble, have a few drinks, eat out. Neither of them had been there before. And it was she who'd wanted to do something exciting.

Excitement, she believed, must be a word belonging to her generation. Her mother had never mentioned the concept to her. What might pass for it in their home came through living next door to Mr. Rodriguez, who would often come home drunk in the middle of the night and would sometimes try to get in his locked front door instead of sleeping in his car. Mrs. Rodriguez would scream at him and the neighborhood about whores and the devil, diseases and lice. Then there was Rudy Rodriguez, their oldest son, who had brought police cars to the street more than once, and Mike, their next oldest, who was a football star at UT-Austin and even tried out for a pro team. She didn't remember her sisters seeming too concerned about the feeling of excitement either. The older one married when she was twenty, and the big thing in her life was a wedding ceremony and reception and her first baby. She never wanted to leave El Paso for even a drive. Her other sister went to college to get married but ended up a schoolteacher and, as far as she knew, was still a virgin.

Sylvia herself had chosen security when there'd been a choice. Her husband now hadn't been her boyfriend then. But he wanted to marry her and had a degree from college and a good job with a future, which was the life she was leading today. He was already a floor manager at a major department store in Huntington Beach, they were paying off a mortgage on a four-bedroom house in an almost new development only a mile from the ocean, and they lived on a stainless street where there was no concept of race or creed and where the gloom of unemployment and bad times she heard about over the color television seemed as distant as Mexico. Though they were by no means rich, they could make all their payments on time, and for her birthday her husband had even bought her a microwave oven she never asked for or wanted.

She didn't often think about the boy she didn't marry. She was in high school, which he'd only been to for two years before he dropped out. He lived wherever anybody would let him if he didn't have money, and sometimes that was in the county jail. He told her he loved her but she probably would have let him even if he hadn't said it. That was a winter night when a windhard hail broke out the windowpane in his rented room off Montana Street. He got up naked, his eyes the only part of him that seemed to have to adjust to the black wind, water cresting his cheekbones and rolling down his back, and he took nails and a hammer from his workbags and made a shutter out of an empty dresser drawer he disassembled with his fist. It was still cold but they were laughing under his blankets because he said there was nothing to worry about, they still had two more drawers with nothing in them.

Ray withdrew all the money from his account. It was, by accident, a thousand for each of their ten years. Not much by Houston standards, but enough to make him feel gold-plated when he visited back home, and it might have been only the beginning. It had crossed his mind more than once to put it down on some land—he imagined building a house near the river, planting some trees, raising thoroughbreds, starting up a ranch not unlike the one his father spent his life working on—but he never kidded himself about how far away he was from that. He didn't know what he'd do with it now. He'd been considering a swimming pool, but he always recalled the lean, unemployed times when he wished he'd had enough of a cushion to wait for the better jobs. Good and bad construction workers, including superintendents, came and went for lots of reasons, and he'd taught himself not to be surprised when he was handed an extra check on pay day with "layoff" stamped on it. This time maybe he could have kept the job, but he didn't offer the company's field boss an excuse for his time off because he didn't want to talk about his wife and children. He didn't know how to explain such things because he'd never learned how and it never occurred to him that he might have to. Layoff checks were to be expected. They always made some sense.

He took the money from the account and cashed his checks. The ten thousand he wanted in hundred-dollar bills. He agreed that he was acting a little crazy but it was a decision as certain as the cash would be in his pocket and the bank manager spent several hours making sure he got it once Ray assured him that he knew exactly what he was doing.

He drank only one beer on the airplane. He sat next to a window in the non-smoking section and no one sat next to him. Sometimes he shut his eyes, but he didn't sleep. When he opened them he'd see the wing of the airplane shudder. There weren't enough clouds to look at, and the earth seemed only slightly more alive than one of his hundred-dollar bills. Thinking like this shamed him somehow, and he prayed he'd be forgiven such a huge ingratitude.

• • •

Sylvia relaxed considerably when she saw the green road sign that told them Las Vegas was 175 miles away. She'd examined her map too many times and her husband had noticed. He'd wanted her to go to the auto club and get a new map and make reservations through it because that was what they paid for. But she insisted that she could do it all herself. Everything about this, even calling for hotel prices and making reservations over toll-free telephone lines, even marking out the simple route on a map, had become like a statement of independence for her, a muscling-up in challenge to what in any mind was a contented, idyllic life. And she took it very seriously. She was determined to have things go her way, to direct the flow of events without suggestions or advice or cautions. She was doing this with "her" money, alloting a certain amount for the hotel, food, entertainment, gas, a certain amount for her husband to gamble with, a certain amount for her gambling. She'd figured all this as a debit in her bookkeeping, but she also figured that her winning would verify something, would mean something, though she had no idea what. Winning was her hope, and though she pretended otherwise, she clung to it religiously.

"Do you see that sign?" her husband said to their son. " 'Eat Gas.' Those oil companies think of everything."

The boy was fidgety and Sylvia told him to go to sleep and when he woke up they'd be there, even though she knew that if he did she'd pay by having to stay up late with him. She could have easily left him at home with the older boy, but she wanted him along for an excuse. With him, they'd have to do their gambling separately, in shifts. She gave her husband another reason for taking the four-year-old along.

"It's great to get on the road, isn't it?" her husband asked her. "And in a big, comfortable car. Who would have thought? Think we'll see Frank Sinatra?"

She smiled. She never doubted that she made a good choice marrying him. He was ordinary in the best ways, watching football games on Monday nights, taking the children to amusement parks every month and her to a restaurant every week or so. His pride would show when they went back to visit their parents, and when someone asked him where they lived, he would say down the street from Carlos Palomino, though in fact they had no idea where the fighter lived, only that it was supposed to be within the same city limits. His small exaggerations like that made up for his unstartling existence, kept him in touch with his neighborhood friends still linked to the less affluent, working class suburb he grew up in. He was a good man, and, most importantly, he loved her.

"It's pretty here," she told him.

He chuckled at her. "I guess."

"In a different way. It's still open. The sky looks like El Paso's."

"I guess I see what you mean. I guess."

• • •

Ray came to gamble, but instead he wandered through casinos and lost money, betting randomly at dice tables the house favorites like the hard ten and hard four and any craps, and, while at the roulette table, the single numbers and always the double zero. Each time he played a twenty-dollar bill from his paychecks and each time a dealer or a croupier would turn his green paper into red chips which would be eased away and clicked into perfect stacks. He was aimless enough even to play the dollar slots, and when he won sixty dollars, his first winning since he got there, he tinkled and spun away the time until every silver dollar was gone on a triple and double and single line play. When he decided he wanted to sit and drink he settled on seven-card stud with a ten dollar buy-in and alternated between whiskey, his Houston drink, and rum and coke, his Juárez drink. He tried to fill flushes when he had three of the same suit and the high hand showed the same face cards, and he would raise with a low pair under and a low pair up and invariably lose to a full house or a flush. During one hand, he stayed in on three raises each on the last two cards when he had a chance of a high straight, and lost to three nines. After this he simply played drunk, seven rounds worth, waiting for more cards that never came to drop in front of him, losing three hundred dollars more. When he finally stumbled through the tall heavy doors of the casino and stood underneath the heaven of hundred-watt bulbs above the main entrance, watching old men with young women exit limousines with two-hundred-watt shines, with the bells and tingles and shuffles, the melody of all this ringing between his ears like a phrase from a song he heard on the car radio when he walked into work, it occurred to him that he didn't have to do it this way, that he could win.

He lay down on the bed of his hotel room, listening to the television he'd left on while he'd been out. The movie was *Lawrence of Arabia* and the voice he heard was Anthony Quinn's. He didn't feel drunk anymore, but very alone, and sad. Those days he'd spent in his empty house were angry, and he'd paced, opening drawers and cabinets like he would find something, waiting like he knew what he was waiting for. He'd cried like his youngest son and he only slept an hour or two at intervals throughout the day and night. He wanted to feel alone, but in the morning newspapers scuffed sidewalks and cars would drive off, children would walk to school. In the afternoon he could hear a neighbor's soap operas if he went to the right window in his house, and a meter man passed through his backyard. In the evening the cars would return and there'd be football, basketball, rock 'n' roll. From midnight to dawn a digital clock whirred. He was in this new world and he could be hidden, but not alone. Here he was. He turned off the television, letting the darkened room loom with images of the wooden steps outside his office, with a picture of his wife changing her clothes near him, of his children boarding an airplane for a stay in El Paso while he and his wife sorted things out, of his own childhood there, the dirt baseball diamonds, the dirt driveway where he pulled the engine from his first car, the girls he loved so purely, the candles he lit on holidays, the stupid fights he won and lost, his marriage and the move from El Paso and his mother's tears, his father's bony handshake—all as distant and dry as that blue sky, as a story he could tell his children who could speak only English.

He heard voices in the hallway. Young men persuading young women to go in. When their door closed, their existence muffled away, and that was good to him. He had even been about to fall into sleep when he heard something that squeezed his heart until he stood up, frightened, and held still for several seconds. He nudged his shoulder into a wall and heard the hymn music coming from the room next door, from a television or radio. Jesus, the lover of my soul, sung by a choir, accompanied by an organ. He went back to bed relieved. He couldn't take any more surprises and for a moment he thought he'd gone over the ledge. He felt very weary now, even thought he would get some sleep, and he stayed on his back, in the center of the king-size bed, getting up many times throughout the night and morning to drink and to piss, expecting sleep any time, resting in the dark.

"What's all this stuff about El Paso?" her husband asked.

"I don't know," Sylvia said like a thief.

"Are you homesick? Is it Christmas? You could go there this Christmas if you want. It's only me that has to be around home this year."

"No."

"Because you don't have to stay home. You could take the boys back with you."

"I don't want to go. I didn't realize I was talking about it that much."

"You could stay those two weeks school's out. I could get an airplane and spend the day."

"I don't want to. Honest. There's just something about Las Vegas that reminds me of it, that's all."

Her husband sighed and fell onto the bed. "You were talking about it before we got here," he reminded her.

Sylvia didn't argue because he was right. She felt embarrassed and wanted the subject changed. "We can all see the Captain and Tennille," she proposed.

"I don't know why you're acting so weird about it. Wanting to be with your family is as Mexican as having babies."

"Let's eat dinner and everything."

"All right," he yawned, stretching on one of the two hard beds in the bright hotel room.

"We'll go make a reservation at that booth we saw in the lobby and you take a nap."

"Good thinking," he said, yawning again.

She took her son's hand and the room key and went out the door and said hello to the two maids, a Black and an Asian, who stopped talking as she and the boy passed almost running.

Once Ray made the decision to win, he knew the first thing to do was to have control, so he began by observing the play at dice tables and cards without drinking or gambling. He passed many innocuous hours and finally took a seat at a seven-card stud game and tested his will. He set a two-hour limit on himself. He didn't play when he got bad hole cards, and when one of the players was on a winning streak he didn't stay in if he had a weak though solid hand. When he held a good hand he bet moderately and raised only the last two deals. When he left the table it was with forty dollars more than he had when he sat down.

Later that evening he removed his envelope with the ten thousand dollars from his safe-deposit box at the hotel and walked it to a Texas Hold 'Em table which required a two-hundred-dollar buy-in. A simple game, each player getting two cards down which he combines with five cards the dealer turns up on the middle of the table, it is also a game of big winners and big losers, and this one was for particularly high stakes, even by Vegas standards. Already a second row of spectators strained to see over those in the first row, who snuggled against the metal railing that partitioned them off from the players, all of whom showed a minimum of a thousand dollars in green twenty-five-dollar chips and red five-dollar ones.

Ray took the seat at the top of the oval and counted out five thousand dollars, which were quickly transformed into chips for the dealer by a young woman, and his swell of stacks beat all but two of the players, an obese New Yorker with a slobbish cigar and a bag of green chips, and a slit-eyed, deep Southerner who hid under a cap and peered above several highrise-like piles.

Ray played conservatively in the beginning, in order to follow the betting. He quickly discovered that there were really only three serious gamblers—the Southerner, who bought a few hands with large raises and was challenged only one time by the New Yorker, whose two pair beat one, and a Hollywood movie type who lost with average hands, but whose pocket was so full of hundred-dollar bills he didn't seem to worry about it, and an Arab who would never show his cards.

After two hours Ray was about eight hundred dollars down. He had won a hand, dropped out of three, and paid to see two. He'd drunk one shot of whiskey early to settle his nerves and it must have worked because, even though he was behind, he felt a confidence he hadn't remembered since he married his wife, since he accepted the job as superintendent. It was something that only happened to a person a few times but which was as palpable as silver dollars in the pocket: he belonged there, an equal to the best, his hidden status hovering over him like a fawning lover. He knew, and he was certain they knew, he was going to walk away a winner.

His chance came about an hour later when he got two tens underneath, spades and diamonds, and the first card the dealer showed was a seven of hearts. The guy from Hollywood bet unusually high, five hundred, and only the Arab and the Southerner, besides himself, stayed. The next card was a two of spades, and he stayed in for the next five-hundred-dollar bet, and for the five hundred more the Southerner used to scare away the other two.

The dealer turned a ten of clubs and Ray met the Southerner's next five hundred with a thousand-dollar raise. When the Southerner notched it up another, he matched it and shoved in all the chips in front of him.

"Let's play 'em up," the Southerner smiled when he called the bet. The table was excited, but no one moved. Ray didn't really understand what he was supposed to do.

"Let's see what ya got there, friend."

"Turn 'em up," suggested the New Yorker. "He wants to negotiate."

He showed his tens. The Southerner had two hearts. It was three tens against a possible flush.

"I'll give ya two to one on the pot," offered the Southerner.

Ray didn't even think it over. He shook his head confidently. Jack of hearts.

"Fifty-fifty," said the Southerner, who'd stood up to see.

Ray shook his head again.

Two of hearts.

The Southerner was immodestly happy and the spectators breathed loudly as he pushed his chair away and reached in for the pot and, nearly hopping, stacked his mound of winnings to new heights. He talked voluably to the players sitting beside him and gave an unsporting stare of triumph at the loser.

Ray counted out four thousand dollars more. He felt more dazed than defeated, weak-kneed but standing. He was more disappointed than angry, not at the Southerner or himself, but at the deeper injustice of things. It did not make sense. It was not fair.

He thought that maybe he should pull out right then as the cards were being dealt around again. If he backed out, he could spare himself more loss. That would be the sensible thing to do considering the realities of unemployment, even in Houston. And chances were that he would be wearing those work bags again. He felt blurred by his insecurity, but in this fuzz he made out a queen on the table to match the queen-four in his hand.

He stayed in, as did the Arab and the moviemaker, as did the Southerner, who seemed to be playing this one for fun while he continued to reorganize his chips. After the dealer turned up a four and an ace, Ray upped the pot by five hundred on his two pair, and all stayed.

The dealer turned over another four and Ray made it another five hundred. The Arab dropped out, the moviemaker saw the bet, and the Southerner raised it another five hundred.

The last card was a king. Ray bet another five hundred on his full house, figuring the Southerner to play for that. The moviemaker considered the stakes and his chances, then threw in his cards.

"That plus five," said the Southerner carelessly.

Ray saw that and bet the rest without hesitating.

"I gotta see this one, amigo," the Southerner said. "Let's see what you can do."

Ray matched his queen-four to the table's queen-two fours.

The Southerner could barely contain himself. He flipped over a king-four and hugged the chips to his corner, crying for some racks to put all his money in. The New Yorker laughed. The other players felt no happiness for him, though they showed no signs of pity for the loser either.

Ray walked evenly to his hotel, contented only by knowing that in this defeat he had not been a fool because they were such strong hands that he couldn't have played them any other way. He couldn't say that about many losses. He'd done this gambling to win, and someone else had the better luck, and only luck. It was not always so simple. His wife, for instance, had left him for a richer man who she'd fallen in love with.

He was not sure what to expect next because he was taken by an unusual mood. Late by work standards, it was still early in Las Vegas. He turned off the lights and opened a window to a windless, cold desert, a range of mountains and below a tall, arching sky. He listened for something but all he got was some hotel machine and puffs of traffic. It was maybe okay that he lost, even justice of a kind. It was fresh like the cold air, like the winter air in El Paso.

Ray Muñoz closed his eyes on the bed. He waited to shiver with some strong emotion. Instead fell asleep in the chilled silence of the sanitized hotel room.

"I don't see how people can do it," her husband said after his night out alone. "It goes too fast and hurts too much."

"Did you win?"

"In a sense. I stopped contributing to the cause."

Sylvia looked away from him.

"You know, I think they've got it rigged, because when I played the dollar slot machines I won right away, on my first pulls. Something like thirty or forty dollars. I thought I had it made, but I never won again after that."

"Is that all you played?" she asked, angry.

"No, I played some blackjack too. It's something, this place. There's so much happening. This man that sat by me was playing twenty dollars a hand and was winning for a long time, but when he started losing he started betting more money. That's how it is here, easy come, easy go. I think the guy was drunk. Did you know that all the drinks are free? Anyway, I couldn't take it. I don't think I can take winning or losing, though it is fun to watch. I wandered all around the casino and counted all the money that other people lost. That felt better than losing all mine."

"Mine," she said seriously.

"Ours," he said automatically. "And I can't waste it. Maybe if it was money someone gave me and told me I *had* to gamble with."

"I did," Sylvia said.

"And then again I doubt if I could do that," he laughed without hearing her. "Hey, we're gonna have to take the baby to the circus shows they have at night. There were these stunt motorcyclists driving inside this ball and it scared the pants off me." He yawned. "I tried to win him a stuffed animal while I was up there. How long's he been asleep?"

"A few hours."

"Too bad they don't have babysitters. It'd be fun to have a drink together." He pulled her down on the bed and even touched her breasts.

"He'll wake up," she said.

He rolled off. "I guess I'm a little drunk already." He looked at the television screen. "What're you watching?"

"I just found it an hour ago. It's a program on how to play the casino games."

"They think of everything, don't they?"

"It's exciting."

"It's not worth the risk though."

"Do you really think that?"

"Yes. I really don't think you can win. Las Vegas exists because people lose. The only money I'd like giving them would be to own a piece of it."

She turned off the television. "I've already seen it twice."

"Leave it on. Maybe there's a Frank Sinatra movie."

Ray slept twelve uninterrupted hours, got up and drank water at the bathroom sink, and slept three more. When the sleep was over, and he shook the blood loose in his veins, he felt what he least expected, like he'd won.

He counted the ten crisp hundred-dollar bills he still had. He counted seven twenties he had in his wallet.

His plan had become very simple. He would go back to El Paso and see his children, he would talk to his brothers and sisters, listen to his mother, visit his father's grave, and, no matter what happened tonight, he would go home a winner.

• • •

Sylvia stood under a wide archway that divided the hotel lobby from the casino. For two days she'd seen and heard this, but now she was by herself, awed by how quiet it really was and how alone it could make her feel.

She wanted very much to age past this stage in her life. She didn't think it was right of her and she felt guilty and spoiled. Had she not been so fortunate, had she made different choices along the way, she knew she would probably want nothing more than what she had, and she would have undoubtedly settled for less.

She had no idea what her purpose was in this. She didn't know what kind of answer this would present her with, what she would do with it. She only knew that winning would be an answer, and that losing would be an answer. She didn't know which would be preferable, and still she was determined to win.

That evening Ray turned the thousand dollars into chips and leaned into a craps table. He played intelligently, and when he didn't feel right, he didn't place any bets. He waited for the dice and a hot hand. He was up, but not making a killing.

Sylvia had not been doing well. She took cards for blackjack and lost, she laid chips on red and black numbers for roulette and lost, though both by the inconclusive nibble of small wagers. She was more short of time than patience or money. And though she had been afraid of craps because the betting was so complicated, and though she was aware that she could just as easily spend her fortune waiting on the click of a ball at a spinning wheel or the snap of a laminated card on a baize table, she knew it had to be the padded tumble of dice.

At first Ray didn't find anything too special about the attractive woman who came to stand across from him, and it was only because he didn't want to bet on a few rolls that he noticed her choosing the poorer odds on the table, like the field and the hard-way numbers. So he watched her, and then he stared at her, and he did this until he felt he had to, until the casino had become nothing more than a faded backdrop of noise and light and color to her. Like the sight of a pretty girlfriend long forgotten, she flushed him with such a strong emotion that it didn't seem a memory but an awakening as conclusive as the one he'd left his hotel with. He stared, certain he didn't know her and never had.

Sylvia had very early become used to men's eyes, and had learned that even though she couldn't ignore them, she could walk away from them. But rather than being distracted by this large man who gawked at her so childlike, she became more focused and sharp. His unwilled admiration was the warmest luck she'd played with all night.

When she was offered the dice by the stickman, Sylvia was down to her last three nickel chips, while Ray was three hundred above his original thousand. When she accepted the dice and bet one five-dollar chip on a pass, Ray put four hundred on the same and then the full extent of the double odds on her point of four, which she threw on the next toss. He put up a thousand on another pass while she let her ten dollars ride and threw a ten. He backed his thousand with two more on the odds, which, like the four, paid two to one. She rolled two times before a four-six combination appeared.

"Winners on the pass line!" the stickman barked. "The table's got a shooter!"

Ray counted out five hundred dollars worth of the chips the dealer gave him in winnings and slid them over to Sylvia. "Please," he said. "Give it back only if we win."

She might have refused, but she was gagged by confusion. She picked up the dice and threw.

"Seven! *Big* winners on the *pass* line!"

Ray wouldn't take back the money he'd left her in the pass line area, and Sylvia considered setting the loan aside in the rack in front of her, but gave into it, to him, and played the line. She had become the one watching now, watching him, and never had she felt so in control and out of control at the same time.

Ray bet on her pass with certainty and when she had a point he took as many come and odds bets as he could get, and she shot lots of numbers. Sylvia let Ray's pass line money ride and made her point three more times in a row, which multiplied into winnings of four thousand dollars. Ray quit when he counted close to forty thousand, and it took racks to carry the chips to the cashier's window.

"Thank you so much," Sylvia said uncomfortably, as though she were standing under her front door porch light. She held out the money she owed him.

"I want you to keep it," he told her in Spanish.

She believed that he was not making some haughty or suave or even the slightest of an insincere gesture. But she did expect him to say something about a drink or food. She'd already thought of how probably she'd have to say no, say something about her husband and son who were waiting, but he did not ask, and it did not seem because he was so overwhelmed by his winnings.

Sylvia checked to see that her husband was asleep beside her and listened for her son's breathing in the bed near them. She touched herself slowly. At first it was her hand and then it was not. At first she made her stiff fingers tingle across her skin, and then her palms flattened and her fingers softened and bent. Sometimes the hand would even reach her face, her lips, her eyes. She was warm and unlonely. She felt young and she liked the familiar cold air settling above the blanket. She knew that she could not leave the window open long, but she let herself enjoy every moment it was.

· · ·

In bed much later that night, Ray was thinking again of Sylvia. He had not cheated on his wife in those ten years of marriage, and though as a young man he had a better than average share of dates, he had not had that many lovers, and those he did have he looked back on as much in defeat as in conquest. Maybe he'd be different this time out. He thought of Sylvia and he felt her as though she were next to him on the vacant side of the bed. He felt her without moving, sexually, and he liked it very much.

Sylvia and Ray stared at one another as he came into the restaurant for break-fast. He'd chosen the place randomly and seeing her again, by chance, inspired some strange confidence in him.

Sylvia didn't want to draw him into a conversation so she looked away. Sitting there, patiently waiting for her husband to eat his meal, tested her until she realized that Ray wasn't going to say anything. Then she felt very alive.

When her husband finished, Sylvia stood, glancing at Ray self-consciously. Her son scooted the wooden chair away from the table noisily and ran out to the other side of the glass door and smashed his face on it to see back inside. He made faces at Ray, who smiled at him from his table.

"Big tip or little?" her husband asked her. "Maybe we should save some to make up for all the losses. We still gotta get home." He left twenty percent.

She couldn't let herself look at Ray on her way out, but she walked down the restaurant's aisle worried about her appearance. When her husband caught up with her, she still couldn't think of what to say.

"Are you feeling okay?" her husband asked.

"Just sleepy is all."

"Too much action without the old man last night, huh? You can nap on the way home."

She took his hand.

"You sure you don't want to go and visit the family for Christmas?"

"No, really, I only wanted to do this. And I had a good time. I always wanted to know about Las Vegas, and now I do." She squeezed his hand.

Outside the restaurant, on the famous Strip, Ray couldn't help but notice the flat plain of black asphalt that belted the underlying desert, couldn't help but realize that the miracle of these steel and concrete casinos and hotels and res-taurants were doomed by the wind and the sun and the sand, couldn't help but feel good that he was moving around in this impermanent place like a winner.

Ron Hansen

WICKEDNESS

RON HANSEN (1947–) is the author, most recently, of the novel *Isn't It Romantic?* and a book of essays called *A Stay Against Confusion: Essays on Faith and Fiction.* Among his other books are *Desperadoes, The Assassination of Jesse James by the Coward Robert Ford, Nebraska, Mariette in Ecstasy, Atticus,* and a children's book, *The Shadowmaker.* A native of Omaha, he received the Award in Literature from the American Academy and Institute of Arts and Letters for *Nebraska,* a collection of short fiction. He is Gerard Manley Hopkins SJ Professor of the Arts and Humanities at Santa Clara University.

At the end of the nineteenth century a girl from Delaware got on a milk train in Omaha and took a green wool seat in the second-class car. August was outside the window, and sunlight was a yellow glare on the trees. Up front, a railway conductor in a navy-blue uniform was gingerly backing down the aisle with a heavy package in a gunnysack that a boy was helping him with. They were talking about an agreeable seat away from the hot Nebraska day that was persistent outside, and then they were setting their cargo across the runnered aisle from the girl and tilting it against the shellacked wooden wall of the railway car before walking back up the aisle and elsewhere into August.

She was sixteen years old and an Easterner just recently hired as a county schoolteacher, but she knew enough about prairie farming to think the heavy package was a crank-and-piston washing machine or a boxed plowshare and coulter, something no higher than the bloody stump where the poultry were chopped with a hatchet and then wildly high-stepped around the yard. Soon, however, there was a juggling movement and the gunnysack slipped aside, and she saw an old man sitting there, his limbs hacked away, and dark holes where his ears ought to have been, the skin pursed at his jaw hinge like pink lips in a kiss. The milk train jerked into a roll through the railway yard, and the old man was jounced so that his gray cheek pressed against the hot window glass. Although he didn't complain, it seemed an uneasy position, and the girl wished she had the courage to get up from her seat and tug the jolting body upright. She instead got to her page in *Quo Vadis* and pretended to be so rapt by the book that she didn't look up again until Columbus, where a doctor with liquorice on his breath sat heavily beside her and openly stared over his newspaper before whispering that the poor man was a carpenter in Genoa who'd been caught out in the great blizzard of 1888. Had she heard of that one?

The girl shook her head.

She ought to look out for their winters, the doctor said. Weather in Nebraska could be the wickedest thing she ever saw.

She didn't know what to say, so she said nothing. And at Genoa a young teamster got on in order to carry out the old man, whose half body was heavy enough that the boy had to yank the gunnysack up the aisle like 60 pounds of mail.

In the year 1888, on the twelfth day of January, a pink sun was up just after seven and southeastern zephyrs of such soft temperature were sailing over the Great Plains that squatters walked their properties in high rubber boots and April jackets and some farmhands took off their Civil War greatcoats to rake silage into the cattle troughs. However, sheep that ate whatever they could the night before raised their heads away from food and sniffed the salt tang in the air. And all that morning streetcar mules were reported to be acting up, nipping each other, jingling the hitch rings, foolishly waggling their dark manes and necks as though beset by gnats and horseflies.

A Danish cattleman named Axel Hansen later said he was near the Snake River and tipping a teaspoon of saleratus into a yearling's mouth when he heard a faint groaning in the north that was like the noise of a high waterfall at a fair distance. Axel looked toward Dakota, and there half the sky was suddenly gray and black and indigo blue with great storm clouds that were seething up as high as the sun and wrangling toward him at horse speed. Weeds were being uprooted, sapling trees were bullwhipping, and the top inches of snow and prairie soil were being sucked up and stirred like the dirty flour that was called red dog. And then the onslaught hit him hard as furniture, flying him onto his back so that when Axel looked up, he seemed to be deep undersea and in icehouse cold. Eddying snow made it hard to breathe any way but sideways, and getting up to just his knees and hands seemed a great attainment. Although his sod house was but a quarter-mile away, it took Axel four hours to get there. Half his face was frozen gray and hard as weather-boarding so the cattleman was speechless until nightfall, and then Axel Hansen simply told his wife, That was not pleasant.

Cow tails stuck out sideways when the wind caught them. Sparrows and crows whumped hard against the windowpanes, their eyes seeking out an escape, their wings fanned out and flattened as though pinned up in an ornithologist's display. Cats died, dogs died, pigeons died. Entire farms of cattle and pigs and geese and chickens were wiped out in a single night. Horizontal snow that was hard and dry as salt dashed and seethed over everything, sloped up like rooftops, tricked its way across creek beds and ditches, milkily purled down city streets, stole shanties and coops and pens from a bleak landscape that was even then called the Great American Desert. Everything about the blizzard seemed to have personality and hateful intention. Especially the cold. At 6 A.M., the temperature at Valentine, Nebraska, was 30 degrees above zero. Half a day later the temperature was 14 below, a drop of 44 degrees and the difference between having toes and not, between staying alive overnight and not, between ordinary concerns and one overriding idea.

Ainslie Classen was hopelessly lost in the whiteness and tilting low under the jamming gale when his right elbow jarred against a joist of his pigsty. He walked around the sty by skating his sore red hands along the upright shiplap and then squeezed inside through the slops trough. The pigs scampered over to him, seeking his protection, and Ainslie put himself among them, getting down in their stink and their body heat, socking them away only when they ganged up or when two or three presumed he was food. Hurt was nailing into his finger joints until he thought to work his hands into the pigs' hot wastes, and smeared some onto his skin. The pigs grunted around him and intelligently snuffled at his body with their pink and tender noses, and Ainslie thought, *You are not me but I am you*, and Ainslie Classen got through the night without shame or injury.

Whereas a Hartington woman took two steps out her door and disappeared until the snow sank away in April and raised her body up from her garden patch.

An Omaha cigar maker got off the Leavenworth Street trolley that night, 50 yards from his own home and 5 yards from another's. The completeness of the blizzard so puzzled him that the cigar maker tramped up and down the block more than 20 times and then slept against a lamp-post and died.

A cattle inspector froze to death getting up on his quarter horse. The next morning he was still tilting the saddle with his upright weight, one cowboy boot just inside the iced stirrup, one bear-paw mitten over the horn and reins. His quarter horse apparently kept waiting for him to complete his mount, and then the quarter horse died too.

A Chicago boy visiting his brother for the holidays was going to a neighbor's farm to borrow a scoop shovel when the night train of blizzard raged in and overwhelmed him. His tracks showed the boy mistakenly slanted past the sod house he'd just come from, and then tilted forward with perhaps the vain hope of running into some shop or shed or railway depot. His body was found four days later and 27 miles from home.

A forty-year-old wife sought out her husband in the open range land near O'Neill and days later was found standing up in her muskrat coat and black bandanna, her scarf-wrapped hands tightly clenching the top strand of rabbit wire that was keeping her upright, her blue eyes still open but cloudily bottled by a half inch of ice, her jaw unhinged as though she'd died yelling out a name.

The 1 A.M. report from the Chief Signal Officer in Washington, D.C., had said Kansas and Nebraska could expect "fair weather, followed by snow, brisk to high southerly winds gradually diminishing in force, becoming westerly and warmer, followed by colder."

Sin Thomas undertook the job of taking Emily Flint home from their Holt County schoolhouse just before noon. Sin's age was sixteen, and Emily was not only six years younger but also practically kin to him, since her stepfather was Sin's older brother. Sin took the girl's hand and they haltingly tilted against the uprighting gale on their walk to a dark horse, gray-maned and gray-tailed with ice. Sin cracked the reins loose of the crowbar tie-up and helped Emily up onto his horse, jumping up onto the croup from a soapbox and clinging the girl to him as though she were groceries he couldn't let spill.

Everything she knew was no longer there. She was in a book without descriptions. She could put her hand out and her hand would disappear. Although Sin knew the general direction to Emily's house, the geography was so duned and drunk with snow that Sin gave up trying to nudge his horse one way or another and permitted its slight adjustments away from the wind. Hours passed and the horse strayed southeast into Wheeler County, and then in misery and pneumonia it stopped, planting its overworked legs like four parts of an argument and slinging its head away from Sin's yanks and then hanging its nose in anguish. Emily hopped down into the snow and held on to the boy's coat as Sin uncinched the saddle and jerked off a green horse blanket and slapped it against his iron leggings in order to crack the ice from it. And then Sin scooped out a deep nook in a snow slope that was as high and steep as the roof of a New Hampshire house. Emily tightly wrapped herself in the green horse blanket and slumped inside the nook in the snow, and the boy crept on top of her and stayed like that, trying not to press into her.

Emily would never say what was said or was cautiously not said that night. She may have been hysterical. In spite of the fact that Emily was out of the wind, she later said that the January night's temperature was like wire-cutting pliers that snipped at her ears and toes and fingertips until the horrible pain became only a nettling and then a kind of sleep and her feet seemed as dead as her shoes. Emily wept, but her tears froze cold as penny nails and her upper lip seemed candlewaxed by her nose and she couldn't stop herself from feeling the difference in the body on top of her. She thought Sin Thomas was responsible, that the night suited his secret purpose, and she so complained of the bitter cold that Sin finally took off his Newmarket overcoat and tailored it around the girl; but sixty years later, when Emily wrote her own account of the ordeal, she forgot to say anything about him giving her his overcoat and only said in an ordinary way that they spent the night inside a snowdrift and that "by morning the storm had subsided."

With daybreak Sin told Emily to stay there and, with or without his New-market overcoat, the boy walked away with the forlorn hope of chancing upon his horse. Winds were still high, the temperature was 35 degrees below zero, and the snow was deep enough that Sin pulled lopsidedly with every step and then toppled over just a few yards away. And then it was impossible for him to get to his knees, and Sin only sank deeper when he attempted to swim up into the high wave of snow hanging over him. Sin told himself that he would try again to get out, but first he'd build up his strength by napping for just a little while. He arranged his body in the snow gully so that the sunlight angled onto it, and then Sin Thomas gave in to sleep and within twenty minutes died.

His body was discovered at noon by a Wheeler County search party, and shortly after that they came upon Emily. She was carried to a nearby house where she slumped in a kitchen chair while girls her own age dipped Emily's hands and feet into pans of ice water. She could look up over a windowsill and see Sin Thomas's body standing upright on the porch, his hands woodenly crossed at his chest, so Emily kept her brown eyes on the pinewood floor and slept that night with jars of hot water against her skin. She could not walk for two months. Even scissoring tired her hands. She took a cashier's job with the Nebraska Farm Implements Company and kept it for forty-five years, staying all her life in Holt County. She died in a wheelchair on a hospital porch in the month of April. She was wearing a glamorous sable coat. She never married.

The T. E. D. Schusters' only child was a seven-year-old boy named Cleo who rode his Shetland pony to the Westpoint school that day and had not shown up on the doorstep by 2 P.M., when Mr. Schuster went down into the root cellar, dumped purple sugar beets onto the earthen floor, and upended the bushel basket over his head as he slung himself against the onslaught in his second try for Westpoint. Hours later Mrs. Schuster was tapping powdered salt onto the night candles in order to preserve the wax when the door abruptly blew open and Mr. Schuster stood there without Cleo and utterly white and petrified with cold. She warmed him up with okra soup and tenderly wrapped his frozen feet and hands in strips of gauze that she'd dipped in kerosene, and they were sitting on milking stools by a red-hot stove, their ankles just touching, only the usual sentiments being expressed, when they heard a clopping on the wooden stoop and looked out to see the dark Shetland pony turned gray and shaggy-bearded with ice, his legs as wobbly as if he'd just been born. Jammed under the saddle skirt was a damp, rolled-up note from the Scottish schoolteacher that said, Cleo is safe. The Schusters invited the pony into the house and bewildered him with praises as Cleo's mother scraped ice from the pony's shag with her own ivory comb, and Cleo's father gave him sugar from the Dresden bowl as steam rose up from the pony's back.

· · ·

Even at 6 o'clock that evening, there was no heat in Mathias Aachen's house, and the seven Aachen children were in whatever stockings and clothing they owned as they put their hands on a Hay-burner stove that was no warmer than soap. When a jar of apricots burst open that night and the iced orange syrup did not ooze out, Aachen's wife told the children, You ought now to get under your covers. While the seven were crying and crowding onto their dirty floor mattresses, she ran the green tent cloth along the iron wire dividing the house and slid underneath horse blankets in Mathias Aachen's gray wool trousers and her own gray dress and a ghastly muskrat coat that in hot weather gave birth to insects.

Aachen said, Every one of us will be dying of cold before morning. Freezing here. In Nebraska.

His wife just lay there, saying nothing.

Aachen later said he sat up bodingly until shortly after 1 P.M., when the house temperature was so exceedingly cold that a gray suede of ice was on the teapot and his pretty girls were whimpering in their sleep. You are not meant to stay here, Aachen thought, and tilted hot candle wax into his right ear and then his left, until he could only hear his body drumming blood. And then Aachen got his Navy Colt and kissed his wife and killed her. And then walked under the green tent cloth and killed his seven children, stopping twice to capture a scuttling boy and stopping once more to reload.

Hattie Benedict was in her Antelope County schoolyard overseeing the noon recess in a black cardigan sweater and gray wool dress when the January blizzard caught her unaware. She had been impatiently watching four girls in flying coats playing Ante I Over by tossing a spindle of chartreuse yarn over the one-room schoolhouse, and then a sharp cold petted her neck and Hattie turned toward the open fields of hoarfrosted scraggle and yellow grass. Just a half mile away was a gray blur of snow underneath a dark sky that was all hurry and calamity, like a nighttime city of sin-black buildings and havoc in the streets. Wind tortured a creekside cottonwood until it cracked apart. A tin water pail rang in a skipping roll to the horse path. One quarter of the tar-paper roof was torn from the schoolhouse and sailed southeast 40 feet. And only then did Hattie yell for the older boys with their cigarettes and clay pipes to hurry in from the prairie 20 rods away, and she was hustling a dallying girl inside just as the snowstorm socked into her Antelope County schoolhouse, shipping the building awry off its timber skids so that the southwest side heavily dropped 6 inches and the oak-plank floor became a slope that Hattie ascended unsteadily while ordering the children to open their *Webster Franklin Fourth Reader* to the Lord's Prayer in verse and to say it aloud. And then Hattie stood by her desk with her pink hands held theatrically to her cheeks as she looked up at the walking noise of bricks being jarred from the chimney and down the roof.

Every window view was as white as if butchers' paper had been tacked up. Winds pounded into the windowpanes and dry window putty trickled onto the unpainted sills. Even the slough grass fire in the Hay-burner stove was sucked high into the tin stack pipe so that the soot on it reddened and snapped. Hattie could only stare. Four of the boys were just about Hattie's age, so she didn't say anything when they ignored the reading assignment and earnestly got up from the wooden benches in order to argue *oughts* and *ought nots* in the cloakroom. She heard the girls saying Amen and then she saw Janusz Vasko, who was fifteen years old and had grown up in Nebraska weather, gravely exiting the cloakroom with a cigarette behind one ear and his right hand raised high overhead. Hattie called on him, and Janusz said the older boys agreed that they could get the little ones home, but only if they went out right away. And before she could even give it thought, Janusz tied his red handkerchief over his nose and mouth and jabbed his orange corduroy trousers inside his antelope boots with a pencil.

Yes, Hattie said, please go, and Janusz got the boys and girls to link themselves together with jump ropes and twine and piano wire, and twelve of Hattie Benedict's pupils walked out into a nothingness that the boys knew from their shoes up and dully worked their way across as though each crooked stump and tilted fence post was a word they could spell in a plain-spoken sentence in a book of practical knowledge. Hours later the children showed up at their homes, aching and crying in raw pain. Each was given cocoa or the green tea of the elder flower and hot bricks were put next to their feet while they napped and newspapers printed their names incorrectly. And then, one by one, the children disappeared from history.

Except for Johan and Alma Lindquist, aged nine and six, who stayed behind in the schoolhouse, owing to the greater distance to their ranch. Hattie opened a week-old Omaha newspaper on her desktop and with caution peeled a spotted yellow apple on it, eating tan slices from her scissor blade as she peered out at children who seemed irritatingly sad and pathetic. She said, You wish you were home.

The Lindquists stared.

Me too, she said. She dropped the apple core onto the newspaper page and watched it ripple with the juice stain. Have you any idea where Pennsylvania is?

East, the boy said. Johan was eating pepper cheese and day-old rye bread from a tin lunch box that sparked with electricity whenever he touched it. And his sister nudged him to show how her yellow hair was beguiled toward her green rubber comb whenever she brought it near.

Hattie was talking in such quick English that she could tell the Lindquists couldn't quite understand it. She kept hearing the snow pinging and pattering against the windowpanes, and the storm howling like clarinets down the stack pipe, but she perceived the increasing cold in the room only when she looked to the Lindquists and saw their Danish sentences grayly blossoming as they spoke. Hattie went into the cloakroom and skidded out the poorhouse box, rummaging from it a Scotch plaid scarf that she wrapped twice around her skull and ears just as a squaw would, and snipping off the fingertips of some red knitted gloves that were only slightly too small. She put them on and then she got into her secondhand coat and Alma whispered to her brother but Hattie said she'd have no whispering, she hated that, she couldn't wait for their kin to show up for them, she had too many responsibilities, and nothing interesting ever happened in the country. Everything was stupid. Everything was work. She didn't even have a girlfriend. She said she'd once been sick for four days, and two by two practically every woman in Neligh mistrustfully visited her rooming house to squint at Hattie and palm her forehead and talk about her symptoms. And then they'd snail out into the hallway and prattle and whisper in the hawk and spit of the German language.

Alma looked at Johan with misunderstanding and terror, and Hattie told them to get out paper and pencils; she was going to say some necessary things and the children were going to write them down. She slowly paced as she constructed a paragraph, one knuckle darkly striping the blackboard, but she couldn't properly express herself. She had forgotten herself so absolutely that she thought forgetting was a yeast in the air; or that the onslaught's only point was to say over and over again that she was next to nothing. Easily bewildered. Easily dismayed. The Lindquists were shying from the crazy woman and concentrating their shame on a nickel pad of Wisconsin paper. And Hattie thought, *You'll give me an ugly name and there will be cartoons and snickering and the older girls will idly slay me with jokes and imitations.*

She explained she was taking them to her rooming house, and she strode purposefully out into the great blizzard as if she were going out to a garden to fetch some strawberries, and Johan dutifully followed, but Alma stayed inside the schoolhouse with her purple scarf up over her mouth and nose and her own dark sandwich of pepper cheese and rye bread clutched to her breast like a prayer book. And then Johan stepped out of the utter whiteness to say Alma had to hurry up, that Miss Benedict was angrily asking him if his sister had forgotten how to use her legs. So Alma stepped out of the one-room schoolhouse, sinking deep in the snow and sloshing ahead in it as she would in a pond until she caught up with Hattie Benedict, who took the Lindquists' hands in her own and walked them into the utter whiteness and night of the afternoon. Seeking to blindly go north to her rooming house, Hattie put her high button shoes in the deep tracks that Janusz and the schoolchildren had made, but she misstepped twice, and that was enough to get her on a screw-tape path over snow bumps and hillocks that took her south and west and very nearly into a great wilderness that was like a sea in high gale.

Hattie imagined herself reaching the Elkhorn River and discovering her rooming house standing high and honorable under the sky's insanity. And then she and the Lindquist children would duck over their teaspoons of tomato soup and soda crackers as the town's brooms and scarecrows teetered over them, hooking their green hands on the boy and girl and saying, Tell us about it. She therefore created a heroine's part for herself and tried to keep to it as she floundered through drifts as high as a four-poster bed in a white room of piety and weeping. Hattie pretended gaiety by saying once, See how it swirls! but she saw that the Lindquists were tucking deep inside themselves as they trudged forward and fell and got up again, the wind drawing tears from their squinting eyes, the hard, dry snow hitting their skin like wildly flying pencils. Hours passed as Hattie tipped away from the press of the wind into country that was a puzzle to her, but she kept saying, Just a little farther, until she saw Alma playing Gretel by secretly trailing her right hand along a high wave of snow in order to secretly let go yet another crumb of her rye bread. And then, just ahead of her, she saw some pepper cheese that the girl dropped some time ago. Hissing spindrifts tore away from the snow swells and spiked her face like sharp pins, but then a door seemed to inch ajar and Hattie saw the slight, dark change of a haystack and she cut toward it, announcing that they'd stay there for the night.

She slashed away an access into the haystack and ordered Alma to crawl inside, but the girl hesitated as if she were still thinking of the gingerbread house and the witch's oven, and Hattie acidly whispered, You'll be a dainty mouthful. She meant it as a joke but her green eyes must have seemed crazy, because the little girl was crying when Hattie got inside the haystack next to her, and then Johan was crying, too, and Hattie hugged the Lindquists to her body and tried to shush them with a hymn by Dr. Watts, gently singing, Hush, my dears, lie still and slumber. She couldn't get her feet inside the haystack, but she couldn't feel them anyway just then, and the haystack was making everything else seem right and possible. She talked to the children about hot pastries and taffy and Christmas presents, and that night she made up a story about the horrible storm being a wicked old man whose only thought was to eat them up, but he couldn't find them in the haystack even though he looked and looked. The old man was howling, she said, because he was so hungry.

At daybreak a party of farmers from Neligh rode out on their high plowhorses to the Antelope County schoolhouse in order to get Hattie and the Lindquist children, but the room was empty and the bluetick hound that was with them kept scratching up rye bread until the party walked along behind it on footpaths that wreathed around the schoolyard and into a haystack 20 rods away where the older boys smoked and spit tobacco juice at recess. The Lindquist girl and the boy were killed by the cold, but Hattie Benedict had stayed alive inside the hay, and she wouldn't come out again until the party of men yanked her by the ankles. Even then she kept the girl's body hugged against one side and the boy's body hugged to the other, and when she was put up on one horse, she stared down at them with green eyes that were empty of thought or understanding and inquired if they'd be okay. Yes, one man said. You took good care of them.

Bent Lindquist ripped down his kitchen cupboards and carpentered his own triangular caskets, blacking them with shoe polish, and then swaddled Alma and Johan in black alpaca that was kindly provided by an elder in the Church of Jesus Christ of Latter-Day Saints. And all that night Danish women sat up with the bodies, sopping the Lindquists' skin with vinegar so as to impede putrefaction.

Hattie Benedict woke up in a Lincoln hospital with sweet oil of spermaceti on her hands and lips, and weeks later a Kansas City surgeon amputated her feet with a polished silver hacksaw in the presence of his anatomy class. She was walking again by June, but she was attached to cork-and-iron shoes and she sighed and grunted with every step. Within a year she grew so overweight that she gave up her crutches for a wicker-backed wheelchair and stayed in Antelope County on a pension of 40 dollars per month, letting her dark hair grow dirty and leafy, reading one popular romance per day. And yet she complained so much about her helplessness, especially in winter, that the Protestant churches took up a collection and Hattie Benedict was shipped by train to Oakland, California, whence she sent postcards saying she'd married a trolley repairman and she hated Nebraska, hated their horrible weather, hated their petty lives.

On Friday the thirteenth some pioneers went to the upper stories of their houses to jack up the windows and crawl out onto snow that was like a jeweled ceiling over their properties. Everything was sloped and planed and caped and whitely furbelowed. One man couldn't get over his boyish delight in tramping about on deer-hide snowshoes at the height of his roof gutters, or that his dogwood tree was forgotten but for twigs sticking out of the snow like a skeleton's fingers. His name was Eldad Alderman, and he jabbed a bamboo fishing pole in four likely spots a couple of feet below his snowshoes before the bamboo finally thumped against the plank roof of his chicken coop. He spent two hours spading down to the coop and then squeezed in through the one window in order to walk among the fowl and count up. Half his sixty hens were alive; the other half were still nesting, their orange beaks lying against their white hackles, sitting there like a dress shop's hats, their pure white eggs not yet cold underneath them. In gratitude to those thirty chickens that withstood the ordeal, Eldad gave them Dutch whey and curds and eventually wrote a letter praising their constitutions in the *American Poultry Yard*.

Anna Shevschenko managed to get oxen inside a shelter sturdily constructed of oak scantling and a high stack of barley straw, but the snow powder was so fine and fiercely penetrating that it sifted through and slowly accumulated on the floor. The oxen tamped it down and inchingly rose toward the oak scantling rafters, where they were stopped as the snow flooded up, and by daybreak were overcome and finally asphyxiated. Widow Schevschenko decided then that an old woman could not keep a Nebraska farm alone, and she left for the East in February.

One man lost 300 Rhode Island Red chickens; another lost 26 Hereford cattle and sold their hides for 2 dollars apiece. Hours after the Hubenka boy permitted 21 hogs to get out of the snowstorm and join their 40 Holsteins in the upper barn, the planked floor in the cattle linter collapsed under the extra weight and the livestock perished. Since even coal picks could no more than chip the earth, the iron-hard bodies were hauled aside until they could be put underground in April, and just about then some Pawnee Indians showed up outside David City. Knowing their manner of living, Mr. Hubenka told them where the carcasses were rotting in the sea wrack of weed tangles and thaw-water jetsam, and the Pawnee rode their ponies onto the property one night and hauled the carrion away.

And there were stories about a Union Pacific train being arrested by snow on a railway siding near Lincoln, and the merchandizers in the smoking car playing euchre, high five, and flinch until sunup; about cowboys staying inside a Hazard bunkhouse for three days and getting bellyaches from eating so many tins of anchovies and saltine crackers; about the Omaha YMCA where shop clerks paged through inspirational pamphlets or played checkers and cribbage or napped in green leather Chesterfield chairs until the great blizzard petered out.

Half a century later, in Atkinson, there was a cranky talker named Bates, who maintained he was the fellow who first thought of attaching the word *blizzard* to the onslaught of high winds and slashing dry snow and ought to be given credit for it. And later, too, a Lincoln woman remembered herself as a little girl peering out through yellowed window paper at a yard and countryside that were as white as the first day of God's creation. And then a great white Brahma bull with street-wide horns trotted up to the house, the night's snow puffing up from his heavy footsteps like soap flakes, gray funnels of air flaring from his nostrils and wisping away in the horrible cold. With a tilt of his head the great bull sought out the hiding girl under a Chesterfield table and, having seen her, sighed and trotted back toward Oklahoma.

Wild turkey were sighted over the next few weeks, their wattled heads and necks just above the snow like dark sticks, some of them petrified that way but others simply waiting for happier times to come. The onslaught also killed prairie dogs, jackrabbits, and crows, and the coyotes that relied upon them for food got so hungry that skulks of them would loiter like juveniles in the yards at night and yearn for scraps and castaways in old songs of agony that were always misunderstood.

• • •

Addie Dillingham was seventeen and irresistible that January day of the great blizzard, a beautiful English girl in an hourglass dress and an ankle-length otter-skin coat that was sculpted brazenly to display a womanly bosom and bustle. She had gently agreed to join an upperclassman at the Nebraska School of Medicine on a journey across the green ice of the Missouri River to Iowa, where there was a party at the Masonic Temple in order to celebrate the final linking of Omaha and Council Bluffs. The medical student was Repler Hitchcock of Council Bluffs—a good companion, a Republican, and an Episcopalian—who yearned to practice electrotherapeutics in Cuernavaca, Mexico. He paid for their three-course luncheon at the Paxton Hotel and then the couple strolled down Douglas Street with 400 other partygoers, who got into cutters and one-horse open sleighs just underneath the iron legs and girders of what would eventually be called the Ak-Sar-Ben Bridge. At a cap-pistol shot the party jerked away from Nebraska and there were champagne toasts and cheers and yahooing, but gradu-ally the party scattered and Addie could only hear the iron shoes of the plow-horse and the racing sleigh hushing across the shaded window glass of river, like those tropical flowers shaped like saucers and cups that slide across the green silk of a pond of their own accord.

At the Masonic Temple there were coconut macaroons and hot syllabub made with cider and brandy, and quadrille dancing on a puncheon floor to songs like the "Butterfly Whirl" and "Cheater Swing" and "The Girl I Left Behind Me." Although the day was getting dark and there was talk about a great snowstorm roistering outside, Addie insisted on staying out on the dance floor until only twenty people remained and the quadrille caller had put away his violin and his sister's cello. Addie smiled and said, Oh what fun! as Repler tidily helped her into her mother's otter-skin coat and then escorted her out into a grand empire of snow that Addie thought was thrilling. And then, al-though the world by then was wrathfully meaning everything it said, she walked alone to the railroad depot at Ninth and Broadway so she could take the one-stop train called The Dummy across to Omaha.

Addie sipped hot cocoa as she passed sixty minutes up close to the rail-road depot's coal stoker oven and some other partygoers sang of Good King Wenceslaus over a parlor organ. And then an old yardman who was sheeped in snow trudged through the high drifts by the door and announced that no more trains would be going out until morning.

Half the couples stranded there had family in Council Bluffs and decided to stay overnight, but the idea of traipsing back to Repler's house and sleeping in his sister's trundle bed seemed squalid to Addie, and she decided to walk the iron railway trestle across to Omaha.

Addie was a half hour away from the Iowa railway yard and up on the tracks over the great Missouri before she had second thoughts. White hatchings and tracings of snow flew at her horizontally. Wind had rippled snow up against the southern girders so that the high white skin was pleated and patterned like oyster shell. Every creosote tic was tented with snow that angled down into dark troughs that Addie could fit a leg through. Everything else was night sky and mystery, and the world she knew had disappeared. And yet she walked out onto the trestle, teetering over to a catwalk and sidestepping along it in high-button shoes, 40 feet above the ice, her left hand taking the yield from one guy wire as her right hand sought out another. Yelling winds were yanking at her, and the iron trestle was swaying enough to tilt her over into nothingness, as though Addie Dillingham were a playground game it was just inventing. Half-way across, her gray tam-o'shanter was snagged out just far enough into space that she could follow its spider-drop into the night, but she only stared at the great river that was lying there moon-white with snow and intractable. Wishing for her to jump.

Years later Addie thought that she got to Nebraska and did not give up and was not overfrightened because she was seventeen and could do no wrong, and accidents and dying seemed a government you could vote against, a mother you could ignore. She said she panicked at one jolt of wind and sank down to her knees up there and briefly touched her forehead to iron that hurt her skin like teeth, but when she got up again, she could see the ink-black stitching of the woods just east of Omaha and the shanties on timber piers just above the Missouri River's jagged stacks of ice. And she grinned as she thought how she would look to a vagrant down there plying his way along a rope in order to assay his trotlines for gar and catfish and then, perhaps, appraising the night as if he'd heard a crazy woman screaming in a faraway hospital room. And she'd be jaun-tily up there on the iron trestle like a new star you could wish on, and as joyous as the last high notes of "The Girl I Left Behind Me."

A. M. Homes

A REAL DOLL

A. M. HOMES (1961–) is the author of the novels *The End of Alice, This Book Will Save Your Life, Music for Torching, In a Country of Mothers,* and *Jack,* and the story collections *The Safety of Objects* and *Things You Should Know.* She is the recipient of numerous awards, including a Guggenheim, National Foundation for the Arts, and New York Foundation for the Arts fellowships. Her work appears in such magazines as *Artforum* and *Vanity Fair,* among others. Her *New Yorker* essay, "The Mistress's Daughter," was excerpted from a memoir of the same title. Homes lives in New York City.

I'm dating Barbie. Three afternoons a week, while my sister is at dance class, I take Barbie away from Ken. I'm practicing for the future.

At first I sat in my sister's room watching Barbie, who lived with Ken, on a doily, on top of the dresser.

I was looking at her but not really looking. I was looking, and all of the sudden realized she was staring at me.

She was sitting next to Ken, his khaki-covered thigh absently rubbing her bare leg. He was rubbing her, but she was staring at me.

"Hi," she said.

"Hello," I said.

"I'm Barbie," she said, and Ken stopped rubbing her leg.

"I know."

"You're Jenny's brother."

I nodded. My head was bobbing up and down like a puppet on a weight.

"I really like your sister. She's sweet," Barbie said. "Such a good little girl. Especially lately, she makes herself so pretty, and she's started doing her nails."

I wondered if Barbie noticed that Miss Wonderful bit her nails and that when she smiled her front teeth were covered with little flecks of purple nail polish. I wondered if she knew Jennifer colored in the chipped chewed spots with purple magic marker, and then sometimes sucked on her fingers so that not only did she have purple flecks of polish on her teeth, but her tongue was the strangest shade of violet.

"So listen," I said. "Would you like to go out for a while? Grab some fresh air, maybe take a spin around the backyard?"

"Sure," she said.

I picked her up by her feet. It sounds unusual but I was too petrified to take her by the waist. I grabbed her by the ankles and carried her off like a Popsicle stick.

As soon as we were out back, sitting on the porch of what I used to call my fort, but which my sister and parents referred to as the playhouse, I started freaking. I was suddenly and incredibly aware that I was out with Barbie. I didn't know what to say.

"So, what kind of a Barbie are you?" I asked.

"Excuse me?"

"Well, from listening to Jennifer I know there's Day to Night Barbie, Magic Moves Barbie, Gift-Giving Barbie, Tropical Barbie, My First Barbie, and more."

"I'm Tropical," she said. I'm Tropical, she said, the same way a person might say I'm Catholic or I'm Jewish. "I came with a one-piece bathing suit, a brush, and a ruffle you can wear so many ways," Barbie squeaked.

She actually squeaked. It turned out that squeaking was Barbie's birth defect. I pretended I didn't hear it.

We were quiet for a minute. A leaf larger than Barbie fell from the maple tree above us and I caught it just before it would have hit her. I half expected her to squeak, "You saved my life. I'm yours, forever." Instead she said, in a perfectly normal voice, "Wow, big leaf."

I looked at her. Barbie's eyes were sparkling blue like the ocean on a good day. I looked and in a moment noticed she had the whole world, the cosmos, drawn in makeup above and below her eyes. An entire galaxy, clouds, stars, a sun, the sea, painted onto her face. Yellow, blue, pink, and a million silver sparkles.

We sat looking at each other, looking and talking and then not talking and looking again. It was a stop-and-start thing with both of us constantly saying the wrong thing, saying anything, and then immediately regretting having said it.

It was obvious Barbie didn't trust me. I asked her if she wanted something to drink.

"Diet Coke," she said. And I wondered why I'd asked.

I went into the house, upstairs into my parents' bathroom, opened the medicine cabinet, and got a couple of Valiums. I immediately swallowed one. I figured if I could be calm and collected, she'd realize I wasn't going to hurt her. I broke another Valium into a million small pieces, dropped some slivers into Barbie's Diet Coke, and swished it around so it'd blend. I figured if we could be calm and collected together, she'd be able to trust me even sooner. I was falling in love in a way that had nothing to do with love.

"So, what's the deal with you and Ken?" I asked later after we'd loosened up, after she'd drunk two Diet Cokes, and I'd made another trip to the medicine cabinet.

She giggled. "Oh, we're just really good friends."

"What's the deal with him really, you can tell me. I mean, is he or isn't he?"

"Ish she or ishn' she," Barbie said, in a slow slurred way, like she was so intoxicated that if they made a Breathalizer for Valium, she'd melt it.

I regretted having fixed her a third Coke. I mean if she o.d.'ed and died Jennifer would tell my mom and dad for sure.

"Is he a faggot or what?"

Barbie laughed and I almost slapped her. She looked me straight in the eye.

"He lusts after me," she said. "I come home at night and he's standing there, waiting. He doesn't wear underwear, you know. I mean, isn't that strange, Ken doesn't own any underwear. I heard Jennifer tell her friend that they don't even make any for him. Anyway, he's always there waiting, and I'm like, Ken we're friends, okay, that's it. I mean, have you ever noticed, he has molded plastic hair. His head and his hair are all one piece. I can't go out with a guy like that. Besides, I don't think he'd be up for it if you know what I mean. Ken is not what you'd call well endowed. . . . All he's got is a little plastic bump, more of a hump, really, and what the hell are you supposed to do with that?"

She was telling me things I didn't think I should hear and all the same, I was leaning into her, like if I moved closer she'd tell me more. I was taking every word and holding it for a minute, holding groups of words in my head like I didn't understand English. She went on and on, but I wasn't listening.

The sun sank behind the playhouse, Barbie shivered, excused herself, and ran around back to throw up. I asked her if she felt okay. She said she was fine, just a little tired, that maybe she was coming down with the flu or something. I gave her a piece of a piece of gum to chew and took her inside.

On the way back to Jennifer's room I did something Barbie almost didn't forgive me for. I did something which not only shattered the moment, but nearly wrecked the possibility of our having a future together.

In the hallway between the stairs and Jennifer's room, I popped Barbie's head into my mouth, like lion and tamer, God and Godzilla.

I popped her whole head into my mouth, and Barbie's hair separated into single strands like Christmas tinsel and caught in my throat, nearly choking me. I could taste layer on layer of makeup, Revlon, Max Factor, and Maybelline. I closed my mouth around Barbie and could feel her breath in mine. I could hear her screams in my throat. Her teeth, white, Pearl Drops, Pepsodent, and the whole Osmond family, bit my tongue and the inside of my cheek like I might accidently bite myself. I closed my mouth around her neck and held her suspended, her feet uselessly kicking the air in front of my face.

Before pulling her out, I pressed my teeth lightly into her neck, leaving marks

Barbie described as scars of her assault, but which I imagined as a New Age necklace of love.

"I have never, ever in my life been treated with such utter disregard," she said as soon as I let her out.

She was lying. I knew Jennifer sometimes did things with Barbie. I didn't mention that once I'd seen Barbie hanging from Jennifer's ceiling fan, spinning around in great wide circles, like some imitation Superman.

"I'm sorry if I scared you."

"Scared me!" she squeaked.

She went on squeaking, a cross between the squeal when you let the air out of a balloon and a smoke alarm with weak batteries. While she was squeaking, the phrase *a head in the mouth is worth two in the bush* started running through my head. I knew it had come from somewhere, started as something else, but I couldn't get it right. *A head in the mouth is worth two in the bush,* again and again, like the punch line to some dirty joke.

"Scared me. Scared me. Scared me!" Barbie squeaked louder and louder until finally she had my attention again. "Have you ever been held captive in the dark cavern of someone's body?"

I shook my head. It sounded wonderful.

"Typical," she said. "So incredibly, typically male."

For a moment I was proud.

"Why do you have to do things you know you shouldn't, and worse, you do them with a light in your eye, like you're getting some weird pleasure that only another boy would understand? You're all the same," she said. "You're all Jack Nicholson."

I refused to put her back in Jennifer's room until she forgave me, until she understood that I'd done what I did with only the truest of feeling, no harm intended.

I heard Jennifer's feet clomping up the stairs. I was running out of time.

"You know I'm really interested in you," I said to Barbie.

"Me too," she said, and for a minute I wasn't sure if she meant she was interested in herself or me.

"We should do this again," I said. She nodded.

I leaned down to kiss Barbie. I could have brought her up to my lips, but somehow it felt wrong. I leaned down to kiss her and the first thing I got was her nose in my mouth. I felt like a St. Bernard saying hello.

No matter how graceful I tried to be, I was forever licking her face. It wasn't a question of putting my tongue in her ear or down her throat, it was simply literally trying not to suffocate her. I kissed Barbie with my back to Ken and then turned around and put her on the doily right next to him. I was tempted to drop her down on Ken, to mash her into him, but I managed to restrain myself.

"That was fun," Barbie said. I heard Jennifer in the hall.

"Later," I said.

Jennifer came into the room and looked at me.

"What?" I said.

"It's my room," she said.

"There was a bee in it. I was killing it for you."

"A bee. I'm allergic to bees. Mom, Mom," she screamed. "There's a bee."

"Mom's not home. I killed it."

"But there might be another one."

"So call me and I'll kill it."

"But if it stings me I might die." I shrugged and walked out. I could feel Barbie watching me leave.

I took a Valium about twenty minutes before I picked her up the next Friday. By the time I went into Jennifer's room, everything was getting easier.

"Hey," I said when I got up to the dresser.

She was there on the doily with Ken, they were back to back, resting against each other, legs stretched out in front of them.

Ken didn't look at me. I didn't care.

"You ready to go?" I asked. Barbie nodded. "I thought you might be thirsty." I handed her the Diet Coke I'd made for her.

I'd figured Barbie could take a little less than an eighth of a Valium without getting totally senile. Basically, I had to give her Valium crumbs since there was no way to cut one that small.

She took the Coke and drank it right in front of Ken. I kept waiting for him to give me one of those I-know-what-you're-up-to-and-I-don't-like-it looks, the kind my father gives me when he walks into my room without knocking and I automatically jump twenty feet in the air.

Ken acted like he didn't even know I was there. I hated him.

"I can't do a lot of walking this afternoon," Barbie said.

I nodded. I figured no big deal since mostly I seemed to be carrying her around anyway.

"My feet are killing me," she said.

I was thinking about Ken.

"Don't you have other shoes?"

My family was very into shoes. No matter what seemed to be wrong my father always suggested it could be cured by wearing a different pair of shoes. He believed that shoes, like tires, should be rotated.

"It's not the shoes," she said. "It's my toes."

"Did you drop something on them?" My Valium wasn't working. I was having trouble making small talk. I needed another one.

"Jennifer's been chewing on them."

"What?"

"She chews on my toes."

"You let her chew your footies?"

I couldn't make sense out of what she was saying. I was thinking about not being able to talk, needing another or maybe two more Valiums, yellow adult-strength Pez.

"Do you enjoy it?" I asked.

"She literally bites down on them, like I'm flank steak or something," Barbie said. "I wish she'd just bite them off and have it over with. This is taking forever. She's chewing and chewing, more like gnawing at me."

"I'll make her stop. I'll buy her some gum, some tobacco or something, a pencil to chew on."

"Please don't say anything. I wouldn't have told you except . . . ," Barbie said.

"But she's hurting you."

"It's between Jennifer and me."

"Where's it going to stop?" I asked.

"At the arch, I hope. There's a bone there, and once she realizes she's bitten the soft part off, she'll stop."

"How will you walk?"

"I have very long feet."

I sat on the edge of my sister's bed, my head in my hands. My sister was biting Barbie's feet off and Barbie didn't seem to care. She didn't hold it against her and in a way I liked her for that. I liked the fact she understood how we all have little secret habits that seem normal enough to us, but which we know better than to mention out loud. I started imagining things I might be able to get away with.

"Get me out of here," Barbie said. I slipped Barbie's shoes off. Sure enough, someone had been gnawing at her. On her left foot the toes were dangling and on the right, half had been completely taken off. There were tooth marks up to her ankles. "Let's not dwell on this," Barbie said.

I picked Barbie up. Ken fell over backwards and Barbie made me straighten him up before we left. "Just because you know he only has a bump doesn't give you permission to treat him badly," Barbie whispered.

I fixed Ken and carried Barbie down the hall to my room. I held Barbie above me, tilted my head back, and lowered her feet into my mouth. I felt like a young sword swallower practicing for my debut. I lowered Barbie's feet and legs into my mouth and then began sucking on them. They smelled like Jennifer and dirt and plastic. I sucked on her stubs and she told me it felt nice.

"You're better than a hot soak," Barbie said. I left her resting on my pillow and went downstairs to get us each a drink.

We were lying on my bed, curled into and out of each other. Barbie was on a pillow next to me and I was on my side facing her. She was talking about men, and as she talked I tried to be everything she said. She was saying she didn't like men who were afraid of themselves. I tried to be brave, to look courageous and secure. I held my head a certain way and it seemed to work. She said she didn't like men who were afraid of femininity, and I got confused.

"Guys always have to prove how boy they really are," Barbie said.

I thought of Jennifer trying to be a girl, wearing dresses, doing her nails, putting makeup on, wearing a bra even though she wouldn't need one for about fifty years.

"You make fun of Ken because he lets himself be everything he is. He doesn't hide anything."

"He doesn't have anything to hide," I said. "He has tan molded plastic hair, and a bump for a dick."

"I never should have told you about the bump."

I lay back on the bed. Barbie rolled over, off the pillow, and rested on my chest. Her body stretched from my nipple to my belly button. Her hands pressed against me, tickling me.

"Barbie," I said.

"Umm humm."

"How do you feel about me?"

She didn't say anything for a minute. "Don't worry about it," she said, and slipped her hand into my shirt through the space between the buttons.

Her fingers were like the ends of toothpicks performing some subtle ancient torture, a dance of boy death across my chest. Barbie crawled all over me like an insect who'd run into one too many cans of Raid.

Underneath my clothes, under my skin, I was going crazy. First off, I'd been kidnapped by my underwear with no way to manually adjust without attracting unnecessary attention.

With Barbie caught in my shirt I slowly rolled over, like in some space shuttle docking maneuver. I rolled onto my stomach, trapping her under me. As slowly and unobtrusively as possible, I ground myself against the bed, at first hoping it would fix things and then again and again, caught by a pleasure/pain principle.

"Is this a water bed?" Barbie asked.

My hand was on her breasts, only it wasn't really my hand, but more like my index finger. I touched Barbie and she made a little gasp, a squeak in reverse. She squeaked backwards, then stopped, and I was stuck there with my hand on her, thinking about how I was forever crossing a line between the haves and the have-nots, between good guys and bad, between men and animals, and there was absolutely nothing I could do to stop myself.

Barbie was sitting on my crotch, her legs flipped back behind her in a position that wasn't human.

At a certain point I had to free myself. If my dick was blue, it was only because it had suffocated. I did the honors and Richard popped out like an escape from maximum security.

"I've never seen anything so big," Barbie said. It was the sentence I dreamed of, but given the people Barbie normally hung out with, namely the bump boy himself, it didn't come as a big surprise.

She stood at the base of my dick, her bare feet buried in my pubic hair. I was almost as tall as she was. Okay, not almost as tall, but clearly we could be related. She and Richard even had the same vaguely surprised look on their faces.

She was on me and I couldn't help wanting to get inside her. I turned Barbie over and was on top of her, not caring if I killed her. Her hands pressed so hard into my stomach that it felt like she was performing an appendectomy.

I was on top, trying to get between her legs, almost breaking her in half. But there was nothing there, nothing to fuck except a small thin line that was supposed to be her ass crack.

I rubbed the thin line, the back of her legs and the space between her legs. I turned Barbie's back to me so I could do it without having to look at her face.

Very quickly, I came. I came all over Barbie, all over her and a little bit in her hair. I came on Barbie and it was the most horrifying experience I ever had. It didn't stay on her. It doesn't stick to plastic. I was finished. I was holding a come-covered Barbie in my hand like I didn't know where she came from.

Barbie said, "Don't stop," or maybe I just think she said that because I read it somewhere. I don't know anymore. I couldn't listen to her. I couldn't even look at her. I wiped myself off with a sock, pulled my clothes on, and then took Barbie into the bathroom.

At dinner I noticed Jennifer chewing her cuticles between bites of tuna-noodle casserole. I asked her if she was teething. She coughed and then started choking to death on either a little piece of fingernail, a crushed potato chip from the casserole, or maybe even a little bit of Barbie footie that'd stuck in her teeth. My mother asked her if she was okay.

"I swallowed something sharp," she said between coughs that were clearly influenced by the acting class she'd taken over the summer.

"Do you have a problem?" I asked her.

"Leave your sister alone," my mother said.

"If there are any questions to ask we'll do the asking," my father said.

"Is everything all right?" my mother asked Jennifer. She nodded. "I think you could use some new jeans," my mother said. "You don't seem to have many play clothes anymore."

"Not to change the subject," I said, trying to think of a way to stop Jennifer from eating Barbie alive.

"I don't wear pants," Jennifer said. "Boys wear pants."

"Your grandma wears pants," my father said.

"She's not a girl."

My father chuckled. He actually fucking chuckled. He's the only person I ever met who could actually fucking chuckle.

"Don't tell her that," he said, chuckling.

"It's not funny," I said.

"Grandma's are pull-ons anyway," Jennifer said. "They don't have a fly. You have to have a penis to have a fly."

"Jennifer," my mother said. "That's enough of that."

I decided to buy Barbie a present. I was at that strange point where I would have done anything for her. I took two buses and walked more than a mile to get to Toys R Us.

Barbie row was aisle 14C. I was a wreck. I imagined a million Barbies and having to have them all. I pictured fucking one, discarding it, immediately grabbing a fresh one, doing it, and then throwing it onto a growing pile in the corner of my room. An unending chore. I saw myself becoming a slave to Barbie. I wondered how many Tropical Barbies were made each year. I felt faint.

There were rows and rows of Kens, Barbies, and Skippers. Funtime Barbie, Jewel Secrets Ken, Barbie Rocker with "Hot Rockin' Fun and Real Dancin' Action." I noticed Magic Moves Barbie, and found myself looking at her carefully, flirtatiously, wondering if her legs were spreadable. "Push the switch and she moves," her box said. She winked at me while I was reading.

The only Tropical I saw was a black Tropical Ken. From just looking at him you wouldn't have known he was black. I mean, he wasn't black like anyone would be black. Black Tropical Ken was the color of a raisin, a raisin all spread out and unwrinkled. He had a short Afro that looked like a wig had been dropped down and fixed on his head, a protective helmet. I wondered if black Ken was really white Ken sprayed over with a thick coating of ironed raisin plastic.

I spread eight black Kens out in a line across the front of a row. Through the plastic window of his box he told me he was hoping to go to dental school. All eight black Kens talked at once. Luckily, they all said the same thing at the same time. They said he really liked teeth. Black Ken smiled. He had the same white Pearl Drops, Pepsodent, Osmond family teeth that Barbie and white Ken had. I thought the entire Mattel family must take really good care of themselves. I figured they might be the only people left in America who actually brushed after every meal and then again before going to sleep.

I didn't know what to get Barbie. Black Ken said I should go for clothing, maybe a fur coat. I wanted something really special. I imagined a wonderful present that would draw us somehow closer.

There was a tropical pool and patio set, but I decided it might make her homesick. There was a complete winter holiday, with an A-frame house, fireplace, snowmobile, and sled. I imagined her inviting Ken away for a weekend without me. The six o'clock news set was nice, but because of her squeak, Barbie's future as an anchorwoman seemed limited. A workout center, a sofa bed and coffee table, a bubbling spa, a bedroom play set. I settled on the grand piano. It was $13.00. I'd always made it a point to never spend more than ten dollars on anyone. This time I figured, what the hell, you don't buy a grand piano every day.

"Wrap it up, would ya," I said at the checkout desk.

From my bedroom window I could see Jennifer in the backyard, wearing her tutu and leaping all over the place. It was dangerous as hell to sneak in and get Barbie, but I couldn't keep a grand piano in my closet without telling someone.

"You must really like me," Barbie said when she finally had the piano un-wrapped.

I nodded. She was wearing a ski suit and skis. It was the end of August and eighty degrees out. Immediately, she sat down and played "Chopsticks."

I looked out at Jennifer. She was running down the length of the deck, jump-ing onto the railing and then leaping off, posing like one of those red flying horses you see on old Mobil gas signs. I watched her do it once and then the second time, her foot caught on the railing, and she went over the edge the hard way. A minute later she came around the edge of the house, limping, her tutu dented and dirty, pink tights ripped at both knees. I grabbed Barbie from the piano bench and raced her into Jennifer's room.

"I was just getting warmed up," she said. "I can play better than that, really."

I could hear Jennifer crying as she walked up the stairs.

"Jennifer's coming," I said. I put her down on the dresser and realized Ken was missing.

"Where's Ken?" I asked quickly.

"Out with Jennifer," Barbie said.

I met Jennifer at her door. "Are you okay?" I asked. She cried harder. "I saw you fall."

"Why didn't you stop me?" she said.

"From falling?"

She nodded and showed me her knees.

"Once you start to fall no one can stop you." I noticed Ken was tucked into the waistband of her tutu.

"They catch you," Jennifer said.

I started to tell her it was dangerous to go leaping around with a Ken stuck in your waistband, but you don't tell someone who's already crying that they did something bad.

I walked her into the bathroom, and took out the hydrogen peroxide. I was a first aid expert. I was the kind of guy who walked around waiting for someone to have a heart attack just so I could practice my CPR technique.

"Sit down," I said.

Jennifer sat down on the toilet without putting the lid down. Ken was stabbing her all over the place and instead of pulling him out, she squirmed around trying to get comfortable like she didn't know what else to do. I took him out for her. She watched as though I was performing surgery or something.

"He's mine," she said.

"Take off your tights," I said.

"No," she said.

"They're ruined," I said. "Take them off."

Jennifer took off her ballet slippers and peeled off her tights. She was wearing my old Underoos with superheroes on them, Spiderman and Superman and Batman all poking out from under a dirty dented tutu. I decided not to say anything, but it looked funny as hell to see a flat crotch in boys' underwear. I had the feeling they didn't bother making underwear for Ken because they knew it looked too weird on him.

I poured peroxide onto her bloody knees. Jennifer screamed into my ear. She bent down and examined herself, poking her purple fingers into the torn skin; her tutu bunched up and rubbed against her face, scraping it. I worked on her knees, removing little pebbles and pieces of grass from the area.

She started crying again.

"You're okay," I said. "You're not dying." She didn't care. "Do you want anything?" I asked, trying to be nice.

"Barbie," she said.

It was the first time I'd handled Barbie in public. I picked her up like she was a complete stranger and handed her to Jennifer, who grabbed her by the hair. I started to tell her to ease up, but couldn't. Barbie looked at me and I shrugged. I went downstairs and made Jennifer one of my special Diet Cokes.

"Drink this," I said, handing it to her. She took four giant gulps and immediately I felt guilty about having used a whole Valium.

"Why don't you give a little to your Barbie," I said. "I'm sure she's thirsty too."

Barbie winked at me and I could have killed her, first off for doing it in front of Jennifer, and second because she didn't know what the hell she was winking about.

I went into my room and put the piano away. I figured as long as I kept it in the original box I'd be safe. If anyone found it, I'd say it was a present for Jennifer.

• • •

Wednesday Ken and Barbie had their heads switched. I went to get Barbie, and there on top of the dresser were Barbie and Ken, sort of. Barbie's head was on Ken's body and Ken's head was on Barbie. At first I thought it was just me.

"Hi," Barbie's head said.

I couldn't respond. She was on Ken's body and I was looking at Ken in a whole new way.

I picked up the Barbie head/Ken and immediately Barbie's head rolled off. It rolled across the dresser, across the white doily past Jennifer's collection of miniature ceramic cats, and *boom* it fell to the floor. I saw Barbie's head rolling and about to fall, and then falling, but there was nothing I could do to stop it. I was frozen, paralyzed with Ken's headless body in my left hand.

Barbie's head was on the floor, her hair spread out underneath it like angel wings in the snow, and I expected to see blood, a wide rich pool of blood, or at least a little bit coming out of her ear, her nose, or her mouth. I looked at her head on the floor and saw nothing but Barbie with eyes like the cosmos looking up at me. I thought she was dead.

"Christ, that hurt," she said. "And I already had a headache from these earrings."

There were little red dot/ball earrings jutting out of Barbie's ears.

"They go right through my head, you know. I guess it takes getting used to," Barbie said.

I noticed my mother's pin cushion on the dresser next to the other Barbie/Ken, the Barbie body, Ken head. The pin cushion was filled with hundreds of pins, pins with flat silver ends and pins with red, yellow, and blue dot/ball ends.

"You have pins in your head," I said to the Barbie head on the floor.

"Is that supposed to be a compliment?"

I was starting to hate her. I was being perfectly clear and she didn't understand me.

I looked at Ken. He was in my left hand, my fist wrapped around his waist. I looked at him and realized my thumb was on his bump. My thumb was pressed against Ken's crotch and as soon as I noticed I got an automatic hard-on, the kind you don't know you're getting, it's just there. I started rubbing Ken's bump and watching my thumb like it was a large-screen projection of a porno movie.

"What are you doing?" Barbie's head said. "Get me up. Help me." I was rubbing Ken's bump/hump with my finger inside his bathing suit. I was standing in the middle of my sister's room, with my pants pulled down.

"Aren't you going to help me?" Barbie kept asking. "Aren't you going to help me?"

In the second before I came, I held Ken's head hole in front of me. I held Ken upside down above my dick and came inside of Ken like I never could in Barbie.

I came into Ken's body and as soon as I was done I wanted to do it again. I wanted to fill Ken and put his head back on, like a perfume bottle. I wanted Ken to be the vessel for my secret supply. I came in Ken and then I remembered he wasn't mine. He didn't belong to me. I took him into the bathroom and soaked him in warm water and Ivory liquid. I brushed his insides with Jennifer's toothbrush and left him alone in a cold-water rinse.

"Aren't you going to help me, aren't you?" Barbie kept asking.

I started thinking she'd been brain damaged by the accident. I picked her head up from the floor.

"What took you so long?" she asked.

"I had to take care of Ken."

"Is he okay?"

"He'll be fine. He's soaking in the bathroom." I held Barbie's head in my hand.

"What are you going to do?"

"What do you mean?" I said.

Did my little incident, my moment with Ken, mean that right then and there some decision about my future life as queerbait had to be made?

"This afternoon. Where are we going? What are we doing? I miss you when I don't see you," Barbie said.

"You see me every day," I said.

"I don't really see you. I sit on top of the dresser and if you pass by, I see you. Take me to your room."

"I have to bring Ken's body back."

I went into the bathroom, rinsed out Ken, blew him dry with my mother's blow dryer, then played with him again. It was a boy thing, we were boys together. I thought sometime I might play ball with him, I might take him out instead of Barbie.

"Everything takes you so long," Barbie said when I got back into the room.

I put Ken back up on the dresser, picked up Barbie's body, knocked Ken's head off, and smashed Barbie's head back down on her own damn neck.

"I don't want to fight with you," Barbie said as I carried her into my room. "We don't have enough time together to fight. Fuck me," she said.

I didn't feel like it. I was thinking about fucking Ken and Ken being a boy. I was thinking about Barbie and Barbie being a girl. I was thinking about Jennifer, switching Barbie and Ken's heads, chewing Barbie's feet off, hanging Barbie from the ceiling fan, and who knows what else.

"Fuck me," Barbie said again.

I ripped Barbie's clothing off. Between Barbie's legs Jennifer had drawn pubic hair in reverse. She'd drawn it upside down so it looked like a fountain spewing up and out in great wide arcs. I spit directly onto Barbie and with my thumb and first finger rubbed the ink lines, erasing them. Barbie moaned.

"Why do you let her do this to you?"

"Jennifer owns me," Barbie moaned.

Jennifer owns me, she said, so easily and with pleasure. I was totally jealous. Jennifer owned Barbie and it made me crazy. Obviously it was one of those relationships that could only exist between women. Jennifer could own her because it didn't matter that Jennifer owned her. Jennifer didn't want Barbie, she had her.

"You're perfect," I said.

"I'm getting fat," Barbie said.

Barbie was crawling all over me, and I wondered if Jennifer knew she was a nymphomaniac. I wondered if Jennifer knew what a nymphomaniac was.

"You don't belong with little girls," I said.

Barbie ignored me.

There were scratches on Barbie's chest and stomach. She didn't say anything about them and so at first I pretended not to notice. As I was touching her, I could feel they were deep, like slices. The edges were rough; my finger caught on them and I couldn't help but wonder.

"Jennifer?" I said, massaging the cuts with my tongue, as though my tongue, like sandpaper, would erase them. Barbie nodded.

In fact, I thought of using sandpaper, but didn't know how I would explain it to Barbie: *You have to lie still and let me rub it really hard with this stuff that's like terrycloth dipped in cement.* I thought she might even like it if I made it into an S&M kind of thing and handcuffed her first.

I ran my tongue back and forth over the slivers, back and forth over the words "copyright 1966 Mattel Inc., Malaysia" tattooed on her back. Tonguing the tattoo drove Barbie crazy. She said it had something to do with scar tissue being extremely sensitive.

Barbie pushed herself hard against me, I could feel her slices rubbing my skin. I was thinking that Jennifer might kill Barbie. Without meaning to she might just go over the line and I wondered if Barbie would know what was happening or if she'd try to stop her.

We fucked, that's what I called it, fucking. In the beginning Barbie said she hated the word, which made me like it even more. She hated it because it was so strong and hard, and she said we weren't fucking, we were making love. I told her she had to be kidding.

"Fuck me," she said that afternoon and I knew the end was coming soon. "Fuck me," she said. I didn't like the sound of the word.

Friday when I went into Jennifer's room, there was something in the air. The place smelled like a science lab, a fire, a failed experiment.

Barbie was wearing a strapless yellow evening dress. Her hair was wrapped into a high bun, more like a wedding cake than something Betty Crocker would whip up. There seemed to be layers and layers of angel's hair spinning in a circle above her head. She had yellow pins through her ears and gold fuck-me shoes that matched the belt around her waist. For a second I thought of the belt and imagined tying her up, but more than restraining her arms or legs, I thought of wrapping the belt around her face, tying it across her mouth.

I looked at Barbie and saw something dark and thick like a scar rising up and over the edge of her dress. I grabbed her and pulled the front of the dress down.

"Hey, big boy," Barbie said. "Don't I even get a hello?"

Barbie's breasts had been sawed at with a knife. There were a hundred marks from a blade that might have had five rows of teeth like shark jaws. And as if that wasn't enough, she'd been dissolved by fire, blue and yellow flames had been pressed against her and held there until she melted and eventually became the fire that burned herself. All of it had been somehow stirred with the lead of a pencil, the point of a pen, and left to cool. Molten Barbie flesh had been left to harden, black and pink plastic swirled together, in the crater Jennifer had dug out of her breasts.

I examined her in detail like a scientist, a pathologist, a fucking medical examiner. I studied the burns, the gouged-out area, as if by looking closely I'd find something, an explanation, a way out.

A disgusting taste came up into my mouth, like I'd been sucking on batteries. It came up, then sank back down into my stomach, leaving my mouth puckered with the bitter metallic flavor of sour saliva. I coughed and spit onto my shirt sleeve, then rolled the sleeve over to cover the wet spot.

With my index finger I touched the edge of the burn as lightly as I could. The round rim of her scar broke off under my finger. I almost dropped her.

"It's just a reduction," Barbie said. "Jennifer and I are even now."

Barbie was smiling. She had the same expression on her face as when I first saw her and fell in love. She had the same expression she always had and I couldn't stand it. She was smiling, and she was burned. She was smiling, and she was ruined. I pulled her dress back up, above the scarline. I put her down carefully on the doily on top of the dresser and started to walk away.

"Hey," Barbie said, "aren't we going to play?"

Mary Hood

HOW FAR SHE WENT

MARY HOOD (1946–), a Georgia native, is the author of the novel *Familiar Heat* and two short story collections, *How Far She Went*, which won the Flannery O'Connor Award for Short Fiction and *The Southern Review*/Louisiana State University Short Fiction Award, and *And Venus Is Blue*, which won the Lillian Smith Book Award, the Townsend Prize for Fiction, and the Dixie Council of Authors and Journalists Author-of-the-Year Award. A recipient of the Whiting Award, she was the John and Renée Grisham Southern Writer-in-Residence at the University of Mississippi and has taught creative writing at Berry College; Reinhardt College; Centre College in Danville, Kentucky; and the University of Georgia.

They had quarreled all morning, squalled all summer about the incidentals: how tight the girl's cut-off jeans were, the "Every Inch a Woman" T-shirt, her choice of music and how loud she played it, her practiced inattention, her sullen look. Her granny wrung out the last boiled dishcloth, pinched it to the line, giving the basin a sling and a slap, the water flying out in a scalding arc onto the Queen Anne's lace by the path, never mind if it bloomed, that didn't make it worth anything except to chiggers, but the girl would cut it by the everlasting armload and cherish it in the old churn, going to that much trouble for a weed but not bending once—unbegged—to pick the nearest bean; she was sulking now. Bored. Displaced.

"And what do you think happens to a chigger if nobody ever walks by his weed?" her granny asked, heading for the house with that sidelong uneager unanswered glance, hoping for what? The surprise gift of a smile? Nothing. The woman shook her head and said it. "Nothing." The door slammed behind her. Let it.

"I hate it here!" the girl yelled then. She picked up a stick and broke it and threw the pieces—one from each hand—at the laundry drying in the noon. Missed. Missed.

Then she turned on her bare, haughty heel and set off high-shouldered into the heat, quick but not far, not far enough—no road was *that* long—only as far as she dared. At the gate, a rusty chain swinging between two lichened posts, she stopped, then backed up the raw drive to make a run at the barrier, lofting, clear-

281

ing it clean, her long hair wild in the sun. Triumphant, she looked back at the house where she caught at the dark window her granny's face in its perpetual eclipse of disappointment, old at fifty. She stepped back, but the girl saw her.

"You don't know me!" the girl shouted, chin high, and ran till her ribs ached.

As she rested in the rattling shade of the willows, the little dog found her. He could be counted on. He barked all the way, and squealed when she pulled the burr from his ear. They started back to the house for lunch. By then the mailman had long come and gone in the old ruts, leaving the one letter folded now to fit the woman's apron pocket.

If bad news darkened her granny's face, the girl ignored it. Didn't talk at all, another of her distancings, her defiances. So it was as they ate that the woman summarized, "Your daddy wants you to cash in the plane ticket and buy you something. School clothes. For here."

Pale, the girl stared, defenseless only an instant before blurting out, "You're lying."

The woman had to stretch across the table to leave her handprint on that blank cheek. She said, not caring if it stung or not, "He's been planning it since he sent you here."

"I could turn this whole house over, dump it! Leave you slobbering over that stinking jealous dog in the dust!" The girl trembled with the vision, with the strength it gave her. It made her laugh. "Scatter the Holy Bible like confetti and ravel the crochet into miles of stupid string! I could! I will! I won't stay here!" But she didn't move, not until her tears rose to meet her color, and then to escape the shame of minding so much she fled. Just headed away, blind. It didn't matter, this time, how far she went.

The woman set her thoughts against fretting over their bickering, just went on unalarmed with chores, clearing off after the uneaten meal, bringing in the laundry, scattering corn for the chickens, ladling manure tea onto the porch flowers. She listened though. She always had been a listener. It gave her a cocked look. She forgot why she had gone into the girl's empty room, that ungirlish, tenuous lodging place with its bleak order, its ready suitcases never unpacked, the narrow bed, the contested radio on the windowsill. The woman drew the cracked shade down between the radio and the August sun. There wasn't anything else to do.

It was after six when she tied on her rough oxfords and walked down the drive and dropped the gate chain and headed back to the creosoted shed where she kept her tools. She took a hoe for snakes, a rake, shears to trim the grass where it grew, and seed in her pocket to scatter where it never had grown at all. She put the tools and her gloves and the bucket in the trunk of the old Chevy, its prime and rust like an Appaloosa's spots through the chalky white finish. She left the trunk open and the tool handles sticking out. She wasn't going far.

The heat of the day had broken, but the air was thick, sultry, weighted with honeysuckle in second bloom and the Nu-Grape scent of kudzu. The maple and poplar leaves turned over, quaking, silver. There wouldn't be any rain. She told the dog to stay, but he knew a trick. He stowed away when she turned her back, leaped right into the trunk with the tools, then gave himself away with exultant barks. Hearing him, her court jester, she stopped the car and welcomed him into the front seat beside her. Then they went on. Not a mile from her gate she turned onto the blue gravel of the cemetery lane, hauled the gearshift into reverse to whoa them, and got out to take the idle walk down to her buried hopes, bending all along to rout out a handful of weeds from between the markers of old acquaintance. She stood there and read, slow. The dog whined at her hem; she picked him up and rested her chin on his head, then he wriggled and whined to run free, contrary and restless as a child.

The crows called strong and bold MOM! MOM! A trick of the ear to hear it like that. She knew it was the crows, but still she looked around. No one called her that now. She was done with that. And what was it worth anyway? It all came to this: solitary weeding. The sinful fumble of flesh, the fear, the listening for a return that never came, the shamed waiting, the unanswered prayers, the perjury on the certificate—hadn't she lain there weary of the whole lie and it only beginning? and a voice telling her, "Here's your baby, here's your girl," and the swaddled package meaning no more to her than an extra anything, something store-bought, something she could take back for a refund.

"Tie her to the fence and give her a bale of hay," she had murmured, drugged, and they teased her, excused her for such a welcoming, blaming the anesthesia, but it went deeper than that; *she* knew, and the *baby* knew: there was no love in the begetting. That was the secret, unforgivable, that not another good thing could ever make up for, where all the bad had come from, like a visitation, a punishment. She knew that was why Sylvie had been wild, had gone to earth so early, and before dying had made this child in sudden wedlock, a child who would be just like her, would carry the hurting on into another generation. A matter of time. No use raising her hand. But she *had* raised her hand. Still wore on its palm the memory of the sting of the collision with the girl's cheek; had she broken her jaw? Her heart? Of course not. She said it aloud: "Takes more than that."

She went to work then, doing what she could with her old tools. She pecked the clay on Sylvie's grave, new-looking, unhealed after years. She tried again, scattering seeds from her pocket, every last possible one of them. Off in the west she could hear the pulpwood cutters sawing through another acre across the lake. Nearer, there was the racket of motorcycles laboring cross-country, insect-like, distracting.

She took her bucket to the well and hung it on the pump. She had half filled it when the bikers roared up, right down the blue gravel, straight at her. She let the bucket overflow, staring. On the back of one of the machines was the girl. Sylvie's girl! Her bare arms wrapped around the shirtless man riding between her thighs. They were first. The second biker rode alone. She studied their strangers' faces as they circled her. They were the enemy, all of them. Laughing. The girl was laughing too, laughing like her mama did. Out in the middle of nowhere the girl had found these two men, some moth-musk about her drawing them (too soon!) to what? She shouted it: "What in God's—" They roared off without answering her, and the bucket of water tipped over, spilling its stain blood-dark on the red dust.

The dog went wild barking, leaping after them, snapping at the tires, and there was no calling him down. The bikers made a wide circuit of the church-yard, then roared straight across the graves, leaping the ditch and landing up-right on the road again, heading off toward the reservoir.

Furious, she ran to her car, past the barking dog, this time leaving him be-hind, driving after them, horn blowing nonstop, to get back what was not theirs. She drove after them knowing what they did not know, that all the roads be-yond that point dead-ended. She surprised them, swinging the Impala across their path, cutting them off; let them hit it! They stopped. She got out, breath-ing hard, and said, when she could, "She's underage." Just that. And put out her claiming hand with an authority that made the girl's arms drop from the man's insolent waist and her legs tremble.

"I was just riding," the girl said, not looking up.

Behind them the sun was heading on toward down. The long shadows of the pines drifted back and forth in the same breeze that puffed the distant sails on the lake. Dead limbs creaked and clashed overhead like the antlers of locked and furious beasts.

"Sheeeut," the lone rider said. "I told you." He braced with his muddy boot and leaned out from his machine to spit. The man the girl had been riding with had the invading sort of eyes the woman had spent her lifetime bolting doors against. She met him now, face to face.

"Right there, missy," her granny said, pointing behind her to the car.

The girl slid off the motorcycle and stood halfway between her choices. She started slightly at the poosh! as he popped another top and chugged the beer in one uptilting of his head. His eyes never left the woman's. When he was through, he tossed the can high, flipping it end over end. Before it hit the ground he had his pistol out and, firing once, winged it into the lake.

"Freaking lucky shot," the other one grudged.

"I don't need luck," he said. He sighted down the barrel of the gun at the woman's head. "POW!" he yelled, and when she recoiled, he laughed. He swung around to the girl; he kept aiming the gun, here, there, high, low, all around. "Y'all settle it," he said, with a shrug.

The girl had to understand him then, had to know him, had to know better. But still she hesitated. He kept looking at her, then away.

"She's fifteen," her granny said. "You can go to jail."

"You can go to hell," he said.

"Probably will," her granny told him. "I'll save you a seat by the fire." She took the girl by the arm and drew her to the car; she backed up, swung around, and headed out the road toward the churchyard for her tools and dog. The whole way the girl said nothing, just hunched against the far door, staring hard-eyed out at the pines going past.

The woman finished watering the seed in, and collected her tools. As she worked, she muttered, "It's your own kin buried here, you might have the decency to glance this way one time ..." The girl was finger-tweezing her eyebrows in the side mirror. She didn't look around as the dog and the woman got in. Her granny shifted hard, sending the tools clattering in the trunk.

When they came to the main road, there were the men. Watching for them. Waiting for them. They kicked their machines into life and followed, close, bumping them, slapping the old fenders, yelling. The girl gave a wild glance around at the one by her door and said, "Gran'ma?" and as he drew his pistol, "Gran'ma!" just as the gun nosed into the open window. She frantically cranked the glass up between her and the weapon, and her granny, seeing, spat, "Fool!" She never had been one to pray for peace or rain. She stamped the accelerator right to the floor.

The motorcycles caught up. Now she braked, hard, and swerved off the road into an alley between the pines, not even wide enough for the school bus, just a fire scrape that came out a quarter mile from her own house, if she could get that far. She slewed on the pine straw, then righted, tearing along the dark tunnel through the woods. She had for the time being bested them; they were left behind. She was winning. Then she hit the wallow where the tadpoles were already five weeks old. The Chevy plowed in and stalled. When she got it cranked again, they were stuck. The tires spattered mud three feet up the near trunks as she tried to spin them out, to rock them out. Useless. "Get out and run!" she cried, but the trees were too close on the passenger side. The girl couldn't open her door. She wasted precious time having to crawl out under the steering wheel. The woman waited but the dog ran on.

They struggled through the dusky woods, their pace slowed by the thick straw and vines. Overhead, in the last light, the martins were reeling free and sure after their prey.

"Why? Why?" the girl gasped, as they lunged down the old deer trail. Behind them they could hear shots, and glass breaking as the men came to the bogged car. The woman kept on running, swatting their way clear through the shoulder-high weeds. They could see the Greer cottage, and made for it. But it was ivied-over, padlocked, the woodpile dry-rotting under its tarp, the electric meterbox empty on the pole. No help there.

The dog, excited, trotted on, yelping, his lips whiteflecked. He scented the lake and headed that way, urging them on with thirsty yips. On the clay shore, treeless, deserted, at the utter limit of land, they stood defenseless, listening to the men coming on, between them and home. The woman pressed her hands to her mouth, stifling her cough. She was exhausted. She couldn't think.

"We can get under!" the girl cried suddenly, and pointed toward the Greers' dock, gap-planked, its walkway grounded on the mud. They splashed out to it, wading in, the woman grabbing up the telltale, tattletale dog in her arms. They waded out to the far end and ducked under. There was room between the foam floats for them to crouch neck-deep.

The dog wouldn't hush, even then; never had yet, and there wasn't time to teach him. When the woman realized that, she did what she had to do. She grabbed him whimpering; held him; held him under till the struggle ceased and the bubbles rose silver from his fur. They crouched there then, the two of them, submerged to the shoulders, feet unsteady on the slimed lake bed. They listened. The sky went from rose to ocher to violet in the cracks over their heads. The motorcycles had stopped now. In the silence there was the glissando of locusts, the dry crunch of boots on the flinty beach, their low man-talk drifting as they prowled back and forth. One of them struck a match.

"—they in these woods we could burn 'em out."

The wind carried their voices away into the pines. Some few words eddied back.

"—lippy old smartass do a little work on her knees besides praying—"

Laughter. It echoed off the deserted house. They were getting closer.

One of them strode directly out to the dock, walked on the planks over their heads. They could look up and see his boot soles. He was the one with the gun. He slapped a mosquito on his bare back and cursed. The carp, roused by the troubling of the waters, came nosing around the dock, guzzling and snorting. The girl and her granny held still, so still. The man fired his pistol into the shadows, and a wounded fish thrashed, dying. The man knelt and reached for it, chuffing out his beery breath. He belched. He pawed the lake for the dead fish, cursing as it floated out of reach. He shot it again, firing at it till it sank and the gun was empty. Cursed that too. He stood then and unzipped and relieved himself of some of the beer. They had to listen to that. To know that about him. To endure that, unprotesting.

Back and forth on shore the other one ranged, restless. He lit another cigarette. He coughed. He called, "Hey! They got away, man, that's all. Don't get your shorts in a wad. Let's go."

"Yeah." He finished. He zipped. He stumped back across the planks and leaped to shore, leaving the dock tilting amid widening ripples. Underneath, they waited.

The bike cranked. The other ratcheted, ratcheted, then coughed, caught, roared. They circled, cut deep ruts, slung gravel, and went. Their roaring died away and away. Crickets resumed and a near frog bic-bic-bicked.

Under the dock, they waited a little longer to be sure. Then they ducked below the water, scraped out from under the pontoon, and came up into free air, slogging toward shore. It had seemed warm enough in the water. Now they shivered. It was almost night. One streak of light still stood reflected on the darkening lake, drew itself thinner, narrowing into a final cancellation of day. A plane winked its way west.

The girl was trembling. She ran her hands down her arms and legs, shedding water like a garment. She sighed, almost a sob. The woman held the dog in her arms; she dropped to her knees upon the random stones and murmured, private, haggard, "Oh, honey," three times, maybe all three times for the dog, maybe once for each of them. The girl waited, watching. Her granny rocked the dog like a baby, like a dead child, rocked slower and slower and was still.

"I'm sorry," the girl said then, avoiding the dog's inert, empty eye.

"It was him or you," her granny said, finally, looking up. Looking her over. "Did they mess with you? With your britches? Did they?"

"No!" Then, quieter, "No, ma'am."

When the woman tried to stand up she staggered, lightheaded, clumsy with the freight of the dog. "No, ma'am," she echoed, fending off the girl's "Let me." And she said again, "It was him or you. I know that. I'm not going to rub your face in it." They saw each other as well as they could in that failing light, in any light.

The woman started toward home, saying, "Around here, we bear our own burdens." She led the way along the weedy shortcuts. The twilight bleached the dead limbs of the pines to bone. Insects sang in the thickets, silencing at their oncoming.

"We'll see about the car in the morning," the woman said. She bore her armful toward her own moth-ridden dusk-to-dawn security light with that country grace she had always had when the earth was reliably progressing underfoot. The girl walked close behind her, exactly where *she* walked, matching her pace, matching her stride, close enough to put her hand forth (if the need arose) and touch her granny's back where the faded voile was clinging damp, the merest gauze between their wounds.

Denis Johnson

CAR CRASH WHILE HITCHHIKING

DENIS JOHNSON (1949–) was born in Munich, West Germany. The son of a U.S. information agent, Johnson had lived in Tokyo, Washington, D.C., Manila, and Munich by the time he was eighteen. He received a BA from the University of Iowa and attended the Iowa Writers' Workshop. When he was nineteen, his first collection of poetry, *The Incognito Lounge*, was selected for the 1982 National Poetry Series. He is the author of the story collection *Jesus' Son* and the novels *Angels, Fiskadoro, The Stars at Noon,* and *Resuscitation of a Hanged Man*. He has received two National Endowment for the Arts Fellowships; a fellowship from the Fine Arts Work Center in Provincetown, Massachusetts; and a Whiting Writers' Award for excellence in fiction and poetry. Mr. Johnson has held a variety of jobs, including teaching at Lake Forest College outside Chicago, waiting tables in Seattle, and teaching creative writing at the state prison in Florence, Arizona. He is currently the Mitte Chair at Texas State University in San Marcos, Texas.

A salesman who shared his liquor and steered while sleeping ... A Cherokee filled with bourbon ... A VW no more than a bubble of hashish fumes, captained by a college student ...

And a family from Marshalltown who head-onned and killed forever a man driving west out of Bethany, Missouri ...

... I rose up sopping wet from sleeping under the pouring rain, and something less than conscious, thanks to the first three of the people I've already named—the salesman and the Indian and the student—all of whom had given me drugs. At the head of the entrance ramp I waited without hope of a ride. What was the point, even, of rolling up my sleeping bag when I was too wet to be let into anybody's car? I draped it around me like a cape. The downpour raked the asphalt and gurgled in the ruts. My thoughts zoomed pitifully. The traveling salesman had fed me pills that made the linings of my veins feel scraped out. My jaw ached. I knew every raindrop by its name. I sensed everything before it happened. I knew a certain Oldsmobile would stop for me even before it slowed, and by the sweet voices of the family inside it I knew we'd have an accident in the storm.

I didn't care. They said they'd take me all the way.

The man and the wife put the little girl up front with them, and left the baby in back with me and my dripping bedroll. "I'm not taking you anywhere very fast," the man said. "I've got my wife and babies here, that's why."

You are the ones, I thought. And I piled my sleeping bag against the left-hand door and slept across it, not caring whether I lived or died. The baby slept free on the seat beside me. He was about nine months old.

. . . But before any of this, that afternoon, the salesman and I had swept down into Kansas City in his luxury car. We'd developed a dangerous cynical camaraderie beginning in Texas, where he'd taken me on. We ate up his bottle of amphetamines, and every so often we pulled off the interstate and bought another pint of Canadian Club and a sack of ice. His car had cylindrical glass holders attached to either door and a white, leathery interior. He said he'd take me home to stay overnight with his family, but first he wanted to stop and see a woman he knew.

Under midwestern clouds like great gray brains we left the superhighway with a drifting sensation and entered Kansas City's rush hour with a sensation of running aground. As soon as we slowed down, all the magic of traveling together burned away. He went on and on about his girlfriend. "I like this girl, I think I love this girl—but I've got two kids and a wife, and there's certain obligations there. And on top of everything else, I love my wife. I'm gifted with love. I love my kids. I love all my relatives." As he kept on, I felt jilted and sad: "I have a boat, a little sixteen-footer. I have two cars. There's room in the backyard for a swimming pool." He found his girlfriend at work. She ran a furniture store, and I lost him there.

The clouds stayed the same until night. Then, in the dark, I didn't see the storm gathering. The driver of the Volkswagen, a college man, the one who stoked my head with all the hashish, let me out beyond the city limits just as it began to rain. Never mind the speed I'd been taking, I was too overcome to stand up. I lay out in the grass off the exit ramp and woke in the middle of a puddle that had filled up around me.

And later, as I've said, I slept in the back seat while the Oldsmobile—the family from Marshalltown—splashed along through the rain. And yet I dreamed I was looking right through my eyelids, and my pulse marked off the seconds of time. The Interstate through western Missouri was, in that era, nothing more than a two-way road, most of it. When a semi truck came toward us and passed going the other way, we were lost in a blinding spray and a warfare of noises such as you get being towed through an automatic car wash. The wipers stood up and lay down across the windshield without much effect. I was exhausted, and after an hour I slept more deeply.

I'd known all along exactly what was going to happen. But the man and his wife woke me up later, denying it viciously.

"Oh—*no!*"

"NO!"

I was thrown against the back of their seat so hard that it broke. I commenced bouncing back and forth. A liquid which I knew right away was human blood flew around-the car and rained down on my head. When it was over I was in the back seat again, just as I had been. I rose up and looked around. Our headlights had gone out. The radiator was hissing steadily. Beyond that, I didn't hear a thing. As far as I could tell, I was the only one conscious. As my eyes adjusted I saw that the baby was lying on its back beside me as if nothing had happened. Its eyes were open and it was feeling its cheeks with its little hands.

In a minute the driver, who'd been slumped over the wheel, sat up and peered at us. His face was smashed and dark with blood. It made my teeth hurt to look at him—but when he spoke, it didn't sound as if any of his teeth were broken.

"What happened?"

"We had a wreck," he said.

"The baby's okay," I said, although I had no idea how the baby was.

He turned to his wife.

"Janice," he said. "Janice, Janice!"

"Is she okay?"

"She's dead!" he said, shaking her angrily.

"No, she's not." I was ready to deny everything myself now.

Their little girl was alive, but knocked out. She whimpered in her sleep. But the man went on shaking his wife.

"Janice!" he hollered.

His wife moaned.

"She's not dead," I said, clambering from the car and running away.

"She won't wake up," I heard him say.

I was standing out here in the night, with the baby, for some reason, in my arms. It must have still been raining, but I remember nothing about the weather. We'd collided with another car on what I now perceived was a two-lane bridge. The water beneath us was invisible in the dark.

Moving toward the other car I began to hear rasping, metallic snores. Somebody was flung halfway out the passenger door, which was open, in the posture of one hanging from a trapeze by his ankles. The car had been broadsided, smashed so flat that no room was left inside of it even for this person's legs, to say nothing of a driver or any other passengers. I just walked right on past.

Headlights were coming from far off. I made for the head of the bridge, waving them to stop with one arm, and clutching the baby to my shoulder with the other.

It was a big semi, grinding its gears as it decelerated. The driver rolled down his window and I shouted up at him. "There's a wreck. Go for help."

"I can't turn around here," he said.

He let me and the baby up on the passenger side, and we just sat there in the cab, looking at the wreckage in his headlights.

"Is everybody dead?" he asked.

"I can't tell who is and who isn't," I admitted.

He poured himself a cup of coffee from a thermos and switched off all but his parking lights.

"What time is it?"

"Oh, it's around quarter after three," he said.

By his manner he seemed to endorse the idea of not doing anything about this. I was relieved and tearful. I'd thought something was required of me, but I hadn't wanted to find out what it was.

When another car showed, coming the opposite direction, I thought I should talk to them. "Can you keep the baby?" I asked the truck driver.

"You'd better hang on to him," the driver said. "It's a boy, isn't it?"

"Well, I think so," I said.

The man hanging out of the wrecked car was still alive as I passed, and I stopped, grown a little more used to the idea now of how really badly broken he was, and made sure there was nothing I could do. He was snoring loudly and rudely. His blood bubbled out of his mouth with every breath. He wouldn't be taking many more. I knew that, but he didn't, and therefore I looked down into the great pity of a person's life on this earth. I don't mean that we all end up dead, that's not the great pity. I mean that he couldn't tell me what he was dreaming, and I couldn't tell him what was real.

Before too long there were cars backed up for a ways at either end of the bridge, and headlights giving a night-game atmosphere in the steaming rubble, and ambulances and cop cars nudging through so that the air pulsed with color. I didn't talk to anyone. My secret was that in this short while I had gone from being the president of this tragedy to being a faceless onlooker at a gory wreck. At some point an officer learned that I was one of the passengers, and took my statement. I don't remember any of this, except that he told me, "Put out your cigarette." We paused in our conversation to watch the dying man being loaded into the ambulance. He was still alive, still dreaming obscenely. The blood ran off of him in strings. His knees jerked and his head rattled.

There was nothing wrong with me, and I hadn't seen anything, but the policeman had to question me and take me to the hospital anyway. The word came over his car radio that the man was now dead, just as we came under the awning of the emergency-room entrance.

I stood in a tiled corridor with my wet sleeping bag bunched against the wall beside me, talking to a man from the local funeral home.

The doctor stopped to tell me I'd better have an X-ray.

"No."

"Now would be the time. If something turns up later . . ."

"There's nothing wrong with me."

Down the hall came the wife. She was glorious, burning. She didn't know yet that her husband was dead. We knew. That's what gave her such power over us. The doctor took her into a room with a desk at the end of the hall, and from under the closed door a slab of brilliance radiated as if, by some stupendous process, diamonds were being incinerated in there. What a pair of lungs! She shrieked as I imagined an eagle would shriek. It felt wonderful to be alive to hear it! I've gone looking for that feeling everywhere.

"There's nothing wrong with me"—I'm surprised I let those words out. But it's always been my tendency to lie to doctors, as if good health consisted only of the ability to fool them.

Some years later, one time when I was admitted to the detox at Seattle General Hospital, I took the same tack.

"Are you hearing unusual sounds or voices?" the doctor asked.

"Help us, oh God, it hurts," the boxes of cotton screamed.

"Not exactly," I said.

"Not exactly," he said. "Now what does that mean."

"I'm not ready to go into all that," I said. A yellow bird fluttered close to my face, and my muscles grabbed. Now I was flopping like a fish. When I squeezed shut my eyes, hot tears exploded from the sockets. When I opened them, I was on my stomach.

"How did the room get so white?" I asked.

A beautiful nurse was touching my skin. "These are vitamins," she said, and drove the needle in.

It was raining. Gigantic ferns leaned over us. The forest drifted down a hill. I could hear a creek rushing down among rocks. And you, you ridiculous people, you expect me to help you.

Edward P. Jones

MARIE

EDWARD P. JONES (1950–), the author of *Lost in the City*, has published stories in *The Paris Review, Ploughshares, Callaloo, Essence,* and elsewhere. His novel *The Known World* received the 2004 Pulitzer Prize for Fiction, and his newest book, *All Aunt Hagar's Children*, was a finalist for the PEN/Faulkner Award. A recipient of an MFA from the University of Virginia, he has taught at Princeton University, George Mason University, Warren Wilson College, Hofstra University, American University, and the University of Virginia. He was awarded a MacArthur Fellowship in 2004.

Every now and again, as if on a whim, the federal government people would write to Marie Delaveaux Wilson in one of those white, stampless envelopes and tell her to come in to their place so they could take another look at her. They, the Social Security people, wrote to her in a foreign language that she had learned to translate over the years, and for all the years she had been receiving the letters the same man had been signing them. Once, because she had something important to tell him, Marie called the number the man always put at the top of the letters, but a woman answered Mr. Smith's telephone and told Marie he was in an all-day meeting. Another time she called and a man said Mr. Smith was on vacation. And finally one day a woman answered and told Marie that Mr. Smith was deceased. The woman told her to wait and she would get someone new to talk to her about her case, but Marie thought it bad luck to have telephoned a dead man and she hung up.

Now, years after the woman had told her Mr. Smith was no more, the letters were still being signed by John Smith. Come into our office at 21st and M streets, Northwest, the letters said in that foreign language. Come in so we can see if you are still blind in one eye, come in so we can see if you are still old and getting older. Come in so we can see if you still deserve to get Supplemental Security Income payments.

She always obeyed the letters, even if the order now came from a dead man, for she knew people who had been temporarily cut off from SSI for not showing up or even for being late. And once cut off, you had to move heaven and earth to get back on.

So on a not unpleasant day in March, she rose in the dark in the morning,

293

even before the day had any sort of character, to give herself plenty of time to bathe, eat, lay out money for the bus, dress, listen to the spirituals on the radio. She was eighty-six years old, and had learned that life was all chaos and painful uncertainty and that the only way to get through it was to expect chaos even in the most innocent of moments. Offer a crust of bread to a sick bird and you often drew back a bloody finger.

John Smith's letter had told her to come in at eleven o'clock, his favorite time, and by nine that morning she had had her bath and had eaten. Dressed by nine thirty. The walk from Claridge Towers at 12th and M down to the bus stop at 14th and K took her about ten minutes, more or less. There was a bus at about ten thirty, her schedule told her, but she preferred the one that came a half hour earlier, lest there be trouble with the ten thirty bus. After she dressed, she sat at her dining room table and went over still again what papers and all else she needed to take. Given the nature of life—particularly the questions asked by the Social Security people—she always took more than they might ask for—her birth certificate, her husband's death certificate, doctors' letters.

One of the last things she put in her pocketbook was a seven-inch or so knife that she had, with the use of a small saw borrowed from a neighbor, serrated on both edges. The knife, she was convinced now, had saved her life about two weeks before. Before then she had often been careless about when she took the knife out with her, and she had never taken it out in daylight, but now she never left her apartment without it, even when going down the hall to the trash drop.

She had gone out to buy a simple box of oatmeal, no more, no less. It was about seven in the evening, the streets with enough commuters driving up 13th Street to make her feel safe. Several yards before she reached the store, the young man came from behind her and tried to rip off her coat pocket where he thought she kept her money, for she carried no purse or pocketbook after five o'clock. The money was in the other pocket with the knife, and his hand caught in the empty pocket long enough for her to reach around with the knife and cut his hand as it came out of her pocket.

He screamed and called her an old bitch. He took a few steps up 13th Street and stood in front of Emerson's Market, examining the hand and shaking off blood. Except for the cars passing up and down 13th Street, they were alone, and she began to pray.

"You cut me," he said, as if he had only been minding his own business when she cut him. "Just look what you done to my hand," he said and looked around as if for some witness to her crime. There was not a great amount of blood, but there was enough for her to see it dripping to the pavement. He seemed to be about twenty, no more than twenty-five, dressed the way they were all dressed nowadays, as if a blind man had matched up all their colors. It occurred to her to say that she had seven grandchildren his age, that by telling him this he would leave her alone. But the more filth he spoke, the more she wanted him only to come toward her again.

"You done crippled me, you old bitch."

"I sure did," she said, without malice, without triumph, but simply the way she would have told him the time of day had he asked and had she known. She gripped the knife tighter, and as she did, she turned her body ever so slightly so that her good eye lined up with him. Her heart was making an awful racket, wanting to be away from him, wanting to be safe at home. I will not be moved, some organ in the neighborhood of the heart told the heart. "And I got plenty more where that come from."

The last words seemed to bring him down some and, still shaking the blood from his hand, he took a step or two back, which disappointed her. I will not be moved, that other organ kept telling the heart. "You just crazy, thas all," he said. "Just a crazy old hag." Then he turned and lumbered up toward Logan Circle, and several times he looked back over his shoulder as if afraid she might be following. A man came out of Emerson's, then a woman with two little boys. She wanted to grab each of them by the arm and tell them she had come close to losing her life. "I saved myself with this here thing," she would have said. She forgot about the oatmeal and took her raging heart back to the apartment. She told herself that she should, but she never washed the fellow's blood off the knife, and over the next few days it dried and then it began to flake off.

Toward ten o'clock that morning Wilamena Mason knocked and let herself in with a key Marie had given her.

"I see you all ready," Wilamena said.

"With the help of the Lord," Marie said. "Want a spot a coffee?"

"No thanks," Wilamena said, and dropped into a chair at the table. "Been drinkin so much coffee lately, I'm gonna turn into coffee. Was up all night with Calhoun."

"How he doin?"

Wilamena told her Calhoun was better that morning, his first good morning in over a week. Calhoun Lambeth was Wilamena's boyfriend, a seventy-five-year-old man she had taken up with six or so months before, not long after he moved in. He was the best-dressed old man Marie had ever known, but he had always appeared to be sickly, even while strutting about with his gold-tipped cane. And seeing that she could count his days on the fingers of her hands, Marie had avoided getting to know him. She could not understand why Wilamena, who could have had any man in Claridge Towers or any other senior citizen building for that matter, would take such a man into her bed. "True love," Wilamena had explained. "Avoid heartache," Marie had said, trying to be kind.

They left the apartment. Marie sought help from no one, lest she come to depend on a person too much. But since the encounter with the young man, Wilamena had insisted on escorting Marie. Marie, to avoid arguments, allowed Wilamena to walk with her from time to time to the bus stop, but no farther.

Nothing fit Marie's theory about life like the weather in Washington. Two days before, the temperature had been in the forties, and yesterday it had dropped to the low twenties then warmed up a bit, with the afternoon bringing snow flurries. Today the weather people on the radio had said it would be warm enough to wear just a sweater, but Marie was wearing her coat. And tomorrow, the weather people said, it would be in the thirties, with maybe an inch or so of snow.

Appointments near twelve o'clock were always risky, because the Social Security people often took off for lunch long before noon and returned sometime after one. And except for a few employees who seemed to work through their lunch hours, the place shut down. Marie had never been interviewed by someone willing to work through the lunch hour. Today, though the appointment was for eleven, she waited until one thirty before the woman at the front of the waiting room told her she would have to come back another day, because the woman who handled her case was not in.

"You put my name down when I came in like everything was all right," Marie said after she had been called up to the woman's desk.

"I know," the woman said, "but I thought that Mrs. Brown was in. They told me she was in. I'm sorry." The woman began writing in a log book that rested between her telephone and a triptych of photographs. She handed Marie a slip and told her again she was sorry.

"Why you have me wait so long if she whatn't here?" She did not want to say too much, appear too upset, for the Social Security people could be unforgiving. And though she was used to waiting three and four hours, she found it especially unfair to wait when there was no one for her at all behind those panels the Social Security people used for offices. "I been here since before eleven."

"I know," the woman behind the desk said. "I know. I saw you there, ma'am, but I really didn't know Mrs. Brown wasn't here." There was a nameplate at the front of the woman's desk and it said Vernelle Wise. The name was surrounded by little hearts, the kind a child might have drawn.

Marie said nothing more and left.

The next appointment was two weeks later, eight thirty, a good hour, and the day before, a letter signed by John Smith arrived to remind her. She expected to be out at least by twelve. Three times before eleven o'clock, Marie asked Vernelle Wise if the man, Mr. Green, who was handling her case, was in that day, and each time the woman assured her that he was. At twelve, Marie ate one of the two oranges and three of the five slices of cheese she had brought. At one, she asked again if Mr. Green was indeed in that day and politely reminded Vernelle Wise that she had been waiting since about eight that morning. Vernelle was just as polite and told her the wait would soon be over.

At one fifteen, Marie began to watch the clock hands creep around the dial. She had not paid much attention to the people about her, but more and more it seemed that others were being waited on who had arrived long after she had gotten there. After asking about Mr. Green at one, she had taken a seat near the front, and as more time went by, she found herself forced to listen to the conversation that Vernelle was having with the other receptionist next to her.

"I told him . . . I told him . . . I said just get your things and leave," said the other receptionist, who didn't have a nameplate.

"Did he leave?" Vernelle wanted to know.

"Oh, no," the other woman said. "Not at first. But I picked up some of his stuff, that Christian Dior jacket he worships. I picked up my cigarette lighter and that jacket, just like I was gonna do something bad to it, and he started movin then."

Vernelle began laughing. "I wish I was there to see that." She was filing her fingernails. Now and again she would look at her fingernails to inspect her work, and if it was satisfactory, she would blow on the nail and on the file. "He back?" Vernelle asked.

The other receptionist eyed her. "What you think?" and they both laughed.

Along about two o'clock Marie became hungry again, but she did not want to eat the rest of her food because she did not know how much longer she would be there. There was a soda machine in the corner, but all sodas gave her gas.

"You-know-who gonna call you again?" the other receptionist was asking Vernelle.

"I hope so," Vernelle said. "He pretty fly. Seemed decent too. It kinda put me off when he said he was a car mechanic. I kinda like kept tryin to take a peek at his fingernails and everything the whole evenin. See if they was dirty or what."

"Well, that mechanic stuff might be good when you get your car back. My cousin's boyfriend used to do that kinda work and he made good money, girl. I mean real good money."

"Hmmmm," Vernelle said. "Anyway, the kids like him, and you know how peculiar they can be."

"Tell me about it. They do the job your mother and father used to do, huh? Only on another level."

"You can say that again," Vernelle said.

Marie went to her and told her how long she had been waiting.

"Listen," Vernelle said, pointing her fingernail file at Marie. "I told you you'll be waited on as soon as possible. This is a busy day. So I think you should just go back to your seat until we call your name." The other receptionist began to giggle.

Marie reached across the desk and slapped Vernelle Wise with all her might. Vernelle dropped the file, which made a cheap tinny sound when it hit the plastic board her chair was on. But no one heard the file because she had begun to cry right away. She looked at Marie as if, in the moment of her greatest need, Marie had denied her. "Oh, oh," Vernelle Wise said through the tears. "Oh, my dear God . . ."

The other receptionist, in her chair on casters, rolled over to Vernelle and put her arm around her. "Security!" the other receptionist hollered. "We need security here!"

The guard at the front door came quickly around the corner, one hand on his holstered gun and the other pointing accusatorially at the people seated in the waiting area. Marie had sat down and was looking at the two women almost sympathetically, as if a stranger had come in, hit Vernelle Wise, and fled.

"She slapped Vernelle!" the other receptionist said.

"Who did it?" the guard said, reaching for the man sitting beside Marie. But when the other receptionist said it was the old lady in the blue coat, the guard held back for the longest time, as if to grab her would be like arresting his own grandmother. He stood blinking and he would have gone on blinking had Marie not stood up.

She was too flustered to wait for the bus and so took a cab home. With both chains, she locked herself in the apartment, refusing to answer the door or the telephone the rest of the day and most of the next. But she knew that if her family or friends received no answer at the door or on the telephone, they would think something had happened to her. So the next afternoon, she began answering the phone and spoke with the chains on, telling Wilamena and others that she had a toothache.

For days and days after the incident she ate very little, asked God to forgive her. She was haunted by the way Vernelle's cheek had felt, by what it was like to invade and actually touch the flesh of another person. And when she thought too hard, she imagined that she was slicing through the woman's cheek, the way she had sliced through the young man's hand. But as time went on she began to remember the man's curses and the purplish color of Vernelle's fingernails, and all remorse would momentarily take flight. Finally, one morning nearly two weeks after she slapped the woman, she woke with a phrase she had not used or heard since her children were small: You whatn't raised that way.

It was the next morning that the thin young man in the suit knocked and asked through the door chains if he could speak with her. She thought that he was a Social Security man come to tear up her card and papers and tell her that they would send her no more checks. Even when he pulled out an identification card showing that he was a Howard University student, she did not believe.

In the end, she told him she didn't want to buy anything, not magazines, not candy, not anything.

"No, no," he said. "I just want to talk to you for a bit. About your life and everything. It's for a project for my folklore course. I'm talking to everyone in the building who'll let me. Please . . . I won't be a bother. Just a little bit of your time."

"I don't have anything worth talkin about," she said. "And I don't keep well these days."

"Oh, ma'am, I'm sorry. But we all got something to say. I promise I won't be a bother."

After fifteen minutes of his pleas, she opened the door to him because of his suit and his tie clip with a bird in flight, and because his long dark-brown fingers reminded her of delicate twigs. But had he turned out to be death with a gun or a knife or fingers to crush her neck, she would not have been surprised. "My name's George. George Carter. Like the president." He had the kind of voice that old people in her young days would have called womanish. "But I was born right here in D.C. Born, bred, and buttered, my mother used to say."

He stayed the rest of the day and she fixed him dinner. It scared her to be able to talk so freely with him, and at first she thought that at long last, as she had always feared, senility had taken hold of her. A few hours after he left, she looked his name up in the telephone book, and when a man who sounded like him answered, she hung up immediately. And the next day she did the same thing. He came back at least twice a week for many weeks and would set his cassette recorder on her coffee table. "He's takin down my whole life," she told Wilamena, almost the way a woman might speak in awe of a new boyfriend.

One day he played back for the first time some of what she told the recorder:

> . . . My father would be sittin there readin the paper. He'd say whenever they put in a new president, "Look like he got the chair for four years." And it got so that's what I saw—this poor man sittin in that chair for four long years while the rest of the world went on about its business. I don't know if I thought he ever did anything, the president. I just knew that he had to sit in that chair for four years. Maybe I thought that by his sittin in that chair and doin nothin else for four years he made the country what it was and that without him sittin there the country wouldn't be what it was. Maybe thas what I got from listenin to my father readin and to my mother askin him questions bout what he was readin. They was like that, you see. . . .

George stopped the tape and was about to put the other side in when she touched his hand.

"No more, George," she said. "I can't listen to no more. Please . . . please, no more." She had never in her whole life heard her own voice. Nothing had been so stunning in a long, long while, and for a few moments before she found herself, her world turned upside down. There, rising from a machine no bigger than her Bible, was a voice frighteningly familiar and yet unfamiliar, talking about a man whom she knew as well as her husbands and her sons, a man dead and buried sixty years. She reached across to George and he handed her the tape. She turned it over and over, as if the mystery of everything could be discerned if she turned it enough times. She began to cry, and with her other hand she lightly touched the buttons of the machine.

Between the time Marie slapped the woman in the Social Security office and the day she heard her voice for the first time, Calhoun Lambeth, Wilamena's boyfriend, had been in and out of the hospital three times. Most evenings when Calhoun's son stayed the night with him, Wilamena would come up to Marie's and spend most of the evening, sitting on the couch that was catty-corner to the easy chair facing the big window. She said very little, which was unlike her, a woman with more friends than hairs on her head and who, at sixty-eight, loved a good party. The most attractive woman Marie knew would only curl her legs up under herself and sip whatever Marie put in her hand. She looked out at the city until she took herself to her apartment or went back down to Calhoun's place. In the beginning, after he returned from the hospital the first time, there was the desire in Marie to remind her friend that she wasn't married to Calhoun, that she should just get up and walk away, something Marie had seen her do with other men she had grown tired of.

Late one night, Wilamena called and asked her to come down to the man's apartment, for the man's son had had to work that night and she was there alone with him and she did not want to be alone with him. "Sit with me a spell," Wilamena said. Marie did not protest, even though she had not said more than ten words to the man in all the time she knew him. She threw on her bathrobe, picked up her keys and serrated knife, and went down to the second floor.

He was propped up on the bed, and he was surprisingly alert and spoke to Marie with an unforced friendliness. She had seen this in other dying people— a kindness and gentleness came over them that was often embarrassing for those around them. Wilamena sat on the side of the bed. Calhoun asked Marie to sit in a chair beside the bed and then he took her hand and held it for the rest of the night. He talked on throughout the night, not always understandable. Wilamena, exhausted, eventually lay across the foot of the bed. Almost everything the man had to say was about a time when he was young and was married for a year or so to a woman in Nicodemus, Kansas, a town where there were only black people. Whether the woman had died or whether he had left her,

Marie could not make out. She only knew that the woman and Nicodemus seemed to have marked him for life.

"You should go to Nicodemus," he said at one point, as if the town was only around the corner. "I stumbled into the place by accident. But you should go on purpose. There ain't much to see, but you should go there and spend some time there."

Toward four o'clock that morning, he stopped talking and moments later he went home to his God. Marie continued holding the dead man's hand and she said the Lord's prayer over and over until it no longer made sense to her. She did not wake Wilamena. Eventually, the sun came through the man's venetian blinds and she heard the croaking of the pigeons congregating on the window ledge. When she finally placed his hand on his chest, the dead man expelled a burst of air that sounded to Marie like a sigh. It occurred to her that she, a complete stranger, was the last thing he had known in the world and that now that he was no longer in the world all she knew of him was that Nicodemus place and a lovesick woman asleep at the foot of his bed. She thought that she was hungry and thirsty, but the more she looked at the dead man and the sleeping woman, the more she realized that what she felt was a sense of loss.

Two days later, the Social Security people sent her a letter, again signed by John Smith, telling her to come to them one week hence. There was nothing in the letter about the slap, no threat to cut off her SSI payments because of what she had done. Indeed, it was the same sort of letter John Smith usually sent. She called the number at the top of the letter, and the woman who handled her case told her that Mrs. White would be expecting her on the day and time stated in the letter. Still, she suspected the Social Security people were planning something for her, something at the very least that would be humiliating. And, right up until the day before the appointment, she continued calling to confirm that it was okay to come in. Often, the person she spoke to after the switchboard woman and before the woman handling her case was Vernelle. "Social Security Administration. This is Vernelle Wise. May I help you?" And each time Marie heard the receptionist identify herself she wanted to apologize. "I whatn't raised that way," she wanted to tell the woman.

George Carter came the day she got the letter to present her with a cassette machine and copies of the tapes she had made about her life. It took quite some time for him to teach her how to use the machine, and after he was gone, she was certain it took so long because she really did not want to know how to use it. That evening, after her dinner, she steeled herself and put a tape marked "Parents; Early Childhood" in the machine.

 . . . *My mother had this idea that everything could be done in Washington, that a human bein could take all they troubles to Washington and things would be set right. I think that was all wrapped up with her notion of the govment, the Supreme Court and the president and the like. "Up there," she would say, "things can be made right." "Up there" was her only words for Washington. All them other cities had names, but Washington didn't need a name. It was just called "up there." I was real small and didn't know any better, so somehow I got to thinkin since things were on the perfect side in Washington, that maybe God lived there. God and his people . . . When I went back home to visit that first time and told my mother all about my livin in Washington, she fell into such a cry, like maybe I had managed to make it to heaven without dyin. Thas how people was back in those days. . . .*

The next morning she looked for Vernelle Wise's name in the telephone book. And for several evenings she would call the number and hang up before the phone had rung three times. Finally, on a Sunday, two days before the appointment, she let it ring and what may have been a little boy answered. She could tell he was very young because he said "Hello" in a too-loud voice, as if he was not used to talking on the telephone.

"Hello," he said. "Hello, who this? Granddaddy, that you? Hello. Hello. I can see you."

Marie heard Vernelle tell him to put down the telephone, then another child, perhaps a girl somewhat older than the boy, came on the line. "Hello. Hello. Who is this?" she said with authority. The boy began to cry, apparently because he did not want the girl to talk if he couldn't. "Don't touch it," the girl said. "Leave it alone." The boy cried louder and only stopped when Vernelle came to the telephone.

"Yes?" Vernelle said. "Yes." Then she went off the line to calm the boy who had again begun to cry. "Loretta," she said, "go get his bottle. . . . Well, look for it. What you got eyes for?"

There seemed to be a second boy, because Vernelle told him to help Loretta look for the bottle. "He always losin things," Marie heard the second boy say. "You should tie everything to his arms." "Don't tell me what to do," Vernelle said. "Just look for that damn bottle."

"I don't lose nofin. I don't," the first boy said. "You got snot in your nose."

"Don't say that," Vernelle said before she came back on the line. "I'm sorry," she said to Marie. "Who is this? . . . Don't you dare touch it if you know what's good for you!" she said. "I wanna talk to Granddaddy," the first boy said. "Loretta, get me that bottle!"

Marie hung up. She washed her dinner dishes. She called Wilamena because she had not seen her all day, and Wilamena told her that she would be up later. The cassette tapes were on the coffee table beside the machine, and she began picking them up, one by one. She read the labels. "Husband No. 1." "Working." "Husband No. 2." "Children." "Race Relations." "Early D.C. Experiences."

"Husband No. 3." She had not played another tape since the one about her mother's idea of what Washington was like, but she could still hear the voice, her voice. Without reading its label, she put a tape in the machine.

> . . . *I never planned to live in Washington, had no idea I would ever even step one foot in this city. This white family my mother worked for, they had a son married and gone to live in Baltimore. He wanted a maid, somebody to take care of his children. So he wrote to his mother and she asked my mother and my mother asked me about goin to live in Baltimore. Well, I was young. I guess I wanted to see the world, and Baltimore was as good a place to start as anywhere. This man sent me a train ticket and I went off to Baltimore. Hadn't ever been kissed, hadn't ever been anything, but here I was goin farther from home than my mother and father put together. . . . Well, sir, the train stopped in Washington, and I thought I heard the conductor say we would be stoppin a bit there, so I got off. I knew I probably wouldn't see no more than that Union Station, but I wanted to be able to say I'd done that, that I step foot in the capital of the United States. I walked down to the end of the platform and looked around, then I peeked into the station. Then I went in. And when I got back, the train and my suitcase was gone. Everything I had in the world on the way to Baltimore. . . .*
>
> *. . . I couldn't calm myself anough to listen to when the redcap said another train would be leavin for Baltimore, I was just that upset. I had a buncha addresses of people we knew all the way from home up to Boston, and I used one precious nickel to call a woman I hadn't seen in years, cause I didn't have the white people in Baltimore number. This woman come and got me, took me to her place. I member like it was yesterday, that we got on this streetcar marked 13th and D NE. The more I rode, the more brighter things got. You ain't lived till you been on a streetcar. The further we went on that streetcar—dead down in the middle of the street—the more I knowed I could never go live in Baltimore. I knowed I could never live in a place that didn't have that streetcar and them clackety-clack tracks. . . .*

She wrapped the tapes in two plastic bags and put them in the dresser drawer that contained all that was valuable to her—birth and death certificates, silver dollars, life insurance policies, pictures of her husbands and the children they had given each other, and the grandchildren those children had given her and the great-grands whose names she had trouble remembering. She set the tapes in a back corner of the drawer, away from the things she needed to get her hands on regularly. She knew that however long she lived, she would not ever again listen to them, for in the end, despite all that was on the tapes, she could not stand the sound of her own voice.

Thom Jones

THE PUGILIST AT REST

THOM JONES (1945–) is the author of three short story collections: *The Pugilist at Rest* (a National Book Award finalist), *Cold Snap,* and *Sonny Liston Was a Friend of Mine.* His stories have appeared in such magazines as *The New Yorker, Playboy, Esquire, GQ,* and *Harper's.* He lives in Olympia, Washington, with his wife and daughter.

Hey Baby got caught writing a letter to his girl when he was supposed to be taking notes on the specs of the M-14 rifle. We were sitting in a stifling hot Quonset hut during the first weeks of boot camp, August 1966, at the Marine Corps Recruit Depot in San Diego. Sergeant Wright snatched the letter out of Hey Baby's hand, and later that night in the squad bay he read the letter to the Marine recruits of Platoon 263, his voice laden with sarcasm. "*Hey, Baby!*" he began, and then as he went into the body of the letter he worked himself into a state of outrage and disgust. It was a letter to *Rosie Rottencrotch,* he said at the end, and what really mattered, what was really at issue and what was of utter importance was not *Rosie Rottencrotch* and her steaming-hot panties but rather the muzzle velocity of the M-14 rifle.

Hey Baby paid for the letter by doing a hundred squat thrusts on the concrete floor of the squad bay, but the main prize he won that night was that he became forever known as Hey Baby to the recruits of Platoon 263—in addition to being a shitbird, a faggot, a turd, a maggot, and other such standard appellations. To top it all off, shortly after the incident, Hey Baby got a Dear John from this girl back in Chicago, of whom Sergeant Wright, myself, and seventy-eight other Marine recruits had come to know just a little.

Hey Baby was not in the Marine Corps for very long. The reason for this was that he started in on my buddy, Jorgeson. Jorgeson was my main man, and Hey Baby started calling him Jorgepussy and began harassing him and pushing him around. He was down on Jorgeson because whenever we were taught some sort of combat maneuver or tactic, Jorgeson would say, under his breath, "You could get *killed* if you try that." Or, "Your ass is *had,* if you do that." You got the feeling that Jorgeson didn't think loving the American flag and defending democratic ideals in Southeast Asia were all that important. He told me that what he really wanted to do was have an artist's loft in the SoHo district of New York City,

304

wear a beret, eat liver sausage sandwiches made with stale baguettes, drink Tokay wine, smoke dope, paint pictures, and listen to the wailing, sorrowful songs of that French singer Edith Piaf, otherwise known as "The Little Sparrow."

After the first half hour of boot camp most of the other recruits wanted to get out, too, but they nourished dreams of surfboards, Corvettes, and blond babes. Jorgeson wanted to be a beatnik and hang out with Jack Kerouac and Neal Cassady, slam down burning shots of amber whiskey, and hear Charles Mingus play real cool jazz on the bass fiddle. He wanted to practice Zen Buddhism, throw the I Ching, eat couscous, and study astrology charts. All of this was foreign territory to me. I had grown up in Aurora, Illinois, and had never heard of such things. Jorgeson had a sharp tongue and was so supercilious in his remarks that I didn't know quite how seriously I should take this talk, but I enjoyed his humor and I did believe he had the sensibilities of an artist. It was not some vague yearning. I believed very much that he could become a painter of pictures. At that point he wasn't putting his heart and soul into becoming a Marine. He wasn't a true believer like me.

Some weeks after Hey Baby began hassling Jorgeson, Sergeant Wright gave us his best speech: "You men are going off to war, and it's not a pretty thing," etc. & etc., "and if Luke the Gook knocks down one of your buddies, a fellow Marine, you are going to risk your life and go in and get that Marine and you are going to bring him out. Not because I said so. No! You are going after that Marine because *you* are a Marine, a member of the most elite fighting force in the world, and that man out there who's gone down is a Marine, and he's your *buddy*. He is your brother! Once you are a Marine, you are *always* a Marine and you will never let another Marine down." Etc. & etc. "You can take a Marine out of the Corps but you can't take the Corps out of a Marine." Etc. & etc. At the time it seemed to me a very good speech, and it stirred me deeply. Sergeant Wright was no candy ass. He was one squared-away dude, and he could call cadence. Man, it puts a lump in my throat when I remember how that man could sing cadence. Apart from Jorgeson, I think all of the recruits in Platoon 263 were proud of Sergeant Wright. He was the real thing, the genuine article. He was a crackerjack Marine.

In the course of training, lots of the recruits dropped out of the original platoon. Some couldn't pass the physical fitness tests and had to go to a special camp for pussies. This was a particularly shameful shortcoming, the most humiliating apart from bed-wetting. Other recruits would get pneumonia, strep throat, infected foot blisters, or whatever, and lose time that way. Some didn't qualify at the rifle range. One would break a leg. Another would have a nervous breakdown (and this was also deplorable). People dropped out right and left. When the recruit corrected whatever deficiency he had, or when he got better, he would be picked up by another platoon that was in the stage of basic training that he had been in when his training was interrupted. Platoon 263 picked up dozens of recruits in this fashion. If everything went well, however, you got through with the whole business in twelve weeks. That's not a long time, but it seemed like a long time. You did not see a female in all that time. You did not see a newspaper or a television set. You did not eat a candy bar. Another thing was the fact that you had someone on top of you, watching every move you made. When it was time to "shit, shower, and shave," you were given just ten minutes, and had to confront lines and so on to complete the entire affair. Head calls were so infrequent that I spent a lot of time that might otherwise have been neutral or painless in the eye-watering anxiety that I was going to piss my pants. We *ran* to chow, where we were faced with enormous steam vents that spewed out a sickening smell of rancid, superheated grease. Still, we entered the mess hall with ravenous appetites, ate a huge tray of food in just a few minutes, and then *ran* back to our company area in formation, choking back the burning bile of a meal too big to be eaten so fast. God forbid that you would lose control and vomit.

If all had gone well in the preceding hours, Sergeant Wright would permit us to smoke one cigarette after each meal. Jorgeson had shown me the wisdom of switching from Camels to Pall Malls—they were much longer, packed a pretty good jolt, and when we snapped open our brushed-chrome Zippos, torched up, and inhaled the first few drags, we shared the overmastering pleasure that tobacco can bring if you use it seldom and judiciously. These were always the best moments of the day—brief respites from the tyrannical repression of recruit training. As we got close to the end of it all Jorgeson liked to play a little game. He used to say to me (with fragrant blue smoke curling out of his nostrils), "If someone said, 'I'll give you ten thousand dollars to do all of this again,' what would you say?" "No way, Jack!" He would keep on upping it until he had John Beresford Tipton, the guy from *The Millionaire*, offering me a check for a million bucks. "Not for any money," I'd say.

While they were all smoldering under various pressures, the recruits were also getting pretty "salty"—they were beginning to believe. They were beginning to think of themselves as Marines. If you could make it through this, the reasoning went, you wouldn't crack in combat. So I remember that I had tears in my eyes when Sergeant Wright gave us the spiel about how a Marine would charge a machine-gun nest to save his buddies, dive on a hand grenade, do whatever it takes—and yet I was ashamed when Jorgeson caught me wiping them away. All of the recruits were teary except Jorgeson. He had these very clear cobalt blue eyes. They were so remarkable that they caused you to notice Jorgeson in a crowd. There was unusual beauty in these eyes, and there was an extraordinary power in them. Apart from having a pleasant enough face, Jorgeson was small and unassuming except for these eyes. Anyhow, when he caught me getting sentimental he gave me this look that penetrated to the core of my being. It was the icy look of absolute contempt, and it caused me to doubt myself. I said, "Man! Can't you get into it? For Christ's sake!"

"I'm not like you," he said. "But I am into it, more than you could ever know. I never told you this before, but I am Kal-El, born on the planet Krypton and rocketed to Earth as an infant, moments before my world exploded. Disguised as a mild-mannered Marine, I have resolved to use my powers for the good of mankind. Whenever danger appears on the scene, truth and justice will be served as I slip into the green U.S.M.C. utility uniform and become Earth's greatest hero."

I got highly pissed and didn't talk to him for a couple of days after this. Then, about two weeks before boot camp was over, when we were running out to the parade field for drill with our rifles at port arms, all assholes and elbows, I saw Hey Baby give Jorgeson a nasty shove with his M-14. Hey Baby was a large and fairly tough young man who liked to displace his aggressive impulses on Jorgeson, but he wasn't as big or as tough as I.

Jorgeson nearly fell down as the other recruits scrambled out to the parade field, and Hey Baby gave a short, malicious laugh. I ran past Jorgeson and caught up to Hey Baby; he picked me up in his peripheral vision, but by then it was too late. I set my body so that I could put everything into it, and with one deft stroke I hammered him in the temple with the sharp edge of the steel butt plate of my M-14. It was not exactly a premeditated crime, although I had been laying to get him. My idea before this had simply been to lay my hands on him, but now I had blood in my eye. I was a skilled boxer, and I knew the temple was a vulnerable spot; the human skull is otherwise hard and durable, except at its base. There was a sickening crunch, and Hey Baby dropped into the ice plants along the side of the company street.

The entire platoon was out on the parade field when the house mouse screamed at the assistant D.I., who rushed back to the scene of the crime to find Hey Baby crumpled in a fetal position in the ice plants with blood all over the place. There was blood from the scalp wound as well as a froth of blood emitting from his nostrils and his mouth. Blood was leaking from his right ear. Did I see skull fragments and brain tissue? It seemed that I did. To tell you the truth, I wouldn't have cared in the least if I had killed him, but like most criminals I was very much afraid of getting caught. It suddenly occurred to me that I could be headed for the brig for a long time. My heart was pounding out of my chest. Yet the larger part of me didn't care. Jorgeson was my buddy, and I wasn't going to stand still and let someone fuck him over.

The platoon waited at parade rest while Sergeant Wright came out of the duty hut and took command of the situation. An ambulance was called, and it came almost immediately. A number of corpsmen squatted down alongside the fallen man for what seemed an eternity. Eventually they took Hey Baby off with a fractured skull. It would be the last we ever saw of him. Three evenings later, in the squad bay, the assistant D.I. told us rather ominously that Hey Baby had recovered consciousness. That's all he said. What did *that* mean? I was worried, because Hey Baby had seen me make my move, but, as it turned out, when he came to he had forgotten the incident and all events of the preceding two weeks. Retrograde amnesia. Lucky for me. I also knew that at least three other recruits had seen what I did, but none of them reported me. Every member of the platoon was called in and grilled by a team of hard-ass captains and a light colonel from the Criminal Investigation Detachment. It took a certain amount of balls to lie to them, yet none of my fellow jarheads reported me. I was well liked and Hey Baby was not. Indeed, many felt that he got exactly what was coming to him.

The other day—Memorial Day, as it happened—I was cleaning some stuff out of the attic when I came upon my old dress-blue uniform. It's a beautiful uniform, easily the most handsome worn by any of the U.S. armed forces. The rich color recalled Jorgeson's eyes for me—not that the color matched, but in the sense that the color of each was so startling. The tunic does not have lapels, of course, but a high collar with red piping and the traditional golden eagle, globe, and anchor insignia on either side of the neck clasp. The tunic buttons are not brassy—although they are in fact made of brass—but are a delicate gold in color, like Florentine gold. On the sleeves of the tunic my staff sergeant's chevrons are gold on red. High on the left breast is a rainbow display of fruit salad representing my various combat citations. Just below these are my marksmanship badges; I shot Expert in rifle as well as pistol.

I opened a sandalwood box and took my various medals out of the large plastic bag I had packed them in to prevent them from tarnishing. The Navy Cross and the two Silver Stars are the best; they are such pretty things they dazzle you. I found a couple of Thai sticks in the sandalwood box as well. I took a whiff of the box and smelled the smells of Saigon—the whores, the dope, the saffron, cloves, jasmine, and patchouli oil. I put the Thai sticks back, recalling the three-day hangover that particular batch of dope had given me more than twenty-three years before. Again I looked at my dress-blue tunic. My most distinctive badge, the crowning glory, and the one of which I am most proud, is the set of Airborne wings. I remember how it was, walking around Oceanside, California—the Airborne wings and the high-and-tight haircut were recognized by all the Marines; they meant you were the crème de la crème, you were a recon Marine.

Recon was all Jorgeson's idea. We had lost touch with each other after boot camp. I was sent to com school in San Diego, where I had to sit in a hot Class A wool uniform all day and learn the Morse code. I deliberately flunked out, and when I was given the perfunctory option for a second shot, I told the colonel, "Hell no, sir. I want to go 003—infantry. I want to be a ground-pounder. I didn't join the service to sit at a desk all day."

I was on a bus to Camp Pendleton three days later, and when I got there I ran into Jorgeson. I had been thinking of him a lot. He was a clerk in headquarters company. Much to my astonishment, he was fifteen pounds heavier, and had grown two inches, and he told me he was hitting the weight pile every night after running seven miles up and down the foothills of Pendleton in combat boots, carrying a rifle and a full field pack. After the usual what's-been-happening? b.s., he got down to business and said, "They need people in Force Recon, what do you think? Headquarters is one boring motherfucker."

I said, "Recon? Paratrooper? You got to be shittin' me! When did you get so gung-ho, man?"

He said, "Hey, you were the one who *bought* the program. Don't fade on me now, God damn it! Look, we pass the physical fitness test and then they send us to jump school at Benning. If we pass that, we're in. And we'll pass. Those doggies ain't got jack. Semper fi, motherfucker! Let's do it."

There was no more talk of Neal Cassady, Edith Piaf, or the artist's loft in SoHo. I said, "If Sergeant Wright could only see you now!"

We were just three days in country when we got dropped in somewhere in the western highlands of the Quang Tri province. It was a routine reconnaissance patrol. It was not supposed to be any kind of big deal at all—just acclimation. The morning after our drop we approached a clear field. I recall that it gave me a funny feeling, but I was too new to fully trust my instincts. *Everything* was spooky; I was fresh meat, F.N.G.—a Fucking New Guy.

Before moving into the field, our team leader sent Hanes—a lance corporal, a short-timer, with only twelve days left before his rotation was over—across the field as a point man. This was a bad omen and everyone knew it. Hanes had two Purple Hearts. He followed the order with no hesitation and crossed the field without drawing fire. The team leader signaled for us to fan out and told me to circumvent the field and hump through the jungle to investigate a small mound of loose red dirt that I had missed completely but that he had picked up with his trained eye. I remember I kept saying, "Where?" He pointed to a heap of earth about thirty yards along the tree line and about ten feet back in the bushes. Most likely it was an anthill, but you never knew—it could have been an N.V.A. tunnel. "Over there," he hissed. "God damn it, do I have to draw pictures for you?"

I moved smartly in the direction of the mound while the rest of the team reconverged to discuss something. As I approached the mound I saw that it was in fact an anthill, and I looked back at the team and saw they were already halfway across the field, moving very fast.

Suddenly there were several loud hollow pops and the cry "Incoming!" Seconds later the first of a half-dozen mortar rounds landed in the loose earth surrounding the anthill. For a millisecond, everything went black. I was blown back and lifted up on a cushion of warm air. At first it was like the thrill of a carnival ride, but it was quickly followed by that stunned, jangly, electric feeling you get when you hit your crazy bone. Like that, but not confined to a small area like the elbow. I felt it shoot through my spine and into all four limbs. A thick plaster of sand and red clay plugged up my nostrils and ears. Grit was blown in between my teeth. If I hadn't been wearing a pair of Ray-Ban aviator shades, I would certainly have been blinded permanently—as it was, my eyes were loaded with grit. (I later discovered that fine red earth was somehow blown in behind the crystal of my pressure-tested Rolex Submariner, underneath my fingernails and toenails, and deep into the pores of my skin.) When I was able to, I pulled out a canteen filled with lemon-lime Kool-Aid and tried to flood my eyes clean. This helped a little, but my eyes still felt like they were on fire. I rinsed them again and blinked furiously.

I rolled over on my stomach in the prone position and leveled my field-issue M-16. A company of screaming N.V.A. soldiers ran into the field, firing as they came—I saw their green tracer rounds blanket the position where the team had quickly congregated to lay out a perimeter, but none of our own red tracers were going out. Several of the Marines had been killed outright by the mortar rounds. Jorgeson was all right, and I saw him cast a nervous glance in my direction. Then he turned to the enemy and began to fire his M-16. I clicked my rifle on to automatic and pulled the trigger, but the gun was loaded with dirt and it wouldn't fire.

Apart from Jorgeson, the only other American putting out any fire was Second Lieutenant Milton, also a fairly new guy, a "cherry," who was down on one knee firing his .45, an exercise in almost complete futility. I assumed that Milton's 16 had jammed, like mine, and watched as AK-47 rounds, having penetrated his flak jacket and then his chest, ripped through the back of his field pack and buzzed into the jungle beyond like a deadly swarm of bees. A few seconds later, I heard the swoosh of an R.P.G. rocket, a dud round that dinged the lieutenant's left shoulder before it flew off in the bush behind him. It took off his whole arm, and for an instant I could see the white bone and ligaments of his shoulder, and the red flesh of muscle tissue, looking very much like fresh prime beef, well marbled and encased in a thin layer of yellowish white adipose tissue that quickly became saturated with dark red blood. What a lot of blood there was. Still, Milton continued to fire his .45. When he emptied his clip, I watched him remove a fresh one from his web gear and attempt to load the pistol with one hand. He seemed to fumble with the fresh clip for a long time, until at last he dropped it, along with his .45. The lieutenant's head slowly sagged forward, but he stayed up on one knee with his remaining arm extended out to the enemy, palm upward in the soulful, heartrending gesture of Al Jolson doing a rendition of "Mammy."

A hail of green tracer rounds buzzed past Jorgeson, but he coolly returned fire in short, controlled bursts. The light, tinny pops from his M-16 did not sound very reassuring, but I saw several N.V.A. go down. AK-47 fire kicked up red dust all around Jorgeson's feet. He was basically out in the open, and if ever a man was totally alone it was Jorgeson. He was dead meat and he had to know it. It was very strange that he wasn't hit immediately.

Jorgeson zigged his way over to the body of a large black Marine who carried an M-60 machine gun. Most of the recon Marines carried grease guns or Swedish Ks; an M-60 was too heavy for traveling light and fast, but this Marine had been big and he had been paranoid. I had known him least of anyone in the squad. In three days he had said nothing to me, I suppose because I was F.N.G., and had spooked him. Indeed, now he was dead. That august seeker of truth, Schopenhauer, was correct: *We are like lambs in a field, disporting themselves under the eye of the butcher, who chooses out first one and then another for his prey. So it is that in our good days we are all unconscious of the evil Fate may have presently in store for us—sickness, poverty, mutilation, loss of sight or reason.*

It was difficult to judge how quickly time was moving. Although my senses had been stunned by the concussion of the mortar rounds, they were, however paradoxical this may seem, more acute than ever before. I watched Jorgeson pick up the machine gun and begin to spread an impressive field of fire back at the enemy. Thuk thuk thuk, thuk thuk thuk, thuk thuk thuk! I saw several more bodies fall, and began to think that things might turn out all right after all. The N.V.A. dropped for cover, and many of them turned back and headed for the tree line. Jorgeson fired off a couple of bandoliers, and after he stopped to load another, he turned back and looked at me with those blue eyes and a smile like "How am I doing?" Then I heard the steelcork pop of an M-79 launcher and saw a rocket grenade explode through Jorgeson's upper abdomen, causing him to do something like a back flip. His M-60 machine gun flew straight up into the air. The barrel was glowing red like a hot poker, and continued to fire in a "cook off" until the entire bandolier had run through.

In the meantime I had pulled a cleaning rod out of my pack and worked it through the barrel of my M-16. When I next tried to shoot, the Tonka-toy son of a bitch remained jammed, and at last I frantically broke it down to find the source of the problem. I had a dirty bolt. Fucking dirt everywhere. With numbed fingers I removed the firing pin and worked it over with a toothbrush, dropping it in the red dirt, picking it up, cleaning it, and dropping it again. My fingers felt like Novocain, and while I could see far away, I was unable to see up close. I poured some more Kool-Aid over my eyes. It was impossible for me to get my weapon clean. Lucky for me, ultimately.

Suddenly N.V.A. soldiers were running through the field shoving bayonets into the bodies of the downed Marines. It was not until an N.V.A. trooper kicked Lieutenant Milton out of his tripod position that he finally fell to the ground. Then the soldiers started going through the dead Marines' gear. I was still frantically struggling with my weapon when it began to dawn on me that the enemy had forgotten me in the excitement of the firefight. I wondered what had happened to Hanes and if he had gotten clear. I doubted it, and hopped on my survival radio to call in an air strike when finally a canny N.V.A. trooper did remember me and headed in my direction most ricky-tick.

With a tight grip on the spoon, I pulled the pin on a fragmentation grenade and then unsheathed my K-bar. About this time Jorgeson let off a horrendous shriek—a gut shot is worse than anything. Or did Jorgeson scream to save my life? The N.V.A. moving in my direction turned back to him, studied him for a moment, and then thrust a bayonet into his heart. As badly as my own eyes hurt, I was able to see Jorgeson's eyes—a final flash of glorious azure before they faded into the unfocused and glazed gray of death. I repinned the grenade, got up on my knees, and scrambled away until finally I was on my feet with a useless and incomplete handful of M-16 parts, and I was running as fast and as hard as I have ever run in my life. A pair of Phantom F-4s came in very low with delayed-action high-explosive rounds and napalm. I could feel the almost unbearable heat waves of the latter, volley after volley. I can still feel it and smell it to this day.

Concerning Lance Corporal Hanes: they found him later, fried to a crisp by the napalm, but it was nonetheless ascertained that he had been mutilated while alive. He was like the rest of us—eighteen, nineteen, twenty years old. What did we know of life? Before Vietnam, Hanes didn't think he would ever die. I mean, yes, he knew that in theory he would die, but he *felt* like he was going to live forever. I know that I felt that way. Hanes was down to twelve days and a wake-up. When other Marines saw a short-timer get greased, it devastated their morale. However, when I saw them zip up the body bag on Hanes I became incensed. Why hadn't Milton sent him back to the rear to burn shit or something when he got so short? Twelve days to go and then mutilated. Fucking Milton! Fucking Second Lieutenant!

Theogenes was the greatest of gladiators. He was a boxer who served under the patronage of a cruel nobleman, a prince who took great delight in bloody spectacles. Although this was several hundred years before the times of those most enlightened of men Socrates, Plato, and Aristotle, and well after the Minoans of Crete, it still remains a high point in the history of Western civilization and culture. It was the approximate time of Homer, the greatest poet who ever lived. Then, as now, violence, suffering, and the cheapness of life were the rule.

The sort of boxing Theogenes practiced was not like modernday boxing with those kindergarten Queensberry Rules. The two contestants were not permitted the freedom of a ring. Instead, they were strapped to flat stones, facing each other nose-to-nose. When the signal was given they would begin hammering each other with fists encased in heavy leather thongs. It was a fight to the death. Fourteen hundred and twenty-five times Theogenes was strapped to the stone and fourteen hundred and twenty-five times he emerged a victor.

Perhaps it is Theogenes who is depicted in the famous Roman statue (based on the earlier Greek original) of "The Pugilist at Rest." I keep a grainy black-and-white photograph of it in my room. The statue depicts a muscular athlete approaching his middle age. He has a thick beard and a full head of curly hair. In addition to the telltale broken nose and cauliflower ears of a boxer, the pugilist has the slanted, drooping brows that bespeak torn nerves. Also, the forehead is piled with scar tissue. As may be expected, the pugilist has the musculature of a fighter. His neck and trapezius muscles are well developed. His shoulders are enormous; his chest is thick and flat, without the bulging pectorals of the body-builder. His back, oblique, and abdominal muscles are highly pronounced, and he has that greatest asset of the modern boxer—sturdy legs. The arms are large, particularly the forearms, which are reinforced with the leather wrappings of the cestus. It is the body of a small heavyweight—lithe rather than bulky, but by no means lacking in power: a Jack Johnson or a Dempsey, say. If you see the authentic statue at the Terme Museum, in Rome, you will see that the seated boxer is really not much more than a light heavyweight. People were small in those days. The important thing was that he was perfectly proportioned.

The pugilist is sitting on a rock with his forearms balanced on his thighs. That he is seated and not pacing implies that he has been through all this many times before. It appears that he is conserving his strength. His head is turned as if he were looking over his shoulder—as if someone had just whispered something to him. It is in this that the "art" of the sculpture is conveyed to the viewer. Could it be that someone has just summoned him to the arena? There is a slight look of befuddlement on his face, but there is no trace of fear. There is an air about him that suggests that he is eager to proceed and does not wish to cause anyone any trouble or to create a delay, even though his life will soon be on the line. Besides the deformities on his noble face, there is also the suggestion of weariness and philosophical resignation. *All the world's a stage, and all the men and women merely players.* Exactly! He knew this more than two thousand years before Shakespeare penned the line. How did he come to be at this place in space and time? Would he rather be safely removed to the countryside—an obscure, stinking peasant shoving a plow behind a mule? Would that be better? Or does he revel in his role? Perhaps he once did, but surely not now. Is this the great Theogenes or merely a journeyman fighter, a former slave or criminal bought by one of the many contractors who for months trained the condemned for their brief moment in the arena? I wonder if Marcus Aurelius loved the "Pugilist" as I do, and came to study it and to meditate before it?

I cut and ran from that field in Southeast Asia. I've read that Davy Crockett, hero of the American frontier, was cowering under a bed when Santa Anna and his soldiers stormed into the Alamo. What is the truth? Jack Dempsey used to get so scared before his fights that he sometimes wet his pants. But look what he did to Willard and to Luis Firpo, the Wild Bull of the Pampas! It was something close to homicide. What is courage? What is cowardice? The magnificent Roberto Duran gave us *"No más,"* but who had a greater fighting heart than Duran?

I got over that first scare and saw that I was something quite other than that which I had known myself to be. Hey Baby proved only my warm-up act. There was a reservoir of malice, poison, and vicious sadism in my soul, and it poured forth freely in the jungles and rice paddies of Vietnam. I pulled three tours. I wanted some payback for Jorgeson. I grieved for Lance Corporal Hanes. I grieved for myself and what I had lost. I committed unspeakable crimes and got medals for it.

It was only fair that I got a head injury myself. I never got a scratch in Vietnam, but I got tagged in a boxing smoker at Pendleton. Fought a bad-ass light heavyweight from artillery. Nobody would fight this guy. He could box. He had all the moves. But mainly he was a puncher—it was said that he could punch with either hand. It was said that his hand speed was superb. I had finished off at least a half rack of Hamm's before I went in with him and started getting hit with head shots I didn't even see coming. They were right. His hand speed *was* superb.

I was twenty-seven years old, smoked two packs a day, was a borderline alcoholic. I shouldn't have fought him—I knew that—but he had been making noise. A very long time before, I had been the middleweight champion of the First Marine Division. I had been a so-called war hero. I had been a recon Marine. But now I was a garrison Marine and in no kind of shape.

He put me down almost immediately, and when I got up I was terribly afraid. I was tight and I could not breathe. It felt like he was hitting me in the face with a ball peen hammer. It felt like he was busting lightbulbs in my face. Rather than one opponent, I saw three. I was convinced his gloves were loaded, and a wave of self-pity ran through me.

I began to move. He made a mistake by expending a lot of energy trying to put me away quickly. I had no intention of going down again, and I knew I wouldn't. My buddies were watching, and I had to give them a good show. While I was afraid, I was also exhilarated; I had not felt this alive since Vietnam. I began to score with my left jab, and because of this I was able to withstand his bull charges and divert them. I thought he would throw his bolt, but in the beginning he was tireless. I must have hit him with four hundred left jabs. It got so that I could score at will, with either hand, but he would counter, trap me on the ropes, and pound. He was the better puncher and was truly hurting me, but I was scoring, and as the fight went on the momentum shifted and I took over. I staggered him again and again. The Marines at ringside were screaming for me to put him away, but however much I tried, I could not. Although I could barely stand by the end, I was sorry that the fight was over. Who had won? The referee raised my arm in victory, but I think it was pretty much a draw. Judging a prizefight is a very subjective thing.

About an hour after the bout, when the adrenaline had subsided, I realized I had a terrible headache. It kept getting worse, and I rushed out of the N.C.O. Club, where I had gone with my buddies to get loaded.

I stumbled outside, struggling to breathe, and I headed away from the company area toward Sheepshit Hill, one of the many low brown foothills in the vicinity. Like a dog who wants to die alone, so it was with me. Everything got swirly, and I dropped in the bushes.

I was unconscious for nearly an hour, and for the next two weeks I walked around like I was drunk, with double vision. I had constant headaches and seemed to have grown old overnight. My health was gone.

I became a very timid individual. I became introspective. I wondered what had made me act the way I had acted. Why had I killed my fellowmen in war, without any feeling, remorse, or regret? And when the war was over, why did I continue to drink and swagger around and get into fistfights? Why did I like to dish out pain, and why did I take positive delight in the suffering of others? Was I insane? Was it too much testosterone? Women don't do things like that. The rapacious Will to Power lost its hold on me. Suddenly I began to feel sympathetic to the cares and sufferings of all living creatures. You lose your health and you start thinking this way.

Has man become any better since the times of Theogenes? The world is replete with badness. I'm not talking about that old routine where you drag out the Spanish Inquisition, the Holocaust, Joseph Stalin, the Khmer Rouge, etc. It happens in our own backyard. Twentieth-century America is one of the most materially prosperous nations in history. But take a walk through an American prison, a nursing home, the slums where the homeless live in cardboard boxes, a cancer ward. Go to a Vietnam vets' meeting, or an A.A. meeting, or an Overeaters Anonymous meeting. *How hollow and unreal a thing is life, how deceitful are its pleasures, what horrible aspects it possesses.* Is the world not rather like a hell, as Schopenhauer, that clearheaded seer—who has helped me transform my suffering into an object of understanding—was so quick to point out? They called him a pessimist and dismissed him with a word, but it is peace and self-renewal that I have found in his pages.

About a year after my fight with the guy from artillery I started having seizures. I suffered from a form of left-temporal-lobe seizure which is sometimes called

Dostoyevski's epilepsy. It's so rare as to be almost unknown. Freud, himself a neurologist, speculated that Dostoyevski was a hysterical epileptic, and that his fits were unrelated to brain damage—psychogenic in origin. Dostoyevski did not have his first attack until the age of twenty-five, when he was imprisoned in Siberia and received fifty lashes after complaining about the food. Freud figured that after Dostoyevski's mock execution, the four years' imprisonment in Siberia, the tormented childhood, the murder of his tyrannical father, etc. & etc.— he had all the earmarks of hysteria, of grave psychological trauma. And Dostoyevski had displayed the trademark features of the psychomotor epileptic long before his first attack. These days physicians insist there is no such thing as the "epileptic personality." I think they say this because they do not want to add to the burden of the epileptic's suffering with an extra stigma. Privately they do believe in these traits. Dostoyevski was nervous and depressed, a tormented hypochondriac, a compulsive writer obsessed with religious and philosophic themes. He was hyperloquacious, raving, etc. & etc. His gambling addiction is well known. By most accounts he was a sick soul.

The peculiar and most distinctive thing about his epilepsy was that in the split second before his fit—in the aura, which is in fact officially a part of the attack—Dostoyevski experienced a sense of felicity, of ecstatic well-being unlike anything an ordinary mortal could hope to imagine. It was the experience of satori. Not the nickel-and-dime satori of Abraham Maslow, but the Supreme. He said that he wouldn't trade ten years of life for this feeling, and I, who have had it, too, would have to agree. I can't explain it, I don't understand it—it becomes slippery and elusive when it gets any distance on you—but I have felt this down to the core of my being. Yes, God exists! But then it slides away and I lose it. I become a doubter. Even Dostoyevski, the fervent Christian, makes an almost airtight case against the possibility of the existence of God in the Grand Inquisitor digression in *The Brothers Karamazov*. It is probably the greatest passage in all of world literature, and it tilts you to the court of the atheist. This is what happens when you approach Him with the intellect.

It is thought that St. Paul had a temporal-lobe fit on the road to Damascus. Paul warns us in First Corinthians that God will confound the intellectuals. It is known that Muhammad composed the Koran after attacks of epilepsy. Black Elk experienced fits before his grand "buffalo" vision. Joan of Arc is thought to have been a left-temporal-lobe epileptic. Each of these in a terrible flash of brain lightning was able to pierce the murky veil of illusion which is spread over all things. Just so did the scales fall from my eyes. It is called the "sacred disease."

But what a price. I rarely leave the house anymore. To avoid falling injuries, I always wear my old boxer's headgear, and I always carry my mouthpiece. Rather more often than the aura where "every common bush is afire with God," I have the typical epileptic aura, which is that of terror and impending doom. If

I can keep my head and think of it, and if there is time, I slip the mouthpiece in and thus avoid biting my tongue. I bit it in half once, and when they sewed it back together it swelled enormously, like a huge red-and-black sausage. I was unable to close my mouth for more than two weeks.

The fits are coming more and more. I'm loaded on Depakene, phenobarbital, Tegretol, Dilantin—the whole shitload. A nurse from the V.A. bought a pair of Staffordshire terriers for me and trained them to watch me as I sleep, in case I have a fit and smother facedown in my bedding. What delightful companions these dogs are! One of them, Gloria, is especially intrepid and clever. Inevitably, when I come to I find that the dogs have dragged me into the kitchen, away from blankets and pillows, rugs, and objects that might suffocate me, and that they have turned me on my back. There's Gloria, barking in my face. Isn't this incredible?

My sister brought a neurosurgeon over to my place around Christmas—not some V.A. butcher but a guy from the university hospital. He was a slick dude in a nine-hundred-dollar suit. He came down on me hard, like a used-car sales-man. He wants to cauterize a small spot in a nerve bundle in my brain. "It's not a lobotomy, it's a *cingulotomy*," he said.

Reckless, desperate, last-ditch psychosurgery is still pretty much unthinkable in the conservative medical establishment. That's why he made a personal visit to my place. A house call. Drumming up some action to make himself a name. "See that bottle of Thorazine?" he said. "You can throw that poison away," he said. "All that amitriptyline. That's garbage, you can toss that, too." He said, "Tell me something. How can you take all of that shit and still walk?" He said, "You take enough drugs to drop an elephant."

He wants to cut me. He said that the feelings of guilt and worthlessness, and the heaviness of a heart blackened by sin, will go away. "It is *not* a lobotomy," he said.

I don't like the guy. I don't trust him. I'm not convinced, but I can't go on like this. If I am not having a panic attack I am engulfed in tedious, unrelenting depression. I am overcome with a deadening sense of languor; I can't *do* any-thing. I wanted to give my buddies a good show! What a goddam fool. I am a goddam fool!

It has taken me six months to put my thoughts in order, but I wanted to do it in case I am a vegetable after the operation. I know that my buddy Jorgeson was a real American hero. I wish that he had lived to be something else, if not a painter of pictures then even some kind of fuck-up with a factory job and four divorces, bankruptcy petitions, in and out of jail. I wish he had been that. I wish he had been *anything* rather than a real American hero. So, then, if I am to feel somewhat *indifferent* to life after the operation, all the better. If not, not.

If I had a more conventional sense of morality I would shitcan those dress blues, and I'd send that Navy Cross to Jorgeson's brother. Jorgeson was the one who won it, who pulled the John Wayne number up there near Khe Sanh and saved my life, although I lied and took the credit for all of those dead N.V.A. He had created a stunning body count—nothing like Theogenes, but Jorgeson only had something like twelve minutes total in the theater of war.

The high command almost awarded me the Medal of Honor, but of course there were no witnesses to what I claimed I had done, and I had saved no one's life. When I think back on it, my tale probably did not sound as credible as I thought it had at the time. I was only nineteen years old and not all that practiced a liar. I figure if they *had* given me the Medal of Honor, I would have stood in the ring up at Camp Las Pulgas in Pendleton and let that light heavyweight from artillery fucking kill me.

Now I'm thinking I might call Hey Baby and ask how he's doing. No shit, a couple of neuropsyches—we probably have a lot in common. I could apologize to him. But I learned from my fits that you don't have to do that. Good and evil are only illusions. Still, I cannot help but wonder sometimes if my vision of the Supreme Reality was any more real than the demons visited upon schizophrenics and madmen. Has it all been just a stupid neurochemical event? Is there no God at all? The human heart rebels against this.

If they fuck up the operation, I hope I get to keep my dogs somehow—maybe stay at my sister's place. If they send me to the nuthouse I lose the dogs for sure.

Jamaica Kincaid

GIRL

JAMAICA KINCAID (1946–) was born and educated in St. John's, Antigua, in the West Indies. Her first book, *At the Bottom of the River*, a collection of stories, received the Morton Dauwen Zabel Award of the American Academy and Institute of Arts and Letters and was nominated for the PEN/Faulkner Award. Ms. Kincaid's other books are *Annie John; A Small Place; Lucy; My Brother*, a finalist for the National Book Award; and *The Autobiography of My Mother*, a nominee for the National Book Critics Circle Award in Fiction, a finalist for the PEN/Faulkner Award, and the winner of the Cleveland Foundation's Anisfield-Wolf Book Award as well as the *Boston Book Review*'s Fisk Fiction Prize. Her stories have appeared in *The New Yorker, Rolling Stone,* and *The Paris Review*. She lives with her husband and two children in Bennington, Vermont.

Wash the white clothes on Monday and put them on the stone heap; wash the color clothes on Tuesday and put them on the clothesline to dry; don't walk barehead in the hot sun; cook pumpkin fritters in very hot sweet oil; soak your little clothes right after you take them off; when buying cotton to make yourself a nice blouse, be sure that it doesn't have gum on it, because that way it won't hold up well after a wash; soak salt fish overnight before you cook it; is it true that you sing benna in Sunday school?; always eat your food in such a way that it won't turn someone else's stomach; on Sundays try to walk like a lady and not like the slut you are so bent on becoming; don't sing benna in Sunday school; you mustn't speak to wharf-rat boys, not even to give directions; don't eat fruits on the street—flies will follow you; *but I don't sing benna on Sundays at all and never in Sunday school;* this is how to sew on a button; this is how to make a buttonhole for the button you have just sewed on; this is how to hem a dress when you see the hem coming down and so to prevent yourself from looking like the slut I know you are so bent on becoming; this is how you iron your father's khaki shirt so that it doesn't have a crease; this is how you iron your father's khaki pants so that they don't have a crease; this is how you grow okra—far from the house, because okra tree harbors red ants; when you are growing dasheen, make sure it gets plenty of water or else it makes your throat itch when you are eating it; this is how you sweep a corner; this is how you sweep a whole house; this is how you sweep a yard; this is how you smile to someone you don't like very much; this is how you smile to someone you don't like at all; this is how you smile to someone you like completely; this is how you set a table for tea; this is how you set a table for dinner; this is how you set a table for dinner with an important guest; this is how you set a table for lunch; this is how you set a table for breakfast; this is how to behave in the presence of men who don't know you very well, and this way they won't recognize immediately the slut I have warned you against becoming; be sure to wash every day, even if it is with your own spit; don't squat down to play marbles—you are not a boy, you know; don't pick people's flowers—you might catch something; don't throw stones at blackbirds, because it might not be a blackbird at all; this is how to make a bread pudding; this is how to make doukona; this is how to make pepper pot; this is how to make a good medicine for a cold; this is how to make a good medicine to throw away a child before it even becomes a child; this is how to catch a fish; this is how to throw back a fish you don't like, and that way something bad won't fall on you; this is how to bully a man; this is how a man bullies you; this is how to love a man, and if this doesn't work there are other ways, and if they don't work don't feel too bad about giving up; this is how to spit up in the air if you feel like it, and this is how to move quick so that it doesn't fall on you; this is how to make ends meet; always squeeze bread to make sure it's fresh; *but what if the baker won't let me feel the bread?;* you mean to say that after all you are really going to be the kind of woman who the baker won't let near the bread?

Jhumpa Lahiri

A TEMPORARY MATTER

JHUMPA LAHIRI (1967–) was born in London, England, and grew up in South Kingstown, Rhode Island. Lahiri received her BA in English literature from Barnard College, then multiple degrees from Boston University: an MA in English, an MA in creative writing, an MA in comparative literature, and a PhD in Renaissance studies. Her collection of stories, *Interpreter of Maladies,* won the Pulitzer Prize for Fiction and the Hemingway Foundation/PEN Award, and her novel, *The Namesake,* was adapted for the film by director Mira Nair. Lahiri currently lives in Brooklyn with her husband and two children.

The notice informed them that it was a temporary matter: for five days their electricity would be cut off for one hour, beginning at eight P.M. A line had gone down in the last snowstorm, and the repairmen were going to take advantage of the milder evenings to set it right. The work would affect only the houses on the quiet tree-lined street, within walking distance of a row of brick-faced stores and a trolley stop, where Shoba and Shukumar had lived for three years.

"It's good of them to warn us," Shoba conceded after reading the notice aloud, more for her own benefit than Shukumar's. She let the strap of her leather satchel, plump with files, slip from her shoulders, and left it in the hallway as she walked into the kitchen. She wore a navy blue poplin raincoat over gray sweatpants and white sneakers, looking, at thirty-three, like the type of woman she'd once claimed she would never resemble.

She'd come from the gym. Her cranberry lipstick was visible only on the outer reaches of her mouth, and her eyeliner had left charcoal patches beneath her lower lashes. She used to look this way sometimes, Shukumar thought, on mornings after a party or a night at a bar, when she'd been too lazy to wash her face, too eager to collapse into his arms. She dropped a sheaf of mail on the table without a glance. Her eyes were still fixed on the notice in her other hand. "But they should do this sort of thing during the day."

"When I'm here, you mean," Shukumar said. He put a glass lid on a pot of lamb, adjusting it so only the slightest bit of steam could escape. Since January he'd been working at home, trying to complete the final chapters of his dissertation on agrarian revolts in India. "When do the repairs start?"

"It says March nineteenth. Is today the nineteenth?" Shoba walked over to the framed corkboard that hung on the wall by the fridge, bare except for a calendar of William Morris wallpaper patterns. She looked at it as if for the first time, studying the wallpaper pattern carefully on the top half before allowing her eyes to fall to the numbered grid on the bottom. A friend had sent the calendar in the mail as a Christmas gift, even though Shoba and Shukumar hadn't celebrated Christmas that year.

"Today then," Shoba announced. "You have a dentist appointment next Friday, by the way."

He ran his tongue over the tops of his teeth; he'd forgotten to brush them that morning. It wasn't the first time. He hadn't left the house at all that day, or the day before. The more Shoba stayed out, the more she began putting in extra hours at work and taking on additional projects, the more he wanted to stay in, not even leaving to get the mail, or to buy fruit or wine at the stores by the trolley stop.

Six months ago, in September, Shukumar was at an academic conference in Baltimore when Shoba went into labor, three weeks before her due date. He hadn't wanted to go to the conference, but she had insisted; it was important to make contacts, and he would be entering the job market next year. She told him that she had his number at the hotel, and a copy of his schedule and flight numbers, and she had arranged with her friend Gillian for a ride to the hospital in the event of an emergency. When the cab pulled away that morning for the airport, Shoba stood waving good-bye in her robe, with one arm resting on the mound of her belly as if it were a perfectly natural part of her body.

Each time he thought of that moment, the last moment he saw Shoba pregnant, it was the cab he remembered most, a station wagon, painted red with blue lettering. It was cavernous compared to their own car. Although Shukumar was six feet tall, with hands too big ever to rest comfortably in the pockets of his jeans, he felt dwarfed in the back seat. As the cab sped down Beacon Street, he imagined a day when he and Shoba might need to buy a station wagon of their own, to cart their children back and forth from music lessons and dentist appointments. He imagined himself gripping the wheel, as Shoba turned around to hand the children juice boxes. Once, these images of parenthood had troubled Shukumar, adding to his anxiety that he was still a student at thirty-five. But that early autumn morning, the trees still heavy with bronze leaves, he welcomed the image for the first time.

A member of the staff had found him somehow among the identical convention rooms and handed him a stiff square of stationery. It was only a telephone number, but Shukumar knew it was the hospital. When he returned to Boston it was over. The baby had been born dead. Shoba was lying on a bed, asleep, in a private room so small there was barely enough space to stand beside her, in a wing of the hospital they hadn't been to on the tour for expectant parents. Her placenta had weakened and she'd had a cesarean, though not quickly enough.

The doctor explained that these things happen. He smiled in the kindest way it was possible to smile at people known only professionally. Shoba would be back on her feet in a few weeks. There was nothing to indicate that she would not be able to have children in the future.

These days Shoba was always gone by the time Shukumar woke up. He would open his eyes and see the long black hairs she shed on her pillow and think of her, dressed, sipping her third cup of coffee already, in her office downtown, where she searched for typographical errors in textbooks and marked them, in a code she had once explained to him, with an assortment of colored pencils. She would do the same for his dissertation, she promised, when it was ready. He envied her the specificity of her task, so unlike the elusive nature of his. He was a mediocre student who had a facility for absorbing details without curiosity. Until September he had been diligent if not dedicated, summarizing chapters, outlining arguments on pads of yellow lined paper. But now he would lie in their bed until he grew bored, gazing at his side of the closet which Shoba always left partly open, at the row of the tweed jackets and corduroy trousers he would not have to choose from to teach his classes that semester. After the baby died it was too late to withdraw from his teaching duties. But his adviser had arranged things so that he had the spring semester to himself. Shukumar was in his sixth year of graduate school. "That and the summer should give you a good push," his adviser had said. "You should be able to wrap things up by next September."

But nothing was pushing Shukumar. Instead he thought of how he and Shoba had become experts at avoiding each other in their three-bedroom house, spending as much time on separate floors as possible. He thought of how he no longer looked forward to weekends, when she sat for hours on the sofa with her colored pencils and her files, so that he feared that putting on a record in his own house might be rude. He thought of how long it had been since she looked into his eyes and smiled, or whispered his name on those rare occasions they still reached for each other's bodies before sleeping.

In the beginning he had believed that it would pass, that he and Shoba would get through it all somehow. She was only thirty-three. She was strong, on her feet again. But it wasn't a consolation. It was often nearly lunchtime when Shukumar would finally pull himself out of bed and head downstairs to the coffeepot, pouring out the extra bit Shoba left for him, along with an empty mug, on the countertop.

Shukumar gathered onion skins in his hands and let them drop into the garbage pail, on top of the ribbons of fat he'd trimmed from the lamb. He ran the water in the sink, soaking the knife and the cutting board, and rubbed a lemon half along his fingertips to get rid of the garlic smell, a trick he'd learned from Shoba. It was seven-thirty. Through the window he saw the sky, like soft black pitch. Uneven banks of snow still lined the sidewalks, though it was warm enough for people to walk about without hats or gloves. Nearly three feet had fallen in the last storm, so that for a week people had to walk single file, in narrow trenches. For a week that was Shukumar's excuse for not leaving the house. But now the trenches were widening, and water drained steadily into grates in the pavement.

"The lamb won't be done by eight," Shukumar said. "We may have to eat in the dark."

"We can light candles," Shoba suggested. She unclipped her hair, coiled neatly at her nape during the days, and pried the sneakers from her feet without untying them. "I'm going to shower before the lights go," she said, heading for the staircase. "I'll be down."

Shukumar moved her satchel and her sneakers to the side of the fridge. She wasn't this way before. She used to put her coat on a hanger, her sneakers in the closet, and she paid bills as soon as they came. But now she treated the house as if it were a hotel. The fact that the yellow chintz armchair in the living room clashed with the blue-and-maroon Turkish carpet no longer bothered her. On the enclosed porch at the back of the house, a crisp white bag still sat on the wicker chaise, filled with lace she had once planned to turn into curtains.

While Shoba showered, Shukumar went into the downstairs bathroom and found a new toothbrush in its box beneath the sink. The cheap, stiff bristles hurt his gums, and he spit some blood into the basin. The spare brush was one of many stored in a metal basket. Shoba had bought them once when they were on sale, in the event that a visitor decided, at the last minute, to spend the night.

It was typical of her. She was the type to prepare for surprises, good and bad. If she found a skirt or a purse she liked she bought two. She kept the bonuses from her job in a separate bank account in her name. It hadn't bothered him. His own mother had fallen to pieces when his father died, abandoning the house he grew up in and moving back to Calcutta, leaving Shukumar to settle it all. He liked that Shoba was different. It astonished him, her capacity to think ahead. When she used to do the shopping, the pantry was always stocked with extra bottles of olive and corn oil, depending on whether they were cooking Italian or Indian. There were endless boxes of pasta in all shapes and colors, zippered sacks of basmati rice, whole sides of lambs and goats from the Muslim butchers at Haymarket, chopped up and frozen in endless plastic bags. Every other Saturday they wound through the maze of stalls Shukumar eventually knew by heart. He watched in disbelief as she bought more food, trailing behind her with canvas bags as she pushed through the crowd, arguing under the morning sun with boys too young to shave but already missing teeth, who twisted up brown paper bags of artichokes, plums, gingerroot, and yams, and dropped them on their scales, and tossed them to Shoba one by one. She didn't mind being jostled, even when she was pregnant. She was tall, and broad-shouldered, with hips that her obstetrician assured her were made for child-bearing. During the drive back home, as the car curved along the Charles, they invariably marveled at how much food they'd bought.

It never went to waste. When friends dropped by, Shoba would throw together meals that appeared to have taken half a day to prepare, from things she had frozen and bottled, not cheap things in tins but peppers she had marinated herself with rosemary, and chutneys that she cooked on Sundays, stirring boiling pots of tomatoes and prunes. Her labeled mason jars lined the shelves of the kitchen, in endless sealed pyramids, enough, they'd agreed, to last for their grandchildren to taste. They'd eaten it all by now. Shukumar had been going through their supplies steadily, preparing meals for the two of them, measuring out cupfuls of rice, defrosting bags of meat day after day. He combed through her cookbooks every afternoon, following her penciled instructions to use two teaspoons of ground coriander seeds instead of one, or red lentils instead of yellow. Each of the recipes was dated, telling the first time they had eaten the dish together. April 2, cauliflower with fennel. January 14, chicken with almonds and sultanas. He had no memory of eating those meals, and yet there they were, recorded in her neat proofreader's hand. Shukumar enjoyed cooking now. It was the one thing that made him feel productive. If it weren't for him, he knew, Shoba would eat a bowl of cereal for her dinner.

Tonight, with no lights, they would have to eat together. For months now they'd served themselves from the stove, and he'd taken his plate into his study, letting the meal grow cold on his desk before shoving it into his mouth without pause, while Shoba took her plate to the living room and watched game shows, or proofread files with her arsenal of colored pencils at hand.

At some point in the evening she visited him. When he heard her approach he would put away his novel and begin typing sentences. She would rest her hands on his shoulders and stare with him into the blue glow of the computer screen. "Don't work too hard," she would say after a minute or two, and head off to bed. It was the one time in the day she sought him out, and yet he'd come to dread it. He knew it was something she forced herself to do. She would look around the walls of the room, which they had decorated together last summer with a border of marching ducks and rabbits playing trumpets and drums. By the end of August there was a cherry crib under the window, a white changing table with mint-green knobs, and a rocking chair with checkered cushions. Shukumar had disassembled it all before bringing Shoba back from the hospital, scraping off the rabbits and ducks with a spatula. For some reason the room did not haunt him the way it haunted Shoba. In January, when he stopped working at his carrel in the library, he set up his desk there deliberately, partly because the room soothed him, and partly because it was a place Shoba avoided.

• • •

Shukumar returned to the kitchen and began to open drawers. He tried to locate a candle among the scissors, the eggbeaters and whisks, the mortar and pestle she'd bought in a bazaar in Calcutta, and used to pound garlic cloves and cardamom pods, back when she used to cook. He found a flashlight, but no batteries, and a half-empty box of birthday candles. Shoba had thrown him a surprise birthday party last May. One hundred and twenty people had crammed into the house—all the friends and the friends of friends they now systematically avoided. Bottles of vinho verde had nested in a bed of ice in the bathtub. Shoba was in her fifth month, drinking ginger ale from a martini glass. She had made a vanilla cream cake with custard and spun sugar. All night she kept Shukumar's long fingers linked with hers as they walked among the guests at the party.

Since September their only guest had been Shoba's mother. She came from Arizona and stayed with them for two months after Shoba returned from the hospital. She cooked dinner every night, drove herself to the supermarket, washed their clothes, put them away. She was a religious woman. She set up a small shrine, a framed picture of a lavender-faced goddess and a plate of marigold petals, on the bedside table in the guest room, and prayed twice a day for healthy grandchildren in the future. She was polite to Shukumar without being friendly. She folded his sweaters with an expertise she had learned from her job in a department store. She replaced a missing button on his winter coat and knit him a beige and brown scarf, presenting it to him without the least bit of ceremony, as if he had only dropped it and hadn't noticed. She never talked to him about Shoba; once, when he mentioned the baby's death, she looked up from her knitting, and said, "But you weren't even there."

It struck him as odd that there were no real candles in the house. That Shoba hadn't prepared for such an ordinary emergency. He looked now for something to put the birthday candles in and settled on the soil of a potted ivy that normally sat on the windowsill over the sink. Even though the plant was inches from the tap, the soil was so dry that he had to water it first before the candles would stand straight. He pushed aside the things on the kitchen table, the piles of mail, the unread library books. He remembered their first meals there, when they were so thrilled to be married, to be living together in the same house at last, that they would just reach for each other foolishly, more eager to make love than to eat. He put down two embroidered place mats, a wedding gift from an uncle in Lucknow, and set out the plates and wineglasses they usually saved for guests. He put the ivy in the middle, the white-edged, star-shaped leaves girded by ten little candles. He switched on the digital clock radio and tuned it to a jazz station.

"What's all this?" Shoba said when she came downstairs. Her hair was wrapped in a thick white towel. She undid the towel and draped it over a chair, allowing her hair, damp and dark, to fall across her back. As she walked absently toward the stove she took out a few tangles with her fingers. She wore a clean pair of sweatpants, a T-shirt, an old flannel robe. Her stomach was flat again, her waist narrow before the flare of her hips, the belt of the robe tied in a floppy knot.

It was nearly eight. Shukumar put the rice on the table and the lentils from the night before into the microwave oven, punching the numbers on the timer.

"You made *rogan josh*," Shoba observed, looking through the glass lid at the bright paprika stew.

Shukumar took out a piece of lamb, pinching it quickly between his fingers so as not to scald himself. He prodded a larger piece with a serving spoon to make sure the meat slipped easily from the bone. "It's ready," he announced.

The microwave had just beeped when the lights went out, and the music disappeared.

"Perfect timing," Shoba said.

"All I could find were birthday candles." He lit up the ivy, keeping the rest of the candles and a book of matches by his plate.

"It doesn't matter," she said, running a finger along the stem of her wineglass. "It looks lovely."

In the dimness, he knew how she sat, a bit forward in her chair, ankles crossed against the lowest rung, left elbow on the table. During his search for the candles, Shukumar had found a bottle of wine in a crate he had thought was empty. He damped the bottle between his knees while he turned in the corkscrew. He worried about spilling, and so he picked up the glasses and held them close to his lap while he filled them. They served themselves, stirring the rice with their forks, squinting as they extracted bay leaves and cloves from the stew. Every few minutes Shukumar lit a few more birthday candles and drove them into the soil of the pot.

"It's like India," Shoba said, watching him tend his makeshift candelabra. "Sometimes the current disappears for hours at a stretch. I once had to attend an entire rice ceremony in the dark. The baby just cried and cried. It must have been so hot."

Their baby had never cried, Shukumar considered. Their baby would never have a rice ceremony, even though Shoba had already made the guest list, and decided on which of her three brothers she was going to ask to feed the child its first taste of solid food, at six months if it was a boy, seven if it was a girl.

"Are you hot?" he asked her. He pushed the blazing ivy pot to the other end of the table, closer to the piles of books and mail, making it even more difficult for them to see each other. He was suddenly irritated that he couldn't go upstairs and sit in front of the computer.

"No. It's delicious," she said, tapping her plate with her fork. "It really is."

He refilled the wine in her glass. She thanked him.

They weren't like this before. Now he had to struggle to say something that interested her, something that made her look up from her plate, or from her proofreading files. Eventually he gave up trying to amuse her. He learned not to mind the silences.

"I remember during power failures at my grandmother's house, we all had to say something," Shoba continued. He could barely see her face, but from her tone he knew her eyes were narrowed, as if trying to focus on a distant object. It was a habit of hers.

"Like what?"

"I don't know. A little poem. A joke. A fact about the world. For some reason my relatives always wanted me to tell them the names of my friends in America. I don't know why the information was so interesting to them. The last time I saw my aunt she asked after four girls I went to elementary school with in Tucson. I barely remember them now."

Shukumar hadn't spent as much time in India as Shoba had. His parents, who settled in New Hampshire, used to go back without him. The first time he'd gone as an infant he'd nearly died of amoebic dysentery. His father, a nervous type, was afraid to take him again, in case something were to happen, and left him with his aunt and uncle in Concord. As a teenager he preferred sailing camp or scooping ice cream during the summers to going to Calcutta. It wasn't until after his father died, in his last year of college, that the country began to interest him, and he studied its history from course books as if it were any other subject. He wished now that he had his own childhood story of India.

"Let's do that," she said suddenly.

"Do what?"

"Say something to each other in the dark."

"Like what? I don't know any jokes."

"No, no jokes." She thought for a minute. "How about telling each other something we've never told before."

"I used to play this game in high school," Shukumar recalled. "When I got drunk."

"You're thinking of truth or dare. This is different. Okay, I'll start." She took a sip of wine. "The first time I was alone in your apartment, I looked in your address book to see if you'd written me in. I think we'd known each other two weeks."

"Where was I?"

"You went to answer the telephone in the other room. It was your mother, and I figured it would be a long call. I wanted to know if you'd promoted me from the margins of your newspaper."

"Had I?"

"No. But I didn't give up on you. Now it's your turn."

He couldn't think of anything, but Shoba was waiting for him to speak. She hadn't appeared so determined in months. What was there left to say to her? He thought back to their first meeting, four years earlier at a lecture hall in Cambridge, where a group of Bengali poets were giving a recital. They'd ended up side by side, on folding wooden chairs. Shukumar was soon bored; he was unable to decipher the literary diction, and couldn't join the rest of the audience as they sighed and nodded solemnly after certain phrases. Peering at the newspaper folded in his lap, he studied the temperatures of cities around the world. Ninety-one degrees in Singapore yesterday, fifty-one in Stockholm. When he turned his head to the left, he saw a woman next to him making a grocery list on the back of a folder, and was startled to find that she was beautiful.

"Okay," he said, remembering. "The first time we went out to dinner, to the Portuguese place, I forgot to tip the waiter. I went back the next morning, found out his name, left money with the manager."

"You went all the way back to Somerville just to tip a waiter?"

"I took a cab."

"Why did you forget to tip the waiter?"

The birthday candles had burned out, but he pictured her face clearly in the dark, the wide tilting eyes, the full grape-toned lips, the fall at age two from her high chair still visible as a comma on her chin. Each day, Shukumar noticed, her beauty, which had once overwhelmed him, seemed to fade. The cosmetics that had seemed superfluous were necessary now, not to improve her but to define her somehow.

"By the end of the meal I had a funny feeling that I might marry you," he said, admitting it to himself as well as to her for the first time. "It must have distracted me."

The next night Shoba came home earlier than usual. There was lamb left over from the evening before, and Shukumar heated it up so that they were able to eat by seven. He'd gone out that day, through the melting snow, and bought a packet of taper candles from the corner store, and batteries to fit the flashlight. He had the candles ready on the countertop, standing in brass holders shaped like lotuses, but they ate under the glow of the copper-shaded ceiling lamp that hung over the table.

When they had finished eating, Shukumar was surprised to see that Shoba was stacking her plate on top of his, and then carrying them over to the sink. He had assumed she would retreat to the living room, behind her barricade of files.

"Don't worry about the dishes," he said, taking them from her hands.

"It seems silly not to," she replied, pouring a drop of detergent onto a sponge. "It's nearly eight o'clock."

His heart quickened. All day Shukumar had looked forward to the lights going out. He thought about what Shoba had said the night before, about looking in his address book. It felt good to remember her as she was then, how bold yet nervous she'd been when they first met, how hopeful. They stood side by side at the sink, their reflections fitting together in the frame of the window. It made him shy, the way he felt the first time they stood together in a mirror. He couldn't recall the last time they'd been photographed. They had stopped attending parties, went nowhere together. The film in his camera still contained pictures of Shoba, in the yard, when she was pregnant.

After finishing the dishes, they leaned against the counter, drying their hands on either end of a towel. At eight o'clock the house went black. Shukumar lit the wicks of the candles, impressed by their long, steady flames.

"Let's sit outside," Shoba said. "I think it's warm still."

They each took a candle and sat down on the steps. It seemed strange to be sitting outside with patches of snow still on the ground. But everyone was out of their houses tonight, the air fresh enough to make people restless. Screen doors opened and closed. A small parade of neighbors passed by with flashlights.

"We're going to the bookstore to browse," a silver-haired man called out. He was walking with his wife, a thin woman in a windbreaker, and holding a dog on a leash. They were the Bradfords, and they had tucked a sympathy card into Shoba and Shukumar's mailbox back in September. "I hear they've got their power."

"They'd better," Shukumar said. "Or you'll be browsing in the dark."

The woman laughed, slipping her arm through the crook of her husband's elbow. "Want to join us?"

"No thanks," Shoba and Shukumar called out together. It surprised Shukumar that his words matched hers.

He wondered what Shoba would tell him in the dark. The worst possibilities had already run through his head. That she'd had an affair. That she didn't respect him for being thirty-five and still a student. That she blamed him for being in Baltimore the way her mother did. But he knew those things weren't true. She'd been faithful, as had he. She believed in him. It was she who had insisted he go to Baltimore. What didn't they know about each other? He knew she curled her fingers tightly when she slept, that her body twitched during bad dreams. He knew it was honeydew she favored over cantaloupe. He knew that when they returned from the hospital the first thing she did when she walked into the house was pick out objects of theirs and toss them into a pile in the hallway: books from the shelves, plants from the windowsills, paintings from walls, photos from tables, pots and pans that hung from the hooks over the stove. Shukumar had stepped out of her way, watching as she moved methodically from room to room. When she was satisfied, she stood there staring at the pile she'd made, her lips drawn back in such distaste that Shukumar had thought she would spit. Then she'd started to cry.

He began to feel cold as he sat there on the steps. He felt that he needed her to talk first, in order to reciprocate.

"That time when your mother came to visit us," she said finally. "When I said one night that I had to stay late at work, I went out with Gillian and had a martini."

He looked at her profile, the slender nose, the slightly masculine set of her jaw. He remembered that night well; eating with his mother, tired from teaching two classes back to back, wishing Shoba were there to say more of the right things because he came up with only the wrong ones. It had been twelve years since his father had died, and his mother had come to spend two weeks with him and Shoba, so they could honor his father's memory together. Each night his mother cooked something his father had liked, but she was too upset to eat the dishes herself, and her eyes would well up as Shoba stroked her hand. "It's so touching," Shoba had said to him at the time. Now he pictured Shoba with Gillian, in a bar with striped velvet sofas, the one they used to go to after the movies, making sure she got her extra olive, asking Gillian for a cigarette. He imagined her complaining, and Gillian sympathizing about visits from in-laws. It was Gillian who had driven Shoba to the hospital.

"Your turn," she said, stopping his thoughts.

At the end of their street Shukumar heard sounds of a drill and the electricians shouting over it. He looked at the darkened facades of the houses lining the street. Candles glowed in the windows of one. In spite of the warmth, smoke rose from the chimney.

"I cheated on my Oriental Civilization exam in college," he said. "It was my last semester, my last set of exams. My father had died a few months before. I could see the blue book of the guy next to me. He was an American guy, a maniac. He knew Urdu and Sanskrit. I couldn't remember if the verse we had to identify was an example of a *ghazal* or not. I looked at his answer and copied it down."

It had happened over fifteen years ago. He felt relief now, having told her.

She turned to him, looking not at his face, but at his shoes—old moccasins he wore as if they were slippers, the leather at the back permanently flattened. He wondered if it bothered her, what he'd said. She took his hand and pressed it. "You didn't have to tell me why you did it," she said, moving closer to him.

They sat together until nine o'clock, when the lights came on. They heard some people across the street clapping from their porch, and televisions being turned on. The Bradfords walked back down the street, eating ice-cream cones and waving. Shoba and Shukumar waved back. Then they stood up, his hand still in hers, and went inside.

Somehow, without saying anything, it had turned into this. Into an exchange of confessions—the little ways they'd hurt or disappointed each other, and themselves. The following day Shukumar thought for hours about what to say to her. He was torn between admitting that he once ripped out a photo of a woman in one of the fashion magazines she used to subscribe to and carried it in his books for a week, or saying that he really hadn't lost the sweater-vest she bought him for their third wedding anniversary but had exchanged it for cash at Filene's, and that he had gotten drunk alone in the middle of the day at a hotel bar. For their first anniversary, Shoba had cooked a ten-course dinner just for him. The vest depressed him. "My wife gave me a sweater-vest for our anniversary," he complained to the bartender, his head heavy with cognac. "What do you expect?" the bartender had replied. "You're married."

As for the picture of the woman, he didn't know why he'd ripped it out. She wasn't as pretty as Shoba. She wore a white sequined dress, and had a sullen face and lean, mannish legs. Her bare arms were raised, her fists around her head, as if she were about to punch herself in the ears. It was an advertisement for stockings. Shoba had been pregnant at the time, her stomach suddenly immense, to the point where Shukumar no longer wanted to touch her. The first time he saw the picture he was lying in bed next to her, watching her as she read. When he noticed the magazine in the recycling pile he found the woman and tore out the page as carefully as he could. For about a week he allowed himself a glimpse each day. He felt an intense desire for the woman, but it was a desire that turned to disgust after a minute or two. It was the closest he'd come to infidelity.

He told Shoba about the sweater on the third night, the picture on the fourth. She said nothing as he spoke, expressed no protest or reproach. She simply listened, and then she took his hand, pressing it as she had before. On the third night, she told him that once after a lecture they'd attended, she let him speak to the chairman of his department without telling him that he had a dab of pâté on his chin. She'd been irritated with him for some reason, and so she'd let him go on and on, about securing his fellowship for the following semester, without putting a finger to her own chin as a signal. The fourth night, she said that she never liked the one poem he'd ever published in his life, in a literary magazine in Utah. He'd written the poem after meeting Shoba. She added that she found the poem sentimental.

Something happened when the house was dark. They were able to talk to each other again. The third night after supper they'd sat together on the sofa, and once it was dark he began kissing her awkwardly on her forehead and her face, and though it was dark he closed his eyes, and knew that she did, too. The fourth night they walked carefully upstairs, to bed, feeling together for the final step with their feet before the landing, and making love with a desperation they had forgotten. She wept without sound, and whispered his name, and traced his eyebrows with her finger in the dark. As he made love to her he wondered what he would say to her the next night, and what she would say, the thought of it exciting him. "Hold me," he said, "hold me in your arms." By the time the lights came back on downstairs, they'd fallen asleep.

The morning of the fifth night Shukumar found another notice from the electric company in the mailbox. The line had been repaired ahead of schedule, it said. He was disappointed. He had planned on making shrimp *malai* for Shoba, but when he arrived at the store he didn't feel like cooking anymore. It wasn't the same, he thought, knowing that the lights wouldn't go out. In the store the shrimp looked gray and thin. The coconut milk tin was dusty and overpriced. Still, he bought them, along with a beeswax candle and two bottles of wine.

She came home at seven-thirty. "I suppose this is the end of our game," he said when he saw her reading the notice.

She looked at him. "You can still light candles if you want." She hadn't been to the gym tonight. She wore a suit beneath the raincoat. Her makeup had been retouched recently.

When she went upstairs to change, Shukumar poured himself some wine and put on a record, a Thelonius Monk album he knew she liked.

When she came downstairs they ate together. She didn't thank him or compliment him. They simply ate in a darkened room, in the glow of a beeswax candle. They had survived a difficult time. They finished off the shrimp. They finished off the first bottle of wine and moved on to the second. They sat together until the candle had nearly burned away. She shifted in her chair, and Shukumar thought that she was about to say something. But instead she blew out the candle, stood up, turned on the light switch, and sat down again.

"Shouldn't we keep the lights off?" Shukumar asked.

She set her plate aside and clasped her hands on the table. "I want you to see my face when I tell you this," she said gently.

His heart began to pound. The day she told him she was pregnant, she had used the very same words, saying them in the same gentle way, turning off the basketball game he'd been watching on television. He hadn't been prepared then. Now he was.

Only he didn't want her to be pregnant again. He didn't want to have to pretend to be happy.

"I've been looking for an apartment and I've found one," she said, narrowing her eyes on something, it seemed, behind his left shoulder. It was nobody's fault, she continued. They'd been through enough. She needed some time alone. She had money saved up for a security deposit. The apartment was on Beacon Hill, so she could walk to work. She had signed the lease that night before coming home.

She wouldn't look at him, but he stared at her. It was obvious that she'd rehearsed the lines. All this time she'd been looking for an apartment, testing the water pressure, asking a Realtor if heat and hot water were included in the rent. It sickened Shukumar, knowing that she had spent these past evenings preparing for a life without him. He was relieved and yet he was sickened. This was what she'd been trying to tell him for the past four evenings. This was the point of her game.

Now it was his turn to speak. There was something he'd sworn he would never tell her, and for six months he had done his best to block it from his mind. Before the ultrasound she had asked the doctor not to tell her the sex of their child, and Shukumar had agreed. She had wanted it to be a surprise.

Later, those few times they talked about what had happened, she said at least they'd been spared that knowledge. In a way she almost took pride in her decision, for it enabled her to seek refuge in a mystery. He knew that she assumed it was a mystery for him, too. He'd arrived too late from Baltimore—when it was all over and she was lying on the hospital bed. But he hadn't. He'd arrived early enough to see their baby, and to hold him before they cremated him. At first he had recoiled at the suggestion, but the doctor said holding the baby might help him with the process of grieving. Shoba was asleep. The baby had been cleaned off, his bulbous lids shut tight to the world.

"Our baby was a boy," he said. "His skin was more red than brown. He had black hair on his head. He weighed almost five pounds. His fingers were curled shut, just like yours in the night."

Shoba looked at him now, her face contorted with sorrow. He had cheated on a college exam, ripped a picture of a woman out of a magazine. He had returned a sweater and got drunk in the middle of the day instead. These were the things he had told her. He had held his son, who had known life only within her, against his chest in a darkened room in an unknown wing of the hospital. He had held him until a nurse knocked and took him away, and he promised himself that day that he would never tell Shoba, because he still loved her then, and it was the one thing in her life that she had wanted to be a surprise.

Shukumar stood up and stacked his plate on top of hers. He carried the plates to the sink, but instead of running the tap he looked out the window. Outside the evening was still warm, and the Bradfords were walking arm in arm. As he watched the couple the room went dark, and he spun around. Shoba had turned the lights off. She came back to the table and sat down, and after a moment Shukumar joined her. They wept together, for the things they now knew.

David Leavitt

TERRITORY

DAVID LEAVITT (1961–) is the author of several story collections, recently brought together as *Collected Stories*. His novels include *The Lost Language of Cranes, While England Sleeps, The Body of Jonah Boyd,* and *The Indian Clerk.* He is a recipient of fellowships from both the Guggenheim Foundation and the National Endowment for the Arts. He is a professor of English at the University of Florida, where he codirects the creative writing program and edits the journal *Subtropics*.

Neil's mother, Mrs. Campbell, sits on her lawn chair behind a card table outside the food co-op. Every few minutes, as the sun shifts, she moves the chair and table several inches back so as to remain in the shade. It is a hundred degrees outside, and bright white. Each time someone goes in or out of the co-op a gust of air-conditioning flies out of the automatic doors, raising dust from the cement.

Neil stands just inside, poised over a water fountain, and watches her. She has on a sun hat, and a sweatshirt over her tennis dress; her legs are bare, and shiny with cocoa butter. In front of her, propped against the table, a sign proclaims: MOTHERS, FIGHT FOR YOUR CHILDREN'S RIGHTS—SUPPORT A NON-NUCLEAR FUTURE. Women dressed exactly like her pass by, notice the sign, listen to her brief spiel, finger pamphlets, sign petitions or don't sign petitions, never give money. Her weary eyes are masked by dark glasses. In the age of Reagan, she has declared, keeping up the causes of peace and justice is a futile, tiresome, and unrewarding effort; it is therefore an effort fit only for mothers to keep up. The sun bounces off the window glass through which Neil watches her. His own reflection lines up with her profile.

Later that afternoon, Neil spreads himself out alongside the pool and imagines he is being watched by the shirtless Chicano gardener. But the gardener, concentrating on his pruning, is neither seductive nor seducible. On the lawn, his mother's large Airedales—Abigail, Lucille, Fern—amble, sniff, urinate. Occasionally, they accost the gardener, who yells at them in Spanish.

After two years' absence, Neil reasons, he should feel nostalgia, regret, gladness upon returning home. He closes his eyes and tries to muster the proper

335

background music for the cinematic scene of return. His rhapsody, however, is interrupted by the noises of his mother's trio—the scratchy cello, whining violin, stumbling piano—as she and Lillian Havalard and Charlotte Feder plunge through Mozart. The tune is cheery, in a Germanic sort of way, and utterly inappropriate to what Neil is trying to feel. Yet it *is* the music of his adolescence; they have played it for years, bent over the notes, their heads bobbing in silent time to the metronome.

It is getting darker. Every few minutes, he must move his towel so as to remain within the narrowing patch of sunlight. In four hours, Wayne, his lover of ten months and the only person he has ever imagined he could spend his life with, will be in this house, where no lover of his has ever set foot. The thought fills him with a sense of grand terror and curiosity. He stretches, tries to feel seductive, desirable. The gardener's shears whack at the ferns; the music above him rushes to a loud, premature conclusion. The women laugh and applaud themselves as they give up for the day. He hears Charlotte Feder's full nasal twang, the voice of a fat woman in a pink pants suit—odd, since she is a scrawny, arthritic old bird, rarely clad in anything other than tennis shorts and a blouse. Lillian is the fat woman in the pink pants suit; her voice is thin and warped by too much crying. Drink in hand, she calls out from the porch, "Hot enough!" and waves. He lifts himself up and nods to her.

The women sit on the porch and chatter; their voices blend with the clink of ice in glasses. They belong to a small circle of ladies all of whom, with the exception of Neil's mother, are widows and divorcées. Lillian's husband left her twenty-two years ago, and sends her a check every month to live on; Charlotte has been divorced twice as long as she was married, and has a daughter serving a long sentence for terrorist acts committed when she was nineteen. Only Neil's mother has a husband, a distant sort of husband, away often on business. He is away on business now. All of them feel betrayed—by husbands, by children, by history.

Neil closes his eyes, tries to hear the words only as sounds. Soon, a new noise accosts him: his mother arguing with the gardener in Spanish. He leans on his elbows and watches them; the syllables are loud, heated, and compressed, and seem on the verge of explosion. But the argument ends happily; they shake hands. The gardener collects his check and walks out the gate without so much as looking at Neil.

He does not know the gardener's name; as his mother has reminded him, he does not know most of what has gone on since he moved away. Her life has gone on, unaffected by his absence. He flinches at his own egoism, the egoism of sons.

"Neil! Did you call the airport to make sure the plane's coming in on time?"

"Yes," he shouts to her. "It is."

"Good. Well, I'll have dinner ready when you get back."

"Mom—"

"What?" The word comes out in a weary wail that is more of an answer than a question.

"What's wrong?" he says, forgetting his original question.

"Nothing's wrong," she declares in a tone that indicates that everything is wrong. "The dogs have to be fed, dinner has to be made, and I've got people here. Nothing's wrong."

"I hope things will be as comfortable as possible when Wayne gets here."

"Is that a request or a threat?"

"Mom—"

Behind her sunglasses, her eyes are inscrutable. "I'm tired," she says. "It's been a long day. I . . . I'm anxious to meet Wayne. I'm sure he'll be wonderful, and we'll all have a wonderful, wonderful time. I'm sorry. I'm just tired."

She heads up the stairs. He suddenly feels an urge to cover himself; his body embarrasses him, as it has in her presence since the day she saw him shirtless and said with delight, "Neil! You're growing hair under your arms!"

Before he can get up, the dogs gather round him and begin to sniff and lick at him. He wriggles to get away from them, but Abigail, the largest and stupidest, straddles his stomach and nuzzles his mouth. He splutters and, laughing, throws her off. "Get away from me, you goddamn dogs," he shouts, and swats at them. They are new dogs, not the dog of his childhood, not dogs he trusts.

He stands, and the dogs circle him, looking up at his face expectantly. He feels renewed terror at the thought that Wayne will be here so soon: Will they sleep in the same room? Will they make love? He has never had sex in his parents' house. How can he be expected to be a lover here, in this place of his childhood, of his earliest shame, in this household of mothers and dogs?

"Dinnertime! Abbylucyferny, Abbylucyferny, dinnertime!" His mother's litany disperses the dogs, and they run for the door.

"Do you realize," he shouts to her, "that no matter how much those dogs love you they'd probably kill you for the leg of lamb in the freezer?"

Neil was twelve the first time he recognized in himself something like sexuality. He was lying outside, on the grass, when Rasputin—the dog, long dead, of his childhood—began licking his face. He felt a tingle he did not recognize, pulled off his shirt to give the dog access to more of him. Rasputin's tongue tickled coolly. A wet nose started to sniff down his body, toward his bathing suit. What he felt frightened him, but he couldn't bring himself to push the dog away. Then his mother called out, "Dinner," and Rasputin was gone, more interested in food than in him.

It was the day after Rasputin was put to sleep, years later, that Neil finally stood in the kitchen, his back turned to his parents, and said, with unexpected ease, "I'm a homosexual." The words seemed insufficient, reductive. For years, he had believed his sexuality to be detachable from the essential him, but now he realized that it was part of him. He had the sudden, despairing sensation that though the words had been easy to say, the fact of their having been aired was incurably damning. Only then, for the first time, did he admit that they were true, and he shook and wept in regret for what he would not be for his mother, for having failed her. His father hung back, silent; he was absent for that moment as he was mostly absent—a strong absence. Neil always thought of him sitting on the edge of the bed in his underwear, captivated by something on television. He said, "It's O.K., Neil." But his mother was resolute; her lower lip didn't quaver. She had enormous reserves of strength to which she only gained access at moments like this one. She hugged him from behind, wrapped him in the childhood smells of perfume and brownies, and whispered, "It's O.K., honey." For once, her words seemed as inadequate as his. Neil felt himself shrunk to an embarrassed adolescent, hating her sympathy, not wanting her to touch him. It was the way he would feel from then on whenever he was in her presence—even now, at twenty-three, bringing home his lover to meet her.

All through his childhood, she had packed only the most nutritious lunches, had served on the PTA, had volunteered at the children's library and at his school, had organized a successful campaign to ban a racist history textbook. The day after he told her, she located and got in touch with an organization called the Coalition of Parents of Lesbians and Gays. Within a year, she was president of it. On weekends, she and the other mothers drove their station wagons to San Francisco, set up their card tables in front of the Bulldog Baths, the Liberty Baths, passed out literature to men in leather and denim who were loath to admit they even had mothers. These men, who would habitually do violence to each other, were strangely cowed by the suburban ladies with their informational booklets, and bent their heads. Neil was a sophomore in college then, and lived in San Francisco. She brought him pamphlets detailing the dangers of bathhouses and back rooms, enemas and poppers, wordless sex in alleyways. His excursion into that world had been brief and lamentable, and was over. He winced at the thought that she knew all his sexual secrets, and vowed to move to the East Coast to escape her. It was not very different from the days when she had campaigned for a better playground, or tutored the Hispanic children in the audiovisual room. Those days, as well, he had run away from her concern. Even today, perched in front of the co-op, collecting signatures for nuclear disarmament, she was quintessentially a mother. And if the lot of mothers was to expect nothing in return, was the lot of sons to return nothing?

Driving across the Dumbarton Bridge on his way to the airport, Neil thinks, I have returned nothing; I have simply returned. He wonders if she would have given birth to him had she known what he would grow up to be.

Then he berates himself: Why should he assume himself to be the cause of her sorrow? She has told him that her life is full of secrets. She has changed since he left home—grown thinner, more rigid, harder to hug. She has given up baking, taken up tennis; her skin has browned and tightened. She is no longer the woman who hugged him and kissed him, who said, "As long as you're happy, that's all that's important to us."

The flats spread out around him; the bridge floats on purple and green silt, and spongy bay fill, not water at all. Only ten miles north, a whole city has been built on gunk dredged up from the bay.

He arrives at the airport ten minutes early, to discover that the plane has landed twenty minutes early. His first view of Wayne is from behind, by the baggage belt. Wayne looks as he always looks—slightly windblown—and is wearing the ratty leather jacket he was wearing the night they met. Neil sneaks up on him and puts his hands on his shoulders; when Wayne turns around, he looks relieved to see him.

They hug like brothers; only in the safety of Neil's mother's car do they dare to kiss. They recognize each other's smells, and grow comfortable again. "I never imagined I'd actually see you out here," Neil says, "but you're exactly the same here as there."

"It's only been a week."

They kiss again. Neil wants to go to a motel, but Wayne insists on being pragmatic. "We'll be there soon. Don't worry."

"We could go to one of the bathhouses in the city and take a room for a couple of aeons," Neil says. "Christ, I'm hard up. I don't even know if we're going to be in the same bedroom."

"Well, if we're not," Wayne says, "we'll sneak around. It'll be romantic."

They cling to each other for a few more minutes, until they realize that people are looking in the car window. Reluctantly, they pull apart. Neil reminds himself that he loves this man, that there is a reason for him to bring this man home.

He takes the scenic route on the way back. The car careers over foothills, through forests, along white four-lane highways high in the mountains. Wayne tells Neil that he sat next to a woman on the plane who was once Marilyn Monroe's psychiatrist's nurse. He slips his foot out of his shoe and nudges Neil's ankle, pulling Neil's sock down with his toe.

"I have to drive," Neil says. "I'm very glad you're here."

There is a comfort in the privacy of the car. They have a common fear of walking hand in hand, of publicly showing physical affection, even in the permissive West Seventies of New York—a fear that they have admitted only to one another. They slip through a pass between two hills, and are suddenly in residential Northern California, the land of expensive ranch-style houses.

As they pull into Neil's mother's driveway, the dogs run barking toward the car. When Wayne opens the door, they jump and lap at him, and he tries to close it again. "Don't worry. Abbylucyferny! Get in the house, damn it!"

His mother descends from the porch. She has changed into a blue flower-print dress, which Neil doesn't recognize. He gets out of the car and halfheart-edly chastises the dogs. Crickets chirp in the trees. His mother looks radiant, even beautiful, illuminated by the headlights, surrounded by the now quiet dogs, like a Circe with her slaves. When she walks over to Wayne, offering her hand, and says, "Wayne, I'm Barbara," Neil forgets that she is his mother.

"Good to meet you, Barbara," Wayne says, and reaches out his hand. Craftier than she, he whirls her around to kiss her cheek.

Barbara! He is calling his mother Barbara! Then he remembers that Wayne is five years older than he is. They chat by the open car door, and Neil shrinks back—the embarrassed adolescent, uncomfortable, unwanted.

So the dreaded moment passes and he might as well not have been there. At dinner, Wayne keeps the conversation smooth, like a captivated courtier seek-ing Neil's mother's hand. A faggot son's sodomist—such words spit into Neil's head. She has prepared tiny meatballs with fresh coriander, fettucine with pesto. Wayne talks about the street people in New York; El Salvador is a tragedy; if only Sadat had lived; Phyllis Schlafly—what can you do?

"It's a losing battle," she tells him. "Every day I'm out there with my card table, me and the other mothers, but I tell you, Wayne, it's a losing battle. Some-times I think us old ladies are the only ones with enough patience to fight."

Occasionally, Neil says something, but his comments seem stupid and clumsy. Wayne continues to call her Barbara. No one under forty has ever called her Barbara as long as Neil can remember. They drink wine; he does not.

Now is the time for drastic action. He contemplates taking Wayne's hand, then checks himself. He has never done anything in her presence to indicate that the sexuality he confessed to five years ago was a reality and not an inven-tion. Even now, he and Wayne might as well be friends, college roommates. Then Wayne, his savior, with a single, sweeping gesture, reaches for his hand, and clasps it, in the midst of a joke he is telling about Saudi Arabians. By the time he is laughing, their hands are joined. Neil's throat contracts; his heart begins to beat violently. He notices his mother's eyes flicker, glance downward; she never breaks the stride of her sentence. The dinner goes on, and every taboo nurtured since childhood falls quietly away.

She removes the dishes. Their hands grow sticky; he cannot tell which fin-gers are his and which Wayne's. She clears the rest of the table and rounds up the dogs.

"Well, boys, I'm very tired, and I've got a long day ahead of me tomorrow, so I think I'll hit the sack. There are extra towels for you in Neil's bathroom, Wayne. Sleep well."

"Good night, Barbara," Wayne calls out. "It's been wonderful meeting you."
They are alone. Now they can disentangle their hands.

"No problem about where we sleep, is there?"

"No," Neil says. "I just can't imagine sleeping with someone in this house."

His leg shakes violently. Wayne takes Neil's hand in a firm grasp and hauls him up.

Later that night, they lie outside, under redwood trees, listening to the hysteria of the crickets, the hum of the pool cleaning itself. Redwood leaves prick their skin. They fell in love in bars and apartments, and this is the first time that they have made love outdoors. Neil is not sure he has enjoyed the experience. He kept sensing eyes, imagined that the neighborhood cats were staring at them from behind a fence of brambles. He remembers he once hid in this spot when he and some of the children from the neighborhood were playing sardines, re- members the intoxication of small bodies packed together, the warm breath of suppressed laughter on his neck. "The loser had to go through the spanking machine," he tells Wayne.

"Did you lose often?"

"Most of the time. The spanking machine never really hurt—just a whirl of hands. If you moved fast enough, no one could actually get you. Sometimes, though, late in the afternoon, we'd get naughty. We'd chase each other and pull each other's pants down. That was all. Boys and girls together!"

"Listen to the insects," Wayne says, and closes his eyes.

Neil turns to examine Wayne's face, notices a single, small pimple. Their lovemaking usually begins in a wrestle, a struggle for dominance, and ends with a somewhat confusing loss of identity—as now, when Neil sees a foot on the grass, resting against his leg, and tries to determine if it is his own or Wayne's.

From inside the house, the dogs begin to bark. Their yelps grow into alarmed falsettos. Neil lifts himself up. "I wonder if they smell something," he says.

"Probably just us," says Wayne.

"My mother will wake up. She hates getting waked up."

Lights go on in the house; the door to the porch opens.

"What's wrong, Abby? What's wrong?" his mother's voice calls softly.

Wayne clamps his hand over Neil's mouth. "Don't say anything," he whispers.

"I can't just—" Neil begins to say, but Wayne's hand closes over his mouth again. He bites it, and Wayne starts laughing.

"What was that?" Her voice projects into the garden. "Hello?" she says.

The dogs yelp louder. "Abbylucyferny, it's O.K., it's O.K." Her voice is soft and panicked. "Is anyone there?" she asks loudly.

The brambles shake. She takes a flashlight, shines it around the garden. Wayne and Neil duck down; the light lands on them and hovers for a few seconds. Then it clicks off and they are in the dark—a new dark, a darker dark, which their eyes must readjust to.

"Let's go to bed, Abbylucyferny," she says gently. Neil and Wayne hear her pad into the house. The dogs whimper as they follow her, and the lights go off.

Once before, Neil and his mother had stared at each other in the glare of bright lights. Four years ago, they stood in the arena created by the headlights of her car, waiting for the train. He was on his way back to San Francisco, where he was marching in a Gay Pride Parade the next day. The train station was next door to the food co-op and shared its parking lot. The co-op, familiar and boring by day, took on a certain mystery in the night. Neil recognized the spot where he had skidded on his bicycle and broken his leg. Through the glass doors, the brightly lit interior of the store glowed, its rows and rows of cans and boxes forming their own horizon, each can illuminated so that even from outside Neil could read the labels. All that was missing was the ladies in tennis dresses and sweatshirts, pushing their carts past bins of nuts and dried fruits.

"Your train is late," his mother said. Her hair fell loosely on her shoulders, and her legs were tanned. Neil looked at her and tried to imagine her in labor with him—bucking and struggling with his birth. He felt then the strange, sexless love for women which through his whole adolescence he had mistaken for heterosexual desire.

A single bright light approached them; it preceded the low, haunting sound of the whistle. Neil kissed his mother, and waved goodbye as he ran to meet the train. It was an old train, with windows tinted a sort of horrible lemon-lime. It stopped only long enough for him to hoist himself on board, and then it was moving again. He hurried to a window, hoping to see her drive off, but the tint of the window made it possible for him to make out only vague patches of light—street lamps, cars, the co-op.

He sank into the hard, green seat. The train was almost entirely empty; the only other passenger was a dark-skinned man wearing bluejeans and a leather jacket. He sat directly across the aisle from Neil, next to the window. He had rough skin and a thick mustache. Neil discovered that by pretending to look out the window he could study the man's reflection in the lemon-lime glass. It was only slightly hazy—the quality of a bad photograph. Neil felt his mouth open, felt sleep closing in on him. Hazy red and gold flashes through the glass pulsed in the face of the man in the window, giving the curious impression of muscle spasms. It took Neil a few minutes to realize that the man was staring at him, or, rather, staring at the back of his head—staring at his staring. The man smiled as though to say, I know exactly what you're staring at, and Neil felt the sickening sensation of desire rise in his throat.

Right before they reached the city, the man stood up and sat down in the seat next to Neil's. The man's thigh brushed deliberately against his own. Neil's eyes were watering; he felt sick to his stomach. Taking Neil's hand, the man said, "Why so nervous, honey? Relax."

Neil woke up the next morning with the taste of ashes in his mouth. He was lying on the floor, without blankets or sheets or pillows. Instinctively, he reached for his pants, and as he pulled them on came face to face with the man from the train. His name was Luis; he turned out to be a dog groomer. His apartment smelled of dog.

"Why such a hurry?" Luis said.

"The parade. The Gay Pride Parade. I'm meeting some friends to march."

"I'll come with you," Luis said. "I think I'm too old for these things, but why not?"

Neil did not want Luis to come with him, but he found it impossible to say so. Luis looked older by day, more likely to carry diseases. He dressed again in a torn T-shirt, leather jacket, bluejeans. "It's my everyday apparel," he said, and laughed. Neil buttoned his pants, aware that they had been washed by his mother the day before. Luis possessed the peculiar combination of hypermasculinity and effeminacy which exemplifies faggotry. Neil wanted to be rid of him, but Luis's mark was on him, he could see that much. They would become lovers whether Neil liked it or not.

They joined the parade midway. Neil hoped he wouldn't meet anyone he knew; he did not want to have to explain Luis, who clung to him. The parade was full of shirtless men with oiled, muscular shoulders. Neil's back ached. There were floats carrying garishly dressed prom queens and cheerleaders, some with beards, some actually looking like women. Luis said, "It makes me proud, makes me glad to be what I am." Neil supposed that by darting into the crowd ahead of him he might be able to lose Luis forever, but he found it difficult to let him go; the prospect of being alone seemed unbearable.

Neil was startled to see his mother watching the parade, holding up a sign. She was with the Coalition of Parents of Lesbians and Gays; they had posted a huge banner on the wall behind them proclaiming: OUR SONS AND DAUGHTERS, WE ARE PROUD OF YOU. She spotted him; she waved, and jumped up and down.

"Who's that woman?" Luis asked.

"My mother. I should go say hello to her."

"O.K.," Luis said. He followed Neil to the side of the parade. Neil kissed his mother. Luis took off his shirt, wiped his face with it, smiled.

"I'm glad you came," Neil said.

"I wouldn't have missed it, Neil. I wanted to show you I cared."

He smiled, and kissed her again. He showed no intention of introducing Luis, so Luis introduced himself.

"Hello, Luis," Mrs. Campbell said. Neil looked away. Luis shook her hand,

and Neil wanted to warn his mother to wash it, warned himself to check with a V.D. clinic first thing Monday.

"Neil, this is Carmen Bologna, another one of the mothers," Mrs. Campbell said. She introduced him to a fat Italian woman with flushed cheeks, and hair arranged in the shape of a clamshell.

"Good to meet you, Neil, good to meet you," said Carmen Bologna. "You know my son, Michael? I'm so proud of Michael! He's doing so well now. I'm proud of him, proud to be his mother I am, and your mother's proud, too!"

The woman smiled at him, and Neil could think of nothing to say but "Thank you." He looked uncomfortably toward his mother, who stood listening to Luis. It occurred to him that the worst period of his life was probably about to begin and he had no way to stop it.

A group of drag queens ambled over to where the mothers were standing. "Michael! Michael!" shouted Carmen Bologna, and embraced a sticklike man wrapped in green satin. Michael's eyes were heavily dosed with green eyeshadow, and his lips were painted pink.

Neil turned and saw his mother staring, her mouth open. He marched over to where Luis was standing, and they moved back into the parade. He turned and waved to her. She waved back; he saw pain in her face, and then, briefly, regret. That day, he felt she would have traded him for any other son. Later, she said to him, "Carmen Bologna really was proud, and, speaking as a mother, let me tell you, you have to be brave to feel such pride."

Neil was never proud. It took him a year to dump Luis, another year to leave California. The sick taste of ashes was still in his mouth. On the plane, he envisioned his mother sitting alone in the dark, smoking. She did not leave his mind until he was circling New York, staring down at the dawn rising over Queens. The song playing in his earphones would remain hovering on the edges of his memory, always associated with her absence. After collecting his baggage, he took a bus into the city. Boys were selling newspapers in the middle of highways, through the windows of stopped cars. It was seven in the morning when he reached Manhattan. He stood for ten minutes on East Thirty-fourth Street, breathed the cold air, and felt bubbles rising in his blood.

Neil got a job as a paralegal—a temporary job, he told himself. When he met Wayne a year later, the sensations of that first morning returned to him. They'd been up all night, and at six they walked across the park to Wayne's apartment with the nervous, deliberate gait of people aching to make love for the first time. Joggers ran by with their dogs. None of them knew what Wayne and he were about to do, and the secrecy excited him. His mother came to mind, and the song, and the whirling vision of Queens coming alive below him. His breath solidified into clouds, and he felt happier than he had ever felt before in his life.

• • •

The second day of Wayne's visit, he and Neil go with Mrs. Campbell to pick up the dogs at the dog parlor. The grooming establishment is decorated with pink ribbons and photographs of the owner's champion pit bulls. A fat, middle-aged woman appears from the back, leading the newly trimmed and fluffed Abigail, Lucille, and Fern by three leashes. The dogs struggle frantically when they see Neil's mother, tangling the woman up in their leashes. "Ladies, behave!" Mrs. Campbell commands, and collects the dogs. She gives Fern to Neil and Abigail to Wayne. In the car on the way back, Abigail begins pawing to get on Wayne's lap.

"Just push her off," Mrs. Campbell says. "She knows she's not supposed to do that."

"You never groomed Rasputin," Neil complains.

"Rasputin was a mutt."

"Rasputin was a beautiful dog, even if he did smell."

"Do you remember when you were a little kid, Neil, you used to make Rasputin dance with you? Once you tried to dress him up in one of my blouses."

"I don't remember that," Neil says.

"Yes. I remember," says Mrs. Campbell. "Then you tried to organize a dog beauty contest in the neighborhood. You wanted to have runners-up—everything."

"A dog beauty contest?" Wayne says.

"Mother, do we have to—"

"I think it's a mother's privilege to embarrass her son," Mrs. Campbell says, and smiles.

When they are about to pull into the driveway, Wayne starts screaming, and pushes Abigail off his lap. "Oh, my God!" he says. "The dog just pissed all over me."

Neil turns around and sees a puddle seeping into Wayne's slacks. He suppresses his laughter, and Mrs. Campbell hands him a rag.

"I'm sorry, Wayne," she says. "It goes with the territory."

"This is really disgusting," Wayne says, swatting at himself with the rag.

Neil keeps his eyes on his own reflection in the rearview mirror and smiles.

At home, while Wayne cleans himself in the bathroom, Neil watches his mother cook lunch—Japanese noodles in soup. "When you went off to college," she says, "I went to the grocery store. I was going to buy you ramen noodles, and I suddenly realized you weren't going to be around to eat them. I started crying right then, blubbering like an idiot."

Neil clenches his fists inside his pockets. She has a way of telling him little sad stories when he doesn't want to hear them—stories of dolls broken by her brothers, lunches stolen by neighborhood boys on the way to school. Now he has joined the ranks of male children who have made her cry.

"Mama, I'm sorry," he says.

She is bent over the noodles, which steam in her face. "I didn't want to say anything in front of Wayne, but I wish you had answered me last night. I was very frightened—and worried."

"I'm sorry," he says, but it's not convincing. His fingers prickle. He senses a great sorrow about to be born.

"I lead a quiet life," she says. "I don't want to be a disciplinarian. I just don't have the energy for these—shenanigans. Please don't frighten me that way again."

"If you were so upset, why didn't you say something?"

"I'd rather not discuss it. I lead a quiet life. I'm not used to getting woken up late at night. I'm not used—"

"To my having a lover?"

"No, I'm not used to having other people around, that's all. Wayne is charming. A wonderful young man."

"He likes you, too."

"I'm sure we'll get along fine."

She scoops the steaming noodles into ceramic bowls. Wayne returns, wearing shorts. His white, hairy legs are a shocking contrast to hers, which are brown and sleek.

"I'll wash those pants, Wayne," Mrs. Campbell says. "I have a special detergent that'll take out the stain."

She gives Neil a look to indicate that the subject should be dropped. He looks at Wayne, looks at his mother; his initial embarrassment gives way to a fierce pride—the arrogance of mastery. He is glad his mother knows that he is desired, glad it makes her flinch.

Later, he steps into the backyard; the gardener is back, whacking at the bushes with his shears. Neil walks by him in his bathing suit, imagining he is on parade.

That afternoon, he finds his mother's daily list on the kitchen table:

TUESDAY

7:00—breakfast
Take dogs to groomer
Groceries (?)

Campaign against Draft—4–7

Buy underwear
Trios—2:00
Spaghetti

Fruit
Asparagus if sale
Peanuts
Milk

Doctor's Appointment (make)
Write Cranston/Hayakawa
re disarmament

Handi-Wraps
Mozart
Abigail
Top Ramen
Pedro

Her desk and trash can are full of such lists; he remembers them from the earliest days of his childhood. He had learned to read from them. In his own life, too, there have been endless lists—covered with check marks and arrows, at least one item always spilling over onto the next day's agenda. From September to November, "Buy plane ticket for Christmas" floated from list to list to list.

The last item puzzles him: Pedro. Pedro must be the gardener. He observes the accretion of names, the arbitrary specifics that give a sense of his mother's life. He could make a list of his own selves: the child, the adolescent, the promiscuous faggot son, and finally the good son, settled, relatively successful. But the divisions wouldn't work; he is today and will always be the child being licked by the dog, the boy on the floor with Luis; he will still be everything he is ashamed of. The other lists—the lists of things done and undone—tell their own truth: that his life is measured more properly in objects than in stages. He knows himself as "jump rope," "book," "sunglasses," "underwear."

"Tell me about your family, Wayne," Mrs. Campbell says that night, as they drive toward town. They are going to see an Esther Williams movie at the local revival house: an underwater musical, populated by mermaids, underwater Rockettes.

"My father was a lawyer," Wayne says. "He had an office in Queens, with a neon sign. I think he's probably the only lawyer in the world who had a neon sign. Anyway, he died when I was ten. My mother never remarried. She lives in Queens. Her great claim to fame is that when she was twenty-two she went on 'The $64,000 Question.' Her category was mystery novels. She made it to sixteen thousand before she got tripped up."

"When I was about ten, I wanted you to go on 'Jeopardy,'" Neil says to his mother. "You really should have, you know. You would have won."

"You certainly loved 'Jeopardy,'" Mrs. Campbell says. "You used to watch it during dinner. Wayne, does your mother work?"

"No," he says. "She lives off investments."

"You're both only children," Mrs. Campbell says. Neil wonders if she is ruminating on the possible connection between that coincidence and their "alternative life style."

The movie theater is nearly empty. Neil sits between Wayne and his mother. There are pillows on the floor at the front of the theater, and a cat is prowling over them. It casts a monstrous shadow every now and then on the screen, disturbing the sedative effect of water ballet. Like a teenager, Neil cautiously reaches his arm around Wayne's shoulder. Wayne takes his hand immediately. Next to them, Neil's mother breathes in, out, in, out. Neil timorously moves his other arm and lifts it behind his mother's neck. He does not look at her, but he can tell from her breathing that she senses what he is doing. Slowly, carefully, he lets his hand drop on her shoulder; it twitches spasmodically, and he jumps, as if he had received an electric shock. His mother's quiet breathing is broken by a gasp; even Wayne notices. A sudden brightness on the screen illuminates the panic in her eyes, Neil's arm frozen above her, about to fall again. Slowly, he lowers his arm until his fingertips touch her skin, the fabric of her dress. He has gone too far to go back now; they are all too far.

Wayne and Mrs. Campbell sink into their seats, but Neil remains stiff, holding up his arms, which rest on nothing. The movie ends, and they go on sitting just like that.

"I'm old," Mrs. Campbell says later, as they drive back home. "I remember when those films were new. Your father and I went to one on our first date. I loved them, because I could pretend that those women underwater were flying—they were so graceful. They really took advantage of Technicolor in those days. Color was something to appreciate. You can't know what it was like to see a color movie for the first time, after years of black-and-white. It's like trying to explain the surprise of snow to an East Coaster. Very little is new anymore, I fear."

Neil would like to tell her about his own nostalgia, but how can he explain that all of it revolves around her? The idea of her life before he was born pleases him. "Tell Wayne how you used to look like Esther Williams," he asks her.

She blushes. "I was told I looked like Esther Williams, but really more like Gene Tierney," she says. "Not beautiful, but interesting. I like to think I had a certain magnetism."

"You still do," Wayne says, and instantly recognizes the wrongness of his comment. Silence and a nervous laugh indicate that he has not yet mastered the family vocabulary.

When they get home, the night is once again full of the sound of crickets.

Mrs. Campbell picks up a flashlight and calls the dogs. "Abbylucyferny, Abbylucyferny," she shouts, and the dogs amble from their various corners. She pushes them out the door to the backyard and follows them. Neil follows her. Wayne follows Neil, but hovers on the porch. Neil walks behind her as she tramps through the garden. She holds out her flashlight, and snails slide from behind bushes, from under rocks, to where she stands. When the snails become visible, she crushes them underfoot. They make a wet, cracking noise, like eggs being broken.

"Nights like this," she says, "I think of children without pants on, in hot South American countries. I have nightmares about tanks rolling down our street."

"The weather's never like this in New York," Neil says. "When it's hot, it's humid and sticky. You don't want to go outdoors."

"I could never live anywhere else but here. I think I'd die. I'm too used to the climate."

"Don't be silly."

"No, I mean it," she says. "I have adjusted too well to the weather."

The dogs bark and howl by the fence. "A cat, I suspect," she says. She aims her flashlight at a rock, and more snails emerge—uncountable numbers, too stupid to have learned not to trust light.

"I know what you were doing at the movie," she says.

"What?"

"I know what you were doing."

"What? I put my arm around you."

"I'm sorry, Neil," she says. "I can only take so much. Just so much."

"What do you mean?" he says. "I was only trying to show affection."

"Oh, affection—I know about affection."

He looks up at the porch, sees Wayne moving toward the door, trying not to listen.

"What do you mean?" Neil says to her.

She puts down the flashlight and wraps her arms around herself. "I remember when you were a little boy," she says. "I remember, and I have to stop remembering. I wanted you to grow up happy. And I'm very tolerant, very understanding. But I can only take so much."

His heart seems to have risen into his throat. "Mother," he says, "I think you know my life isn't your fault. But for God's sake, don't say that your life is my fault."

"It's not a question of fault," she says. She extracts a Kleenex from her pocket and blows her nose. "I'm sorry, Neil. I guess I'm just an old woman with too much on her mind and not enough to do." She laughs halfheartedly. "Don't worry. Don't say anything," she says. "Abbylucyferny, Abbylucyferny, time for bed!"

He watches her as she walks toward the porch, silent and regal. There is the pad of feet, the clinking of dog tags as the dogs run for the house.

He was twelve the first time she saw him march in a parade. He played the tuba, and as his elementary-school band lumbered down the streets of their then small town she stood on the sidelines and waved. Afterward, she had taken him out for ice cream. He spilled some on his red uniform, and she swiped at it with a napkin. She had been there for him that day, as well as years later, at that more memorable parade; she had been there for him every day.

Somewhere over Iowa, a week later, Neil remembers this scene, remembers other days, when he would find her sitting in the dark, crying. She had to take time out of her own private sorrow to appease his anxiety. "It was part of it," she told him later. "Part of being a mother."

"The scariest thing in the world is the thought that you could unknowingly ruin someone's life," Neil tells Wayne. "Or even change someone's life. I hate the thought of having such control. I'd make a rotten mother."

"You're crazy," Wayne says. "You have this great mother, and all you do is complain. I know people whose mothers have disowned them."

"Guilt goes with the territory," Neil says.

"Why?" Wayne asks, perfectly seriously.

Neil doesn't answer. He lies back in his seat, closes his eyes, imagines he grew up in a house in the mountains of Colorado, surrounded by snow—endless white snow on hills. No flat places, and no trees; just white hills. Every time he has flown away, she has come into his mind, usually sitting alone in the dark, smoking. Today she is outside at dusk, skimming leaves from the pool.

"I want to get a dog," Neil says.

Wayne laughs. "In the city? It'd suffocate."

The hum of the airplane is druglike, dazing. "I want to stay with you a long time," Neil says.

"I know." Imperceptibly, Wayne takes his hand.

"It's very hot there in the summer, too. You know, I'm not thinking about my mother now."

"It's O.K."

For a moment, Neil wonders what the stewardess or the old woman on the way to the bathroom will think, but then he laughs and relaxes.

Later, the plane makes a slow circle over New York City, and on it two men hold hands, eyes closed, and breathe in unison.

Kelly Link

STONE ANIMALS

KELLY LINK is the author of *Magic for Beginners* and *Stranger Things Happen*. Her stories have appeared in *The Best American Short Stories, McSweeney's Mammoth Treasury of Thrilling Tales, Conjunctions, A Public Space,* and elsewhere. Her honors include three Nebula Awards and an NEA Fellowship. She lives in Northampton, Massachusetts.

Henry asked a question. He was joking.

"As a matter of fact," the real estate agent snapped, "it is."

It was not a question she had expected to be asked. She gave Henry a goofy, appeasing smile and yanked at the hem of the skirt of her pink linen suit, which seemed as if it might, at any moment, go rolling up her knees like a window shade. She was younger than Henry, and sold houses that she couldn't afford to buy.

"It's reflected in the asking price, of course," she said. "Like you said."

Henry stared at her. She blushed.

"I've never seen anything," she said. "But there are stories. Not stories that I know. I just know there are stories. If you believe that sort of thing."

"I don't," Henry said. When he looked over to see if Catherine had heard, she had her head up the tiled fireplace, as if she were trying it on, to see whether it fit. Catherine was six months pregnant. Nothing fit her except for Henry's baseball caps, his sweatpants, his T-shirts. But she liked the fireplace.

Carleton was running up and down the staircase, slapping his heels down hard, keeping his head down and his hands folded around the banister. Carleton was serious about how he played. Tilly sat on the landing, reading a book, legs poking out through the railings. Whenever Carleton ran past, he thumped her on the head, but Tilly never said a word. Carleton would be sorry later, and never even know why.

Catherine took her head out of the fireplace. "Guys," she said. "Carleton, Tilly. Slow down a minute and tell me what you think. Think King Spanky will be okay out here?"

"King Spanky is a cat, Mom," Tilly said. "Maybe we should get a dog, you know, to help protect us." She could tell by looking at her mother that they were

351

going to move. She didn't know how she felt about this, except she had plans for the yard. A yard like that needed a dog.

"I don't like big dogs," said Carleton, six years old and small for his age. "I don't like this staircase. It's too big."

"Carleton," Henry said. "Come here. I need a hug."

Carleton came down the stairs. He lay down on his stomach on the floor and rolled, noisily, floppily, slowly, over to where Henry stood with the real estate agent. He curled like a dead snake around Henry's ankles. "I don't like those dogs outside," he said.

"I know it looks like we're out in the middle of nothing, but if you go down through the backyard, cut through that stand of trees, there's this little path. It takes you straight down to the train station. Ten-minute bike ride," the agent said. Nobody ever remembered her name, which was why she had to wear too-tight skirts. She was, as it happened, writing a romance novel, and she spent a lot of time making up pseudonyms, just in case she ever finished it. Ophelia Pink. Matilde Hightower. LaLa Treeble. Or maybe she'd write gothics. Ghost stories. But not about people like these. "Another ten minutes on that path and you're in town."

"What dogs, Carleton?" Henry said.

"I think they're lions, Carleton," said Catherine. "You mean the stone ones beside the door? Just like the lions at the library. You love those lions, Carleton. Patience and Fortitude?"

"I've always thought they were rabbits," the real estate agent said. "You know, because of the ears. They have big ears." She flopped her hands and then tugged at her skirt, which would not stay down. "I think they're pretty valuable. The guy who built the house had a gallery in New York. He knew a lot of sculptors."

Henry was struck by that. He didn't think he knew a single sculptor.

"I don't like the rabbits," Carleton said. "I don't like the staircase. I don't like this room. It's too big. I don't like *her*."

"Carleton," Henry said. He smiled at the real estate agent.

"I don't like the house," Carleton said, clinging to Henry's ankles. "I don't like houses. I don't want to live in a house."

"Then we'll build you a teepee out on the lawn," Catherine said. She sat on the stairs beside Tilly, who shifted her weight, almost imperceptibly, towards Catherine. Catherine sat as still as possible. Tilly was in fourth grade and difficult in a way that girls weren't supposed to be. Mostly she refused to be cuddled or babied. But she sat there, leaning on Catherine's arm, emanating saintly fragrances: peacefulness, placidness, goodness. *I want this house*, Catherine said, moving her lips like a silent movie heroine, to Henry, so that neither Carleton nor the agent, who had bent over to inspect a piece of dust on the floor, could see. "You can live in your teepee, and we'll invite you to come over for lunch. You like lunch, don't you? Peanut butter sandwiches?"

"I don't," Carleton said, and sobbed once.

But they bought the house anyway. The real estate agent got her commission. Tilly rubbed the waxy, stone ears of the rabbits on the way out, pretending that they already belonged to her. They were as tall as she was, but that wouldn't always be true. Carleton had a peanut butter sandwich.

The rabbits sat on either side of the front door. Two stone animals sitting on cracked, mossy haunches. They were shapeless, lumpish, patient in a way that seemed not worn down, but perhaps never really finished in the first place. There was something about them that reminded Henry of Stonehenge. Catherine thought of topiary shapes; *The Velveteen Rabbit*; soldiers who stand guard in front of palaces and never even twitch their noses. Maybe they could be donated to a museum. Or broken up with jackhammers. They didn't suit the house at all.

"So what's the house like?" said Henry's boss. She was carefully stretching rubber bands around her rubber band ball. By now the rubber band ball was so big, she had to get special extra-large rubber bands from the art department. She claimed it helped her think. She had tried knitting for a while, but it turned out that knitting was too utilitarian, too feminine. Making an enormous ball out of rubber bands struck the right note. It was something a man might do.

It took up half of her desk. Under the fluorescent office lights it had a peeled red liveliness. You almost expected it to shoot forward and out the door. The larger it got, the more it looked like some kind of eyeless, hairless, legless animal. Maybe a dog. A Carleton-sized dog, Henry thought, although not a Carleton-sized rubber band ball.

Catherine joked sometimes about using the carleton as a measure of unit.

"Big," Henry said. "Haunted."

"Really?" his boss said. "So's this rubber band." She aimed a rubber band at Henry and shot him in the elbow. This was meant to suggest that she and Henry were good friends, and just goofing around, the way good friends did. But what it really meant was that she was angry at him. "Don't leave me," she said.

"I'm only two hours away." Henry put up his hand to ward off rubber bands. "Quit it. We talk on the phone, we use email. I come back to town when you need me in the office."

"You're sure this is a good idea?" his boss said. She fixed her reptilian, watery gaze on him. She had problematical tear ducts. Though she could have had a minor surgical procedure to fix this, she'd chosen not to. It was a tactical advantage, the way it spooked people.

It didn't really matter that Henry remained immune to rubber bands and crocodile tears. She had backup strategies. She thought about which would be most effective while Henry pitched his stupid idea all over again.

Henry had the movers' phone number in his pocket, like a talisman. He wanted to take it out, wave it at The Crocodile, say, Look at this! Instead he said, "For nine years, we've lived in an apartment next door to a building that smells like urine. Like someone built an entire building out of bricks made of compressed red pee. Someone spit on Catherine in the street last week. This old Russian lady in a fur coat. A kid rang our doorbell the other day and tried to sell us gas masks. Door-to-door gas mask salesmen. Catherine bought one. When she told me about it, she burst into tears. She said she couldn't figure out if she was feeling guilty because she'd bought a gas mask, or if it was because she hadn't bought enough for everyone."

"Good Chinese food," his boss said. "Good movies. Good bookstores. Good dry cleaners. Good conversation."

"Treehouses," Henry said. "I had a treehouse when I was a kid."

"You were never a kid," his boss said.

"Three bathrooms. Crown moldings. We can't even see our nearest neighbor's house. I get up in the morning, have coffee, put Carleton and Tilly on the bus, and go to work in my pajamas."

"What about Catherine?" The Crocodile put her head down on her rubber band ball. Possibly this was a gesture of defeat.

"There was that thing. Catherine's whole department is leaving. Like rats deserting a sinking ship. Anyway, Catherine needs a change. And so do I," Henry said. "We've got another kid on the way. We're going to garden. Catherine'll teach ESOL, find a book group, write her book. Teach the kids how to play bridge. You've got to start them early."

He picked a rubber band off the floor and offered it to his boss. "You should come out and visit some weekend."

"I never go upstate," The Crocodile said. She held on to her rubber band ball. "Too many ghosts."

"Are you going to miss this? Living here?" Catherine said. She couldn't stand the way her stomach poked out. She couldn't see past it. She held up her left foot to make sure it was still there, and pulled the sheet off Henry.

"I love the house," Henry said.

"Me too," Catherine said. She was biting her fingernails. Henry could hear her teeth going *click, click*. Now she had both feet up in the air. She wiggled them around. Hello, feet.

"What are you doing?"

She put them down again. On the street outside, cars came and went, pushing smears of light along the ceiling, slow and fast at the same time. The baby was wriggling around inside her, kicking out with both feet like it was swimming across the English Channel, the Pacific. Kicking all the way to China. "Did you buy that story about the former owners moving to France?"

"I don't believe in France," Henry said. *"Je ne crois pas en France."*

"Neither do I," Catherine said. "Henry?"

"What?"

"Do you love the house?"

"I love the house."

"I love it more than you do," Catherine said, although Henry hated it when she said things like that. "What do you love best?"

"That room in the front," Henry said. "With the windows. Our bedroom. Those weird rabbit statues."

"Me too," Catherine said, although she didn't. "I love those rabbits."

Then she said, "Do you ever worry about Carleton and Tilly?"

"What do you mean?" Henry said. He looked at the alarm clock: it was 4 A.M. "Why are we awake right now?"

"Sometimes I worry that I love one of them better," Catherine said. "Like I might love Tilly better. Because she used to wet the bed. Because she's always so angry. Or Carleton, because he was so sick when he was little."

"I love them both the same," Henry said.

He didn't even know he was lying. Catherine knew, though. She knew he was lying, and she knew he didn't even know it. Most of the time she thought that it was okay. As long as he thought he loved them both the same, and acted as if he did, that was good enough.

"Well, do you ever worry that you love them more than me?" she said. "Or that I love them more than I love you?"

"Do you?" Henry said.

"Of course," Catherine said. "I have to. It's my job."

She found the gas mask in a box of wineglasses, and also six recent issues of *The New Yorker,* which she still might get a chance to read someday. She put the gas mask under the sink and *The New Yorker*s in the sink. Why not? It was her sink. She could put anything she wanted into it. She took the magazines out again and put them into the refrigerator, just for fun.

Henry came into the kitchen, holding silver candlesticks and a stuffed armadillo, which someone had made into a purse. It had a shoulder strap made out of its own skin. You opened its mouth and put things inside it, lipstick and subway tokens. It had pink gimlet eyes and smelled strongly of vinegar. It belonged to Tilly, although how it had come into her possession was unclear. Tilly claimed she'd won it at school in a contest involving donuts. Catherine thought it more likely Tilly had either stolen it or (slightly preferable) found it in someone's trash. Now Tilly kept her most valuable belongings inside the purse, to keep them safe from Carleton, who was covetous of the precious things—because they were small, and because they belonged to Tilly—but afraid of the armadillo.

"I've already told her she can't take it to school for at least the first two weeks. Then we'll see." She took the purse from Henry and put it with the gas mask under the sink.

"What are they doing?" Henry said. Framed in the kitchen window, Carleton and Tilly hunched over the lawn. They had a pair of scissors and a notebook and a stapler.

"They're collecting grass." Catherine took dishes out of a box, put the Bubble Wrap aside for Tilly to stomp, and stowed the dishes in a cabinet. The baby kicked like it knew all about Bubble Wrap. "Whoa, Fireplace," she said. "We don't have a dancing license in there."

Henry put out his hand, rapped on Catherine's stomach. *Knock, knock.* It was Tilly's joke. Catherine would say, "Who's there?" and Tilly would say, Candlestick's here. Fat Man's here. Box. Hammer. Milk shake. Clarinet. Mousetrap. Fiddlestick. Tilly had a whole list of names for the baby. The real estate agent would have approved.

"Where's King Spanky?" Henry said.

"Under our bed," Catherine said. "He's up in the box frame."

"Have we unpacked the alarm clock?" Henry said.

"Poor King Spanky," Catherine said. "Nobody to love except an alarm clock. Come upstairs and let's see if we can shake him out of the bed. I've got a present for you."

The present was in a U-Haul box exactly like all the other boxes in the bedroom, except that Catherine had written HENRY'S PRESENT on it instead of LARGE FRONT BEDROOM. Inside the box were Styrofoam peanuts and then a smaller box from Takashimaya. The Takashimaya box was fastened with a silver ribbon. The tissue paper inside was dull gold, and inside the tissue paper was a green silk robe with orange sleeves and heraldic animals in orange and gold thread. "Lions," Henry said.

"Rabbits," Catherine said.

"I didn't get you anything," Henry said.

Catherine smiled nobly. She liked giving presents better than getting presents. She'd never told Henry, because it seemed to her that it must be selfish in some way she'd never bothered to figure out. Catherine was grateful to be married to Henry, who accepted all presents as his due; who looked good in the clothes that she bought him; who was vain, in an easygoing way, about his good looks. Buying clothes for Henry was especially satisfying now, while she was pregnant and couldn't buy them for herself.

She said, "If you don't like it, then I'll keep it. Look at you, look at those sleeves. You look like the emperor of Japan."

They had already colonized the bedroom, making it full of things that belonged to them. There was Catherine's mirror on the wall, and their mahogany wardrobe, their first real piece of furniture, a wedding present from Catherine's great-aunt. There was their serviceable, queen-sized bed with King Spanky lodged up inside it, and there was Henry, spinning his arms in the wide orange sleeves, like an embroidered windmill. Henry could see all of these things in the mirror, and behind him, their lawn and Tilly and Carleton, stapling grass into their notebook. He saw all of these things and he found them good. But he couldn't see Catherine. When he turned around, she stood in the doorway, frowning at him. She had the alarm clock in her hand.

"Look at you," she said again. It worried her, the way something, someone, *Henry,* could suddenly look like a place she'd never been before. The alarm began to ring and King Spanky came out from under the bed, trotting over to Catherine. She bent over, awkwardly—ungraceful, ungainly, so clumsy, so fucking awkward, being pregnant was like wearing a fucking suitcase strapped across your middle—put the alarm clock down on the ground, and King Spanky hunkered down in front of it, his nose against the ringing glass face.

And that made her laugh again. Henry loved Catherine's laugh. Downstairs, their children slammed a door open, ran through the house, carrying scissors, both Catherine and Henry knew, and slammed another door open and were outside again, leaving behind the smell of grass. There was a store in New York where you could buy a perfume that smelled like that.

Catherine and Carleton and Tilly came back from the grocery store with a tire, a rope to hang it from, and a box of pancake mix for dinner. Henry was online, looking at a jpeg of a rubber band ball. There was a message too. The Crocodile needed him to come into the office. It would be just a few days. Someone was setting fires and there was no one smart enough to see how to put them out except for him. They were his accounts. He had to come in and save them. She knew Catherine and Henry's apartment hadn't sold; she'd checked with their listing agent. So surely it wouldn't be impossible, not impossible, only inconvenient.

He went downstairs to tell Catherine. "That *witch*," she said, and then bit her lip. "She called the listing agent? I'm sorry. We talked about this. Never mind. Just give me a moment."

Catherine inhaled. Exhaled. Inhaled. If she were Carleton, she would hold her breath until her face turned red and Henry agreed to stay home, but then again, it never worked for Carleton. "We ran into our new neighbors in the grocery store. She's about the same age as me. Liz and Marcus. One kid, older, a girl, um, I think her name was Alison, maybe from a first marriage—potential babysitter, which is really good news. Liz is a lawyer. Gorgeous. Reads Oprah books. He likes to cook."

"So do I," Henry said.

"You're better looking," Catherine said. "So do you have to go back tonight, or can you take the train in the morning?"

"The morning is fine," Henry said, wanting to seem agreeable.

Carleton appeared in the kitchen, his arms pinned around King Spanky's middle. The cat's front legs stuck straight out, as if Carleton were dowsing. King Spanky's eyes were closed. His whiskers twitched Morse code. "What are you wearing?" Carleton said.

"My new uniform," Henry said. "I wear it to work."

"Where do you work?" Carleton said, testing.

"I work at home," Henry said. Catherine snorted.

"He looks like the king of rabbits, doesn't he? The plenipotentiary of Rabbitaly," she said, no longer sounding particularly pleased about this.

"He looks like a princess," Carleton said, now pointing King Spanky at Henry like a gun.

"Where's your grass collection?" Henry said. "Can I see it?"

"No," Carleton said. He put King Spanky on the floor, and the cat slunk out of the kitchen, heading for the staircase, the bedroom, the safety of the bedsprings, the beloved alarm clock, the beloved. The beloved may be treacherous, greasy-headed and given to evil habits, or else it can be a man in his late forties who works too much, or it can be an alarm clock.

"After dinner," Henry said, trying again, "we could go out and find a tree for your tire swing."

"No," Carleton said, regretfully. He lingered in the kitchen, hoping to be asked a question to which he could say yes.

"Where's your sister?" Henry said.

"Watching television," Carleton said. "I don't like the television here."

"It's too big," Henry said, but Catherine didn't laugh.

Henry dreams he is the king of the real estate agents. Henry loves his job. He tries to sell a house to a young couple with twitchy noses and big dark eyes. Why does he always dream that he's trying to sell things?

The couple stare at him nervously. He leans towards them as if he's going to whisper something in their silly, expectant ears. It's a secret he's never told anyone before. It's a secret he didn't even know that he knew. "Let's stop fooling," he says. "You can't afford to buy this house. You don't have any money. You're rabbits."

"Where do you work?" Carleton said, in the morning, when Henry called from Grand Central.

"I work at home," Henry said. "Home where we live now, where you are. Eventually. Just not today. Are you getting ready for school?"

Carleton put the phone down. Henry could hear him saying something to Catherine. "He says he's not nervous about school," she said. "He's a brave kid."

"I kissed you this morning," Henry said, "but you didn't wake up. There were all these rabbits on the lawn. They were huge. King Spanky–sized. They were just sitting there like they were waiting for the sun to come up. It was funny, like some kind of art installation. But it was kind of creepy too. Think they'd been there all night?"

"Rabbits? Can they have rabies? I saw them this morning when I got up," Catherine said. "Carleton didn't want to brush his teeth this morning. He says something's wrong with his toothbrush."

"Maybe he dropped it in the toilet, and he doesn't want to tell you," Henry said.

"Maybe you could buy a new toothbrush and bring it home," Catherine said. "He doesn't want one from the drugstore here. He wants one from New York."

"Where's Tilly?" Henry said.

"She says she's trying to figure out what's wrong with Carleton's toothbrush. She's still in the bathroom," Catherine said.

"Can I talk to her for a second?" Henry said.

"Tell her she needs to get dressed and eat her Cheerios," Catherine said. "After I drive them to school, Liz is coming over for coffee. Then we're going to go out for lunch. I'm not unpacking another box until you get home. Here's Tilly."

"Hi," Tilly said. She sounded as if she were asking a question.

Tilly never liked talking to people on the telephone. How were you supposed to know if they were really who they said they were? And even if they were who they claimed to be, they didn't know whether you were who you said you were. You could be someone else. They might give away information about you, and not even know it. There were no protocols. No precautions.

She said, "Did you brush your teeth this morning?"

"Good morning, Tilly," her father (if it was her father) said. "My toothbrush was fine. Perfectly normal."

"That's good," Tilly said. "I let Carleton use mine."

"That was very generous," Henry said.

"No problem," Tilly said. Sharing things with Carleton wasn't like having to share things with other people. It wasn't really like sharing things at all. Carleton belonged to her, like the toothbrush. "Mom says that when we get home today, we can draw on the walls in our rooms if we want to, while we decide what color we want to paint them."

"Sounds like fun," Henry said. "Can I draw on them too?"

"Maybe," Tilly said. She had already said too much. "Gotta go. Gotta eat breakfast."

"Don't be worried about school," Henry said.

"I'm not worried about school," Tilly said.

"I love you," Henry said.

"I'm real concerned about this toothbrush," Tilly said.

He closed his eyes only for a minute. Just for a minute. When he woke up, it was dark and he didn't know where he was. He stood up and went over to the door, almost tripping over something. It sailed away from him in an exuberant, rollicking sweep. According to the clock on his desk, it was 4 A.M. Why was it always 4 A.M.? There were four messages on his cell phone, all from Catherine.

He checked train schedules online. Then he sent Catherine a fast email.

Fell asleep @ midnight? Mssed trains. Awake now, going to keep on working. Pttng out fires. Take the train home early afternoon? Still lv me?

Before he went back to work, he kicked the rubber band ball back down the hall towards The Crocodile's door.

Catherine called him at 8:45.

"I'm sorry," Henry said.

"I bet you are," Catherine said.

"I can't find my razor. I think The Crocodile had some kind of tantrum and tossed my stuff."

"Carleton will love that," Catherine said. "Maybe you should sneak in the house and shave before dinner. He had a hard day at school yesterday."

"Maybe I should grow a beard," Henry said. "He can't be afraid of everything, all the time. Tell me about the first day of school."

"We'll talk about it later," Catherine said. "Liz just drove up. I'm going to be her guest at the gym. Just make it home for dinner."

At 6 A.M. Henry emailed Catherine again. "Srry. Accidentally startd avalanche while puttng out fires. Wait up for me? How ws 2nd day of school?" She didn't write him back. He called and no one picked up the phone. She didn't call.

He took the last train home. By the time it reached the station, he was the only one left in his car. He unchained his bicycle and rode it home in the dark. Rabbits pelted across the footpath in front of his bike. There were rabbits foraging on his lawn. They froze as he dismounted and pushed the bicycle across the grass. The lawn was rumpled; the bike went up and down over invisible depressions that he supposed were rabbit holes. There were two short fat men standing in the dark on either side of the front door, waiting for him, but when he came closer, he remembered that they were stone rabbits. "Knock, knock," he said.

The real rabbits on the lawn tipped their ears at him. The stone rabbits waited for the punch line, but they were just stone rabbits. They had nothing better to do.

The front door wasn't locked. He walked through the downstairs rooms, putting his hands on the backs and tops of furniture. In the kitchen, cut-down boxes leaned in stacks against the wall, waiting to be recycled or remade into cardboard houses and spaceships and tunnels for Carleton and Tilly.

Catherine had unpacked Carleton's room. Night-lights in the shape of bears and geese and cats were plugged into every floor outlet. There were little low-watt table lamps as well—hippo, robot, gorilla, pirate ship. Everything was soaked in a tender, peaceable light, translating Carleton's room into something more than a bedroom: something luminous, numinous, Carleton's cartoony Midnight Church of Sleep.

Tilly was sleeping in the other bed.

Tilly would never admit that she sleepwalked, the same way that she would never admit that she sometimes still wet the bed. But she refused to make friends. Making friends would have meant spending the night in strange houses. Tomorrow morning she would insist that Henry or Catherine must have carried her from her room, put her to bed in Carleton's room for reasons of their own.

Henry knelt down between the two beds and kissed Carleton on the forehead. He kissed Tilly, smoothed her hair. How could he not love Tilly better? He'd known her longer. She was so brave, so angry.

On the walls of Carleton's bedroom, Henry's children had drawn a house. A cat nearly as big as the house. There was a crown on the cat's head. Trees or flowers with pairs of leaves that pointed straight up, still bigger, and a stick figure on a stick bicycle, riding past the trees. When he looked closer, he thought that maybe the trees were actually rabbits. The wall smelled like Fruit Loops. Someone had written *Henry Is A Rat Fink! Ha Ha!* He recognized his wife's handwriting.

"Scented markers," Catherine said. She stood in the door, holding a pillow against her stomach. "I was sleeping downstairs on the sofa. You walked right past and didn't see me."

"The front door was unlocked," Henry said.

"Liz says nobody ever locks their doors out here," Catherine said. "Are you coming to bed, or were you just stopping by to see how we were?"

"I have to go back in tomorrow," Henry said. He pulled a toothbrush out of his pocket and showed it to her. "There's a box of Krispy Kreme donuts on the kitchen counter."

"Delete the donuts," Catherine said. "I'm not that easy." She took a step towards him and accidentally kicked King Spanky. The cat yowled. Carleton woke up. He said, "Who's there? Who's there?"

"It's me," Henry said. He knelt beside Carleton's bed in the light of the Winnie the Pooh lamp. "I brought you a new toothbrush."

Carleton whimpered.

"What's wrong, spaceman?" Henry said. "It's just a toothbrush." He leaned towards Carleton and Carleton scooted back. He began to scream.

In the other bed, Tilly was dreaming about rabbits. When she'd come home from school, she and Carleton had seen rabbits, sitting on the lawn as if they had kept watch over the house all the time that Tilly had been gone. In her dream they were still there. She dreamed she was creeping up on them. They opened their mouths, wide enough to reach inside like she was some kind of rabbit dentist, and so she did. She put her hand around something small and cold and hard. Maybe it was a ring, a diamond ring. Or a. Or. It was a. She couldn't wait to show Carleton. Her arm was inside the rabbit all the way to her shoulder. Someone put their little cold hand around her wrist and yanked. Somewhere her mother was talking. She said—

"It's the beard."

Catherine couldn't decide whether to laugh or cry or scream like Carleton. That would surprise Carleton, if she started screaming too. "Shoo! Shoo, Henry—go shave and come back as quick as you can, or else he'll never go back to sleep."

"Carleton, honey," she was saying as Henry left the room. "It's your dad. It's not Santa Claus. It's not the big bad wolf. It's your dad. Your dad just forgot. Why don't you tell me a story? Or do you want to go watch your daddy shave?"

Catherine's hot water bottle was draped over the tub. Towels were heaped on the floor. Henry's things had been put away behind the mirror. It made him feel tired, thinking of all the other things that still had to be put away. He washed his hands, then looked at the bar of soap. It didn't feel right. He put it back on the sink, bent over and sniffed it and then tore off a piece of toilet paper, used the toilet paper to pick up the soap. He threw it in the trash and unwrapped a new bar of soap. There was nothing wrong with the new soap. There was nothing wrong with the old soap either. He was just tired. He washed his hands and lathered up his face, shaved off his beard and watched the little bristles of hair wash down the sink. When he went to show Carleton his brand-new face, Catherine was curled up in bed beside Carleton. They were both asleep. They were still asleep when he left the house at five thirty the next morning.

• • •

"Where are you?" Catherine said.

"I'm on my way home. I'm on the train." The train was still in the station. They would be leaving any minute. They had been leaving any minute for the last hour or so, and before that, they had had to get off the train twice, and then back on again. They had been assured there was nothing to worry about. There was no bomb threat. There was no bomb. The delay was only temporary. The people on the train looked at each other, trying to seem as if they were not looking. Everyone had their cell phones out.

"The rabbits are out on the lawn again," Catherine said. "There must be at least fifty or sixty. I've never counted rabbits before. Tilly keeps trying to go outside to make friends with them, but as soon as she's outside, they all go bouncing away like beach balls. I talked to a lawn specialist today. He says we need to do something about it, which is what Liz was saying. Rabbits can be a big problem out here. They've probably got tunnels and warrens all through the yard. It could be a problem. Like living on top of a sinkhole. But Tilly is never going to forgive us. She knows something's up. She says she doesn't want a dog anymore. It would scare away the rabbits. Do you think we should get a dog?"

"So what do they do? Put out poison? Dig up the yard?" Henry said. The man in the seat in front of him got up. He took his bags out of the luggage rack and left the train. Everyone watched him go, pretending they were not.

"He was telling me they have these devices, kind of like ultrasound equipment. They plot out the tunnels, close them up, and then gas the rabbits. It sounds gruesome," Catherine said. "And this kid, this baby has been kicking the daylights out of me. All day long it's kick, kick, jump, kick, like some kind of martial artist. He's going to be an angry kid, Henry. Just like his sister. Her sister. Or maybe I'm going to give birth to rabbits."

"As long as they have your eyes and my chin," Henry said.

"I've gotta go," Catherine said. "I have to pee again. All day long it's the kid jumping, me peeing, Tilly getting her heart broken because she can't make friends with the rabbits, me worrying because she doesn't want to make friends with other kids, just with rabbits, Carleton asking if today he has to go to school, does he have to go to school tomorrow, why am I making him go to school when everybody there is bigger than him, why is my stomach so big and fat, why does his teacher tell him to act like a big boy? Henry, why are we doing this again? Why am I pregnant? And where are you? Why aren't you here? What about our deal? Don't you want to be here?"

"I'm sorry," Henry said. "I'll talk to The Crocodile. We'll work something out."

"I thought you wanted this too, Henry. Don't you?"

"Of course," Henry said. "Of course I want this."

"I've gotta go," Catherine said again. "Liz is bringing some women over.

We're finally starting that book club. We're going to read *Fight Club*. Her step-daughter Alison is going to look after Tilly and Carleton for me. I've already talked to Tilly. She promises she won't bite or hit or make Alison cry."

"What's the trade? A few hours of bonus TV?"

"No," Catherine said. "Something's up with the TV."

"What's wrong with the TV?"

"I don't know," Catherine said. "It's working fine. But the kids won't go near it. Isn't that great? It's the same thing as the toothbrush. You'll see when you get home. I mean, it's not just the kids. I was watching the news earlier, and then I had to turn it off. It wasn't the news. It was the TV."

"So it's the downstairs bathroom and the coffeemaker and Carleton's toothbrush and now the TV?"

"There's some other stuff as well, since this morning. Your office, apparently. Everything in it—your desk, your bookshelves, your chair, even the paper clips."

"That's probably a good thing, right? I mean, that way they'll stay out of there."

"I guess," Catherine said. "The thing is, I went and stood in there for a while and it gave me the creeps too. So now I can't pick up email. And I had to throw out more soap. And King Spanky doesn't love the alarm clock anymore. He won't come out from under the bed when I set it off."

"The alarm clock too?"

"It does sound different," Catherine said. "Just a little bit different. Or maybe I'm insane. This morning, Carleton told me that he knew where our house was. He said we were living in a secret part of Central Park. He said he recognizes the trees. He thinks that if he walks down that little path, he'll get mugged. I've really got to go, Henry, or I'm going to wet my pants, and I don't have time to change again before everyone gets here."

"I love you," Henry said.

"Then why aren't you here?" Catherine said victoriously. She hung up and ran down the hallway towards the downstairs bathroom. But when she got there, she turned around. She went racing up the stairs, pulling down her pants as she went, and barely got to the master bedroom bathroom in time. All day long she'd gone up and down the stairs, feeling extremely silly. There was nothing wrong with the downstairs bathroom. It's just the fixtures. When you flush the toilet or run water in the sink. She doesn't like the sound the water makes.

Several times now, Henry had come home and found Catherine painting rooms, which was a problem. The problem was that Henry kept going away. If he didn't keep going away, he wouldn't have to keep coming home. That was Catherine's point. Henry's point was that Catherine wasn't supposed to be painting rooms while she was pregnant. Pregnant women weren't supposed to breathe around paint fumes.

Catherine solved this problem by wearing the gas mask while she painted. She had known the gas mask would come in handy. She told Henry she promised to stop painting as soon as he started working at home, which was the plan. Meanwhile, she couldn't decide on colors. She and Carleton and Tilly spent hours looking at paint strips with colors that had names like Sangria, Peat Bog, Tulip, Tantrum, Planetarium, Galactica, Tea Leaf, Egg Yolk, Tinker Toy, Gauguin, Susan, Envy, Aztec, Utopia, Wax Apple, Rice Bowl, Cry Baby, Fat Lip, Green Banana, Trampoline, Finger Nail. It was a wonderful way to spend time. They went off to school, and when they got home, the living room would be Harp Seal instead of Full Moon. They'd spend some time with that color, getting to know it, ignoring the television, which was haunted (*haunted* wasn't the right word, of course, but Catherine couldn't think what the right word was) and then a couple of days later, Catherine would go buy some more primer and start again. Carleton and Tilly loved this. They begged her to repaint their bedrooms. She did.

She wished she could eat paint. Whenever she opened a can of paint her mouth watered. When she'd been pregnant with Carleton, she hadn't been able to eat anything except for olives and hearts of palm and dry toast. When she'd been pregnant with Tilly, she'd eaten dirt, once, in Central Park. Tilly thought they should name the baby after a paint color Chalk, or Dilly Dilly, or Keelhauled. Lapis Lazulily. Knock, knock.

Catherine kept meaning to ask Henry to take the television and put it in the garage. Nobody ever watched it now. They'd had to stop using the microwave as well, and a colander, some of the flatware, and she was keeping an eye on the toaster. She had a premonition, or an intuition. It didn't feel wrong, not yet, but she had a feeling about it. There was a gorgeous pair of earrings that Henry had given her—how was it possible to be spooked by a pair of diamond earrings?—and yet. Carleton wouldn't play with his Lincoln Logs, and so they were going to the Salvation Army, and Tilly's armadillo purse had disappeared. Tilly hadn't said anything about it, and Catherine hadn't wanted to ask.

Sometimes, if Henry wasn't coming home, Catherine painted after Carleton and Tilly went to bed. Sometimes Tilly would walk into the room where Catherine was working, Tilly's eyes closed, her mouth open, a tourist-somnambulist. She'd stand there, with her head cocked towards Catherine. If Catherine spoke to her, she never answered, and if Catherine took her hand, she would follow Catherine back to her own bed and lie down again. But sometimes Catherine let Tilly stand there and keep her company. Tilly was never so attentive, so *present*, when she was awake. Eventually she would turn and leave the room and Catherine would listen to her climb back up the stairs. Then she would be alone again.

. . .

Catherine dreams about colors. It turns out her marriage was the same color she had just painted the foyer. Velveteen Fade. Leonard Felter, who had had an ongoing affair with two of his graduate students, several adjuncts, two tenured faculty members, brought down Catherine's entire department, and saved Catherine's marriage, would make a good lipstick or nail polish. Peach Nooky. There's The Crocodile, a particularly bilious Eau De Vil, a color that tastes bad when you say it. Her mother, who had always been disappointed by Catherine's choices, turned out to have been a beautiful, rich, deep chocolate. Why hadn't Catherine ever seen that before? Too late, too late. It made her want to cry.

Liz and she are drinking paint, thick and pale as cream. "Have some more paint," Catherine says. "Do you want sugar?"

"Yes, lots," Liz says. "What color are you going to paint the rabbits?"

Catherine passes her the sugar. She hasn't even thought about the rabbits, except which rabbits does Liz mean, the stone rabbits or the real rabbits? How do you make them hold still?

"I got something for you," Liz says. She's got Tilly's armadillo purse. It's full of paint strips. Catherine's mouth fills with saliva.

Henry dreams he has an appointment with the exterminator. "You've got to take care of this," he says. "We have two small children. These things could be rabid. They might carry plague."

"See what I can do," the exterminator says, sounding glum. He stands next to Henry. He's an odd-looking, twitchy guy. He has big ears. They contemplate the skyscrapers that poke out of the grass like obelisks. The lawn is teeming with skyscrapers. "Never seen anything like this before. Never wanted to see anything like this. But if you want my opinion, it's the house that's the real problem—"

"Never mind about my wife," Henry says. He squats down beside a knee-high art-deco skyscraper, and peers into a window. A little man looks back at him and shakes his fists, screaming something obscene. Henry flicks a finger at the window, almost hard enough to break it. He feels hot all over. He's never felt this angry before in his life, not even when Catherine told him that she'd accidentally slept with Leonard Felter. The little bastard is going to regret what he just said, whatever it was. He lifts his foot.

The exterminator says, "I wouldn't do that if I were you. You have to dig them up, get the roots. Otherwise, they just grow back. Like your house. Which is really just the tip of the iceberg lettuce, so to speak. You've probably got seventy, eighty stories underground. You gone down on the elevator yet? Talked to the people living down there? It's your house, and you're just going to let them live there rent-free? Mess with your things like that?"

"What?" Henry says, and then he hears helicopters, fighter planes the size of hummingbirds. "Is this really necessary?" he says to the exterminator.

The exterminator nods. "You have to catch them off guard."

"Maybe we're being hasty," Henry says. He has to yell to be heard above the noise of the tiny, tinny, furious planes. "Maybe we can settle this peacefully."

"Hemree," the interrogator says, shaking his head. "You called me in because I'm the expert, and you knew you needed help."

Henry wants to say "You're saying my name wrong." But he doesn't want to hurt the undertaker's feelings.

The alligator keeps on talking. "Listen up, Hemreeee, and shut up about negotiations and such, because if we don't take care of this right away, it may be too late. This isn't about homeownership, or lawn care, Hemreeeeee, this is war. The lives of your children are at stake. The happiness of your family. Be brave. Be strong. Just hang on to your rabbit and fire when you see delight in their eyes."

He woke up. "Catherine," he whispered. "Are you awake? I was having this dream."

Catherine laughed. "That's the phone, Liz," she said. "It's probably Henry, saying he'll be late."

"Catherine," Henry said. "Who are you talking to?"

"Are you mad at me, Henry?" Catherine said. "Is that why you won't come home?"

"I'm right here," Henry said.

"You take your rabbits and your crocodiles and get out of here," Catherine said. "And then come straight home again."

She sat up in bed and pointed her finger. "I am sick and tired of being spied on by rabbits!"

When Henry looked, something stood beside the bed, rocking back and forth on its heels. He fumbled for the light, got it on, and saw Tilly, her mouth open, her eyes closed. She looked larger than she ever did when she was awake. "It's just Tilly," he said to Catherine, but Catherine lay back down again. She put her pillow over her head. When he picked Tilly up, to carry her back to bed, she was warm and sweaty, her heart racing as if she had been running through all the rooms of the house.

He walked through the house. He rapped on walls, testing. He put his ear against the floor. No elevator. No secret rooms, no hidden passageways.

There isn't even a basement.

Tilly has divided the yard in half. Carleton is not allowed in her half, unless she gives permission.

From the bottom of her half of the yard, where the trees run beside the driveway, Tilly can barely see the house. She's decided to name the yard Matilda's Rabbit Kingdom. Tilly loves naming things. When the new baby is born, her mother has promised that she can help pick out the real names, although there will only be two real names, a first one and a middle. Tilly doesn't understand why there can only be two. *Oishi* means "delicious" in Japanese. That would make a good name, either for the baby or for the yard, because of the grass. She knows the yard isn't as big as Central Park, but it's just as good, even if there aren't any pagodas or castles or carriages or people on roller skates. There's plenty of grass. There are hundreds of rabbits. They live in an enormous underground city, maybe a city just like New York. Maybe her dad can stop working in New York, and come work under the lawn instead. She could help him, go to work with him. She could be a biologist, like Jane Goodall, and go and live underground with the rabbits. Last year her ambition had been to go and live secretly in the Metropolitan Museum of Art, but someone has already done that, even if it's only in a book. Tilly feels sorry for Carleton. Everything he ever does, she'll have already been there. She'll already have done that.

Tilly has left her armadillo purse sticking out of a rabbit hole. First she made the hole bigger; then she packed the dirt back in around the armadillo so that only the shiny, peeled snout poked out. Carleton digs it out again with his stick. Maybe Tilly meant him to find it. Maybe it was a present for the rabbits, except what is it doing here, in his half of the yard? When he lived in the apartment, he was afraid of the armadillo purse, but there are better things to be afraid of out here. But be careful, Carleton. Might as well be careful. The armadillo purse says Don't touch me. So he doesn't. He uses his stick to pry open the snap-mouth, dumps out Tilly's most valuable things, and with his stick pushes them one by one down the hole. Then he puts his ear to the rabbit hole so that he can hear the rabbits say thank you. Saying thank you is polite. But the rabbits say nothing. They're holding their breath, waiting for him to go away. Carleton waits too. Tilly's armadillo, empty and smelly and haunted, makes his eyes water.

Someone comes up and stands behind him. "I didn't do it," he says. "They fell."

But when he turns around, it's the girl who lives next door. Alison. The sun is behind her and makes her shine. He squints. "You can come over to my house if you want to," she says. "Your mom says. She's going to pay me fifteen bucks an hour, which is way too much. Are your parents really rich or something? What's that?"

"It's Tilly's," he says. "But I don't think she wants it anymore."

She picks up Tilly's armadillo. "Pretty cool," she says. "Maybe I'll keep it for her."

Deep underground, the rabbits stamp their feet in rage.

• • •

Catherine loves the house. She loves her new life. She's never understood people who get stuck, become unhappy, can't change, can't adapt. So she's out of a job. So what? She'll find something else to do. So Henry can't leave his job yet, won't leave his job yet. So the house is haunted. That's okay. They'll work through it. She buys some books on gardening. She plants a rosebush and a climbing vine in a pot. Tilly helps. The rabbits eat off all the leaves. They bite through the vine.

"Shit," Catherine says when she sees what they've done. She shakes her fists at the rabbits on the lawn. The rabbits flick their ears at her. They're laughing, she knows it. She's too big to chase after them.

"Henry, wake up. Wake up."

"I'm awake," he said, and then he was. Catherine was crying: noisy, wet, ugly sobs. He put his hand out and touched her face. Her nose was running.

"Stop crying," he said. "I'm awake. Why are you crying?"

"Because you weren't here," she said. "And then I woke up and you were here, but when I wake up tomorrow morning you'll be gone again. I miss you. Don't you miss me?"

"I'm sorry," he said. "I'm sorry I'm not here. I'm here now. Come here."

"No," she said. She stopped crying, but her nose still leaked. "And now the dishwasher is haunted. We have to get a new dishwasher before I have this baby. You can't have a baby and not have a dishwasher. And you have to live here with us. Because I'm going to need some help this time. Remember Carleton, how fucking hard that was."

"He was one cranky baby," Henry said. When Carleton was three months old, Henry had realized that they'd misunderstood something. Babies weren't babies—they were land mines; bear traps; wasp nests. They were a noise, which was sometimes even not a noise, but merely a listening for a noise; they were a damp, chalky smell; they were the heaving, jerky, sticky manifestation of not-sleep. Once Henry had stood and watched Carleton in his crib, sleeping peacefully. He had not done what he wanted to do. He had not bent over and yelled in Carleton's ear. Henry still hadn't forgiven Carleton, not yet, not entirely, not for making him feel that way.

"Why do you have to love your job so much?" Catherine said.

"I don't know," Henry said. "I don't love it."

"Don't lie to me," Catherine said.

"I love you better," Henry said. He does, he does, he does loves Catherine better. He's already made that decision. But she isn't even listening.

"Remember when Carleton was little and you would get up in the morning and go to work and leave me all alone with them?" Catherine poked him in the side. "I used to hate you. You'd come home with takeout, and I'd forget I hated you, but then I'd remember again, and I'd hate you even more because it was so easy for you to trick me, to make things okay again, just because for an hour I could sit in the bathtub and eat Chinese food and wash my hair."

"You used to carry an extra shirt with you, when you went out," Henry said. He put his hand down inside her T-shirt, on her fat, full breast. "In case you leaked."

"You can't touch that breast," Catherine said. "It's haunted." She blew her nose on the sheets.

Catherine's friend Lucy owns an online boutique, Nice Clothes for Fat People. There's a woman in Tarrytown who knits stretchy, sexy Argyle sweaters exclusively for NCFP, and Lucy has an appointment with her. She wants to stop off and see Catherine afterwards, before she has to drive back to the city again. Catherine gives her directions, and then begins to clean house, feeling out of sorts. She's not sure she wants to see Lucy right now. Carleton has always been afraid of Lucy, which is embarrassing. And Catherine doesn't want to talk about Henry. She doesn't want to explain about the downstairs bathroom. She had planned to spend the day painting the wood trim in the dining room, but now she'll have to wait.

The doorbell rings, but when Catherine goes to answer it, no one is there. Later on, after Tilly and Carleton have come home, it rings again, but no one is there. It rings and rings, as if Lucy is standing outside, pressing the bell over and over again. Finally Catherine pulls out the wire. She tries calling Lucy's cell phone, but can't get through. Then Henry calls. He says that he's going to be late.

Liz opens the front door, yells, "Hello, anyone home! You've got to see your rabbits, there must be thousands of them. Catherine, is something wrong with your doorbell?"

Henry's bike, so far, was okay. He wondered what they'd do if the Toyota suddenly became haunted. Would Catherine want to sell it? Would resale value be affected? The car and Catherine and the kids were gone when he got home, so he put on a pair of work gloves and went through the house with a cardboard box, collecting all the things that felt haunted. A hairbrush in Tilly's room, an old pair of Catherine's tennis shoes. A pair of Catherine's underwear that he finds at the foot of the bed. When he picked them up he felt a sudden shock of longing for Catherine, like he'd been hit by some kind of spooky lightning. It hit him in the pit of the stomach, like a cramp. He dropped them in the box.

The silk kimono from Takashimaya. Two of Carleton's night-lights. He opened the door to his office, put the box inside. All the hair on his arms stood up. He closed the door.

Then he went downstairs and cleaned paintbrushes. If the paintbrushes were becoming haunted, if Catherine was throwing them out and buying new ones, she wasn't saying. Maybe he should check the Visa bill. How much were they spending on paint, anyway?

Catherine came into the kitchen and gave him a hug. "I'm glad you're home," she said. He pressed his nose into her neck and inhaled. "I left the car running—I've got to pee. Would you go pick up the kids for me?"

"Where are they?" Henry said.

"They're over at Liz's. Alison is babysitting them. Do you have money on you?"

"You mean I'll meet some neighbors?"

"Wow, sure," Catherine said. "If you think you're ready. Are you ready? Do you know where they live?"

"They're our neighbors, right?"

"Take a left out of the driveway, go about a quarter of a mile, and they're the red house with all the trees in front."

But when he drove up to the red house and went and rang the doorbell, no one answered. He heard a child come running down a flight of stairs and then stop and stand in front of the door. "Carleton? Alison?" he said. "Excuse me, this is Catherine's husband, Henry. Carleton and Tilly's dad." The whispering stopped. He waited for a bit. When he crouched down and lifted the mail slot, he thought he saw someone's feet, the hem of a coat, something furry? A dog? Someone standing very still, just to the right of the door? Carleton, playing games. "I see you," he said, and wiggled his fingers through the mail slot. Then he thought maybe it wasn't Carleton after all. He got up quickly and went back to the car. He drove into town and bought more soap.

Tilly was standing in the driveway when he got home, her hands on her hips. "Hi, Dad," she said. "I'm looking for King Spanky. He got outside. Look what Alison found."

She held out a tiny toy bow strung with what looked like dental floss, an arrow as small as a needle.

"Be careful with that," Henry said. "It looks sharp. Archery Barbie, right? So did you guys have a good time with Alison?"

"Alison's okay," Tilly said. She belched. "'Scuse me. I don't feel very good."

"What's wrong?" Henry said.

"My stomach is funny," Tilly said. She looked up at him, frowned, and then vomited all over his shirt, his pants.

"Tilly!" he said. He yanked off his shirt, used a sleeve to wipe her mouth. The vomit was foamy and green.

"It tastes horrible," she said. She sounded surprised. "Why does it always taste so bad when you throw up?"

"So that you won't go around doing it for fun," he said. "Are you going to do it again?"

"I don't think so," she said, making a face.

"Then I'm going to go wash up and change clothes. What were you eating, anyway?"

"Grass," Tilly said.

"Well, no wonder," Henry said. "I thought you were smarter than that, Tilly. Don't do that anymore."

"I wasn't planning to," Tilly said. She spat in the grass.

When Henry opened the front door, he could hear Catherine talking in the kitchen. "The funny thing is," she said, "none of it was true. It was just made up, just like something Carleton would do. Just to get attention."

"Dad," Carleton said. He was jumping up and down on one foot. "Want to hear a song?"

"I was looking for you," Henry said. "Did Alison bring you home? Do you need to go to the bathroom?"

"Why aren't you wearing any clothes?" Carleton said.

Someone in the kitchen laughed, as if they had heard this.

"I had an accident," Henry said, whispering. "But you're right, Carleton, I should go change." He took a shower, rinsed and wrung out his shirt, put on clean clothes, but by the time he got downstairs, Catherine and Carleton and Tilly were eating Cheerios for dinner. They were using paper bowls, plastic spoons, as if it were a picnic. "Liz was here, and Alison, but they were going to a movie," she said. "They said they'd meet you some other day. It was awful—when they came in the door, King Spanky went rushing outside. He's been watching the rabbits all day. If he catches one, Tilly is going to be so upset."

"Tilly's been eating grass," Henry said.

Tilly rolled her eyes. As if.

"Not again!" Catherine said. "Tilly, real people don't eat grass. Oh, look, fantastic, there's King Spanky. Who let him in? What's he got in his mouth?"

King Spanky sits with his back to them. He coughs and something drops to the floor, maybe a frog, or a baby rabbit. It goes scrabbling across the floor, half-leaping, dragging one leg. King Spanky just sits there, watching as it disappears under the sofa. Carleton freaks out. Tilly is shouting "Bad King Spanky! Bad cat!" When Henry and Catherine push the sofa back, it's too late, there's just King Spanky and a little blob of sticky blood on the floor.

Catherine would like to write a novel. She'd like to write a novel with no children in it. The problem with novels with children in them is that bad things will happen either to the children or else to the parents. She wants to write something funny, something romantic.

It isn't very comfortable to sit down now that she's so big. She's started writing on the walls. She writes in pencil. She names her characters after paint colors. She imagines them leading beautiful, happy, useful lives. No haunted toasters. No mothers no children no crocodiles no photocopy machines no Leonard Felters. She writes for two or three hours, and then she paints the walls again before anyone gets home. That's always the best part.

"I need you next weekend," The Crocodile said. Her rubber band ball sat on the floor beside her desk. She had her feet up on it, in an attempt to show it who was boss. The rubber band ball was getting too big for its britches. Someone was going to have to teach it a lesson, send it a memo.

She looked tired. Henry said, "You don't need me."

"I do," The Crocodile said, yawning. "I *do*. The clients want to take you out to dinner at the Four Seasons when they come in to town. They want to go see musicals with you. *Rent. Phantom of the Cabaret Lion.* They want to go to Coney Island with you and eat hot dogs. They want to go out to trendy bars and clubs and pick up strippers and publicists and performance artists. They want to talk about poetry, philosophy, sports, politics, their lousy relationships with their fathers. They want to ask you for advice about their love lives. They want you to come to the weddings of their children and make toasts. You're indispensable, honey. I hope you know that."

"Catherine and I are having some problems with rabbits," Henry said. The rabbits were easier to explain than the other thing. "They've taken over the yard. Things are a little crazy."

"I don't know anything about rabbits," The Crocodile said, digging her pointy heels into the flesh of the rubber band ball until she could feel the red rubber blood come running out. She pinned Henry with her beautiful, watery eyes.

"Henry." She said his name so gently that he had to lean forward to hear what she was saying.

She said, "You have the best of both worlds. A wife and children who adore you, a beautiful house in the country, a secure job at a company that depends on you, a boss who appreciates your talents, clients who think you're the shit. You *are* the shit, Henry, and the thing is, you're probably thinking that no one deserves to have all this. You think you have to make a choice. You think you have to give up something. But you don't have to give up anything, Henry, and anyone who tells you otherwise is a fucking rabbit. Don't listen to them. You can have it all. You *deserve* to have it all. You love your job. Do you love your job?"

"I love my job," Henry says. The Crocodile smiles at him tearily.

It's true. He loves his job.

When Henry came home, it must have been after midnight, because he never got home before midnight. He found Catherine standing on a ladder in the kitchen, one foot resting on the sink. She was wearing her gas mask, a black cotton sports bra, and a pair of black sweatpants rolled down so he could see she wasn't wearing any underwear. Her stomach stuck out so far, she had to hold her arms at a funny angle to run the roller up and down the wall in front of her. Up and down in a V. Then fill the V in. She had painted the kitchen ceiling a shade of purple so dark, it almost looked black. Midnight Eggplant.

Catherine has been buying paints from a specialty catalog. All the colors are named after famous books, *Madame Bovary, Forever Amber, Fahrenheit 451, Tin Drum, A Curtain of Green, Twenty Thousand Leagues Beneath the Sea.* She was painting the walls *Catch-22*, a novel she'd taught over and over again to undergraduates. It always went over well. The paint color was nice too. She couldn't decide if she missed teaching. The thing about teaching and having children is that you always ended up treating your children like undergraduates, and your undergraduates like children. There was a particular tone of voice. She'd even used it on Henry a few times, just to see if it worked.

All the cabinets were fenced around with masking tape, like a crime scene. The room stank of new paint.

Catherine took off the gas mask and said, "Tilly picked it out. What do you think?" Her hands were on her hips. Her stomach poked out at Henry. The gas mask had left a ring of white and red around her eyes and chin.

Henry said, "How was the dinner party?"

"We had fettuccine. Liz and Marcus stayed and helped me do the dishes."

("Is something wrong with your dishwasher?" "No. I mean, yes. We're getting a new one.")

She had had a feeling. It had been a feeling like déjà vu, or being drunk, or falling in love. Like teaching. She had imagined an audience of rabbits out on the lawn, watching her dinner party. A classroom of rabbits, watching a documentary. Rabbit television. Her skin had felt electric.

"So she's a lawyer?" Henry said.

"You haven't even met them yet," Catherine said, suddenly feeling possessive. "But I like them. I really, really like them. They wanted to know all about us. You. I think they think that either we're having marriage problems or that you're imaginary. Finally I took Liz upstairs and showed her your stuff in the closet. I pulled out the wedding album and showed them photos."

"Maybe we could invite them over on Sunday? For a cookout?" Henry said.

"They're away next weekend," Catherine said. "They're going up to the mountains on Friday. They have a house up there. They've invited us. To come along."

"I can't," Henry said. "I have to take care of some clients next weekend. Some big shots. We're having some cash flow problems. Besides, are you allowed to go away? Did you check with your doctor, what's his name again, Dr. Marks?"

"You mean, did I get my permission slip signed?" Catherine said. Henry put his hand on her leg and held on. "Dr. Marks said I'm shipshape. Those were his exact words. Or maybe he said tip-top. It was something alliterative."

"Well, I guess you ought to go, then," Henry said. He rested his head against her stomach. She let him. He looked so tired. "Before Golf Cart shows up. Or what is Tilly calling the baby now?"

"She's around here somewhere," Catherine said. "I keep putting her back in her bed and she keeps getting out again. Maybe she's looking for you."

"Did you get my email?" Henry said. He was listening to Catherine's stomach. He wasn't going to stop touching her unless she told him to.

"You know I can't check email on your computer anymore," Catherine said.

"This is so stupid," Henry said. "This house isn't haunted. There isn't any such thing as a haunted house."

"It isn't the house," Catherine said. "It's the stuff we brought with us. Except for the downstairs bathroom, and that might just be a draft, or an electrical problem. The house is fine. I love the house."

"Our stuff is fine," Henry said. "I love our stuff."

"If you really think our stuff is fine," Catherine said, "then why did you buy a new alarm clock? Why do you keep throwing out the soap?"

"It's the move," Henry said. "It was a hard move."

"King Spanky hasn't eaten his food in three days," Catherine said. "At first I thought it was the food, and I bought new food and he came down and ate it and I realized it wasn't the food, it was King Spanky. I couldn't sleep all night, knowing he was up under the bed. Poor spooky guy. I don't know what to do. Take him to the vet? What do I say? Excuse me, but I think my cat is haunted? Anyway, I can't get him out of the bed. Not even with the old alarm clock, the haunted one."

"I'll try," Henry said. "Let me try and see if I can get him out." But he didn't move. Catherine tugged at a piece of his hair and he put up his hand. She gave him her roller. He popped off the cylinder and bagged it and put it in the freezer, which was full of paintbrushes and other rollers. He helped Catherine down from the ladder. "I wish you would stop painting."

"I can't," she said. "It has to be perfect. If I can just get it right, then everything will go back to normal and stop being haunted and the rabbits won't tunnel under the house and make it fall down, and you'll come home and stay home, and our neighbors will finally get to meet you and they'll like you and you'll like them, and Carleton will stop being afraid of everything, and Tilly will fall asleep in her own bed, and stay there, and—"

"Hey," Henry said. "It's all going to work out. It's all good. I really like this color."

"I don't know," Catherine said. She yawned. "You don't think it looks too old-fashioned?"

They went upstairs and Catherine took a bath while Henry tried to coax King Spanky out of the bed. But King Spanky wouldn't come out. When Henry got down on his hands and knees, and stuck the flashlight under the bed, he could see King Spanky's eyes, his tail hanging down from the box frame.

Out on the lawn the rabbits were perfectly still. Then they sprang up in the air, turning and dropping and landing and then freezing again. Catherine stood at the window of the bathroom, toweling her hair. She turned the bathroom light off, so that she could see them better. The moonlight picked out their shining eyes, the moon-colored fur, each hair tipped in paint. They were playing some rabbit game like leapfrog. Or they were dancing the quadrille. Fighting a rabbit war. Did rabbits fight wars? Catherine didn't know. They ran at each other and then turned and darted back, jumping and crouching and rising up on their back legs. A pair of rabbits took off like racehorses, sailing through the air and over a long curled shape in the grass. Then back over again. She put her face against the window. It was Tilly, stretched out against the grass, Tilly's legs and feet bare and white.

"Tilly," she said, and ran out of the bathroom, wearing only the towel around her hair.

"What is it?" Henry said as Catherine darted past him, and down the stairs. He ran after her, and by the time she had opened the front door, was kneeling beside Tilly, the wet grass tickling her thighs and her belly. Henry was there, too, and he picked up Tilly and was carrying her back into the house. They wrapped her in a blanket and put her in her bed, and because neither of them wanted to sleep in the bed where King Spanky was hiding, they lay down on the sofa in the family room, curled up against each other. When they woke up in the morning, Tilly was asleep in a ball at their feet.

For a whole minute or two, last year, Catherine thought she had it figured out. She was married to a man whose specialty was solving problems, salvaging bad situations. If she did something dramatic enough, if she fucked up badly enough, it would save her marriage. And it did, except that once the problem was solved and the marriage was saved and the baby was conceived and the house was bought, then Henry went back to work.

She stands at the window in the bedroom and looks out at all the trees. For a minute she imagines that Carleton is right, and they are living in Central Park and Fifth Avenue is just right over there. Henry's office is just a few blocks away. All those rabbits are just tourists.

Henry wakes up in the middle of the night. There are people downstairs. He can hear women talking, laughing, and he realizes Catherine's book club must have come over. He gets out of bed. It's dark. What time is it anyway? But the alarm clock is haunted again. He unplugs it. As he comes down the stairs, a voice says, "Well, will you look at that!" and then, "Right under his nose the whole time!"

Henry walks through the house, turning on lights. Tilly stands in the middle of the kitchen. "May I ask who's calling?" she says. She's got Henry's cell phone tucked between her shoulder and her face. She's holding it upside down. Her eyes are open, but she's asleep.

"Who are you talking to?" Henry says.

"The rabbits," Tilly says. She tilts her head, listening. Then she laughs. "Call back later," she says. "He doesn't want to talk to you. Yeah. Okay." She hands Henry his phone. "They said it's no one you know."

"Are you awake?" Henry says.

"Yes," Tilly says, still asleep. He carries her back upstairs. He makes a bed out of pillows in the hall closet and lays her down across them. He tucks a blanket around her. If she refuses to wake up in the same bed that she goes to sleep in, then maybe they should make it a game. If you can't beat them, join them.

Catherine hadn't had an affair with Leonard Felter. She hadn't even slept with him. She had just said she had, because she was so mad at Henry. She could have slept with Leonard Felter. The opportunity had been there. And he had been magical, somehow: the only member of the department who could make the photocopier make copies, and he was nice to all of the secretaries. Too nice, as it turned out. And then, when it turned out that Leonard Felter had been fucking everyone, Catherine had felt she couldn't take it back. So she and Henry had gone to therapy together. Henry had taken some time off work. They'd taken the kids to Yosemite. They'd gotten pregnant. She'd been remorseful for something she hadn't done. Henry had forgiven her. Really, she'd saved their marriage. But it had been the sort of thing you could do only once.

If someone has to save the marriage a second time, it will have to be Henry.

Henry went looking for King Spanky. They were going to see the vet: he had the cat cage in the car, but no King Spanky. It was early afternoon, and the rabbits were out on the lawn. Up above, a bird hung, motionless, on a hook of air. Henry craned his head, looking up. It was a big bird, a hawk maybe. It circled, once, twice, again, and then dropped like a stone, towards the rabbits. The rabbits didn't move. There was something about the way they waited, as if this were all a game. The bird dropped through the air, folded like a knife, and then it jerked, tumbled, fell. The wings loose. The bird smashed into the grass and feathers flew up. The rabbits moved closer, as if investigating.

Henry went to see for himself. The rabbits scattered, and the lawn was empty. No rabbits, no bird. But there, down in the trees, beside the bike path, Henry saw something move. King Spanky swung his tail angrily, slunk into the woods.

When Henry came out of the woods, the rabbits were back, guarding the lawn again and Catherine was calling his name. "Where were you?" she said. She was wearing her gas mask around her neck, and there was a smear of paint on her arm. Whiskey Horse. She'd been painting the linen closet.

"King Spanky took off," Henry said. "I couldn't catch him. I saw the weirdest thing—this bird was going after the rabbits, and then it fell—"

"Marcus came by," Catherine said. Her cheeks were flushed. He knew that if he touched her, her skin would be hot. "He stopped by to see if you wanted to go play golf."

"Who wants to play golf?" Henry said. "I want to go upstairs with you. Where are the kids?"

"Alison took them into town, to see a movie," Catherine said. "I'm going to pick them up at three."

Henry lifted the gas mask off her neck, fitted it around her face. He unbuttoned her shirt, undid the clasp of her bra. "Better take this off," he said. "Better take all your clothes off. I think they're haunted."

"You know what would make a great paint color? Can't believe no one has done this yet. Yellow Sticky. What about King Spanky?" Catherine said. She sounded like Darth Vader, maybe on purpose, and Henry thought it was sexy: Darth Vader, pregnant, with his child. She put her hand against his chest and shoved. Not too hard, but harder than she meant to. It turned out that painting had given her some serious muscle. That will be a good thing when she has another kid to haul around.

"Yellow Sticky. That's great. Forget King Spanky," Henry said. "King Spanky is a terrible name for a paint color."

Catherine was painting Tilly's room Lavender Fist. It was going to be a surprise. But when Tilly saw it, she burst into tears. "Why can't you just leave it alone?" she said. "I liked it the way it was."

"I thought you liked purple," Catherine said, astounded. She took off her gas mask.

"I hate purple," Tilly said. "And I hate you. You're so fat. Even Carleton thinks so."

"Tilly!" Catherine said. She laughed. "I'm pregnant, remember?"

"That's what you think," Tilly said. She ran out of the room and across the hall. There were crashing noises, the sounds of things breaking.

"Tilly!" Catherine said.

Tilly stood in the middle of Carleton's room. All around her lay broken night-lights, lamps, broken lightbulbs. The carpet was dusted in glass. Tilly's feet were bare and Catherine looked down, realized that she wasn't wearing shoes either. "Don't move, Tilly," she said.

"They were haunted," Tilly said, and began to cry.

• • •

"So how come your dad's never home?" Alison said.

"I don't know," Carleton said. "Guess what? Tilly broke all my night-lights?"

"Yeah," Alison said. "You must be pretty mad."

"No, it's good that she did," Carleton said, explaining. "They were haunted. Tilly didn't want me to be afraid."

"But aren't you afraid of the dark?" Alison said.

"Tilly said I shouldn't be," Carleton said. "She said the rabbits stay awake all night, that they make sure everything is okay, even when it's dark. Tilly slept outside once, and the rabbits protected her."

"So you're going to stay with us this weekend," Alison said.

"Yes," Carleton said.

"But your dad isn't coming," Alison said.

"No," Carleton said. "I don't know."

"Want to go higher?" Alison said. She pushed the swing and sent him soaring.

When Henry puts his hand against the wall in the living room, it gives a little, as if the wall is pregnant. The paint under the paint is wet. He walks around the house, running his hands along the walls. Catherine has been painting a mural in the foyer. She's painted trees and trees and trees. Golden trees with brown leaves and green leaves and red leaves, and reddish trees with purple leaves and yellow leaves and pink leaves. She's even painted some leaves on the wooden floor, as if the trees are dropping them. "Catherine," he says. "You have got to stop painting the damn walls. The rooms are getting smaller."

Nobody says anything back. Catherine and Tilly and Carleton aren't home. It's the first time Henry has spent the night alone in his house. He can't sleep. There's no television to watch. Henry throws out all of Catherine's paintbrushes. But when Catherine gets home, she'll just buy new ones.

He sleeps on the couch, and during the night someone comes and stands and watches him sleep. Tilly. Then he wakes up and remembers that Tilly isn't there.

The rabbits watch the house all night long. It's their job.

Tilly is talking to the rabbits. It's cold outside, and she's lost her gloves. "What's your name?" she says. "Oh, you beauty. You beauty." She's on her hands and knees. Carleton watches from his side of the yard.

"Can I come over?" he says. "Can I please come over?"

Tilly ignores him. She gets down on her hands and knees, moving even closer to the rabbits. There are three of them, one of them almost close enough to touch. If she moved her hand, slowly, maybe she could grab it by the ears. Maybe she can catch it and train it to live inside. They need a pet rabbit. King

Spanky is haunted. He spends most of his time outside. Her parents keep their bedroom door shut so that King Spanky can't get in.

"Good rabbit," Tilly says. "Just stay still. Stay still."

The rabbits flick their ears. Carleton begins to sing a song Alison has taught them, a skipping song. Carleton is such a girl. Tilly puts out her hand. There's something tangled around the rabbit's neck, like a piece of string or a leash. She wiggles closer, holding out her hand. She stares and stares and can hardly believe her eyes. There's a person, a little man sitting behind the rabbit's ears, holding on to the rabbit's fur and the piece of knotted string, with one hand. His other hand is cocked back, like he's going to throw something. He's looking right at her—his hand flies forward and something hits her hand. She pulls her hand back, astounded. "Hey!" she says, and she falls over on her side and watches the rabbits go springing away. "Hey, you! Come back!"

"What?" Carleton yells. He's frantic. "What are you doing? Why won't you let me come over?"

She closes her eyes, just for a second. Shut up, Carleton. Just shut up. Her hand is throbbing and she lies down, holds her hand up to her face. Shut. Up.

When she wakes up, Carleton is sitting beside her. "What are you doing on my side?" she says, and he shrugs.

"What are you doing?" he says. He rocks back and forth on his knees. "Why did you fall over?"

"None of your business," she says. She can't remember what she was doing. Everything looks funny. Especially Carleton. "What's wrong with you?"

"Nothing's wrong with me," Carleton says, but something is wrong. She studies his face and begins to feel sick, as if she's been eating grass. Those sneaky rabbits! They've been distracting her, and now, while she wasn't paying attention, Carleton's become haunted.

"Oh yes it is," Tilly says, forgetting to be afraid, forgetting her hand hurts, getting angry instead. She's not the one to blame. This is her mother's fault, her father's fault, and it's Carleton's fault too. How could he have let this happen? "You just don't know it's wrong. I'm going to tell Mom."

Haunted Carleton is still a Carleton who can be bossed around. "Don't tell," he begs.

Tilly pretends to think about this, although she's already made up her mind. Because what can she say? Either her mother will notice that something's wrong or else she won't. Better to wait and see. "Just stay away from me," she tells Carleton. "You give me the creeps."

Carleton begins to cry, but Tilly is firm. He turns around, walks slowly back to his half of the yard, still crying. For the rest of the afternoon, he sits beneath the azalea bush at the edge of his side of the yard, and cries. It gives Tilly the creeps. Her hand throbs where something has stung it. The rabbits are all hiding underground. King Spanky has gone hunting.

• • •

"What's up with Carleton?" Henry said, coming downstairs. He couldn't stop yawning. It wasn't that he was tired, although he was tired. He hadn't given Carleton a good-night kiss, just in case it turned out he was coming down with a cold. He didn't want Carleton to catch it. But it looked like Carleton, too, was already coming down with something.

Catherine shrugged. Paint samples were balanced across her stomach like she'd been playing solitaire. All weekend long, away from the house, she'd thought about repainting Henry's office. She'd never painted a haunted room before. Maybe if you mixed the paint with a little bit of holy water? She wasn't sure: What was holy water, anyway? Could you buy it? "Tilly's being mean to him," she said. "I wish they would make some friends out here. He keeps talking about the new baby, about how he'll take care of it. He says it can sleep in his room. I've been trying to explain babies to him, about how all they do is sleep and eat and cry."

"And get bigger," Henry said.

"That too," Catherine said. "So did he go to sleep okay?"

"Eventually," Henry said. "He's just acting really weird."

"How is that different from usual?" Catherine said. She yawned. "Is Tilly finished with her homework?"

"I don't know," Henry said. "You know, just weird. Different weird. Maybe he's going through a weird spell. Tilly wanted me to help her with her math, but I couldn't get it to come out right. So what's up with my office?"

"I cleared it out," Catherine said. "Alison and Liz came over and helped. I told them we were going to redecorate. Why is it that we're the only ones who notice everything is fucking haunted around here?"

"So where'd you put my stuff?" Henry said. "What's up?"

"You're not working here now," Catherine pointed out. She didn't sound angry, just tired. "Besides, it's all haunted, right? So I took your computer into the shop, so they could have a look at it. I don't know, maybe they can unhaunt it."

"Well," Henry said. "Okay. Is that what you told them? It's haunted?"

"Don't be ridiculous," Catherine said. She discarded a paint strip. Too lemony. "So I heard about the bomb scare on the radio."

"Yeah," Henry said. "The subways were full of kids with crew cuts and machine guns. And they evacuated our building for about an hour. We all went and stood outside, holding on to our laptops like idiots, just in case. The Crocodile carried out her rubber band ball, which must weigh about thirty pounds. It kind of freaked people out, even the firemen. I thought the bomb squad was going to blow it up. So tell me about your weekend."

"Tell me about yours," Catherine said.

"You know," Henry said. "Those clients are assholes. But they don't know they're assholes, so it's almost okay. You just have to feel sorry for them. They don't get it. You have to explain how to have fun, and then they get anxious, so they drink a lot and so you have to drink too. Even The Crocodile got drunk. She did this weird wriggly dance to a Pete Seeger song. So what's their place like?"

"It's nice," Catherine said. "You know, really nice."

"So you had a good weekend? Carleton and Tilly had a good time?"

"It was really nice," Catherine said. "No, really, it was great. I had a fucking great time. So you're sure you can make it home for dinner on Thursday."

It wasn't a question.

"Carleton looks like he might be coming down with something," Henry said. "Here. Do you think I feel hot? Or is it cold in here?"

Catherine said, "You're fine. It's going to be Liz and Marcus and some of the women from the book group and their husbands, and what's her name, the real estate agent. I invited her too. Did you know she's written a book? I was going to do that! I'm getting the new dishwasher tomorrow. No more paper plates. And the lawn care specialist is coming on Monday to take care of the rabbits. I thought I'd drop off King Spanky at the vet, take Tilly and Carleton back to the city, stay with Lucy for two or three days—did you know she tried to find this place and got lost? She's supposed to come up for dinner too—just in case the poison doesn't go away right away, you know, or in case we end up with piles of dead rabbits on the lawn. Your job is to make sure there are no dead rabbits when I bring Tilly and Carleton back."

"I guess I can do that," Henry said.

"You'd better," Catherine said. She stood up with some difficulty, came and leaned over his chair. Her stomach bumped into his shoulder. Her breath was hot. Her hands were full of strips of color. "Sometimes I wish that instead of working for The Crocodile, you were having an affair with her. I mean, that way you'd come home when you're supposed to. You wouldn't want me to be suspicious."

"I don't have any time to have affairs," Henry said. He sounded put out. Maybe he was thinking about Leonard Felter. Or maybe he was picturing The Crocodile naked. The Crocodile wearing stretchy red rubber sex gear. Catherine imagined telling Henry the truth about Leonard Felter. I didn't have an affair. Did not. I made it up. Is that a problem?

"That's exactly what I mean," Catherine said. "You'd better be here for dinner. You live here, Henry. You're my husband. I want you to meet our friends. I want you to be here when I have this baby. I want you to fix what's wrong with the downstairs bathroom. I want you to talk to Tilly. She's having a rough time. She won't talk to me about it."

"Tilly's fine," Henry said. "We had a long talk tonight. She said she's sorry she broke all of Carleton's night-lights. I like the trees, by the way. You're not going to paint over them, are you?"

"I had all this leftover paint," Catherine said. "I was getting tired of just slapping paint on with the rollers. I wanted to do something fancier."

"You could paint some trees in my office, when you paint my office."

"Maybe," Catherine said. "Ooof, this baby won't stop kicking me." She lay down on the floor in front of Henry, and lifted her feet into his lap. "Rub my feet. I've still got so much fucking paint. But once your office is done, I'm done with the painting. Tilly told me to stop it or else. She keeps hiding my gas mask. Will you be here for dinner?"

"I'll be here for dinner," Henry said, rubbing her feet. He really meant it. He was thinking about the exterminator, about rabbit corpses scattered all across the lawn, like a war zone. Poor rabbits. What a mess.

After they went to see the therapist, after they went to Yosemite and came home again, Henry said to Catherine, "I don't want to talk about it anymore. I don't want to talk about it ever again. Can we not talk about it?"

"Talk about what?" Catherine said. But she had almost been sorry. It had been so much work. She'd had to invent so many details that eventually it began to seem as if she hadn't made it up after all. It was too strange, too confusing, to pretend it had never happened, when, after all, it *had* never happened.

Catherine is dressing for dinner. When she looks in the mirror, she's as big as a cruise ship. A water tower. She doesn't look like herself at all. The baby kicks her right under the ribs.

"Stop that," she says. She's sure the baby is going to be a girl. Tilly won't be pleased. Tilly has been extra good all day. She helped make the salad. She set the table. She put on a nice dress.

Tilly is hiding from Carleton under a table in the foyer. If Carleton finds her, Tilly will scream. Carleton is haunted, and nobody has noticed. Nobody cares except Tilly. Tilly says names for the baby, under her breath. Dollop. Shampool. Custard. Knock, knock. The rabbits are out on the lawn, and King Spanky has gotten under the bed again, and he won't come out, not for a million haunted alarm clocks.

Her mother has painted trees all along the wall under the staircase. They don't look like real trees. They aren't real colors. It doesn't look like Central Park at all. In among the trees, her mother has painted a little door. It isn't a real door, except that when Tilly goes over to look at it, it is real. There's a doorknob, and when Tilly turns it, the door opens. Underneath the stairs, there's another set of stairs, little dirt stairs, going down. On the third stair, there's a rabbit sitting there, looking up at Tilly. It hops down, one step, and then another. Then another.

"Rumpled Stiltskin!" Tilly says to the rabbit. "Lipstick!"

Catherine goes to the closet to get out Henry's pink shirt. What's the name of that real estate agent? Why can't she ever remember? She lays the shirt on the bed and then stands there for a moment, stunned. It's too much. The pink shirt is haunted. She pulls out all of Henry's suits, his shirts, his ties. All haunted. Every fucking thing is haunted. Even the fucking shoes. When she pulls out the drawers, socks, underwear, handkerchiefs, everything, it's all spoiled. All haunted. Henry doesn't have a thing to wear. She goes downstairs, gets trash bags, and goes back upstairs again. She begins to dump clothes into the trash bags.

She can see Carleton framed in the bedroom window. He's chasing the rabbits with a stick. She hoists open the window, leans out, yells, "Stay away from those fucking rabbits, Carleton! Do you hear me?"

She doesn't recognize her own voice.

Tilly is running around downstairs somewhere. She's yelling too, but her voice gets farther and farther away, fainter and fainter. She's yelling, "Hairbrush! Zeppelin! Torpedo! Marmalade!"

The doorbell rings.

The Crocodile started laughing. "Okay, Henry. Calm down."

He fired off another rubber band. "I mean it," he said. "I'm late. I'll be late. She's going to kill me."

"Tell her it's my fault," The Crocodile said. "So they started dinner without you. Big deal."

"I tried calling," Henry said. "Nobody answered." He had an idea that the phone was haunted now. That's why Catherine wasn't answering. They'd have to get a new phone. Maybe the lawn specialist would know a house specialist. Maybe somebody could do something about this. "I should go home," he said. "I should go home right now." But he didn't get up. "I think we've gotten ourselves into a mess, me and Catherine. I don't think things are good right now."

"Tell someone who cares," The Crocodile suggested. She wiped at her eyes. "Get out of here. Go catch your train. Have a great weekend. See you on Monday."

So Henry goes home, he has to go home, but of course he's late, it's too late. The train is haunted. The closer they get to his station, the more haunted the train gets. None of the other passengers seem to notice. And of course, his bike turns out to be haunted, too. He leaves it at the station and he walks home in the dark, down the bike path. Something follows him home. Maybe it's King Spanky.

Here's the yard, and here's his house. He loves his house, how it's all lit up. You can see right through the windows, you can see the living room, which Catherine has painted Ghost Crab. The trim is Rat Fink. Catherine has worked so hard. The driveway is full of cars, and inside, people are eating dinner. They're admiring Catherine's trees. They haven't waited for him, and that's fine. His neighbors: he loves his neighbors. He's going to love them as soon as he meets them. His wife is going to have a baby any day now. His daughter will stop walking in her sleep. His son isn't haunted. The moon shines down and paints the world a color he's never seen before. Oh, Catherine, wait till you see this. Shining lawn, shining rabbits, shining world. The rabbits are out on the lawn. They've been waiting for him, all this time, they've been waiting. Here's his rabbit, his very own rabbit. Who needs a bike? He sits on his rabbit, legs pressed against the warm, silky, shining flanks, one hand holding on to the rabbit's fur, the knotted string around its neck. He has something in his other hand, and when he looks, he sees it's a spear. All around him, the others are sitting on their rabbits, waiting patiently, quietly. They've been waiting for a long time, but the waiting is almost over. In a little while, the dinner party will be over and the war will begin.

Reginald McKnight

THE KIND OF LIGHT
THAT SHINES ON TEXAS

REGINALD MCKNIGHT (1956–), a 1981 Thomas J. Watson Fellow, is a short story author and novelist. He has won the O. Henry Award, the Drue Heinz Literature Prize, a Bread Loaf Fellowship, the Whiting Writer's Award, and the Addison M. Metcalf Award. His works include *Moustapha's Eclipse, I Get on the Bus, The Kind of Light That Shines on Texas, White Boys,* and *He Sleeps.* In addition to writing, McKnight has been a professor of English at the University of Maryland, College Park; Carnegie Mellon University; and the University of Michigan, Ann Arbor. He is currently the Hamilton Holmes Professor of English at the University of Georgia in Athens.

I never liked Marvin Pruitt. Never liked him, never knew him, even though there were only three of us in the class. Three black kids. In our school there were fourteen classrooms of thirty-odd white kids (in '66, they considered Chicanos provisionally white) and three or four black kids. Primary school in primary colors. Neat division. Alphabetized. They didn't stick us in the back, or arrange us by degrees of hue, apartheidlike. This was real integration, a ten-to-one ratio as tidy as upper-class landscaping. If it all worked, you could have ten white kids all to yourself. They could talk to you, get the feel of you, scrutinize you bone deep if they wanted to. They seldom wanted to, and that was fine with me for two reasons. The first was that their scrutiny was irritating. How do you comb your hair—why do you comb your hair—may I please touch your hair—were the kinds of questions they asked. This is no way to feel at home. The second reason was Marvin. He embarrassed me. He smelled bad, was at least two grades behind, was hostile, dark skinned, homely, close-mouthed. I feared him for his size, pitied him for his dress, watched him all the time. Marveled at him, mystified, astonished, uneasy.

He had the habit of spitting on his right arm, juicing it down till it would glisten. He would start in immediately after taking his seat when we'd finished with the Pledge of Allegiance, "The Yellow Rose of Texas," "The Eyes of Texas Are upon You," and "Mistress Shady." Marvin would rub his spit-flecked arm with his left hand, rub and roll as if polishing an ebony pool cue. Then he would

386

rest his head in the crook of his arm, sniffing, huffing deep like black-jacket boys huff bagsful of acrylics. After ten minutes or so, his eyes would close, heavy. He would sleep till recess. Mrs. Wickham would let him.

There was one other black kid in our class. A girl they called Ah-so. I never learned what she did to earn this name. There was nothing Asian about this big-shouldered girl. She was the tallest, heaviest kid in school. She was quiet, but I don't think any one of us was subtle or sophisticated enough to nickname our classmates according to any but physical attributes. Fat kids were called Porky or Butterball, skinny ones were called Stick or Ichabod. Ah-so was big, thick, and African. She would impassively sit, sullen, silent as Marvin. She wore the same dark blue pleated skirt every day, the same ruffled white blouse every day. Her skin always shone as if worked by Marvin's palms and fingers. I never spoke one word to her, nor she to me.

Of the three of us, Mrs. Wickham called only on Ah-so and me. Ah-so never answered one question, correctly or incorrectly, so far as I can recall. She wasn't stupid. When asked to read aloud she read well, seldom stumbling over long words, reading with humor and expression. But when Wickham asked her about Farmer Brown and how many cows, or the capital of Vermont, or the date of this war or that, Ah-so never spoke. Not one word. But you always felt she could have answered those questions if she'd wanted to. I sensed no tension, embarrassment, or anger in Ah-so's reticence. She simply refused to speak. There was something unshakable about her, some core so impenetrably solid, you got the feeling that if you stood too close to her she could eat your thoughts like a black star eats light. I didn't despise Ah-so as I despised Marvin. There was nothing malevolent about her. She sat like a great icon in the back of the classroom, tranquil, guarded, sealed up, watchful. She was close to sixteen, and it was my guess she'd given up on school. Perhaps she was just obliging the wishes of her family, sticking it out till the law could no longer reach her.

There were at least half a dozen older kids in our class. Besides Marvin and Ah-so there was Oakley, who sat behind me, whispering threats into my ear; Varna Willard with the large breasts; Eddie Limon, who played bass for a high school rock band; and Lawrence Ridderbeck, who everyone said had a kid and a wife. You couldn't expect me to know anything about Texan educational practices of the 1960s, so I never knew why there were so many older kids in my sixth-grade class. After all, I was just a boy and had transferred into the school around midyear. My father, an air force sergeant, had been sent to Viet Nam. The air force sent my mother, my sister, Claire, and me to Connolly Air Force Base, which during the war housed "unaccompanied wives." I'd been to so many different schools in my short life that I ceased wondering about their differences. All I knew about the Texas schools is that they weren't afraid to flunk you.

Yet though I was only twelve then, I had a good idea why Wickham never once called on Marvin, why she let him snooze in the crook of his polished arm. I knew why she would press her lips together, and narrow her eyes at me whenever I correctly answered a question, rare as that was. I know why she badgered Ah-so with questions everyone knew Ah-so would never even consider answering. Wickham didn't like us. She wasn't gross about it, but it was clear she didn't want us around. She would prove her dislike day after day with little stories and jokes. "I just want to share with you all," she would say, "a little riddle my daughter told me at the supper table th'other day. Now, where do you go when you injure your knee?" Then one, two, or all three of her pets would say for the rest of us, "We don't know, Miz Wickham," in that skin-chilling way suckasses speak, "where?" "Why, to Africa," Wickham would say, "where the knee grows."

The thirty-odd white kids would laugh, and I would look across the room at Marvin. He'd be asleep. I would glance back at Ah-so. She'd be sitting still as a projected image, staring down at her desk. I, myself, would smile at Wickham's stupid jokes, sometimes fake a laugh. I tried to show her that at least one of us was alive and alert, even though her jokes hurt. I sucked ass, too, I suppose. But I wanted her to understand more than anything that I was not like her other nigra children, that I was worthy of more than the nonattention and the negative attention she paid Marvin and Ah-so. I hated her, but never showed it. No one could safely contradict that woman. She knew all kinds of tricks to demean, control, and punish you. And she could swing her two-foot paddle as fluidly as a big-league slugger swings a bat. You didn't speak in Wickham's class unless she spoke to you first. You didn't chew gum, or wear "hood" hair. You didn't drag your feet, curse, pass notes, hold hands with the opposite sex. Most especially, you didn't say anything bad about the Aggies, Governor Connolly, LBJ, Sam Houston, or Waco. You did the forbidden and she would get you. It was that simple.

She never got me, though. Never gave her reason to. But she could have invented reasons. She did a lot of that. I can't be sure, but I used to think she pitied me because my father was in Viet Nam and my uncle A.J. had recently died there. Whenever she would tell one of her racist jokes, she would always glance at me, preface the joke with, "Now don't you nigra children take offense. This is all in fun, you know. I just want to share with you all something Coach Gilchrest told me th'other day." She would tell her joke, and glance at me again. I'd giggle, feeling a little queasy. "I'm half Irish," she would chuckle, "and you should hear some of those Irish jokes." She never told any, and I never really expected her to. I just did my Tom-thing. I kept my shoes shined, my desk neat, answered her questions as best I could, never brought gum to school, never cursed, never slept in class. I wanted to show her we were not all the same.

I tried to show them all, all thirty-odd, that I was different. It worked to some degree, but not very well. When some article was stolen from someone's locker or desk, Marvin, not I, was the first accused. I'd be second. Neither Marvin, nor Ah-so nor I were ever chosen for certain classroom honors—"Pledge leader," "flag holder," "noise monitor," "paper passer outer," but Mrs. Wickham once let me be "eraser duster." I was proud. I didn't even care about the cracks my fellow students made about my finally having turned the right color. I had done something that Marvin, in the deeps of his never-ending sleep, couldn't even dream of doing. Jack Preston, a kid who sat in front of me, asked me one day at recess whether I was embarrassed about Marvin. "Can you believe that guy?" I said. "He's like a pig or something. Makes me sick."

"Does it make you ashamed to be colored?"

"No," I said, but I meant yes. Yes, if you insist on thinking us all the same. Yes, if his faults are mine, his weaknesses inherent in me.

"I'd be," said Jack.

I made no reply. I was ashamed. Ashamed for not defending Marvin and ashamed that Marvin even existed. But if it had occurred to me, I would have asked Jack whether he was ashamed of being white because of Oakley. Oakley, "Oak Tree," Kelvin "Oak Tree" Oakley. He was sixteen and proud of it. He made it clear to everyone, including Wickham, that his life's ambition was to stay in school one more year, till he'd be old enough to enlist in the army. "Them slopes got my brother," he would say. "I'mna sign up and git me a few slopes. Gonna kill them bastards deader'n shit." Oakley, so far as anyone knew, was and always had been the oldest kid in his family. But no one contradicted him. He would, as anyone would tell you, "snap yer neck jest as soon as look at you." Not a boy in class, excepting Marvin and myself, had been able to avoid Oakley's pink bellies, Texas titty twisters, moon pie punches, or worse. He didn't bother Marvin, I suppose, because Marvin was closer to his size and age, and because Marvin spent five sixths of the school day asleep. Marvin probably never crossed Oakley's mind. And to say that Oakley hadn't bothered me is not to say he had no intention of ever doing so. In fact, this haphazard sketch of hairy fingers, slash of eyebrow, explosion of acne, elbows, and crooked teeth, swore almost daily that he'd like to kill me.

Naturally, I feared him. Though we were about the same height, he outweighed me by no less than forty pounds. He talked, stood, smoked, and swore like a man. No one, except for Mrs. Wickham, the principal, and the coach, ever laid a finger on him. And even Wickham knew that the hot lines she laid on him merely amused him. He would smile out at the classroom, goofy and bashful, as she laid down the two, five, or maximum ten strokes on him. Often he would wink, or surreptitiously flash us the thumb as Wickham worked on him. When she was finished, Oakley would walk so cool back to his seat you'd think he was on wheels. He'd slide into his chair, sniff the air, and say, "Somethin's burnin. Do y'all smell smoke? I swanee, I smell smoke and fahr back here." If he had made these cracks and never threatened me, I might have grown to admire

Oakley, even liked him a little. But he hated me, and took every opportunity during the six-hour school day to make me aware of this. "Some Sambo's gittin his ass broke open one of these days," he'd mumble. "I wanna fight somebody. Need to keep in shape till I git to Nam."

I never said anything to him for the longest time. I pretended not to hear him, pretended not to notice his sour breath on my neck and ear. "Yep," he'd whisper. "Coonies keep y' in good shape for slope killin." Day in, day out, that's the kind of thing I'd pretend not to hear. But one day when the rain dropped down like lead balls, and the cold air made your skin look plucked, Oakley whispered to me, "My brother tells me it rains like this in Nam. Maybe I oughta go out at recess and break your ass open today. Nice and cool so you don't sweat. Nice and wet to clean up the blood." I said nothing for at least half a minute, then I turned half right and said, "Thought you said your brother was dead." Oakley, silent himself, for a time, poked me in the back with his pencil and hissed, "*Yer* dead." Wickham cut her eyes our way, and it was over.

It was hardest avoiding him in gym class. Especially when we played murderball. Oakley always aimed his throws at me. He threw with unblinking intensity, his teeth gritting, his neck veining, his face flushing, his black hair sweeping over one eye. He could throw hard, but the balls were squishy and harmless. In fact, I found his misses more intimidating than his hits. The balls would whizz by, thunder against the folded bleachers. They rattled as though a locomotive were passing through them. I would duck, dodge, leap as if he were throwing grenades. But he always hit me, sooner or later. And after a while I noticed that the other boys would avoid throwing at me, as if I belonged to Oakley.

One day, however, I was surprised to see that Oakley was throwing at everyone else but me. He was uncommonly accurate, too; kids were falling like tin cans. Since no one was throwing at me, I spent most of the game watching Oakley cut this one and that one down. Finally, he and I were the only ones left on the court. Try as he would, he couldn't hit me, nor I him. Coach Gilchrest blew his whistle and told Oakley and me to bring the red rubber balls to the equipment locker. I was relieved I'd escaped Oakley's stinging throws for once. I was feeling triumphant, full of myself. As Oakley and I approached Gilchrest, I thought about saying something friendly to Oakley: Good game, Oak Tree, I would say. Before I could speak, though, Gilchrest said, "All right boys, there's five minutes left in the period. Y'all are so good, looks like, you're gonna have to play like men. No boundaries, no catch outs, and you gotta hit your opponent three times in order to win. Got me?"

We nodded.

"And you're gonna use these," said Gilchrest, pointing to three volleyballs at his feet. "And you better believe they're pumped full. Oates, you start at that end of the court. Oak Tree, you're at th'other end. Just like usual, I'll set the balls at mid-court, and when I blow my whistle I want y'all to haul your cheeks to the middle and th'ow for all you're worth. Got me?" Gilchrest nodded at our nods, then added, "Remember, no boundaries, right?"

I at my end, Oakley at his, Gilchrest blew his whistle. I was faster than Oakley and scooped up a ball before he'd covered three quarters of his side. I aimed, threw, and popped him right on the knee. "One-zip!" I heard Gilchrest shout. The ball bounced off his knee and shot right back into my hands. I hurried my throw and missed. Oakley bent down, clutched the two remaining balls. I remember being amazed that he could palm each ball, run full out, and throw left-handed or right-handed without a shade of awkwardness. I spun, ran, but one of Oakley's throws glanced off the back of my head. "One-one!" hollered Gilchrest. I fell and spun on my ass as the other ball came sailing at me. I caught it. "He's out!" I yelled. Gilchrest's voice boomed, "No catch outs. Three hits. Three hits." I leapt to my feet as Oakley scrambled across the floor for another ball. I chased him down, leapt, and heaved the ball hard as he drew himself erect. The ball hit him dead in the face, and he went down flat. He rolled around, cupping his hands over his nose. Gilchrest sped to his side, helped him to his feet, asked him whether he was OK. Blood flowed from Oakley's nose, dripped in startlingly bright spots on the floor, his shoes, Gilchrest's shirt. The coach removed Oakley's T-shirt and pressed it against the big kid's nose to stanch the bleeding. As they walked past me toward the office I mumbled an apology to Oakley, but couldn't catch his reply. "You watch your filthy mouth, boy," said Gilchrest to Oakley.

The locker room was unnaturally quiet as I stepped into its steamy atmosphere. Eyes clicked in my direction, looked away. After I was out of my shorts, had my towel wrapped around me, my shower kit in hand, Jack Preston and Brian Nailor approached me. Preston's hair was combed slick and plastic looking. Nailor's stood up like frozen flames. Nailor smiled at me with his big teeth and pale eyes. He poked my arm with a finger. "You fucked up," he said.

"I tried to apologize."

"Won't do you no good," said Preston.

"I swanee," said Nailor.

"It's part of the game," I said. "It was an accident. Wasn't my idea to use volleyballs."

"Don't matter," Preston said. "He's jest lookin for an excuse to fight you."

"I never done nothing to him."

"Don't matter," said Nailor. "He don't like you."

"Brian's right, Clint. He'd jest as soon kill you as look at you."

"I never done nothing to him."

"Look," said Preston, "I know him pretty good. And jest between you and me, it's 'cause you're a city boy—"

"Whadda you mean? I've never—"

"He don't like your clothes—"

"And he don't like the fancy way you talk in class."

"What fancy—"

"I'm tellin him, if you don't mind, Brian."

"Tell him then."

"He don't like the way you say 'tennis shoes' instead of sneakers. He don't like coloreds. A whole bunch a things, really."

"I never done nothing to him. He's got no reason—"

"*And,*" said Nailor, grinning, "*and,* he says you're a stuck-up rich kid." Nailor's eyes had crow's-feet, bags beneath them. They were a man's eyes.

"My dad's a sergeant," I said.

"You chicken to fight him?" said Nailor.

"Yeah, Clint, don't be chicken. Jest go on and git it over with. He's whupped pert near ever'body else in the class. It ain't so bad."

"Might as well, Oates."

"Yeah, yer pretty skinny, but yer jest about his height. Jest git 'im in a headlock and don't let go."

"Goddamn," I said, "he's got no reason to—"

Their eyes shot right and I looked over my shoulder. Oakley stood at his locker, turning its tumblers. From where I stood I could see that a piece of cotton was wedged up one of his nostrils, and he already had the makings of a good shiner. His acne burned red like a fresh abrasion. He snapped the locker open and kicked his shoes off without sitting. Then he pulled off his shorts, revealing two paddle stripes on his ass. They were fresh red bars speckled with white, the white speckles being the reverse impression of the paddle's suction holes. He must not have watched his filthy mouth while in Gilchrest's presence. Behind me, I heard Preston and Nailor pad to their lockers.

Oakley spoke without turning around. "Somebody's gonna git his skinny black ass kicked, right today, right after school." He said it softly. He slipped his jock off, turned around. I looked away. Out the corner of my eye I saw him stride off, his hairy nakedness a weapon clearing the younger boys from his path. Just before he rounded the corner of the shower stalls, I threw my toilet kit to the floor and stammered, "I—I never did nothing to you, Oakley." He stopped, turned, stepped closer to me, wrapping his towel around himself. Sweat streamed down my rib cage. It felt like ice water. "You wanna go at it right now, boy?"

"I never did nothing to you." I felt tears in my eyes. I couldn't stop them even though I was blinking like mad. "Never."

He laughed. "You busted my nose, asshole."

"What about before? What'd I ever do to you?"

"See you after school, Coonie." Then he turned away, flashing his acne-spotted back like a semaphore. "Why?" I shouted. "Why you wanna fight me?"

Oakley stopped and turned, folded his arms, leaned against a toilet stall. "Why you wanna fight *me*, Oakley?" I stepped over the bench. "What'd I do? Why me?" And then unconsciously, as if scratching, as if breathing, I walked toward Marvin, who stood a few feet from Oakley, combing his hair at the mirror. "Why not him?" I said. "How come you're after *me* and not *him?*" The room froze. Froze for a moment that was both evanescent and eternal, somewhere between an eye blink and a week in hell. No one moved, nothing happened; there was no sound at all. And then it was as if all of us at the same moment looked at Marvin. He just stood there, combing away, the only body in motion, I think. He combed his hair and combed it, as if seeing only his image, hearing only his comb scraping his scalp. I knew he'd heard me. There's no way he could not have heard me. But all he did was slide the comb into his pocket and walk out the door.

"I got no quarrel with Marvin," I heard Oakley say. I turned toward his voice, but he was already in the shower.

I was able to avoid Oakley at the end of the school day. I made my escape by asking Mrs. Wickham if I could go to the rest room.

"'Rest room,'" Oakley mumbled. "It's a damn toilet, sissy."

"Clinton," said Mrs. Wickham. "Can you *not* wait till the bell rings? It's almost three o'clock."

"No ma'am," I said. "I won't make it."

"Well, I should make you wait just to teach you to be more mindful about . . . hygiene . . . uh, things." She sucked in her cheeks, squinted. "But I'm feeling charitable today. You may go." I immediately left the building, and got on the bus. "Ain't you a little early?" said the bus driver, swinging the door shut. "Just left the office," I said. The driver nodded, apparently not giving me a second thought. I had no idea why I'd told her I'd come from the office, or why she found it a satisfactory answer. Two minutes later the bus filled, rolled, and shook its way to Connolly Air Base. When I got home, my mother was sitting in the living room, smoking her Slims, watching her soap opera. She absently asked me how my day had gone and I told her fine. "Hear from Dad?" I said.

"No, but I'm sure he's fine." She always said that when we hadn't heard from him in a while. I suppose she thought I was worried about him, or that I felt vulnerable without him. It was neither. I just wanted to discuss something with my mother that we both cared about. If I spoke with her about things that happened at school, or on my weekends, she'd listen with half an ear, say something like, "Is that so?" or "You don't say?" I couldn't stand that sort of thing. But when I mentioned my father, she treated me a bit more like an adult, or at least someone who was worth listening to. I didn't want to feel like a boy that afternoon. As I turned from my mother and walked down the hall I thought about the day my father left for Viet Nam. Sharp in his uniform, sure behind his aviator specs, he slipped a cigar from his pocket and stuck it in mine. "Not till I get back," he said. "We'll have us one when we go fishing. Just you and me, out on the lake all day, smoking and casting and sitting. Don't let Mama see it. Put it in y'back pocket." He hugged me, shook my hand, and told me I was the man of the house now. He told me he was depending on me to take good care of my mother and sister. "Don't you let me down, now, hear?" And he tapped his thick finger on my chest. "You almost as big as me. Boy, you something else." I believed him when he told me those things. My heart swelled big enough to swallow my father, my mother, Claire. I loved, feared, and respected myself, my manhood. That day I could have put all of Waco, Texas, in my heart. And it wasn't till about three months later that I discovered I really wasn't the man of the house, that my mother and sister, as they always had, were taking care of me.

For a brief moment I considered telling my mother about what had happened at school that day, but for one thing, she was deep down in the halls of *General Hospital,* and never paid you much mind till it was over. For another thing, I just wasn't the kind of person—I'm still not, really—to discuss my problems with anyone. Like my father I kept things to myself, talked about my problems only in retrospect. Since my father wasn't around I consciously wanted to be like him, doubly like him, I could say. I wanted to be the man of the house in some respect, even if it had to be in an inward way. I went to my room, changed my clothes, and laid out my homework. I couldn't focus on it. I thought about Marvin, what I'd said about him or done to him—I couldn't tell which. I'd done something to him, said something about him; said something about and done something to myself. *How come you're after me and not him?* I kept trying to tell myself I hadn't meant it that way. *That* way. I thought about approaching Marvin, telling him what I really meant was that he was more Oakley's age and weight than I. I would tell him I meant I was no match for Oakley. *See, Marvin, what I meant was that he wants to fight a colored guy, but is afraid to fight you 'cause you could beat him.* But try as I did, I couldn't for a moment convince myself that Marvin would believe me. I meant it *that* way and no other. Everybody heard. Everybody knew. That afternoon I forced myself to confront the notion that tomorrow I would probably have to fight both Oakley and Marvin. I'd have to be two men.

I rose from my desk and walked to the window. The light made my skin look orange, and I started thinking about what Wickham had told us once about light. She said that oranges and apples, leaves and flowers, the whole multicolored world, was not what it appeared to be. The colors we see, she said, look like they do only because of the light or ray that shines on them. "The color of the thing isn't what you see, but the light that's reflected off it." Then she shut out the lights and shone a white light lamp on a prism. We watched the pale splay of colors on the projector screen; some people oohed and aahed. Suddenly, she switched on a black light and the color of everything changed. The prism colors vanished, Wickham's arms were purple, the buttons of her dress were as orange as hot coals, rather than the blue they had been only seconds before. We were all very quiet. "Nothing," she said, after a while, "is really what it appears to be." I didn't really understand then. But as I stood at the window, gazing at my orange skin, I wondered what kind of light I could shine on Marvin, Oakley, and me that would reveal us as the same.

I sat down and stared at my arms. They were dark brown again. I worked up a bit of saliva under my tongue and spat on my left arm. I spat again, then rubbed the spittle into it, polishing, working till my arm grew warm. As I spat, and rubbed, I wondered why Marvin did this weird, nasty thing to himself, day after day. Was he trying to rub away the black, or deepen it, doll it up? And if he did this weird nasty thing for a hundred years, would he spit-shine himself invisible, rolling away the eggplant skin, revealing the scarlet muscle, blue vein, pink and yellow tendon, white bone? Then disappear? Seen through, all colors, no colors. Spitting and rubbing. Is this the way you do it? I leaned forward, sniffed the arm. It smelled vaguely of mayonnaise. After an hour or so, I fell asleep.

I saw Oakley the second I stepped off the bus the next morning. He stood outside the gym in his usual black penny loafers, white socks, high-water jeans, T-shirt, and black jacket. Nailor stood with him, his big teeth spread across his bottom lip like playing cards. If there was anyone I felt like fighting, that day, it was Nailor. But I wanted to put off fighting for as long as I could. I stepped toward the gymnasium, thinking that I shouldn't run, but if I hurried I could beat Oakley to the door and secure myself near Gilchrest's office. But the moment I stepped into the gym, I felt Oakley's broad palm clap down on my shoulder. "Might as well stay out here, Coonie," he said. "I need me a little target practice." I turned to face him and he slapped me, one-two, with the back, then the palm of his hand, as I'd seen Bogart do to Peter Lorre in *The Maltese Falcon*. My heart went wild. I could scarcely breathe. I couldn't swallow.

"Call me a nigger," I said. I have no idea what made me say this. All I know is that it kept me from crying. "Call me a nigger, Oakley."

"Fuck you, ya black-ass slope." He slapped me again, scratching my eye. "I don't do what coonies tell me."

"Call me a nigger."

"Outside, Coonie."

"Call me one. Go ahead!"

He lifted his hand to slap me again, but before his arm could swing my way, Marvin Pruitt came from behind me and calmly pushed me aside. "Git out my way, boy," he said. And he slugged Oakley on the side of his head. Oakley stumbled back, stiff-legged. His eyes were big. Marvin hit him twice more, once again to the side of the head, once to the nose. Oakley went down and stayed down. Though blood was drawn, whistles blowing, fingers pointing, kids hollering, Marvin just stood there, staring at me with cool eyes. He spat on the ground, licked his lips, and just stared at me, till Coach Gilchrest and Mr. Calderon tackled him and violently carried him away. He never struggled, never took his eyes off me.

Nailor and Mrs. Wickham helped Oakley to his feet. His already fattened nose bled and swelled so that I had to look away. He looked around, bemused, walleyed, maybe scared. It was apparent he had no idea how bad he was hurt. He didn't blink. He didn't even touch his nose. He didn't look like he knew much of anything. He looked at me, looked me dead in the eye, in fact, but didn't seem to recognize me.

That morning, like all other mornings, we said the Pledge of Allegiance, sang "The Yellow Rose of Texas," "The Eyes of Texas Are upon You," and "Mistress Shady." The room stood strangely empty without Oakley, and without Marvin, but at the same time you could feel their presence more intensely somehow. I felt like I did when I'd walk into my mother's room and could smell my father's cigars or cologne. He was more palpable, in certain respects, than when there in actual flesh. For some reason, I turned to look at Ah-so, and just this once I let my eyes linger on her face. She had a very gentle-looking face, really. That surprised me. She must have felt my eyes on her because she glanced up at me for a second and smiled, white teeth, downcast eyes. Such a pretty smile. That surprised me too. She held it for a few seconds, then let it fade. She looked down at her desk, and sat still as a photograph.

David Means

THE SECRET GOLDFISH

DAVID MEANS (1961–), born and raised in Michigan, is the author of three short story collections, including *Assorted Fire Events*, winner of the *Los Angeles Times* Book Prize and finalist for the National Book Critics Circle Award. His latest book, *The Secret Goldfish*, was short-listed for the Frank O'Connor International Short Story Award. Means's work has recently appeared in *The O. Henry Prize 2006; Best American Short Stories 2005*; and *Best American Mystery Stories, 2005; Zoetrope; Harper's;* and *The New Yorker*. He lives in Nyack, New York, and teaches writing at Vassar College.

He had a weird growth along his dorsal fin, and that gape-mouth grimace you see in older fish. Way too big for his tank, too, having outgrown the standard goldfish age limit. Which is what? About one month? He was six years old— outlandishly old for a fish. One afternoon, Teddy, as he was called then, now just Ted, took notice of the condition of Fish's tank: a wedge of sunlight plunged through the window of his bedroom and struck the water's surface, disappearing. The water was so clotted it had become a solid mass, a putty within which Fish was presumably swimming, or dead. Most likely dead. Where's Fish? Where's Fish? Teddy yelled to his mom. She came into his room, caught sight of the tank, and gave a small yelp. Once again, a fish had been neglected.

Everyone knows the story. The kids beg and plead: Please, please get us a fish (or a dog), we'll feed it, we will, honest, we'll take care of it and you won't have to do a single thing. We'll clean the tank walls with the brush and make sure the filter charcoal is replaced regularly and refill the water when it evaporates. Please, please, we can handle it, we're old enough now, we are, it'll be so much fun, it will, so much fun. But in the end they don't. They dump too much food in no matter how often they're told to be careful, to use just a pinch, and even after they've read Biblical-sounding fables about the fish who ate too much and grew too large for its bowl, shattering the sides, they watch gleefully while he consumes like mad, unable to stop. It's fun to watch him eat, to witness the physical manifestation of a fact: the level of Fish's hunger is permanently set to high. In the metaphysics of the fish universe, gluttony is not a sin. The delicate wafers of food fall lightly onto the water, linger on the surface tension, and are

397

broken apart on infinitely eager lips. She overfeeds, too (on the days when she's pretty sure the kids haven't fed him). Her shaking mechanics are sloppy. The light flakes become moist, collude, collect their inertia, and all too often fall out of the can in a large clump. Really, she hasn't neglected the poor fish. "Neglect" seems a word too heavy with submerged intent. Something was bound to slip to the side amid the chaos of the domestic arena. But Fish has sustained himself in terrible conditions. He is the king of all goldfish survivors.

Her own childhood goldfish—named Fred—ended his days in Grayling Pond, a hole near her house in northern Michigan, dug out by the state D.N.R. on a pond-production grant. (Why the Great Lakes state needed more ponds is anyone's guess.) Garnished with a wide band of lily pads, the water a pale yellow, speckled with skeeter-bug ripples, the pond was close to becoming a marsh. Hope you survive, Fred, her father had said as he slopped the fish out of the pail and into the pond. She did not forget the sight of her beloved fish as he slipped from the lip of the bucket and rode the glassine tube of water into the pond. The rest of the summer she imagined his orange form—brilliantly bright and fluorescent against the glimmer of water—in a kind of slow-motion replay. Dumbest animals on earth, she remembered her father adding. Nothing dumber than a carp. Except maybe a catfish, or your goddam mother.

Not long after that afternoon at Grayling Pond, her father left the house in a fit of rage. Gone for good, her mother said. Thank Christ. Then, a few months later, he was killed in a freak accident, crushed between hunks of ice and the hull of a container ship in Duluth. Superior's slush ice was temperamental that winter, chewing up the coastline, damaging bulkheads. Her father had signed on as one of the men who went down with poles and gave furtive pokes and prods, in the tradition of those Michigan rivermen who had once dislodged logjams with their peaveys and pike poles, standing atop the timber in their spiked boots, sparring with magnificent forces. Accounts varied, but the basic story was that the ice shifted, some kind of crevasse formed, and he slipped in. Then the lake gave a heave and his legs were crushed, clamped in the jaw of God's stupid justice. As she liked to imagine it, he had just enough time to piece together a little prayer asking for forgiveness for being a failure of a father ("Dear Heavenly Father, forgive me for my huge failings as a father to my dear daughter and even more for my gaping failure as a husband to my wife") and for dumping Fred ("and for getting rid of that fish my daughter loved more than me"), and then to watch as the pale winter sun slipped quickly away while the other men urged him to remain calm and told him that he'd be fine and they'd have him out in a minute or so, while knowing for certain that they wouldn't.

Long after her father was gone, she imagined Fred lurking in the lower reaches of Grayling Pond, in the coolest pockets, trying to conserve his energy. Sometimes, when she was cleaning upstairs and dusting Teddy's room, she would pause in the deep, warm, silent heart of a suburban afternoon and watch Fish as he dangled asleep, wide-eyed, unmoving, just fluffing his fins softly on occasion. One time she even tried it herself, standing still, suspended in the dense fluid of an unending array of demanding tasks—cleaning, cooking, washing, grocery shopping, snack-getting—while outside the birds chirped and the traffic hissed past on the parkway.

The marriage had fallen apart abruptly. Her husband—who worked in the city as a corporate banker and left the house each morning at dawn with the *Times*, still wrapped in its bright-blue delivery bag, tucked beneath his arm—had betrayed his vows. One evening, he'd arrived home from work with what seemed to be a new face: his teeth were abnormally white. He'd had them bleached in the city. (In retrospect, she saw that his bright teeth were the first hint of his infidelity.) He had found a dentist on Park Avenue. Soon he was coming home late on some nights and not at all on others, under the vague pretense of work obligations. In Japan, he explained, people sleep overnight in town as a sign of their dedication to business; they rent cubicles just wide enough for a body, like coffins, he said, and for days when he did not return she thought of those small compartments and she chose to believe him. (Of course I know about the Japanese, she had said, emphatically.) Then one night she found him in the bathroom with a bar of soap, rubbing it gently against his wedding ring. It's too tight, he said. I'm just trying to loosen it. When others were perplexed by the fact that she had not deduced his infidelity, picked up on the clues, during those fall months, she felt compelled (though she never did) to describe the marriage in all of its long complexity—fifteen years—starting with the honeymoon in Spain: the parador in Chinchón, outside Madrid, that had once been a monastery, standing naked with him at the balcony door in the dusky night air listening to the sounds of the village and the splash of the pool. She had given up her career for the relationship, for the family. She had given up plenty in order to stay home for Teddy's and Annie's formative years, to make sure those brain synapses formed correctly, to be assured that the right connections were fused. (Because studies had made it clear that a kid's success depends on the first few years. It was important to develop the fine motor skills, to have the appropriate hand play, not to mention critical reasoning skills, before the age of four!) So, yes, she guessed the whole decision to give herself over to the domestic job had been an act of free will, but now it felt as though the act itself had been carried out in the conditions of betrayal that would eventually unfold before her.

Fish had come into the family fold in a plastic Baggie of water, bulging dangerously, knotted at the top, with a mate, Sammy, who would end up a floater two days later. Pet Universe had given free goldfish to all the kids on a preschool field trip. In less than a year, Fish had grown too big for his starter bowl and begun to tighten his spiralled laps, restricted in his movements by his gathering bulk and the glass walls of the bowl. Then he graduated to a classic five-gallon bowl, where, in the course of the next few years, he grew, until one afternoon, still deep in what seemed to be a stable domestic situation, with the kids off at school, she went out to Pet Universe and found a large tank and some water-prep drops and a filter unit, one that sat on the rim and produced a sleek, foun-tainlike curl of water, and some turquoise gravel and a small figurine to keep the fish company: a cartoonish pirate galleon—a combination of Mark Twain riv-erboat and man-of-war—with an exaggerated bow and an orange plastic paddle wheel that spun around in the tank's currents until it gobbed up and stuck. The figurine, which was meant to please the eyes of children, had that confused mix of design that put commercial viability ahead of the truth. Teddy and Annie hated it. Ultimately, the figure served one purpose. It rearranged the conceptual space of the tank and gave the illusion that Fish now had something to do, something to work around, during his languorous afternoon laps, and she found herself going in to watch him, giving deep philosophical consideration to his actions: Did Fish remember that he had passed that way before? Was he aware of his eternal hell, caught in the tank's glass grip? Or did he feel wondrously free, swimming—for all he knew—in Lake Superior, an abundant, wide field of water, with some glass obstructions here and there? Was he basically free of wants, needs, and everything else? Did he wonder at the food miraculously ap-pearing atop the surface tension, food to be approached with parted lips?

One evening, after observing Fish, when she was at the sink looking out the window at the yard, she saw her husband there, along the south side, holding his phone to his ear and lifting his free hand up and down from his waist in a slight flapping gesture that she knew indicated that he was emotionally agi-tated.

Shortly after that, the tank began to murk up. Through the dim months of January and February, the filter clotted, the flow stopped, and stringy green silk grew on the lip of the waterfall. The murk thickened. In the center of the dark-ness, Fish swam in random patterns and became a sad, hopeless entity curled into his plight. He was no longer fooled by his short-term memory into think-ing that he was eternally free. Nor was he bored by the repetitive nature of his laps, going around the stupid ship figurine, sinking down into the gravel, picking—typical bottom-feeder—for scraps. Instead, he was lost in the eternal roar of an isotropic universe, flinging himself wildly within the expanding big bang of tank murk. On occasion, he found his way to the light and rubbed his eye against the glass, peering out in a judgmental way. But no one was there to see him. No one seemed available to witness these outward glances. Until the day when Teddy, now just Ted, noticed and said, Mom, Mom, the tank, and she went and cleaned it, but only after she had knocked her knuckle a few times on the glass and seen that he was alive, consumed in the dark but moving and seemingly healthy. Then she felt awe at the fact that life was sustainable even under the most abhorrent conditions. She felt a fleeting connection between this awe and the possibility that God exists. But then she reminded herself that it was only Fish. Just frickin' Fish, she thought. Here I am so weepy and sad, trying to make sense of my horrible situation, that something like this will give me hope. Of course, she was probably also thinking back to that afternoon, watching her father sluice Fred down into the warm waters of the shallow pond in Michigan. Her memory of it was profoundly clear. The vision of the fish itself—pristine and orange—travelling through the water as it spilled from the bucket was exact and perfect.

She set to work scooping out the water with an old Tupperware bowl, replacing it in increments so the chlorine would evaporate, driving to Pet Universe to get another cotton filter, some water-clarifying drops, and a pound sack of activated charcoal nuggets. She disassembled the pump mechanism—a small magnet attached to a ring of plastic that hovered, embraced by a larger magnet. Somehow the larger magnet cooperated with the magnet on the plastic device and used physical laws of some sort to suck the water up and through the filter, where it cascaded over the wide lip and twisted as it approached the surface. It seemed to her as her fingers cleaned the device that it was not only a thing of great simplicity and beauty but also something much deeper, a tool meant to sustain Fish's life and, in turn, his place in the family. The afternoon was clear, blue-skied, wintry bright—and out the kitchen window she saw the uncut lawn, dark straw brown, matted down in van Gogh swirls, frosted with cold. Past the lawn, the woods, through which she could see the cars moving on the parkway, stood stark and brittle in the direct implications of the winter light. It was a fine scene, embarrassingly suburban, but certainly fine. Back upstairs, she saw Fish swimming jauntily in his new conditions and she was pretty sure that he was delighted, moving with swift strokes from one end of the tank to the other, skirting the figurine professionally, wagging his back fin—what was that called? was it the caudal fin?—fashionably, like a cabaret dancer working her fan. A beautiful tail, unfurling in a windswept motion in the clearing water. When she leaned down for a closer look, it became apparent that the fin was much, much larger than it seemed when it was in action and twining in on itself. When Fish paused, it swayed open beautifully—a fine, healthy, wide carp tail. Along his sides, he had the usual scars of an abused fish, a wound or two, a missing scale, a new, smaller growth of some kind down near his anal fin. But otherwise he seemed big, brutally healthy, still blinking off the shock of the sudden glare.

Then the tank fell back into its murk, got worse, stank up, and became, well, completely, utterly, fantastically murky. Here one might note tangentially: if, as Aristotle claims, poetry is something of graver import than history—partly because of the naturalness of its statements—then Fish was more important than any domestic history, because Fish was poetic, in that he had succumbed to the darkness that had formed around him, and yet he was unwilling to die— or, rather, he *did not* die. He kept himself alive. He kept at it. Somehow he gathered enough oxygen from the water—perhaps by staying directly under the trickle that made its way over the lip of the filter. Of course, by nature he was a bottom-feeder, a mudfish, accustomed to slime and algae and to an environment that, for other fish, would be insufferable. No trout could sustain itself in these conditions. Not even close. A good brookie would've gone belly up long ago. A brookie would want cool pockets of a fast-moving stream, sweet riffles, bubbling swirls, to live a good life. But Fish stood in his cave of slime, graver than the history of the household into which his glass enclave had been placed: Dad packing his suitcases, folding and refolding his trousers and taking his ties off the electric tie rack and carefully folding them inside sheets of tissue, and then taking his shoes and putting each pair, highly glossed oxfords (he was one of the few to make regular use of the shoeshine stand at Grand Central), into cotton drawstring sacks, and then emptying his top dresser drawer, taking his cufflinks, his old wallets, and a few other items. All of this stuff, the history of the house, the legal papers signed and sealed and the attendant separation agreement and, of course, the divorce that left her the house—all this historical material was transpiring outside the gist of Fish. He could chart his course and touch each corner of the tank and still not know shit. But he understood something. That much was clear. The world is a mucky mess. It gets clotted up, submerged in its own gunk. End of story.

He brushed softly against the beard of algae that hung from the filter device, worked his way over to the figurine, leaned his flank against her side, and felt the shift of temperature as night fell—Teddy liked to sleep with the window cracked a bit—and the oxygen content increased slightly as the water cooled. During the day, the sun cranked through the window, the tank grew warm, and he didn't move at all, unless someone came into the room and knocked on the tank or the floor, and then he jerked forward slightly before quickly settling down. A few times the downstairs door slammed hard enough to jolt him awake. Or there was a smashing sound from the kitchen. Or voices. "What in the world should we do?" "I would most certainly like this to be amicable, for the sake of the kids." Or a shoe striking the wall in the adjacent master bedroom. At times he felt a kinship with the figurine, as if another carp were there alongside him, waiting, hovering. Other times he felt a slight kinship with the sides of the tank, which touched his gill flaps when he went in search of light. God, if only he knew that he, Fish, was at the very center of the domestic arena, holding court with his own desire to live. He might have died happily right there! But he was not a symbolic fish. He seemed to have no desire to stand as the tragic hero in this drama.

• • •

Sent out, told to stay out, the kids were playing together down in the yard so that, inside, the two central figures, Dad and Mom, might have one final talk. The kids were standing by the playhouse—which itself was falling to decrepitude, dark-gray smears of mildew growing on its fake logs—pretending to be a mom and a dad themselves, although they were a bit too old and self-conscious for playacting. Perhaps they were old enough to know that they were faking it on two levels, regressing to a secondary level of playacting they'd pretty much rejected but playing Mom and Dad anyway, Teddy saying, I'm gonna call my lawyer if you don't settle with me, and Annie responding, in her high sweet voice, I knew you'd lawyer up on me, I just knew it, and then both kids giggling in that secretive, all-knowing way they have. Overhead, the tree branches were fuzzed with the first buds of spring, but it was still a bit cold, and words hovered in vapor from their mouths and darkness was falling fast over the trees, and beyond the trees the commuter traffic hissed unnoticed.

If you were heading south on the Merritt Parkway on the afternoon of April 3rd, and you happened to look to your right through the trees after Exit 35, you might've seen them, back beyond the old stone piles, the farm fences that no longer held significance except maybe as a reminder of the Robert Frost poem about good fences and good neighbors and all of that: two kids leaning against an old playhouse while the house behind them appeared cozy, warm, and, clearly, expensive. A fleeting tableau without much meaning to the commuting folk aside from the formulaic economics of the matter: near the parkway = reduced value, but an expensive area + buffer of stone walls + old trees + trendiness of area = more value.

There is something romantic and heartening about seeing those homes through the trees from the vantage of the parkway—those safe, confided Connecticut lives. Inside the house, the secret goldfish is going about his deeply moving predicament, holding his life close to the gills, subdued by the dark but unwilling to relinquish his cellular activities, the Krebs cycle still spinning its carbohydrate breakdown. The secret goldfish draws close to the center of the cosmos. In the black hole of familial carelessness, he awaits the graceful moment when the mother, spurred on by Teddy, will give yet another soft shriek. She'll lean close to the glass and put her eye there to search for Fish. Fish will be there, of course, hiding in the core of the murk near the figurine, playing possum, so that she will, when she sees him, feel the pitiful sinking in her gut—remembering the preschool field trip to Pet Universe—and a sorrow so deep it will send her to her knees to weep. She'll think of the sad little pet funeral she hoped to perform when Fish died (when Fish's sidekick died, Dad flushed him away): a small but deeply meaningful moment in the backyard, with the trowel, digging a shoebox-size hole, putting the fish in, performing a small rite ("Dear Lord, dear Heavenly Father, dear Fish God, God of Fish, in Fish's name we gather here to put our dear fish to rest"), and then placing atop the burial mound a big rock painted with the word FISH. It would be a moment designed to teach the children the ways of loss, and the soft intricacies of seeing something that was once alive now dead, and to clarify that sharp defining difference, to smooth it over a bit, so that they will remember the moment and know, later, recalling it, that she was a good mother, the kind who would hold pet funerals.

But Fish is alive. His big old carp gills clutch and lick every tiny trace of oxygen from the froth of depravity in the inexplicably determinate manner that only animals have. He will have nothing to do with this household. And later that evening, once Dad is gone, they'll hold a small party to celebrate his resurrection, because they had assumed—as was natural in these circumstances—that he was dead, or near enough death to be called dead, having near-death visions, as the dead are wont: that small pinpoint of light at the end of the tunnel and visions of an existence as a fish in some other ethery world, a better world for a fish, with fresh clear water bursting with oxygen and other carp large and small in communal bliss and just enough muck and mud for good pickings. After the celebration, before bedtime, they'll cover the top of the clean tank in plastic wrap and, working together, moving slowly with the unison of pallbearers, being careful not to slosh the water, carry it down the stairs to the family room, where with a soft patter of congratulatory applause they'll present Fish with a new home, right next to the television set.

Susan Minot

LUST

SUSAN MINOT (1956–) was born in Boston and grew up in Manchester-by-the-Sea. Her first novel, *Monkeys*, received the Prix Femina Étranger in France. Her short stories have been selected for inclusion in *The Best American Short Stories, Pushcart Prize,* and *The O. Henry Awards.* She also wrote the screenplay for Bernardo Bertolucci's *Stealing Beauty.* She lives in New York City and Maine.

Leo was from a long time ago, the first one I ever saw nude. In the spring before the Hellmans filled their pool, we'd go down there in the deep end, with baby oil, and like that. I met him the first month away at boarding school. He had a halo from the campus light behind him. I flipped.

Roger was fast. In his illegal car, we drove to the reservoir, the radio blaring, talking fast, fast, fast. He was always going for my zipper. He got kicked out sophomore year.

By the time the band got around to playing "Wild Horses," I had tasted Bruce's tongue. We were clicking in the shadows on the other side of the amplifier, out of Mrs. Donovan's line of vision. It tasted like salt, with my neck bent back, because we had been dancing so hard before.

Tim's line: "I'd like to see you in a bathing suit." I knew it was his line when he said the exact same thing to Annie Hines.

You'd go on walks to get off campus. It was raining like hell, my sweater as sopped as a wet sheep. Tim pinned me to a tree, the woods light brown and dark brown, a white house half hidden with the lights already on. The water was as loud as a crowd hissing. He made certain comments about my forehead, about my cheeks.

We started off sitting at one end of the couch and then our feet were squished against the armrest and then he went over to turn off the TV and came back after he had taken off his shirt and then we slid onto the floor and he got up again to close the door, then came back to me, a body waiting on the rug.

You'd try to wipe off the table or to do the dishes and Willie would untuck your shirt and get his hands up under in front, standing behind you, making puffy noises in your ear.

He likes it when I wash my hair. He covers his face with it and if I start to say something, he goes, "Shush."

For a long time, I had Philip on the brain. The less they noticed you, the more you got them on the brain.

My parents had no idea. Parents never really know what's going on, especially when you're away at school most of the time. If she met them, my mother might say, "Oliver seems nice" or "I like that one" without much of an opinion. If she didn't like them, "He's a funny fellow, isn't he?" or "Johnny's perfectly nice but a drink of water." My father was too shy to talk to them at all unless they played sports and he'd ask them about that.

The sand was almost cold underneath because the sun was long gone. Eben piled a mound over my feet, patting around my ankles, the ghostly surf rumbling behind him in the dark. He was the first person I ever knew who died, later that summer, in a car crash. I thought about it for a long time.

"Come here," he says on the porch.
    I go over to the hammock and he takes my wrist with two fingers.
    "What?"
    He kisses my palm then directs my hand to his fly.

Songs went with whichever boy it was. "Sugar Magnolia" was Tim, with the line "Rolling in the rushes / down by the riverside." With "Darkness Darkness," I'd picture Philip with his long hair. Hearing "Under My Thumb" there'd be the smell of Jamie's suede jacket.

We hid in the listening rooms during study hall. With a record cover over the door's window, the teacher on duty couldn't look in. I came out flushed and heady and back at the dorm was surprised how red my lips were in the mirror.

One weekend at Simon's brother's, we stayed inside all day with the shades down, in bed, then went out to Store 24 to get some ice cream. He stood at the magazine rack and read through *MAD* while I got butterscotch sauce, craving something sweet.

I could do some things well. Some things I was good at, like math or painting or even sports, but the second a boy put his arm around me, I forgot about wanting to do anything else, which felt like a relief at first until it became like sinking into a muck.

It was different for a girl.

When we were little, the brothers next door tied up our ankles. They held the door of the goat house and wouldn't let us out till we showed them our underpants. Then they'd forget about being after us and when we played whiffle ball, I'd be just as good as they were.

Then it got to be different. Just because you have on a short skirt, they yell from the cars, slowing down for a while, and if you don't look, they screech off and call you a bitch.

"What's the matter with me?" they say, point-blank.
    Or else, "Why won't you go out with me? I'm not asking you to get married," about to get mad.
    Or it'd be, trying to be reasonable, in a regular voice, "Listen, I just want to have a good time."
    So I'd go because I couldn't think of something to say back that wouldn't be obvious, and if you go out with them, you sort of have to do something.

I sat between Mack and Eddie in the front seat of the pickup. They were having a fight about something. I've a feeling about me.

Certain nights you'd feel a certain surrender, maybe if you'd had wine. The surrender would be forgetting yourself and you'd put your nose to his neck and feel like a squirrel, safe, at rest, in a restful dream. But then you'd start to slip from that and the dark would come in and there'd be a cave. You make out the dim shape of the windows and feel yourself become a cave, filled absolutely with air, or with a sadness that wouldn't stop.

Teenage years. You know just what you're doing and don't see the things that start to get in the way.

Lots of boys, but never two at the same time. One was plenty to keep you in a state. You'd start to see a boy and something would rush over you like a fast storm cloud and you couldn't possibly think of anyone else. Boys took it differently. Their eyes perked up at any little number that walked by. You'd act like you weren't noticing.

The joke was that the school doctor gave out the pill like aspirin. He didn't ask you anything. I was fifteen. We had a picture of him in assembly, holding up an IUD shaped like a T. Most girls were on the pill, if anything, because they couldn't handle a diaphragm. I kept the dial in my top drawer like my mother and thought of her each time I tipped out the yellow tablets in the morning before chapel.

If they were too shy, I'd be more so. Andrew was nervous. We stayed up with his family album, sharing a pack of Old Golds. Before it got light, we turned on the TV. A man was explaining how to plant seedlings. His mouth jerked to the side in a tic. Andrew thought it was a riot and kept imitating him. I laughed to be polite. When we finally dozed off, he dared to put his arm around me, but that was it.

You wait till they come to you. With half fright, half swagger, they stand one step down. They dare to touch the button on your coat then lose their nerve and quickly drop their hand so you—you'd do anything for them. You touch their cheek.

The girls sit around in the common room and talk about boys, smoking their heads off.
   "What are you complaining about?" says Jill to me when we talk about problems.
   "Yeah," says Giddy. "You always have a boyfriend."
   I look at them and think, As if.

I thought the worst thing anyone could call you was a cock-teaser. So, if you flirted, you had to be prepared to go through with it. Sleeping with someone was perfectly normal once you had done it. You didn't really worry about it. But there were other problems. The problems had to do with something else entirely.

Mack was during the hottest summer ever recorded. We were renting a house on an island with all sorts of other people. No one slept during the heat wave, walking around the house with nothing on which we were used to because of the nude beach. In the living room, Eddie lay on top of a coffee table to cool off. Mack and I, with the bedroom door open for air, sweated and sweated all night.

"I can't take this," he said at three A.M. "I'm going for a swim." He and some guys down the hall went to the beach. The heat put me on edge. I sat on a cracked chest by the open window and smoked and smoked till I felt even worse, waiting for something—I guess for him to get back.

One was on a camping trip in Colorado. We zipped our sleeping bags together, the coyotes' hysterical chatter far away. Other couples murmured in other tents. Paul was up before sunrise, starting a fire for breakfast. He wasn't much of a talker in the daytime. At night, his hand leafed about in the hair at my neck.

There'd be times when you overdid it. You'd get carried away. All the next day, you'd be in a total fog, delirious, absent-minded, crossing the street and nearly getting run over.

The more girls a boy has, the better. He has a bright look, having reaped fruits, blooming. He stalks around, sure-shouldered, and you have the feeling he's got more in him, a fatter heart, more stories to tell. For a girl, with each boy it's as though a petal gets plucked each time.

Then you start to get tired. You begin to feel diluted, like watered-down stew.

Oliver came skiing with us. We lolled by the fire after everyone had gone to bed. Each creak you'd think was someone coming downstairs. The silver loop bracelet he gave me had been a present from his girlfriend before.

On vacations, we went skiing, or you'd go south if someone invited you. Some people had apartments in New York that their families hardly ever used. Or summer houses, or older sisters. We always managed to find someplace to go.

We made the plan at coffee hour. Simon snuck out and met me at Main Gate after lights-out. We crept to the chapel and spent the night in the balcony. He tasted like onions from a submarine sandwich.

The boys are one of two ways: either they can't sit still or they don't move. In front of the TV, they won't budge. On weekends they play touch football while we sit on the sidelines, picking blades of grass to chew on, and watch. We're always watching them run around. We shiver in the stands, knocking our boots together to keep our toes warm, and they whizz across the ice, chopping their sticks around the puck. When they're in the rink, they refuse to look at you, only eyeing each other beneath low helmets. You cheer for them but they don't look up, even if it's a face-off when nothing's happening, even if they're doing drills before any game has started at all.

• • •

Dancing under the pink tent, he bent down and whispered in my ear. We slipped away to the lawn on the other side of the hedge. Much later, as he was leaving the buffet with two plates of eggs and sausage, I saw the grass stains on the knees of his white pants.

Tim's was shaped like a banana, with a graceful curve to it. They're all different. Willie's like a bunch of walnuts when nothing was happening, another's as thin as a thin hot dog. But it's like faces; you're never really surprised.

Still, you're not sure what to expect.

I look into his face and he looks back. I look into his eyes and they look back at mine. Then they look down at my mouth so I look at his mouth, then back to his eyes then, backing up, at his whole face. I think, Who? Who are you? His head tilts to one side.
    I say, "Who are you?"
    "What do you mean?"
    "Nothing."
    I look at his eyes again, deeper. Can't tell who he is, what he thinks.
    "What?" he says. I look at his mouth.
    "I'm just wondering," I say and go wandering across his face. Study the chin line. It's shaped like a persimmon.
    "Who are you? What are you thinking?"
    He says, "What the hell are you talking about?"

Then they get mad after, when you say enough is enough. After, when it's easier to explain that you don't want to. You wouldn't dream of saying that maybe you weren't really ready to in the first place.

Gentle Eddie. We waded into the sea, the waves round and plowing in, buffalo-headed, slapping our thighs. I put my arms around his freckled shoulders and he held me up, buoyed by the water, and rocked me like a sea shell.

I had no idea whose party it was, the apartment jam-packed, stepping over people in the hallway. The room with the music was practically empty, the bare floor, me in red shoes. This fellow slides onto one knee and takes me around the waist and we rock to jazzy tunes, with my toes pointing heavenward, and waltz and spin and dip to "Smoke Gets in Your Eyes" or "I'll Love You Just for Now." He puts his head to my chest, runs a sweeping hand down my inside thigh and we go loose-limbed and sultry and as smooth as silk and I stamp my red heels and he takes me into a swoon. I never saw him again after that but I thought, I could have loved that one.

You wonder how long you can keep it up. You begin to feel as if you're showing through, like a bathroom window that only lets in grey light, the kind you can't see out of.

They keep coming around. Johnny drives up at Easter vacation from Baltimore and I let him in the kitchen with everyone sound asleep. He has friends waiting in the car.

"What are you, crazy? It's pouring out there," I say.

"It's okay," he says. "They understand."

So he gets some long kisses from me, against the refrigerator, before he goes because I hate those girls who push away a boy's face as if she were made out of Ivory soap, as if she's that much greater than he is.

The note on my cubby told me to see the headmaster. I had no idea for what. He had received complaints about my amorous displays on the town green. It was Willie that spring. The headmaster told me he didn't care what I did but that Casey Academy had a reputation to uphold in the town. He lowered his glasses on his nose. "We've got twenty acres of woods on this campus," he said. "If you want to smooch with your boyfriend, there are twenty acres for you to do it out of the public eye. You read me?"

Everybody'd get weekend permissions for different places, then we'd all go to someone's house whose parents were away. Usually there'd be more boys than girls. We raided the liquor closet and smoked pot at the kitchen table and you'd never know who would end up where, or with whom. There were always disasters. Ceci got bombed and cracked her head open on the banister and needed stitches. Then there was the time Wendel Blair walked through the picture window at the Lowes' and got slashed to ribbons.

He scared me. In bed, I didn't dare look at him. I lay back with my eyes closed, luxuriating because he knew all sorts of expert angles, his hands never fumbling, going over my whole body, pressing the hair up and off the back of my head, giving an extra hip shove, as if to say *There*. I parted my eyes slightly, keeping the screen of my lashes low because it was too much to look at him, his mouth loose and pink and parted, his eyes looking through my forehead, or kneeling up, looking through my throat. I was ashamed but couldn't look him in the eye.

· · ·

You wonder about things feeling a little off-kilter. You begin to feel like a piece of pounded veal.

At boarding school, everyone gets depressed. We go in and see the housemother, Mrs. Gunther. She got married when she was eighteen. Mr. Gunther was her high school sweetheart, the only boyfriend she ever had.
"And you knew you wanted to marry him right off?" we ask her.
She smiles and says, "Yes."
"They always want something from you," says Jill, complaining about her boyfriend.
"Yeah," says Giddy. "You always feel like you have to deliver something."
"You do," says Mrs. Gunther. "Babies."

After sex, you curl up like a shrimp, something deep inside you ruined, slammed in a place that sickens at slamming, and slowly you fill up with an overwhelming sadness, an elusive gaping worry. You don't try to explain it, filled with the knowledge that it's nothing after all, everything filling up finally and absolutely with death. After the briskness of loving, loving stops. And you roll over with death stretched out alongside you like a feather boa, or a snake, light as air, and you . . . you don't even ask for anything or try to say something to him because it's obviously your own damn fault. You haven't been able to—to what? To open your heart. You open your legs but can't, or don't dare anymore, to open your heart.

It starts this way:
You stare into their eyes. They flash like all the stars are out. They look at you seriously, their eyes at a low burn and their hands no matter what starting off shy and with such a gentle touch that the only thing you can do is take that tenderness and let yourself be swept away. When, with one attentive finger they tuck the hair behind your ear, you—
You do everything they want.
Then comes after. After when they don't look at you. They scratch their balls, stare at the ceiling. Or if they do turn, their gaze is altogether changed. They are surprised. They turn casually to look at you, distracted, and get a mild distracted surprise. You're gone. Their blank look tells you that the girl they were fucking is not there anymore. You seem to have disappeared.

Rick Moody

BOYS

RICK MOODY (1961–) is the author, most recently, of *The Diviners*, a novel, and a collection of novellas entitled *Right Livelihoods*.

Boys enter the house, boys enter the house. Boys, and with them the ideas of boys (ideas leaden, reductive, inflexible), enter the house. Boys, two of them, wound into hospital packaging, boys with infant pattern baldness, slung in the arms of parents, boys dreaming of breasts, enter the house. Twin boys, kettles on the boil, boys in hideous vinyl knapsacks that young couples from Edison, NJ, wear on their shirt fronts, knapsacks coated with baby saliva and staphylococcus and milk vomit, enter the house. Two boys, one striking the other with a rubberized hot dog, enter the house. Two boys, one of them striking the other with a willow switch about the head and shoulders, the other crying, enter the house. Boys enter the house, speaking nonsense. Boys enter the house, calling for Mother. On a Sunday, in May, a day one might nearly describe as *perfect*, an ice cream truck comes slowly down the lane, chimes inducing salivation, and children run after it, not long after which boys dig a hole in the backyard and bury their younger sister's dolls *two feet down*, so that she will never find these dolls and these dolls will *rot in hell*, after which boys enter the house. Boys, trailing after their father like he is the Second Goddamned Coming of Christ Goddamned Almighty, enter the house, repair to the basement to watch baseball. Boys enter the house, site of devastation, and repair immediately to the kitchen, where they mix lighter fluid, vanilla pudding, drain-opening lye, balsamic vinegar, blue food coloring, calamine lotion, cottage cheese, ants, a plastic lizard that one of them received in his Xmas stocking, tacks, leftover mashed potatoes, Spam, frozen lima beans, and chocolate syrup in a medium-sized saucepan and heat over a low flame until thick, afterwards transferring the contents of this saucepan into a Pyrex lasagna dish, baking the Pyrex lasagna dish in the oven for nineteen minutes before attempting to persuade their sister that she should *eat the mixture;* later they smash three family heirlooms (the last, a glass egg, *intentionally*) in a two-and-a-half-hour stretch, whereupon they are sent to their bedroom, until freed, in each case thirteen minutes after. Boys enter the house, starchy in pressed shirts and flannel pants that *itch so bad*, fresh from Sunday School instruction, blond and brown locks (respectively) plastered down, but

413

even so with a number of cowlicks protruding at odd angles, disconsolate and humbled, uncertain if boyish things—such as shooting at the neighbor's dog with a pump action bb gun and gagging the fat boy up the street with a bandanna and showing their shriveled boy-penises to their younger sister—are exempted from the commandment to *Love the Lord thy God with all thy heart and with all thy soul, and with all thy might, and thy neighbor as thyself.* Boys enter the house in baseball gear (only one of the boys can hit): in their spikes, in mismatched tube socks that smell like Stilton cheese. Boys enter the house in soccer gear. Boys enter the house carrying skates. Boys enter the house with lacrosse sticks, and, soon after, tossing a lacrosse ball lightly in the living room they destroy a lamp. One boy enters the house sporting basketball clothes, the other wearing jeans and a sweatshirt. One boy enters the house bleeding profusely and is taken out to get stitches, the other watches. Boys enter the house at the end of term carrying report cards, sneak around the house like spies of foreign nationality, looking for a place to hide the report cards for the time being (under the toaster? in a medicine cabinet?). One boy with a black eye enters the house, one boy without. Boys with acne enter the house and squeeze and prod large skin blemishes in front of their sister. Boys with acne treatment products hidden about their persons enter the house. Boys, standing just up the street, sneak cigarettes behind a willow in the Elys' yard, wave smoke away from their natural fibers, hack terribly, experience nausea, then enter the house. Boys call each other *retard, homo, geek,* and, later, *Neckless Thug, Theater Fag,* and enter the house exchanging further epithets. Boys enter the house with nose hair clippers, chase sister around the house threatening to depilate her eyebrows. She cries. Boys attempt to induce girls to whom they would not have spoken only six or eight months prior to enter the house with them. Boys enter the house with girls efflorescent and homely, and attempt to induce girls to sneak into their bedroom, as they still share a single bedroom; girls refuse. Boys enter the house, go to separate bedrooms. Boys, with their father (an arm around each of them), enter the house, but of the monologue preceding and succeeding this entrance, not a syllable is preserved. Boys enter the house having masturbated in a variety of locales. Boys enter the house having masturbated in train station bathrooms, in forests, in beach houses, in football bleachers at night under the stars, in cars (under a blanket), in the shower, backstage, on a plane, the boys masturbate constantly, identically, three times a day in some cases, desire like a madness upon them, at the mere sound of certain words, words that sound like other words, *interrogative* reminding them of *intercourse, beast* reminding them of *breast, sects* reminding them of *sex,* and so forth, the boys are not very smart yet, and, as they enter the house, they feel, as always, immense shame at the scale of this *self-abusive cogitation,* seeing a classmate, seeing a billboard, seeing a fire hydrant, seeing things that should not induce thoughts of masturbation (their sister, e.g.) and then thinking of masturbation anyway. Boys enter the house, go to their rooms, remove sexually explicit magazines from hidden stashes, put on loud music, feel despair. Boys enter the house worried; they argue. The boys are ugly, they are failures, they will never be loved, they enter the house. Boys enter the house and kiss their mother, who feels differently, now they have outgrown her. Boys enter the house, kiss their mother, she explains the seriousness of their sister's difficulty, *her diagnosis.* Boys enter the house, having attempted to locate the spot in their yard where the dolls were buried, eight or nine years prior, without success; they go to their sister's room, sit by her bed. Boys enter the house and tell their completely bald sister jokes about baldness. Boys hold either hand of their sister, laying aside differences, having trudged grimly into the house. Boys skip school, enter house, hold vigil. Boys enter the house after their parents have both gone off to work, sit with their sister and with their sister's nurse. Boys enter the house carrying cases of beer. Boys enter the house, very worried now, didn't know more worry was possible. Boys enter the house carrying controlled substances, neither having told the other that he is carrying a controlled substance, though an intoxicated posture seems appropriate under the circumstances. Boys enter the house *weeping* and hear weeping around them. Boys enter the house, embarrassed, silent, anguished, keening, afflicted, angry, woeful, *grief-stricken.* Boys enter the house on vacation, each clasps the hand of the other with genuine warmth, the one wearing dark colors and having shaved a portion of his head, the other having grown his hair out longish and wearing, uncharacteristically, a tie-dyed shirt. Boys enter the house on vacation and argue bitterly about politics (other subjects are no longer discussed), one boy supporting the Maoist insurgency in a certain Southeast Asian country, one believing that *to change the system you need to work inside it;* one boy threatens to *beat the living shit out of the other,* refuses crème brûlée, though it is created by his mother in order to keep the peace. One boy writes home and thereby enters the house only through a mail slot: he argues that the other boy is *crypto-fascist,* believing that *the market can seek its own level on questions of ethics and morals;* boys enter the house on vacation and announce future professions; boys enter the house on vacation and change their minds about professions; boys enter the house on vacation and one boy brings home a *sweetheart,* but throws a tantrum when it is suggested that the *sweetheart* will have to retire on the folding bed in the basement; the other boy, having no *sweetheart,* is distant and withdrawn, preferring to talk late into the night about family members gone from this world. Boys enter the house several weeks apart. Boys enter the house on days of heavy rain. Boys enter the house, in different calendar years, and upon entering, the boys seem to do nothing but compose manifestos, for the benefit of parents; they follow their mother around the place, having fashioned their manifestos in celebration of brand-new independence: *Mom, I like to lie in bed late into the morning watching game shows,* or, *I'm never going to date anyone but artists from now on, mad girls, dreamers, practicers of black magic,* or *A man should eat bologna, sliced meats are important,* or, *An Amer-*

ican should bowl at least once a year, but these manifestos apply only for brief spells, after which they are reversed or discarded. Boys don't enter the house, at all, except as ghostly afterimages of younger selves, fleeting images of sneakers dashing up a staircase; soggy towels on the floor of the bathroom; blue jeans coiled like asps in the basin of the washing machine; boys as an absence of boys, blissful at first, you put a thing down on a spot, put this book down, come back later, *it's still there;* you buy a box of cookies, eat three, later three are missing. Nevertheless, when boys next enter the house, which they ultimately must do, it's a relief, even if it's only in preparation for weddings of acquaintances from boyhood, one boy has a beard, neatly trimmed, the other has rakish sideburns, one boy wears a hat, the other boy thinks hats are ridiculous, one boy wears khakis pleated at the waist, the other wears denim, but each changes into his suit (one suit fits well, one is a little tight), as though suits are *the* liminary marker of adulthood. Boys enter the house after the wedding and they are slapping each other on the back and yelling at anyone who will listen, *It's a party!* One boy enters the house, carried by friends, having been arrested (after the wedding) for driving while intoxicated, complexion ashen; the other boy tries to keep his mouth shut: the car is on its side in a ditch, the car has the top half of a tree broken over its bonnet, the car has struck another car which has in turn struck a third, *Everyone will have seen.* One boy misses his brother horribly, misses the past, misses a time worth being nostalgic over, *a time that never existed,* back when they set their sister's playhouse on fire; the other boy avoids all mention of that time; each of them is once the boy who enters the house alone, missing the other, each is devoted and each callous, and each plays his part on the telephone, over the course of months. Boys enter the house with fishing gear, according to prearranged date and time, arguing about whether to use *lures* or *live bait,* in order to meet their father for the *fishing adventure,* after which boys enter the house again, almost immediately, with live bait, having settled the question; boys boast of having caught fish in the past, though no fish has ever been caught: *Remember when the blues were biting?* Boys enter the house carrying their father, slumped. Happens so fast. Boys rush into the house leading EMTs to the couch in the living room where the body lies, boys enter the house, boys enter the house, boys enter the house. Boys hold open the threshold, awesome threshold that has welcomed them when they haven't even been able to welcome themselves, that threshold which welcomed them when they *had* to be taken in, here is its tarnished knocker, here is its euphonious bell, here's where the boys had to sand the door down because it never would hang right in the frame, here are the scuff marks from when boys were on the wrong side of the door *demanding,* here's where there were once milk bottles for the milkman, here's where the newspaper always landed, here's the mail slot, here's the light on the front step, illuminated, here's where the boys are standing, as that beloved man is carried out. Boys, no longer boys, exit.

Bharati Mukherjee

THE MANAGEMENT OF GRIEF

BHARATI MUKHERJEE (1940–) is the author of the novels *Leave It to Me*, *The Holder of the World*, *Jasmine*, *Wife*, *The Tiger's Daughter*, *Desirable Daughters*, and *The Tree Bride;* the short-story collections *Darkness* and *The Middleman and Other Stories;* and the nonfiction books, *Days and Nights in Calcutta* and *The Sorrow and the Terror* (both coauthored with Clark Blaise). She has been awarded many grants and honors, including the National Book Critics Circle Award for Best Fiction (for *The Middleman and Other Stories*), a Guggenheim Fellowship, an NEA grant, and a Canada Council Senior Arts Fellowship. She is currently professor of English at the University of California, Berkeley.

A woman I don't know is boiling tea the Indian way in my kitchen. There are a lot of women I don't know in my kitchen, whispering and moving tactfully. They open doors, rummage through the pantry, and try not to ask me where things are kept. They remind me of when my sons were small, on Mother's Day or when Vikram and I were tired, and they would make big, sloppy omelets. I would lie in bed pretending I didn't hear them.

Dr. Sharma, the treasurer of the Indo-Canada Society, pulls me into the hallway. He wants to know if I am worried about money. His wife, who has just come up from the basement with a tray of empty cups and glasses, scolds him. "Don't bother Mrs. Bhave with mundane details." She looks so monstrously pregnant her baby must be days overdue. I tell her she shouldn't be carrying heavy things. "Shaila," she says, smiling, "this is the fifth." Then she grabs a teenager by his shirttails. He slips his Walkman off his head. He has to be one of her four children; they have the same domed and dented foreheads. "What's the official word now?" she demands. The boy slips the headphones back on. "They're acting evasive, Ma. They're saying it could be an accident or a terrorist bomb."

All morning, the boys have been muttering, Sikh bomb, Sikh bomb. The men, not using the word, bow their heads in agreement. Mrs. Sharma touches her forehead at such a word. At least they've stopped talking about space debris and Russian lasers.

Two radios are going in the dining room. They are tuned to different stations. Someone must have brought the radios down from my boys' bedrooms. I haven't gone into their rooms since Kusum came running across the front lawn in her bathrobe. She looked so funny, I was laughing when I opened the door.

The big TV in the den is being whizzed through American networks and cable channels.

"Damn!" some man swears bitterly. "How can these preachers carry on like nothing's happened?" I want to tell him we're not that important. You look at the audience, and at the preacher in his blue robe with his beautiful white hair, the potted palm trees under a blue sky, and you know they care about nothing.

The phone rings and rings. Dr. Sharma's taken charge. "We're with her," he keeps saying. "Yes, yes, the doctor has given calming pills. Yes, yes, pills are having necessary effect." I wonder if pills alone explain this calm. Not peace, just a deadening quiet. I was always controlled, but never repressed. Sound can reach me, but my body is tensed, ready to scream. I hear their voices all around me. I hear my boys and Vikram cry, "Mommy, Shaila!" and their screams insulate me, like headphones.

The woman boiling water tells her story again and again. "I got the news first. My cousin called from Halifax before six A.M., can you imagine? He'd gotten up for prayers and his son was studying for medical exams and he heard on a rock channel that something had happened to a plane. They said first it had disappeared from the radar, like a giant eraser just reached out. His father called me, so I said to him, what do you mean, 'something bad'? You mean a hijacking? And he said, *Behn*, there is no confirmation of anything yet, but check with your neighbors because a lot of them must be on that plane. So I called poor Kusum straight away. I knew Kusum's husband and daughter were booked to go yesterday."

Kusum lives across the street from me. She and Satish had moved in less than a month ago. They said they needed a bigger place. All these people, the Sharmas and friends from the Indo-Canada Society, had been there for the housewarming. Satish and Kusum made tandoori on their big gas grill and even the white neighbors piled their plates high with that luridly red, charred, juicy chicken. Their younger daughter had danced, and even our boys had broken away from the Stanley Cup telecast to put in a reluctant appearance. Everyone took pictures for their albums and for the community newspapers—another of our families had made it big in Toronto—and now I wonder how many of those happy faces are gone. "Why does God give us so much if all along He intends to take it away?" Kusum asks me.

I nod. We sit on carpeted stairs, holding hands like children. "I never once told him that I loved him," I say. I was too much the well-brought-up woman. I was so well brought up I never felt comfortable calling my husband by his first name.

"It's all right," Kusum says. "He knew. My husband knew. They felt it. Modern young girls have to say it because what they feel is fake."

Kusum's daughter Pam runs in with an overnight case. Pam's in her McDonald's uniform. "Mummy! You have to get dressed!" Panic makes her cranky. "A reporter's on his way here."

"Why?"

"You want to talk to him in your bathrobe?" She starts to brush her mother's long hair. She's the daughter who's always in trouble. She dates Canadian boys and hangs out in the mall, shopping for tight sweaters. The younger one, the goody-goody one according to Pam, the one with a voice so sweet that when she sang *bhajans* for Ethiopian relief even a frugal man like my husband wrote out a hundred-dollar check, *she* was on that plane. *She* was going to spend July and August with grandparents because Pam wouldn't go. Pam said she'd rather waitress at McDonald's. "If it's a choice between Bombay and Wonderland, I'm picking Wonderland," she'd said.

"Leave me alone," Kusum yells. "You know what I want to do? If I didn't have to look after you now, I'd hang myself."

Pam's young face goes blotchy with pain. "Thanks," she says, "don't let me stop you."

"Hush," pregnant Mrs. Sharma scolds Pam. "Leave your mother alone. Mr. Sharma will tackle the reporters and fill out the forms. He'll say what has to be said."

Pam stands her ground. "You think I don't know what Mummy's thinking? *Why her?* That's what. That's sick! Mummy wishes my little sister were alive and I were dead."

Kusum's hand in mine is trembly hot. We continue to sit on the stairs.

She calls before she arrives, wondering if there's anything I need. Her name is Judith Templeton and she's an appointee of the provincial government. "Multiculturalism?" I ask, and she says "partially," but that her mandate is bigger. "I've been told you knew many of the people on the flight," she says. "Perhaps if you'd agree to help us reach the others . . . ?"

She gives me time at least to put on tea water and pick up the mess in the front room. I have a few *samosas* from Kusum's housewarming that I could fry up, but then I think, why prolong this visit?

Judith Templeton is much younger than she sounded. She wears a blue suit with a white blouse and a polka-dot tie. Her blond hair is cut short, her only jewelry is pearl-drop earrings. Her briefcase is new and expensive looking, a gleaming cordovan leather. She sits with it across her lap. When she looks out the front windows onto the street, her contact lenses seem to float in front of her light blue eyes.

"What sort of help do you want from me?" I ask. She has refused the tea, out of politeness, but I insist, along with some slightly stale biscuits.

"I have no experience," she admits. "That is, I have an M.S.W. and I've worked in liaison with accident victims, but I mean I have no experience with a tragedy of this scale—"

"Who could?" I ask.

"—and with the complications of culture, language, and customs. Someone mentioned that Mrs. Bhave is a pillar—because you've taken it more calmly."

At this, perhaps, I frown, for she reaches forward, almost to take my hand. "I hope you understand my meaning, Mrs. Bhave. There are hundreds of people in Metro directly affected, like you, and some of them speak no English. There are some widows who've never handled money or gone on a bus, and there are old parents who still haven't eaten or gone outside their bedrooms. Some houses and apartments have been looted. Some wives are still hysterical. Some husbands are in shock and profound depression. We want to help, but our hands are tied in so many ways. We have to distribute money to some people, and there are legal documents—these things can be done. We have interpreters, but we don't always have the human touch, or maybe the right human touch. We don't want to make mistakes, Mrs. Bhave, and that's why we'd like to ask you to help us."

"More mistakes, you mean," I say.

"Police matters are not in my hands," she answers.

"Nothing I can do will make any difference," I say. "We must all grieve in our own way."

"But you are coping very well. All the people said, Mrs. Bhave is the strongest person of all. Perhaps if the others could see you, talk with you, it would help them."

"By the standards of the people you call hysterical, I am behaving very oddly and very badly, Miss Templeton." I want to say to her, *I wish I could scream, starve, walk into Lake Ontario, jump from a bridge.* "They would not see me as a model. I do not see myself as a model."

I am a freak. No one who has ever known me would think of me reacting this way. This terrible calm will not go away.

She asks me if she may call again, after I get back from a long trip that we all must make. "Of course," I say. "Feel free to call, anytime."

Four days later, I find Kusum squatting on a rock overlooking a bay in Ireland. It isn't a big rock, but it juts sharply out over water. This is as close as we'll ever get to them. June breezes balloon out her sari and unpin her knee-length hair. She has the bewildered look of a sea creature whom the tides have stranded.

It's been one hundred hours since Kusum came stumbling and screaming across my lawn. Waiting around the hospital, we've heard many stories. The police, the diplomats, they tell us things thinking that we're strong, that knowledge is helpful to the grieving, and maybe it is. Some, I know, prefer ignorance, or their own versions. The plane broke into two, they say. Unconsciousness was instantaneous. No one suffered. My boys must have just finished their breakfasts. They loved eating on planes, they loved the smallness of plates, knives, and forks. Last year they saved the airline salt and pepper shakers. Half an hour more and they would have made it to Heathrow.

Kusum says that we can't escape our fate. She says that all those people—our husbands, my boys, her girl with the nightingale voice, all those Hindus, Christians, Sikhs, Muslims, Parsis, and atheists on that plane—were fated to die together off this beautiful bay. She learned this from a swami in Toronto.

I have my Valium.

Six of us "relatives"—two widows and four widowers—chose to spend the day today by the waters instead of sitting in a hospital room and scanning photographs of the dead. That's what they call us now: relatives. I've looked through twenty-seven photos in two days. They're very kind to us, the Irish are very understanding. Sometimes understanding means freeing a tourist bus for this trip to the bay, so we can pretend to spy our loved ones through the glassiness of waves or in sun-speckled cloud shapes.

I could die here, too, and be content.

"What is that, out there?" She's standing and flapping her hands, and for a moment I see a head shape bobbing in the waves. She's standing in the water, I on the boulder. The tide is low, and a round, black, head-sized rock has just risen from the waves. She returns, her sari end dripping and ruined, and her face is a twisted remnant of hope, the way mine was a hundred hours ago, still laughing but inwardly knowing that nothing but the ultimate tragedy could bring two women together at six o'clock on a Sunday morning. I watch her face sag into blankness.

"That water felt warm, Shaila," she says at length.

"You can't," I say. "We have to wait for our turn to come."

I haven't eaten in four days, haven't brushed my teeth.

"I know," she says. "I tell myself I have no right to grieve. They are in a better place than we are. My swami says depression is a sign of our selfishness."

Maybe I'm selfish. Selfishly I break away from Kusum and run, sandals slapping against stones, to the water's edge. What if my boys aren't lying pinned under the debris? What if they aren't stuck a mile below that innocent blue chop? What if, given the strong currents . . .

Now I've ruined my sari, one of my best. Kusum has joined me, knee deep in water that feels to me like a swimming pool. I could settle in the water, and my husband would take my hand and the boys would slap water in my face just to see me scream.

"Do you remember what good swimmers my boys were, Kusum?"

"I saw the medals," she says.

One of the widowers, Dr. Ranganathan from Montreal, walks out to us, carrying his shoes in one hand. He's an electrical engineer. Someone at the hotel mentioned his work is famous around the world, something about the place where physics and electricity come together. He has lost a huge family, something indescribable. "With some luck," Dr. Ranganathan suggests to me, "a good swimmer could make it safely to some island. It is quite possible that there may be many, many microscopic islets scattered around."

"You're not just saying that?" I tell Dr. Ranganathan about Vinod, my elder son. Last year he took diving as well.

"It's a parent's duty to hope," he says. "It is foolish to rule out possibilities that have not been tested. I myself have not surrendered hope."

Kusum is sobbing once again. "Dear lady," he says, laying his free hand on her arm, and she calms down.

"Vinod is how old?" he asks me. He's very careful, as we all are. *Is*, not was.

"Fourteen. Yesterday he was fourteen. His father and uncle were going to take him down to the Taj and give him a big birthday party. I couldn't go with them because I couldn't get two weeks off from my stupid job in June." I process bills for a travel agent. June is a big travel month.

Dr. Ranganathan whips the pockets of his suit jacket inside out. Squashed roses, in darkening shades of pink, float on the water. He tore the roses off creepers in somebody's garden. He didn't ask anyone if he could pluck the roses, but now there's been an article about it in the local papers. When you see an Indian person, it says, please give them flowers.

"A strong youth of fourteen," he says, "can very likely pull to safety a younger one."

My sons, though four years apart, were very close. Vinod wouldn't let Mithun drown. *Electrical engineering*, I think, foolishly perhaps: this man knows important secrets of the universe, things closed to me. Relief spins me lightheaded. No wonder my boys' photographs haven't turned up in the gallery of photos of the recovered dead. "Such pretty roses," I say.

"My wife loved pink roses. Every Friday I had to bring a bunch home. I used to say, Why? After twenty-odd years of marriage you're still needing proof positive of my love?" He has identified his wife and three of his children. Then others from Montreal, the lucky ones, intact families with no survivors. He chuckles as he wades back to shore. Then he swings around to ask me a question. "Mrs. Bhave, you are wanting to throw in some roses for your loved ones? I have two big ones left."

But I have other things to float: Vinod's pocket calculator; a half-painted model B-52 for my Mithun. They'd want them on their island. And for my husband? For him I let fall into the calm, glassy waters a poem I wrote in the hospital yesterday. Finally he'll know my feelings for him.

"Don't tumble, the rocks are slippery," Dr. Ranganathan cautions. He holds out a hand for me to grab.

Then it's time to get back on the bus, time to rush back to our waiting posts on hospital benches.

Kusum is one of the lucky ones. The lucky ones flew here, identified in multiplicate their loved ones, then will fly to India with the bodies for proper ceremonies. Satish is one of the few males who surfaced. The photos of faces we saw on the walls in an office at Heathrow and here in the hospital are mostly of women. Women have more body fat, a nun said to me matter-of-factly. They float better.

Today I was stopped by a young sailor on the street. He had loaded bodies, he'd gone into the water when—he checks my face for signs of strength—when the sharks were first spotted. I don't blush, and he breaks down. "It's all right," I say. "Thank you." I heard about the sharks from Dr. Ranganathan. In his orderly mind, science brings understanding, it holds no terror. It is the shark's duty. For every deer there is a hunter, for every fish a fisherman.

The Irish are not shy; they rush to me and give me hugs and some are crying. I cannot imagine reactions like that on the streets of Toronto. Just strangers, and I am touched. Some carry flowers with them and give them to any Indian they see.

After lunch, a policeman I have gotten to know quite well catches hold of me. He says he thinks he has a match for Vinod. I explain what a good swimmer Vinod is.

"You want me with you when you look at photos?" Dr. Ranganathan walks ahead of me into the picture gallery. In these matters, he is a scientist, and I am grateful. It is a new perspective. "They have performed miracles," he says. "We are indebted to them."

The first day or two the policemen showed us relatives only one picture at a time; now they're in a hurry, they're eager to lay out the possibles, and even the probables.

The face on the photo is of a boy much like Vinod; the same intelligent eyes, the same thick brows dipping into a V. But this boy's features, even his cheeks, are puffier, wider, mushier.

"No." My gaze is pulled by other pictures. There are five other boys who look like Vinod.

The nun assigned to console me rubs the first picture with a fingertip. "When they've been in the water for a while, love, they look a little heavier." The bones under the skin are broken, they said on the first day—try to adjust your memories. It's important.

"It's not him. I'm his mother. I'd know."

"I know this one!" Dr. Ranganathan cries out, and suddenly, from the back of the gallery, "And this one!" I think he senses that I don't want to find my boys. "They are the Kutty brothers. They were also from Montreal." I don't mean to be crying. On the contrary, I am ecstatic. My suitcase in the hotel is packed heavy with dry clothes for my boys.

The policeman starts to cry. "I am so sorry, I am so sorry, ma'am. I really thought we had a match."

With the nun ahead of us and the policeman behind, we, the unlucky ones without our children's bodies, file out of the makeshift gallery.

From Ireland most of us go on to India. Kusum and I take the same direct flight to Bombay, so I can help her clear customs quickly. But we have to argue with a man in uniform. He has large boils on his face. The boils swell and glow with sweat as we argue with him. He wants Kusum to wait in line and he refuses to take authority because his boss is on a tea break. But Kusum won't let her coffins out of sight, and I shan't desert her though I know that my parents, elderly and diabetic, must be waiting in a stuffy car in a scorching lot.

"You bastard!" I scream at the man with the popping boils. Other passengers press closer. "You think we're smuggling contraband in those coffins!"

Once upon a time we were well-brought-up women; we were dutiful wives who kept our heads veiled, our voices shy and sweet.

In India, I become, once again, an only child of rich, ailing parents. Old friends of the family come to pay their respects. Some are Sikh, and inwardly, involuntarily, I cringe. My parents are progressive people; they do not blame communities for a few individuals.

In Canada it is a different story now.

"Stay longer," my mother pleads. "Canada is a cold place. Why would you want to be by yourself?" I stay.

Three months pass. Then another.

"Vikram wouldn't have wanted you to give up things!" they protest. They call my husband by the name he was born with. In Toronto he'd changed to Vik so the men he worked with at his office would find his name as easy as Rod or Chris. "You know, the dead aren't cut off from us!"

My grandmother, the spoiled daughter of a rich zamindar, shaved her head with rusty razor blades when she was widowed at sixteen. My grandfather died of childhood diabetes when he was nineteen, and she saw herself as the harbinger of bad luck. My mother grew up without parents, raised indifferently by an uncle, while her true mother slept in a hut behind the main estate house and took her food with the servants. She grew up a rationalist. My parents abhor mindless mortification.

The zamindar's daughter kept stubborn faith in Vedic rituals; my parents rebelled. I am trapped between two modes of knowledge. At thirty-six, I am too old to start over and too young to give up. Like my husband's spirit, I flutter between worlds.

Courting aphasia, we travel. We travel with our phalanx of servants and poor relatives. To hill stations and to beach resorts. We play contract bridge in dusty gymkhana clubs. We ride stubby ponies up crumbly mountain trails. At tea dances, we let ourselves be twirled twice round the ballroom. We hit the holy spots we hadn't made time for before. In Varanasi, Kalighat, Rishikesh, Hardwar, astrologers and palmists seek me out and for a fee offer me cosmic consolations.

Already the widowers among us are being shown new bride candidates. They cannot resist the call of custom, the authority of their parents and older brothers. They must marry; it is the duty of a man to look after a wife. The new wives will be young widows with children, destitute but of good family. They will make loving wives, but the men will shun them. I've had calls from the men over crackling Indian telephone lines. "Save me," they say, these substantial, educated, successful men of forty. "My parents are arranging a marriage for me." In a month they will have buried one family and returned to Canada with a new bride and partial family.

I am comparatively lucky. No one here thinks of arranging a husband for an unlucky widow.

Then, on the third day of the sixth month into this odyssey, in an abandoned temple in a tiny Himalayan village, as I make my offering of flowers and sweetmeats to the god of a tribe of animists, my husband descends to me. He is squatting next to a scrawny sadhu in moth-eaten robes. Vikram wears the vanilla suit he wore the last time I hugged him. The sadhu tosses petals on a butter-fed flame, reciting Sanskrit mantras, and sweeps his face of flies. My husband takes my hands in his.

You're beautiful, he starts. Then, *What are you doing here?*

Shall I stay? I ask. He only smiles, but already the image is fading. *You must finish alone what we started together.* No seaweed wreathes his mouth. He speaks too fast, just as he used to when we were an envied family in our pink split-level. He is gone.

In the windowless altar room, smoky with joss sticks and clarified butter lamps, a sweaty hand gropes for my blouse. I do not shriek. The sadhu arranges his robe. The lamps hiss and sputter out.

When we come out of the temple, my mother says, "Did you feel something weird in there?"

My mother has no patience with ghosts, prophetic dreams, holy men, and cults.

"No," I lie. "Nothing."

But she knows that she's lost me. She knows that in days I shall be leaving.

· · ·

Kusum's put up her house for sale. She wants to live in an ashram in Hardwar. Moving to Hardwar was her swami's idea. Her swami runs two ashrams, the one in Hardwar and another here in Toronto.

"Don't run away," I tell her.

"I'm not running away," she says. "I'm pursuing inner peace. You think you or that Ranganathan fellow are better off?"

Pam's left for California. She wants to do some modeling, she says. She says when she comes into her share of the insurance money she'll open a yoga-cum-aerobics studio in Hollywood. She sends me postcards so naughty I daren't leave them on the coffee table. Her mother has withdrawn from her and the world.

The rest of us don't lose touch, that's the point. Talk is all we have, says Dr. Ranganathan, who has also resisted his relatives and returned to Montreal and to his job, alone. He says, Whom better to talk with than other relatives? We've been melted down and recast as a new tribe.

He calls me twice a week from Montreal. Every Wednesday night and every Saturday afternoon. He is changing jobs, going to Ottawa. But Ottawa is over a hundred miles away, and he is forced to drive two hundred and twenty miles a day from his home in Montreal. He can't bring himself to sell his house. The house is a temple, he says; the king-sized bed in the master bedroom is a shrine. He sleeps on a folding cot. A devotee.

There are still some hysterical relatives. Judith Templeton's list of those needing help and those who've "accepted" is in nearly perfect balance. Acceptance means you speak of your family in the past tense and you make active plans for moving ahead with your life. There are courses at Seneca and Ryerson we could be taking. Her gleaming leather briefcase is full of college catalogues and lists of cultural societies that need our help. She has done impressive work, I tell her.

"In the textbooks on grief management," she replies—I am her confidante, I realize, one of the few whose grief has not sprung bizarre obsessions—"there are stages to pass through: rejection, depression, acceptance, reconstruction." She has compiled a chart and finds that six months after the tragedy, none of us still rejects reality, but only a handful are reconstructing. "Depressed acceptance" is the plateau we've reached. Remarriage is a major step in reconstruction (though she's a little surprised, even shocked, over *how* quickly some of the men have taken on new families). Selling one's house and changing jobs and cities is healthy.

How to tell Judith Templeton that my family surrounds me, and that like creatures in epics, they've changed shapes? She sees me as calm and accepting but worries that I have no job, no career. My closest friends are worse off than I. I cannot tell her my days, even my nights, are thrilling.

She asks me to help with families she can't reach at all. An elderly couple in Agincourt whose sons were killed just weeks after they had brought their parents over from a village in Punjab. From their names, I know they are Sikh. Judith Templeton and a translator have visited them twice with offers of money for airfare to Ireland, with bank forms, power-of-attorney forms, but they have refused to sign, or to leave their tiny apartment. Their sons' money is frozen in the bank. Their sons' investment apartments have been trashed by tenants, the furnishings sold off. The parents fear that anything they sign or any money they receive will end the company's or the country's obligations to them. They fear they are selling their sons for two airline tickets to a place they've never seen.

The high-rise apartment is a tower of Indians and West Indians, with a sprinkling of Orientals. The nearest bus-stop kiosk is lined with women in saris. Boys practice cricket in the parking lot. Inside the building, even I wince a bit from the ferocity of onion fumes, the distinctive and immediate Indianness of frying ghee, but Judith Templeton maintains a steady flow of information. These poor old people are in imminent danger of losing their place and all their services.

I say to her, "They are Sikh. They will not open up to a Hindu woman." And what I want to add is, as much as I try not to, I stiffen now at the sight of beards and turbans. I remember a time when we all trusted each other in this new country, it was only the new country we worried about.

The two rooms are dark and stuffy. The lights are off, and an oil lamp sputters on the coffee table. The bent old lady has let us in, and her husband is wrapping a white turban over his oiled, hip-length hair. She immediately goes to the kitchen, and I hear the most familiar sound of an Indian home, tap water hitting and filling a teapot.

They have not paid their utility bills, out of fear and inability to write a check. The telephone is gone; electricity and gas and water are soon to follow. They have told Judith their sons will provide. They are good boys, and they have always earned and looked after their parents.

We converse a bit in Hindi. They do not ask about the crash and I wonder if I should bring it up. If they think I am here merely as a translator, then they may feel insulted. There are thousands of Punjabi speakers, Sikhs, in Toronto to do a better job. And so I say to the old lady, "I too have lost my sons, and my husband, in the crash."

Her eyes immediately fill with tears. The man mutters a few words which sound like a blessing. "God provides and God takes away," he says.

I want to say, But only men destroy and give back nothing. "My boys and my husband are not coming back," I say. "We have to understand that."

Now the old woman responds. "But who is to say? Man alone does not decide these things." To this her husband adds his agreement.

Judith asks about the bank papers, the release forms. With a stroke of the pen, they will have a provincial trustee to pay their bills, invest their money, send them a monthly pension.

"Do you know this woman?" I ask them.

The man raises his hand from the table, turns it over, and seems to regard each finger separately before he answers. "This young lady is always coming here, we make tea for her, and she leaves papers for us to sign." His eyes scan a pile of papers in the corner of the room. "Soon we will be out of tea, then will she go away?"

The old lady adds, "I have asked my neighbors and no one else gets *angrezi* visitors. What have we done?"

"It's her job," I try to explain. "The government is worried. Soon you will have no place to stay, no lights, no gas, no water."

"Government will get its money. Tell her not to worry, we are honorable people."

I try to explain the government wishes to give money, not take. He raises his hand. "Let them take," he says. "We are accustomed to that. That is no problem."

"We are strong people," says the wife. "Tell her that."

"Who needs all this machinery?" demands the husband. "It is unhealthy, the bright lights, the cold air on a hot day, the cold food, the four gas rings. God will provide, not government."

"When our boys return," the mother says.

Her husband sucks his teeth. "Enough talk," he says.

Judith breaks in. "Have you convinced them?" The snaps on her cordovan briefcase go off like firecrackers in that quiet apartment. She lays the sheaf of legal papers on the coffee table. "If they can't write their names, an X will do— I've told them that."

Now the old lady has shuffled to the kitchen and soon emerges with a pot of tea and two cups. "I think my bladder will go first on a job like this," Judith says to me, smiling. "If only there was some way of reaching them. Please thank her for the tea. Tell her she's very kind."

I nod in Judith's direction and tell them in Hindi, "She thanks you for the tea. She thinks you are being very hospitable but she doesn't have the slightest idea what it means."

I want to say, Humor her. I want to say, My boys and my husband are with me too, more than ever. I look in the old man's eyes and I can read his stubborn, peasant's message: *I have protected this woman as best I can. She is the only person I have left. Give to me or take from me what you will, but I will not sign for it. I will not pretend that I accept.*

In the car, Judith says, "You see what I'm up against? I'm sure they're lovely people, but their stubbornness and ignorance are driving me crazy. They think signing a paper is signing their sons' death warrants, don't they?"

I am looking out the window. I want to say, *In our culture, it is a parent's duty to hope.*

"Now, Shaila, this next woman is a real mess. She cries day and night, and she refuses all medical help. We may have to—"

"Let me out at the subway," I say.

"I beg your pardon?" I can feel those blue eyes staring at me.

It would not be like her to disobey. She merely disapproves, and slows at a corner to let me out. Her voice is plaintive. "Is there anything I said? Anything I did?"

I could answer her suddenly in a dozen ways, but I choose not to. "Shaila? Let's talk about it," I hear, then slam the door.

A wife and mother begins her new life in a new country, and that life is cut short. Yet her husband tells her, Complete what we have started. We, who stayed out of politics and came halfway around the world to avoid religious and political feuding, have been the first in the New World to die from it. I no longer know what we started, nor how to complete it. I write letters to the editors of local papers and to members of Parliament. Now at least they admit it was a bomb. One MP answers back, with sympathy, but with a challenge. You want to make a difference? Work on a campaign. Work on mine. Politicize the Indian voter.

My husband's old lawyer helps me set up a trust. Vikram was a saver and a careful investor. He had saved the boys' boarding school and college fees. I sell the pink house at four times what we paid for it and take a small apartment downtown. I am looking for a charity to support.

We are deep in the Toronto winter, gray skies, icy pavements. I stay indoors, watching television. I have tried to assess my situation, how best to live my life, to complete what we began so many years ago. Kusum has written me from Hardwar that her life is now serene. She has seen Satish and has heard her daughter sing again. Kusum was on a pilgrimage, passing through a village, when she heard a young girl's voice, singing one of her daughter's favorite *bhajans.* She followed the music through the squalor of a Himalayan village, to a hut where a young girl, an exact replica of her daughter, was fanning coals under the kitchen fire. When she appeared, the girl cried out, "Ma!" and ran away. What did I think of that?

I think I can only envy her.

Pam didn't make it to California, but writes me from Vancouver. She works in a department store, giving makeup hints to Indian and Oriental girls. Dr.

Ranganathan has given up his commute, given up his house and job, and accepted an academic position in Texas, where no one knows his story and he has vowed not to tell it. He calls me now once a week.

I wait, I listen and I pray, but Vikram has not returned to me. The voices and the shapes and the nights filled with visions ended abruptly several weeks ago.

I take it as a sign.

One rare, beautiful, sunny day last week, returning from a small errand on Yonge Street, I was walking through the park from the subway to my apartment. I live equidistant from the Ontario Houses of Parliament and the University of Toronto. The day was not cold, but something in the bare trees caught my attention. I looked up from the gravel, into the branches and the clear blue sky beyond. I thought I heard the rustling of larger forms, and I waited a moment for voices. Nothing.

"What?" I asked.

Then as I stood in the path looking north to Queen's Park and west to the university, I heard the voices of my family one last time. *Your time has come,* they said. *Go, be brave.*

I do not know where this voyage I have begun will end. I do not know which direction I will take. I dropped the package on a park bench and started walking.

Antonya Nelson

FEMALE TROUBLE

ANTONYA NELSON (1961–) was born in Wichita, Kansas. She received an MFA in creative writing from the University of Arizona in 1986. Her first story collection, *The Expendables*, won the Flannery O'Connor Award for Short Fiction in 1990. She is the author of four other short story collections, including *Some Fun* (Scribner, 2006), and three novels (*Talking in Bed*, *Nobody's Girl*, and *Living to Tell*). She shares the Cullen Chair in Creative Writing at the University of Houston with her husband, Robert Boswell, and lives in New Mexico, Texas, and Colorado.

McBride found himself at the Pima County psychiatric hospital in the middle of the day. "Don't visit me here," Daisy told him. She slid her palms over her frizzy white hair as if to keep it from flying off like dandelion fluff. "It embarrasses me, these crazy people make me ashamed."

"I thought you wanted to see me. I thought that was the point. Why else are you in Tucson?" Daisy, McBride's girlfriend of the year before, had been discovered on the highway near the Triple T truck stop carrying a portable typewriter, trying to hitch a ride. Native New Yorker, she'd never learned to drive; maybe that was why McBride had assumed she would stay in Salt Lake City, where he'd left her. He certainly preferred to think of that chapter as a closed one, a place he had chosen against.

Daisy said, "I want to see you when I'm normal again. I just feel like you're staring at me, at my flabby skin and everything." She began jerking her shoulders in some simulation of crying but her eyes remained dry. McBride did not wish to touch her. She'd taken on an institutional smell and her sweatsuit hid any physical charm. Her eyes had lost whatever snappish wit they'd once held, glazed with depression and the medication used to treat it. McBride reached to hold her and felt she was made of something more inert than her former substance, dull as clay, and pale as an albino, as if she'd been dipped in bleach. In the past, she'd been burnished, tanned twice weekly in a salon coffin, hair dyed golden and frowsily restrained with combs and barrettes, a Victoria's Secret kind of girl, pubic hair dyed to match.

Had his leaving her brought about such thorough transformation? He felt like asking her. He was sort of flattered, sort of appalled.

When she'd fallen in love with him she'd gone to his apartment and climbed into his bed and waited for him to come home. She was a free spirit with a crush, a mission, a taste for disaster. His roommate had greeted him in the kitchen that late night, wearing boxers and socks, whispering as he stepped daintily on tiptoes, "There's a *girl* in your bed" with such admiration and awe that McBride seemed stripped of very many options. A naked girl between your sheets was not a thing to take lightly.

"Drunk?" he asked, pulling off his own clothes.

His roommate had given an elaborate impatient shrug and shiver: who cared? Or: of course drunk; you had to ask?

Was she desperate? No—devoted. Spontaneous. Outrageous. A girl on fire, burning so that you wanted to stand in the radiating glow, a girl on the verge, confident in not caring. The prospect of death did not deter her. She was up for whatever.

And this had led her here, McBride supposed, later and after, immolation imminent. The Arizona desert was forgiving in February, springlike by eastern standards. They sat in the building's courtyard. A general wooden catatonia in the human population—patients and orderlies both—made the Adirondack chairs seem full of personality, resting at jaunty angles and in conversational clusters over the evergreen grass. Other visitors carried Styrofoam cups of coffee to other patients, crossing the lawn quickly, trying to be spry in the face of lethargy. McBride felt trapped by his past, and kept sneaking covert glances at his watch. His tapping foot ached for an accelerator.

What he remembered about Daisy was sex. Even when he'd stopped loving her, he'd wanted to fuck her. They'd been strangers their first night together, Daisy waiting for him drunk on that crowded single mattress. His roommate's awe, "There's a *girl* in your bed." Like a gift, like an animal in a gunnysack, and on fire, in heat.

Was there a word for the way you winced, recalling a former affection, that place in your rib cage that briefly collapsed, your glance that no longer lingered but skimmed over her face like a skipped stone over water?

Now Daisy said, "Look," and pointed toward the hospital entrance. "Family theater." They watched a woman wrench herself free of the guiding hands of an older couple, her parents, McBride guessed, the three of them sharing a lankiness. Their daughter was easily in her forties, long-limbed and angry, crossing her arms defiantly and refusing to enter the front doors. McBride was sympathetic to the parents, who looked harried and doomed, as if they hadn't slept in days. Daisy said, "Old farts just want to get rid of her." McBride supposed that was true but he didn't blame them.

When the woman suddenly sprinted down the walk toward the street the parents began shouting. The woman ran like a dancer, straight into the street without looking. Her mother screamed, putting her hands to her cheeks. Cars weaved around the daughter as she stood between lanes but nobody stopped driving. Nobody in Tucson ever stopped driving. The woman stood facing traffic like the oblivious prow of a ship. McBride looked to the orderlies, who'd jumped up yet made no move toward action.

"Help her," Daisy said to him, pushing his elbow from the chair arm. He rose and started reluctantly for the street, jogging in such a way that his teeth hurt. When he reached the woman she took his arm as if she'd been waiting for him, her partner on their dance stage. She stared at him with clear unmedicated eyes, startled like a deer, pretty and skittish.

"What am I doing?" she asked.

McBride told her what he'd seen as he escorted her up the walk. They passed her parents, who simply watched as if at a wedding.

"*You'd* never do a thing like this," she informed McBride as they entered the building's foyer. She held his arm lightly, with long shaking fingers. A group had clustered at the commotion and now drifted away disappointed at the tame outcome.

"A thing like what?"

"Like impulsive behavior. It's a feminine trait."

McBride recalled a similar complaint Daisy had made when he refused to try sushi or inhale an illicit powder. No, he wouldn't eat raw fish, or snort an alien drug. Nor would he bolt, barefooted, into traffic.

"Party pooper," Daisy called him. "Wet blanket. Coward." What was so brave about taking risks, he'd asked her. What separated it from stepping off a cliff?

"You step off holding my hand," she'd said, popping a pill, removing a garment, switching off the headlights at high speed on a dark highway. But he'd wanted a bungee, a net, a loophole.

The woman's parents had followed them inside and now stood deferentially behind McBride. The woman let loose of his arm, surrendering to her parents. "This way," she said quietly, leading them toward the admissions desk.

Daisy had her eyes closed when McBride got back to their chairs. "I'm not asleep," she told him.

McBride sat on the arm of the chair, ready to leave.

"Fix everything?" she asked acidly; this was like her, to tell him to do something, then ridicule him for doing it.

"I should go," he said.

"You should," she agreed, starting to not-cry again.

"I'll come back."

"I'll be here."

At home that evening McBride's current girlfriend Martha sat on newspapers painting chairs. In her spare time she decorated secondhand furniture; her house was full of it, colorful as a toy store. Yellow snakes wound up the spindles of one chair, blue tulips drawn freehand popped along the arms of another. Sad music came from a bedroom, the mournful wailing of loons. Martha's gray head was tilted and her tongue was lodged beneath her upper lip in concentration. There was the odor of hearty food beneath the paint fumes, that and the burnt herby smell of marijuana, which she'd smoked earlier. The ordinariness of the evening, the simple and somehow unbelievable normalness of it—the way McBride could accept a healthy woman in the house where he lived doing something so utterly charming as painting furniture and cooking food—should have made him happy. Instead, he was irritated by the tableau. He felt domesticated, as if it had happened against his will. Time with Daisy, however brief, had left something under his skin.

"How was she?" Martha asked.

"Drugged. Nuts. I ended up dragging some other woman out of the street in front of the hospital."

"Alive?"

"More or less." He told her about the morning while she worked her brush around in her patient, stoned method. The room grew dim and she quit, leaning back on her hands, legs splayed open lazily. She was the first woman McBride had ever known who was not at war with her body: she liked it, it liked her. She walked around in the world unself-conscious inside of it, completely casual with its shortcomings as well as its gifts. Fond, as if of a beloved pet.

"Oh, Daisy," McBride said, trying to sound as if he could dismiss his old girlfriend, laboring to evoke that useful wince that meant he was over her, ashamed of former passion. "How was *your* day?"

Martha quoted some of her accident victims' depositions to cheer him up. She worked in the police court downtown taking statements from bad drivers. This was only one of her jobs. She also interviewed rape victims for a professor at the University of Arizona, having some talent at listening. She was thirty-six, six years older than McBride, prematurely gray, and had lived with a number of men so she knew how to do it. Calmly. With a great deal of forbearance and humor. Even her name: Martha. Not Muffy, not Marti, nothing cute or hip, an old-fashioned name designating a person with both feet on the ground. She said, " 'Coming home I drove into the wrong house and collided with a tree I don't have.' "

McBride smiled. Martha smiled, too, and rose to extract whatever she had cooked from the oven, which had the bloody odor of red meat and mushrooms. Wine. He suspected she made up depositions but she swore they were authentic. Her favorite went: "I had been driving for forty years when I fell asleep at the wheel and hit a telephone pole." The rape victims she and McBride had agreed not to discuss.

They ate on the front porch in the breeze of an oscillating fan. Even in February, the birds went on and on, noisy as a coffee klatch. The next-door neighbor the transvestite came out, as he always did, as the sun fell, lips a red bow, bosom an emphatic bolster. His era was the fifties: floral, with forgiving hemlines.

"Imagine going through all the nonsense he must go through to look like that," McBride had once mistakenly said. The shaving, the plucking, the makeup, the heels: torture. Martha had thrown her head back to laugh. She could really laugh. "Just imagine," she'd said.

They waved, as usual. The pretense seemed to be that two people shared the little house next door, a man and a woman who were never seen together yet wore the same shoe size. "What*ever*," McBride muttered, also as usual. Martha liked her funky neighborhood. She liked the tree full of umbrellas as well as the lawn art on the corner, toasters and blenders and microwave ovens set out as ornaments among the plastic flowers and spinning pinwheels. She liked the car with toys glued onto its chassis. She had told McBride, when he complained of the weirdness, that as he grew older he would treasure the odd, shun the ordinary, grow easy as she with eccentricity. It would not threaten him so.

Personally, McBride thought that Martha lived among the bizarre in order not to feel so bizarre herself, normal by comparison. Plus, her neighbors' obvious dilemmas distracted her from her own, which was that she wanted a baby. Women were on timetables, cycles, deadlines. That ticking clock, bomb or alarm, irked McBride. His gender had forever, plenitude, a wealth of progeny waiting in the wings. Babies, like the rape interviews, was a topic best avoided.

Predictably, he dreamed about Daisy that night. He was in his old house, the one he'd grown up in in Oklahoma City. In the dream Daisy lived around the corner from his parents. She rented a small sunny room. McBride visited her there and she kissed him on the cheek. He woke feeling tender toward her. It had been such a sweet kiss, so innocent and discrete, like the kiss of a child, free of history or future, and it had such melancholy force that McBride woke in a state of pure desire, which impelled his waking Martha to make love with her, his fantasy life blurred by dream. Perhaps when he came, it was into the memory of his sleeping vision of Daisy. The memory—combined, Martha and Daisy, sanity and sickness—carried him through the day, their faces next to his, his sexual past shoved against his sexual present, an interesting friction.

He visited Daisy again a week later. The tenderness of his dream had faded. Her depression made him impatient. This aspect of Daisy seemed to him an enormous weakness and he did not tolerate weakness well, trying to get a handle on his own. She wore the same sweatsuit, the same muzzy expression, the same drained pallor. Today it was cloudy but they sat in the same hopeful Adirondack chairs outside, staring at the front door as if the drama they'd witnessed last time might also replay itself, the middle-aged woman fleeing her parents, the need to run into traffic. McBride was annoyed to discover he had on the identical shirt he'd worn then, too.

Without apparent emotion, Daisy said, "I'm pregnant I think."

McBride looked hard at her, trying to figure where the sensible part of her went when the other part came out.

"Don't worry," she continued, "it's not yours."

"It *couldn't* be," he said.

"True." She said nothing for a while, then added, "I could have had your baby after you moved away. I could have left her in Salt Lake, given her up to the Mormons to raise. Don't men ever wonder what happens to their sperm? I'd worry, if I were a man, but men—it's all just hit and run."

What occurred to McBride was that all the nasty forces of nature had female pronouns, typhoons and tornadoes and those mythic creatures, the Furies and Sirens. They were powerful, and they sent you reeling, they trapped you.

"Daisy, what are you going to do?"

"I don't know." She shook her fluffy head. "I have to get off of these drugs if I'm pregnant, that's for sure. But what else? You got me." She picked at the chipped green paint on her chair arm for a few minutes in silence. Then added, "There were two men in Salt Lake. We all three lived together, very French movie. Either one could be the dad, though they'd both suck at it."

McBride said, "You know, your life is kind of crisis-oriented, have you noticed that?"

She lifted her face to the brightest cloud, the one that hid the sun, and said, sullenly, "No," and then wouldn't say another word.

Two men. The image of Daisy at the fulcrum of a threesome wouldn't leave McBride. Somehow this wrinkle intrigued him, against his will. What kind of sleeping arrangements had prevailed? Was there an alpha male, stud one, stud two? Some homosexual stuff? How did the three of them behave at breakfast, sitting together over coffee in their underwear and ruffled hair?

At home Martha attempted to cheer him. "To avoid hitting the bumper of the car in front, I struck the pedestrian."

McBride told her, "I'm starting to believe these reports of yours."

Martha feigned shock, sucking on a joint. "You mean you didn't before?"

"Not before Daisy."

"Daisy," Martha said, looking bemused, annoyed in the unthreatened way a strong woman does in the face of a puny one.

"She lived with two men at once, she says."

"She's done everything, that gal, all the things I always thought I would do. It's disappointing to realize how staid I've become." But she smiled. Her complacency didn't really trouble her—look at what surrounded her, arty furniture, queer neighbors, clacking birds.

The pregnancy part went unmentioned, but the next time he visited the hospital Martha wanted to come with him. She insisted. She drove. For someone who evaluated car accidents for a living she handled an automobile very badly, swerving arrogantly through traffic, refusing to do head checks, one palm ever ready on the horn. She had lapses but mostly Martha was reliable, grown up. Now that he'd become one it surprised McBride how few adults were grown-ups. It still seemed all seventh grade, and you had to keep on your toes.

Daisy had dressed for McBride's visit this week. Someone—some anal-retentive obsessive-compulsive with a lot of time on her hands—had lassoed Daisy's wild hair into tiny braids which crisscrossed her shapely skull in a flattering style. The sweatsuit had been traded for black jeans and a glossy button-down shirt, under which her breasts bobbed. She'd smeared makeup over the sores around her mouth and the dark circles beneath her eyes, and she looked like a country-western singer ready to make a comeback. Next to her, Martha seemed far too robust, big and indestructible, like a Hereford beside an impala. McBride saw that the visit was going to go wrong in a way he hadn't anticipated.

Women intimidated Daisy; even in the sanest of moments she didn't like them, though she pretended otherwise. Without the possibility of an encounter ending in sex, Daisy was a bit at sea. McBride sat on the grass before the willing Adirondack chairs where the women sat leaning back, faces to the sun. He thought of triangles, the two women here together only because of him; the two men in Salt Lake maybe waiting to hear from Daisy, wandering around the house wondering what they were doing together, stuck with each other and a legally binding lease. Because he could come up with nothing to say in front of Martha, McBride understood he was not innocent in his current relationship with Daisy, a fact that made him tired of himself.

Martha said, "So how are you feeling?"

Daisy took the finger she was chewing from her mouth and said, "Sad. I'm having an abortion tomorrow and that makes me *really* sad, even though I don't think I'm ready for a child."

McBride felt Martha appraising him, compiling all the data, his not telling her about the baby, his phony forgetfulness on the matter. Then she nodded at Daisy. "That's understandable. I'm just now feeling ready for a child."

"You have time. You're not old."

"I *am* old, but it's nice of you to say. I've had three abortions and every time I think, I just saved another kid from being fucked-up. It's one way not to feel bad."

"Well, tomorrow I'll save my second from being fucked-up."

McBride was grateful he hadn't fathered any of these fetuses. Both women looked down at him, their expressions identical: what good was he, there on the grass? He didn't want to donate his sperm to Martha's desire, and though he was in the position of footstool, they couldn't even put their feet up on him.

"Coffee," he said, hopping to. And once he'd left them together he did not want to return and so roamed the hospital halls.

The place was poorly funded, understaffed, cheaply built and maintained. It was not old enough to seem gothically romantic nor new enough to appear at least clean and modern. In all the popular spots, the carpet was worn through; the furniture was crooked, broken plastic from the seventies, and the windows were smudged with years' worth of fingerprints, people pressing against the glass, longing to escape the big box they seemed to find themselves trapped inside. Everywhere televisions, laugh tracks and commercials fading in and out of every open doorway as McBride passed. Was there anything more representative of illness and confinement than daytime TV, anything more definitively the killing of time? This first floor was public; the upper ones required speaking with a station manager. To avoid returning to Martha and Daisy— he could see them from the second floor window near the elevator, still talking together in the sun, Daisy tilted back with her eyes closed, Martha watching her—he gave himself the challenge of lying his way past a station manager. The fourth was Daisy's floor; the higher one went, the crazier the occupants.

But it was no challenge at all. He merely mentioned Daisy's name and was pointed in the direction of her room. The woman at the desk didn't even have him sign in. He opened her dresser drawers and looked in her closet. Nothing but the portable typewriter she'd been found with on the highway. Also some odd articles of clothing, obviously stuff that had been donated, discards. Plain white underpants, high-waisted and modest, nothing like what she'd worn before. A picture of Jesus over her headboard, eyes pitched upward, just as exasperated as anyone else who had to deal with Daisy.

"I didn't know you were a patient here."

McBride whirled, caught. At the doorway stood the woman from the street, arms crossed as if chilly. She resembled Audrey Hepburn, he thought, willowy, frail, and jittery as a stray. "I'm not," he said, recovering. "I'm waiting for Daisy."

"Daisy." She said it skeptically. "Well, I'm glad you're not a patient because I would feel bad about not struggling more if you were. Couldn't have let another inmate be my undoing."

McBride smiled because she seemed to be joking but she didn't return the smile. She simply walked away, as if he'd made the wrong answer, the bones of her ribs and hips visible beneath her gray dress. From the hallway, he looked back outside. The Adirondack chairs were abandoned, big yawning laps.

Somehow Daisy wound up at McBride's house. This was because it was officially, legally, Martha's house, and Martha had invited her. She didn't believe Daisy was crazy. Confused, yes. In trouble, yes. Maybe even more trouble than craziness but not crazy. The thing on the highway, with the typewriter? McBride whispered this in their bedroom after Daisy had fallen asleep on the study couch.

"She was pregnant," Martha said. "Overwrought."

"She still is pregnant."

"True. But that's only till tomorrow. Then we work on getting her off the heavy-duty meds."

"What makes you want to do this? You don't even know her."

"She's your friend," Martha said simply. She wore a large white nightgown with ruffles and lace, matronly on her though it would have seemed sexy and Victorian on someone else, someone skinny, anorexic, or strung out like a junkie, like the woman at the hospital, like Daisy.

"She might still be in love with me," McBride warned Martha in the dark.

Martha laughed and wouldn't stop. It was lusty, gutsy laughter, and McBride didn't like it.

"What's funny? She might be."

"Oh, you sound so serious, like you wouldn't be able to defend yourself." She held her hands above her head as if shielding herself from an oncoming train. "Stop, stop! Don't love me." She laughed again. "Gimme a break. You're a big strong man, capable of fending off a crazy woman's love."

"You said she wasn't crazy."

"She shows all the signs of molestation."

"Naturally. She's a tabloid story, waiting to happen."

"I'm pretty sure she's been sexually abused."

"Only with permission," McBride said. "Only because she wanted to be."

"You don't believe that." In fact he did believe it, but best to keep that to himself. Best to leave that can of worms in the cupboard. On this subject they could not have an agreeable conversation. Martha had interviewed over a hundred rape victims, her specific interest in their notions of dress and how they felt about their bodies, before and after. She and McBride lay with thoughts of rape between them, a few moments of respectful silence. She believed he was better than he was; often he did not feel like dispelling this.

Then she rolled on top of him and became heavy. She loved to start sex this way, covering him like a blanket, breathing into his neck, heat, comfort. Her bed she'd made herself, headboard a pilfered road sign from high school days. Her friends had wanted DIP or PROCEED WITH CAUTION or MEN AT WORK, but what had Martha stolen? SOFT SHOULDER.

"The act of rape and the act of love are the same gesture," she'd told him once, explaining the messiness, the warring, scarring horror.

"Insert tab A into slot B," McBride said, deflecting, going for the joke.

"No, I mean that something twisted and confusing like that is called a paradox."

"A pair of ducks?" He didn't want to be educated; he knew he'd fail the final exam. He'd had it with complexity.

"A pair of fucked ducks."

There was something between McBride's girlfriends and it began to grow, like a romance, as if they had secrets. Daisy had only to say a word and the two of them would be uncontrollably amused, laughing so hard they couldn't speak. McBride vaguely remembered this about her, how she pulled you into her private chamber, made you feel that only you and she lived there, in the heady and ticklish dark. Her bratty sense of humor was surfacing, now that she'd stepped down from her meds. As well as her readiness to lie. "My brother was sexually ambivalent," she said, when the transvestite next door walked out one evening.

"Before or after the heroin overdose?" McBride said flatly. "Or maybe that was your cousin? She's always got a relative or ex-boyfriend to one-up with," he explained to Martha, who blinked at him, unmoved as a lizard.

"You're just jealous of my radar," Daisy claimed.

"Gaydar," Martha amended. And there they were, hysterical again.

There'd been no abortion, a decision made without McBride's input. One of those roommates in Utah had sent some little seed out innocent in the world, trapped and growing now inside crazy Daisy.

Meanwhile McBride continued to visit the county hospital. He went to see Claire. Claire: tall, and faintly British.

"Why are you here?" she asked him.

He shook his head. She never smiled, never let loose of a somehow reassuring seriousness. She was very somber. You could say anything. She never evaded. "Why are *you* here?" he asked.

"I can't keep house," she said. "I forget to eat. I take walks and get lost. I leave the doors unlocked. My parents' television and video camera and every single CD they owned were stolen last time they left me alone." Her parents were on an extended vacation in Greece. When they traveled, Claire stayed at the hospital.

"You're not sick," McBride told her, "you're just forgetful. If forgetfulness were an illness, the whole city would be in a straitjacket."

"I'm pathologically forgetful," Claire said. "I forget so I can hurt my parents."

"But not consciously?"

"Of course not consciously. They're retired, so this vacation they're taking is from me. Do you understand? They are sitting on a beach, a million miles away from their troubles. Meaning me. I am their troubles."

Then it was summer and McBride began sleeping with Claire. She put on her shoes and they signed her out and drove to a motel on the highway not far from the hospital. Coincidentally, it was across the street from the Triple T truck stop where Daisy had been found. Twenty-five dollars, no questions asked. The cash exchange without receipt or bill, no evidence, no residue. What McBride liked about the Sands Motel was its air-conditioning—no swampy evaporative cooler here—which worked beautifully. Otherwise, the rooms were typically hideous and disturbing. They would not let you forget they'd accommodated hundreds of strangers before you, some sogginess in the carpet, lingering odor of cigarette, ripped sheet where someone else's toenail had pierced through. Claire in sex was the same as Claire in conversation: thoroughly confrontational, right there. "I've heard that this is the most sensitive spot on a man," she might say, pressing the pad of her thumb against his perineum.

"Yes," he would breathe, lifted as if upon a salty sea wave. "You heard right."

She had a thespian's voice, or a smoker's, and she hummed when she was up against McBride, melancholy and rousing as a distant train whistle. She alone called him by his first name, murmuring it. "Your name is like a kiss," she claimed, illustrating by placing it in the hollow of his throat; "Peter," she said, humming lungs, mouth releasing warm air. After sex she lay quietly on his chest and slept, a small smile on her lips. He nestled his palm against her scalp. She had a dainty head. Everywhere her bones were close to the surface, where her fair skin showed tiny blue veins, a network of hairline cracks, porcelain. When he pulled his hand away, her fine black hair shivered with static electricity. In sleep, she looked like what she must have looked like as a child, that smile like a dim memory, as if she were happy.

As he stroked her hair and the painfully knobby knuckles of her spinal column, he wondered why it was he had begun fucking older women. He thought he'd matured, but maybe younger women just didn't like him anymore. Was he more complicated, or more desperate? "We love each other's damage," Martha had once said, to explain their relationship. Apparently, Martha loved his, whatever it was. But only now did McBride actually follow her meaning. He couldn't have said that he loved Claire, but he felt ready to go to the mat for her. To protect this brief easy sleep. To defend her against her parents, for example, if need be, against her own self-loathing.

"You don't have to worry about suicide," she told him one day as he dropped her off after.

McBride had not, until that moment, given it a thought but from then on, of course, he thought of it frequently.

"She hates me," McBride told Martha, referring to Daisy. What he meant was that he hated her.

He and Martha had met for lunch downtown near the courthouse where McBride was laying brick. The summer had become so hot that the workday began at 5 A.M., ending by 1:00. Martha chewed her taco before answering. "She thinks you take me for granted."

"*I* take you for granted? The total stranger who's not even helping with bills, let alone *house*keeping, thinks *I'm* taking you for granted?" He was outraged; then he remembered his affair with Claire and calmed down. The checks and balances of intimacy.

Martha smiled. "I have a feeling she's got a kind of crush on me, frankly. I think she thinks I saved her. She's had enough of men, for a while."

He didn't say that he didn't believe Daisy *could* capture a man, these days, so changed was her body, skin, appeal. She had an aura of illness, contagion, that only a maternal impulse could love. "How do I take you for granted?"

"I didn't say you did; Daisy said it."

"But why does she think so?"

Martha leaned forward over the paper wrappings of their lunch, looked at him with her healthy hazel eyes. "She says you used to be much more physical with her than you are with me."

"You listen to this stuff?" His voice was louder than he intended; the lawyers at the next table shifted. Daisy was right, and it made him want to go kill her.

Martha leaned back. "I'm not worried about us. I like you, I think you like me. We laugh enough, even though we don't fuck as often as we used to." She tilted her head, squinted; she could wait. "You asked me what Daisy thought and I told you, but it doesn't bother me. So don't fret."

McBride found Daisy in Martha's sewing room, asleep on the Hide-a-Bed. When he sat beside her she woke without alarm; nothing in human nature would surprise her.

She propped herself sleepily on an elbow, letting the sheet drop to reveal she wore a soiled spaghetti strap T-shirt, nipples large and brown through the sheer material, abdomen like a cantaloupe. "I was thinking you might come to me someday, Mac," she said, placing a warm hand on his thigh.

McBride stood abruptly. "I'm not seducing you," he told her. "I want you out of here, in fact. If you're well enough to think I'd sleep with you, you're well enough to get the fuck out."

"I know you're sleeping with someone else," Daisy said, her eyes leveraging the threat. She would tell. She would ruin his life. There was no correct response so he simply stared at her, hating her. Then she began crying, and it was all McBride could do to keep from throwing a tantrum himself. Her face before him—quivering chapped lips, fair eyebrows full of acne—seemed to want to be struck. What did she expect from him? It enraged him to see her sobbing; he felt like grabbing her by the shoulders and flinging her back against the couch. How dare she know his secret? She looked up from under her hair and suddenly smiled through her tears, as if she'd caught on to a trick. She was a slutty, easy girl, and McBride could not deny the appeal. He remembered her in bed: her pleasure came only in extremity, at the very moment that might mark pain.

She liked to bite and be bitten, hair clutched and yanked. Now she reached a hand for his kneecap and spread her fingers slowly, as if she might insinuate herself just this way throughout his system. Infuriated, McBride lurched away, stumbled onto the floor. She followed, into his lap, and they were wrestling, Daisy sinking her teeth first into his arm and next his neck, hard enough for his nerves to trill. He put a knee between her legs and forced her arms apart. Below him, crucified, she breathed deeply, a strand of saliva across her cheek. The fact that her T-shirt and underwear did not cover her made McBride aware of her odor, which was powerful, unwashed and sexual. Rank, with a need to be hurt, and him not so far from obliging.

"Go away," he told her desperately. "Please. Go. Away." He felt his swelling erection as a betrayal—but of whom? What?

She rolled out from under him and curled toward the dark cavern beneath the bed like an animal. From the back she looked just like she always had, sinuous, nocturnal.

In the bathroom McBride tilted his head and checked the spot she'd bitten on his neck in the mirror. There were tiny broken capillaries but they looked enough like razor burn to reassure him his struggle with Daisy would go undiscovered. His heart, he noted, was beating so hard he could see it in his chest, in his reflection, pulsing there like a mouse in his pocket.

"If you want to make love with me, you can't do it with anyone else," Claire told him the next day as she ran her fingers over the bite marks on his arm. Leave it to the woman he didn't live with to sniff out his deception. "I know you live with Martha, but that doesn't necessarily mean you make love with her."

"We have sex," McBride told her, wondering why he found it necessary to convince her of this fact while obscuring others.

"Sex with someone you live with is more like masturbation," she said. "Just some warm object to rub on until you come. Do-it-yourself sex."

"I'm a do-it-your-selfer from way back," McBride said, wanting the punch line, wanting to stay out of the deep well, out of the tricky web. Women were so prone to abstraction, to pitching you into outer space. They were not afraid of the dark, the absence of gravity.

"Fucking her isn't necessarily making love," Claire said. "*We* make love." Then she fell into her postcoital nap, a little gift her body gave her, exhausted childish sleep.

He took home Claire's theory and tried it on the next time he and Martha had sex. In the living room, Daisy watched television, a habit she'd adopted at the psychiatric hospital and had not given up. She sat around the house indulging an adolescent appetite, Cheetos and Skittles, Count Chocula.

"Where are you?" Martha whispered in his face, holding it in her plump fingers, peering inside him, nose to nose. She was stoned, a state that made her want orgasm and honesty. McBride thought of Claire's words and Daisy's pregnant breasts while he worked his penis inside Martha. Where was he, indeed?

"You can go," she breathed into his ear, his mature girlfriend with her solid legs around his hips, feet locked behind him, "but you have to come back."

The next time he visited the hospital, Claire had been moved to a new ward. They were doing what an aide called a suicide watch. Claire had been caught sawing at her wrists, using a plastic knife, but still. "Those things have serrated edges, man," the aide said. "Ser*rated*," he repeated.

McBride found her tranquilized, staring apathetically at a *New York Review of Books* tabloid. "I can't read this," she said. "The words are floating around like boats." Her wrists were wrapped with gauze, bright clean bracelets. "I feel poisoned," she declared, sailing the book review across the room like a Frisbee. "They're trying to kill me." Considering her behavior, McBride couldn't hold it against the hospital.

"Why?" he asked, hoping simplicity would be his strong suit.

"Why not, you big asshole? That's the real question." She drew a soppy breath, her fine features blue, as if she weren't getting enough oxygen. She cried in the slow, drugged way of hopeless sedation. *Asshole* was not really part of her vocabulary. That was the drugs talking.

"Baby," he said, embracing her, careful of her bandages.

"That's what I need," she said, "a term of endearment. *Muffin. Kitten.*"

"Maybe you should eat? You look kind of . . ."

"I hate fat," Claire said flatly. "I work hard to be thin. I *don't* eat, in order to be thin."

"That's kind of sick."

She simply stared at him, waiting for something she didn't know to emerge from his mouth. "Your girlfriend is fat," she added. It wasn't a good moment. McBride liked her better when she wasn't catty. Also, he was too tempted to respond in kind, to be catty with her. They could get nasty together, it turned out, eat each other's spleen. "She's got a big *tush,* that girlfriend of yours."

"Where are mom and dad?"

"Flying home, wringing their . . ." She held out her own hands, illustrating by twisting her palms, wrists stiff in their wrapping. "They don't have a notion what to do."

"What should *I* do?" he asked.

"Save me," she said, collapsing against him. She wanted to take him with her, he thought. She was drowning, and if he did not escape this clutch, he would wind up washed ashore somewhere, bloated and cold.

• • •

"You can't save her," he told Martha that very night, referring to Daisy, hoping he was right. Daisy, seven months pregnant, had disappeared into south Tucson. The three of them had been eating Mexican food across from the greyhound track; they'd made money betting on those strange creatures, then celebrated with burritos and beer, Daisy on her best behavior, sipping a soda, consuming protein and calcium, like a good mother. But after the bathroom run, she was gone.

Their waiter gave an elaborate shrug, his mustache a wriggling caterpillar on his upper lip.

"Fucking Daisy," McBride said, vindicated. She could not be saved, see? "I guess we have to call the police." He got ahead of himself, saw himself standing around with a cop describing his lunatic ex-girlfriend, driving through danger-ous south Tucson looking for a fuzzy-headed pregnant woman . . . but Martha was giving him such a glance full of disappointment and impatience that he returned to the present moment, Corona bottles, coagulated quesadilla.

"It scares me how much you hate her. You used to love her."

"Come on, Martha, she's manipulative and dishonest and so totally fucked-up . . ." Wasn't the evidence capable of speaking for itself? Furthermore, he refused to believe he'd ever loved Daisy. No one could prove it.

"We have to find her," Martha said, rising from their booth. "You pay, I'll be out on Fourth Ave., walking."

"You can't walk on Fourth—" But she was through the door, and the waiter was handing McBride the ticket, shrugging again, apologetic.

They fought while they searched for Daisy. McBride considered how efficient the situation was—usually a fight required so much energy, such a commitment of time, the yelling part, the pulling-the-phone-out-of-the-wall part, the walk-around-the-block part, the silent thoughtful part, the making up part, the crying and fucking, headache and hangover, raked-over-the-coals, run-through-the-wringer, launched-into-space, deep-in-the-hole part. Hours could go by; a person could lose a day. So it was good, in his opinion, to be occupied with the quest for Daisy while they had their squabble. The problem was that Martha had more experience fighting, a more logical mind-set, and made points like a lawyer. Like a public defender, the type doing pro bono business, the righteous path of the Good Samaritan. She took the moral high road—Daisy in trouble, loyalty, humanity—which left McBride with the inevitable role of bastard. Add to this the affair with suicidal Claire, and you had the picture of a man in a futile argument, perhaps about to be dumped by a nice woman in whose nice house he was living, driving badly in a bad neighborhood, to boot.

He found himself hoping they would see Daisy out there in the dark.

But Daisy was gone for five days, and the fight with Martha wasn't resolved even after all that time. Somehow the stages had gotten messed up; they couldn't progress past sullen silence with each other. Martha was *disappointed* in him. He couldn't make himself fix it. She had every right to be *disappointed* in him. As much as he'd once lusted after Daisy, he now reviled her; that was what troubled Martha, the degree to which love could flip to hate. "Paradox," he wanted to tell her savagely. "That old saw."

He avoided Claire. He abandoned her by telling himself he was being true to Martha.

Daisy managed to phone them up from Phoenix, where a truck driver had left her after buying her a new wardrobe and giving her a stack of *Watchtowers* to contemplate. His name was Buck, and Daisy entered the house referring to his kindness constantly.

Martha hugged her wayward stray, patting Daisy's back maternally; McBride resisted the urge to punch her in the face.

"You're not a burden," Martha insisted when Daisy tried to explain her running away. "I want you to stay with me, even after the baby. I love babies." Embracing, the two women looked decidedly freakish, in McBride's opinion. "You're just bored," Martha insisted. "You need some meaningful activity during these last weeks. Maybe I could teach you how to drive?"

They settled on shopping. Neither of them was a mall type, which made the trip that much more thrilling. Daisy came home wearing her old perfume again, an expensive scent, describable in the way of fine wine: the amber plushness of pears, velvet, oak, wealth. McBride remembered it with equal parts revulsion and nostalgia.

"*Hos*talgia," he thought: sick desire.

That night, when he couldn't get into the spirit of a fashion show featuring maternity clothes and hair clips, Martha accused him of impersonating an adult. Abruptly she threw him a curve, direct from her stoned keenness. "Are you in love with someone else?"

"What?"

She waited.

"No," he croaked, wanting to ask if Daisy had told her something, knowing that would backfire. "No," he repeated, unconvincingly. Just a week ago it would have been a lie, but how could he explain now? The timing made him want to laugh like a madman.

"I'm sleeping in the sewing room tonight," Martha said, taking her pillow.

"Maybe you should fuck Daisy!" he blurted.

"Maybe I should," she agreed, calmly, leveling an unashamed glance in his direction.

Where did women get it, that composure, that open-minded fluid sense that not only might anything happen, but that it might be amazing? McBride could all too easily envision Daisy and Martha naked together, tongue to nape of neck, breast to breast, quivering haunch to ropy one, the homecoming embrace pushed to a climax. It was pretty, candlelit, its sound track full of saxophone.

Men with men: who could look upon it with anything but perplexity? Erections bobbing between them like those annoying trick snakes, coiled in a peanut can, unsealed and sent sproinging in your face. Ha ha. Meanwhile in the background, sound track a circus organ grinder, perhaps a kazoo.

He lay awake alone beneath the SOFT SHOULDER sign thinking of Martha. Was she trying to make him her little boy? Punish him? Improve him? "You know what your problem is?" she'd once told him, laughing yet serious. "You have gag reflex."

"Meaning?"

"Meaning, you can't deal." She did not suffer from this impediment. Why had she attached herself to *him*? Only lately had he wondered—was he a project, not unlike flaky Daisy, someone shell-shocked and deemed for whatever reason worthy of Martha's concern? He didn't want to be her project. He preferred to think of himself as her willing plaything, the party boy, the one who could choose to leave the party. He paid rent, he stocked beer and toilet paper, he had volition.

"You're a coward," Martha told him in the morning. Overnight, she seemed to have chosen against him. She didn't even seem concerned enough to be hurt. Just that disappointed. "You won't commit to anything. The hard parts embarrass you. You feel like everything's a scene instead of just another opportunity to get close to someone. That's what is unforgivable. You're terrible in a crisis. You just want the easy parts, none of the work."

He could not not think of Claire, but what he said was, "Is this about having a baby?"

"This is about *you*," Martha said. "A topic with which you should be fairly familiar. This is about a woman you not only left behind like some dog on the highway, but about whom you won't say one kind word." McBride had to marvel: even angry she wouldn't leave her prepositions dangling. "Not one," said Martha. "I can't get over what a jerk you seem to be. Actually, what I can't get over is that I'm in love with a jerk. I should know better."

"I love you, too," he said quickly.

Martha sighed. "That is *so* not the point."

Meanwhile, Claire's parents sprang her from the psych hospital, which meant that McBride had to sit in their living room drinking iced tea making small talk with them before taking Claire to the motel across from the Triple T. He was conducting an experiment, testing his maturity, trying to recapture what seemed to have scurried off. Were his intentions honorable? her parents' faces asked, forlorn, unsure how to behave if the answer were no. The scars on Claire's wrists were disconcerting, raised welts with tiny suture holes on either side.

"Will those go away?" he asked at the motel, putting his lips on her scars, working at not being disgusted.

"How should I know?" Claire was naked now, but what she'd removed were seafoam green scrubs, as if qualified to dress like a doctor, having hung around them for a while.

"Why so testy?" McBride asked, checking his watch. The iced tea and chat had seriously cut into their time. When Claire smacked him, he didn't know if it was for the question or the looking at the watch. She was one unpredictable girl. They made love then, and following, went through the requisite small sleep.

Leaving McBride to think. Who did he love? Could he ask his women to put in bids for him, sell himself to the one who turned in the most impressive vita? Was he looking for a particular kind of woman and had to have these three to provide one whole? He considered the virtues of each—Martha's good humor and stability, Claire's startling honesty and tragic openness, Daisy's wild sexuality and obsessiveness—and understood their individual appeal as well as their limitations. But perhaps it was having three of them that really excited him. His affection was maybe like a dropped watermelon, three rocking wet seedy parts. Or like a trident. He pictured his penis, three-pronged instead of one.

Or maybe he needed the compounded guilt each relationship made him feel, especially as it related to the other two. High drama had its own charm, like living on a fault plane.

Claire's parents sat right where they'd been left, on plush Barcaloungers before the television. Their iced tea glasses still full of tea, diluted, sweating puddles. The strange stasis that had apparently prevailed here while McBride had been off in a rutting fever, ravishing their middle-aged daughter in a cheesy motel gave him pause. *This* gave him pause—her father looking sad, her mother looking sadder—not the preceding insanity.

He would not be back. His last look at Claire was like his first: she with her parents, sullen, struggling.

He arrived home to find Daisy entertaining the transvestite. They sat in the chairs that McBride and Martha had used to sit in, in the breeze from the oscillating fan. The transvestite had left lipstick prints on a hand-thrown coffee mug. In his large palms, the cup was dwarfed, silly. His nails, unpainted, were smooth, on the verge of being long, and his knuckles, McBride took a moment to notice, were shaved. Unbelievable. The man stayed seated as he extended one of these hands for a shake, like a lady.

"Alberta," he announced. "Your neighbor."

"We've seen you around," McBride said, gripping a little too firmly, a little too masculinely.

"I love the furniture! Your wife is a*maz*ing with a paintbrush!"

"Not his wife," Daisy was quick to say. "How was *your* day, Mackle?" she asked coquettishly, grinning up at him, employing a long-ago pet name, reminding him of others: *Prozac*, because he'd pulled her out of a depression, way back when. *Moon Pie*, he'd called her. And meant it.

"I gotta pee," McBride said, exiting. Entering. Well, here was his house but where was his confidence about belonging in it? On the porch sat the man, the woman, the soon-to-be baby, a fundamental threesome unrelated and weird. "You're not strong enough to accept the limitations of others," insightful Martha had informed him. He wished she would quit knowing him so well, stop being so smart. Why *did* she love a jerk like him? Was that the weakness he would have to object to? He felt like a rung bell, jangling in a lonesome tower, village idiot down below yanking his chain.

"Did you know it was going to be black?" McBride asked Martha.

"I knew it was a fifty-fifty chance." Martha was flushed, wearing a set of green scrubs like the ones Claire owned. Six women had attended Daisy's labor and delivery, Daisy screaming like a tortured crow, the rest of them murmuring and assuring, room of pigeons. The baby, a perfectly healthy girl, was purple as a Nigerian. McBride could only gawk. No one else was fazed; their role was to adore, congratulate, rally. Martha cradled the baby in such a manner that McBride finally understood he would have to leave her. Already that baby meant more to her than he did, or could. Never had a decision been clearer. It made him feel oddly selfless, to see his responsibility.

"Isn't she amazing?" Martha positively glowed, face ruddy with effort, good work, the species' only real priority. She could have been the mother herself, with her wide hips and open heart.

"Unbelievable," McBride said. He looked at the tiny bundle in her arms, dark and constricted. Hard to believe she'd grow up to wear cheap jewelry and eat junk food. Let boys put their hands between her thighs. "Reminds me of an eggplant," he told Martha.

She looked at him as if through the retracting lens of a spyglass: good-bye. "You're so cold," she said, turning back to the room of women.

The deal is, it always goes from bad to worse. The living trajectory, birth to death, going up means coming down. Like that.

McBride told himself these things as he drove to the hospital emergency room a week after Donatella's birth. Claire had jumped from one of Tucson's few overpasses into the traffic below. Everything was broken, head to toe; she would die. She lay now unconscious while a team of experts tried to put her back together. McBride was not innocent in this, as he had not seen her for more than a month, pretending he was tired, pretending he felt guilty about deceiving Martha, pretending he had problems as profound as hers. How was it that affection turned, tiny tender gears no longer meshing, gone suddenly, overnight, eroded with pity? Sour with scorn? When her mother called, three in the morning, Martha had handed him the phone with a single scathing word, that one that had been like a kiss: *Peter*. They'd just failed to have sex, McBride pumping furiously, stiff as a stick of dynamite, unable to explode.

Now he screamed into the ER parking lot, horrified. One more portion of his life, another member in his tribe of female troubles, gone haywire. You build complication like a house of cards, geometrical, tricky, fragile. And like a child, you then like to step aside and stamp your feet, watch as it folds up on itself, flat one-dimensional deck. Dead.

Oh, those parents. Once again, sitting unmoving, identical drinks before them, same condensation. On the television: television. His intentions hadn't been honorable, apparently, after all. Had she wanted to die for love, or its lack? She lay in the highly technical, highly temporary ICU, wrapped, strapped, tracheotomy tube in her neck, metal bolt in her skull, suction hose in her mouth, monitors around her like a recording studio, flashing numbers, graphs. Crust of rusty blood here and there, and her beautiful eyelashes, like folded fragile spider legs, wilted on those pale cheeks. Did this sleep replicate the one she fell into after sex? McBride swooned. Fainting wasn't what he had imagined. He was aware of himself crashing, vital fluids rushing from head, hands, feet to pool and churn in his stomach. His thought was that he would vomit, and be left empty as a pocket. And there was the nurse, the woman who, like a mother, materialized beside him at just the proper moment to smooth his brow, bring him 'round.

He held Claire's letter to him, unopened, missive from the grave, given over by the parents. Her heart, in his hands. On his porch sat four females, lover, ex-girlfriend, her black infant, and the neighbor who counted himself among the girls. Where did McBride fit? He could not be what they required. Nothing to do but squeeze out, he had already been squeezed out.

And he was glad, he told himself. Glad for his simple body, its fixtures out in the open, the expression on his face projecting exactly what was behind it in his head. What was it with women and all this hidden equipment? They dressed up, made up, faked orgasms, cried when happy, laughed when bitter, stirred up protoplasmic stews of life and then pulled aces from sleeves, wreaked havoc all the wide world over, forever refusing to come clean.

That was how he wanted to feel, driving his car with his worldly possessions: clean. Free. Was that the same as being cold? Cowardly? He'd left Salt Lake

City and he could leave Tucson; the West was full of cities where his slate would be blank, his plate would be empty. There was a girl out there, he could almost see her, radiant, blonde, a healthy hiker a few years younger than he, straight teeth, muscular calves, sentimental taste in music. He would find *her* . . . but how did that accident claim go, the one that had amused him not so long ago? "I saw a slow moving, sad-faced old gentleman as he bounded off the roof of my car . . ." Nothing to do but plunge on. Set the cruise control, lower the windows, raise the radio, stay between the broken yellow lines, and don't look back. No no no.

Joyce Carol Oates

THE TRANSLATION

JOYCE CAROL OATES (1938–), a member of the American Academy of Arts and Letters since 1978, is the author of the novels *Blonde, We Were the Mulvaneys, Middle Age: A Romance, Black Water, The Falls, Missing Mom,* and most recently *The Gravedigger's Daughter.* Among her story collections is *High Lonesome: New and Selected Stories 1966–2006.* She is a recipient of the National Book Award, the Prix Femina, the PEN/Malamud Award, and most recently the *Chicago Tribune* Lifetime Achievement Award in Literature.

What were the words for *woman, man, love, freedom, fate?*—in this strange land where the architecture and the countryside and the sea with its dark choppy waters and the very air itself seemed to Oliver totally foreign, unearthly? He must have fallen in love with the woman at once, after fifteen minutes' conversation. Such perversity was unlike him. He had loved a woman twenty years before; had perhaps loved two or even three women in his lifetime; but had never fallen in love, had never been *in love;* such melodramatic passion was not his style. He had only spoken with her for fifteen minutes at the most, and not directly: through the translator assigned to him. He did not know her at all. Yet, that night, he dreamed of rescuing her.

"I am struck and impressed," he said politely, addressing the young woman introduced to him as a music teacher at the high school and a musician—a violist—herself, "with the marvelous old buildings here . . . the church that is on the same street as my hotel . . . yes? . . . you know it? . . . and with the beauty of the parks, the trees and flowers, everything so well-tended, and the manner of the people I have encountered . . . they are friendly but not effusive; they appear so very . . . so very healthy," he said, hearing his voice falter, realizing that he was being condescending; as if it surprised him, the fact that people in this legendary, long-suffering nation were not very different from people anywhere. But his translator translated the speech and the young woman appeared to agree, nodding, smiling as if to encourage him. Thank God, he had not offended her. "I am very grateful to have been allowed a visa," he said. "I have never visited a country that has struck me in such a way . . . an immediate sense of, of . . . how shall I put it . . . of something like nostalgia . . . do you know the expression, the meaning? . . . nostalgia . . . emotion for something once possessed but now lost, perhaps not now even accessible through memory. . . ."

If he was making a fool of himself with this speech, and by so urgently staring at the woman, Alisa, the others did not appear to notice; they listened intently, even greedily, as Oliver's young translator repeated his words, hardly pausing for breath. He was a remarkable young man, probably in his early twenties, and Oliver had the idea that the translator's presence and evident good will toward him were freeing his tongue, giving him a measure of happiness for the first time since he had left the United States. For the first time, really, in many years. It was marvelous, magical, to utter his thoughts aloud and to hear, then, their instantaneous translation into a foreign language—to sit with his translator at his left hand, watching the effect of his words upon his listeners' faces as they were translated. An eerie, uncanny experience . . . unsettling and yet exciting in a way Oliver could not have explained. He had not liked the idea of relying upon a translator; one of his failings, one of the disappointments of his life, had always been a certain shyness or coolness in his character, which it was evidently his fate not to alter, and he had supposed that travel into a country as foreign as this one, and as formally antagonistic to the United States, would be especially difficult since he knew nothing of the language. But in fact the translator was like a younger brother to him, like a son. There was an intimacy between them and a pleasurable freedom, even an unembarrassed lyricism in Oliver's remarks that he could not possibly have anticipated.

Of course his mood was partly attributable to the cognac and to the close, crowded, overheated room in which the reception was being held and to his immediate attraction for the dusky-haired, solemn young woman with the name he could not pronounce—*Alisa* was as close as he could come to it; he would have to ask the translator to write it out for him when they returned to the hotel. It would not last, his mood of gaiety. But for the present moment he was very happy, merely to hear these people speak their language, a melodic play of explosive consonants and throaty vowels; it hardly mattered that his translator could manage to translate only a fraction of what was being said. Oliver was happy, almost euphoric. He was intoxicated. He had to restrain himself from taking one of Alisa's delicate hands in his own and squeezing it, to show how taken he was by her. *I know you are suffering in this prison-state of yours*, he wanted to whisper to her, *and I want, I want to do something for you . . . want to rescue you, save you, change your life. . . .*

The Director of the Lexicographic Institute was asking him a courteous, convoluted question about the current state of culture in his own nation, and everyone listened, frowning as if with anxiety, while, with one part of his mind, Oliver made several statements. His translator took them up at once, transformed them into those eerie, exquisite sounds; the Director nodded gravely,

emphatically; the others nodded; it seemed to be about what they had anticipated. One of the men, white-haired, diminutive, asked something in a quaver-
ing voice, and Oliver's translator hesitated before repeating it. "Dr. Crlejevec is
curious to know—is it true that your visual artists have become artists merely of
the void—that is, of death—they are exclusively morbid, they have turned their
backs on life?" The translator blushed, not quite meeting Oliver's gaze, as if he
were embarrassed by the question. But the question did not annoy Oliver. Not
in the least. He disliked much of contemporary art anyway and welcomed the
opportunity to express his feelings warmly, knowing what he said would endear
him to these people. It pleased him most of all that Alisa listened so closely. Her
long, nervous fingers toyed with a cameo broach she wore at her throat; her gray
eyes were fixed upon his face. "Art moves in a certain tendril-like manner . . . in
many directions, though at a single point in history one direction is usually
stressed and acclaimed . . . like the evolutionary gropings of nature, to my way
of thinking. Do you see? The contemporary pathway is but a tendril, a feeler, an
experimental gesture . . . because it is obsessed with death and the void and the
annihilation of self it will necessarily die . . . it pronounces its own death sentence."

The words were translated; the effect was instantaneous; Oliver's pronounce-
ment seemed to meet with approval. The Director, however, posed another
question. He was a huge man in his fifties, with a ruddy, beefy face and rather
coarse features, though his voice seemed to Oliver quite cultured. ". . . But in the
meantime, does it not do damage? . . . to the unformed, that is, to the young, the
susceptible . . . does it not do irreparable damage, such deathly art?"

Oliver's high spirits could not be diminished. He only pretended to be thinking seriously before he answered, "Not at all! In my part of the world, 'serious'
art is ignored by the masses; the unformed, the young, the susceptible are hardly
aware of its existence!"

He had expected his listeners to laugh. But they did not laugh. The young
woman murmured something, shaking her head. Oliver's translator said to him,
"She says she is shocked . . . unless, of course, you are joking."

The conversation shifted. Oliver was taken to other groups of people, was
introduced by his translator, was made to feel important, honored. From time to
time he glanced back at the young woman—when he saw her preparing to
leave, he was stricken; he wanted to tell his translator to stop her, but of course
that would have been indecorous. *I want to do something for you. Anything. I
want* . . . But it would have been indecorous.

"She is a fine person, very hard-working, very trustworthy," Liebert was saying
slowly. "Not my friend or even acquaintance, but my sister's . . . my older sister,
who was her classmate. She is a very accomplished violist, participated in a

festival last spring in Moscow, but also a very fine teacher here, very hardwork-ing, very serious."

"Is she married?" Oliver asked.

They were being driven in a shiny black taxicab along an avenue of trees in blossom—acacia, lime—past buildings of all sizes, some very old, some dis-concertingly new, of glass and poured concrete and steel, and from time to time the buildings fell back and a monument appeared, sudden, grandiose, rather pompous—not very old either, Oliver noted. Postwar.

"There is some difficulty, yes," the translator said, "with the husband ... and with the father as well. But I do not know, really. I am not an acquaintance of hers, as I said. She lives her life, I live mine. We meet a few times a year, at gatherings like the one last night ... she too does translations, though not into English. Into German exclusively."

"Then she is married? You mentioned a husband ... ?"

Liebert looked out the window, as if embarrassed by Oliver's interest. He was not unwilling to talk about the young woman, but not willing either. For the first time in their three days' acquaintance, Oliver felt the young man's stubborn nature. "They have not been together in one place for many years, as I under-stand it," he said. "The husband, not an acquaintance of my own, is some years older than she ... a doctor, I believe ... a research specialist in an area I know nothing of. He is in another city. He has been in another city, and Alisa in this city, for many years."

"I'm sorry to hear that," Oliver said sincerely. "She struck me as sweet, vul-nerable ... possibly a little lonely? I don't like to think that she may be un-happy."

Liebert shrugged his shoulders.

"Unhappy, so?" he murmured.

They drove through a square and Oliver's attention was drawn to an im-mense portrait of a man's face: a poster three stories high.

"Amazing!" he said without irony.

"It is not amazing, it is ordinary life," Liebert said. "We live here."

"... She isn't unhappy then? No more than most?"

"There is not the—what is the word?—the compulsion to analyze such things, such states of mind," Liebert said with a vague air of reproach. "It is enough to complete the day—working hard, carrying out one's obligations. You understand? Leisure would only result in morbid self-scrutiny and the void, the infatuation with the void, which is your fate."

"My fate?" Oliver said. "Not mine. Don't confuse me with anyone else."

Liebert mumbled an apology.

They drove on in silence for a few minutes. They were approaching a hilly area north of the city; in the near distance were mountains of a peculiar magenta color, partly obscured by mist. Oliver still felt that uncharacteristic euphoria, as if he were in a dream, a kind of paradise, and on all sides miracles ringed him in. He had not been prepared for the physical beauty of this place, or for the liveliness of its people. And his translator, Liebert, was quite a surprise. He spoke English with very little accent, clear-voiced, boyish, attentive to Oliver's every hesitation or expression of curiosity, exactly as if he could read Oliver's thoughts. He evidently took it as his solemn duty to make Oliver comfortable in every way. His manner was both shy and composed, childlike and remarkably mature. He had a sweet, melancholy, shadowed face with a thick head of dark curly hair and a widow's peak above a narrow forehead; his cheekbones were Slavic; his complexion was pale but with a faint rosy cast to it, as if the blood hummed warmly close beneath the skin. Large brown eyes, a long nose, ears too large for his slender face . . . something about him put Oliver in mind of a nocturnal animal, quick, furtive, naturally given to silence. In general he had an ascetic appearance. No doubt he was very poor, in his ill-fitting tweed suit and scuffed brown shoes, his hair crudely cut, so short that it emphasized the thinness of his neck and the prominence of his Adam's apple. Not handsome, perhaps, but attractive in his own way. Oliver liked him very much.

"If you would like, perhaps another meeting could be arranged," he said softly. "That is, it would not be impossible."

"Another meeting? With her?"

"If you would like," Liebert said.

Love: loss of equilibrium. Imbalance. Something fundamental to one's being, an almost physical certainty of self, is violated. Oliver had loved women in the past and he had felt, even, this distressing physical urgency, this anxiety, before; but it had never blossomed so quickly, based on so little evidence. The night of the reception at the Institute he had slept poorly, rehearsing in his sleep certain phrases he would say to Alisa, pleading with her, begging her. For what? And why? She was a striking woman, perhaps not beautiful; it was natural that he might be attracted to her, though his experiences with women in recent years had been disappointing. But the intensity of his feeling worried him. It was exactly as if something foreign to his nature had infiltrated his system, had found him vulnerable, had shot his temperature up by several degrees. And he rejoiced in it, despite his worry and an obscure sense of shame. He really rejoiced in it. He woke, poured himself some of the sweet-tasting brandy he had left on his night table, lay back upon the goose-feather pillows, and thought of her. Was it possible he could see her again? Under what pretext? He was leaving in four days. Possibly he could extend his visit. Possibly not.

He recalled her bony, broad cheekbones, the severity of her gaze, her rather startled smile. A stranger. One of many strangers. In this phase of his life, Oliver thought, he met only strangers; he had no wish to see people he knew.

I love you. I want . . . what do I want? . . . I want to know more about you.

A mistake, but he could not resist pouring more brandy into the glass. It tasted like sweet, heavy syrup at first and then, after a few seconds, like pure alcohol, blistering, acidic. One wished to obliterate the strong taste with the sweet—the impulse was to sip a little more.

According to his clock in its small leather traveling case it was three-fifteen.

I want . . . what do I want? he murmured aloud.

Liebert translated for Oliver: "She says that the 'extravagance' you speak of in Androv's chronicles . . . and in our literature generally . . . is understood here as exaggeration . . . metaphors? . . . metaphors, yes, for interior states. But we ourselves, we are not extravagant in our living."

"Of course I only know Androv's work in translation," Oliver said quickly. "It reads awkwardly, rather like Dreiser? . . . do you know the name, the novelist? . . . one of our distinguished American novelists, no longer so popular as he once was . . . I was enormously impressed with the stubbornness, the resiliency, the audacity of Androv's characters, and despite his technique of exaggeration they seemed to me very lifelike." He paused, in order to give Liebert the opportunity to translate. He was breathing quickly, watching Alisa's face. They were having a drink in the hotel lounge, a dim, quiet place where morose potted plants of a type Oliver did not recognize grew more than six feet high, drooping over the half dozen marble tables. Oliver was able to see his own reflection in a mirror across the room; the mirror looked smoky, webbed as if with a spider's web; his own face hovered there indistinct and pale. His constant, rather nervous smile was not visible.

In the subdued light of the hotel lounge Alisa seemed to him more beautiful than before. Her dark hair was drawn back and fastened in an attractive French twist; it was not done carelessly into a bun or a knot, the way many local women wore their hair; it shone with good health. She wore a white blouse and, again, the old-fashioned cameo broach, and a hip-length sweater of some coarse dark wool, and a nondescript skirt that fell well below her knees. Her eyes were slightly slanted, almond-shaped, dark, glistening; her cheekbones, like Liebert's, were prominent. Oliver guessed her to be about thirty-five, a little older than he had thought. But striking—very striking. Every movement of hers charmed him. Her mixture of shyness and composure, her quick contralto voice, her habit of glancing from Oliver to Liebert to Oliver again, almost flirtatiously—he knew he was staring rudely at her, but he could not look away.

"She says—Of course we have a reputation for audacity; how else could we have survived? The blend of humor and morbidity . . . the bizarre tall tales . . . 'deaths and weddings,' if you are familiar with the allusion? . . . no? . . . she is referring to the third volume of *The Peasants*," Liebert murmured. Oliver nodded as if he were following all this. In fact he had lost track of the conversation; the woman fascinated him; he was vexed with the thought that he had seen her somewhere before, had in some way known her before. . . . And he had read only the first two volumes of Androv's massive work. "From the early fifteenth century, as you know, most of the country has been under foreign dominion . . . the most harsh, the Turks . . . centuries of oppression . . . between 1941 and 1945 alone there were two million of us murdered. . . . Without the 'extravagance' and even the mania of high spirits, how could we have survived?"

"I know, I understand, I am deeply sympathetic," Oliver said at once.

He could not relax, though he had had two drinks that afternoon. Something was urgent, crucial—he must not fail—but he could not quite comprehend what he must do. An American traveler, not really a tourist, prominent enough in his own country to merit the designation of "cultural emissary"—the State Department's term, not his own—he heard his own accent and his own predictable words with a kind of revulsion, as if, here, in this strange, charming country, the personality he had created for himself over a forty-three-year period were simply inadequate: shallow, superficial, hypocritical. He had not suffered. He could pretend knowledge and sympathy, but of course he was an impostor; he had not suffered except in the most ordinary of ways—an early, failed marriage; a satisfactory but not very exciting profession; the stray, undefined disappointments of early middle age. He listened to the woman's low, beautifully modulated voice, and to his translator's voice; he observed their perfect manners, their rather shabby clothing, and judged himself inferior. He hoped they would not notice. Liebert, who had spent so many patient hours with him, must sense by now his own natural superiority; must have some awareness of the irony of their relative positions. Oliver hoped the young man would not resent him, would not turn bitterly against him before the visit came to a conclusion. It seemed to him an ugly fact of life: that he, Oliver, had money, had a certain measure of prestige, however lightly he valued it, and had, most of all, complete freedom to travel anywhere he wished. The vast earth was his—as much of it as he cared to explore. Other cultures, other ways of life were open to his investigation. Even the past was his, for he could visit places of antiquity, could assemble countless books and valuable objects, could pursue any interest of his to its culmination. As the editor and publisher of a distinguished magazine, which featured essays on international culture, with as little emphasis as possible upon politics, Oliver was welcome nearly anywhere; he knew several languages—French, Italian, Spanish—and if he did not know a country's language a skillful interpreter was assigned to him and there was rarely any difficulty. Though he was accustomed to think of himself as colorless, as a failure—as a young man he had wanted to be a poet and a playwright—it was nevertheless true that he was a public success, and that he had a certain amount

of power. Alisa and Liebert, however, were powerless; in a sense they were pris--
oners.

Of course they proclaimed their great satisfaction with postwar events. The
Nazis had been driven back, another world power had come to their aid, the
government under which they now lived was as close to perfection as one might
wish. Compared to their tumultuous, miserable past, how sunny their present
seemed!—of course they were happy. But they were prisoners just the same.
They could not leave their country. It might even be the case that they could
not leave this particular city without good cause. Oliver happened to know
that nearly one-third of the population was involved, on one level or another, in
espionage—neighbors reporting on neighbors, relatives on relatives, students
on teachers, teachers on supervisors, friends on friends. It was a way of life. As
Liebert had said the other day, it was nothing other than ordinary life for
them.

Oliver knew. He knew. The two of them were fortunate just to have jobs that
weren't manual; they were fortunate to be as free as they were, talking with an
American. He believed he could gauge their fate in the abstract, in the collective, no matter that the two were really strangers to him. He knew and he did
sympathize and, in spite of his better judgment, he wished he could help
them.

At dusk they walked three abreast along the sparsely lit boulevard, the main
street of the city; Oliver was to be taken to a workingman's café; he was tired of
the hotel food, the expensive dinners. They spoke now of the new buildings that
were being erected, south of the city, along the sea cliff; they told Oliver that he
must take time to visit one of the excavations farther to the south—he would
see Roman ornaments, coins, grave toys, statuary. "Alisa says—the evidence of
other centuries and other civilizations is so close to us," Liebert murmured, "we
are unable to place too much emphasis upon the individual, the ephemeral. Do
you see? I have often thought along those lines myself."

"Yes, I suppose so—I suppose that's right," Oliver said slowly.

Alisa said something to him, looking up at him. Liebert, on his right side,
translated at once: "Future generations are as certain as the past—there is a
continuity—there is a progress, an evolution. It is clear, it is scientifically de-
monstrable."

"Is it?" Oliver said, for a moment wondering if it might be so. "Yes—that's
possible—I'm sure that's possible."

Liebert translated his words and Alisa laughed.

"Why is she laughing? What did you say?" Oliver asked, smiling.

"I said—only what you said. I translated your words faithfully," Liebert said
rather primly.

"She has such a ready, sweet laugh," Oliver said. "She's so charming, so unconscious of herself. . . . Ask her, Liebert, where she's from . . . where she went to school . . . where she lives . . . what her life is like."

"All that?" Liebert asked. "So much!"

"But we have all evening, don't we?" Oliver said plaintively. ". . . All night?"

That day he had been a guest at the District Commissioner's home, for a two-hour luncheon. He had been driven to the village where the poet Hisjak had been born. Along with another guest of honor, an Italian novelist, he had been shown precious documents—the totally illegible manuscripts of an unknown writer, unknown at least to Oliver—kept in a safe in a museum. The first two evenings of his visit had been spent at endless dinners. He had witnessed a troupe of youthful dancers in rehearsal; he had admired the many statues of heroes placed about the city; he had marveled over the Byzantine domes, the towers and vaulting roofs and fountains. But his hours with Alisa and Liebert were by far the most enjoyable; he knew he would never forget them.

They ate a thick, greasy stew of coarse beef and vegetables, and many slices of whole-grain bread and butter, and drank two bottles of wine, of a dry, tart nature, quite unfamiliar to Oliver. The three of them sat at a corner table in an utterly unimpressive restaurant; it was crude and brightly lit and noisy as an American diner. At first the other patrons took notice of them, but as time passed and the restaurant grew noisier they were able to speak without being overheard. Oliver was very happy. He felt strangely free, like a child. The food was delicious; he kept complimenting them, and asking Liebert to tell the waitress, and even to tell the cook; the bread, especially, seemed extraordinary—he insisted that he had never tasted bread so good. "How can I leave? Where can I go from here?" he said jokingly. They were served small, flaky tarts for dessert, and Oliver ate his in two or three bites, though he was no longer hungry and the oversweet taste, apricots and brandy and raw dark sugar, was not really to his liking.

"You are all so wonderful . . ." he said.

Alisa sat across from him, Liebert sat to his left. The table was too small for their many dishes and glasses and silverware. They laughed together like old friends, easily, intimately. Alisa showed her gums as she laughed—no self-consciousness about her—utterly natural, direct. Her eyes narrowed to slits and opened wide again, sparkling. The wine had brought a flush to her cheeks. Liebert too was expansive, robust. He no longer played the role of the impoverished, obsequious student. Sometimes he spoke to Oliver without feeling the necessity to translate his English for Alisa; sometimes he and Alisa exchanged remarks, and though Oliver did not know what they were saying, or why they laughed so merrily, he joined them in their laughter. Most of the time, however, Liebert translated back and forth from Oliver to Alisa, from Alisa to Oliver, rapidly, easily, always with genuine interest. Oliver liked the rhythm that was established: like a game, like a piece of music, like the bantering of love. Oliver's words in English translated into Alisa's language, Alisa's words translated into Oliver's language, magically. Surely it was magic. Oliver asked Alisa about her background, about the village she had grown up in; he asked her about her parents, about her work. It turned out that her father had been a teacher also, a music teacher at one of the colleges—"very distinguished and well loved"—but he had become ill, there was no treatment available, he had wanted to return to his home district to die. Oliver listened sympathetically. There was more to it, he supposed, there was something further about it . . . but he could not inquire. And what about the husband? But he could not inquire; he did not dare.

"You are all so remarkably free of bitterness," he said.

Liebert translated. Alisa replied. Liebert hesitated before saying: "Why should we be bitter? We live with complexity. You wish simplicity in your life . . . good divided sharply from evil, love divided from hate . . . beauty from ugliness. We have always been different. We live with complexity; we would not recognize the world otherwise."

Oliver was staring at Alisa. "Did you really say that?" he asked.

"Of course she said that. Those words exactly," Liebert murmured.

"She's so . . . she's so very . . . I find her so very charming," Oliver said weakly. "Please don't translate! Please. Do you see? It's just that I find her so . . . I admire her without reservation," he said, squeezing Liebert's arm. "I find it difficult to reply to her. Central Europe is baffling to me; I expected to be meeting quite different kinds of people; your closed border, your wartime consciousness that seems never to lift, your reputation for . . . for certain inexplicable . . ." Both Liebert and Alisa were watching him, expressionless. He fell silent. Absurdly, he had been about to speak of the innumerable arrests and imprisonments, even of the tortures reported in the West, but it seemed to him now that perhaps these reports were lies. He did not know what to believe.

"Freedom and constraint cannot be sharply divided, the one from the other," Liebert said coldly. "Freedom is a relative thing. It is relative to the context, to the humanity it serves . . . shelters. For instance, your great American cities, they are so famed, they are 'free'; you would boast citizens can come and go as they wish . . . each in his automobile—isn't that so? But, in fact, we know that your people are terrified of being hurt by one another. They are terrified of being killed by their fellow citizens. In this way," Liebert said, smiling, "in this way it must be judged that the nature of freedom is not so simple. But it is always political."

"There's a difference between self-imposed restrictions and . . . and the restrictions of a state like yours," Oliver said, obscurely hurt, blinking. He had no interest in defending his nation. He did not care about it at all, not at the moment. "But perhaps you are correct, the issue is always political, even when it is baffling and obscure. . . . In America we have too much freedom and the individual is free to hurt others, this is an excess of . . . am I speaking too quickly? . . . this is an excess rather than . . . But I don't wish to talk of such things," he said softly. "Not tonight. It is more important, our being together. Do you agree? Yes? Ask Alisa—does she agree?"

They agreed. They laughed together like old friends.

"Alisa says—We must live our lives in the interstices of the political state," Liebert said slyly, "like sparrows who make their nests on window ledges or street lamps. They are happy there until the happiness stops. We are happy, until it stops. But perhaps it will not stop for many years—who can predict? Political oppression is no more a disaster than an accident on the highway or a fatal disease or being born crippled—"

"Disaster is disaster," Oliver said thickly. "What do we care? There isn't time. I must leave in a few days. . . . I admire you both so very, very much. You're noble, you're brave, you're attractive . . . she is beautiful, isn't she? . . . beautiful! I've never met anyone so intelligent and beautiful at the same time, so vivacious, good-natured. . . . Will you tell her that? Please?"

Liebert turned to her and spoke. She lowered her head, fussed with her hair, reddened slightly, frowned. A long moment passed. She glanced shyly at Oliver. Seeing the desperation in his eyes, she managed to smile.

"Thank you," Oliver whispered. "Thank you both so very much."

Something was stinging him.

Bedbugs?

His arms were curiously leaden; he could not move; he could not rake his nails against his sides, his abdomen, his buttocks, his back. He groaned but did not wake. The stinging became a single sweeping flame that covered his body, burned fiercely.

"Alisa?" he said. "Are you here? Are you hiding?"

He was in the Old City, the City of Stone. Much of it had been leveled during the war, but there were ancient buildings—fortresses, inns, cathedrals. The weight of time. The weight of the spirit. On all sides voices were chattering in that exquisite, teasing language he could not decipher. They were mocking him, jeering at him. They knew him very well. He was to be led to their shrine, where a miracle would be performed. The holy saint of Toskinjevec, patron saint of lepers, epileptics, the crippled and the insane and the fanatic. . . . He was being hurried along the cobblestone streets. There were heavy oak doors with iron hinges; there were rusted latches and locks; walls slime-green with mold, beginning to crumble. Footsteps rang and echoed. Liebert held his hand, murmured words of comfort, stroked his head. He wanted only to obey. "Where is she? Is she already there?" he whispered. Liebert told him to be still—he must not speak! Someone was following them. Someone wished to hurt them. Oliver saw, in a panic, the greenish-copper steeple of an old church; he could take refuge in its ruins; no one would find them there. The main part of the building had been reduced to rubble. A wall remained and on this wall were posters of the great President—charmingly candid shots that showed the man with one of his children, and in a peasant's costume, and with a rifle raised to his shoulder, one eye squinted shut, and on the ledge above a waterfall, his arm raised in a salute to the crowd gathered below. Oliver hurried. Someone would stand guard for them—one of the men he had seen in the restaurant, had seen without really considering; a young black-haired man who had been playing chess with a friend, and who had not glanced up a single time at Oliver and his friends. But now he would stand guard. Now he was to be trusted.

They descended into a cellar. Everywhere there were slabs of stone, broken plasterboard, broken glass. Weeds grew abundantly in the cracks. "Hurry," Liebert urged, dragging him forward. Then Oliver was with her, clutching at her. By a miracle they were together. He kissed her desperately, recklessly. She pretended to resist. "No, there isn't time, there isn't enough time," he begged, "no, don't stop me. . . ." She went limp; she put her arms around his neck; they struggled together, panting, while the young translator urged them on, anxious, a little annoyed. Oliver's entire body stung. Waves of heat swept over him and broke into tiny bits so that he groaned aloud. He wanted her so violently, he was so hungry for her, for her or for something. . . . "How can I bring you with me?" he said. "I love you, I won't surrender you." She spoke in short melodic phrases. He could not understand. Now she too was anxious, clutching at him, pressing herself against him. Oliver could not bear it. He was going mad. Then, out of the corner of his eye, he happened to see someone watching them. The police! . . . But no, it was a poorly dressed old man, a cripple, peering at them from behind a broken wall. He was deformed: his legs were mere stumps. Oliver stared, in a panic. He could not believe what he saw. Behind the old man were two or three others, half crawling, pushing themselves along through the debris by the exertions of their arms, their legs cut off at the thigh. They were bearded, wide-eyed, gaping, moronic. He understood that they were moronic. Oliver tried to lead Alisa away, but she resisted. Evidently the men were from a nearby hospital and were harmless. They had been arrested in an abortive uprising of some sort, years before, and punished in ways fitting their audacity; but now they were harmless, harmless. . . .

His sexual desire died at once. The dream died at once.

He could not sleep. The dream had left him terrified and nauseous.

During the past few years life had thinned out for Oliver. It had become insubstantial, unreal, too spontaneous to have much value. Mere details, pieces, ugly tiny bits. Nothing was connected and nothing made sense. Was this "life"?—an idle pointless flow? He had watched it, knowing that one must be attentive, one must be responsible. But he had not really believed in it. There was no internal necessity, no order, only that jarring spontaneity, a world of slivers and teasing fragments. Ugly and illusory.

Here, however, things seemed different. He could breathe here. There were travelers who could not accept the reality of the countries they visited, and who yearned, homesick, for their own country, for their own language; but Oliver was not one of them. He would not have cared—not for a moment!—if the past were eradicated, his home country destroyed and erased from history.

He poured brandy into a glass, his fingers steady.

"Would I mourn . . . ? Never."

The dream had frightened him, but it was fading now. It was not important. He had had too much to eat, too much to drink. His emotional state was unnatural. Love was an imbalance: he was temporarily out of control. But he would be all right. He had faith in himself.

The woman lived in a one-room apartment, Liebert had informed him. She shared it with another teacher at the high school, a woman. Should Oliver wish to visit her there—how could it be arranged? She could not come to the hotel. That was out of the question. Liebert had muttered something about the possibility of the other woman going to visit her family . . . though this would involve some expenses . . . she would need money. It would be awkward, but it could be arranged. If so, then Alisa would be alone and Oliver would be welcome to visit her. There might be danger, still. Or was there no danger? Oliver really did not know.

"And what of her husband?" Oliver had asked hesitantly.

"Ah—there is no risk. The man is in a hospital at Kanleža, in the mountains . . . he is receiving treatment for emotional maladjustment . . . a very sad case. Very sad. It is tragic, but he is no risk; do not worry about him," Liebert said softly.

They looked at each other for a moment. Oliver warmed, reddened. He did not know if he was terribly ashamed or simply excited.

"I love her," he whispered. "I can't help it."

Liebert might not have heard, he had spoken so softly. But he did not ask Oliver to repeat his words.

"How much money would the woman need?" Oliver asked helplessly.

They had been here, in this room. The money had changed hands and Liebert had gone and Oliver had undressed at once, exhausted from the evening, from all the eating and drinking and talking. He had wanted only to sleep. His fate was decided, he would meet Alisa the following day, he would extend his visit for another week perhaps, in order to see her every day; but now he must sleep, he was sick with exhaustion. And so he had slept. But dreams disturbed him: in them he was trying to speak, trying to make himself understood, while strangers mocked and jeered. The last dream, of Alisa and the deformed old men, was the most violent of all, a nightmare of the sort he had not had for years. When he woke, he felt debased, poisoned. It was as if a poison of some sort had spread throughout his body.

He sat up, leafing through a guidebook in English, until dawn.

"But I don't understand. Where is Mr. Liebert?"

His new translator was a stout, perspiring man in his fifties, no more than five feet four inches tall. He wore a shiny black suit with a vest and oversized buttons, of black plastic. Baldness had enlarged his round face. His eyebrows were snarled and craggy, his lips pale, rubbery. With a shrug of his shoulders he dismissed Liebert. "Who knows? There was important business. Back home, called away. Not your concern."

He smiled. Oliver stared, thinking: He's a nightmare. He's from a nightmare. But the man was real, the bright chilly morning was real, Oliver's dismay and alarm were real. He tried to protest, saying that he had liked Liebert very much, the two of them had understood each other very well; but the new translator merely smiled stupidly, as before. "I am your escort now and your translator," he repeated.

Oliver made several telephone calls, but there was nothing to be done.

"I do not have the acquaintance of Mr. Liebert," the new translator said as they walked out together. One eyelid descended in a wink. "But there is no lack of sympathy. It is all the same. —A nice day, isn't it? That is acacia tree in blossom; is lovely, eh? Every spring."

The man's accent was guttural. Oliver could not believe his bad luck. He walked in a trance, thinking of Alisa, of Liebert—Liebert, who had been so charming, so quick. It did not seem possible that this had happened.

That day he saw the posters of his dream. He saw a tarnished coppery-green steeple rising above a ruined church. He saw, in the distance, long, low, curiously narrow strips of cloud or mist rising from the sea, reaching into the lower part of the city. Beside him, the squat, perspiring man chattered in babyish English, translated signs and menus, kept asking Oliver in his mechanical chirping voice, "It is nice, eh? Spring day. Good luck." From time to time he winked at Oliver as if there were a joke between them.

Oliver shuddered.

The city looked different. There was too much traffic—buses, motorbikes, vans of one kind or another—and from the newer section of the city, where a number of one-story factories had been built, there came invisible clouds of poison. The sky was mottled; though it was May fifteenth, it was really quite cold.

"Where is Liebert?" Oliver asked, more than once. "He and I were friends . . . we understood each other. . . ."

They went to a folk museum where they joined another small group. Oliver tried to concentrate. He smiled, he was courteous as always, he made every effort to be civil. But the banalities!—the idiotic lies! His translator repeated what was said in a thick, dull voice, passing no judgment—as Liebert would have done, slyly—and Oliver was forced to reply, to say something. He stammered, he heard his voice proclaiming the most asinine things—bald, blunt compliments, flattery. Seven or eight men in a group for an endless luncheon, exchanging banalities, hypocritical praise, chatter about the weather and the blossoming trees and the National Ballet. The food was too rich, and when Oliver's came to him it was already lukewarm. The butter was unsalted and tasteless. One of the men, a fat, pompous official, exactly like an official in a political cartoon, smoked a cigar and the smoke drifted into Oliver's face. He tried to bring up the subject of his first translator but was met with uncomprehending stares.

Afterward he was taken, for some reason, to the offices of the Ministry of Agriculture; he was introduced to the editor of a series of agricultural pamphlets; it was difficult for him to make sense of what was being said. Some of these people spoke English as well as his translator, and he had the idea that others merely pretended not to know English. There was a great deal of chatter. He thought of Alisa and felt suddenly exhausted. He would never get to her now—it was impossible. Beside him the fat sweating man kept close watch. What was being said?—words. He leaned against a gritty windowsill, staring absently out at the innumerable rooftops, the ugly chimneys and water tanks, the banal towers. He remembered the poison of his dream and could taste it in the air now; the air of this city was remarkably polluted.

"You are tired now? Too much visit? You rest, eh?"

"Yes."

"You leave soon, it was said? Day after tomorrow?"

"Yes. I think so."

There were streetcars and factory whistles. Automobile horns. In the street someone stared rudely at him. Oliver wondered what these people saw—a tall, sandy-haired man in his early forties, distracted, haggard, rather vain in his expensive clothes? They looked at his clothes, not at him. At his shoes. They did not see him at all; they had no use for him.

"You are maybe sick . . . ?"

"A little. I think. Yes."

"Ah!" he said, in a parody of sympathy. "You go to room, rest. Afterward perk up. Afterward there is plan for evening—yes? All set?"

"Evening? I thought this evening was free—"

The man winked. "She is friend—old friend. Sympathizes you."

"I don't understand," Oliver stammered.

"All understand. All sympathize one another," the man said cheerfully.

• • •

"Is wealthy? Own several automobiles? What about house—houses? Parents are living? How many brothers and sisters? Is married, has children? How many? Names?"

The three of them sat together, not in Alisa's room but in another café. Oliver was paying for their drinks. He was paying for everything. The woman's curt, rude questions were being put to him in clusters and he managed to answer, as succinctly as possible, trying not to show his despair. When his translator repeated Oliver's answers, Alisa nodded emphatically, always the same way, her eyes bright, deliberately widened. Wisps of hair had come loose about her forehead; it annoyed Oliver that she did not brush them away. She was a little drunk, her laughter was jarring, she showed her gums when she laughed—he could hardly bear to watch her.

"Say like our country very much? Good. New place going up—there is new company, Volkswagen—many new jobs. When you come back, another year, lots new things. You are friendly, always welcome. Very nice. Good to know...."

The conversation seemed to rattle on without Oliver's intervention. He heard his voice, heard certain simple-minded replies. Alisa and the fat man laughed merrily. They were having a fine time. Oliver drank because he had nothing else to do; whenever he glanced at his watch, the others looked at it also, with childish, open avarice. Time did not pass. He dreaded any mention of the room, of the alleged roommate who had left town, but he had the idea that if he refused to mention it, the others would not mention it either. They were having too good a time drinking. They murmured to each other in their own language and broke into peals of laughter, and other patrons, taking notice, grinned as if sharing their good spirits.

"Is nice place? All along here, this street. Yes? Close to hotel. All close. She says—Is wife of yours pretty? Young? Is not jealous, you on long trip, take airplane? Any picture of wife? Babies?"

"No wife," Oliver said wearily. "No babies."

"No—? Is not married."

"Is not," Oliver said.

"Not *love?* Not once?"

"Not," he said.

The two of them exchanged incredulous looks. Then they laughed again and Oliver sat, silent, while their laughter washed about him.

Being driven to the airport he saw, on the street, a dark-haired cyclist pedaling energetically—a young long-nosed handsome boy in a pullover sweater—Liebert—his heart sang: *Liebert.* But of course it was not Liebert. It was a stranger, a boy of about seventeen, no one Oliver knew. Then, again, at the airport he saw him. Again it was Liebert. A mechanic in coveralls, glimpsed in a

468 / JOYCE CAROL OATES

doorway, solemn, dark-eyed, with a pronounced widow's peak and prominent cheekbones: Liebert. He wanted to push his way through the crowd to him. To his translator. He wanted to touch him again, wanted to squeeze his hands, his arm. But of course the young man was a stranger—his gaze was dull, his mouth slack. Oliver stared at him just the same. His plane was loading; it was time for him to leave, yet he stood there, paralyzed.

"What will I do for the rest of my life . . . ?" he called to the boy.

Tim O'Brien

THE THINGS THEY CARRIED

TIM O'BRIEN (1946–) is the winner of the 1979 National Book Award for Fiction for his novel *Going After Cacciato*. He is also the author of *In the Lake of the Woods*, named Best Work of Fiction in 1994 by *Time* magazine; *The Things They Carried*, a finalist for the Pulitzer Prize and the National Book Critics Circle Award; as well as *If I Die in a Combat Zone, Box Me Up and Ship Me Home*, a Vietnam memoir. His most recent novel is *July, July*. He is currently a visiting professor and endowed chair at Southwest Texas State University where he teaches in the Creative Writing Program.

First Lieutenant Jimmy Cross carried letters from a girl named Martha, a junior at Mount Sebastian College in New Jersey. They were not love letters, but Lieutenant Cross was hoping, so he kept them folded in plastic at the bottom of his rucksack. In the late afternoon, after a day's march, he would dig his foxhole, wash his hands under a canteen, unwrap the letters, hold them with the tips of his fingers, and spend the last hour of light pretending. He would imagine romantic camping trips into the White Mountains in New Hampshire. He would sometimes taste the envelope flaps, knowing her tongue had been there. More than anything, he wanted Martha to love him as he loved her, but the letters were mostly chatty, elusive on the matter of love. She was a virgin, he was almost sure. She was an English major at Mount Sebastian, and she wrote beautifully about her professors and roommates and midterm exams, about her respect for Chaucer and her great affection for Virginia Woolf. She often quoted lines of poetry; she never mentioned the war, except to say, Jimmy, take care of yourself. The letters weighed 10 ounces. They were signed Love, Martha, but Lieutenant Cross understood that Love was only a way of signing and did not mean what he sometimes pretended it meant. At dusk, he would carefully return the letters to his rucksack. Slowly, a bit distracted, he would get up and move among his men, checking the perimeter, then at full dark he would return to his hole and watch the night and wonder if Martha was a virgin.

The things they carried were largely determined by necessity. Among the necessities or near-necessities were P-38 can openers, pocket knives, heat tabs, wristwatches, dog tags, mosquito repellent, chewing gum, candy, cigarettes, salt tablets, packets of Kool-Aid, lighters, matches, sewing kits, Military Payment Certificates, C rations, and two or three canteens of water. Together, these items weighed between 15 and 20 pounds, depending upon a man's habits or rate of metabolism. Henry Dobbins, who was a big man, carried extra rations; he was especially fond of canned peaches in heavy syrup over pound cake. Dave Jensen, who practiced field hygiene, carried a toothbrush, dental floss, and several hotel-sized bars of soap he'd stolen on R&R in Sydney, Australia. Ted Lavender, who was scared, carried tranquilizers until he was shot in the head outside the village of Than Khe in mid-April. By necessity, and because it was SOP, they all carried steel helmets that weighed 5 pounds including the liner and camouflage cover. They carried the standard fatigue jackets and trousers. Very few carried underwear. On their feet they carried jungle boots—2.1 pounds—and Dave Jensen carried three pairs of socks and a can of Dr. Scholl's foot powder as a precaution against trench foot. Until he was shot, Ted Lavender carried six or seven ounces of premium dope, which for him was a necessity. Mitchell Sanders, the RTO, carried condoms. Norman Bowker carried a diary. Rat Kiley carried comic books. Kiowa, a devout Baptist, carried an illustrated New Testament that had been presented to him by his father, who taught Sunday school in Oklahoma City, Oklahoma. As a hedge against bad times, however, Kiowa also carried his grandmother's distrust of the white man, his grandfather's old hunting hatchet. Necessity dictated. Because the land was mined and booby-trapped, it was SOP for each man to carry a steel-centered, nylon-covered flak jacket, which weighed 6.7 pounds, but which on hot days seemed much heavier. Because you could die so quickly, each man carried at least one large compress bandage, usually in the helmet band for easy access. Because the nights were cold, and because the monsoons were wet, each carried a green plastic poncho that could be used as a raincoat or groundsheet or make-shift tent. With its quilted liner, the poncho weighed almost two pounds, but it was worth every ounce. In April, for instance, when Ted Lavender was shot, they used his poncho to wrap him up, then to carry him across the paddy, then to lift him into the chopper that took him away.

They were called legs or grunts.

To carry something was to hump it, as when Lieutenant Jimmy Cross humped his love for Martha up the hills and through the swamps. In its intransitive form, to hump meant to walk, or to march, but it implied burdens far beyond the intransitive.

Almost everyone humped photographs. In his wallet, Lieutenant Cross carried two photographs of Martha. The first was a Kodacolor snapshot signed Love, though he knew better. She stood against a brick wall. Her eyes were gray and neutral, her lips slightly open as she stared straight-on at the camera. At night, sometimes, Lieutenant Cross wondered who had taken the picture, because he knew she had boyfriends, because he loved her so much, and because he could see the shadow of the picture-taker spreading out against the brick wall. The second photograph had been clipped from the 1968 Mount Sebastian yearbook. It was an action shot—women's volleyball—and Martha was bent horizontal to the floor, reaching, the palms of her hands in sharp focus, the tongue taut, the expression frank and competitive. There was no visible sweat. She wore white gym shorts. Her legs, he thought, were almost certainly the legs of a virgin, dry and without hair, the left knee cocked and carrying her entire weight, which was just over one hundred pounds. Lieutenant Cross remembered touching that left knee. A dark theater, he remembered, and the movie was *Bonnie and Clyde,* and Martha wore a tweed skirt, and during the final scene, when he touched her knee, she turned and looked at him in a sad, sober way that made him pull his hand back, but he would always remember the feel of the tweed skirt and the knee beneath it and the sound of the gunfire that killed Bonnie and Clyde, how embarrassing it was, how slow and oppressive. He remembered kissing her good night at the dorm door. Right then, he thought, he should've done something brave. He should've carried her up the stairs to her room and tied her to the bed and touched that left knee all night long. He should've risked it. Whenever he looked at the photographs, he thought of new things he should've done.

What they carried was partly a function of rank, partly of field specialty.

As a first lieutenant and platoon leader, Jimmy Cross carried a compass, maps, code books, binoculars, and a .45-caliber pistol that weighed 2.9 pounds fully loaded. He carried a strobe light and the responsibility for the lives of his men.

As an RTO, Mitchell Sanders carried the PRC-25 radio, a killer, 26 pounds with its battery.

As a medic, Rat Kiley carried a canvas satchel filled with morphine and plasma and malaria tablets and surgical tape and comic books and all the things a medic must carry, including M&M's for especially bad wounds, for a total weight of nearly 20 pounds.

As a big man, therefore a machine gunner, Henry Dobbins carried the M-60, which weighed 23 pounds unloaded, but which was almost always loaded. In addition, Dobbins carried between 10 and 15 pounds of ammunition draped in belts across his chest and shoulders.

As PFCs or Spec 4s, most of them were common grunts and carried the standard M-16 gas-operated assault rifle. The weapon weighed 7.5 pounds unloaded, 8.2 pounds with its full 20-round magazine. Depending on numerous factors, such as topography and psychology, the riflemen carried anywhere from 12 to 20 magazines, usually in cloth bandoliers, adding on another 8.4 pounds at minimum, 14 pounds at maximum. When it was available, they also carried

M-16 maintenance gear—rods and steel brushes and swabs and tubes of LSA oil—all of which weighed about a pound. Among the grunts, some carried the M-79 grenade launcher, 5.9 pounds unloaded, a reasonably light weapon except for the ammunition, which was heavy. A single round weighed 10 ounces. The typical load was 25 rounds. But Ted Lavender, who was scared, carried 34 rounds when he was shot and killed outside Than Khe, and he went down under an exceptional burden, more than 20 pounds of ammunition, plus the flak jacket and helmet and rations and water and toilet paper and tranquilizers and all the rest, plus the unweighed fear. He was dead weight. There was no twitching or flopping. Kiowa, who saw it happen, said it was like watching a rock fall, or a big sandbag or something—just boom, then down—not like the movies where the dead guy rolls around and does fancy spins and goes ass over teakettle—not like that, Kiowa said, the poor bastard just flat-fuck fell. Boom. Down. Nothing else. It was a bright morning in mid-April. Lieutenant Cross felt the pain. He blamed himself. They stripped off Lavender's canteens and ammo, all the heavy things, and Rat Kiley said the obvious, the guy's dead, and Mitchell Sanders used his radio to report one U.S. KIA and to request a chopper. Then they wrapped Lavender in his poncho. They carried him out to a dry paddy, established security, and sat smoking the dead man's dope until the chopper came. Lieutenant Cross kept to himself. He pictured Martha's smooth young face, thinking he loved her more than anything, more than his men, and now Ted Lavender was dead because he loved her so much and could not stop thinking about her. When the dustoff arrived, they carried Lavender aboard. Afterward they burned Than Khe. They marched until dusk, then dug their holes, and that night Kiowa kept explaining how you had to be there, how fast it was, how the poor guy just dropped like so much concrete. Boom-down, he said. Like cement.

In addition to the three standard weapons—the M-60, M-16, and M-79—they carried whatever presented itself, or whatever seemed appropriate as a means of killing or staying alive. They carried catch-as-catch-can. At various times, in various situations, they carried M-14s and CAR-15s and Swedish Ks and grease guns and captured AK-47s and Chi-Coms and RPGs and Simonov carbines and black market Uzis and .38-caliber Smith & Wesson handguns and 66 mm LAWs and shotguns and silencers and blackjacks and bayonets and C-4 plastic explosives. Lee Strunk carried a slingshot; a weapon of last resort, he called it. Mitchell Sanders carried brass knuckles. Kiowa carried his grandfather's feathered hatchet. Every third or fourth man carried a Claymore antipersonnel mine—3.5 pounds with its firing device. They all carried fragmentation grenades—14 ounces each. They all carried at least one M-18 colored smoke grenade—24 ounces. Some carried CS or tear gas grenades. Some carried white phosphorus grenades. They carried all they could bear, and then some, including a silent awe for the terrible power of the things they carried.

In the first week of April, before Lavender died, Lieutenant Jimmy Cross received a good-luck charm from Martha. It was a simple pebble, an ounce at most. Smooth to the touch, it was a milky white color with flecks of orange and violet, oval-shaped, like a miniature egg. In the accompanying letter, Martha wrote that she had found the pebble on the Jersey shoreline, precisely where the land touched water at high tide, where things came together but also separated. It was this separate-but-together quality, she wrote, that had inspired her to pick up the pebble and to carry it in her breast pocket for several days, where it seemed weightless, and then to send it through the mail, by air, as a token of her truest feelings for him. Lieutenant Cross found this romantic. But he wondered what her truest feelings were, exactly, and what she meant by separate-but-together. He wondered how the tides and waves had come into play on that afternoon along the Jersey shoreline when Martha saw the pebble and bent down to rescue it from geology. He imagined bare feet. Martha was a poet, with the poet's sensibilities, and her feet would be brown and bare, the toenails unpainted, the eyes chilly and somber like the ocean in March, and though it was painful, he wondered who had been with her that afternoon. He imagined a pair of shadows moving along the strip of sand where things came together but also separated. It was phantom jealousy, he knew, but he couldn't help himself. He loved her so much. On the march, through the hot days of early April, he carried the pebble in his mouth, turning it with his tongue, tasting sea salt and moisture. His mind wandered. He had difficulty keeping his attention on the war. On occasion he would yell at his men to spread out the column, to keep their eyes open, but then he would slip away into daydreams, just pretending, walking barefoot along the Jersey shore, with Martha, carrying nothing. He would feel himself rising. Sun and waves and gentle winds, all love and lightness.

What they carried varied by mission.

When a mission took them to the mountains, they carried mosquito netting, machetes, canvas tarps, and extra bug juice.

If a mission seemed especially hazardous, or if it involved a place they knew to be bad, they carried everything they could. In certain heavily mined AOs, where the land was dense with Toe Poppers and Bouncing Betties, they took turns humping a 28-pound mine detector. With its headphones and big sensing plate, the equipment was a stress on the lower back and shoulders, awkward to handle, often useless because of the shrapnel in the earth, but they carried it anyway, partly for safety, partly for the illusion of safety.

On ambush, or other night missions, they carried peculiar little odds and ends. Kiowa always took along his New Testament and a pair of moccasins for silence. Dave Jensen carried night-sight vitamins high in carotene. Lee Strunk carried his slingshot; ammo, he claimed, would never be a problem. Rat Kiley carried brandy and M&M's candy. Until he was shot, Ted Lavender carried the starlight scope, which weighed 6.3 pounds with its aluminum carrying case. Henry Dobbins carried his girlfriend's pantyhose wrapped around his neck as a comforter. They all carried ghosts. When dark came, they would move out single file across the meadows and paddies to their ambush coordinates, where they would quietly set up the Claymores and lie down and spend the night waiting.

Other missions were more complicated and required special equipment. In mid-April, it was their mission to search out and destroy the elaborate tunnel complexes in the Than Khe area south of Chu Lai. To blow the tunnels, they carried one-pound blocks of pentrite high explosives, four blocks to a man, 68 pounds in all. They carried wiring, detonators, and battery-powered clackers. Dave Jensen carried earplugs. Most often, before blowing the tunnels, they were ordered by higher command to search them, which was considered bad news, but by and large they just shrugged and carried out orders. Because he was a big man, Henry Dobbins was excused from tunnel duty. The others would draw numbers. Before Lavender died there were 17 men in the platoon, and whoever drew the number 17 would strip off his gear and crawl in headfirst with a flashlight and Lieutenant Cross's .45-caliber pistol. The rest of them would fan out as security. They would sit down or kneel, not facing the hole, listening to the ground beneath them, imagining cobwebs and ghosts, whatever was down there—the tunnel walls squeezing in—how the flashlight seemed impossibly heavy in the hand and how it was tunnel vision in the very strictest sense, compression in all ways, even time, and how you had to wiggle in—ass and elbows—a swallowed-up feeling—and how you found yourself worrying about odd things: Will your flashlight go dead? Do rats carry rabies? If you screamed, how far would the sound carry? Would your buddies hear it? Would they have the courage to drag you out? In some respects, though not many, the waiting was worse than the tunnel itself. Imagination was a killer.

On April 16, when Lee Strunk drew the number 17, he laughed and muttered something and went down quickly. The morning was hot and very still. Not good, Kiowa said. He looked at the tunnel opening, then out across a dry paddy toward the village of Than Khe. Nothing moved. No clouds or birds or people. As they waited, the men smoked and drank Kool-Aid, not talking much, feeling sympathy for Lee Strunk but also feeling the luck of the draw. You win some, you lose some, said Mitchell Sanders, and sometimes you settle for a rain check. It was a tired line and no one laughed.

Henry Dobbins ate a tropical chocolate bar. Ted Lavender popped a tran-quilizer and went off to pee.

After five minutes, Lieutenant Jimmy Cross moved to the tunnel, leaned down, and examined the darkness. Trouble, he thought—a cave-in maybe. And then suddenly, without willing it, he was thinking about Martha. The stresses and fractures, the quick collapse, the two of them buried alive under all that weight. Dense, crushing love. Kneeling, watching the hole, he tried to concen-trate on Lee Strunk and the war, all the dangers, but his love was too much for him, he felt paralyzed, he wanted to sleep inside her lungs and breathe her blood and be smothered. He wanted her to be a virgin and not a virgin, all at once. He wanted to know her. Intimate secrets: Why poetry? Why so sad? Why that grayness in her eyes? Why so alone? Not lonely, just alone—riding her bike across campus or sitting off by herself in the cafeteria—even dancing, she danced alone—and it was the aloneness that filled him with love. He remem-bered telling her that one evening. How she nodded and looked away. And how, later, when he kissed her, she received the kiss without returning it, her eyes wide open, not afraid, not a virgin's eyes, just flat and uninvolved.

Lieutenant Cross gazed at the tunnel. But he was not there. He was buried with Martha under the white sand at the Jersey shore. They were pressed to-gether, and the pebble in his mouth was her tongue. He was smiling. Vaguely, he was aware of how quiet the day was, the sullen paddies, yet he could not bring himself to worry about matters of security. He was beyond that. He was just a kid at war, in love. He was twenty-four years old. He couldn't help it.

A few moments later Lee Strunk crawled out of the tunnel. He came up grinning, filthy but alive. Lieutenant Cross nodded and closed his eyes while the others clapped Strunk on the back and made jokes about rising from the dead.

Worms, Rat Kiley said. Right out of the grave. Fuckin' zombie.

The men laughed. They all felt great relief.

Spook city, said Mitchell Sanders.

Lee Strunk made a funny ghost sound, a kind of moaning, yet very happy, and right then, when Strunk made that high happy moaning sound, when he went *Ahhooooo*, right then Ted Lavender was shot in the head on his way back from peeing. He lay with his mouth open. The teeth were broken. There was a swollen black bruise under his left eye. The cheekbone was gone. Oh shit, Rat Kiley said, the guy's dead. The guy's dead, he kept saying, which seemed profound—the guy's dead. I mean really.

The things they carried were determined to some extent by superstition. Lieu-tenant Cross carried his good-luck pebble. Dave Jensen carried a rabbit's foot. Norman Bowker, otherwise a very gentle person, carried a thumb that had been presented to him as a gift by Mitchell Sanders. The thumb was dark brown, rubbery to the touch, and weighed four ounces at most. It had been cut from a VC corpse, a boy of fifteen or sixteen. They'd found him at the bottom of an irrigation ditch, badly burned, flies in his mouth and eyes. The boy wore black shorts and sandals. At the time of his death he had been carrying a pouch of rice, a rifle, and three magazines of ammunition.

You want my opinion, Mitchell Sanders said, there's a definite moral here.

He put his hand on the dead boy's wrist. He was quiet for a time, as if counting a pulse, then he patted the stomach, almost affectionately, and used Kiowa's hunting hatchet to remove the thumb.

Henry Dobbins asked what the moral was.

Moral?

You know. *Moral.*

Sanders wrapped the thumb in toilet paper and handed it across to Norman Bowker. There was no blood. Smiling, he kicked the boy's head, watched the flies scatter, and said, It's like with that old TV show—Paladin. Have gun, will travel.

Henry Dobbins thought about it.

Yeah, well, he finally said. I don't see no moral.

There it *is,* man.

Fuck off.

They carried USO stationery and pencils and pens. They carried Sterno, safety pins, trip flares, signal flares, spools of wire, razor blades, chewing tobacco, liberated joss sticks and statuettes of the smiling Buddha, candles, grease pencils, *The Stars and Stripes,* fingernail clippers, Psy Ops leaflets, bush hats, bolos, and much more. Twice a week, when the resupply choppers came in, they carried hot chow in green mermite cans and large canvas bags filled with iced beer and soda pop. They carried plastic water containers, each with a two-gallon capacity. Mitchell Sanders carried a set of starched tiger fatigues for special occasions. Henry Dobbins carried Black Flag insecticide. Dave Jensen carried empty sandbags that could be filled at night for added protection. Lee Strunk carried tanning lotion. Some things they carried in common. Taking turns, they carried the big PRC-77 scrambler radio, which weighed 30 pounds with its battery. They shared the weight of memory. They took up what others could no longer bear. Often, they carried each other, the wounded or weak. They carried infections. They carried chess sets, basketballs, Vietnamese-English dictionaries, insignia of rank, Bronze Stars and Purple Hearts, plastic cards imprinted with the Code of Conduct. They carried diseases, among them malaria and dysentery. They carried lice and ringworm and leeches and paddy algae and various rots and molds. They carried the land itself—Vietnam, the place, the soil—a powdery orange-red dust that covered their boots and fatigues and faces. They carried the sky. The whole atmosphere, they carried it, the humidity, the monsoons, the stink of fungus and decay, all of it, they carried gravity. They moved like mules. By daylight they took sniper fire, at night they were mortared, but it was not battle, it was just the endless march, village to village, without purpose, nothing won or lost. They marched for the sake of the march. They plodded along slowly, dumbly, leaning forward against the heat, unthinking, all blood and bone, simple grunts, soldiering with their legs, toiling up the hills and down into the paddies and across the rivers and up again and down, just humping, one step and then the next and then another, but no volition, no will, because it was automatic, it was anatomy, and the war was entirely a matter of posture and carriage, the hump was everything, a kind of inertia, a kind of emptiness, a dullness of desire and intellect and conscience and hope and human sensibility. Their principles were in their feet. Their calculations were biological. They had no sense of strategy or mission. They searched the villages without knowing what to look for, not caring, kicking over jars of rice, frisking children and old men, blowing tunnels, sometimes setting fires and sometimes not, then forming up and moving on to the next village, then other villages, where it would always be the same. They carried their own lives. The pressures were enormous. In the heat of early afternoon, they would remove their helmets and flak jackets, walking bare, which was dangerous but which helped ease the strain. They would often discard things along the route of march. Purely for comfort, they would throw away rations, blow their Claymores and grenades, no matter, because by nightfall the resupply choppers would arrive with more of the same, then a day or two later still more, fresh watermelons and crates of ammunition and sunglasses and woolen sweaters—the resources were stunning—sparklers for the Fourth of July, colored eggs for Easter—it was the great American war chest—the fruits of science, the smokestacks, the canneries, the arsenals at Hartford, the Minnesota forests, the machine shops, the vast fields of corn and wheat—they carried like freight trains; they carried it on their backs and shoulders—and for all the ambiguities of Vietnam, all the mysteries and unknowns, there was at least the single abiding certainty that they would never be at a loss for things to carry.

After the chopper took Lavender away, Lieutenant Jimmy Cross led his men into the village of Than Khe. They burned everything. They shot chickens and dogs, they trashed the village well, they called in artillery and watched the wreckage, then they marched for several hours through the hot afternoon, and then at dusk, while Kiowa explained how Lavender died, Lieutenant Cross found himself trembling.

He tried not to cry. With his entrenching tool, which weighed five pounds, he began digging a hole in the earth.

He felt shame. He hated himself. He had loved Martha more than his men, and as a consequence Lavender was now dead, and this was something he would have to carry like a stone in his stomach for the rest of the war.

All he could do was dig. He used his entrenching tool like an ax, slashing, feeling both love and hate, and then later, when it was full dark, he sat at the bottom of his foxhole and wept. It went on for a long while. In part, he was grieving for Ted Lavender, but mostly it was for Martha, and for himself, because she belonged to another world, which was not quite real, and because she was a junior at Mount Sebastian College in New Jersey, a poet and a virgin and uninvolved, and because he realized she did not love him and never would.

Like cement, Kiowa whispered in the dark. I swear to God—boom, down. Not a word.

I've heard this, said Norman Bowker.

A pisser, you know? Still zipping himself up. Zapped while zipping.

All right, fine. That's enough.

Yeah, but you had to see it, the guy just—

I *heard,* man. Cement. So why not shut the fuck *up?*

Kiowa shook his head sadly and glanced over at the hole where Lieutenant Jimmy Cross sat watching the night. The air was thick and wet. A warm dense fog had settled over the paddies and there was the stillness that precedes rain.

After a time Kiowa sighed.

One thing for sure, he said. The lieutenant's in some deep hurt. I mean that crying jag—the way he was carrying on—it wasn't fake or anything, it was real heavy-duty hurt. The man cares.

Sure, Norman Bowker said.

Say what you want, the man does care.

We all got problems.

Not Lavender.

No, I guess not, Bowker said. Do me a favor, though.

Shut up?

That's a smart Indian. Shut up.

Shrugging, Kiowa pulled off his boots. He wanted to say more, just to lighten up his sleep, but instead he opened his New Testament and arranged it beneath his head as a pillow. The fog made things seem hollow and unattached. He tried not to think about Ted Lavender, but then he was thinking how fast it was, no drama, down and dead, and how it was hard to feel anything except surprise. It seemed unchristian. He wished he could find some great sadness, or even anger, but the emotion wasn't there and he couldn't make it happen. Mostly he felt pleased to be alive. He liked the smell of the New Testament under his cheek, the leather and ink and paper and glue, whatever the chemicals were. He liked hearing the sounds of night. Even his fatigue, it felt fine, the stiff muscles and the prickly awareness of his own body, a floating feeling. He enjoyed not being dead. Lying there, Kiowa admired Lieutenant Jimmy Cross's capacity for grief. He wanted to share the man's pain, he wanted to care as Jimmy Cross cared. And yet when he closed his eyes, all he could think was Boom-down, and all he could feel was the pleasure of having his boots off and the fog curling in around him and the damp soil and the Bible smells and the plush comfort of night.

After a moment Norman Bowker sat up in the dark.

What the hell, he said. You want to talk, *talk*. Tell it to me.

Forget it.

No, man, go on. One thing I hate, it's a silent Indian.

For the most part they carried themselves with poise, a kind of dignity. Now and then, however, there were times of panic, when they squealed or wanted to squeal but couldn't, when they twitched and made moaning sounds and covered their heads and said Dear Jesus and flopped around on the earth and fired their weapons blindly and cringed and sobbed and begged for the noise to stop and went wild and made stupid promises to themselves and to God and to their mothers and fathers, hoping not to die. In different ways, it happened to all of them. Afterward, when the firing ended, they would blink and peek up. They would touch their bodies, feeling shame, then quickly hiding it. They would force themselves to stand. As if in slow motion, frame by frame, the world would take on the old logic—absolute silence, then the wind, then sunlight, then voices. It was the burden of being alive. Awkwardly, the men would reassemble themselves, first in private, then in groups, becoming soldiers again. They would repair the leaks in their eyes. They would check for casualties, call in dustoffs, light cigarettes, try to smile, clear their throats and spit and begin cleaning their weapons. After a time someone would shake his head and say, No lie, I almost shit my pants, and someone else would laugh, which meant it was bad, yes, but the guy had obviously not shit his pants, it wasn't that bad, and in any case nobody would ever do such a thing and then go ahead and talk about it. They would squint into the dense, oppressive sunlight. For a few moments, perhaps, they would fall silent, lighting a joint and tracking its passage from man to man, inhaling, holding in the humiliation. Scary stuff, one of them might say. But then someone else would grin or flick his eyebrows and say, Roger-dodger, almost cut me a new asshole, *almost*.

There were numerous such poses. Some carried themselves with a sort of wistful resignation, others with pride or stiff soldierly discipline or good humor or macho zeal. They were afraid of dying but they were even more afraid to show it.

They found jokes to tell.

They used a hard vocabulary to contain the terrible softness. *Greased* they'd say. *Offed, lit up, zapped while zipping*. It wasn't cruelty, just stage presence. They were actors. When someone died, it wasn't quite dying, because in a curious way it seemed scripted, and because they had their lines mostly memorized, irony mixed with tragedy, and because they called it by other names, as if to encyst and destroy the reality of death itself. They kicked corpses. They cut off thumbs. They talked grunt lingo. They told stories about Ted Lavender's supply of tranquilizers, how the poor guy didn't feel a thing, how incredibly tranquil he was.

There's a moral here, said Mitchell Sanders.

They were waiting for Lavender's chopper, smoking the dead man's dope.

The moral's pretty obvious, Sanders said, and winked. Stay away from drugs. No joke, they'll ruin your day every time.

Cute, said Henry Dobbins.

Mind blower, get it? Talk about wiggy. Nothing left, just blood and brains.

They made themselves laugh.

There it is, they'd say. Over and over—there it is, my friend, there it is—as if the repetition itself were an act of poise, a balance between crazy and almost crazy, knowing without going, there it is, which meant be cool, let it ride, because Oh yeah, man, you can't change what can't be changed, there it is, there it absolutely and positively and fucking well *is.*

They were tough.

They carried all the emotional baggage of men who might die. Grief, terror, love, longing—these were intangibles, but the intangibles had their own mass and specific gravity, they had tangible weight. They carried shameful memories. They carried the common secret of cowardice barely restrained, the instinct to run or freeze or hide, and in many respects this was the heaviest burden of all, for it could never be put down, it required perfect balance and perfect posture. They carried their reputations. They carried the soldier's greatest fear, which was the fear of blushing. Men killed, and died, because they were embarrassed not to. It was what had brought them to the war in the first place, nothing positive, no dreams of glory or honor, just to avoid the blush of dishonor. They died so as not to die of embarrassment. They crawled into tunnels and walked point and advanced under fire. Each morning, despite the unknowns, they made their legs move. They endured. They kept humping. They did not submit to the obvious alternative, which was simply to close the eyes and fall. So easy, really. Go limp and tumble to the ground and let the muscles unwind and not speak and not budge until your buddies picked you up and lifted you into the chopper that would roar and dip its nose and carry you off to the world. A mere matter of falling, yet no one ever fell. It was not courage, exactly; the object was not valor. Rather, they were too frightened to be cowards.

By and large they carried these things inside, maintaining the masks of composure. They sneered at sick call. They spoke bitterly about guys who had found release by shooting off their own toes or fingers. Pussies, they'd say. Candyasses. It was fierce, mocking talk, with only a trace of envy or awe, but even so the image played itself out behind their eyes.

They imagined the muzzle against flesh. So easy: squeeze the trigger and blow away a toe. They imagined it. They imagined the quick, sweet pain, then the evacuation to Japan, then a hospital with warm beds and cute geisha nurses.

And they dreamed of freedom birds.

At night, on guard, staring into the dark, they were carried away by jumbo jets. They felt the rush of takeoff. *Gone!* they yelled. And then velocity—wings and engines—a smiling stewardess—but it was more than a plane, it was a real bird, a big sleek silver bird with feathers and talons and high screeching. They were flying. The weights fell off; there was nothing to bear. They laughed and held on tight, feeling the cold slap of wind and altitude, soaring, thinking *It's over, I'm gone!*—they were naked, they were light and free—it was all lightness, bright and fast and buoyant, light as light, a helium buzz in the brain, a giddy bubbling in the lungs as they were taken up over the clouds and the war, beyond duty, beyond gravity and mortification and global entanglements—*Sin loi!* they yelled. *I'm sorry, motherfuckers, but I'm out of it, I'm goofed, I'm on a space cruise, I'm gone!*—and it was a restful, unencumbered sensation, just riding the light waves, sailing that big silver freedom bird over the mountains and oceans, over America, over the farms and great sleeping cities and cemeteries and highways and the golden arches of McDonald's, it was flight, a kind of fleeing, a kind of falling, falling higher and higher, spinning off the edge of the earth and beyond the sun and through the vast, silent vacuum where there were no burdens and where everything weighed exactly nothing—*Gone!* they screamed. *I'm sorry but I'm gone!*—and so at night, not quite dreaming, they gave themselves over to lightness, they were carried, they were purely borne.

On the morning after Ted Lavender died, First Lieutenant Jimmy Cross crouched at the bottom of his foxhole and burned Martha's letters. Then he burned the two photographs. There was a steady rain falling, which made it difficult, but he used heat tabs and Sterno to build a small fire, screening it with his body, holding the photographs over the tight blue flame with the tips of his fingers.

He realized it was only a gesture. Stupid, he thought. Sentimental, too, but mostly just stupid.

Lavender was dead. You couldn't burn the blame.

Besides, the letters were in his head. And even now, without photographs, Lieutenant Cross could see Martha playing volleyball in her white gym shorts and yellow T-shirt. He could see her moving in the rain.

When the fire died out, Lieutenant Cross pulled his poncho over his shoulders and ate breakfast from a can.

There was no great mystery, he decided.

In those burned letters Martha had never mentioned the war, except to say,

Jimmy, take care of yourself. She wasn't involved. She signed the letters Love, but it wasn't love, and all the fine lines and technicalities did not matter. Virginity was no longer an issue. He hated her. Yes, he did. He hated her. Love, too, but it was a hard, hating kind of love.

The morning came up wet and blurry. Everything seemed part of everything else, the fog and Martha and the deepening rain.

He was a soldier, after all.

Half smiling, Lieutenant Jimmy Cross took out his maps. He shook his head hard, as if to clear it, then bent forward and began planning the day's march. In ten minutes, or maybe twenty, he would rouse the men and they would pack up and head west, where the maps showed the country to be green and inviting. They would do what they had always done. The rain might add some weight, but otherwise it would be one more day layered upon all the other days.

He was realistic about it. There was that new hardness in his stomach. He loved her but he hated her.

No more fantasies, he told himself.

Henceforth, when he thought about Martha, it would be only to think that she belonged elsewhere. He would shut down the daydreams. This was not Mount Sebastian, it was another world, where there were no pretty poems or midterm exams, a place where men died because of carelessness and gross stupidity. Kiowa was right. Boom-down, and you were dead, never partly dead.

Briefly, in the rain, Lieutenant Cross saw Martha's gray eyes gazing back at him.

He understood.

It was very sad, he thought. The things men carried inside. The things men did or felt they had to do.

He almost nodded at her, but didn't.

Instead he went back to his maps. He was now determined to perform his duties firmly and without negligence. It wouldn't help Lavender, he knew that, but from this point on he would comport himself as an officer. He would dispose of his good-luck pebble. Swallow it, maybe, or use Lee Strunk's slingshot, or just drop it along the trail. On the march he would impose strict field discipline. He would be careful to send out flank security, to prevent straggling or bunching up, to keep his troops moving at the proper pace and at the proper interval. He would insist on clean weapons. He would confiscate the remainder of Lavender's dope. Later in the day, perhaps, he would call the men together and speak to them plainly. He would accept the blame for what had happened to Ted Lavender. He would be a man about it. He would look them in the eyes, keeping his chin level, and he would issue the new SOPs in a calm, impersonal tone of voice, a lieutenant's voice, leaving no room for argument or discussion. Commencing immediately, he'd tell them, they would no longer abandon equipment along the route of march. They would police up their acts. They would get their shit together, and keep it together, and maintain it neatly and in good working order.

He would not tolerate laxity. He would show strength, distancing himself.

Among the men there would be grumbling, of course, and maybe worse, because their days would seem longer and their loads heavier, but Lieutenant Jimmy Cross reminded himself that his obligation was not to be loved but to lead. He would dispense with love; it was not now a factor. And if anyone quarreled or complained, he would simply tighten his lips and arrange his shoulders in the correct command posture. He might give a curt little nod. Or he might not. He might just shrug and say, Carry on, then they would saddle up and form into a column and move out toward the villages west of Than Khe.

Daniel Orozco

ORIENTATION

DANIEL OROZCO (1957–) was born and raised in San Francisco. His stories have appeared in the *Best American Short Stories*, *Best American Mystery Stories*, and *Pushcart Prize* anthologies, and in *Harper's*, *McSweeney's*, *Zoetrope All-Story*, and others. He is the recipient of a National Endowment for the Arts fellowship, and currently teaches in the Creative Writing Program at the University of Idaho.

Those are the offices and these are the cubicles. That's my cubicle there, and this is your cubicle. This is your phone. Never answer your phone. Let the Voicemail System answer it. This is your Voicemail System Manual. There are no personal phone calls allowed. We do, however, allow for emergencies. If you must make an emergency phone call, ask your supervisor first. If you can't find your supervisor, ask Phillip Spiers, who sits over there. He'll check with Clarissa Nicks, who sits over there. If you make an emergency phone call without asking, you may be let go.

These are your In and Out boxes. All the forms in your In box must be logged in by the date shown in the upper left-hand corner, initialed by you in the upper right-hand corner, and distributed to the Processing Analyst whose name is numerically coded in the lower left-hand corner. The lower right-hand corner is left blank. Here's your Processing Analyst Numerical Code Index. And here's your Forms Processing Procedures Manual.

You must pace your work. What do I mean? I'm glad you asked that. We pace our work according to the eight-hour workday. If you have twelve hours of work in your In box, for example, you must compress that work into the eight-hour day. If you have one hour of work in your In box, you must expand that work to fill the eight-hour day. That was a good question. Feel free to ask questions. Ask too many questions, however, and you may be let go.

That is our receptionist. She is a temp. We go through receptionists here. They quit with alarming frequency. Be polite and civil to our temps. Learn their names. Invite them to lunch occasionally. But don't get close to them, as it only makes it more difficult when they leave. And they always leave. You can be sure of that.

The men's room is over there. The women's room is over there. John La-

Fountaine, who sits over there, uses the women's room occasionally. He says it is accidental. We know better, but we let it pass. John LaFountaine is harmless, his forays into the forbidden territory of the women's room simply a benign thrill, a faint blip on the dull flat line of his life.

Russell Nash, who sits in the cubicle to your left, is in love with Amanda Pierce, who sits in the cubicle to your right. They ride the same bus together after work. For Amanda Pierce, it is just a tedious bus ride made less tedious by the idle nattering of Russell Nash. But for Russell Nash, it is the highlight of his day. It is the highlight of his life. Russell Nash has put on forty pounds, and grows fatter with each passing month, nibbling on chips and cookies while peeking glumly over the partitions at Amanda Pierce, and gorging himself at home on cold pizza and ice cream while watching adult videos on TV.

Amanda Pierce, in the cubicle to your right, has a six-year-old son named Jamie, who is autistic. Her cubicle is plastered from top to bottom with the boy's crayon artwork—sheet after sheet of precisely drawn concentric circles and ellipses, in black and yellow. She rotates them every other Friday. Be sure to comment on them. Amanda Pierce also has a husband, who is a lawyer. He subjects her to an escalating array of painful and humiliating sex games, to which Amanda Pierce reluctantly submits. She comes to work exhausted and freshly wounded each morning, wincing from the abrasions on her breasts, or the bruises on her abdomen, or the second-degree burns on the backs of her thighs.

But we're not supposed to know any of this. Do not let on. If you let on, you may be let go.

Amanda Pierce, who tolerates Russell Nash, is in love with Albert Bosch, who sits over there. Albert Bosch, who only dimly registers Amanda Pierce's existence, has eyes only for Ellie Tapper, who sits over there. Ellie Tapper, who hates Albert Bosch, would walk through fire for Curtis Lance. But Curtis Lance hates Ellie Tapper. Isn't the world a funny place? Not in the ha-ha sense, of course.

Anika Bloom sits in that cubicle. Last year, while reviewing quarterly reports in a meeting with Barry Hacker, Anika Bloom's left palm began to bleed. She fell into a trance, stared into her hand, and told Barry Hacker when and how his wife would die. We laughed it off. She was, after all, a new employee. But Barry Hacker's wife is dead. So unless you want to know exactly when and how you'll die, never talk to Anika Bloom.

Colin Heavey sits in that cubicle over there. He was new once, just like you. We warned him about Anika Bloom. But at last year's Christmas Potluck, he felt sorry for her when he saw that no one was talking to her. Colin Heavey brought her a drink. He hasn't been himself since. Colin Heavey is doomed. There's nothing he can do about it, and we are powerless to help him. Stay away from Colin Heavey. Never give any of your work to him. If he asks to do something, tell him you have to check with me. If he asks again, tell him I haven't gotten back to you.

This is the Fire Exit. There are several on this floor, and they are marked accordingly. We have a Floor Evacuation Review every three months, and an Escape Route Quiz once a month. We have our Biannual Fire Drill twice a year, and our Annual Earthquake Drill once a year. These are precautions only. These things never happen.

For your information, we have a comprehensive health plan. Any catastrophic illness, any unforeseen tragedy is completely covered. All dependents are completely covered. Larry Bagdikian, who sits over there, has six daughters. If anything were to happen to any of his girls, or to all of them, if all six were to simultaneously fall victim to illness or injury—stricken with a hideous degenerative muscle disease or some rare toxic blood disorder, sprayed with semiautomatic gunfire while on a class field trip, or attacked in their bunk beds by some prowling nocturnal lunatic—if any of this were to pass, Larry's girls would all be taken care of. Larry Bagdikian would not have to pay one dime. He would have nothing to worry about.

We also have a generous vacation and sick leave policy. We have an excellent disability insurance plan. We have a stable and profitable pension fund. We get group discounts for the symphony, and block seating at the ballpark. We get commuter ticket books for the bridge. We have Direct Deposit. We are all members of Costco.

This is our kitchenette. And this, this is our Mr. Coffee. We have a coffee pool, into which we each pay two dollars a week for coffee, filters, sugar, and CoffeeMate. If you prefer Cremora or half-and-half to CoffeeMate, there is a special pool for three dollars a week. If you prefer Sweet'N'Low to sugar, there is special pool for two-fifty a week. We do not do decaf. You are allowed to join the coffee pool of your choice, but you are not allowed to touch the Mr. Coffee.

This is the microwave oven. You are allowed to *heat* food in the microwave oven. You are not, however, allowed to *cook* food in the microwave oven.

We get one hour for lunch. We also get one fifteen-minute break in the morning, and one fifteen-minute break in the afternoon. Always take your breaks. If you skip a break, it is gone forever. For your information, your break is a privilege, not a right. If you abuse the break policy, we are authorized to rescind your breaks. Lunch, however, is a right, not a privilege. If you abuse the lunch policy, our hands will be tied, and we will be forced to look the other way. We will not enjoy that.

This is the refrigerator. You may put your lunch in it. Barry Hacker, who sits over there, steals food from this refrigerator. His petty theft is an outlet for his grief. Last New Year's Eve, while kissing his wife, a blood vessel burst in her brain. Barry Hacker's wife was two months pregnant at the time, and lingered in a coma for half a year before dying. It was a tragic loss for Barry Hacker. He hasn't been himself since. Barry Hacker's wife was a beautiful woman. She was also completely covered. Barry Hacker did not have to pay one dime. But his dead wife haunts him. She haunts all of us. We have seen her, reflected in the monitors of our computers, moving past our cubicles. We have seen the dim shadow of her face in our photocopies. She pencils herself in in the reception-ist's appointment book, with the notation: To see Barry Hacker. She has left messages in the receptionist's Voicemail box, messages garbled by the electronic chirrups and buzzes in the phone line, her voice echoing from an immense distance within the ambient hum. But the voice is hers. And beneath her voice, beneath the tidal whoosh of static and hiss, the gurgling and crying of a baby can be heard.

In any case, if you bring a lunch, put a little something extra in the bag for Barry Hacker. We have four Barrys in this office. Isn't that a coincidence?

This is Matthew Payne's office. He is our Unit Manager, and his door is al-ways closed. We have never seen him, and you will never see him. But he is here. You can be sure of that. He is all around us.

This is the Custodian's Closet. You have no business in the Custodian's Closet.

And this, this is our Supplies Cabinet. If you need supplies, see Curtis Lance. He will log you in on the Supplies Cabinet Authorization Log, then give you a Supplies Authorization Slip. Present your pink copy of the Supplies Authoriza-tion Slip to Ellie Tapper. She will log you in on the Supplies Cabinet Key Log, then give you the key. Because the Supplies Cabinet is located outside the Unit Manager's office, you must be very quiet. Gather your supplies quietly. The Supplies Cabinet is divided into four sections. Section One contains letterhead stationery, blank paper and envelopes, memo and notepads, and so on. Section Two contains pens and pencils and typewriter and printer ribbons, and the like. In Section Three we have erasers, correction fluids, transparent tapes, glue sticks, et cetera. And in Section Four we have paper clips and pushpins and scissors and razor blades. And here are the spare blades for the shredder. Do not touch the shredder, which is located over there. The shredder is of no concern to you.

Gwendolyn Stich sits in that office there. She is crazy about penguins, and collects penguin knickknacks: penguin posters and coffee mugs and stationery, penguin stuffed animals, penguin jewelry, penguin sweaters and tee shirts and socks. She has a pair of penguin fuzzy slippers she wears when working late at the office. She has a tape cassette of penguin sounds which she listens to for relaxation. Her favorite colors are black and white. She has personalized license plates that read: PEN GWEN. Every morning, she passes through all the cu-bicles to wish each of us a *good* morning. She brings Danish on Wednesdays for Hump Day morning break, and doughnuts on Fridays for T.G.I.F. afternoon break. She organizes the Annual Christmas Potluck and is in charge of the Birthday List. Gwendolyn Stich's door is always open to all of us. She will always lend an ear and put in a good word for you; she will always give you a hand or the shirt off her back or a shoulder to cry on. Because her door is always open, she hides and cries in a stall in the women's room. And John LaFountaine—who, enthralled when a woman enters, sits quietly in his stall with his knees to his chest—John LaFountaine has heard her vomiting in there. We have come upon Gwendolyn Stich huddled in the stairwell, shivering in the updraft, sipping a Diet Mr. Pibb and hugging her knees. She does not let any of this interfere with her work. If it interfered with her work, she might have to be let go.

Kevin Howard sits in that cubicle over there. He is a serial killer, the one they call the Carpet Cutter, responsible for the mutilations across town. We're not supposed to know that, so do not let on. Don't worry. His compulsion inflicts itself on strangers only, and the routine established is elaborate and unwavering. The victim must be a white male, a young adult no older than thirty, heavy-set, with dark hair and eyes, and the like. The victim must be chosen at random, before sunset, from a public place; the victim is followed home and must put up a struggle, et cetera. The carnage inflicted is precise: the angle and direction of the incisions, the layering of skin and muscle tissue, the rearrangement of the visceral organs, and so on. Kevin Howard does not let any of this interfere with his work. He is, in fact, our fastest typist. He types as if he were on fire. He has a secret crush on Gwendolyn Stich and leaves a red-foil-wrapped Hershey's Kiss on her desk every afternoon. But he hates Anika Bloom and keeps well away from her. In his presence, she has uncontrollable fits of shaking and trembling. Her left palm does not stop bleeding.

In any case, when Kevin Howard gets caught, act surprised. Say that he seemed like a nice person, a bit of a loner, perhaps, but always quiet and polite.

This is the photocopier room. And this, this is our view. It faces southwest. West is down there, toward the water. North is back there. Because we are on the seventeenth floor, we are afforded a magnificent view. Isn't it beautiful? It overlooks the park, where the tops of those trees are. You can see a segment of the bay between those two buildings there. You can see the sun set in the gap between those two buildings over there. You can see this building reflected in the glass panels of that building across the way. There. See? That's you, waving. And look there. There's Anika Bloom in the kitchenette, waving back.

Enjoy this view while photocopying. If you have problems with the photocopier, see Russell Nash. If you have any questions, ask your supervisor. If you can't find your supervisor, ask Phillip Spiers. He sits over there. He'll check with Clarissa Nicks. She sits over there. If you can't find them, feel free to ask me. That's my cubicle. I sit in there.

Julie Orringer

PILGRIMS

JULIE ORRINGER (1973–) is the author of the short story collection *How to Breathe Underwater*, a *New York Times* Notable Book and the winner of the Northern California BookAward. A graduate of Cornell University and the Iowa Writers' Workshop, Orringer was a Truman Capote Fellow in the Stegner Program at Stanford. Her stories have appeared in *The Paris Review*, *McSweeney's*, *Ploughshares*, *Zoetrope: All-Story*, *The Pushcart Prize Anthology*, *The Best New American Voices*, and *The Best American Non-Required Reading*. With the assistance of a grant from the National Endowment for the Arts, she is working on a novel set in Budapest and Paris in the late 1930s.

It was Thanksgiving Day and hot, because this was New Orleans; they were driving uptown to have dinner with strangers. Ella pushed at her loose tooth with the tip of her tongue and fanned her legs with the hem of her velvet dress. On the seat beside her, Benjamin fidgeted with his shirt buttons. He had worn his pilgrim costume, brown shorts and a white shirt and yellow paper buckles taped to his shoes. In the front seat their father drove without a word, while their mother dozed against the window glass. She wore a blue dress and a strand of jade beads and a knit cotton hat beneath which she was bald.

Three months earlier, Ella's father had explained what chemotherapy was, and how it would make her mother better. He had even taken Ella to the hospital once when her mother had a treatment. She remembered it like a filmstrip from school, a series of connected images she wished she didn't have to watch: her mother with an IV needle in her arm, the steady drip from the bag of orange liquid, her father speaking softly to himself as he paced the room, her mother shaking so hard she had to be tied down.

At night Ella and her brother tapped a secret code against the wall that separated their rooms: one knock, I'm afraid; two knocks, Don't worry; three knocks, Are you still awake? four, Come quick. And then there was the Emergency Signal, a stream of knocks that kept on coming, which meant her brother could hear their mother and father crying in their bedroom. If it went on for more than a minute, Ella would give four knocks and her brother would run to her room and crawl under the covers.

There were changes in the house, healing rituals which required Ella's mother to go outside and embrace trees or lie facedown on the grass. Sometimes she did a kind of Asian dance that looked like karate. She ate bean paste and Japanese vegetables, or sticky brown rice wrapped in seaweed. And now they were going to have dinner with people they had never met, people who ate seaweed and brown rice every day of their lives.

They drove through the Garden District, where Spanish moss hung like beards from the trees. Once during Mardi Gras, Ella had ridden a trolley here with her brother and grandmother, down to the French Quarter where they'd eaten beignets at Café du Monde. She wished she were sitting in one of those wrought-iron chairs and shaking powdered sugar onto a beignet. How much better than to be surrounded by strangers, eating food that tasted like the bottom of the sea.

They turned onto a side street, and her father studied the directions. "It should be at the end of this block," he said.

Ella's mother shifted in her seat. "Where are we?" she asked, her voice dreamy with painkillers.

"Almost there," said Ella's father.

They pulled to the curb in front of a white house with sagging porches and a trampled lawn. Vines covered the walls and moss grew thick and green between the roof slates. Under the porte cochere stood a beat-up Honda and a Volkswagen with mismatched side panels. A faded bigwheel lay on its side on the walk.

"Come on," their father said, and gave them a tired smile. "Time for fun." He got out of the car and opened the doors for Ella and her mother, sweeping his arm chauffeurlike as they climbed out.

Beside the front door was a tarnished doorbell in the shape of a lion's head. "Push it," her father said. Ella pushed. A sound like churchbells echoed inside the house.

Then the door swung open and there was Mister Kaplan, a tall man with wiry orange hair and big dry-looking teeth. He shook hands with Ella's parents, so long and vigorously it seemed to Ella he might as well say *Congratulations*.

"And you must be Ben and Ella," he said, bending down.

Ella gave a mute nod. Her brother kicked at the doorjamb.

"Well, come on in," he said. "I have a tree castle out back."

Benjamin's face came up, twisted with skepticism. "A what?"

"The kids are back there. They'll show you," he said.

"What an interesting foyer," their mother said. She bent down to look at the brass animals on the floor, a turtle and a jackal and a llama. Next to the animals stood a blue vase full of rusty metal flowers. A crystal chandelier dangled from the ceiling, its arms hung with dozens of God's-eyes and tiny plastic babies from Mardi Gras king cakes. On a low wooden shelf against the wall, pair after pair of canvas sandals and sneakers and Birkenstocks were piled in a heap. A crayoned sign above it said SHOES OFF NOW!

Ella looked down at her feet. She was wearing her new patent-leather Mary Janes.

"Your socks are nice too," her father said, and touched her shoulder. He stepped out of his own brown loafers and set them on top of the pile. Then he knelt before Ella's mother and removed her pumps. "Shoes off," he said to Ella and Ben.

"Even me?" Ben said. He looked down at his paper buckles.

Their father took off Ben's shoes and removed the paper buckles, tape intact. Then he pressed one buckle onto each of Ben's socks. "There," he said.

Ben looked as if he might cry.

"Everyone's in the kitchen," Mister Kaplan said. "We're all cooking."

"Marvelous," said Ella's mother. "We love to cook."

They followed him down a cavern of a hall, its walls decorated with sepia-toned photographs of children and parents, all of them staring stone-faced from their gilt frames. They passed a sweep of stairs, and a room with nothing in it but straw mats and pictures of blue Indian goddesses sitting on beds of cloud.

"What's that room?" Benjamin said.

"Meditation room," Mister Kaplan said, as if it were as commonplace as a den.

The kitchen smelled of roasting squash and baked apples and spices. There was an old brick oven and a stove with so many burners it looked as if it had been stolen from a restaurant. At the kitchen table men and women with long hair and loose clothes sliced vegetables or stirred things into bowls. Some of them wore knitted hats like her mother, their skin dull-gray, their eyes purple-shaded underneath. To Ella it seemed they could be relatives of her mother's, shameful cousins recently discovered.

A tall woman with a green scarf around her waist came over and embraced Ella's mother, then bent down to hug Ella and Benjamin. She smelled of smoky perfume. Her wide eyes skewed in different directions as if she were watching two movies projected into opposite corners of the room. Ella did not know how to look at her.

"We're so happy you decided to come," the woman said. "I'm Delilah, Eddy's sister."

"Who's Eddy?" said Ben.

"Mister Kaplan," their father said.

"We use our real names here," Delilah said. "No one is a mister."

She led their parents over to the long table and put utensils into their hands. Their mother was to mix oats into a pastry crust, and their father to chop carrots, something Ella had never seen him do. He looked around in panic, then hunched over and began cutting a carrot into clumsy pieces. He kept glancing at the man to his left, a bearded man with a shaved head, as if to make sure he was doing it right.

Delilah gave Ella and Benjamin hard cookies that tasted like burnt rice. It seemed Ella would have to chew forever. Her loose tooth waggled in its socket.

"The kids are all out back," Delilah said. "There's plenty of time to play before dinner."

"What kids?" Benjamin asked.

"You'll see," said Delilah. She tilted her head at Ella, one of her eyes moving over Ella's velvet dress. "Here's a little trick I learned when I was a girl," she said. In one swift movement she took the back hem of the dress, brought it up between Ella's knees, and tucked it into the sash. "Now you're wearing shorts," she said.

Ella didn't feel like she was wearing shorts. As soon as Delilah turned away, she pulled her skirt out of her sash and let it fall around her legs.

The wooden deck outside was cluttered with Tinkertoys and clay flowerpots and Little Golden Books. Ella heard children screaming and laughing nearby. As she and Benjamin moved to the edge of the deck, there was a rustle in the bushes and a skinny boy leaped out and pointed a suction-cup arrow at them. He stood there breathing hard, his hair full of leaves, his chest bare. "You're on duty," he said.

"Me?" Benjamin said.

"Yes, you. Both of you." He motioned them off the porch with his arrow and took them around the side of the house. There, built into a sprawling oak, was the biggest, most sophisticated tree house Ella had ever seen. There were tiny rooms of sagging plywood, and rope ladders hanging down from doors, and a telescope and a fireman's pole and a red net full of leaves. From one wide platform—almost as high as the top of the house—it seemed you could jump down onto a huge trampoline. Even higher was a kind of crow's nest, a little circular platform built around the trunk. A red-painted sign on the railing read DAGNER! Ella could hear the other children screaming but she couldn't see them. A collie dog barked crazily, staring up at the tree.

"Take off your socks! That's an order," the skinny boy said.

Benjamin glanced at Ella. Ella shrugged. It seemed ridiculous to walk around outside in socks. She bent and peeled off her anklets. Benjamin carefully removed his Pilgrim buckles and put them in his pocket, then sat down and took off his socks. The skinny boy grabbed the socks from their hands and tucked them into the waistband of his shorts.

The mud was thick and cold between Ella's toes, and pecan shells bit her feet as the boy herded them toward the tree house. He prodded Ella toward a ladder of prickly-looking rope. When she stepped onto the first rung, the ladder swung toward the tree and her toes banged against the trunk. The skinny boy laughed.

"Go on," he said. "Hurry up. And no whining."

The rope burned her hands and feet as she ascended. The ladder seemed to go on forever. Ben followed below, making the rope buck and sway as they climbed. At the top there was a small square opening, and Ella thrust both her arms inside and pulled herself into a dark coop. As she stood, her head knocked against something dangling from the ceiling on a length of string. It was a bird's skull, no bigger than a walnut. Dozens of others hung from the ceiling around her. Benjamin huddled at her side.

"Sick," he said.

"Don't look," Ella said.

The suction-cup arrow came up through the hole in the floor.

"Keep going," said the boy. "You're not there yet."

"Go where?" Ella said.

"Through the wall."

Ella brushed the skulls out of her way and leveled her shoulder against one of the walls. It creaked open like a door. Outside, a tree limb as thick as her torso extended up to another plywood box, this one much larger than the first. Ella dropped to her knees and crawled upward. Benjamin followed.

Apparently this was the hostage room. Four kids stood in the semidarkness, wide-eyed and still as sculptures, each bound at the ankles and wrists with vine handcuffs. Two of the kids, a boy and a girl, were so skinny that Ella could see the outlines of bones in their arms and legs. Their hair was patchy and ragged, their eyes black and almond-shaped. In the corner, a white-haired boy in purple overalls whimpered softly to himself. And at the center of the room a girl Benjamin's age stood tied to the tree trunk with brown string. She had the same wild gray eyes and leafy hair as the boy with the arrow.

"It's mine, it's *my* tree house," she said as Ella stared at her.

"Is Mister Kaplan your dad?" Benjamin said.

"My dat-*tee*," the girl corrected him.

"Where's your mom?"

"She died," said the girl, and looked him fiercely in the eye.

Benjamin sucked in his breath and glanced at Ella.

Ella wanted to hit this girl. She bent down close to the girl's face, making her eyes small and mean. "If this is so your tree house," Ella said, "then how come you're tied up?"

"It's *jail*," the girl spat. "In jail you get tied up."

"We could untie you," said Benjamin. He tugged at one of her bonds.

The girl opened her mouth and let out a scream so shrill Ella's eardrums buzzed. Once, as her father had pulled into the driveway at night, he had trapped a rabbit by the leg beneath the wheel of his car; the rabbit had made a sound like that. Benjamin dropped the string and moved against Ella, and the children with ragged hair laughed and jumped on the platform until it crackled and groaned. The boy in purple overalls cried in his corner.

Benjamin put his lips to Ella's ear. "I don't understand it here," he whispered.

There was a scuffle at the door, and the skinny boy stepped into the hostage room. "All right," he said. "Who gets killed?"

"Kill those kids, Peter," the girl said, pointing to Benjamin and Ella.

"Us?" Benjamin said.

"Who do you think?" said the boy.

He poked them in the back with his suction-cup arrow and moved them toward the tree trunk, where rough boards formed a ladder to the next level. Ella and Benjamin climbed until they had reached a narrow platform, and then Peter pushed them to the edge. Ella looked down at the trampoline. It was a longer drop than the high dive at the public pool. She looked over her shoulder and Peter glared at her. Down below the collie barked and barked, his black nose pointed up at them.

Benjamin took Ella's hand and closed his eyes. Then Peter shoved them from behind, and they stumbled forward into space.

There was a moment of terrifying emptiness, nothing but air beneath Ella's feet. She could hear the collie's bark getting closer as she fell. She slammed into the trampoline knees first, then flew, shrieking, back up into the air. When she hit the trampoline a second time, Benjamin's head knocked against her chin. He stood up rubbing his head, and Ella tasted salt in her mouth. Her loose tooth had slipped its roots. She spat it into her palm and studied its jagged edge.

"Move," Peter called from above. The boy in purple overalls was just climbing up onto the platform. Peter pulled him forward until his toes curled over the edge.

"I lost my tooth!" Ella yelled.

"Get off!"

Benjamin scrambled off the trampoline. Ella crawled to the edge, the tooth gleaming and red-rimmed between her fingers, and then the trampoline lurched with the weight of the boy in purple overalls. The tooth flew from her hand and into the bushes, too small to make a sound when it hit.

When she burst into the house crying, blood streaming from her mouth, the long-haired men and women dropped their mixing spoons and went to her. She twisted away from them, looking frantically for her mother and father, but they were nowhere to be seen. There was no way to explain that she wasn't hurt, that she was upset because her tooth was gone and because everything about that house made her want to run away and hide. The adults, their faces creased with worry, pulled her to the sink and held her mouth open. The woman with skewed eyes, Delilah, pressed a tissue against the space where her tooth had been. Ella could smell onions and apples on her hands.

"The time was right," she said. "The new tooth's already coming in."

"Whose is she?" one of the men asked.

Delilah told him the names of Ella's parents. It was strange to hear those familiar words, *Ann* and *Gary*, in the mouths of these long-haired strangers.

"Your mother is upstairs," Delilah said, her eyes swiveling toward some distant hidden room. "She felt a little swimmy-headed. Your dad just brought her some special tea. Maybe we should let her rest, hmm?"

Ella slipped out from beneath Delilah's hand and ran to the hall, remembering the stairway she'd seen earlier. There it was before her, a curve of glossy steps leading to nowhere she knew. Her mother's cough drifted down from one of the bedroom doors. Ella put a foot onto the first stair, feeling the eyes of the adults on her back. No one said anything to stop her. After a moment, she began to climb.

In the upstairs hallway, toys and kids' shoes lay strewn across the floor, and crumpled pants and shirts and dresses lay in a musty-smelling heap. Two naked Barbies sprawled in a frying pan. A record player sat in the middle of the hall, its vacant turntable spinning. Ella stepped over the cord and went into the first room, a small room with a sleeping bag on the bare mattress ticking. In a cage on the nightstand, a white rat scrabbled at a cardboard tube. A finger-painted sign above the bed said CLARIES ROOM. Her mother's cough rose again from down the hall, and she turned and ran toward the sound.

In a room whose blue walls and curtains made everything look as if it were underwater, her mother lay pale and coughing on a bed piled high with pillows. Her father sat on the edge of the bed, his hands raised in the air, thumbs hooked together and palms spread wide. For a moment Ella had no idea what he was doing. Then she saw the shadow of her father's hands against the wall, in the light of a blue-shaded lamp. A shock of relief went through her.

"Tweet, tweet," Ella said.

"Right," her father said. "A birdy."

Ella's mother turned toward her and smiled, more awake, more like her real self than earlier. "Do another one, Gary," she said.

Ella's father twisted his hands into a new shape in the air.

"A dog?" Ella said.

"A fish!" said her mother.

"No," he said, and adjusted his hands. "It's a horsie, see?"

"A horsie?" said Ella's mother. "With fins?"

That made Ella laugh a little.

"Hey," her mother said. "Come here, you. Smile again."

Ella did as she was told.

"You lost your tooth!"

"It's gone," Ella said. She climbed onto the bed to explain, but as she flopped down on the mattress her mother's face contracted with pain.

"Please don't bounce," her mother said. She touched the place where her surgery had been.

Ella's father gave her a stern look and lifted her off the bed. "Your mom's sleepy," he said. "You should run back downstairs now."

"She's always sleepy," Ella said, looking down at her muddy feet. She thought of her tooth lying out in the weeds, and how she'd have nothing to put under her pillow for the tooth fairy.

Her mother began to cry.

Ella's father went to the window and stared down into the yard, his breath fogging the glass. "Go ahead, Ella," he said. "We just need a few minutes."

"My tooth," Ella said. She knew she should leave, but couldn't.

"It'll grow back bigger and stronger," her father said.

She could see he didn't understand what had happened. If only her mother would stop crying she could explain everything. In the blue light her mother looked cold and far away, pressed under the weight of tons of water.

"I'll be down soon," her mother said, sniffling. "Go out and play."

Ella opened her mouth to form some protest, but no words came out.

"Go on, now," her father said.

"It fell in a bush!" she wailed, then turned and ran downstairs.

The other children had come in by then. Her brother stood in line at the down-stairs bathroom to wash before dinner, comparing fingernail dirt with the boy in purple overalls. Hands deep in the pockets of her velvet dress, Ella wandered through the echoing hall into a room lined from floor to ceiling with books. Many of the titles were in other languages, some even written in different alphabets. She recognized *D'Aulaires' Greek Mythology* and *The Riverside Shakespeare* and *Grimm's Fairy Tales*. Scattered around on small tables and decorative stands were tiny human figurines with animal heads: horse-man, giraffe-man, panther-man. On one table sat an Egyptian beetle made of milky green stone, and beside him a real beetle, shiny as metal, who flew at Ella's face when she reached to touch his shell. She batted him away with the back of her hand.

And then, just above where the beetle had fallen, Ella saw a shelf without any books at all. It was low, the height of her knees, with a frayed blue scarf pinned against its back wall. Burnt-down candles stood on either side of a black lacquer box, and on top of this box stood a glass filled with red water.

Ella reached for the glass, and someone behind her screamed.

She turned around. Clarie stood in the doorway, dress unbuttoned at one shoulder, face smeared with mud.

"Don't touch that," she said.

Ella took a step back. "I wasn't going to."

Clarie's eyes seemed to ignite as she bent down and took the glass in both hands. She held it near a lamp, so the light shone through it and cast a red oval upon the wall.

"It's my mother," she said.

For dinner there was a roasted dome of something that looked like meat but wasn't. It was springy and steaming, and when Mister Kaplan cut it open Ella could see that it was stuffed with rice and yams. Benjamin tried to hide under the table, but their father pulled him up by the arms and set him in his place. He prodded his wedge of roast until it slid onto the tablecloth. Then he began to cry quietly.

"The kids aren't vegetarian," their father said, in apology to the men and women at the table. He picked up the slice of roast with his fingers and put it back on Ben's plate. The other men and women held their forks motionless above their own plates, looking at Ella's mother and father with pity.

"Look, Ben," said Delilah. "It's called seitan. Wheat gluten. The other kids love it."

The boy and girl with almond-shaped eyes and ragged hair stopped in mid-chew. The girl looked at Benjamin and narrowed her eyes.

"I don't eat gluten," Benjamin said.

"Come on, now," their father said. "It's great."

Ella's mother pressed her fingers against her temples. She hadn't touched her own dinner. Ella, sitting beside her, took a bite of wheat gluten. It was almost like meat, firm and savory, and the stuffing was flavored with forest-smelling spices. As she glanced around the table she thought of the picture of the First Thanksgiving on the bulletin board at school: the smiling Pilgrims eating turkey and squash, the stern-faced Native Americans looking as if they knew the worst was yet to come. Who among them that night were the Native Americans? Who were the Pilgrims? The dark old house was like a wilderness around them, the wind sighing through its rooms.

"I jumped on the trampoline," said the boy with ragged hair, pulling on the sleeve of the woman next to him. "That boy did a flip." He pointed at Peter, who was smashing rice against his plate with his thumb. "He tied his sister to the tree."

Mister Kaplan set down his fork. He looked sideways at Peter, his mouth pressed into a stern line. "I told you never to do that again," he said. He sounded angry, but his voice was quiet, almost a whisper.

"She made me!" Peter said, and plunged a spoon into his baked squash.

Mister Kaplan's eyes went glossy and faraway. He stared off at the blank wall above Ella's mother's head, drifting away from the noise and chatter of the dinner table. Next to him Delilah shuttled her mismatched eyes back and forth.

Ella's mother straightened in her chair. "Ed," she called softly.

Mister Kaplan blinked hard and looked at her.

"Tell us about your Tai Chi class."

"What," he said.

"Your Tai Chi class."

"You know, I don't really want to talk right now." He pushed back his chair and went into the kitchen. There was the sound of water and then the clink of dishes in the sink. Delilah shook her head. The other adults looked down at their plates. Ella's mother wiped the corners of her mouth with her napkin and crossed her arms over her chest.

"Does anyone want more rice?" Ella's father asked.

"I think we're all thinking about Lena," said the man with the shaved head.

"I know I am," said Delilah.

"Infinity to infinity," said the man. "Dust into star."

The men and women looked at each other, their eyes carrying some message Ella couldn't understand. They clasped each other's hands and bent their heads. "Infinity to infinity," they repeated. "Dust into star."

"Matter into energy," said the man. "Identity into oneness."

"Matter into energy," everyone said. Ella glanced at her father, whose jaw was set hard, unmoving. Her mother's lips formed the words, but no sound came out. Ella thought of the usual Thanksgivings at her uncle Bon's, where everyone talked and laughed at the table and they ate turkey and dressing and sweet potatoes with marshmallows melted on top. She closed her eyes and held her breath, filling her chest with a tightness that felt like magic power. If she tried hard enough could she transport them all, her mother and father, Benjamin and herself, to that other time? She held her breath until it seemed she would explode, then let it out in a rush. She opened her eyes. Nothing had changed. Peter kicked the table leg, and the collie, crouched beside Clarie's chair, whimpered his unease. Ella could see Clarie's hand on his collar, her knuckles bloodless as stones.

Mister Kaplan returned with a platter of baked apples. He cleared his throat, and everyone turned to look at him. "Guess what we forgot," he said. "I spent nearly an hour peeling these things." He held the platter aloft, waiting.

"Who wants some nice baked apples?" he said. "Baked apples. I peeled them."

No one said a word.

After dinner the adults drifted into the room with the straw mats and Indian goddesses. Ella understood that the children were not invited, but she lingered in the doorway to see what would happen. Mister Kaplan bent over a tiny brass dish and held a match to a black cone. A wisp of smoke curled toward the ceiling, and after a moment Ella smelled a dusty, flowery scent. Her mother and father and the rest of the adults sat cross-legged on the floor, not touching each other. A low hum began to fill the room like something with weight and substance. Ella saw her father raise an eyebrow at her mother, as if to ask if these people were serious. But her mother's shoulders were bent in meditation, her mouth open with the drone of the mantra, and Ella's father sighed and let his head fall forward.

Someone pinched Ella's shoulder and she turned around. Peter stood behind her, his eyes small and cold. "Come on," he said. "You're supposed to help clean up."

In the kitchen the children stacked dirty dishes on the counter and ran water in the sink. The boy and girl with almond eyes climbed up onto a wide wooden stepstool and began to scrub dishes. Peter scraped all the scraps into an aluminum pan and gave it to Clarie, who set it on the floor near the dog's water dish. The collie fell at the leftover food with sounds that made Ella sick to her stomach. Clarie stood next to him and stroked his tail.

Then Benjamin came into the kitchen carrying the glass of red water. "Somebody forgot this under the table," he said.

Again there was the dying-rabbit screech. Clarie batted her palms against the sides of her head. "No!" she shrieked. "Put it down!"

Benjamin's eyes went wide, and he set the glass on the kitchen counter. "I don't want it," he said.

The boy in purple overalls squinted at the glass. "Looks like Kool-Aid," he said.

"She gets all crazy," said Peter. "Watch." Peter lifted the glass high into the air, and Clarie ran toward him. "You can't have it," he said.

Clarie jumped up and down in fury, her hands flapping like limp rags. Her mouth opened but no sound came out. Then she curled her fingers into claws and scratched at Peter's arms and chest until he twisted away. He ran across the kitchen and onto the deck, holding the glass in the air, and Clarie followed him, screaming.

The ragged-haired brother and sister looked at each other, arms gloved in white bubbles. In one quick movement they were off the stool, shaking suds around the kitchen. "Come on!" said the boy. "Let's go watch!"

Benjamin grabbed Ella's hand and pulled her toward the screen door. The children pushed out onto the deck and then ran toward the tree castle, where Clarie and her brother were climbing the first rope ladder. It was dark now, and floodlights on the roof of the house illuminated the entire castle, its rooms silver-gray and ghostly, its ropes and nets swaying in a rising breeze. The children gathered on the grass near the trampoline.

Peter held the glass as he climbed, the red water sloshing against its sides.

"Come and get it," he crooned. He reached the first room, and they heard the wall-door scrape against the trunk as he pushed it open. Then he moved out onto the oak limb, agile as the spider monkeys Ella had seen at the zoo. He might as well have had a tail.

Clarie crawled behind him, her hands scrabbling at the bark. Peter howled at the sky as he reached the hostage room.

Benjamin moved toward Ella and pressed his head against her arm. "I want to go home," he said.

"Shh," Ella said. "We can't."

High above, Peter climbed onto the platform from which they had jumped earlier. Still holding the glass, he pulled himself up the tree trunk to the crow's nest. High up on that small, railed platform, where the tree branches became thin and sparse, he stopped. Below him Clarie scrambled onto the jumping platform. She looked out across the yard as if unsure of where he had gone. "Up here," Peter said, holding the glass high.

Ella could hear Clarie grunting as she pulled herself up into the crow's nest. She stood and reached for the glass, her face a small moon in the dark. A few acorns scuttled off the crow's-nest platform.

"Give it!" she cried again.

Peter stood looking at her for a moment in the dark. "You really want it?"

"Peter!"

He swept the glass through the air. The water flew out in an arc, ruby-colored against the glare of the floodlights. Clarie leaned out as if to catch it between her fingers, and with a splintering crack she broke through the railing. Her dress fluttered silently as she fell, and her white hands grasped at the air. There was a quiet instant, the soft sound of water falling on grass. Then, with a shock Ella felt in the soles of her feet, Clarie hit the ground. The girl with the ragged hair screamed.

Clarie lay beside the trampoline, still as sleep, her neck bent at an impossible angle. Ella wanted to look away, but couldn't. The other children, even Benjamin, moved to where Clarie lay and circled around, some calling her name, some just looking. Peter slid down the fireman's pole and stumbled across the lawn toward his sister. He pushed Benjamin aside. With one toe he nudged Clarie's shoulder, then knelt and rolled her over. A bare bone glistened from her wrist. The boy in purple overalls threw up onto the grass.

Ella turned and ran toward the house. She banged the screen door open and skidded across the kitchen floor into the hall. At the doorway of the meditation room she stopped, breathing hard. The parents sat just as she had left them, eyes closed, mouths open slightly, their sound beating like a living thing, their thumbs and forefingers circled into perfect O's. She could smell the heat of them rising in the room and mingling with the scent of the incense. Her father's chin rested on his chest as if he had fallen asleep. Beside him her mother looked drained of blood, her skin so white she seemed almost holy.

"Mom," Ella whispered. "Mom."

Ella's mother turned slightly and opened her eyes. For a moment she seemed between two worlds, her eyes unfocused and distant. Then she blinked and looked at Ella. She shook her head no.

"Please," Ella said, but her mother closed her eyes again. Ella stood there for a long time watching her, but she didn't move or speak. Finally Ella turned and went back outside.

By the time she reached the tree castle Peter had dragged Clarie halfway across the lawn. He turned his eyes on Ella, and she stared back at him. The sound of the mantra continued unbroken from the house. Peter hoisted Clarie again under the arms and dragged her to the bushes, her bare feet bumping over the grass. Then he rolled her over until she was hidden in shadow. He pulled her dress down so it covered her thighs, and turned her head toward the fence that bordered the backyard.

"Get some leaves and stuff," he said. "We have to cover her."

Ella would not move. She took Benjamin's hand, but he pulled away from her and wandered across the lawn, pulling up handfuls of grass. She watched the children pick up twigs, Spanish moss, leaves, anything they could find. The boy in purple overalls gathered cedar bark from a flower bed, and Peter dragged fallen branches out of the underbrush near the fence. They scattered everything they found over Clarie's body. In five minutes they had covered her entirely.

"Go back inside," Peter said. "If anyone cries or says anything, I'll kill them."

Ella turned to go, and that was when she saw her tooth, a tiny white pebble in the weeds. She picked it up and rubbed it clean. Then she knelt beside Clarie, clearing away moss and leaves until she found Clarie's hand. She dropped the tooth into the palm and closed the fingers around it. A shiver spread through her chest, and she covered the hand again. Then she put her arm around Benjamin and they all went back inside. Drawn by the sound of the chanting, they wandered into the hall. All around them hung the yellow photographs, the stony men and women and children looking down at them with sad and knowing eyes. In an oval of black velvet one girl in a white dress held the string of a wooden duck, her lips open as if she were about to speak. Her eyes had the wildness of Clarie's eyes, her legs the same bowed curve.

At last there was a rustle from the meditation room, and the adults drifted out into the hall. They blinked at the light and rubbed their elbows and knees. Ella's mother and father linked arms and moved toward their children. Benjamin gave a hiccup. His eyes looked strange, the pupils huge, the whites flat and dry. Their mother noticed right away. "We'd better get going," she said to Ella's father. "Ben's tired."

She went into the foyer and pulled their shoes from the pile. Mr. Kaplan followed, looking around in bewilderment, as if he could not believe people were leaving. He patted Benjamin on the head and asked Ella's mother if she wanted to take some leftover food. Ella's mother shook her head no. Her father thanked Mister Kaplan for his hospitality. Somewhere toward the back of the house the dog began to bark. Ella pulled Benjamin through the front door, barefoot, and her parents followed them to the car.

All the way past the rows of live oaks, past the cemetery where the little tombs stood like grounded boats, past the low flat shotgun houses with their flaking roofs, Benjamin sat rigid on the backseat and cried without a sound. Ella felt the sobs leaving his chest in waves of hot air. She closed her eyes and followed the car in her mind down the streets that led to their house, until it seemed they had driven past their house long ago and were moving on to a place where strange beds awaited them, where they would fall asleep thinking of dark forests and wake to the lives of strangers.

ZZ Packer

BROWNIES

ZZ PACKER (1973–) is the author of *Drinking Coffee Elsewhere*. Her short stories have been published in *The New Yorker, Harper's, Ploughshares,* and *Zoetrope* and have been anthologized in *Best American Short Stories 2000* and *2003*. She is the recipient of a Guggenheim Fellowship and was named by *Granta* as one of the Best American Writers under forty.

By our second day at Camp Crescendo, the girls in my Brownie troop had decided to kick the asses of each and every girl in Brownie Troop 909. Troop 909 was doomed from the first day of camp; they were white girls, their complexions a blend of ice cream: strawberry, vanilla. They turtled out from their bus in pairs, their rolled-up sleeping bags chromatized with Disney characters: Sleeping Beauty, Snow White, Mickey Mouse; or the generic ones cheap parents bought: washed-out rainbows, unicorns, curly eyelashed frogs. Some clutched Igloo coolers and still others held on to stuffed toys like pacifiers, looking all around them like tourists determined to be dazzled.

Our troop was wending its way past their bus, past the ranger station, past the colorful trail guide drawn like a treasure map, locked behind glass.

"Man, did you smell them?" Arnetta said, giving the girls a slow once-over. "They smell like Chihuahuas. Wet Chihuahuas." Their troop was still at the entrance, and though we had passed them by yards, Arnetta raised her nose in the air and grimaced.

Arnetta said this from the very rear of the line, far away from Mrs. Margolin, who always strung our troop behind her like a brood of obedient ducklings. Mrs. Margolin even looked like a mother duck—she had hair cropped close to a small ball of a head, almost no neck, and huge, miraculous breasts. She wore enormous belts that looked like the kind that weight lifters wear, except hers would be cheap metallic gold or rabbit fur or covered with gigantic fake sunflowers, and often these belts would become nature lessons in and of themselves. "See," Mrs. Margolin once said to us, pointing to her belt, "this one's made entirely from the feathers of baby pigeons."

The belt layered with feathers was uncanny enough, but I was more disturbed by the realization that I had never actually seen a baby pigeon. I searched weeks for one, in vain—scampering after pigeons whenever I was downtown with my father.

But nature lessons were not Mrs. Margolin's top priority. She saw the position of troop leader as an evangelical post. Back at the A.M.E. church where our Brownie meetings were held, Mrs. Margolin was especially fond of imparting religious aphorisms by means of acrostics—"Satan" was the "Serpent Always Tempting and Noisome"; she'd refer to the "Bible" as "Basic Instructions Before Leaving Earth." Whenever she quizzed us on these, expecting to hear the acrostics parroted back to her, only Arnetta's correct replies soared over our vague mumblings.

"Jesus?" Mrs. Margolin might ask expectantly, and Arnetta alone would dutifully answer, "Jehovah's Example, Saving Us Sinners."

Arnetta always made a point of listening to Mrs. Margolin's religious talk and giving her what she wanted to hear. Because of this, Arnetta could have blared through a megaphone that the white girls of Troop 909 were "wet Chihuahuas" without so much as a blink from Mrs. Margolin. Once, Arnetta killed the troop goldfish by feeding it a french fry covered in ketchup, and when Mrs. Margolin demanded that she explain what had happened, claimed the goldfish had been eyeing her meal for hours, then the fish—giving in to temptation— had leapt up and snatched a whole golden fry from her fingertips.

"Serious Chihuahua," Octavia added, and though neither Arnetta nor Octavia could spell "Chihuahua," had ever seen a Chihuahua, trisyllabic words had gained a sort of exoticism within our fourth-grade set at Woodrow Wilson Elementary. Arnetta and Octavia would flip through the dictionary, determined to work the vulgar-sounding ones like "Djibouti" and "asinine" into conversation. "Caucasian Chihuahuas," Arnetta said.

That did it. The girls in my troop turned elastic: Drema and Elise doubled up on one another like inextricably entwined kites; Octavia slapped her belly; Janice jumped straight up in the air, then did it again, as if to slam-dunk her own head. They could not stop laughing. No one had laughed so hard since a boy named Martez had stuck a pencil in the electric socket and spent the whole day with a strange grin on his face.

"Girls, girls," said our parent helper, Mrs. Hedy. Mrs. Hedy was Octavia's mother, and she wagged her index finger perfunctorily, like a windshield wiper. "Stop it, now. Be good." She said this loud enough to be heard, but lazily, bereft of any feeling or indication that she meant to be obeyed, as though she could say these words again at the exact same pitch if a button somewhere on her were pressed. But the rest of the girls didn't stop; they only laughed louder. It was the word "Caucasian" that got them all going. One day at school, about a month before the Brownie camping trip, Arnetta turned to a boy wearing impossibly high-ankled floodwater jeans and said, "What are you? Caucasian?" The word took off from there, and soon everything was Caucasian. If you ate too fast you ate like a Caucasian, if you ate too slow you ate like a Caucasian. The biggest feat anyone at Woodrow Wilson could do was to jump off the swing in midair, at the highest point in its arc, and if you fell (as I had, more than once) instead of landing on your feet, knees bent Olympic gymnast–style, Arnetta and Octavia were prepared to comment. They'd look at each other with the silence of passengers who'd narrowly escaped an accident, then nod their heads, whispering with solemn horror, "Caucasian."

Even the only white kid in our school, Dennis, got in on the Caucasian act. That time when Martez stuck a pencil in the socket, Dennis had pointed and yelled, "That was so Caucasian!" When you lived in the south suburbs of Atlanta, it was easy to forget about whites. Whites were like those baby pigeons: real and existing, but rarely seen or thought about. Everyone had been to Rich's to go clothes shopping, everyone had seen white girls and their mothers coocooing over dresses; everyone had gone to the downtown library and seen white businessmen swish by importantly, wrists flexed in front of them to check the time as though they would change from Clark Kent into Superman at any second. But those images were as fleeting as cards shuffled in a deck, whereas the ten white girls behind us—invaders, Arnetta would later call them—were instantly real and memorable, with their long, shampoo commercial hair, straight as spaghetti from the box. This alone was reason for envy and hatred. The only black girl most of us had ever seen with hair that long was Octavia, whose hair hung past her butt like a Hawaiian hula dancer's. The sight of Octavia's mane prompted other girls to listen to her reverentially, as though whatever she had to say would somehow activate their own follicles. For example, when, on the first day of camp, Octavia made as if to speak, and everyone fell silent. "Nobody," Octavia said, "calls us niggers." At the end of that first day, when half of our troop made their way back to the cabin after tag-team restroom visits, Arnetta said she'd heard one of the Troop 909 girls call Daphne a nigger. The other half of the girls and I were helping Mrs. Margolin clean up the pots and pans from the campfire ravioli dinner. When we made our way to the restrooms to wash up and brush our teeth, we met up with Arnetta midway.

"Man, I completely heard the girl," Arnetta reported. "Right, Daphne?"

Daphne hardly ever spoke, but when she did, her voice was petite and tinkly, the voice one might expect from a shiny new earring. She'd written a poem once, for Langston Hughes Day, a poem brimming with all the teacher-winning ingredients—trees and oceans, sunsets and moons—but what cinched the poem for the grown-ups, snatching the win from Octavia's musical ode to Grandmaster Flash and the Furious Five, were Daphne's last lines:

You are my father, the veteran / When you cry in the dark / It rains and rains and rains in my heart.

She'd always worn clean, though faded, jumpers and dresses when Chic jeans were the fashion, but when she went up to the dais to receive her prize journal, pages trimmed in gold, she wore a new dress with a velveteen bodice and a taffeta skirt as wide as an umbrella. All the kids clapped, though none of them understood the poem. I'd read encyclopedias the way others read comics, and I didn't get it. But those last lines pricked me, they were so eerie, and as my father and I ate cereal, I'd whisper over my Froot Loops, like a mantra, "You are my father, the veteran. You are my father, the veteran, the veteran, the veteran," until my father, who acted in plays as Caliban and Othello and was not a veteran, marched me up to my teacher one morning and said, "Can you tell me what's wrong with this kid?"

I thought Daphne and I might become friends, but I think she grew spooked by me whispering those lines to her, begging her to tell me what they meant, and I soon understood that two quiet people like us were better off quiet alone.

"Daphne? Didn't you hear them call you a nigger?" Arnetta asked, giving Daphne a nudge.

The sun was setting behind the trees, and their leafy tops formed a canopy of black lace for the flame of the sun to pass through. Daphne shrugged her shoulders at first, then slowly nodded her head when Arnetta gave her a hard look.

Twenty minutes later, when my restroom group returned to the cabin, Arnetta was still talking about Troop 909. My restroom group had passed by some of the 909 girls. For the most part, they deferred to us, waving us into the restrooms, letting us go even though they'd gotten there first.

We'd seen them, but from afar, never within their orbit enough to see whether their faces were the way all white girls appeared on TV—ponytailed and full of energy, bubbling over with love and money. All I could see was that some of them rapidly fanned their faces with their hands, though the heat of the day had long passed. A few seemed to be lolling their heads in slow circles, half purposefully, as if exercising the muscles of their necks, half ecstatically, like Stevie Wonder.

"We can't let them get away with that," Arnetta said, dropping her voice to a laryngitic whisper. "We can't let them get away with calling us niggers. I say we teach them a lesson." She sat down cross-legged on a sleeping bag, an embittered Buddha, eyes glimmering acrylic-black. "We can't go telling Mrs. Margolin, either. Mrs. Margolin'll say something about doing unto others and the path of righteousness and all. Forget that shit." She let her eyes flutter irreverently till they half closed, as though ignoring an insult not worth returning. We could all hear Mrs. Margolin outside, gathering the last of the metal campware.

Nobody said anything for a while. Usually people were quiet after Arnetta spoke. Her tone had an upholstered confidence that was somehow both regal and vulgar at once. It demanded a few moments of silence in its wake, like the ringing of a church bell or the playing of taps. Sometimes Octavia would ditto or dissent to whatever Arnetta had said, and this was the signal that others could speak. But this time Octavia just swirled a long cord of hair into pretzel shapes.

"Well?" Arnetta said. She looked as if she had discerned the hidden severity of the situation and was waiting for the rest of us to catch up. Everyone looked from Arnetta to Daphne. It was, after all, Daphne who had supposedly been called the name, but Daphne sat on the bare cabin floor, flipping through the pages of the Girl Scout handbook, eyebrows arched in mock wonder, as if the handbook were a catalogue full of bright and startling foreign costumes. Janice broke the silence. She clapped her hands to broach her idea of a plan. "They gone be sleeping," she whispered conspiratorially, "then we gone sneak into they cabin, then we'll put daddy longlegs in they sleeping bags. Then they'll wake up. Then we gone beat 'em up till they're as flat as frying pans!" She jammed her fist into the palm of her hand, then made a sizzling sound.

Janice's country accent was laughable, her looks homely, her jumpy acrobatics embarrassing to behold. Arnetta and Octavia volleyed amused, arrogant smiles whenever Janice opened her mouth, but Janice never caught the hint, spoke whenever she wanted, fluttered around Arnetta and Octavia futilely offering her opinions to their departing backs. Whenever Arnetta and Octavia shooed her away, Janice loitered until the two would finally sigh and ask, "What is it, Miss Caucasoid? What do you want?"

"Shut up, Janice," Octavia said, letting a fingered loop of hair fall to her waist as though just the sound of Janice's voice had ruined the fun of her hair twisting.

Janice obeyed, her mouth hung open in a loose grin, unflappable, unhurt.

"All right," Arnetta said, standing up. "We're going to have a secret meeting and talk about what we're going to do."

Everyone gravely nodded her head. The word *secret* had a built-in importance, the modifier form of the word carried more clout than the noun. A secret meant nothing; it was like gossip: just a bit of unpleasant knowledge about someone who happened to be someone other than yourself. A secret meeting, or a secret club was entirely different.

That was when Arnetta turned to me as though she knew that doing so was both a compliment and a charity.

"Snot, you're not going to be a bitch and tell Mrs. Margolin, are you?"

I had been called "Snot" ever since first grade, when I'd sneezed in class and two long ropes of mucus had splattered a nearby girl. "Hey," I said. "Maybe you didn't hear them right—I mean—"

"Are you gonna tell on us or not?" was all Arnetta wanted to know, and by the time the question was asked, the rest of our Brownie troop looked at me as though they'd already decided their course of action, me being the only impediment.

Camp Crescendo used to double as a high-school-band and field hockey camp until an arcing field hockey ball landed on the clasp of a girl's metal barrette, knifing a skull nerve and paralyzing the right side of her body. The camp closed down for a few years and the girl's teammates built a memorial, filling the spot on which the girl fell with hockey balls, on which they had painted— all in nail polish—get-well tidings, flowers, and hearts. The balls were still stacked there, like a shrine of ostrich eggs embedded in the ground.

On the second day of camp, Troop 909 was dancing around the mound of hockey balls, their limbs jangling awkwardly, their cries like the constant summer squeal of an amusement park. There was a stream that bordered the field hockey lawn, and the girls from my troop settled next to it, scarfing down the last of lunch: sandwiches made from salami and slices of tomato that had gotten waterlogged from the melting ice in the cooler. From the stream bank, Arnetta eyed the Troop 909 girls, scrutinizing their movements to glean inspiration for battle.

"Man," Arnetta said, "we could bumrush them right now if that damn lady would leave."

The 909 troop leader was a white woman with the severe pageboy hairdo of an ancient Egyptian. She lay on a picnic blanket, sphinxlike, eating a banana, sometimes holding it out in front of her like a microphone. Beside her sat a girl slowly flapping one hand like a bird with a broken wing. Occasionally, the leader would call out the names of girls who'd attempted leapfrogs and flips, or of girls who yelled too loudly or strayed far from the circle.

"I'm just glad Big Fat Mama's not following us here," Octavia said. "At least we don't have to worry about her." Mrs. Margolin, Octavia assured us, was having her Afternoon Devotional, shrouded in mosquito netting, in a clearing she'd found. Mrs. Hedy was cleaning mud from her espadrilles in the cabin.

"I handled them." Arnetta sucked on her teeth and proudly grinned. "I told her we was going to gather leaves."

"Gather leaves," Octavia said, nodding respectfully. "That's a good one. Especially since they're so mad-crazy about this camping thing." She looked from ground to sky, sky to ground. Her hair hung down her back in two braids like a squaw's. "I mean, I really don't know why it's even called camping—all we ever do with Nature is find some twigs and say something like, 'Wow, this fell from a tree.'" She then studied her sandwich. With two disdainful fingers, she picked out a slice of dripping tomato, the sections congealed with red slime. She pitched it into the stream embrowned with dead leaves and the murky effigies of other dead things, but in the opaque water, a group of small silver-brown fish appeared. They surrounded the tomato and nibbled.

"Look!" Janice cried. "Fishes! Fishes!" As she scrambled to the edge of the stream to watch, a covey of insects threw up tantrums from the wheatgrass and nettle, a throng of tiny electric machines, all going at once. Octavia sneaked up behind Janice as if to push her in. Daphne and I exchanged terrified looks. It seemed as though only we knew that Octavia was close enough—and bold enough—to actually push Janice into the stream. Janice turned around quickly, but Octavia was already staring serenely into the still water as though she was gathering some sort of courage from it. "What's so funny?" Janice said, eyeing them all suspiciously.

Elise began humming the tune to "Karma Chameleon," all the girls joining in, their hums light and facile. Janice also began to hum, against everyone else, the high-octane opening chords of "Beat It." "I love me some Michael Jackson," Janice said when she'd finished humming, smacking her lips as though Michael Jackson were a favorite meal. "I will marry Michael Jackson."

Before anyone had a chance to impress upon Janice the impossibility of this, Arnetta suddenly rose, made a sun visor of her hand, and watched Troop 909 leave the field hockey lawn.

"Dammit!" she said. "We've got to get them alone."

"They won't ever be alone," I said. All the rest of the girls looked at me, for I usually kept quiet. If I spoke even a word, I could count on someone calling me Snot. Everyone seemed to think that we could beat up these girls; no one entertained the thought that they might fight back. "The only time they'll be unsupervised is in the bathroom."

"Oh shut up, Snot," Octavia said.

But Arnetta slowly nodded her head. "The bathroom," she said. "The bathroom," she said, again and again. "The bathroom! The bathroom!"

According to Octavia's watch, it took us five minutes to hike to the restrooms, which were midway between our cabin and Troop 909's. Inside, the mirrors above the sinks returned only the vaguest of reflections, as though someone had taken a scouring pad to their surfaces to obscure the shine. Pine needles, leaves, and dirty, flattened wads of chewing gum covered the floor like a mosaic. Webs of hair matted the drain in the middle of the floor. Above the sinks and below the mirrors, stacks of folded white paper towels lay on a long metal counter. Shaggy white balls of paper towels sat on the sink tops in a line like corsages on display. A thread of floss snaked from a wad of tissues dotted with the faint red-pink of blood. One of those white girls, I thought, had just lost a tooth.

Though the restroom looked almost the same as it had the night before, it somehow seemed stranger now. We hadn't noticed the wooden rafters coming together in great Vs. We were, it seemed, inside a whale, viewing the ribs of the roof of its mouth. "Wow. It's a mess," Elise said.

"You can say that again."

Arnetta leaned against the doorjamb of a restroom stall. "This is where they'll be again," she said. Just seeing the place, just having a plan seemed to satisfy her. "We'll go in and talk to them. You know, 'How you doing? How long'll you be here?' That sort of thing. Then Octavia and I are gonna tell them what happens when they call any one of us a nigger."

"I'm going to say something, too," Janice said.

Arnetta considered this. "Sure," she said. "Of course. Whatever you want."

Janice pointed her finger like a gun at Octavia and rehearsed the line she'd thought up, " 'We're gonna teach you a lesson!' That's what I'm going to say." She narrowed her eyes like a TV mobster. " 'We're gonna teach you little girls a lesson!' "

With the back of her hand, Octavia brushed Janice's finger away. "You couldn't teach me to shit in a toilet."

"But," I said, "what if they say, 'We didn't say that? We didn't call anyone an N-I-G-G-E-R.' "

"Snot," Arnetta said, and then sighed. "Don't think. Just fight. If you even know how."

Everyone laughed except Daphne. Arnetta gently laid her hand on Daphne's shoulder. "Daphne. You don't have to fight. We're doing this for you."

Daphne walked to the counter, took a clean paper towel, and carefully unfolded it like a map. With it, she began to pick up the trash all around. Everyone watched.

"C'mon," Arnetta said to everyone. "Let's beat it." We all ambled toward the doorway, where the sunshine made one large white rectangle of light. We were immediately blinded, and we shielded our eyes with our hands and our forearms.

"Daphne?" Arnetta asked. "Are you coming?"

We all looked back at the bending girl, the thin of her back hunched like the back of a custodian sweeping a stage, caught in limelight. Stray strands of her hair were lit near-transparent, thin fiber-optic threads. She did not nod yes to the question, nor did she shake her head no. She abided, bent. Then she began again, picking up leaves, wads of paper, the cotton fluff innards from a torn stuffed toy. She did it so methodically, so exquisitely, so humbly, she must have been trained. I thought of those dresses she wore, faded and old, yet so pressed and clean. I then saw the poverty in them; I then could imagine her mother, cleaning the houses of others, returning home, weary.

"I guess she's not coming."

We left her and headed back to our cabin, over pine needles and leaves, taking the path full of shade.

"What about our secret meeting?" Elise asked.

Arnetta enunciated her words in a way that defied contradiction: "We just had it."

It was nearing our bedtime, but the sun had not yet set. "Hey, your mama's coming," Arnetta said to Octavia when she saw Mrs. Hedy walk toward the cabin, sniffling. When Octavia's mother wasn't giving bored, parochial orders, she sniffled continuously, mourning an imminent divorce from her husband. She might begin a sentence, "I don't know what Robert will do when Octavia and I are gone. Who'll buy him cigarettes?" and Octavia would hotly whisper, "Mama," in a way that meant: Please don't talk about our problems in front of everyone. Please shut up.

But when Mrs. Hedy began talking about her husband, thinking about her husband, seeing clouds shaped like the head of her husband, she couldn't be quiet, and no one could dislodge her from the comfort of her own woe. Only one thing could perk her up—Brownie songs. If the girls were quiet, and Mrs. Hedy was in her dopey, sorrowful mood, she would say, "Y'all know I like those songs, girls. Why don't you sing one?" Everyone would groan, except me and Daphne. I, for one, liked some of the songs.

"C'mon, everybody," Octavia said drearily. "She likes the Brownie song best."

We sang, loud enough to reach Mrs. Hedy:

"I've got something in my pocket; / It belongs across my face. / And I keep it very close at hand / In a most convenient place. I'm sure you couldn't guess it / If you guessed a long, long while. So I'll take it out and put it on / It's a great big Brownie smile!"

The Brownie song was supposed to be sung cheerfully, as though we were elves in a workshop, singing as we merrily cobbled shoes, but everyone except me hated the song so much that they sang it like a maudlin record, played on the most sluggish of rpms.

"That was good," Mrs. Hedy said, closing the cabin door behind her. "Wasn't that nice, Linda?"

"Praise God," Mrs. Margolin answered without raising her head from the chore of counting out Popsicle sticks for the next day's craft session.

"Sing another one," Mrs. Hedy said. She said it with a sort of joyful aggression, like a drunk I'd once seen who'd refused to leave a Korean grocery.

"God, Mama, get over it," Octavia whispered in a voice meant only for Arnetta, but Mrs. Hedy heard it and started to leave the cabin.

"Don't go," Arnetta said. She ran after Mrs. Hedy and held her by the arm. "We haven't finished singing." She nudged us with a single look. "Let's sing the 'Friends Song.' For Mrs. Hedy." Although I liked some of the songs, I hated this one:

Make new friends / But keep the o-old, / One is silver / And the other gold.

If most of the girls in the troop could be any type of metal, they'd be bunched-up wads of tinfoil, maybe, or rusty iron nails you had to get tetanus shots for.

"No, no, no," Mrs. Margolin said before anyone could start in on the "Friends

Song." "An uplifting song. Something to lift her up and take her mind off all these earthly burdens."

Arnetta and Octavia rolled their eyes. Everyone knew what song Mrs. Margolin was talking about, and no one, no one, wanted to sing it.

"Please, no," a voice called out. "Not 'The Doughnut Song.'"

"Please not 'The Doughnut Song,'" Octavia pleaded.

"I'll brush my teeth two times if I don't have to sing 'The Doughnut—'"

"Sing!" Mrs. Margolin demanded.

We sang:

"Life without Jesus is like a do-ough-nut! / Like a do-ooough-nut! / Like a do-ooough-nut! / Life without Jesus is like a do-ough-nut! / There's a hole in the middle of my soul!"

There were other verses, involving other pastries, but we stopped after the first one and cast glances toward Mrs. Margolin to see if we could gain a reprieve. Mrs. Margolin's eyes fluttered blissfully. She was half asleep.

"Awww," Mrs. Hedy said, as though giant Mrs. Margolin were a cute baby, "Mrs. Margolin's had a long day."

"Yes indeed," Mrs. Margolin answered. "If you don't mind, I might just go to the lodge where the beds are. I haven't been the same since the operation."

I had not heard of this operation, or when it had occurred, since Mrs. Margolin had never missed the once-a-week Brownie meetings, but I could see from Daphne's face that she was concerned, and I could see that the other girls had decided that Mrs. Margolin's operation must have happened long ago in some remote time unconnected to our own. Nevertheless, they put on sad faces. We had all been taught that adulthood was full of sorrow and pain, taxes and bills, dreaded work and dealings with whites, sickness and death. I tried to do what the others did. I tried to look silent.

"Go right ahead, Linda," Mrs. Hedy said. "I'll watch the girls." Mrs. Hedy seemed to forget about divorce for a moment; she looked at us with dewy eyes, as if we were mysterious, furry creatures. Meanwhile, Mrs. Margolin walked through the maze of sleeping bags until she found her own. She gathered a neat stack of clothes and pajamas slowly, as though doing so was almost painful. She took her toothbrush, her toothpaste, her pillow. "All right!" Mrs. Margolin said, addressing us all from the threshold of the cabin. "Be in bed by nine." She said it with a twinkle in her voice, letting us know she was allowing us to be naughty and stay up till nine-fifteen.

"C'mon everybody," Arnetta said after Mrs. Margolin left. "Time for us to wash up."

Everyone watched Mrs. Hedy closely, wondering whether she would insist on coming with us since it was night, making a fight with Troop 909 nearly impossible. Troop 909 would soon be in the bathroom, washing their faces, brushing their teeth—completely unsuspecting of our ambush.

"We won't be long," Arnetta said. "We're old enough to go to the restrooms by ourselves."

Ms. Hedy pursed her lips at this dilemma. "Well, I guess you Brownies are almost Girl Scouts, right?"

"Right!"

"Just one more badge," Drema said.

"And about," Octavia droned, "a million more cookies to sell."

Octavia looked at all of us. Now's our chance, her face seemed to say, but our chance to do what, I didn't exactly know.

Finally, Mrs. Hedy walked to the doorway, where Octavia stood dutifully waiting to say good-bye but looking bored doing it. Mrs. Hedy held Octavia's chin. "You'll be good?"

"Yes, Mama."

"And remember to pray for me and your father? If I'm asleep when you get back?"

"Yes, Mama."

When the other girls had finished getting their toothbrushes and washcloths and flashlights for the group restroom trip, I was drawing pictures of tiny birds with too many feathers. Daphne was sitting on her sleeping bag, reading.

"You're not going to come?" Octavia asked.

Daphne shook her head.

"I'm gonna stay, too," I said. "I'll go to the restroom when Daphne and Mrs. Hedy go."

Arnetta leaned down toward me and whispered so that Mrs. Hedy, who'd taken over Mrs. Margolin's task of counting Popsicle sticks, couldn't hear. "No, Snot. If we get in trouble, you're going to get in trouble with the rest of us."

We made our way through the darkness by flashlight. The tree branches that had shaded us just hours earlier, along the same path, now looked like arms sprouting menacing hands. The stars sprinkled the sky like spilled salt. They seemed fastened to the darkness, high up and holy, their places fixed and definite as we stirred beneath them.

Some, like me, were quiet because we were afraid of the dark; others were talking like crazy for the same reason.

"Wow!" Drema said, looking up. "Why are all the stars out here? I never see stars back on Oneida Street."

"It's a camping trip, that's why," Octavia said. "You're supposed to see stars on camping trips."

Janice said, "This place smells like my mother's air freshener."

"These woods are pine," Elise said. "Your mother probably uses pine air freshener."

Janice mouthed an exaggerated "Oh," nodding her head as though she just then understood one of the world's great secrets. No one talked about fighting.

Everyone was afraid enough just walking through the infinite deep of the woods. Even though I didn't fight to fight, was afraid of fighting, I felt I was part of the rest of the troop; like I was defending something. We trudged against the slight incline of the path, Arnetta leading the way.

"You know," I said, "their leader will be there. Or they won't even be there. It's dark already. Last night the sun was still in the sky. I'm sure they're already finished."

Arnetta acted as if she hadn't heard me. I followed her gaze with my flashlight, and that's when I saw the squares of light in the darkness. The bathroom was just ahead.

But the girls were there. We could hear them before we could see them.

"Octavia and I will go in first so they'll think there's just two of us, then wait till I say, 'We're gonna teach you a lesson,'" Arnetta said. "Then, bust in. That'll surprise them."

"That's what I was supposed to say," Janice said.

Arnetta went inside, Octavia next to her. Janice followed, and the rest of us waited outside.

They were in there for what seemed like whole minutes, but something was wrong. Arnetta hadn't given the signal yet. I was with the girls outside when I heard one of the Troop 909 girls say, "NO. That did NOT happen!"

That was to be expected, that they'd deny the whole thing. What I hadn't expected was the voice in which the denial was said. The girl sounded as though her tongue were caught in her mouth. "That's a BAD word!" the girl continued. "We don't say BAD words!"

"Let's go in," Elise said.

"No," Drema said, "I don't want to. What if we get beat up?"

"Snot?" Elise turned to me, her flashlight blinding. It was the first time anyone had asked my opinion, though I knew they were just asking because they were afraid.

"I say we go inside, just to see what's going on."

"But Arnetta didn't give us the signal," Drema said. "She's supposed to say, 'We're gonna teach you a lesson,' and I didn't hear her say it."

"C'mon," I said. "Let's just go in."

We went inside. There we found the white girls—about five girls huddled up next to one big girl. I instantly knew she was the owner of the voice we'd heard. Arnetta and Octavia inched toward us as soon as we entered.

"Where's Janice?" Elise asked, then we heard a flush. "Oh."

"I think," Octavia said, whispering to Elise, "they're retarded."

"We ARE NOT retarded!" the big girl said, though it was obvious that she was. That they all were. The girls around her began to whimper.

"They're just pretending," Arnetta said, trying to convince herself. "I know they are."

Octavia turned to Arnetta. "Arnetta. Let's just leave."

Janice came out of a stall, happy and relieved, then she suddenly remembered her line, pointed to the big girl, and said, "We're gonna teach you a lesson."

"Shut up, Janice," Octavia said, but her heart was not in it. Arnetta's face was set in a lost, deep scowl. Octavia turned to the big girl and said loudly, slowly, as if they were all deaf, "We're going to leave. It was nice meeting you, okay? You don't have to tell anyone that we were here. Okay?"

"Why not?" said the big girl, like a taunt. When she spoke, her lips did not meet, her mouth did not close. Her tongue grazed the roof of her mouth, like a little pink fish. "You'll get in trouble. I know. I know."

Arnetta got back her old cunning. "If you said anything, then you'd be a tattletale."

The girl looked sad for a moment, then perked up quickly. A flash of genius crossed her face. "I like tattletale."

"It's all right, girls. It's gonna be all right!" the 909 troop leader said. All of Troop 909 burst into tears. It was as though someone had instructed them all to cry at once. The troop leader had girls under her arm, and all the rest of the girls crowded about her. It reminded me of a hog I'd seen on a field trip, where all the little hogs gathered about the mother at feeding time, latching onto her teats. The 909 troop leader had come into the bathroom, shortly after the big girl had threatened to tell. Then the ranger came; then, once the ranger had radioed the station, Mrs. Margolin arrived with Daphne in tow.

The ranger had left the restroom area, but everyone else was huddled just outside, swatting mosquitoes.

"Oh. They will apologize," Mrs. Margolin said to the 909 troop leader, but she said this so angrily, I knew she was speaking more to us than to the other troop leader. "When their parents find out, every one a them will be on punishment."

"It's all right, it's all right," the 909 troop leader reassured Mrs. Margolin. Her voice lilted in the same way it had when addressing the girls. She smiled the whole time she talked. She was like one of those TV-cooking-show women who talk and dice onions and smile all at the same time.

"See. It could have happened. I'm not calling your girls fibbers or anything." She shook her head ferociously from side to side, her Egyptian-style pageboy flapping against her cheeks like heavy drapes. "It could have happened. See. Our girls are not retarded. They are delayed learners." She said this in a syrupy instructional voice, as though our troop might be delayed learners as well. "We're from the Decatur Children's Academy. Many of them just have special needs."

"Now we won't be able to walk to the bathroom by ourselves!" the big girl said.

"Yes you will," the troop leader said, "but maybe we'll wait till we get back to Decatur—"

"I don't want to wait!" the girl said. "I want my Independence badge!"

The girls in my troop were entirely speechless. Arnetta looked stoic, as though she were soon to be tortured but was determined not to appear weak. Mrs. Margolin pursed her lips solemnly and said, "Bless them, Lord. Bless them."

In contrast, the Troop 909 leader was full of words and energy. "Some of our girls are echolalic—" She smiled and happily presented one of the girls hanging on to her, but the girl widened her eyes in horror, and violently withdrew herself from the center of attention, sensing she was being sacrificed for the village sins. "Echolalic," the troop leader continued. "That means they will say whatever they hear, like an echo—that's where the word comes from. It comes from 'echo.'" She ducked her head apologetically. "I mean, not all of them have the most progressive of parents, so if they heard a bad word, they might have repeated it. But I guarantee it would not have been intentional."

Arnetta spoke. "I saw her say the word. I heard her." She pointed to a small girl, smaller than any of us, wearing an oversized T-shirt that read: "Eat Bertha's Mussels."

The troop leader shook her head and smiled. "That's impossible. She doesn't speak. She can, but she doesn't."

Arnetta furrowed her brow. "No. It wasn't her. That's right. It was her."

The girl Arnetta pointed to grinned as though she'd been paid a compliment. She was the only one from either troop actually wearing a full uniform: the mocha-colored A-line shift, the orange ascot, the sash covered with badges, though all the same one—the Try-It patch. She took a few steps toward Arnetta and made a grand sweeping gesture toward the sash. "See," she said, full of self-importance, "I'm a Brownie." I had a hard time imagining this girl calling anyone a "nigger"; the girl looked perpetually delighted, as though she would have cuddled up with a grizzly if someone had let her.

On the fourth morning, we boarded the bus to go home. The previous day had been spent building miniature churches from Popsicle sticks. We hardly left the cabin. Mrs. Margolin and Mrs. Hedy guarded us so closely, almost no one talked for the entire day.

Even on the day of departure from Camp Crescendo, all was serious and silent. The bus ride began quietly enough. Arnetta had to sit beside Mrs. Margolin; Octavia had to sit beside her mother. I sat beside Daphne, who gave me her prize journal without a word of explanation.

"You don't want it?"

She shook her head no. It was empty.

Then Mrs. Hedy began to weep. "Octavia," Mrs. Hedy said to her daughter without looking at her, "I'm going to sit with Mrs. Margolin. All right?"

Arnetta exchanged seats with Mrs. Hedy. With the two women up front,

Elise felt it safe to speak. "Hey," she said, then she set her face into a placid, vacant stare, trying to imitate that of a Troop 909 girl. Emboldened, Arnetta made a gesture of mock pride toward an imaginary sash, the way the girl in full uniform had done. Then they all made a game of it, trying to do the most exaggerated imitations of the Troop 909 girls, all without speaking, all without laughing loud enough to catch the women's attention.

Daphne looked down at her shoes, white with sneaker polish. I opened the journal she'd given me. I looked out the window, trying to decide what to write, searching for lines, but nothing could compare with what Daphne had written, "My father, the veteran," my favorite line of all time. It replayed itself in my head, and I gave up trying to write.

By then, it seemed that the rest of the troop had given up making fun of the girls in Troop 909. They were now quietly gossiping about who had passed notes to whom in school. For a moment the gossiping fell off, and all I heard was the hum of the bus as we sped down the road and the muffled sounds of Mrs. Hedy and Mrs. Margolin talking about serious things.

"You know," Octavia whispered, "why did we have to be stuck at a camp with retarded girls? You know?"

"You know why," Arnetta answered. She narrowed her eyes like a cat. "My mama and I were in the mall in Buckhead, and this white lady just kept looking at us. I mean, like we were foreign or something. Like we were from China."

"What did the woman say?" Elise asked.

"Nothing," Arnetta said. "She didn't say nothing."

A few girls quietly nodded their heads.

"There was this time," I said, "when my father and I were in the mall and—"

"Oh shut up, Snot," Octavia said.

I stared at Octavia, then rolled my eyes from her to the window. As I watched the trees blur, I wanted nothing more than to be through with it all: the bus ride, the troop, school—all of it. But we were going home. I'd see the same girls in school the next day. We were on a bus, and there was nowhere else to go.

"Go on, Laurel," Daphne said to me. It seemed like the first time she'd spoken the whole trip, and she'd said my name. I turned to her and smiled weakly so as not to cry, hoping she'd remember when I'd tried to be her friend, thinking maybe that her gift of the journal was an invitation of friendship. But she didn't smile back. All she said was, "What happened?"

I studied the girls, waiting for Octavia to tell me to shut up again before I even had a chance to utter another word, but everyone was amazed that Daphne had spoken. The bus was silent. I gathered my voice. "Well," I said. "My father and I were in this mall, but I was the one doing the staring." I stopped and glanced from face to face. I continued. "There were these white people dressed like Puritans or something, but they weren't Puritans. They were Mennonites. They're these people who, if you ask them to do a favor, like paint your porch or something, they have to do it. It's in their rules."

"That sucks," someone said.

"C'mon," Arnetta said. "You're lying."

"I am not."

"How do you know that's not just some story someone made up?" Elise asked, her head cocked full of daring. "I mean, who's gonna do whatever you ask?"

"It's not made up. I know because when I was looking at them, my father said, 'See those people? If you ask them to do something, they'll do it. Anything you want.'"

No one would call anyone's father a liar—then they'd have to fight the person. But Drema parsed her words carefully. "How does your father know that's not just some story? Huh?"

"Because," I said, "he went up to the man and asked him would he paint our porch, and the man said yes. It's their religion."

"Man, I'm glad I'm a Baptist," Elise said, shaking her head in sympathy for the Mennonites.

"So did the guy do it?" Drema asked, scooting closer to hear if the story got juicy.

"Yeah," I said. "His whole family was with him. My dad drove them to our house. They all painted our porch. The woman and girl were in bonnets and long, long skirts with buttons up to their necks. The guy wore this weird hat and these huge suspenders."

"Why," Arnetta asked archly, as though she didn't believe a word, "would someone pick a porch? If they'll do anything, why not make them paint the whole house? Why not ask for a hundred bucks?"

I thought about it, and then remembered the words my father had said about them painting our porch, though I had never seemed to think about his words after he'd said them.

"He said," I began, only then understanding the words as they uncoiled from my mouth, "it was the only time he'd have a white man on his knees doing something for a black man for free." I now understood what he meant, and why he did it, though I didn't like it. When you've been made to feel bad for so long, you jump at the chance to do it to others. I remembered the Mennonites bending the way Daphne had bent when she was cleaning the restroom. I remembered the dark blue of their bonnets, the black of their shoes. They painted the porch as though scrubbing a floor.

I was already trembling before Daphne asked quietly, "Did he thank them?"

I looked out the window. I could not tell which were the thoughts and which were the trees. "No," I said, and suddenly knew there was something mean in the world that I could not stop.

Arnetta laughed. "If I asked them to take off their long skirts and bonnets and put on some jeans, would they do it?"

And Daphne's voice, quiet, steady: "Maybe they would. Just to be nice."

E. Annie Proulx

THE HALF-SKINNED STEER

E. ANNIE PROULX (1935–) is the author of three short-story collections, *Heart Songs and Other Stories*, *Close Range*, and *Bad Dirt*. She has also written four novels: *Postcards*, *The Shipping News*, *Accordion Crimes*, and *That Old Ace in the Hole*. Her most recent novel is *Cloud Bird*. Her books have been translated into twenty languages. Winner of a Pulitzer Prize, a National Book Award, an *Irish Times* International Fiction Prize, and a PEN/Faulkner Award, she lives and writes in Wyoming.

In the long unfurling of his life, from tight-wound kid hustler in a wool suit riding the train out of Cheyenne to geriatric limper in this spooled-out year, Mero had kicked down thoughts of the place where he began, a so-called ranch on strange ground at the south hinge of the Big Horns. He'd got himself out of there in 1936, had gone to a war and come back, married and married again (and again), made money in boilers and air-duct cleaning and smart investments, retired, got into local politics and out again without scandal, never circled back to see the old man and Rollo bankrupt and ruined because he knew they were.

They called it a ranch and it had been, but one day the old man said it was impossible to run cows in such tough country where they fell off cliffs, disappeared into sinkholes, gave up large numbers of calves to marauding lions, where hay couldn't grow but leafy spurge and Canada thistle throve, and the wind packed enough sand to scour windshields opaque. The old man wangled a job delivering mail, but looked guilty fumbling bills into his neighbors' mailboxes.

Mero and Rollo saw the mail route as a defection from the work of the ranch, work that fell on them. The breeding herd was down to eighty-two and a cow wasn't worth more than fifteen dollars, but they kept mending fence, whittling ears and scorching hides, hauling cows out of mudholes and hunting lions in the hope that sooner or later the old man would move to Ten Sleep with his woman and his bottle and they could, as had their grandmother Olive when Jacob Corn disappointed her, pull the place taut. That bird didn't fly and Mero wound up sixty years later as an octogenarian vegetarian widower pumping an Exercycle in the living room of a colonial house in Woolfoot, Massachusetts.

One of those damp mornings the nail-driving telephone voice of a woman said she was Louise, Tick's wife, and summoned him back to Wyoming. He didn't know who she was, who Tick was, until she said, Tick Corn, your brother Rollo's son, and that Rollo had passed on, killed by a waspy emu though prostate cancer was waiting its chance. Yes, she said, you bet Rollo still owned the ranch. Half of it anyway. Me and Tick, she said, we been pretty much running it the last ten years.

An emu? Did he hear right?

Yes, she said. Well, of course you didn't know. You heard of Down Under Wyoming?

He had not. And thought, what kind of name was Tick? He recalled the bloated grey insects pulled off the dogs. This tick probably thought he was going to get the whole damn ranch and bloat up on it. He said, what the hell was this about an emu? Were they all crazy out there?

That's what the ranch was now, she said, Down Under Wyoming. Rollo'd sold the place way back when to the Girl Scouts, but one of the girls was dragged off by a lion and the G.S.A. sold out to the Banner ranch next door who ran cattle on it for a few years, then unloaded it on a rich Australian businessman who started Down Under Wyoming but it was too much long-distance work and he'd had bad luck with his manager, a feller from Idaho with a pawnshop rodeo buckle, so he'd looked up Rollo and offered to swap him a half-interest if he'd run the place. That was back in 1978. The place had done real well. Course we're not open now, she said, it's winter and there's no tourists. Poor Rollo was helping Tick move the emus to another building when one of them turned on a dime and come right for him with its big razor claws. Emus is bad for claws.

I know, he said. He watched the nature programs on television.

She shouted as though the telephone lines were down all across the country, Tick got your number off the computer. Rollo always said he was going to get in touch. He wanted you to see how things turned out. He tried to fight it off with his cane but it laid him open from belly to breakfast.

Maybe, he thought, things hadn't finished turning out. Impatient with this game he said he would be at the funeral. No point talking about flights and meeting him at the airport, he told her, he didn't fly, a bad experience years ago with hail, the plane had looked like a waffle iron when it landed. He intended to drive. Of course he knew how far it was. Had a damn fine car, Cadillac, always drove Cadillacs, Gislaved tires, interstate highways, excellent driver, never had an accident in his life knock on wood, four days, he would be there by Saturday afternoon. He heard the amazement in her voice, knew she was plotting his age, figuring he had to be eighty-three, a year or so older than Rollo, figuring he must be dotting around on a cane too, drooling the tiny days away, she was probably touching her own faded hair. He flexed his muscular arms, bent his knees, thought he could dodge an emu. He would see his brother dropped in a red Wyoming hole. That event could jerk him back; the dazzled rope of light-ning against the cloud is not the downward bolt, but the compelled upstroke through the heated ether.

He had pulled away at the sudden point when it seemed the old man's girl-friend—now he couldn't remember her name—had jumped the track, Rollo goggling at her bloody bitten fingers, nails chewed to the quick, neck veins like wires, the outer forearms shaded with hairs, and the cigarette glowing, smoke curling up, making her wink her bulged mustang eyes, a teller of tales of hard deeds and mayhem. The old man's hair was falling out, Mero was twenty-three and Rollo twenty and she played them all like a deck of cards. If you admired horses you'd go for her with her arched neck and horsy buttocks, so high and haunchy you'd want to clap her on the rear. The wind bellowed around the house, driving crystals of snow through the cracks of the warped log door and all of them in the kitchen seemed charged with some intensity of purpose. She'd bal-anced that broad butt on the edge of the dog food chest, looking at the old man and Rollo, now and then rolling her glossy eyes over at Mero, square teeth nip-ping a rim of nail, sucking the welling blood, drawing on her cigarette.

The old man drank his Everclear stirred with a peeled willow stick for the bitter taste. The image of him came sharp in Mero's mind as he stood at the hall closet contemplating his hats; should he bring one for the funeral? The old man had had the damnedest curl to his hat brim, a tight roll on the right where his doffing or donning hand gripped it and a wavering downslope on the left like a shed roof. You could recognize him two miles away. He wore it at the table lis-tening to the woman's stories about Tin Head, steadily emptying his glass until he was nine-times-nine drunk, his gangstery face loosening, the crushed rodeo nose and scar-crossed eyebrows, the stub ear dissolving as he drank. Now he must be dead fifty years or more, buried in the mailman sweater.

The girlfriend started a story, yeah, there was this guy named Tin Head down around Dubois when my dad was a kid. Had a little ranch, some horses, cows, kids, a wife. But there was something funny about him. He had a metal plate in his head from falling down some cement steps.

Plenty of guys has them, said Rollo in a challenging way.

She shook her head. Not like his. His was made out of galvy and it eat at his brain.

The old man held up the bottle of Everclear, raised his eyebrows at her: Well, darlin?

She nodded, took the glass from him and knocked it back in one swallow. Oh, that's not gonna slow *me* down, she said.

Mero expected her to neigh.

So what then, said Rollo, picking at the horse shit under his boot heel. What about Tin Head and his galvanized skull-plate?

I heard it this way, she said. She held out her glass for another shot of Everclear and the old man poured it and she went on.

Mero had thrashed all that ancient night, dreamed of horse breeding or hoarse breathing, whether the act of sex or bloody, cut-throat gasps he didn't know. The next morning he woke up drenched in stinking sweat, looked at the ceiling and said aloud, it could go on like this for some time. He meant cows and weather as much as anything, and what might be his chances two or three states over in any direction. In Woolfoot, riding the Exercycle, he thought the truth was somewhat different: he'd wanted a woman of his own without scrounging the old man's leftovers.

What he wanted to know now, tires spanking the tar-filled road cracks and potholes, funeral homburg sliding on the backseat, was if Rollo had got the girlfriend away from the old man, thrown a saddle on her and ridden off into the sunset?

The interstate, crippled by orange pylons, forced traffic into single lanes, broke his expectation of making good time. His Cadillac, boxed between semis with hissing air brakes, snuffled huge rear tires, framed a looming Peterbilt in the back window. His thoughts clogged as if a comb working through his mind had stuck against a snarl. When the traffic eased and he tried to cover some ground the highway patrol pulled him over. The cop, a pimpled, mustached specimen with mismatched eyes, asked his name, where he was going. For the minute he couldn't think what he was doing there. The cop's tongue dapped at the scraggy mustache while he scribbled.

Funeral, he said suddenly. Going to my brother's funeral.

Well you take it easy, Gramps, or they'll be doing one for you.

You're a little polecat, aren't you, he said, staring at the ticket, at the pathetic handwriting, but the mustache was a mile gone, peeling through the traffic as Mero had peeled out of the ranch road that long time ago, squinting through the abraded windshield. He might have made a more graceful exit but urgency had struck him as a blow on the humerus sends a ringing jolt up the arm. He believed it was the horse-haunched woman leaning against the chest and Rollo fixed on her, the old man swilling Everclear and not noticing or, if noticing, not caring, that had worked in him like a key in an ignition. She had long greystreaked braids, Rollo could use them for reins.

Yah, she said, in her low and convincing liar's voice. I'll tell you, on Tin Head's ranch things went wrong. Chickens changed color overnight, calves was born with three legs, his kids was piebald and his wife always crying for blue dishes. Tin Head never finished nothing he started, quit halfway through a job every time. Even his pants was half-buttoned so his wienie hung out. He was a mess with the galvy plate eating at his brain and his ranch and his family was a mess. But, she said. They had to eat, didn't they, just like anybody else?

I hope they eat pies better than the ones you make, said Rollo, who didn't like the mouthful of pits that came with the chokecherries.

His interest in women began a few days after the old man had said, take this guy up and show him them Indan drawrings, jerking his head at the stranger. Mero had been eleven or twelve at the time, no older. They rode along the creek and put up a pair of mallards who flew downstream and then suddenly reappeared, pursued by a goshawk who struck the drake with a sound like a handclap. The duck tumbled through the trees and into deadfall trash and the hawk shot as swiftly away as it had come.

They climbed through the stony landscape, limestone beds eroded by wind into fantastic furniture, stale gnawed breadcrusts, tumbled bones, stacks of dirty folded blankets, bleached crab claws and dog teeth. He tethered the horses in the shade of a stand of limber pine and led the anthropologist up through the stiff-branched mountain mahogany to the overhang. Above them reared corroded cliffs brilliant with orange lichen, pitted with holes and ledges darkened by millennia of raptor feces.

The anthropologist moved back and forth scrutinizing the stone gallery of red and black drawings: bison skulls, a line of mountain sheep, warriors carrying lances, a turkey stepping into a snare, a stick man upside-down dead and falling, red ochre hands, violent figures with rakes on their heads that he said were feather headdresses, a great red bear dancing forward on its hind legs, concentric circles and crosses and latticework. He copied the drawings in his notebook, saying rubba-dubba a few times.

That's the sun, said the anthropologist who resembled an unfinished drawing himself, pointing at an archery target, ramming his pencil into the air as though tapping gnats. That's an atlatl and that's a dragonfly. There we go. You know what this is; and he touched a cloven oval, rubbing the cleft with his dusty fingers. He got down on his hands and knees, pointed out more, a few dozen.

A horseshoe?

A horseshoe! The anthropologist laughed. No boy, it's a vulva. That's what all of these are. You don't know what that is, do you? You go to school on Monday and look it up in the dictionary.

It's a symbol, he said. You know what a symbol is?

Yes, said Mero, who had seen them clapped together in the high school marching band. The anthropologist laughed and told him he had a great future, gave him a dollar for showing him the place. Listen, kid, the Indians did it just like anybody else, he said.

He had looked the word up in the school dictionary, slammed the book closed in embarrassment, but the image was fixed for him (with the brassy background sound of a military march), blunt ochre tracing on stone, and no fleshy examples ever conquered his belief in the subterranean stony structure of female genitalia, the pubic bone a proof, except for the old man's girlfriend whom he imagined down on all fours, entered from behind and whinnying like a mare, a thing not of geology but flesh.

Thursday night, balked by detours and construction, he was on the outskirts of Des Moines and no farther. In the cinderblock motel room he set the alarm but his own stertorous breathing woke him before it rang. He was up at five-fifteen, eyes aflame, peering through the vinyl drapes at his snow-hazed car flashing blue under the motel sign SLEEP SLEEP. In the bathroom he mixed the packet of instant motel coffee and drank it black without ersatz sugar or chemical cream. He wanted the caffeine. The roots of his mind felt withered and punky.

A cold morning, light snow slanting down: he unlocked the Cadillac, started it and curved into the vein of traffic, all semis, double- and triple-trailers. In the headlights' red glare he missed the westbound ramp and got into torn-up muddy streets, swung right and right again, using the motel's SLEEP sign as a landmark, but he was on the wrong side of the interstate and the sign belonged to a different motel.

Another mudholed lane took him into a traffic circle of commuters sucking coffee from insulated cups, pastries sliding on dashboards. Halfway around the hoop he spied the interstate entrance ramp, veered for it, collided with a panel truck emblazoned STOP SMOKING! HYPNOSIS THAT WORKS!, was rammed from behind by a stretch limo, the limo in its turn rear-ended by a yawning hydro-blast operator in a company pickup.

He saw little of this, pressed into his seat by the air bag, his mouth full of a rubbery, dusty taste, eyeglasses cutting into his nose. His first thought was to blame Iowa and those who lived in it. There were a few round spots of blood on his shirt cuff.

A star-spangled Band-Aid over his nose, he watched his crumpled car, pouring dark fluids onto the highway, towed away behind a wrecker. A taxi took him, his suitcase, the homburg funeral hat, in the other direction to Posse Motors where lax salesmen drifted like disorbited satellites and where he bought a secondhand Cadillac, black like the wreck, but three years older and the upholstery not cream leather but sun-faded velour. He had the good tires from the wreck brought over and mounted. He could do that if he liked, buy cars like packs of cigarettes and smoke them up. He didn't care for the way it handled out on the highway, throwing itself abruptly aside when he twitched the wheel and he guessed it might have a bent frame. Damn, he'd buy another for the return trip. He could do what he wanted.

He was half an hour past Kearney, Nebraska, when the full moon rose, an absurd visage balanced in his rearview mirror, above it a curled wig of a cloud, filamented edges like platinum hairs. He felt his swollen nose, palped his chin, tender from the stun of the air bag. Before he slept that night he swallowed a glass of hot tap water enlivened with whiskey, crawled into the damp bed. He had eaten nothing all day yet his stomach coiled at the thought of road food.

He dreamed that he was in the ranch house but all the furniture had been removed from the rooms and in the yard troops in dirty white uniforms fought. The concussive reports of huge guns were breaking the window glass and forcing the floorboards apart so that he had to walk on the joists and below the disintegrating floors he saw galvanized tubs filled with dark, coagulated fluid.

On Saturday morning, with four hundred miles in front of him, he swallowed a few bites of scorched eggs, potatoes painted with canned *salsa verde*, a cup of yellow coffee, left no tip, got on the road. The food was not what he wanted. His breakfast habit was two glasses of mineral water, six cloves of garlic, a pear. The sky to the west hulked sullen, behind him smears of tinselly orange shot through with blinding streaks. The thick rim of sun bulged against the horizon.

He crossed the state line, hit Cheyenne for the second time in sixty years. There was neon, traffic and concrete, but he knew the place, a railroad town that had been up and down. That other time he had been painfully hungry, had gone into the restaurant in the Union Pacific station although he was not used to restaurants and ordered a steak, but when the woman brought it and he cut into the meat the blood spread across the white plate and he couldn't help it, he saw the beast, mouth agape in mute bawling, saw the comic aspects of his revulsion as well, a cattleman gone wrong.

Now he parked in front of a phone booth, locked the car although he stood only seven feet away, and telephoned the number Tick's wife had given him. The ruined car had had a phone. Her voice roared out of the earpiece.

We didn't hear so we wondered if you changed your mind.

No, he said, I'll be there late this afternoon. I'm in Cheyenne now.

The wind's blowing pretty hard. They're saying it could maybe snow. In the mountains. Her voice sounded doubtful.

I'll keep an eye on it, he said.

He was out of town and running north in a few minutes.

The country poured open on each side, reduced the Cadillac to a finger-snap. Nothing had changed, not a goddamn thing, the empty pale place and its roaring wind, the distant antelope as tiny as mice, landforms shaped true to the past. He felt himself slip back, the calm of eighty-three years sheeted off him like water, replaced by a young man's scalding anger at a fool world and the fools in it. What a damn hard time it had been to hit the road. You don't know what it was like, he told his ex-wives until they said they did know, he'd pounded it into their ears two hundred times, the poor youth on the street holding up a sign asking for work, and the job with the furnace man, *yatata yatata ya.* Thirty miles out of Cheyenne he saw the first billboard, DOWN UNDER WYOMING, *Western Fun the Western Way,* over a blown-up photograph of kangaroos hopping through the sagebrush and a blond child grinning in a manic imitation of pleasure. A diagonal banner warned, *Open May 31.*

So what, Rollo had said to the old man's girlfriend, what about that Mr. Tin Head? Looking at her, not just her face, but up and down, eyes moving over her like an iron over a shirt and the old man in his mailman's sweater and lopsided hat tasting his Everclear and not noticing or not caring, getting up every now and then to lurch onto the porch and water the weeds. When he left the room the tension ebbed and they were only ordinary people to whom nothing happened. Rollo looked away from the woman, leaned down to scratch the dog's ears, saying, Snarleyow Snapper, and the woman brought a dish to the sink and ran water on it, yawning. When the old man came back to his chair, the Everclear like sweet oil in his glass, glances resharpened and inflections of voice again carried complex messages.

Well well, she said, tossing her braids back, every year Tin Head butchers one of his steers, and that's what they'd eat all winter long, boiled, fried, smoked, fricasseed, burned and raw. So one time he's out there by the barn and he hits the steer a good one with the axe and it drops stun down. He ties up the back legs, hoists it up and sticks it, shoves the tub under to catch the blood. When it's bled out pretty good he lets it down and starts skinning it, starts with the head, cuts back of the poll down past the eye to the nose, peels the hide back. He don't cut the head off but keeps on skinning, dewclaws to hock up the inside of the thigh and then to the cod and down the middle of the belly to brisket to tail. Now he's ready to start siding, working that tough old skin off. But siding is hard work—(the old man nodded)—and he gets the hide off about halfway and starts thinking about dinner. So he leaves the steer half-skinned there on the ground and he goes into the kitchen, but first he cuts out the tongue which is his favorite dish all cooked up and eats cold with Mrs. Tin Head's mustard in a forget-me-not teacup. Sets it on the ground and goes in to dinner. Dinner is chicken and dumplins, one of them changed-color chickens started out white and ended up blue, yessir, blue as your old daddy's eyes.

She was a total liar. The old man's eyes were murk brown.

Onto the high plains sifted the fine snow, delicately clouding the air, a rare dust, beautiful, he thought, silk gauze, but there was muscle in the wind rocking the heavy car, a great pulsing artery of the jet stream swooping down from the sky to touch the earth. Plumes of smoke rose hundreds of feet into the air, elegant fountains and twisting snow devils, shapes of veiled Arab women and ghost riders dissolving in white fume. The snow snakes writhing across the asphalt straightened into rods. He was driving in a rushing river of cold whiteout foam. He could see nothing, trod on the brake, the wind buffeting the car, a bitter, hard-flung dust hissing over metal and glass. The car shuddered. And as suddenly as it had risen the wind dropped and the road was clear; he could see a long, empty mile.

How do you know when there's enough of anything? What trips the lever that snaps up the STOP sign? What electrical currents fizz and crackle in the brain to shape the decision to quit a place? He had listened to her damn story and the dice had rolled. For years he believed he had left without hard reason and suffered for it. But he'd learned from television nature programs that it had been time for him to find his own territory and his own woman. How many women were out there! He had married three or four of them and sampled plenty.

With the lapping subtlety of incoming tide the shape of the ranch began to gather in his mind; he could recall the intimate fences he'd made, taut wire and perfect corners, the draws and rock outcrops, the watercourse valley steepening, cliffs like bones with shreds of meat on them rising and rising, and the stream plunging suddenly underground, disappearing into subterranean darkness of blind fish, shooting out of the mountain ten miles west on a neighbor's place, but leaving their ranch some badland red country as dry as a cracker, steep canyons with high caves suited to lions. He and Rollo had shot two early in that winter close to the overhang with the painted vulvas. There were good caves up there from a lion's point of view.

He traveled against curdled sky. In the last sixty miles the snow began again. He climbed out of Buffalo. Pallid flakes as distant from each other as galaxies flew past, then more and in ten minutes he was crawling at twenty miles an hour, the windshield wipers thumping like a stick dragged down the stairs.

The light was falling out of the day when he reached the pass, the blunt mountains lost in snow, the greasy hairpin turns ahead. He drove slowly and steadily in a low gear; he had not forgotten how to drive a winter mountain. But the wind was up again, rocking and slapping the car, blotting out all but whipping snow and he was sweating with the anxiety of keeping to the road, dizzy with the altitude. Twelve more miles, sliding and buffeted, before he reached Ten Sleep where streetlights glowed in revolving circles like van Gogh's sun. There had not been electricity when he left the place. In those days there were seventeen black, lightless miles between the town and the ranch, and now the long arch of years compressed into that distance. His headlights picked up a sign: 20 MILES TO DOWN UNDER WYOMING. Emus and bison leered above the letters.

He turned onto the snowy road marked with a single set of tracks, faint but still discernible, the heater fan whirring, the radio silent, all beyond the headlights blurred. Yet everything was as it had been, the shape of the road achingly familiar, sentinel rocks looming as they had in his youth. There was an eerie dream quality in seeing the deserted Farrier place leaning east as it had leaned sixty years ago, the Banner ranch gate, where the companionable tracks he had been following turned off, the gate ghostly in the snow but still flying its wrought iron flag, unmarked by the injuries of weather, and the taut five-strand fences and dim shifting forms of cattle. Next would come the road to their ranch, a left-hand turn just over the crest of a rise. He was running now on the unmarked road through great darkness.

Winking at Rollo the girlfriend said, yes, she had said, yes sir, Tin Head eats half his dinner and then he has to take a little nap. After a while he wakes up again and goes outside stretching his arms and yawning, says, guess I'll finish skinning out that steer. But the steer ain't there. It's gone. Only the tongue, laying on the ground all covered with dirt and straw, and the tub of blood and the dog licking at it.

It was her voice that drew you in, that low, twangy voice, wouldn't matter if she was saying the alphabet, what you heard was the rustle of hay. She could make you smell the smoke from an unlit fire.

How could he not recognize the turnoff to the ranch? It was so clear and sharp in his mind: the dusty crimp of the corner, the low section where the snow drifted, the run where willows slapped the side of the truck. He went a mile, watching for it, but the turn didn't come up, then watched for the Bob Kitchen place two miles beyond, but the distance unrolled and there was nothing. He made a three-point turn and backtracked. Rollo must have given up the old entrance road, for it wasn't there. The Kitchen place was gone to fire or wind. If he didn't find the turn it was no great loss; back to Ten Sleep and scout a motel. But he hated to quit when he was close enough to spit, hated to retrace black miles on a bad night when he was maybe twenty minutes away from the ranch.

He drove very slowly, following his tracks, and the ranch entrance appeared on the right although the gate was gone and the sign down. That was why he'd missed it, that and a clump of sagebrush that obscured the gap.

He turned in, feeling a little triumph. But the road under the snow was rough and got rougher until he was bucking along over boulders and slanted rock and knew wherever he was it was not right.

He couldn't turn around on the narrow track and began backing gingerly, the window down, craning his stiff neck, staring into the redness cast by the tail-lights. The car's right rear tire rolled up over a boulder, slid and sank into a quaggy hole. The tires spun in the snow, but he got no purchase.

I'll sit here, he said aloud. I'll sit here until it's light and then walk down to the Banner place and ask for a cup of coffee. I'll be cold but I won't freeze to death. It played like a joke the way he imagined it with Bob Banner opening the door and saying, why, it's Mero, come on in and have some java and a hot bis-cuit, before he remembered that Bob Banner would have to be 120 years old to play that role. He was maybe three miles from Banner's gate, and the Banner ranch house was another seven miles beyond the gate. Say a ten-mile hike at altitude in a snowstorm. On the other hand he had half a tank of gas. He could run the car for a while, then turn it off, start it again all through the night. It was bad luck, but that's all. The trick was patience.

He dozed half an hour in the wind-rocked car, woke shivering and cramped. He wanted to lie down. He thought perhaps he could put a flat rock under the goddamn tire. Never say die, he said, feeling around the passenger-side floor for the flashlight in his emergency bag, then remembering the wrecked car towed away, the flares and car phone and AAA card and flashlight and matches and candle and Power Bars and bottle of water still in it, and probably now in the damn tow-driver's damn wife's car. He might get a good enough look anyway in the snow-reflected light. He put on his gloves and the heavy overcoat, got out and locked the car, sidled around to the rear, bent down. The taillights lit the snow beneath the rear of the car like a fresh bloodstain. There was a cradle-sized depression eaten out by the spinning tire. Two or three flat ones might get him out, or small round ones, he was not going to insist on the perfect stone. The wind tore at him, the snow was certainly drifting up. He began to shuffle on the road, feeling with his feet for rocks he could move, the car's even throb-bing promising motion and escape. The wind was sharp and his ears ached. His wool cap was in the damn emergency bag.

My lord, she continued, Tin Head is just startled to pieces when he don't see that steer. He thinks somebody, some neighbor don't like him, plenty of them, come and stole it. He looks around for tire marks or footprints but there's noth-ing except old cow tracks. He puts his hand up to his eyes and stares away. Nothing in the north, the south, the east, but way over there in the west on the side of the mountain he sees something moving stiff and slow, stumbling along. It looks raw and it's got something bunchy and wet hanging down over its hindquarters. Yah, it was the steer, never making no sound. And just then it stops and it looks back. And all that distance Tin Head can see the raw meat of the head and the shoulder muscles and the empty mouth without no tongue open wide and its red eyes glaring at him, pure teetotal hate like arrows coming at him, and he knows he is done for and all of his kids and their kids is done for, and that his wife is done for and that every one of her blue dishes has got to break, and the dog that licked the blood is done for, and the house where they lived has to blow away or burn up and every fly or mouse in it.

There was a silence and she added, that's it. And it all went against him, too.

That's it? said Rollo. That's all there is to it?

Yet he knew he was on the ranch, he felt it and he knew this road, too. It was not the main ranch road but some lower entrance he could not quite recollect that cut in below the river. Now he remembered that the main entrance gate was on a side road that branched off well before the Banner place. He found a good stone, another, wondering which track this could be; the map of the ranch in his memory was not as bright now, but scuffed and obliterated as though trodden. The remembered gates collapsed, fences wavered, while the badland features swelled into massive prominence. The cliffs bulged into the sky, lions snarled, the river corkscrewed through a stone hole at a tremendous rate and boulders cascaded from the heights. Beyond the barbwire something moved.

He grasped the car door handle. It was locked. Inside, by the dashboard glow, he could see the gleam of the keys in the ignition where he'd left them to keep the car running. It was almost funny. He picked up a big two-handed rock and smashed it on the driver's-side window, slipped his arm in through the hole, into the delicious warmth of the car, a contortionist's reach, twisting behind the steering wheel and down, and had he not kept limber with exercise and nut cutlets and green leafy vegetables he never could have reached the keys. His fingers grazed and then grasped the keys and he had them. This is how they sort the men out from the boys, he said aloud. As his fingers closed on the keys he glanced at the passenger door. The lock button stood high. And even had it been locked as well, why had he strained to reach the keys when he had only to lift the lock button on the driver's side? Cursing, he pulled out the rubber floor mats and arranged them over the stones, stumbled around the car once more. He was dizzy, tremendously thirsty and hungry, opened his mouth to snow-flakes. He had eaten nothing for two days but the burned eggs that morning. He could eat a dozen burned eggs now.

The snow roared through the broken window. He put the car in reverse and slowly trod the gas. The car lurched and steadied in the track and once more he was twisting his neck, backing in the red glare, twenty feet, thirty, but slipping and spinning; there was too much snow. He was backing up an incline that had seemed level on the way in but showed itself now as a remorselessly long hill studded with rocks and deep in snow. His incoming tracks twisted like rope. He forced out another twenty feet spinning the tires until they smoked, and the rear wheels slewed sideways off the track and into a two-foot ditch, the engine died and that was it. It was almost a relief to have reached this point where the celestial fingernails were poised to nip his thread. He dismissed the ten-mile distance to the Banner place: it might not be that far, or maybe they had pulled the ranch closer to the main road. A truck might come by. Shoes slipping, coat buttoned awry, he might find the mythical Grand Hotel in the sagebrush.

On the main road his tire tracks showed as a faint pattern in the pearly apricot light from the risen moon, winking behind roiling clouds of snow. His blurred shadow strengthened whenever the wind eased. Then the violent country showed itself, the cliffs rearing at the moon, the snow smoking off the prairie like steam, the white flank of the ranch slashed with fence cuts, the sagebrush glittering and along the creek black tangles of willow bunched like dead hair. There were cattle in the field beside the road, their plumed breaths catching the moony glow like comic strip dialogue balloons.

He walked against the wind, his shoes filled with snow, feeling as easy to tear as a man cut from paper. As he walked he noticed one from the herd inside the fence was keeping pace with him. He walked more slowly and the animal lagged. He stopped and turned. It stopped as well, huffing vapor, regarding him, a strip of snow on its back like a linen runner. It tossed its head and in the howling, wintry light he saw he'd been wrong again, that the half-skinned steer's red eye had been watching for him all this time.

Stacey Richter

THE CAVEMEN IN THE HEDGES

STACEY RICHTER (1965–) is the author of two short story collections, *My Date with Satan* and *Twin Study*. Her stories have been widely anthologized and have won many prizes, including four Pushcart Prizes and the National Magazine Award. Find out more about her work at www.staceyrichter.com.

There are cavemen in the hedges again. I take the pellet gun from the rack beside the door and go out back and try to run them off. These cavemen are tough sons of bitches who are impervious to pain, but they love anything shiny, so I load the gun up with golden Mardi Gras beads my girlfriend, Kim, keeps in a bowl on the dresser and aim toward their ankles. There are two of them, hairy and squat, grunting around inside a privet hedge I have harassed with great labor into a series of rectilinear shapes. It takes the cavemen a while to register the beads. It's said that they have poor eyesight, and of all the bullshit printed in the papers about the cavemen in the past few months, this at least seems to be true. They crash through the branches, doing something distasteful. Maybe they're eating garbage. After a while they notice the beads and crawl out, covered in leaves, and start loping after them. They chase them down the alley, occasionally scooping up a few and whining to each other in that high-pitched way they have when they get excited, like little kids complaining.

I take a few steps off the edge of the patio and aim toward the Andersons' lot. The cavemen scramble after the beads, their matted backs receding into the distance.

"What is it?" Kim stands behind me and touches my arm. She's been staying indoors a lot lately, working on the house, keeping to herself. She hasn't said so, but it's pretty obvious the cavemen scare her.

"A couple of furry motherfuckers."

"I think they are," she says.

"What?"

"Motherfuckers. Without taboos. It's disgusting." She shivers and heads back inside.

After scanning the treetops, I follow. There haven't been any climbers reported so far, but they are nothing if not unpredictable. Inside, I find Kim sitting on the kitchen floor, arranging our spices alphabetically. She's transferring them out of their grocery-store bottles and into nicer ones, plain glass, neatly labeled. Kim has been tirelessly arranging things for the last four years—first the contents of our apartment on Pine Avenue, then, as her interior decorating business took off, other people's places, and lately our own house, since we took the plunge and bought it together last September. She finishes with fenugreek and picks up the galanga.

I go to the living room and put on some music. It's a nice, warm Saturday and if it weren't for the cavemen, we'd probably be spending it outdoors.

"Did you lock it?"

I tell her yes. I get a beer from the fridge and watch her. She's up to Greek seasonings. Her slim back is tense under her stretchy black top. The music kicks in and we don't say much for a few minutes. The band is D.I., and they're singing: "Johnny's got a problem and it's out of control!" We used to be punk rockers, Kim and I, back in the day. Now we are homeowners. When the kids down the street throw loud parties, we immediately dial 911.

"The thing that gets me," I say, "is how puny they are."

"What do they want?" asks Kim. Her hair is springing out of its plastic clamp, and she looks like she's going to cry. "What the fuck do they want with us?"

When the cavemen first appeared, they were assumed to be homeless examples of modern man. But it soon became obvious that even the most broken-down and mentally ill homeless guy wasn't *this* hairy. Or naked, hammer-browed, and short. And they didn't rummage through garbage cans and trash piles with an insatiable desire for spherical, shiny objects, empty shampoo bottles, and foam packing peanuts.

A reporter from KUTA had a hunch and sent a paleontologist from the university out to do a little fieldwork. For some reason I was watching the local news that night, and I remember this guy—typical academic, bad haircut, bad teeth—holding something in a take-out box. He said it was *scat*. Just when you think the news can't get any more absurd, there's a guy on TV, holding a turd in his hands, telling you the hairy people scurrying around the bike paths and Dumpsters of our fair burg are probably Neanderthal, from the Middle Paleolithic period, and that they have been surviving on a diet of pizza crusts, unchewed insects, and pigeon eggs.

People started calling them cavemen, though they were both male and female and tended to live in culverts, heavy brush, and freeway underpasses, rather than caves. Or they lived wherever—they turned up in weird places. The security guard at the Ice-O-Plex heard an eerie yipping one night. He flipped on the lights and found a half dozen of them sliding around the rink like otters. At least we knew another thing about them. They loved ice.

Facts about the cavemen have been difficult to establish. It is unclear if they're protected by the law. It is unclear if they are responsible for their actions. It has been determined that they're a nuisance to property and a threat to themselves. They will break into cars and climb fences to gain access to swimming pools, where they drop to all fours to drink. They will snatch food out of trucks or bins and eat out of trash cans. They avoid modern man as a general rule but are becoming bolder by the hour. The university students attempting to study them have had difficulties, though they've managed to discover that the cavemen cannot be taught or tamed and are extremely difficult to contain. They're strong for their size. It's hard to hurt them but they're simple to distract. They love pink plastic figurines and all things little-girl pretty. They love products perfumed with synthetic woodsy or herbal scents. You can shoot at them with rubber bullets all day and they'll just stand there, scratching their asses, but if you wave a little bottle of Barbie bubble bath in front of them they'll follow you around like a dog. They do not understand deterrence. They understand desire.

Fathers, lock up your daughters.

Kim sits across from me at the table, fingering the stem of her wineglass and giving me The Look. She gets The Look whenever I confess that I'm not ready to get married yet. The Look is a peculiar expression, pained and brave, like Kim has swallowed a bee but she isn't going to let on.

"It's fine," she says. "It's not like I'm all goddamn *ready* either."

I drain my glass and sigh. Tonight she's made a fennel-basil lasagna, lit candles, and scratched the price tag off the wine. Kim and I have been together for ten years, since we were twenty-three, and she's still a real firecracker, brainy, blond, and bitchy. What I have in Kim is one of those cute little women with a swishy ponytail who cuts people off in traffic while swearing like a Marine. She's a fierce one, grinding her teeth all night long, grimly determined, though the object of her determination is usually vague or unclear. I've never wanted anyone else. And I've followed her instructions. I've nested. I mean, we bought a house together. We're co-borrowers on a thirty-year mortgage. Isn't that commitment enough?

Oh no, I can see it is not. She shoots me The Look a couple more times and begins grabbing dishes off the table and piling them in the sink. Kim wants the whole ordeal: a white dress, bridesmaids stuffed into taffeta, a soft rain of cherry blossoms. I want none of it. The whole idea of marriage makes me want to pull a dry-cleaning bag over my head. I miss our punk rock days, Kim and me and our loser friends playing in bands, hawking spit at guys in BMWs, shooting drugs . . . and living in basements with anarchy tattoos poking through the rips in our clothing. Those times are gone and we've since established real credit ratings, I had the circled-A tattoo lasered off my neck, but. But. I feel like marriage would exterminate the last shred of the rebel in me. For some reason, I think of marriage as a living death.

Or, I don't know, maybe I'm just a typical guy, don't want to pay for the cow if I can get the milk for free.

Kim is leaning in the open doorway, gazing out at the street, sucking on a cigarette. She doesn't smoke much anymore, but every time I tell her I'm not ready she rips through a pack in a day and a half. "They'd probably ruin it anyway," she says, watching a trio of cavemen out on the street, loping along, sniffing the sidewalk. They fan out and then move back together to briefly touch one another's ragged, dirty brown fur with their noses. The one on the end, lighter-boned with small, pale breasts poking out of her chest hair, stops dead in her tracks and begins making a cooing sound at the sky. It must be a full moon. Then she squats and pees a silver puddle onto the road.

Kim stares at her. She forgets to take a drag and ash builds on the end of her cigarette. I know her; I know what she's thinking. She's picturing hordes of cavemen crashing the reception, grabbing canapés with their fists, rubbing their crotches against the floral arrangements. That would never do. She's too much of a perfectionist to ever allow that.

When I first saw the cavemen scurrying around town, I have to admit I was horrified. It was like when kids started to wear those huge pants—I couldn't get used to it, I couldn't get over the shock. But now I have hopes Kim will let the marriage idea slide for a while. For this reason I am somewhat grateful to the cavemen.

It rains for three days and the railroad underpasses flood. The washes are all running and on the news there are shots of SUVs bobbing in the current because some idiot ignored the DO NOT ENTER WHEN FLOODED sign and tried to gun it through four feet of rushing water. A lot of cavemen have been driven out of their nests and the incident level is way up. They roam around the city hungry and disoriented. We keep the doors locked at all times. Kim has a few stashes of sample-sized shampoo bottles around the house. She says she'll toss them out like trick-or-treat candy if any cavemen come around hassling her. So far, we haven't had any trouble.

Our neighbors, the Schaefers, haven't been so lucky. Kim invites them over for dinner one night, even though she knows I can't stand them. The Schaefers are these lonely, New Age hippies who are always staggering toward us with eager, too-friendly looks on their faces, arms outstretched, like they're going to grab our necks and start sucking. I beg Kim not to invite them, but at this stage in the game she seems to relish annoying me. They arrive dressed in gauzy robes. It turns out Winsome has made us a hammock out of hemp in a grasping attempt to secure our friendship. I tell her it's terrific and take it into the spare room where I stuff it in a closet, fully aware that by morning all of our coats are going to smell like bongwater.

When I return, everyone is sipping wine in the living room while the storm wets down the windows. Winsome is describing how she found a dead cave-baby in their backyard.

"It must not have been there for long," she says, her huge, oil-on-velvet eyes welling up with tears, "because it just looked like it was sleeping, and it wasn't very stiff. Its mother had wrapped it in tinsel, like for Christmas."

"Ick," says Kim. "How can you cry for those things?"

"It looked so vulnerable." Winsome leans forward and touches Kim's knee. "I sensed it had a spirit. I mean, they're human or protohuman or whatever."

"I don't care," says Kim. "I think they're disgusting."

"Isn't that kind of judgmental?"

"I think we should try to understand them," chimes in Evan, smoothing down his smock—every inch the soulful, sandal-wearing, sensitive man. "In a sense, they're us. If we understood why that female caveman wrapped her baby in tinsel, perhaps we'd know a little more about ourselves."

"I don't see why people can't just say 'cavewoman,'" snaps Kim. " 'Female caveman' is weird, like 'male nurse.' Besides, they are not us. We're supposed to have won. You know, survival of the fittest."

"It might be that it's time we expanded our definition of 'humanity,'" intones Evan. "It might be that it's time we welcome all creatures on planet Earth."

I'm so incredibly annoyed by Evan that I have to go into the bathroom and splash cold water on my face. When I get back, Kim has herded the Schaefers into the dining room, where she proceeds to serve us a deluxe vegetarian feast: little kabobs of tofu skewered along with baby turnips, green beans, rice, and steamed leaf of something or other. Everything is lovely, symmetrical, and delicious, as always. The house looks great. Kim has cleaned and polished and organized the contents of each room until it's like living in a furniture store. The Schaefers praise everything and Kim grumbles her thanks. The thing about Kim is she's a wonderful cook, a great creator of ambiance, but she has a habit of getting annoyed with her guests, as if no one could ever be grateful enough for her efforts. We drain a couple more bottles of wine and after a while I notice that Kim has become fed up with the Schaefers too. She starts giving them The Look.

"Seriously," she begins, "do you two even like being married?"

They exchange a glance.

"No, c'mon, really. It's overrated, right?" Kim pulls the hair off her face and I can see how flushed she is, how infuriated. "I think all that crap about biological clocks and baby lust, it's all sexist propaganda meant to keep women in line."

"Well, I haven't noticed any conspiracy," offers Winsome, checking everyone's face to make sure she's not somehow being disagreeable. "I think marriage is just part of the journey."

"Ha," says Kim. "Ha ha ha." She leans across the table, swaying slightly. "I know," she pronounces, "that you don't believe that hippie shit. I can tell," she whispers, "how fucking lost you really are."

Then she stands, picks up her glass, and weaves toward the back door. "I have to go check the basement."

We stare at the space where Kim was for a while. Winsome is blinking rapidly and Evan keeps clearing his throat. I explain we have an unfinished basement that's been known to fill with water when it rains, and that the only entrance to it is outside in the yard, and that Kim probably wants to make sure that everything's okay down there. They nod vigorously. I can tell they're itching to purify our home with sticks of burning sage.

While Kim is gone I take them into the living room and show them my collection of LPs. I pull out my rare purple vinyl X-Ray Specs record, and after considering this for a while, Winsome informs me that purple is a healing color. We hear a couple of bangs under the house. I toy with the idea of checking on Kim, but then I recall the early days of our courtship, before all this house-beautiful crap, when Kim used to hang out the window of my 1956 hearse, which was also purple, and scream "Anarchy now!" and "Destroy!" while lobbing rocks through smoked-glass windows into corporate lobbies. It's difficult to worry about a girl like that.

It doesn't take long for the Schaefers and me to run out of small talk. I have no idea how to get them to go home; social transitions are Kim's jurisdiction. We sit there nodding at each other like idiots until Kim finally straggles back inside. She's muddy, soaked to the bone, and strangely jolly. She says there's about a foot of water in the basement and that she was walking around in there and it's like a big honking wading pool. She giggles. The Schaefers stare with horror at the puddle spreading around her feet onto our nice oak floors. I put my arm around her and kiss her hair. She smells like wet dog.

I come home from work a few days later and find Kim unloading a Toys "R" Us bag. I notice a diamond tiara/necklace set with huge, divorcée-sized fake jewels stuck to a panel of pink cardboard. Again, she seems happy, which is odd for Kim. In fact, she's taken to singing around the house in this new style where she doesn't sing actual words, she goes "nar nar nar" like some demented little kid. It drives me crazy, in particular when the game is on, so I tell her to fucking please cut it out. She glares at me and storms off into the backyard. I let her pout for a while, but I'm in the mood to make an effort, so I eventually go out and find her standing on a chair, hanging over the hedge, gazing at the alley. I lean in beside her and see a caveman shambling off with a red bandana tied around his neck, like a puppy.

"That's weird."

"Look at his butt."

I look. There's a big blob of pink bubble gum stuck in his fur.

"God," says Kim, "isn't that pitiful?"

I ask her what we're having for dinner. She looks at me blankly and says I don't know, what are we having for dinner. I tell her I'll cook, and when I get back from picking up the pizza she's nowhere to be found. I walk from one empty room to another while the hairs on my arms start to tingle. I have to say, there's a peculiar feeling building in the household. Things are in a state of slight disarray. There's a candy bar wrapper on the coffee table, and the bag from the toy store is on the kitchen floor. I yell Kim's name. When she doesn't appear I turn on the TV and eat a few slices straight from the box. For some reason that starts to bother me, so I get up and get a plate, silverware, and a paper napkin. Kim walks in a little while later. She's wet from the waist down and all flushed, as if she's been doing calisthenics.

"I was bailing out the basement!" she says, with great verve, like basement bailing is a terrific new sport. Her hair is tangled around her head and she's sucking on a strand of it. She is smiling away. She says: "I'm worried about letting all that water just stand down there!"

But she doesn't look worried.

On the news one night, a psychic with a flashlight shining up under his chin explains there's a time portal in the condemned Pizza Hut by the freeway. Though the mayor whines he wasn't elected to buckle to the whim of every nutbar with an opinion, there are televised protests featuring people shaking placards proclaiming the Pizza Hut ground zero of unnatural evil, and finally they just bulldoze it to shut everyone up. A while after that, the incident levels start to drop. It seems that the cavemen are thinning out. They are not brainy enough for our world, and they can't stop extinguishing themselves. They tumble into swimming pools and drown. They walk through plate glass windows and sever their arteries. They fall asleep under eighteen-wheelers and wander onto runways and get mauled by pit bulls.

It looks like we're the dominant species after all; rock smashes scissors, Homo sapiens kicks Homo sapiens neanderthalensis's ass.

As the caveman population drops, the ominous feeling around town begins to lift. You can feel it in the air: women jog by themselves instead of in pairs. People barbecue large cuts of meat at dusk. The cavemen, it seems, are thinning out everywhere except around our house. I come home from work and walk through the living room and peek out the back window just in time to see a tough, furry leg disappear through a hole in the hedge. The hole is new. When I go outside and kick around in the landscaping, I find neat little stashes of rhinestones and fake pearls, Barbie shoes, and folded squares of foil wrapping paper. They can't see that well, but have the ears of a dog and flee as soon as I rustle the window shades. One time, though, I peel back the shade silently and catch a pair skipping in circles around the clothesline. One of them is gripping something purple and hairy, and when I go out there later I find a soiled My Little Pony doll on the ground. They are not living up to their reputation as club-swinging brutes. More than anything, they resemble feral little girls.

Also, our house has become an unbelievable mess. Kim walks through the door and drops the mail on the coffee table, where it remains for days until I remove it. There are panties on the bathroom floor and water glasses on top of the television and scraps of food on the kitchen counter. I ask Kim what's going on and she just says she's sick of that anal constant-housekeeping-bullshit, and if I want it clean, I can clean it myself. She looks straight at me and says this, without flinching, without any signs of deference or anger or subtle backing away that had always let me know, in nonverbal but gratifying ways, that I had the upper hand in the relationship. She tosses an orange peel on the table before marching outside and descending into the basement.

I stand there in the kitchen, which smells like sour milk, shaking my head and trying to face up to the increasingly obvious fact that my girlfriend of ten years is having an affair, and that her lover is a Neanderthal man from the Pleistocene epoch. They rendezvous in our moldy, water-stained basement where he takes her on the cement floor beneath a canopy of spiderwebs, grunting over her with his animallike body, or perhaps behind her, so that when she comes back inside there are thick, dark hairs stuck all over her shirt and she smells like a cross between some musky, woodland animal gland and Herbal Essences shampoo. Furthermore, she's stopped shaving her legs.

The next day, I duck out of the office claiming I have a doctor's appointment and zip back home around noon. I open the door with my key and creep inside. I don't know what I'm looking for. I think I half expect to find Kim in bed with one of those things, and that he'll pop up and start "trying to reason" with me in a British accent. What I find instead is an empty house. Kim's car is gone. I poke around, stepping over mounds of dirty clothes, then head out back and take the stairs to the basement. When I pull the door open, the first thing to hit me is the smell of mold and earth. I pace from one side to the other and shine my flashlight around, but I don't see anything suspicious, just an old metal weight-lifting bench with a plastic bucket sitting on top. Maybe, I think, I'm making this whole thing up in my head. Maybe Kim just goes down there because she needs some time to herself.

But then on my way out, I spot something. On the concrete wall beside the door, several feet up, my flashlight picks out a pattern of crude lines. They appear to have been made with charcoal or maybe some type of crayon. When I take a few steps back, I can see it's a drawing, a cave painting of some sort. It's red and black with the occasional pom-pom of dripping orange that looks like it was made by someone who doesn't understand spray paint.

I stand there for two or three minutes trying to figure out what the painting is about, then spend another fifteen trying to convince myself my interpretation is wrong. The picture shows half a dozen cars in a V-shaped formation bearing down on a group of cavemen. The cavemen's flailing limbs suggest flight or panic; obviously, they're in danger of being flattened by the cars. Above them, sketched in a swift, forceful manner, floats a huge, godlike figure with very long arms. One arm cradles the fleeing cavemen while the other blocks the cars. This figure is flowing and graceful and has a big ponytail sprouting from the top of her head. Of course, it's meant to be Kim. Who else?

I go upstairs and sit at the kitchen table, elbowing away half a moldy canta-loupe, and hold my head in my hands. I was hoping it was nothing—a casual flirtation at most—but a guy who makes a cave painting for a girl is probably in love with the girl. And girls love to be loved, even high-strung ones like Kim. I admit I'm hurt, but my hurt switches to anger and my anger to resolve. I can fight this thing. I can win her back. I know her; I know what to do.

I put on rubber gloves and start cleaning everything, thoroughly and with strong-smelling products, the way Kim likes things cleaned. I do the laundry and iron our shirts and line everything up neatly in the closet. I get down on my knees and wipe the baseboards, then up on a chair to dust the lightbulbs. I pull a long clot of hair out of the drain. There's a picture of us in Mexico in a silver frame on top of the medicine cabinet. I pick it up and think: that is my woman! It's civilization versus base instinct, and I vow to deploy the strongest weapon at my disposal: my evolutionarily superior traits. I will use my patience, my fa-cility with machinery and tools, my complex problem-solving skills. I will bathe often and floss my teeth. I will cook with gas.

A little after five Kim walks in and drops the mail on the coffee table. She looks around the house, at the gleaming neatness, smiling slightly and going "nar nar nar" to the tune of "Nobody Does It Better." I stand there in my clean-est suit with my arms hanging at my sides and gaze at her, in her little profes-sional outfit, pretty and sexy in an I-don't-know-it-but-I-do way, clutching her black purse, her hair pulled back with one of those fabric hair things.

"God, I can't believe you cleaned," she says, and walks through the kitchen and out of the house into the yard and slams the basement door behind her.

Kim is so happy. The worst part is she's so disgustingly happy and I could never make her happy all by myself and I don't particularly like her this way. For a couple of weeks she walks around in a delirious haze. She spins around on the porch with her head thrown back and comments on the shape of the clouds. She asks why haven't I bothered to take in the pretty, pretty sunset, all blue and gold. Like I fucking care, I say, forgetting my pledge to be civil. It's as though someone has dumped a bottle of pancake syrup over her head—she has no nastiness left, no edge, no resentment. Her hair is hanging loose and she has dirty feet and bad breath. She smiles all the time. This is not the girl I originally took up with.

Of course, I'm heartsick; I'm torn up inside. Even so, I do my best to act all patient and evolutionarily superior. I keep the house clean enough to lick. I start to cook elaborate meals the minute I get home from work. I groom myself until I'm sleek as a goddamn seal. I aim for a Fred Astaire/James Bond hybrid: smooth, sophisticated, oozing suaveness around the collar and cuffs—the kind of guy who would never fart in front of a woman, at least not audibly. She has a big, inarticulate lug already. I want to provide her with an option.

Kim takes it all for granted, coming and going as she pleases, wandering away from the house without explanation, hanging out in the basement with the door locked and brushing off my questions about what the hell she's doing down there, and with whom. She doesn't listen when I talk to her and eats standing in front of the refrigerator with the door open, yelling between bites that it's time for me to go to the store and get more milk. One evening I watch her polish off a plate of appetizers I have made for her, melon balls wrapped in prosciutto, downing them one after another like airline peanuts. When she's finished, she unbuttons the top button of her pants and ambles out the door and lets it slam without so much as a glance back at me. Without so much as a thank-you.

I trot out after her, figuring it's about time I give her a suave, patient lecture, but I'm not fast enough and she slams the basement door in my face. I pound and scream for a while before giving up and going up into the yard to wait. The night is very still. There's a full moon and the hedges glow silver on the top and then fade to blue at the bottom. I get a glass of iced tea and pull a chair off the patio, thinking to myself that she can't stay down there forever. I think about how maybe I'll catch the caveguy when he comes out too. Maybe I can tie on an apron and offer them both baby wieners on a toothpick.

After a while I hear a rustling in the hedges. At that moment I'm too miserable to be aware of the specifics of what's going on around me, so I'm startled as hell when a cavegirl pops out of the hedge, backlit in the moonlight, and begins walking toward me with a slow, hesitant gate. I sit there, taking shallow breaths, not sure whether or not I should be afraid. She has a low brow and a tucked, abbreviated chin, like Don Knotts's, but her limbs are long and sinewy. When she gets closer I see that she looks a lot stronger than a human woman does, and of course she's naked. Her breasts are like perfect human pinup breasts with bunny fur growing all over them. I can't unstick my eyes from them as they bob toward me, moving closer, until they come to a stop less than an arm's length from my chin. They are simultaneously furry and plump and I really want to bite them. But not hard.

She leans in closer. I hold very still as she reaches out with a leathery hand

and begins to stroke my lapel. She lowers her head to my neck and sniffs. On the exhale I discover that cavegirl breath smells just like moss. She prods me a few times with her fingertips; after she's had enough of that she just rubs the fabric of my suit and sniffs my neck while sort of kneading me rhythmically, like a purring cat. It's pretty obvious she likes my suit—a shiny sharkskin number I've hauled out of the back of the closet in the interest of wooing Kim—and I guess she likes my cologne too. For a minute I feel special and chosen, but then it occurs to me that there's something sleazy and impersonal about her attention. I'm probably just a giant, shiny, sandalwood-scented object to her. The moon is behind her so I can't see her that clearly, but then she shifts and I get a better view of her face and I realize she's young. Really young. I feel like a creep for wanting to feel her up, more because she's about fourteen than because she's a Neanderthal.

She swings a leg over and settles her rump onto my thigh, lapdance-style.

I say: "Whoa there, Jailbait."

The cavegirl leaps up like she's spring-loaded. She stops a few feet away and stares at me. I stare back. She tilts her head from side to side in puzzlement. The moon shines down. I reach into my glass and draw out a crescent-shaped piece of ice, moving with aching slowness, and offer it to her on a flat palm. She considers this ice cube for a good long time. I hold my arm as still as possible while freezing water trickles off my elbow and my muscles start to seize. Then, after a few false lunges, she snatches it from my hand.

"Nar," she says. Just that. Then she darts back into the hedge with her prize.

I remain in the moonlight for a while, shaking with excitement. I feel almost high. It's like I've touched a wild animal; I've communicated with it—an animal that's somehow human, somehow like me. I'm totally giddy.

This is probably how it was with Kim and her guy when they first met.

I guess I'm a complete failure with every category of female because the cavegirl does not come back. Even worse, Kim continues to treat me like I'm invisible. It's painfully clear that my strategy of suaveness isn't working. So I say screw evolution. What's it ever done for me? I go out drinking with the guys and allow the house to return to a state of nature. The plates in the sink turn brown. I shower every other day, every third. Kim and I go days without speaking to each other. By this time there are hardly any cavemen left around town; the count is running at one or two dozen. I go to the bars and everyone is lounging with their drinks, all relaxed and relieved that the cavemen aren't really an issue anymore, while I continue to stew in my own miserable interspecies soap opera. I don't even want to talk to anyone about it. What could I say? Hey buddy, did I mention my girlfriend has thrown me over for the Missing Link? It's humiliating.

One hungover afternoon I decide to skip the bars and come straight home from the office. Kim, naturally, is not around, though this barely registers. I've lost interest in tracking her whereabouts. But when I go into the kitchen, I catch sight of her through the window, standing outside, leaning against the chinaberry tree. It looks like she's sick or something. She's trying to hold herself up but keeps doubling over anyway. I go outside and find her braced against the tree, sobbing from deep in her belly while a string of snot swings from her nose. She's pale and spongy and smudged with dirt and I get the feeling she's been standing there crying all afternoon. She's clutching something. A red bandana. So it was him. The one with gum on his butt.

"Where is he?"

"He's gone," she whispers, and gives me a sad, dramatic, miniseries smile. "They're all gone."

Her sobs begin anew. I pat her on the back.

So she's curled over crying and I'm patting her thinking well, well: now that the other boyfriend is gone she's all mine again. Immediately I'm looking forward to putting the whole caveman ordeal behind us and having a regular life like we had before. I see all sorts of normal activities looming in the distance like a mirage, including things we always made fun of, like procreating and playing golf. She blows her nose in the bandana. I put my arm around her. She doesn't shake it off.

I should wait I know, I should go slow; but I can see the opening, the niche all vacant and waiting for me. I feel absolutely compelled to exploit it right away, before some other guy does. I turn to Kim and say: "Babe, let's just forget about this whole caveman thing and go back to the way it was before. I'm willing to forgive you. Let's have a normal life without any weird creatures in it, okay?"

She's still hiccuping and wiping her nose but I observe a knot of tension building in her shoulders, the little wrinkles of a glare starting around the edge of her eyes. I realize I'm in grave danger of eliciting The Look. It dawns on me that my strategy is a failure and I'd better think fast. So I bow to the inevitable. I've always known I couldn't put it off forever.

I take a deep breath and drop to one knee and tell her I love her and I can't live without her and beg her to marry me while kissing her hand. She's hiccuping and trying to pull her hand away, but in the back of my mind I'm convinced that this is going to work and of course she'll say yes. I've never made an effort like this before; I've only told her I love her two or three times total, in my life. It's inconceivable that this effort won't be rewarded. Plus, I know her. She lives for this. This is exactly what she wants.

I look up at her from my kneeling position. Her hair is greasy and her face is smeared with dirt and snot, but she's stopped crying. I see that she has created a new Look. It involves a shaking of the head while simultaneously pushing the lips outward, like she's crushed a wasp between her teeth and is about to spit it out. It's a look of pity, pity mixed with superiority; pity mixed with superiority and blended with dislike.

"I don't want a normal life without any creatures in it," Kim says, her voice ragged from crying, but contemptuous nonetheless. "I want an extraordinary life, with everything in it."

The Look fades. She brings her dirty, snotty face to mine and kisses me on the forehead and turns and walks away, leaving me on my knees. I stumble into the house after her. I can smell a trail of scent where she's passed by, cinnamon and sweat and fabric softener, but though I run through the house after her, and out into the street, I don't see her anywhere, not all night. Not the night after that. Never again.

Some psychic with a towel on his head says the cavemen passed through his drive-through palm-reading joint on their way back to the Pleistocene epoch, and I finally go over and ask him if he saw Kim with them. He has me write him a check and then says, Oh yeah, I did see her! She was at the front of this line of female cavemen and she was all festooned with beads and tinsel, like she was some sort of goddess! He says it in this bullshit way, but after some reflection I decide even charlatans may see strange and wondrous things, as we all had during the time the cavemen were with us, and then report them so that they sound like a totally improbable lie.

It's bizarre, the way time changes things. Now that the cavemen are gone, it seems obvious that their arrival was the kind of astonishing event people measure their entire lives by; and now that Kim is gone it seems clear that she was astonishing too, regal and proud, like she's represented in the cave painting. I once thought of her as sort of a burden, a pain-in-the-ass responsibility, but now I think of her as the one good thing I had in my life, an intense woman with great reserves of strength, forever vanished.

Or, I don't know; maybe I'm just a typical guy, don't know what I have until it walks out on me.

I've been trying to get over her, but I can't stop wallowing in it. One night we hold a drum circle on the site of the old Pizza Hut, and I swear that after this night, I'll force myself to stop thinking about her. This drum circle is the largest yet, maybe a couple of hundred people milling around, having the kind of conversations people have these days—you know, they were annoyed and frightened by the cavemen when they were here, but now that they're gone they just want them back, they want that weird, vivid feeling, the newness of the primitive world, et cetera. My job is to tend the fire. There's a six-foot pyramid of split pine in the middle of the circle, ready to go. At the signal I throw on a match. The wood is soaked in lighter fluid and goes up with a whoosh. Everyone starts to bang on their drums, or garbage can lids, or whatever percussive dingus they've dragged along, while I stand there poking the flames, periodically squirting in plumes of lighter fluid, as the participants wail and drum and cry and dance.

We are supposedly honoring the cavemen with this activity, but in truth no one ever saw the cavemen making fires or dancing or playing any sort of musical instrument. Apparently the original Neanderthal did these things; they also ate one another's brains and worshipped the skulls of bears, though no one seems anxious to resurrect these particular hobbies. Still, I admit I get kind of into it. Standing there in the middle, sweating, with the sound of the drumming surrounding me while the fire crackles and pops, it's easy to zone out. For a moment I imagine what it might be like to live in an uncivilized haze of sweat and hunger and fear and desire, to never plan, to never speak or think in words—but then the smell of lighter fluid snaps me back to how artificial this whole drum circle is, how prearranged and ignited with gas.

Later, when the fire has burned out, some New Age hardcores roll around in the ashes and pray for the cavemen to come back, our savage brothers, our hairy predecessors, et cetera, but of course they don't come back. Those guys look stupid, covered in ash. When the sun comes up, everyone straggles away. I get into my hatchback and listen to bad news on the radio as I drive home.

George Saunders

SEA OAK

GEORGE SAUNDERS (1958–) is the author of the short story collections *Pastoralia, CivilWarLand in Bad Decline* and, most recently, *In Persuasion Nation.* He is also the author of the novella-length illustrated fable *The Brief and Frightening Reign of Phil,* the *New York Times* bestselling children's book *The Very Persistent Gappers of Frip* (illustrated by Lane Smith), and a forthcoming book of selected nonfiction, *The Braindead Megaphone.* A 2006 MacArthur Fellow, he teaches in the Creative Writing Program at Syracuse University.

At six Mr. Frendt comes on the P.A. and shouts, "Welcome to Joysticks!" Then he announces Shirts Off. We take off our flight jackets and fold them up. We take off our shirts and fold them up. Our scarves we leave on. Thomas Kirster's our beautiful boy. He's got long muscles and bright-blue eyes. The minute his shirt comes off two fat ladies hustle up the aisle and stick some money in his pants and ask will he be their Pilot. He says sure. He brings their salads. He brings their soups. My phone rings and the caller tells me to come see her in the Spitfire mock-up. Does she want me to be her Pilot? I'm hoping. Inside the Spitfire is Margie, who says she's been diagnosed with Chronic Shyness Syndrome, then hands me an Instamatic and offers me ten bucks for a close-up of Thomas's tush.

Do I do it? Yes I do.

It could be worse. It is worse for Lloyd Betts. Lately he's put on weight and his hair's gone thin. He doesn't get a call all shift and waits zero tables and winds up sitting on the P-51 wing, playing solitaire in a hunched-over position that gives him big gut rolls.

I Pilot six tables and make forty dollars in tips plus five an hour in salary.

After closing we sit on the floor for Debriefing. "There are times," Mr. Frendt says, "when one must move gracefully to the next station in life, like for example certain women in Africa or Brazil, I forget which, who either color their faces or don some kind of distinctive headdress upon achieving menopause. Are you with me? One of our ranks must now leave us. No one is an island in terms of being thought cute forever, and so today we must say good-bye to our friend Lloyd. Lloyd, stand up so we can say good-bye to you. I'm sorry. We are all so very sorry."

"Oh God," says Lloyd. "Let this not be true."

But it's true. Lloyd's finished. We give him a round of applause, and Frendt gives him a Farewell Pen and the contents of his locker in a trash bag and out he goes. Poor Lloyd. He's got a wife and two kids and a sad little duplex on Self-Storage Parkway

"It's been a pleasure!" he shouts desperately from the doorway, trying not to burn any bridges.

What a stressful workplace. The minute your Cute Rating drops you're a goner. Guests rank us as Knockout, Honeypie, Adequate, or Stinker. Not that I'm complaining. At least I'm working. At least I'm not a Stinker like Lloyd.

I'm a solid Honeypie/Adequate, heading home with forty bucks cash.

At Sea Oak there's no sea and no oak, just a hundred subsidized apartments and a rear view of FedEx. Min and Jade are feeding their babies while watching *How My Child Died Violently*. Min's my sister. Jade's our cousin. *How My Child Died Violently* is hosted by Matt Merton, a six-foot-five blond who's always giving the parents shoulder rubs and telling them they've been sainted by pain. Today's show features a ten-year-old who killed a five-year-old for refusing to join his gang. The ten-year-old strangled the five-year-old with a jump rope, filled his mouth with baseball cards, then locked himself in the bathroom and wouldn't come out until his parents agreed to take him to FunTimeZone, where he confessed, then dove screaming into a mesh cage full of plastic balls. The audience is shrieking threats at the parents of the killer while the parents of the victim urge restraint and forgiveness to such an extent that finally the audience starts shrieking threats at them too. Then it's a commercial. Min and Jade put down the babies and light cigarettes and pace the room while studying aloud for their GEDs. It doesn't look good. Jade says "regicide" is a virus. Min locates Biafra one planet from Saturn. I offer to help and they start yelling at me for condescending.

"You're lucky, man!" my sister says. "You did high school. You got your frigging diploma. We don't. That's why we have to do this GED shit. If we had our diplomas we could just watch TV and not be all distracted."

"Really," says Jade. "Now shut it, chick! We got to study. Show's almost on."

They debate how many sides a triangle has. They agree that Churchill was in opera. Matt Merton comes back and explains that last week's show on suicide, in which the parents watched a reenactment of their son's suicide, was a healing process for the parents, then shows a video of the parents admitting it was a healing process.

My sister's baby is Troy. Jade's baby is Mac. They crawl off into the kitchen and Troy gets his finger caught in the heat vent. Min rushes over and starts pulling.

"Jesus freaking Christ!" screams Jade. "Watch it! Stop yanking on him and get the freaking Vaseline. You're going to give him a really long arm, man!"

Troy starts crying. Mac starts crying. I go over and free Troy no problem. Meanwhile Jade and Min get in a slap fight and nearly knock over the TV

"Yo, chick!" Min shouts at the top of her lungs. "I'm sure you're slapping me? And then you knock over the freaking TV? Don't you care?"

"I care!" Jade shouts back. "You're the slut who nearly pulled off her own kid's finger for no freaking reason, man!"

Just then Aunt Bernie comes in from DrugTown in her DrugTown cap and hobbles over and picks up Troy and everything calms way down.

"No need to fuss, little man," she says. "Everything's fine. Everything's just hunky-dory."

"Hunky-dory," says Min, and gives Jade one last pinch.

Aunt Bernie's a peacemaker. She doesn't like trouble. Once this guy backed over her foot at FoodKing and she walked home with ten broken bones. She never got married, because Grandpa needed her to keep house after Grandma died. Then he died and left all his money to a woman none of us had ever heard of, and Aunt Bernie started in at DrugTown. But she's not bitter. Sometimes she's so nonbitter it gets on my nerves. When I say Sea Oak's a pit she says she's just glad to have a roof over her head. When I say I'm tired of being broke she says Grandpa once gave her pencils for Christmas and she was so thrilled she sat around sketching horses all day on the backs of used envelopes. Once I asked was she sorry she never had kids and she said no, not at all, and besides, weren't we her kids?

And I said yes we were.

But of course we're not.

For dinner it's beanie-wienies. For dessert it's ice cream with freezer burn.

"What a nice day we've had," Aunt Bernie says once we've got the babies in bed.

"Man, what an optometrist," says Jade.

Next day is Thursday, which means a visit from Ed Anders from the Board of Health. He's in charge of ensuring that our penises never show. Also that we don't kiss anyone. None of us ever kisses anyone or shows his penis except Sonny Vance, who does both, because he's saving up to buy a FaxIt franchise. As for our Penile Simulators, yes, we can show them, we can let them stick out the top of our pants, we can even periodically dampen our tight pants with spray bottles so our Simulators really contour, but our real penises, no, those have to stay inside our hot uncomfortable oversized Simulators.

"Sorry fellas, hi fellas," Anders says as he comes wearily in. "Please know I don't like this any better than you do. I went to school to learn how to inspect meat, but this certainly wasn't what I had in mind. Ha ha!"

He orders a Lindbergh Enchilada and eats it cautiously, as if it's alive and he's afraid of waking it. Sonny Vance is serving soup to a table of hairstylists on a bender and for a twenty shoots them a quick look at his unit.

Just then Anders glances up from his Lindbergh.

"Oh for crying out loud," he says, and writes up a Shutdown and we all get sent home early. Which is bad. Every dollar counts. Lately I've been sneaking toilet paper home in my briefcase. I can fit three rolls in. By the time I get home they're usually flat and don't work so great on the roller but still it saves a few bucks.

I clock out and cut through the strip of forest behind FedEx. Very pretty. A raccoon scurries over a fallen oak and starts nibbling at a rusty bike. As I come out of the woods I hear a shot. At least I think it's a shot. It could be a backfire. But no, it's a shot, because then there's another one, and some kids sprint across the courtyard yelling that Big Scary Dawgz rule.

I run home. Min and Jade and Aunt Bernie and the babies are huddled behind the couch. Apparently they had the babies outside when the shooting started. Troy's walker got hit. Luckily he wasn't in it. It's supposed to look like a duck but now the beak's missing.

"Man, fuck this shit!" Min shouts.

"Freak this crap you mean," says Jade. "You want them growing up with shit-mouths like us? Crap-mouths I mean?"

"I just want them growing up, period," says Min.

"Boo-hoo, Miss Dramatic," says Jade.

"Fuck off, Miss Ho," shouts Min.

"I mean it, jagoff, I'm not kidding," shouts Jade, and punches Min in the arm.

"Girls, for crying out loud!" says Aunt Bernie. "We should be thankful. At least we got a home. And at least none of them bullets actually hit nobody."

"No offense, Bernie?" says Min. "But you call this a freaking home?"

Sea Oak's not safe. There's an ad hoc crackhouse in the laundry room and last week Min found some brass knuckles in the kiddie pool. If I had my way I'd move everybody up to Canada. It's nice there. Very polite. We went for a weekend last fall and got a flat tire and these two farmers with bright-red faces insisted on fixing it, then springing for dinner, then starting a college fund for the babies. They sent us the stock certificates a week later, along with a photo of all of us eating cobbler at a diner. But moving to Canada takes bucks. Dad's dead and left us nada and Ma now lives with Freddie, who doesn't like us, plus he's not exactly rich himself. He does phone polls. This month he's asking divorced women how often they backslide and sleep with their exes. He gets ten bucks for every completed poll.

So not lucrative, and Canada's a moot point.

I go out and find the beak of Troy's duck and fix it with Elmer's.

"Actually you know what?" says Aunt Bernie. "I think that looks even more like a real duck now. Because sometimes their beaks are cracked? I seen one like that downtown."

"Oh my God," says Min. "The kid's duck gets shot in the face and she says we're lucky."

"Well, we are lucky," says Bernie.

"Somebody's beak is cracked," says Jade.

"You know what I do if something bad happens?" Bernie says. "I don't think about it. Don't take it so serious. It ain't the end of the world. That's what I do. That's what I always done. That's how I got where I am."

My feeling is, Bernie, I love you, but where are you? You work at DrugTown for minimum. You're sixty and own nothing. You were basically a slave to your father and never had a date in your life.

"I mean, complain if you want," she says. "But I think we're doing pretty darn good for ourselves."

"Oh, we're doing great," says Min, and pulls Troy out from behind the couch and brushes some duck shards off his sleeper.

Joysticks reopens on Friday. It's a madhouse. They've got the fog on. A bridge club offers me fifteen bucks to oil-wrestle Mel Turner. So I oil-wrestle Mel Turner. They offer me twenty bucks to feed them chicken wings from my hand. So I feed them chicken wings from my hand. The afternoon flies by. Then the evening. At nine the bridge club leaves and I get a sorority. They sing intelligent nasty songs and grope my Simulator and say they'll never be able to look their boyfriends' meager genitalia in the eye again. Then Mr. Frendt comes over and says phone. It's Min. She sounds crazy. Four times in a row she shrieks get home. When I tell her calm down, she hangs up. I call back and no one answers. No biggie. Min's prone to panic. Probably one of the babies is puky. Luckily I'm on FlexTime.

"I'll be back," I say to Mr. Frendt.

"I look forward to it," he says.

I jog across the marsh and through FedEx. Up on the hill there's a light from the last remaining farm. Sometimes we take the boys to the adjacent car wash to look at the cow. Tonight however the cow is elsewhere.

At home Min and Jade are hopping up and down in front of Aunt Bernie, who's sitting very very still at one end of the couch.

"Keep the babies out!" shrieks Min. I don't want them seeing something dead!"

"Shut up, man!" shrieks Jade. "Don't call her something dead!"

She squats down and pinches Aunt Bernie's cheek.

"Aunt Bernie?" she shrieks. "Fuck!"

"We already tried that like twice, chick!" shrieks Min. "Why are you doing that shit again? Touch her neck and see if you can feel that beating thing!"

"Shit shit shit!" shrieks Jade.

I call 911 and the paramedics come out and work hard for twenty minutes, then give up and say they're sorry and it looks like she's been dead most of the afternoon. The apartment's a mess. Her money drawer's empty and her family photos are in the bathtub.

"Not a mark on her," says a cop.

"I suspect she died of fright," says another. "Fright of the intruder?"

"My guess is yes," says a paramedic.

"Oh God," says Jade. "God, God, God."

I sit down beside Bernie. I think: I am so sorry. I'm sorry I wasn't here when it happened and sorry you never had any fun in your life and sorry I wasn't rich enough to move you somewhere safe. I remember when she was young and wore pink stretch pants and made us paper chains out of DrugTown receipts while singing "Froggie Went A-Courting." All her life she worked hard. She never hurt anybody. And now this.

Scared to death in a crappy apartment.

Min puts the babies in the kitchen but they keep crawling out. Aunt Bernie's in a shroud on this sort of dolly and on the couch are a bunch of forms to sign.

We call Ma and Freddie. We get their machine.

"Ma, pick up!" says Min. "Something bad happened! Ma, please freaking pick up!"

But nobody picks up.

So we leave a message.

Lobton's Funeral Parlor is just a regular house on a regular street. Inside there's a rack of brochures with titles like "Why Does My Loved One Appear Somewhat Larger?" Lobton looks healthy. Maybe too healthy. He's wearing a yellow golf shirt and his biceps keep involuntarily flexing. Every now and then he touches his delts as if to confirm they're still big as softballs.

"Such a sad thing," he says.

"How much?" asks Jade. "I mean, like for basic. Not superfancy."

"But not crappy either," says Min. "Our aunt was the best."

"What price range were you considering?" says Lobton, cracking his knuckles. We tell him and his eyebrows go up and he leads us to something that looks like a moving box.

"Prior to usage we'll moisture-proof this with a spray lacquer," he says. "Makes it look quite woodlike."

"That's all we can get?" says Jade. "Cardboard?"

"I'm actually offering you a slight break already," he says, and does a kind of push-up against the wall. "On account of the tragic circumstances. This is Sierra Sunset. Not exactly cardboard. More of a fiberboard."

"I don't know," says Min. "Seems pretty gyppy."

"Can we think about it?" says Ma.

"Absolutely," says Lobton. "Last time I checked this was still America."

I step over and take a closer look. There are staples where Aunt Bernie's spine would be. Down at the foot there's some writing about Folding Tab A into Slot B.

"No freaking way," says Jade. "Work your whole life and end up in a May-flower box? I doubt it."

We've got zip in savings. We sit at a desk and Lobton does what he calls a Credit Calc. If we pay it out monthly for seven years we can afford the Amber Mist, which includes a double-thick balsa box and two coats of lacquer and a one-hour wake.

"But seven years, jeez," says Ma.

"We got to get her the good one," says Min. "She never had anything nice in her life."

So Amber Mist it is.

We bury her at St. Leo's, on the hill up near BastCo. Her part of the graveyard's pretty plain. No angels, no little rock houses, no flowers, just a bunch of flat stones like parking bumpers and here and there a Styrofoam cup. Father Brian says a prayer and then one of us is supposed to talk. But what's there to say? She never had a life. Never married, no kids, work work work. Did she ever go on a cruise? All her life it was buses. Buses buses buses. Once she went with Ma on a bus to Quigley, Kansas, to gamble and shop at an outlet mall. Someone broke into her room and stole her clothes and took a dump in her suitcase while they were at the Roy Clark show. That was it. That was the extent of her tourism. After that it was DrugTown, night and day. After fifteen years as Cashier she got demoted to Greeter. People would ask where the cold remedies were and she'd point to some big letters on the wall that said Cold Remedies.

Freddie, Ma's boyfriend, steps up and says he didn't know her very long but she was an awful nice lady and left behind a lot of love, etc. etc. blah blah blah. While it's true she didn't do much in her life, still she was very dear to those of us who knew her and never made a stink about anything but was always content with whatever happened to her, etc. etc. blah blah blah.

Then it's over and we're supposed to go away.

"We gotta come out here like every week," says Jade.

"I know I will," says Min.

"What, like I won't?" says Jade. "She was so freaking nice."

"I'm sure you swear at a grave," says Min.

"Since when is freak a swear, chick?" says Jade.

"Girls," says Ma.

"I hope I did okay in what I said about her," says Freddie in his full-of-crap way, smelling bad of English Navy. "Actually I sort of surprised myself."

"Bye-bye, Aunt Bernie," says Min.

"Bye-bye, Bern," says Jade.

"Oh my dear sister," says Ma.

I scrunch my eyes tight and try to picture her happy, laughing, poking me in the ribs. But all I can see is her terrified on the couch. It's awful. Out there, somewhere, is whoever did it. Someone came in our house, scared her to death, watched her die, went through our stuff, stole her money. Someone who's still living, someone who right now might be having a piece of pie or running an errand or scratching his ass, someone who, if he wanted to, could drive west for three days or whatever and sit in the sun by the ocean.

We stand a few minutes with heads down and hands folded.

Afterward Freddie takes us to Trabanti's for lunch. Last year Trabanti died and three Vietnamese families went in together and bought the place, and it still serves pasta and pizza and the big oil of Trabanti is still on the wall but now from the kitchen comes this very pretty Vietnamese music and the food is somehow better.

Freddie proposes a toast. Min says remember how Bernie always called lunch dinner and dinner supper? Jade says remember how when her jaw clicked she'd say she needed oil?

"She was a excellent lady," says Freddie.

"I already miss her so bad," says Ma.

"I'd like to kill that fuck that killed her," says Min.

"How about let's don't say fuck at lunch," says Ma.

"It's just a word, Ma, right?" says Min. "Like pluck is just a word? You don't mind if I say pluck? Pluck pluck pluck?"

"Well, shit's just a word too," says Freddie. "But we don't say it at lunch."

"Same with puke," says Ma.

"Shit puke, shit puke," says Min.

The waiter clears his throat. Ma glares at Min.

"I love you girls' manners," Ma says.

"Especially at a funeral," says Freddie.

"This ain't a funeral," says Min.

"The question in my mind is what you kids are gonna do now," says Freddie. "Because I consider this whole thing a wake-up call, meaning it's time for you to pull yourselfs up by the bootstraps like I done and get out of that dangerous craphole you're living at."

"Mr. Phone Poll speaks," says Min.

"Anyways it ain't that dangerous," says Jade.

"A woman gets killed and it ain't that dangerous?" says Freddie.

"All's we need is a dead bolt and a eyehole," says Min.

"What's a bootstrap," says Jade.

"It's like a strap on a boot, you doof," says Min.

"Plus where we gonna go?" says Min. "Can we move in with you guys?"

"I personally would love that and you know that," says Freddie. "But who would not love that is our landlord."

"I think what Freddie's saying is it's time for you girls to get jobs," says Ma.

"Yeah right, Ma," says Min. "After what happened last time?"

When I first moved in, Jade and Min were working the info booth at HardwareNiche. Then one day we picked the babies up at day care and found Troy sitting naked on top of the washer and Mac in the yard being nipped by a Pekingese and the day-care lady sloshed and playing KillerBirds on Nintendo.

So that was that. No more HardwareNiche.

"Maybe one could work, one could baby-sit?" says Ma.

"I don't see why I should have to work so she can stay home with her baby," says Min.

"And I don't see why I should have to work so she can stay home with her baby," says Jade.

"It's like a freaking veece versa," says Min.

"Let me tell you something," says Freddie. "Something about this country. Anybody can do anything. But first they gotta try. And you guys ain't. Two don't work and one strips naked? I don't consider that trying. You kids make squat. And therefore you live in a dangerous craphole. And what happens in a dangerous craphole? Bad tragic shit. It's the freaking American way—you start out in a dangerous craphole and work hard so you can someday move up to a somewhat less dangerous craphole. And finally maybe you get a mansion. But at this rate you ain't even gonna make it to the somewhat less dangerous craphole."

"Like you live in a mansion," says Jade.

"I do not claim to live in no mansion," says Freddie. "But then again I do not live in no slum. The other thing I also do not do is strip naked."

"Thank God for small favors," says Min.

"Anyways he's never actually naked," says Jade.

Which is true. I always have on at least a T-back.

"No wonder we never take these kids out to a nice lunch," says Freddie.

"I do not even consider this a nice lunch," says Min.

For dinner Jade microwaves some Stars-n-Flags. They're addictive. They put sugar in the sauce and sugar in the meat nuggets. I think also caffeine. Someone told me the brown streaks in the Flags are caffeine. We have like five bowls each.

After dinner the babies get fussy and Min puts a mush of ice cream and Hershey's syrup in their bottles and we watch *The Worst That Could Happen*, a half-hour of computer simulations of tragedies that have never actually occurred but theoretically could. A kid gets hit by a train and flies into a zoo, where he's eaten by wolves. A man cuts his hand off chopping wood and while wandering around screaming for help is picked up by a tornado and dropped on a preschool during recess and lands on a pregnant teacher.

"I miss Bernie so bad," says Min.

"Me too," Jade says sadly.

The babies start howling for more ice cream.

"That is so cute," says Jade. "They're like, *Give it the fuck up!*"

"We'll give it the fuck up, sweeties, don't worry," says Min. "We didn't forget about you."

Then the phone rings. It's Father Brian. He sounds weird. He says he's sorry to bother us so late. But something strange has happened. Something bad. Something sort of, you know, unspeakable. Am I sitting? I'm not but I say I am.

Apparently someone has defaced Bernie's grave.

My first thought is there's no stone. It's just grass. How do you deface grass? What did they do, pee on the grass on the grave? But Father's nearly in tears.

So I call Ma and Freddie and tell them to meet us, and we get the babies up and load them into the K-car.

"Deface," says Jade on the way over. "What does that mean, deface?"

"It means like fucked it up," says Min.

"But how?" says Jade. "I mean, like what did they do?"

"We don't know, dumbass," says Min. "That's why we're going there."

"And why?" says Jade. "Why would someone do that?"

"Check out Miss Shreelock Holmes," says Min. "Someone done that because someone is a asshole."

"Someone is a big-time asshole," says Jade.

Father Brian meets us at the gate with a flashlight and a golf cart.

"When I saw this," he says." I literally sat down in astonishment. Nothing like this has ever happened here. I am so sorry. You seem like nice people."

We're too heavy and the wheels spin as we climb the hill, so I get out and jog alongside.

"Okay, folks, brace yourselves," Father says, and shuts off the engine.

Where the grave used to be is just a hole. Inside the hole is the Amber Mist, with the top missing. Inside the Amber Mist is nothing. No Aunt Bernie.

"What the hell," says Jade. "Where's Bernie?"

"Somebody stole Bernie?" says Min.

"At least you folks have retained your feet," says Father Brian. "I'm telling you I literally sat right down. I sat right down on that pile of dirt. I dropped as if shot. See that mark? That's where I sat."

On the pile of grave dirt is a butt-shaped mark.

The cops show up and one climbs down in the hole with a tape measure and a camera. After three or four flashes he climbs out and hands Ma a pair of blue pumps.

"Her little shoes," says Ma. "Oh my God."

"Are those them?" says Jade.

"Those are them," says Min.

"I am freaking out," says Jade.

"I am totally freaking out," says Min.

"I'm gonna sit," says Ma, and drops into the golf cart.

"What I don't get is who'd want her?" says Min.

"She was just this lady," says Jade.

"Typically it's teens?" one cop says. "Typically we find the loved one nearby? Once we found the loved one nearby with, you know, a cigarette between its lips, wearing a sombrero? These kids today got a lot more nerve than we ever did. I never would've dreamed of digging up a dead corpse when I was a teen. You might tip over a stone, sure, you might spray-paint something on a crypt, you might, you know, give a wino a hotfoot."

"But this, jeez," says Freddie. "This is a entirely different ballgame."

"Boy howdy," says the cop, and we all look down at the shoes in Ma's hands.

Next day I go back to work. I don't feel like it but we need the money. The grass is wet and it's hard getting across the ravine in my dress shoes. The soles are slick. Plus they're too tight. Several times I fall forward on my briefcase. Inside the briefcase are my T-backs and a thing of mousse.

Right off the bat I get a tableful of MediBen women seated under a banner saying BEST OF LUCK, BEATRICE, NO HARD FEELINGS. I take off my shirt and serve their salads. I take off my flight pants and serve their soups. One drops a dollar on the floor and tells me feel free to pick it up.

I pick it up.

"Not like that, not like that," she says. "Face the other way, so when you bend we can see your crack."

I've done this about a million times, but somehow I can't do it now.

I look at her. She looks at me.

"What?" she says. "I'm not allowed to say that? I thought that was the whole point."

"That is the whole point, Phyllis," says another lady. "You stand your ground."

"Look," Phyllis says. "Either bend how I say or give back the dollar. I think that's fair."

"You go, girl," says her friend.

I give back the dollar. I return to the Locker Area and sit awhile. For the first time ever, I'm voted Stinker. There are thirteen women at the MediBen table and they all vote me Stinker. Do the MediBen women know my situation? Would they vote me Stinker if they did? But what am I supposed to do, go out and say, Please ladies, my aunt just died, plus her body's missing?

Mr. Frendt pulls me aside.

"Perhaps you need to go home," he says. "I'm sorry for your loss. But I'd like to encourage you not to behave like one of those Comanche ladies who bite off their index fingers when a loved one dies. Grief is good, grief is fine, but too much grief, as we all know, is excessive. If your aunt's death has filled your mouth with too many bitten-off fingers, for crying out loud, take a week off, only don't take it out on our Guests, they didn't kill your dang aunt."

But I can't afford to take a week off. I can't even afford to take a few days off.

"We really need the money," I say.

"Is that my problem?" he says. "Am I supposed to let you dance without vigor just because you need the money? Why don't I put an ad in the paper for all sad people who need money? All the town's sad could come here and strip. Good-bye. Come back when you feel halfway normal."

From the pay phone I call home to see if they need anything from the Food-SoQuik.

"Just come home," Min says stiffly. "Just come straight home."

"What is it?" I say.

"Come home," she says.

Maybe someone's found the body. I imagine Bernie naked, Bernie chopped in two, Bernie posed on a bus bench. I hope and pray that something only mildly bad's been done to her, something we can live with.

At home the door's wide open. Min and Jade are sitting very still on the couch, babies in their laps, staring at the rocking chair, and in the rocking chair is Bernie. Bernie's body.

Same perm, same glasses, same blue dress we buried her in.

What's it doing here? Who could be so cruel? And what are we supposed to do with it?

Then she turns her head and looks at me.

"Sit the fuck down," she says.

In life she never swore.

I sit. Min squeezes and releases my hand, squeezes and releases, squeezes and releases.

"You, mister," Bernie says to me, "are going to start showing your cock. You'll show it and show it. You go up to a lady, if she wants to see it, if she'll pay to see it, I'll make a thumbprint on the forehead. You see the thumbprint, you ask. I'll try to get you five a day, at twenty bucks a pop. So a hundred bucks a day. Seven hundred a week. And that's cash, so no taxes. No withholding. See? That's the beauty of it."

She's got dirt in her hair and dirt in her teeth and her hair is a mess and her tongue when it darts out to lick her lips is black.

"You, Jade," she says. "Tomorrow you start work. Andersen Labels, Fifth and Rivera. Dress up when you go. Wear something nice. Show a little leg. And don't chomp your gum. Ask for Len. At the end of the month, we take the money you made and the cock money and get a new place. Somewhere safe. That's part one of Phase One. You, Min. You baby-sit. Plus you quit smoking. Plus you learn how to cook. No more food out of cans. We gotta eat right to look our best. Because I am getting me so many lovers. Maybe you kids don't know this but I died a freaking virgin. No babies, no lovers. Nothing went in, nothing came out. Ha ha! Dry as a bone, completely wasted, this pretty little thing God gave me between my legs. Well I am going to have lovers now, you fucks! Like in the movies, big shoulders and all, and a summer house, and nice trips, and in the morning in my room a big vase of flowers, and I'm going to get my nipples hard standing in the breeze from the ocean, eating shrimp from a cup, you sons of bitches, while my lover watches me from the veranda, his big shoulders shining, all hard for me, that's one damn thing I will guarantee you kids! Ha ha! You think I'm joking? I ain't freaking joking. I never got nothing! My life was shit! I was never even up in a freaking plane. But that was that life and this is this life. My new life. Cover me up now! With a blanket. I need my beauty rest. Tell anyone I'm here, you all die. Plus they die. Whoever you tell, they die. I kill them with my mind. I can do that. I am very freaking strong now. I got powers! So no visitors. I don't exactly look my best. You got it? You all got it?"

We nod. I go for a blanket. Her hands and feet are shaking and she's grinding her teeth and one falls out.

"Put it over me, you fuck, all the way over!" she screams, and I put it over her.

We sneak off with the babies and whisper in the kitchen.

"It looks like her," says Min.

"It is her," I say.

"It is and it ain't," says Jade.

"We better do what she says," Min says.

"No shit," Jade says.

All night she sits in the rocker under the blanket, shaking and swearing.

All night we sit in Min's bed, fully dressed, holding hands.

"See how strong I am!" she shouts around midnight, and there's a cracking sound, and when I go out the door's been torn off the microwave but she's still sitting in the chair.

• • •

In the morning she's still there, shaking and swearing.

"Take the blanket off!" she screams. "It's time to get this show on the road."

I take the blanket off. The smell is not good. One ear is now in her lap. She keeps absentmindedly sticking it back on her head.

"You, Jade!" she shouts. "Get dressed. Go get that job. When you meet Len, bend forward a little. Let him see down your top. Give him some hope. He's a sicko, but we need him. You, Min! Make breakfast. Something homemade. Like biscuits."

"Why don't you make it with your powers?" says Min.

"Don't be a smartass!" screams Bernie. "You see what I did to that microwave?"

"I don't know how to make freaking biscuits," Min wails.

"You know how to read, right?" Bernie shouts. "You ever heard of a recipe? You ever been in the grave? It sucks so bad! You regret all the things you never did. You little bitches are gonna have a very bad time in the grave unless you get on the stick, believe me! Turn down the thermostat! Make it cold. I like cold. Something's off with my body. I don't feel right."

I turn down the thermostat. She looks at me.

"Go show your cock!" she shouts. "That is the first part of Phase One. After we get the new place, that's the end of the first part of Phase Two. You'll still show your cock, but only three days a week. Because you'll start community college. Pre-law. Pre-law is best. You'll be a whiz. You ain't dumb. And Jade'll work weekends to make up for the decrease in cock money. See? See how that works? Now get out of here. What are you gonna do?"

"Show my cock?" I say.

"Show your cock, that's right," she says, and brushes back her hair with her hand, and a huge wad comes out, leaving her almost bald on one side.

"Oh God," says Min. "You know what? No way me and the babies are staying here alone."

"You ain't alone," says Bernie. "I'm here."

"Please don't go," Min says to me.

"Oh, stop it," Bernie says, and the door flies open and I feel a sort of invisible fist punching me in the back.

Outside it's sunny. A regular day. A guy's changing his oil. The clouds are regular clouds and the sun's the regular sun and the only nonregular thing is that my clothes smell like Bernie, a combo of wet cellar and rotten bacon.

Work goes well. I manage to keep smiling and hide my shaking hands, and my midshift rating is Honeypie. After lunch this older woman comes up and says I look so much like a real Pilot she can hardly stand it.

On her head is a thumbprint. Like Ash Wednesday, only sort of glowing.

I don't know what to do. Do I just come out and ask if she wants to see my cock? What if she says no? What if I get caught? What if I show her and she doesn't think it's worth twenty bucks?

Then she asks if I'll surprise her best friend with a birthday table dance. She points out her friend. A pretty girl, no thumbprint. Looks somehow familiar.

We start over and at about twenty feet I realize it's Angela.

Angela Silveri.

We dated senior year. Then Dad died and Ma had to take a job at Patty-Melt Depot. From all the grease Ma got a bad rash and could barely wear a blouse. Plus Min was running wild. So Angela would come over and there'd be Min getting high under a tarp on the carport and Ma sitting in her bra on a kitchen stool with a fan pointed at her gut. Angela had dreams. She had plans. In her notebook she pasted a picture of an office from the J. C. Penney catalogue and under it wrote, *My (someday?) office.* Once we saw this black Porsche and she said very nice but make hers red. The last straw was Ed Edwards, a big drunk, one of Dad's cousins. Things got so bad Ma rented him the utility room. One night Angela and I were making out on the couch late when Ed came in soused and started peeing in the dishwasher.

What could I say? He's only barely related to me? He hardly ever does that?

Angela's eyes were like these little pies.

I walked her home, got no kiss, came back, cleaned up the dishwasher as best I could. A few days later I got my class ring in the mail and a copy of *The Prophet.*

You will always be my first love, she'd written inside. *But now my path converges to a higher ground. Be well always. Walk in joy. Please don't think me cruel, it's just that I want so much in terms of accomplishment, plus I couldn't believe that guy peed right on your dishes.*

No way am I table dancing for Angela Silveri. No way am I asking Angela Silveri's friend if she wants to see my cock. No way am I hanging around here so Angela can see me in my flight jacket and T-backs and wonder to herself how I went so wrong etc. etc.

I hide in the kitchen until my shift is done, then walk home very, very slowly because I'm afraid of what Bernie's going to do to me when I get there.

Min meets me at the door. She's got flour all over her blouse and it looks like she's been crying.

"I can't take any more of this," she says. "She's like falling apart. I mean shit's falling off her. Plus she made me bake a freaking pie."

On the table is a very lumpy pie. One of Bernie's arms is now disconnected and lying across her lap.

"What are you thinking of!" she shouts. "You didn't show your cock even once? You think it's easy making those thumbprints? You try it, smartass! Do you or do you not know the plan? You gotta get us out of here! And to get us out, you gotta use what you got. And you ain't got much. A nice face. And a decent unit. Not huge, but shaped nice."

"Bernie, God," says Min.

"What, Miss Priss?" shouts Bernie, and slams the severed arm down hard on her lap, and her other ear falls off.

"I'm sorry, but this is too fucking sickening," says Min. "I'm going out."

"What's sickening?" says Bernie. "Are you saying I'm sickening? Well, I think you're sickening. So many wonderful things in life and where's your mind? You think with your lazy ass. Whatever life hands you, you take. You're not going anywhere. You're staying home and studying."

"I'm what?" says Min. "Studying what? I ain't studying. Chick comes into my house and starts ordering me to study? I freaking doubt it."

"You don't know nothing!" Bernie says. "What fun is life when you don't know nothing? You can't find your own town on the map. You can't name a single president. When we go to Rome you won't know nothing about the history. You're going to study the World Book. Do we still have those World Books?"

"Yeah right," says Min. "We're going to Rome."

"We'll go to Rome when he's a lawyer," says Bernie.

"Dream on, chick," says Min. "And we'll go to Mars when I'm a stockbreaker."

"Don't you dare make fun of me!" Bernie shouts, and our only vase goes flying across the room and nearly nails Min in the head.

"She's been like this all day," says Min.

"Like what?" shouts Bernie. "We had a perfectly nice day."

"She made me help her try on my bras," says Min.

"I never had a nice sexy bra," says Bernie.

"And now mine are all ruined," says Min. "They got this sort of goo on them."

"You ungrateful shit!" shouts Bernie. "Do you know what I'm doing for you? I'm saving your boy. And you got the nerve to say I made goo on your bras! Troy's gonna get caught in a crossfire in the courtyard. In September. September eighteenth. He's gonna get thrown off his little trike. With one leg twisted under him and blood pouring out of his ear. It's a freaking prophecy. You know that word? It means prediction. You know that word? You think I'm bullshitting? Well I ain't bullshitting. I got the power. Watch this: All day Jade sat licking labels at a desk by a window. Her boss bought everybody subs for lunch. She's bringing some home in a green bag."

"That ain't true about Troy, is it?" says Min. "Is it? I don't believe it."

"Turn on the TV!" Bernie shouts. "Give me the changer."

I turn on the TV. I give her the changer. She puts on *Nathan's Body Shop*.

Nathan says washboard abs drive the women wild. Then there's a close-up of his washboard abs.

"Oh yes," says Bernie. "Them are for me. I'd like to give those a lick. A lick and a pinch. I'd like to sort of straddle those things."

Just then Jade comes through the door with a big green bag.

"Oh God," says Min.

"Told you so!" says Bernie, and pokes Min in the ribs. "Ha ha! I really got the power!"

"I don't get it," Min says, all desperate. "What happens? Please. What happens to him? You better freaking tell me."

"I already told you," Bernie says. "He'll fly about fifteen feet and live about three minutes."

"Bernie, God," Min says, and starts to cry. "You used to be so nice."

"I'm still so nice," says Bernie, and bites into a sub and takes off the tip of her finger and starts chewing it up.

Just after dawn she shouts out my name.

"Take the blanket off," she says. "I ain't feeling so good."

I take the blanket off. She's basically just this pile of parts: both arms in her lap, head on the arms, heel of one foot touching the heel of the other, all of it sort of wrapped up in her dress.

"Get me a washcloth," she says. "Do I got a fever? I feel like I got a fever. Oh, I knew it was too good to be true. But okay. New plan. New plan. I'm changing the first part of Phase One. If you see two thumbprints, that means the lady'll screw you for cash. We're in a fix here. We gotta speed this up. There ain't gonna be nothing left of me. Who's gonna be my lover now?"

The doorbell rings.

"Son of a bitch," Bernie snarls.

It's Father Brian with a box of doughnuts. I step out quick and close the door behind me. He says he's just checking in. Perhaps we'd like to talk? Perhaps we're feeling some residual anger about Bernie's situation? Which would of course be completely understandable. Once when he was a young priest someone broke in and drew a mustache on the Virgin Mary with a permanent marker, and for weeks he was tortured by visions of bending back the finger of the vandal until he or she burst into tears of apology.

"I knew that wasn't appropriate," he says. "I knew that by indulging in that fantasy I was honoring violence. And yet it gave me pleasure. I also thought of catching them in the act and boinking them in the head with a rock. I also thought of jumping up and down on their backs until something in their spinal column cracked. Actually I had about a million ideas. But you know what I did instead? I scrubbed and scrubbed our Holy Mother, and soon she was as good as new. Her statue, I mean. She herself of course is always good as new."

From inside comes the sound of breaking glass. Breaking glass and then something heavy falling, and Jade yelling and Min yelling and the babies crying.

"Oops, I guess?" he says. "I've come at a bad time? Look, all I'm trying to do is urge you, if at all possible, to forgive the perpetrators, as I forgave the perpetrator that drew on my Virgin Mary. The thing lost, after all, is only your aunt's body, and what is essential, I assure you, is elsewhere, being well taken care of."

I nod. I smile. I say thanks for stopping by. I take the doughnuts and go back inside.

The TV's broke and the refrigerator's tipped over and Bernie's parts are strewn across the living room like she's been shot out of a cannon.

"She tried to get up," says Jade.

"I don't know where the hell she thought she was going," says Min.

"Come here," the head says to me, and I squat down. "That's it for me. I'm fucked. As per usual. Always the bridesmaid, never the bride. Although come to think of it I was never even the freaking bridesmaid. Look, show your cock. It's the shortest line between two points. The world ain't giving away nice lives. You got a trust fund? You a genius? Show your cock. It's what you got. And remember: Troy in September. On his trike. One leg twisted. Don't forget. And also. Don't remember me like this. Remember me like how I was that night we all went to Red Lobster and I had that new perm. Ah Christ. At least buy me a stone."

I rub her shoulder, which is next to her foot.

"We loved you," I say.

"Why do some people get everything and I got nothing?" she says. "Why? Why was that?"

"I don't know," I say.

"Show your cock," she says, and dies again.

We stand there looking down at the pile of parts. Mac crawls toward it and Min moves him back with her foot.

"This is too freaking much," says Jade, and starts crying.

"What do we do now?" says Min.

"Call the cops," Jade says.

"And say what?" says Min.

We think about this awhile.

I get a Hefty bag. I get my winter gloves.

"I ain't watching," says Jade.

"I ain't watching either," says Min, and they take the babies into the bedroom.

I close my eyes and wrap Bernie up in the Hefty bag and twistie-tie the bag shut and lug it out to the trunk of the K-car. I throw in a shovel. I drive up to

St. Leo's. I lower the bag into the hole using a bungee cord, then fill the hole back in.

Down in the city are the nice houses and the so-so houses and the lovers making out in dark yards and the babies crying for their moms, and I wonder if, other than Jesus, this has ever happened before. Maybe it happens all the time. Maybe there's angry dead all over, hiding in rooms, covered with blankets, bossing around their scared, embarrassed relatives. Because how would we know?

I for sure don't plan on broadcasting this.

I smooth over the dirt and say a quick prayer: If it was wrong for her to come back, forgive her, she never got beans in this life, plus she was trying to help us.

At the car I think of an additional prayer: But please don't let her come back again.

When I get home the babies are asleep and Jade and Min are watching a phone-sex infomercial, three girls in leather jumpsuits eating bananas in slo-mo while across the screen runs a constant disclaimer: Not Necessarily the Girls Who Man the Phones! Not Necessarily the Girls Who Man the Phones!

"Them chicks seem to really be enjoying those bananas," says Min in a thin little voice.

"I like them jumpsuits though," says Jade.

"Yeah them jumpsuits look decent," says Min.

Then they look up at me. I've never seen them so sad and beat and sick.

"It's done," I say.

Then we hug and cry and promise never to forget Bernie the way she really was, and I use some Resolve on the rug and they go do some reading in their World Books.

Next day I go in early. I don't see a single thumbprint. But it doesn't matter. I get with Sonny Vance and he tells me how to do it. First you ask the woman would she like a private tour. Then you show her the fake P-40, the Gallery of Historical Aces, the shower stall where we get oiled up, etc. etc. and then in the hall near the rest room you ask if there's anything else she'd like to see. It's sleazy. It's gross. But when I do it I think of September. September and Troy in the crossfire, his little leg bent under him etc. etc.

Most say no but quite a few say yes.

I've got a place picked out at a complex called Swan's Glen. They've never had a shooting or a knifing and the public school is great and every Saturday they have a nature walk for kids behind the clubhouse.

For every hundred bucks I make, I set aside five for Bernie's stone.

What do you write on something like that? LIFE PASSED HER BY? DIED DISAPPOINTED? CAME BACK TO LIFE BUT FELL APART? All true, but too sad, and no way I'm writing any of those.

BERNIE KOWALSKI, it's going to say: BELOVED AUNT.

Sometimes she comes to me in dreams. She never looks good. Sometimes she's wearing a dirty smock. Once she had on handcuffs. Once she was naked and dirty and this mean cat was clawing its way up her front. But every time it's the same thing.

"Some people get everything and I got nothing," she says. "Why? Why did that happen?"

Every time I say I don't know.

And I don't.

Joan Silber

MY SHAPE

JOAN SILBER (1945–) is the author of the novels *Lucky Us*, *In the City*, and *Household Words*—which won the PEN/Hemingway Award—as well as a short story collection, *In My Other Life*. Her short story collection *Ideas of Heaven* (W. W. Norton, 2004) was a finalist for the National Book Award and the Story Prize. Her stories have appeared in *The O. Henry Prize Stories 2007*, *The O. Henry Prize Stories 2003*, *The New Yorker*, *Ploughshares*, *The Paris Review*, *Pushcart Prize XXV*, and *Pushcart Prize XXVIII*. Her next novel will be published by Norton in 2008. Silber has received an award from the American Academy of Arts and Letters and grants from the Guggenheim Foundation, the NEA, and the New York Foundation on the Arts. She lives in New York City and currently teaches at Sarah Lawrence College.

I had my own ideas about a higher purpose, but not enough ideas. I could have used more. When I was in my early teens, I used to go to the bus station in my city and think about panhandling money to get a ticket to Las Vegas. A wide sky of nightclubs glittering in the middle of the desert sounded beautiful to me. I wanted beauty. I'd sit on a bench and do my homework in the bus station, and then I'd go home.

What did I want before this? I took ballet lessons twice a week in the gym of my grammar school and liked the arabesques and the leaping and even the strictness of Miss Allaben drilling us in the six positions. I worked hard at ballet until I began to grow a figure in my leotard. My other hobby was attending services in churches and synagogues all around Cincinnati, where we lived. My parents were a mixed marriage (Jewish and Catholic, a big deal then) and had solved the alleged difficulty of this by not following any religion. So I was a fascinated tourist in any house of worship, and would go anywhere I could get taken. The whole notion of *worship* knocked me out. I saw Jews kissing their fingers and touching them to the velvet cover of the Torah, I saw Catholics kneeling with their mouths open in practiced readiness for the Host, I saw Greek Orthodox placing their lips on icons as if they could not bear to pass them without this seal of adoration. I would emerge blinking into the daylight, shocked at my friends' laughter over what had gone on in there—the choirmaster's bad haircut, the tedium of the sermon, the utter ridiculousness of somebody's mother's hat. I listened, harder than anyone else, to words never said in daily conversation—beseech, transfigure, abounding, mercy. The rapped chest, the bowed head, the murmured Dear Lord. I could not get over people doing this together, the gestures of submission that went on within these walls.

Then the congregation got up and walked outside. Since no one—not my friends or family or even the clergy themselves—seemed to take this to heart the way I did, I had to keep quiet, like a spy with encoded notes or a tippler sipping a flask in the ladies' room. I made up perky reasons for wanting to go each week, "just to see how people are really all alike."

After a while, I heard myself making fun of it with the others, and I stopped going. All at once, suddenly, cold turkey. I turned my back on the whole thing. So. Then I grew the mounded body that was to be my adult shape. I came from a family of women with large breasts, and by fourteen I had my own set, which I sheathed in satin brassieres that made them point forward in military cones. Torpedo tits they were called (by us girls too). Everyone knew that grown men became entirely helpless at the sight of cleavage, the compressed hills rising gloriously above a strapless gown. This fashion in bodies has faded, but I was glad of it then. It is true that in junior high the boys yelled dirty comments (they mooed like cows, they made milking gestures with their hands), but I believed that these immature oafs, as we called them, liked me.

By the time I was out of school, everyone seemed to be telling me that I might enjoy certain privileges if I played my cards right. Once that idea got unpacked, it was more complicated than I guessed—what these privileges were and where contempt hid in the granting of them and what had to be paid for them anyway. People think they know all about this now, but they don't, not exactly. I wanted to be an actress. I was too silly and shallow to be any good at acting, but I could keep my composure onstage, which is something. I was given small parts in summer stock, the hooker or the stenographer or the cigarette girl in the nightclub scene. The summer after my first year of college, I worked in the Twin Pines Theatre. I slept with the bullying director, a fierce-browed man in his forties who had sex with a lot of us and didn't give anybody a bigger part for it. Sleeping your way to the top is a bit of a myth, in my experience.

I liked acting, at that age. You got to dwell on feelings, which were all I dwelt on then anyway, and turn them over, play them out. We had long discussions: Would a child afraid of her father show the fear in public? Would a man who was in love with a woman talk more loudly when she entered the room? Those who'd had real training (I was not one of them) spoke with scorn about actors who "indicated," who tried to display a response without actually feeling it. An audience could always tell. What was new to me here was the idea that insincerity was visible. I understood from this that in real life I was not getting away with as much as I thought.

But otherwise I was a little jerk. I was so hungry for glamour that I put a

white streak in my brown hair, I wore short-shorts and wedge heels, I drank
banana daiquiris until I threw up. I thought the director was going to find himself attracted to me again and we might have a legendary romance, although I
could hardly talk to him. I didn't know anything.

One of the other women told me about a job on a cruise liner. If I could
dance a little, which I was always saying I could, I might be one of the girls
strutting around in sequins in the musical revues they put on to keep the passengers from jumping overboard in boredom. I could get to Europe, to the Ca-
ribbean. They didn't pay you much but you ate well.

The woman who told me this was the director's new cookie, and I was not
sure what she was really saying to me and in what spirit. We're artists, you're the
showgirl, etc. But perhaps she did want to give me something. And I worked
on cruise ships for years. I went to Nassau and Jamaica and Venezuela and
through the Greek islands. I worked in clubs in Miami too, walking around
with a big feathered headdress on and the edges of my buns hanging out the
back of my satin outfit. I lived with a bartender who was irresistible when he
wasn't a repetitious, unintelligent drunk, and with an older man I never liked.
I was twenty-seven—getting old for this stuff—when I got work on a ship
going through the Mediterranean, along the French Riviera and Monaco and
Liguria.

It was a French ship and that was how I met my husband, who was the ship's
purser. He was a soft-eyed man with a whimsical blond mustache, who looked
wonderful in the white uniform of the cruise line; everyone on the ship had a
crush on Jean-Pierre. He was really just a boy. He was older than I was by a year,
and he had poise and good sense, but he was not very worldly. I seemed to
dazzle him, which was certainly nice. And I fell for him, his genial flirting and
his down-and-dirty ardor in bed.

There is an hour on any ship when twilight turns everything a bright and
glowing blue and the horizon disappears, the sea and the sky are the same. The
line between air and water is so apparently incidental that a largeness of vision
comes over everyone; the ship floats on the sky, until night falls and everything
is swallowed in the dark. I have memories of being very happy with Jean-Pierre
while standing out on the lower deck in that blueness, before the ship's lights
came on. He asked if I looked like my mother or my father, and if I was close
to them (I certainly was not). He wanted to know if I could ever live away from
my family and my country for good, if I had ever thought of such a thing,
and I saw myself moving toward a destiny as interesting as any I could have
wished.

I had very little to leave behind, when I went with him to live in St-Malo, the
ancient walled city in Brittany where he had grown up. Jean-Pierre acted utterly
proud to have nabbed me. When he introduced me to people, he always repeated my name, *Ah-lice,* with a certain delighted pause before it, and his trans-

lations to me included goofy compliments no one had really said ("my cousin says you are the flower of America"). We were staying in an apartment that belonged to his uncle, two doors from a fish market whose scent I did not even mind. We married a month after he brought me there. It was a pretty town, high on a bluff, but it had been bombed badly in the war and not all of it had been built back. The rainy beaches were filled in summer with dogs and children running around on the sand. Signs insisted it was *strictement défendu* to bring unleashed dogs anywhere on the premises, and I was amused to see that none of its citizens paid attention.

His family was not unkind to me either, despite the fact that I tried their patience with my meager French and seemed dopey to them in general. Their friendliness was to ask me about Mickey Mouse and Elvis Presley, and in the childishness of these questions my language skills got better. At the endlessly long family dinners on Sundays, I could yammer my answers.

I had a running joke with Jean-Pierre about all the idioms English speakers have for anything sexy or duplicitous—French kisses, French leave, Frenching the bed, French ticklers. We were pretty jolly, the two of us. When we went back on the ship together, I was full of rich confidence. I beamed at the corny banter of old men and their wives, I danced like a proverbial house on fire. I wrote letters to my family from our ports of call, Corsica, Sardinia, Malta. *Allo, chère maman*, I said, I'm having more fun than I can tell you. *Baisers* to everyone, from Alice the blushing bride.

After Easter, when we went back to St-Malo, the town was full of tourists from other parts of France, and I would chat with them across the tables in cafés. People there didn't do that, but I thought they should, and I got them going. In the winter, when Jean-Pierre was hired for another tour of duty, there was no job for me on his ship, and he said maybe I could just stay home without him this once. I had worked since I was nineteen, and this offer of leisure seemed wonderful to me.

But I went a little crazy, by myself like that. I was no longer a novelty to his family and they had conversations I could not follow. In the dank and icy months, I walked around in a heavy, dressy cape and told the children I had a gun underneath it; I told Jean-Pierre's mother she was so cheap that she fed us horse meat; I tried to hitchhike to Rennes but I came back after fifty creepy kilometers on the road with a dead-silent truck driver. Once I got drunk and stood on a table in a café, singing "Blue Monday" and looking down at the patrons. By the time Jean-Pierre got back, I was mopey and fat; I had gained twenty pounds. I had become a thing the French really hate, a blowsy woman. What could we do then? We fought, quite nastily. He seemed stuffy and spiteful, not like someone I knew at all. He said everyone had told him I was a selfish baby but he had said, oh, no, I was devoted to him. We made up and spent two days straight in bed (our desire never cut so deep as then). We went on excursions to Caen and to Mont St-Michel, which even I knew was a famous abbey, although I had stopped caring about churches. We walked across the causeway to get there, and that was the part I liked, walking into the sea. We gave parties for his friends and I made American foods—fried chicken, cole slaw, macaroni salad. The wives began to think I was a big, loose, amiable fool. Jean-Pierre got work in a shipping firm in St-Malo.

For my thirtieth birthday we went to Paris. I had never been there before, and much of it thrilled me—the cakelike elegance of the buildings, the determined verve of people in the streets—and me, Alice, walking through it with my handsome French husband. But I felt too, in the thick of those groomed and confident crowds, the discomfort outsiders often know in Paris, the dawning sense that this is not, really, for us at all—we will never be this stylish or this knowing.

I came back to St-Malo in an agony of thwarted hopes. I thought that all my prettiness, all the gifts I'd been so pleased to have, had gotten me nothing at all. What did I want so desperately? What in the world is *glamour*, what did I mean by that? A heightening of the ordinary, an entry into the club of splendor, a feast of endorsed sensations? Whatever it was, my anguish in wanting it was almost more than I could stand. I suffered blindly. Dolly of silly notions that I was, I wept real tears.

I knew I couldn't stay there weeping. I wasn't bound or indentured, it was the twentieth century. But I wept like that for another year—a shrew to Jean-Pierre and a puzzle to the town. I had one affair, with a humorless older cousin of his, and Jean-Pierre had lovers. In the end, I took the train to Paris and got a cheap ticket on a charter flight, and I left—after weeks of ugliness with Jean-Pierre's family (I might have handled that part better). I went to New York to dance and sing in Broadway shows.

What was I thinking? That it was my last chance. I had never been to New York, and I didn't know how to go about any of it. I showed up for one audition and waited in an outer room crowded with women much younger than I was. In the studio, I could keep in step, when they had us copy a sequence of dance moves, but I was not really dancing. I could sing on key, but in a watery, underpowered warble. I sang *"Je Ne Regrette Rien,"* which made the casting people smile wryly.

This did not make me want any of this less. I thought I had never worked hard enough for anything before (this part was right). *Being in a show* seemed like the exalted professional use of the body, the gold spun from sweat. In *Variety* I saw an ad run by a man who coached performers for musical auditions—twenty years' experience, proven methods. I was so happy after I called him—I was taking charge of my life, as I meant to do. I walked back to the Y where I was staying and I celebrated by eating a steak at the coffee shop next door. I can remember chewing it happily, sitting alone at a table in private joy, putting little charred pink-brown bits of it on my fork with the baked potato, reading a *Vogue* magazine as I ate. I liked food in America.

I was late getting to the coach's the next day. The studio was on Tenth Avenue, further west than I'd been before, and I had not realized how far this was from the subway.

"Should I bother with you?" he said when he opened the door. "What do you think?"

"Oh, yes," I said, tittering and dimpling. "Please."

He was a tall man who had probably once been handsome; he was stark and sinewy now. His dance studio was on the sixth floor of an office building, and the room smelled of old wood and mildewed drapes. I had to display myself for him. That is, I had to strip down to a leotard (I did this in a corner, awkwardly sliding out of my skirt) and follow him in a few dance steps, then perform them again while he looked glumly at me. Next he sat down at the piano and asked me to sing "Three Blind Mice."

"You remember that one, right?"

I tried to carry it off as jauntily as I could. Then he had me sing "Frère Jacques," which I at least did with a decent accent.

"Not much of a singer, are you?" he said.

I shrugged cutely, but I was very miserable. "I can be a dancer," I said. "Don't you think?"

"Maybe. How much do you want it?" He glowered at me from over the piano, a scratched black upright with a hoarse tone.

I answered that question with so much fervor that he smiled, a thing he rarely did, as it turned out.

His name was Duncan Fischbach and I was to spend many hours in his studio. At first it was like any dance class—he demonstrated some steps, and we did them together, and then we linked a few of these sequences, which I was supposed to remember. "Listen to me, are you listening?" he said. "The word *oops* does not get you anywhere in this world, no matter how big a rack you've got on you."

I laughed a little. Women did not take umbrage in any club I'd worked in.

"I hate a giggler," he said. "Do it again till you get it right."

I did the steps again. He circled around me, checking. "Your balance is bad," he said. "Stand on your right foot and don't move until I tell you." I stood for as long as I could, swerving and dipping and regaining my center. "You have to do better than that," he said.

I had to jump in place for fifteen minutes without losing the beat. I had to run around the room and change direction on a dime. I had to hold a number of positions for long spells of time—a split, a high kick, a stretch to my toes with my butt in the air. All of them were exposing, implicitly sexual positions, and I felt like a crude cartoon, twisting and straining, muscles trembling. Nonetheless I was proud of my discipline in the regimen this strange *maître* was drilling me in. I did get more limber.

At my age I had no chance of getting anywhere, Fischbach said, unless I practiced at least seven hours a day. Minimum. I could not do much in my closet of a room at the Y, so I paid to use Fischbach's studio in the evening hours. I was given a key, and I went into that room, with its old-gym smells, always afraid that he was going to appear, but he did not. My body grew lighter and trimmer. I was skipping meals to save money, as the savings I had brought with me ran lower. I had taken a vow to myself not to look for other work. I was so lonely my voice cracked from disuse when I spoke, but I was elated too in a starved and ghostly way.

Sometimes I went to shows (or halves of shows—I walked in at intermission, the one way to go for free). Things had been changing in the theater; the hit shows of the decade were *Hair* and *Jesus Christ Superstar*. They were okay, but I liked the older ones better—*Gypsy, Guys and Dolls, Oklahoma!*—an earlier style of full-throated, tip-tappy entertainment. Most musicals gave me pleasure, but it was not a fan's love for them that made me knock myself out. I saw them as a way to be in a parade of dazzling motion, to be a lovely dancing version of my-self, without the rawness of the clubs. The best of me (I believed) was in that lineup, slim-legged and tight-waisted, too delightful to keep under wraps. That parade, which is always passing through this world, was what I was made for, I thought. I could not bear to have it go by without me. It hurt me to think it might have slipped by already, that I might be too old. I probably was too old.

Fischbach had other students. A few times I met women going in or out, girls with pearly lipstick and pixie bangs. Never any men. I couldn't tell what his own desires were, which gender he liked, or whether he couldn't stand the thought of doing anything with anybody. There was no gallantry in him—the tools of his trade were mockery and command—and he was uncharmed by fe-maleness in general. He was a strong dancer himself, not miraculously light on his feet but muscular and sure; his lines were always clear. He called me an oaf, a potato, a slob, a blight, a hippopotamus.

He believed in tests for me, rehearsals of my resolve, as if the strongest desire had to win, simple as that, in any instance. "Pop quiz," he would say. "If a direc-tor asked you to stand on your head with a dead fish in your mouth, what would you do? If someone stepped on your hand in the middle of a number, how would you act? If you were in California and had to get to a performance in New York and no planes were flying, what would you do? If your grandmother wanted you to stay at her bedside in California, what would you tell her?" There were no trick answers, but the recitation of responses was my practice in "men-tal clarity."

Sometimes I called France collect and talked to Jean-Pierre on the phone. The life I'd had there seemed cushioned and soft, a child's tented garden. When

Jean-Pierre was friendly (sometimes he was not), I would get off the phone and shed tears. I would sit in my room at the Y and have to talk myself back into doing my exercises. How had I, who had once been loved and had a home, thrown myself into this pit?

This could not go on forever. Fischbach had forbidden me to go near any audition until he said I was ready, but I had had thirty-six sessions with him. Week after week. On Labor Day weekend he was going away (did he have friends? it was hard to imagine) and he would do a special extra-long class with me before he left on Friday afternoon.

I was a little late, and he said, "I might have known. Do you have any idea at all what traffic is going to be like this afternoon? Any clue at all?"

"I'll dance fast," I murmured brightly. This was the wrong joke to make, because it gave him the idea to have me do routines in double time. He hammered at the piano with his fingers angled like claws. I was beet-red and sweating heavily when we stopped.

"Now that you're warmed up," he said.

He took up a wooden yardstick from the corner. For a second I believed that he was going to hit me with it. "You know the limbo?" he said. "Did the frogs limbo in your part of La Belle Frogland?"

He held the stick out stiffly, like a traffic gate. "Under," he said. "Lean back. Go with your pelvis first."

I had done this before, as a teenager in Cincinnati. "Oops," I said now, as I bent my knees and cakewalked under the ruler, my shoulders and head going last. It had been much jollier with a line of guffawing kids and calypso music on the hi-fi.

"Again," Fischbach said.

He lowered the stick. I wriggled under. The silence was not pleasant.

"Again," he said. The move meant thrusting my private parts at him—that was the whole comedy of this game—and for once I was not happy to be doing that. Fischbach kept his face impassive; he looked stony and perhaps a little bored.

"Again," he said.

I had to spread my knees wider to keep my footing.

"Again," he said.

I tried to angle one hip lower and twist my torso under the stick, which made me lose my balance. I righted myself by holding on to Fischbach's arm.

"No," he said, and shook me away. I skidded and landed hard on my tailbone.

"You didn't last very long," he said.

"Yes, I did."

"Stay, don't move. I have floor work for you."

He walked to the far wall. "Okay," he said. "Come to me. On your hands and knees."

"What?"

"Just a little crawling. Fast as you can. It's a good workout. Don't argue." I was going to argue, but then he told me not to. I thought I would just get it over quickly—I put my palms flat on the floor and I lunged and scuttled forward, like a swimmer in a race. My bare knees scraped the floor, but I kept thinking I was almost there. Soon, soon. This was a nightmare, but if I did what I had to properly, it would be finished.

"Very good," Fischbach said, when I had reached him. "Very nice. Don't get up, sweetheart."

I sat on the floor, cross-legged, waiting. *Sweetheart*, he said that?

"One last thing," he said. "Then you're ready." I actually nodded.

"Lick my shoe."

"What?"

"You need to do this. You pick. The right or the left."

He was wearing white canvas tennis shoes. I looked at his feet and I looked up at him. His face had almost no expression, but his eyes, in their hooded sockets, were fixed on me, to let me know that I had to do this. I respected (that is almost the right word) the clarity of his will. You might have thought we were both in the service of a great idea. For a moment I did think that. I lowered my head and I touched my tongue to the tip of his shoe, just once. The roughness left a dry spot on my tongue.

I was crying, of course, when I looked up at him. Not a mild flow of tears, but helpless, snotty sobs. Fischbach stayed poker-faced. He really did believe in some theory of severity and triumph, some grand dedication, but there was nothing at its center. He did not care whether I danced or not, or whether anyone did. There was no divine substance he was burning me down to. While I was crying, I understood clearly that I was never going to be a dancer in any Broadway show. Not now, not later. I saw too that I didn't want it so much really. It was as if I suddenly remembered a thing that had been blocked by distraction and interruption. I sat on the floor in my soaked leotard and I was sick with disappointment to be someone who didn't want this. My crying naturally disgusted Fischbach, although it could not have been a surprise to him, I could not have been the first to break down in his studio. (Unless I was the first he was able to push that far, a truly painful thought.)

"Okay, okay. We're done," he said.

He went over and rolled the casing down on the piano keys. I could see that he was trying to carry out these last moments with what he thought of as style. "Get your stuff together," he said. "I'm in a hurry. Don't dawdle like you do."

He got his dungaree jacket off the chair and put it on, tugging at the bottom of it and turning up the collar. "Are you listening?" he said. "Move it. Chop-chop. It's time." He seemed pathetic to me, bossing around a woman who was stretched out on the floor in a fit of weeping. Where could that ever get him? I didn't move—that was my one tiny piece of resistance—and he said, "I'm waiting." He stood over me for some minutes. At last he said, "Never mind. You can lock up when you leave." I left the door open, in fact, and I never mailed him the keys either.

And so I went back to Jean-Pierre. He met my plane in Paris, and he looked wonderful to me, with his soft eyes and his cropped sandy hair, his topcoat flapping in the wind. He seemed very happy to see me, and he didn't rebuke me or ask me terrible questions. Later he was less kind. His family never treated me with any warmth after I came back.

Everyone did notice how slender and strong I was. I could not explain to them how I had stretched and kicked and *plié*'d and tied myself in knots in that stuffy studio, tearing and rebuilding the muscle fibers, pushing myself past the threshold of strain. Once I was back in Britanny, those hours in the studio seemed heroic—*I* seemed heroic, in my submission to the regimen, my single-pointed efforts. And for what? For a vision that was laughable even to me and had made me come back ashamed.

But I did come back a less silly woman. I did not plague Jean-Pierre about things he could do nothing about. And I tried to keep up my training. I would put on a record of *Wonderful Town!* and strut across the kitchen floor to Rosalind Russell. My niece and her friends, who saw me through the window, wanted me to teach them. I began to give lessons to little girls in "jazz dancing" and also tap, which they requested. I liked children and might have had them with Jean-Pierre if we had gotten along better. I could get my class looking like a line of Shirley Temples, all shuffling-off-to-Buffalo in their patent leather shoes, merry and mostly in step, and afterward I helped them on with their little coats.

When the class got too big for any room in our house, I rented a room in the *mairie,* where the town's municipal offices were. It was quite a grand room, with molded plaster garlands along the ceiling and a nice parquet floor. It tickled me to have "The Pajama Game" pouring through its august spaces. Adults wanted to come too to the class, so I had an evening group of solid housewives and lithe young office workers and even a few men. I was a fad, perhaps, but people had fun.

I could not have lived on what I made from my dance classes, but they kept me afloat. Some girls came year after year, and their sisters too. Every fall I worried I wouldn't have students, but I always did. And I was allied with what Americans used to call physical culture. I went hiking in the valley of the Rance, I went to Paris for yoga weekends. Jean-Pierre laughed the first time he saw me in hiking boots; he said I looked like a Valkyrie in shorts.

I liked my muscles more than he did, and they weren't ungainly either. The littlest girls used to beg me to show them a *grand jeté*—and I could jump and land without much thud or bobble even in the later years. The classes were the best part of my week. When Jean-Pierre fell in love with someone else and we split up at last, I was not altogether at a loss. I had something I could do, an occupation. I could not, however, stay in the town.

I went to Paris, to brood and idle for a few weeks before going home to the States. It was not a happy time. I was appalled to think my marriage really was broken forever and I was sorry for the messes we had made. I walked through the whole city of Paris, from Sacre Coeur to Montparnasse, from the Chaillot Palace to the Jardin des Plantes, trying as hard as I might (not hard enough) to keep from stuffing myself with food and drinking a whole bottle of wine every night. I chatted too much with waiters and ticket-takers and all the people in my yoga class.

We were doing the shoulder stand in yoga when I kicked someone behind me by mistake. He was a very polite Parisian in his late forties, who told me not to worry for a single second, it was good for his health to get clipped in the jaw now and then. I was not usually that clumsy. We whispered back and forth about how this was a more dangerous sport than soccer, but at least (he said) you didn't have violent yoga fans. After class he took me out for a very good lunch.

I liked him right away, most people did. He was a history teacher in a *lycée*, a widower with a grown son, with an interest in Zen Buddhism and Duke Ellington. I stayed in Paris because of him—Giles was his name—one week longer and then another week. People say Paris is expensive but you can get by if you know how. After it was plain that I was not going to leave the city any time soon, I began to teach beginners' classes in the yoga studio. I was living with Giles by then in the 7th *arrondissement,* in an old apartment with a rocky sofa and an armoire as big as a stable.

We had a simple, almost rustic life. In the evenings we stayed in, without TV or too much outside company; we read and we listened to music. On weekends we had *pique-niques* in the park when the weather was good, or we played long, companionable rounds of honeymoon bridge. You might have thought we were old people, except that the sex was frank and lively. Quite lively.

Sometimes in the early days I went with him to talks by one of his Buddhist teachers, although they never really seized my imagination. I did learn to meditate, and the followers were certainly a smart group. Giles never pressed any of his enthusiasms on me, except for a habit of buying me cheap Japanese sandals, which he insisted on liking. How could a person scold him? He was always able to consider the most outlandish idea without arguing and was unshocked by anything I told him.

Ten years after we first started living together, I went home to the States to visit. My family made a fuss and then ignored me. I had become one of those ex-pats who didn't know who David Letterman was and who held her knife and fork like a European. When I flew back to Paris a week early, I told everyone I was never leaving France again. Giles's son called me *la convertie*.

At the yoga school we always got a number of Americans in the classes, and I could see they envied my unfazed command of this city and its folkways. It amused me that I of all people had become some worldly personage with good bearing and a forthright gaze, like a type out of Henry James.

I might have turned out a lot worse. I tried not to be vain around the students, not to be some fluttery old bird in drawstring pants. I worried about Giles's health, which was not as strong as it might have been. Otherwise my complaints were truly minor. When Giles had a heart attack last summer, I came to know clearly what minor was.

I was not always good during his illness. In the hospital, I cried out when I saw the tubes clamped over his nostrils. On my visits, I held his hand and gazed at him, while everyone else chattered to him in their usual voluble way. In our apartment I didn't want to answer the door or the phone. I wouldn't go outside at all, except to visit Giles. People came to check on me—Liane, the head of the yoga studio, and Giles's son and his wife. "Get up now," Liane said. "Get yourself dressed." What a nuisance I was to everyone, what trouble.

When Giles came home again I was better. I cleaned myself up, I cleaned the house. I nestled on the couch with him, I brought him cups of *tisane*, I went out to shop. And I went back to teaching yoga, which helped me greatly. The difficulty of certain poses was especially useful. I had to concentrate and I had to be exact. Giles himself got lively again within a few weeks and claimed he felt the same as before. Better even.

In the months right after he was ill, when I'd begun working again, I began practicing a kind of Tibetan meditation called *tonglen.* In its later levels, you send relief and spaciousness, on your outtake of breath, to someone who has done you an injury. Naturally I picked Duncan Fischbach. I have never had another enemy. I'm sure no thought of me has crossed his mind for decades; I was one clumsy student among many for him. How our limits vexed him. He couldn't bear how little we could do. Broken athlete, he must be now, empty shell—who would need relief sent more than he would? I sit with my famous bust rising and falling as I breathe; he would laugh if he saw me. But I do think of him, in short spells and sometimes longer.

TONY'S STORY

LESLIE MARMON SILKO (1948–) was born in Albuquerque, New Mexico, of Laguna Pueblo, Mexican, and white descent. Silko grew up at the Pueblo of Laguna, located in west central New Mexico. She attended a Catholic school in Albuquerque. In 1969 she received a bachelor's degree in English from the University of New Mexico, where she later taught creative writing and a course in oral traditions. Silko's books include *Storyteller; Almanac of the Dead; Yellow Woman; Yellow Woman and the Beauty of the Spirit; Ceremony;* and, most recently, *Gardens in the Dunes.*

ONE

It happened one summer when the sky was wide and hot and the summer rains did not come; the sheep were thin, and the tumbleweeds turned brown and died. Leon came back from the army. I saw him standing by the Ferris wheel across from the people who came to sell melons and chili on San Lorenzo's Day. He yelled at me, "Hey Tony—over here!" I was embarrassed to hear him yell so loud, but then I saw the wine bottle with the brown-paper sack crushed around it.

"How's it going, buddy?"

He grabbed my hand and held it tight like a white man. He was smiling. "It's good to be home again. They asked me to dance tomorrow—it's only the Corn Dance, but I hope I haven't forgotten what to do."

"You'll remember—it will all come back to you when you hear the drum." I was happy, because I knew that Leon was once more a part of the pueblo. The sun was dusty and low in the west, and the procession passed by us, carrying San Lorenzo back to his niche in the church.

"Do you want to get something to eat?" I asked.

Leon laughed and patted the bottle. "No, you're the only one who needs to eat. Take this dollar—they're selling hamburgers over there." He pointed past the merry-go-round to a stand with cotton candy and a snow-cone machine.

It was then that I saw the cop pushing his way through the crowds of people gathered around the hamburger stand and bingo-game tent; he came steadily toward us. I remembered Leon's wine and looked to see if the cop was watching us; but he was wearing dark glasses and I couldn't see his eyes.

He never said anything before he hit Leon in the face with his fist. Leon collapsed into the dust, and the paper sack floated in the wine and pieces of glass. He didn't move and blood kept bubbling out of his mouth and nose. I could hear a siren. People crowded around Leon and kept pushing me away. The tribal policemen knelt over Leon, and one of them looked up at the state cop and asked what was going on. The big cop didn't answer. He was staring at the little patterns of blood in the dust near Leon's mouth. The dust soaked up the blood almost before it dripped to the ground—it had been a very dry summer. The cop didn't leave until they laid Leon in the back of the paddy wagon.

The moon was already high when we got to the hospital in Albuquerque. We waited a long time outside the emergency room with Leon propped between us. Siow and Gaisthea kept asking me, "What happened, what did Leon say to the cop?" and I told them how we were just standing there, ready to buy hamburgers—we'd never even seen him before. They put stitches around Leon's mouth and gave him a shot; he was lucky, they said—it could've been a broken jaw instead of broken teeth.

TWO

They dropped me off near my house. The moon had moved lower into the west and left the close rows of houses in long shadows. Stillness breathed around me, and I wanted to run from the feeling behind me in the dark; the stories about witches ran with me. That night I had a dream—the big cop was pointing a long bone at me—they always use human bones, and the whiteness flashed silver in the moonlight where he stood. He didn't have a human face—only little, round, white-rimmed eyes on a black ceremonial mask.

Leon was better in a few days. But he was bitter, and all he could talk about was the cop. "I'll kill the big bastard if he comes around here again," Leon kept saying.

With something like the cop it is better to forget, and I tried to make Leon understand. "It's over now. There's nothing you can do."

I wondered why men who came back from the army were troublemakers on the reservation. Leon even took it before the pueblo meeting. They discussed it, and the old men decided that Leon shouldn't have been drinking. The interpreter read a passage out of the revised pueblo law-and-order code about possessing intoxicants on the reservation, so we got up and left.

Then Leon asked me to go with him to Grants to buy a roll of barbed wire for his uncle. On the way we stopped at Cerritos for gas, and I went into the store for some pop. He was inside. I stopped in the doorway and turned around before he saw me, but if he really was what I feared, then he would not need to see me—he already knew we were there. Leon was waiting with the truck engine running almost like he knew what I would say.

"Let's go—the big cop's inside."

Leon gunned it and the pickup skidded back on the highway. He glanced back in the rear-view mirror. "I didn't see his car."

"Hidden," I said.

Leon shook his head. "He can't do it again. We are just as good as them."

The guys who came back always talked like that.

THREE

The sky was hot and empty. The half-grown tumbleweeds were dried-up flat and brown beside the highway, and across the valley heat shimmered above wilted fields of corn. Even the mountains high beyond the pale sandrock mesas were dusty blue. I was afraid to fall asleep so I kept my eyes on the blue mountains—not letting them close—soaking in the heat; and then I knew why the drought had come that summer.

Leon shook me. "He's behind us—the cop's following us!"

I looked back and saw the red light on top of the car whirling around, and I could make out the dark image of a man, but where the face should have been there were only the silvery lenses of the dark glasses he wore.

"Stop, Leon! He wants us to stop!"

Leon pulled over and stopped on the narrow gravel shoulder.

"What in the hell does he want?" Leon's hands were shaking.

Suddenly the cop was standing beside the truck, gesturing for Leon to roll down his window. He pushed his head inside, grinding the gum in his mouth; the smell of Doublemint was all around us.

"Get out. Both of you."

I stood beside Leon in the dry weeds and tall yellow grass that broke through the asphalt and rattled in the wind. The cop studied Leon's driver's license. I avoided his face—I knew that I couldn't look at his eyes, so I stared at his black half-Wellingtons, with the black uniform cuffs pulled over them; but my eyes kept moving, upward past the black gun belt. My legs were quivering, and I tried to keep my eyes away from his. But it was like the time when I was very little and my parents warned me not to look into the masked dancers' eyes because they would grab me, and my eyes would not stop.

"What's your name?" His voice was high-pitched and it distracted me from the meaning of the words.

I remember Leon said, "He doesn't understand English so good," and finally I said that I was Antonio Sousea, while my eyes strained to look beyond the silver frosted glasses that he wore; but only my distorted face and squinting eyes reflected back.

And then the cop stared at us for a while, silent; finally he laughed and chewed his gum some more slowly. "Where were you going?"

"To Grants." Leon spoke English very clearly. "Can we go now?"

Leon was twisting the key chain around his fingers, and I felt the sun everywhere. Heat swelled up from the asphalt and when cars went by, hot air and motor smell rushed past us.

"I don't like smart guys, Indian. It's because of you bastards that I'm here. They transferred me here because of Indians. They thought there wouldn't be as many for me here. But I find them." He spit his gum into the weeds near my foot and walked back to the patrol car. It kicked up gravel and dust when he left.

We got back in the pickup, and I could taste sweat in my mouth, so I told Leon that we might as well go home since he would be waiting for us up ahead.

"He can't do this," Leon said. "We've got a right to be on this highway."

I couldn't understand why Leon kept talking about "rights," because it wasn't "rights" that he was after, but Leon didn't seem to understand; he couldn't remember the stories that old Teofilo told.

I didn't feel safe until we turned off the highway and I could see the pueblo and my own house. It was noon, and everybody was eating—the village seemed empty—even the dogs had crawled away from the heat. The door was open, but there was only silence, and I was afraid that something had happened to all of them. Then as soon as I opened the screen door the little kids started crying for more Kool-Aid, and my mother said "no," and it was noisy again like always. Grandfather commented that it had been a fast trip to Grants, and I said "yeah" and didn't explain because it would've only worried them.

"Leon goes looking for trouble—I wish you wouldn't hang around with him." My father didn't like trouble. But I knew that the cop was something terrible, and even to speak about it risked bringing it close to all of us; so I didn't say anything.

That afternoon Leon spoke with the Governor, and he promised to send letters to the Bureau of Indian Affairs and to the State Police Chief. Leon seemed satisfied with that. I reached into my pocket for the arrowhead on the piece of string.

"What's that for?"

I held it out to him. "Here, wear it around your neck—like mine. See? Just in case," I said, "for protection."

"You don't believe in *that*, do you?" He pointed to a .30-30 leaning against the wall. "I'll take this with me whenever I'm in the pickup."

"But you can't be sure that it will kill one of them."

Leon looked at me and laughed. "What's the matter," he said, "have they brainwashed you into believing that a .30-30 won't kill a white man?" He handed back the arrowhead. "Here, you wear two of them."

FOUR

Leon's uncle asked me if I wanted to stay at the sheep camp for a while. The lambs were big, and there wouldn't be much for me to do, so I told him I would. We left early, while the sun was still low and red in the sky. The highway was empty, and I sat there beside Leon imagining what it was like before there were highways or even horses. Leon turned off the highway onto the sheep-camp road that climbs around the sandstone mesas until suddenly all the trees are piñons.

Leon glanced in the rear-view mirror. "He's following us!"

My body began to shake and I wasn't sure if I would be able to speak. "There's no place left to hide. It follows us everywhere."

Leon looked at me like he didn't understand what I'd said. Then I looked past Leon and saw that the patrol car had pulled up beside us; the piñon branches were whipping and scraping the side of the truck as it tried to force us off the road. Leon kept driving with the two right wheels in the rut—bumping and scraping the trees. Leon never looked over at it so he couldn't have known how the reflections kept moving across the mirror-lenses of the dark glasses. We were in the narrow canyon with pale sandstone close on either side—the canyon that ended with a spring where willows and grass and tiny blue flowers grow.

"We've got to kill it, Leon. We must burn the body to be sure."

Leon didn't seem to be listening. I kept wishing that old Teofilo could have been there to chant the proper words while we did it. Leon stopped the truck and got out—he still didn't understand what it was. I sat in the pickup with the .30-30 across my lap, and my hands were slippery.

The big cop was standing in front of the pickup, facing Leon. "You made your mistake, Indian. I'm going to beat the shit out of you." He raised the billy club slowly. "I like to beat Indians with this."

He moved toward Leon with the stick raised high, and it was like the long bone in my dream when he pointed it at me—a human bone painted brown to look like wood, to hide what it really was; they'll do that, you know—carve the bone into a spoon and use it around the house until the victim comes within range.

The shot sounded far away and I couldn't remember aiming. But he was motionless on the ground and the bone wand lay near his feet. The tumble-weeds and tall yellow grass were sprayed with glossy, bright blood. He was on his back, and the sand between his legs and along his left side was soaking up the dark, heavy blood—it had not rained for a long time, and even the tumble-weeds were dying.

"Tony! You killed him—you killed the cop!"

"Help me! We'll set the car on fire."

Leon acted strange, and he kept looking at me like he wanted to run. The head wobbled and swung back and forth, and the left hand and the legs left individual trails in the sand. The face was the same. The dark glasses hadn't fallen off and they blinded me with their hot-sun reflections until I pushed the body into the front seat.

The gas tank exploded and the flames spread along the underbelly of the car. The tires filled the wide sky with spirals of thick black smoke.

"My God, Tony. What's wrong with you? That's a state cop you killed." Leon was pale and shaking.

I wiped my hands on my Levis. "Don't worry, everything is O.K. now, Leon. It's killed. They sometimes take on strange forms."

The tumbleweeds around the car caught fire, and little heatwaves shimmered up toward the sky; in the west, rain clouds were gathering.

Susan Sontag

THE WAY WE LIVE NOW

SUSAN SONTAG (1933–2004) is the author of numerous books of fiction and nonfiction, including the novels *In America* and *The Volcano Lover;* the play, *Alice in Bed;* the collection of stories, *I, etcetera;* and the collection of essays, *Illness as Metaphor and AIDS and Its Metaphors.* Ms. Sontag died in New York City on December 28, 2004.

At first he was just losing weight, he felt only a little ill, Max said to Ellen, and he didn't call for an appointment with his doctor, according to Greg, because he was managing to keep on working at more or less the same rhythm, but he did stop smoking, Tanya pointed out, which suggests he was frightened, but also that he wanted, even more than he knew, to be healthy, or healthier, or maybe just to gain back a few pounds, said Orson, for he told her, Tanya went on, that he expected to be climbing the walls (isn't that what people say?) and found, to his surprise, that he didn't miss cigarettes at all and revelled in the sensation of his lungs being ache-free for the first time in years. But did he have a good doctor, Stephen wanted to know, since it would have been crazy not to go for a checkup after the pressure was off and he was back from the conference in Helsinki, even if by then he was feeling better. And he said, to Frank, that he would go, even though he was indeed frightened, as he admitted to Jan, but who wouldn't be frightened now, though, odd as that might seem, he hadn't been worrying until recently, he avowed to Quentin, it was only in the last six months that he had the metallic taste of panic in his mouth, because becoming seriously ill was something that happened to other people, a normal delusion, he observed to Paolo, if one was thirty-eight and had never had a serious illness; he wasn't, as Jan confirmed, a hypochondriac. Of course, it was hard not to worry, everyone was worried, but it wouldn't do to panic, because, as Max pointed out to Quentin, there wasn't anything one could do except wait and hope, wait and start being careful, be careful, and hope. And even if one did prove to be ill, one shouldn't give up, they had new treatments that promised an arrest of the disease's inexorable course, research was progressing. It seemed that everyone was in touch with everyone else several times a week, checking in, I've never spent so many hours at a time on the phone, Stephen said to Kate, and when I'm exhausted after the two or three calls made to me, giving me the latest, instead of switching off the phone to give myself a respite I tap out the number of another friend or acquaintance, to pass on the news. I'm not sure I can afford to think so much about it, Ellen said, and I suspect my own motives, there's something morbid I'm getting used to, getting excited by, this must be like what people felt in London during the Blitz. As far as I know, I'm not at risk, but you never know, said Aileen. This thing is totally unprecedented, said Frank. But don't you think he ought to see a doctor, Stephen insisted. Listen, said Orson, you can't force people to take care of themselves, and what makes you think the worst, he could be just run-down, people still do get ordinary illnesses, awful ones, why are you assuming it has to be *that*. But all I want to be sure, said Stephen, is that he understands the options, because most people don't, that's why they won't see a doctor or have the test, they think there's nothing one can do. But is there anything one can do, he said to Tanya (according to Greg), I mean what do I gain if I go to the doctor; if I'm really ill, he's reported to have said, I'll find out soon enough.

And when he was in the hospital, his spirits seemed to lighten, according to Donny. He seemed more cheerful than he had been in the last months, Ursula said, and the bad news seemed to come almost as a relief, according to Ira, as a truly unexpected blow, according to Quentin, but you'd hardly expect him to have said the same thing to all his friends, because his relation to Ira was so different from his relation to Quentin (this according to Quentin, who was proud of their friendship), and perhaps he thought Quentin wouldn't be undone by seeing him weep, but Ira insisted that couldn't be the reason he behaved so differently with each, and that maybe he was feeling less shocked, mobilizing his strength to fight for his life, at the moment he saw Ira but overcome by feelings of hopelessness when Quentin arrived with flowers, because anyway the flowers threw him into a bad mood, as Quentin told Kate, since the hospital room was choked with flowers, you couldn't have crammed another flower into that room, but surely you're exaggerating, Kate said, smiling, everybody likes flowers. Well, who wouldn't exaggerate at a time like this, Quentin said sharply. Don't you think *this* is an exaggeration. Of course I do, said Kate gently, I was only teasing, I mean I didn't mean to tease. I know that, Quentin said, with tears in his eyes, and Kate hugged him and said well, when I go this evening I guess I won't bring flowers, what does he want, and Quentin said, according to Max, what he likes best is chocolate. Is there anything else, asked Kate, I mean like chocolate but not chocolate. Licorice, said Quentin, blowing his nose. And besides that. Aren't *you* exaggerating now, Quentin said, smiling. Right, said Kate, so if I want to bring him a whole raft of stuff, besides chocolate and licorice, what else. Jelly beans, Quentin said.

· · ·

He didn't want to be alone, according to Paolo, and lots of people came in the first week, and the Jamaican nurse said there were other patients on the floor who would be glad to have the surplus flowers, and people weren't afraid to visit, it wasn't like the old days, as Kate pointed out to Aileen, they're not even segregated in the hospital any more, as Hilda observed, there's nothing on the door of his room warning visitors of the possibility of contagion, as there was a few years ago; in fact, he's in a double room and, as he told Orson, the old guy on the far side of the curtain (who's clearly on the way out, said Stephen) doesn't even have the disease, so, as Kate went on, you really should go and see him, he'd be happy to see you, he likes having people visit, you aren't not going because you're afraid, are you. Of course not, Aileen said, but I don't know what to say, I think I'll feel awkward, which he's bound to notice, and that will make him feel worse, so I won't be doing him any good, will I. But he won't notice anything, Kate said, patting Aileen's hand, it's not like that, it's not the way you imagine, he's not judging people or wondering about their motives, he's just happy to see his friends. But I never was really a friend of his, Aileen said, you're a friend, he's always liked you, you told me he talks about Nora with you, I know he likes me, he's even attracted to me, but he respects you. But, according to Wesley, the reason Aileen was so stingy with her visits was that she could never have him to herself, there were always others there already and by the time they left still others had arrived, she'd been in love with him for years, and I can understand, said Donny, that Aileen should feel bitter that if there could have been a woman friend he did more than occasionally bed, a woman he really loved, and my God, Victor said, who had known him in those years, he was crazy about Nora, what a heartrending couple they were, two surly angels, then it couldn't have been she.

And when some of the friends, the ones who came every day, waylaid the doctor in the corridor, Stephen was the one who asked the most informed questions, who'd been keeping up not just with the stories that appeared several times a week in the *Times* (which Greg confessed to have stopped reading, unable to stand it any more) but with articles in the medical journals published here and in England and France, and who knew socially one of the principal doctors in Paris who was doing some much-publicized research on the disease, but his doctor said little more than that the pneumonia was not life-threatening, the fever was subsiding, of course he was still weak but he was responding well to the antibiotics, that he'd have to complete his stay in the hospital, which entailed a minimum of twenty-one days on the I.V., before she could start him on the new drug, for she was optimistic about the possibility of getting him into the protocol; and when Victor said that if he had so much trouble eating (he'd say to everyone, when they coaxed him to eat some of the hospital meals, that

588 / SUSAN SONTAG

food didn't taste right, that he had a funny metallic taste in his mouth) it couldn't be good that friends were bringing him all that chocolate, the doctor just smiled and said that in these cases the patient's morale was also an important factor, and if chocolate made him feel better she saw no harm in it, which worried Stephen, as Stephen said later to Donny, because they wanted to believe in the promises and taboos of today's high-tech medicine but here this reassuringly curt and silver-haired specialist in the disease, someone quoted frequently in the papers, was talking like some oldfangled country G.P. who tells the family that tea with honey or chicken soup may do as much for the patient as penicillin, which might mean, as Max said, that they were just going through the motions of treating him, that they were not sure about what to do, or rather, as Xavier interjected, that they didn't know what the hell they were doing, that the truth, the real truth, as Hilda said, upping the ante, was that they didn't, the doctors, really have any hope.

Oh, no, said Lewis, I can't stand it, wait a minute, I can't believe it, are you sure, I mean are they sure, have they done all the tests, it's getting so when the phone rings I'm scared to answer because I think it will be someone telling me someone else is ill; but did Lewis really not know until yesterday, Robert said testily, I find that hard to believe, everybody is talking about it, it seems impossible that someone wouldn't have called Lewis; and perhaps Lewis did know, was for some reason pretending not to know already, because, Jan recalled, didn't Lewis say something months ago to Greg, and not only to Greg, about his not looking well, losing weight, and being worried about him and wishing he'd see a doctor, so it couldn't come as a total surprise. Well, everybody is worried about everybody now, said Betsy, that seems to be the way we live, the way we live now. And, after all, they were once very close, doesn't Lewis still have the keys to his apartment, you know the way you let someone keep the keys after you've broken up, only a little because you hope the person might just saunter in, drunk or high, late some evening, but mainly because it's wise to have a few sets of keys strewn around town, if you live alone, at the top of a former commercial building that, pretentious as it is, will never acquire a doorman or even a resident superintendent, someone whom you can call on for the keys late one night if you find you've lost yours or have locked yourself out. Who else has keys, Tanya inquired, I was thinking somebody might drop by tomorrow before coming to the hospital and bring some treasures, because the other day, Ira said, he was complaining about how dreary the hospital room was, and how it was like being locked up in a motel room, which got everybody started telling funny stories about motel rooms they'd known, and at Ursula's story, about the Luxury Budget Inn in Schenectady, there was an uproar of laughter around his bed, while he watched them in silence, eyes bright with fever, all the while, as Victor recalled, gobbling that damned chocolate. But, according to Jan, whom Lewis's keys enabled to tour the swank of his bachelor lair with an eye to bringing over some art consolation to brighten up the hospital room, the Byzantine icon wasn't on the wall over his bed, and that was a puzzle until Orson remembered that he'd recounted without seeming upset (this disputed by Greg) that the boy he'd recently gotten rid of had stolen it, along with four of the *maki-e* lacquer boxes, as if these were objects as easy to sell on the street as a TV or a stereo. But he's always been very generous, Kate said quietly, and though he loves beautiful things isn't really attached to them, to things, as Orson said, which is unusual in a collector, as Frank commented, and when Kate shuddered and tears sprang to her eyes and Orson inquired anxiously if he, Orson, had said something wrong, she pointed out that they'd begun talking about him in a retrospective mode, summing up what he was like, what made them fond of him, as if he were finished, completed, already a part of the past.

Perhaps he was getting tired of having so many visitors, said Robert, who was, as Ellen couldn't help mentioning, someone who had come only twice and was probably looking for a reason not to be in regular attendance, but there could be no doubt, according to Ursula, that his spirits had dipped, not that there was any discouraging news from the doctors, and he seemed now to prefer being alone a few hours of the day; and he told Donny that he'd begun keeping a diary for the first time in his life, because he wanted to record the course of his mental reactions to this astonishing turn of events, to do something parallel to what the doctors were doing, who came every morning and conferred at his bedside about his body, and that perhaps it wasn't so important what he wrote in it, which amounted, as he said wryly to Quentin, to little more than the usual banalities about terror and amazement that this was happening to him, to him also, plus the usual remorseful assessments of his past life, his pardonable superficialities, capped by resolves to live better, more deeply, more in touch with his work and his friends, and not to care so passionately about what people thought of him, interspersed with admonitions to himself that in this situation his will to live counted more than anything else and that if he really wanted to live, and trusted life, and liked himself well enough (down, ol' debbil Thanatos!), he *would* live, he would be an exception; but perhaps all this, as Quentin ruminated, talking on the phone to Kate, wasn't the point, the point was that by the very keeping of the diary he was accumulating something to reread one day, slyly staking out his claim to a future time, in which the diary would be an object, a relic, in which he might not actually reread it, because he would want to have put this ordeal behind him, but the diary would be there in the drawer of his stupendous Majorelle desk, and he could already, he did actually say to Quentin one late sunny afternoon, propped up in the hospital bed, with the stain of chocolate framing one corner of a heartbreaking smile, see himself in the penthouse, the October sun streaming through those clear windows instead of this streaked one, and the diary, the pathetic diary, safe inside the drawer.

It doesn't matter about the treatment's side effects, Stephen said (when talking to Max), I don't know why you're so worried about that, every strong treatment has some dangerous side effects, it's inevitable, you mean otherwise the treatment wouldn't be effective, Hilda interjected, and anyway, Stephen went on doggedly, just because there *are* side effects it doesn't mean he has to get them, or all of them, each one, or even some of them. That's just a list of all the possible things that could go wrong, because the doctors have to cover themselves, so they make up a worst-case scenario, but isn't what's happening to him, and to so many other people, Tanya interrupted, a worst-case scenario, a catastrophe no one could have imagined, it's too cruel, and isn't everything a side effect, quipped Ira, even *we* are all side effects, but we're not bad side effects, Frank said, he likes having his friends around, and we're helping each other, too; because his illness sticks us all in the same glue, mused Xavier, and, whatever the jealousies and grievances from the past that have made us wary and cranky with each other, when something like this happens (the sky is falling, the sky is falling!) you understand what's really important. I agree, Chicken Little, he is reported to have said. But don't you think, Quentin observed to Max, that being as close to him as we are, making time to drop by the hospital every day, is a way of our trying to define ourselves more firmly and irrevocably as the well, those who aren't ill, who aren't going to fall ill, as if what's happened to him couldn't happen to us, when in fact the chances are that before long one of us will end up where he is, which is probably what he felt when he was one of the cohort visiting Zack in the spring (you never knew Zack, did you?), and, according to Clarice, Zack's widow, he didn't come very often, he said he hated hospitals, and didn't feel he was doing Zack any good, that Zack would see on his face how uncomfortable he was. Oh, he was one of those, Aileen said. A coward. Like me.

And after he was sent home from the hospital, and Quentin had volunteered to move in and was cooking meals and taking telephone messages and keeping the mother in Mississippi informed, well, mainly keeping her from flying to New York and heaping her grief on her son and confusing the household routine with her oppressive ministrations, he was able to work an hour or two in his study, on days he didn't insist on going out, for a meal or a movie, which tired him. He seemed optimistic, Kate thought, his appetite was good, and what he said, Orson reported, was that he agreed when Stephen advised him that the main thing was to keep in shape, he was a fighter, right, he wouldn't be who he was if he weren't, and was he ready for the big fight, Stephen asked rhetorically (as Max told it to Donny), and he said you bet, and Stephen added it could be a lot worse, you could have gotten the disease two years ago, but now so many scientists are working on it, the American team and the French team, everyone bucking for that Nobel Prize a few years down the road, that all you have to do is stay healthy for another year or two and then there will be good treatment, real treatment. Yes, he said, Stephen said, my timing is good. And Betsy, who had been climbing on and rolling off macrobiotic diets for a decade, came up with a Japanese specialist she wanted him to see but thank God, Donny reported, he'd had the sense to refuse, but he did agree to see Victor's visualization therapist, although what could one possibly visualize, said Hilda, when the point of visualizing disease was to see it as an entity with contours, borders, here rather than there, something limited, something you were the host of, in the sense that you could disinvite the disease, while this was so total; or would be, Max said. But the main thing, said Greg, was to see that he didn't go the macrobiotic route, which might be harmless for plump Betsy but could only be devastating for him, lean as he'd always been, with all the cigarettes and other appetite-suppressing chemicals he'd been welcoming into his body for years; and now was hardly the time, as Stephen pointed out, to be worried about cleaning up his act, and eliminating the chemical additives and other pollutants that we're all blithely or not so blithely feasting on, blithely since we're healthy, healthy as we can be; so far, Ira said. Meat and potatoes is what I'd be happy to see him eating, Ursula said wistfully. And spaghetti and clam sauce, Greg added. And thick cholesterol-rich omelettes with smoked mozzarella, suggested Yvonne, who had flown from London for the weekend to see him. Chocolate cake, said Frank. Maybe not chocolate cake, Ursula said, he's already eating so much chocolate.

And when, not right away but still only three weeks later, he was accepted into the protocol for the new drug, which took considerable behind-the-scenes lobbying with the doctors, he talked less about being ill, according to Donny, which seemed like a good sign, Kate felt, a sign that he was not feeling like a victim, feeling not that he *had* a disease but, rather, was living *with* a disease (that was the right cliché, wasn't it?), a more hospitable arrangement, said Jan, a kind of cohabitation which implied that it was something temporary, that it could be terminated, but terminated how, said Hilda, and when you say hospitable, Jan, I hear hospital. And it was encouraging, Stephen insisted, that from the start, at least from the time he was finally persuaded to make the telephone call to his doctor, he was willing to say the name of the disease, pronounce it often and easily, as if it were just another word, like boy or gallery or cigarette or money or deal, as in no big deal, Paolo interjected, because, as Stephen continued, to utter the name is a sign of health, a sign that one has accepted being who one is, mortal, vulnerable, not exempt, not an exception after all, it's a sign that one is willing, truly willing, to fight for one's life. And we must say the name, too, and often, Tanya added, we mustn't lag behind him in honesty, or let him feel that, the effort of honesty having been made, it's something done with and he can go on to other things. One is so much better prepared to help him, Wesley replied. In a way he's fortunate, said Yvonne, who had taken care of a problem at the New York store and was flying back to London this evening, sure, fortunate, said Wesley, no one is shunning him, Yvonne went on, no one's afraid to hug him or kiss him lightly on the mouth, in London we are, as usual, a few years behind you, people I know, people who would seem to be not even remotely at risk, are just terrified, but I'm impressed by how cool and rational you all are; you find us cool, asked Quentin. But I have to say, he's reported to have said, I'm terrified, I find it very hard to read (and you know how he loves to read, said Greg; yes, reading is his television, said Paolo) or to think, but I don't feel hysterical. I feel quite hysterical, Lewis said to Yvonne. But you're able to *do* something for him, that's wonderful, how I wish I could stay longer, Yvonne answered, it's rather beautiful, I can't help thinking, this utopia of friendship you've assembled around him (this pathetic utopia, said Kate), so that the disease, Yvonne concluded, is not, any more, out there. Yes, don't you think we're more at home here, with him, with the disease, said Tanya, because the imagined disease is so much worse than the reality of him, whom we all love, each in our fashion, having it. I know for me his getting it has quite demystified the disease, said Jan, I don't feel afraid, spooked, as I did before he became ill, when it was only news about remote acquaintances, whom I never saw again after they became ill. But you know you're not going to come down with the disease, Quentin said, to which Ellen replied, on her behalf, that's not the point, and possibly untrue, my gynaecologist says that everyone is at risk, everyone who has a sexual life, because sexuality is a chain that links each of us to many others, unknown others, and now the great chain of being has become a chain of death as well. It's not the same for you, Quentin insisted, it's not the same for you as it is for me or Lewis or Frank or Paolo or Max, I'm more and more frightened, and I have every reason to be. I don't think about whether I'm at risk or not, said Hilda, I know that I was afraid to know someone with the disease, afraid of what I'd see, what I'd feel, and after the first day I came to the hospital I felt so relieved. I'll never feel that way, that fear, again; he doesn't seem different from me. He's not, Quentin said.

According to Lewis, he talked more often about those who visited more often, which is natural, said Betsy, I think he's even keeping a tally. And among those who came or checked in by phone every day, the inner circle as it were, those who were getting more points, there was still a further competition, which was what was getting on Betsy's nerves, she confessed to Jan; there's always that vulgar jockeying for position around the bedside of the gravely ill, and though we all feel suffused with virtue at our loyalty to him (speak for yourself, said Jan), to the extent that we're carving time out of every day, or almost every day, though some of us are dropping out, as Xavier pointed out, aren't we getting at least as much out of this as he is. Are we, said Jan. We're rivals for a sign from him of special pleasure over a visit, each stretching for the brass ring of his favor, wanting to feel the most wanted, the true nearest and dearest, which is inevitable with someone who doesn't have a spouse and children or an official in-house lover, hierarchies that no one would dare contest, Betsy went on, so we are the family he's founded, without meaning to, without official titles and ranks (we, we, snarled Quentin); and is it so clear, though some of us, Lewis and Quentin and Tanya and Paolo, among others, are ex-lovers and all of us more or less than friends, which one of us he prefers, Victor said (now it's us, raged Quentin), because sometimes I think he looks forward more to seeing Aileen, who has visited only three times, twice at the hospital and once since he's been home, than he does you or me; but, according to Tanya, after being very disappointed that Aileen hadn't come, now he was angry, while, according to Xavier, he was not really hurt but touchingly passive, accepting Aileen's absence as something he somehow deserved. But he's happy to have people around, said Lewis; he says when he doesn't have company he gets very sleepy, he sleeps (according to Quentin), and then perks up when someone arrives, it's important that he not feel ever alone. But, said Victor, there's one person he hasn't heard from, whom he'd probably like to hear from more than most of us; but she didn't just vanish, even right after she broke away from him, and he knows exactly where she lives now, said Kate, he told me he put in a call to her last Christmas Eve, and she said it's nice to hear from you and Merry Christmas, and he was shattered, according to Orson, and furious and disdainful, according to Ellen (what do you expect of her, said Wesley, she was burned out), but Kate wondered if maybe he hadn't phoned Nora in the middle of a sleepless night, what's the time difference, and Quentin said no, I don't think so, I think he wouldn't want her to know.

And when he was feeling even better and had regained the pounds he'd shed right away in the hospital, though the refrigerator started to fill up with organic wheat germ and grapefruit and skimmed milk (he's worried about his cholesterol count, Stephen lamented), and told Quentin he could manage by himself now, and did, he started asking everyone who visited how he looked, and everyone said he looked great, so much better than a few weeks ago, which didn't jibe with what anyone had told him at that time; but then it was getting harder and harder to know how he looked, to answer such a question honestly when among themselves they wanted to be honest, both for honesty's sake and (as Donny thought) to prepare for the worst, because he'd been looking like *this* for so long, at least it seemed so long, that it was as if he'd always been like this, how did he look before, but it was only a few months, and those words, pale and wan-looking and fragile, hadn't they always applied? And one Thursday Ellen, meeting Lewis at the door of the building, said, as they rode up together in the elevator, how is he *really?* But you see how he is, Lewis said tartly, he's fine, he's perfectly healthy, and Ellen understood that of course Lewis didn't think he was perfectly healthy but that he wasn't worse, and that was true, but wasn't it, well, almost heartless to talk like that. Seems inoffensive to me, Quentin said, but I know what you mean, I remember once talking to Frank, somebody, after all, who has volunteered to do five hours a week of office work at the Crisis Center (I know, said Ellen), and Frank was going on about this guy, diagnosed almost a year ago, and so much further along, who'd been complaining to Frank on the phone about the indifference of some doctor, and had gotten quite abusive about the doctor, and Frank was saying there was no reason to be so upset, the implication being that *he,* Frank, wouldn't behave so irrationally, and I said, barely able to control my scorn, but Frank, Frank, he has every reason to be upset, he's dying, and Frank said, said according to Quentin, oh, I don't like to think about it that way.

And it was while he was still home, recuperating, getting his weekly treatment, still not able to do much work, he complained, but, according to Quentin, up and about most of the time and turning up at the office several days a week, that bad news came about two remote acquaintances, one in Houston and one in Paris, news that was intercepted by Quentin on the ground that it could only depress him, but Stephen contended that it was wrong to lie to him, it was so important for him to live in the truth; that had been one of his first victories, that he was candid, that he was even willing to crack jokes about the disease, but Ellen said it wasn't good to give him this end-of-the-world feeling, too many people were getting ill, it was becoming such a common destiny that maybe some of the will to fight for his life would be drained out of him if it seemed to be as natural as, well, death. Oh, Hilda said, who didn't know personally either the one in Houston or the one in Paris, but knew *of* the one in Paris, a pianist who specialized in twentieth-century Czech and Polish music, I have his records, he's such a valuable person, and, when Kate glared at her, continued defensively, I know every life is equally sacred, but that *is* a thought, another thought, I mean, all these valuable people who aren't going to have their normal four score as it is now, these people aren't going to be replaced, and it's such a loss to the culture. But this isn't going to go on for ever, Wesley said, it can't, they're bound to come up with something (they, they, muttered Stephen), but did you ever think, Greg said, that if some people don't die, I mean even if they can keep them alive (they, they, muttered Kate), they continue to be carriers, and that means, if you have a conscience, that you can never make love, make love fully, as you'd been wont—wantonly, Ira said—to do. But it's better than dying, said

Frank. And in all his talk about the future, when he allowed himself to be hope-ful, according to Quentin, he never mentioned the prospect that even if he didn't die, if he were so fortunate as to be among the first generation of the disease's survivors, never mentioned, Kate confirmed, that whatever happened it was over, the way he had lived until now, but, according to Ira, he did think about it, the end of bravado, the end of folly, the end of trusting life, the end of taking life for granted, and of treating life as something that, samurai-like, he thought himself ready to throw away lightly, impudently; and Kate recalled, sighing, a brief exchange she'd insisted on having as long as two years ago, hud-dling on a banquette covered with steel-grey industrial carpet on an upper level of The Prophet and toking up for their next foray on to the dance floor: she'd said hesitantly, for it felt foolish asking a prince of debauchery to, well, take it easy, and she wasn't keen on playing big sister, a role, as Hilda confirmed, he inspired in many women, are you being careful, honey, you know what I mean. And he replied, Kate went on, no, I'm not, listen, I can't, I just can't, sex is too important to me, always has been (he started talking like that, according to Vic-tor, after Nora left him), and if I get it, well, I get it. But he wouldn't talk like that now, would he, said Greg; he must feel awfully foolish now, said Betsy, like someone who went on smoking, saying I can't give up cigarettes, but when the bad X-ray is taken even the most besotted nicotine addict can stop on a dime. But sex isn't like cigarettes, is it, said Frank, and, besides, what good does it do to remember that he was reckless, said Lewis angrily, the appalling thing is that you just have to be unlucky once, and wouldn't he feel even worse if he'd stopped three years ago and had come down with it anyway, since one of the most terrifying features of the disease is that you don't know when you con-tracted it, it could have been ten years ago, because surely this disease has ex-isted for years and years, long before it was recognized; that is, named. Who knows how long (I think a lot about that, said Max) and who knows (I know what you're going to say, Stephen interrupted) how many are going to get it.

I'm feeling fine, he's reported to have said whenever someone asked him how he was, which was almost always the first question anyone asked. Or: I'm feeling better, how are you? But he said other things, too. I'm playing leapfrog with myself, he is reported to have said, according to Victor. And: There must be a way to get something positive out of this situation, he's reported to have said to Kate. How American of him, said Paolo. Well, said Betsy, you know the old American adage: When you've got a lemon, make lemonade. The one thing I'm sure I couldn't take, Jan said he said to her, is becoming disfigured, but Stephen hastened to point out the disease doesn't take that form very often any more, its profile is mutating, and, in conversation with Ellen, wheeled up words like blood-brain barrier; I never thought there was a barrier *there*, said Jan. But he mustn't know about Max, Ellen said, that would really depress him, please don't tell him, he'll have to know, Quentin said grimly, and he'll be furious not to have been told. But there's time for that, when they take Max off the respirator, said Ellen; but isn't it incredible, Frank said, Max was fine, not feeling ill at all, and then to wake up with a fever of a hundred and five, unable to breathe, but that's the way it often starts, with absolutely no warning, Stephen said, the disease has so many forms. And when, after another week had gone by, he asked Quentin where Max was, he didn't question Quentin's account of a spree in the Bahamas, but then the number of people who visited regularly was thinning out, partly because the old feuds that had been put aside through the first hospitalization and the return home had resurfaced, and the flickering enmity between Lewis and Frank exploded, even though Kate did her best to mediate between them, and also because he himself had done something to loosen the bonds of love that united the friends around him, by seeming to take them all for granted, as if it were perfectly normal for so many people to carve out so much time and attention for him, visit him every few days, talk about him incessantly on the phone with each other; but, according to Paolo, it wasn't that he was less grateful, it was just something he was getting used to, the visits. It had become, with time, a more ordinary kind of situation, a kind of ongoing party, first at the hospital and now since he was home, barely on his feet again, it being clear, said Robert, that I'm on the B list; but Kate said, that's absurd, there's no list; and Victor said, but there is, only it's not he, it's Quentin who's drawing it up. He wants to see us, we're helping him, we have to do it the way he wants, he fell down yesterday on the way to the bathroom, he mustn't be told about Max (but he already knew, according to Donny), it's getting worse.

When I was home, he is reported to have said, I was afraid to sleep, as I was dropping off each night it felt like just that, as if I were falling down a black hole, to sleep felt like giving in to death, I slept every night with the light on; but here, in the hospital, I'm less afraid. And to Quentin he said, one morning, the fear rips through me, it tears me open; and, to Ira, it presses me together, squeezes me toward myself. Fear gives everything its hue, its high. I feel so, I don't know how to say it, exalted, he said to Quentin. Calamity is an amazing high, too. Sometimes I feel *so* well, so powerful, it's as if I could jump out of my skin. Am I going crazy, or what? Is it all this attention and coddling I'm getting from everybody, like a child's dream of being loved? Is it the drugs? I know it sounds crazy but sometimes I think this is a *fantastic* experience, he said shyly; but there was also the bad taste in the mouth, the pressure in the head and at the back of the neck, the red, bleeding gums, the painful, if pink-lobed, breathing, and his ivory pallor, color of white chocolate. Among those who wept when told over the phone that he was back in the hospital were Kate and Stephen (who'd been called by Quentin), and Ellen, Victor, Aileen, and Lewis (who were called by Kate), and Xavier and Ursula (who were called by Stephen). Among those who didn't weep were Hilda, who said that she'd just learned that her seventy-five-year-old aunt was dying of the disease, which she'd contracted from a transfusion given during her successful double bypass of five years ago, and Frank and Donny and Betsy, but this didn't mean, according to Tanya, that they weren't moved and appalled, and Quentin thought they might not be coming soon to the hospital but would send presents; the room, he was in a private room this time, was filling up with flowers, and plants, and books, and tapes. The high tide of barely suppressed acrimony of the last weeks at home subsided into the routines of hospital visiting, though more than a few resented Quentin's having charge of the visiting book (but it was Quentin who had the idea, Lewis pointed out); now, to insure a steady stream of visitors, preferably no more than two at a time (this, the rule in all hospitals, wasn't enforced here, at least on his floor; whether out of kindness or inefficiency, no one could decide), Quentin had to be called first, to get one's time slot, there was no more casual dropping by. And his mother could no longer be prevented from taking a plane and installing herself in a hotel near the hospital; but he seemed to mind her daily presence less than expected, Quentin said; said Ellen it's we who mind, do you suppose she'll stay long. It was easier to be generous with each other visiting him here in the hospital, as Donny pointed out, than at home, where one minded never being alone with him; coming here, in our twos and twos, there's no doubt about what our role is, how we should be, collective, funny, distracting, undemanding, light, it's important to be light, for in all this dread there is gaiety, too, as the poet said, said Kate. (His eyes, his glittering eyes, said Lewis.) His eyes looked dull, extinguished, Wesley said to Xavier, but Betsy said his face, not just his eyes, looked soulful, warm; whatever is there, said Kate, I've never been so aware of his eyes; and Stephen said, I'm afraid of what my eyes show, the way I watch him, with too much intensity, or a phony kind of casualness, said Victor. And, unlike at home, he was clean-shaven each morning, at whatever hour they visited him; his curly hair was always combed; but he complained that the nurses had changed since he was here the last time, and that he didn't like the change, he wanted everyone to be the same. The room was furnished now with some of his personal effects (odd word for one's things, said Ellen), and Tanya brought drawings and a letter from her nine-year-old dyslexic son, who was writing now, since she'd purchased a computer; and Donny brought champagne and some helium balloons, which were anchored to the foot of his bed; tell me about something that's going on, he said, waking up from a nap to find Donny and Kate at the side of his bed, beaming at him; tell me a story, he said wistfully, said Donny, who couldn't think of anything to say; you're the story, Kate said. And Xavier brought an eighteenth-century Guatemalan wooden statue of St. Sebastian with upcast eyes and open mouth, and when Tanya said what's that, a tribute to eros past, Xavier said where I come from Sebastian is venerated as a protector against pestilence.

Pestilence symbolized by arrows? Symbolized by arrows. All people remember is the body of a beautiful youth bound to a tree, pierced by arrows (of which he always seems oblivious, Tanya interjected), people forget that the story continues, Xavier continued, that when the Christian women came to bury the martyr they found him still alive and nursed him back to health. And he said, according to Stephen, I didn't know St. Sebastian didn't die. It's undeniable, isn't it, said Kate on the phone to Stephen, the fascination of the dying. It makes me ashamed. We're learning how to die, said Hilda, I'm not ready to learn, said Aileen; and Lewis, who was coming straight from the other hospital, the hospital where Max was still being kept in I.C.U., met Tanya getting out of the elevator on the tenth floor, and as they walked together down the shiny corridor past the open doors, averting their eyes from the other patients sunk in their beds, with tubes in their noses, irradiated by the bluish light from the television sets, the thing I can't bear to think about, Tanya said to Lewis, is someone dying with the TV on.

He has that strange, unnerving detachment now, said Ellen, that's what upsets me, even though it makes it easier to be with him. Sometimes he was querulous. I can't stand them coming in here taking my blood every morning, what are they doing with all that blood, he is reported to have said; but where was his anger, Jan wondered. Mostly he was lovely to be with, always saying how are *you*, how are you feeling. He's so sweet now, said Aileen. He's so nice, said Tanya. (Nice, nice, groaned Paolo.) At first he was very ill, but he was rallying, according to Stephen's best information, there was no fear of his not recovering this time, and the doctor spoke of his being discharged from the hospital in another ten days if all went well, and the mother was persuaded to fly back to Mississippi, and Quentin was readying the penthouse for his return. And he was still writing his diary, not showing it to anyone, though Tanya, first to arrive one late-winter morning, and finding him dozing, peeked, and was horrified, according to Greg, not by anything she read but by a progressive change in his handwriting: in the recent pages, it was becoming spidery, less legible, and some lines of script wandered and tilted about the page. I was thinking, Ursula said to Quentin, that the difference between a story and a painting or photograph is that in a story you can write, He's still alive. But in a painting or a photo you can't show 'still.' You can just show him being alive. He's still alive, Stephen said.

Amy Tan

TWO KINDS

AMY TAN (1952–) was born in the United States to immigrant parents from China. Her novels are *The Joy Luck Club, The Kitchen God's Wife, The Hundred Secret Senses, The Bonesetter's Daughter,* and *Saving Fish from Drowning,* all *New York Times* bestsellers and the recipients of various awards. She is also the author of a memoir, *The Opposite of Fate;* two children's books, *The Moon Lady* and *The Chinese Siamese Cat;* and numerous articles for magazines, including *The New Yorker, Harper's,* and *National Geographic.* Her current work includes writing a new novel, collaborating on an original television pilot with director Wayne Wang and cowriter Ron Bass, and creating the libretto for *The Bonesetter's Daughter,* which premieres in September 2008 with the San Francisco Opera. Ms. Tan's other musical work for the stage is limited to serving as lead rhythm dominatrix, backup singer, and second tambourine with the literary garage band, the Rock Bottom Remainders, whose members include Stephen King, Dave Barry, and Scott Turow. In spite of their dubious talent, their yearly gigs have managed to raise over a million dollars for literacy programs. Ms. Tan lives in San Francisco and New York with her husband, Lou DeMattei, and their two Yorkshire terriers, Bubba Zo and Lilliput.

My mother believed you could be anything you wanted to be in America. You could open a restaurant. You could work for the government and get good retirement. You could buy a house with almost no money down. You could become rich. You could become instantly famous.

"Of course you can be prodigy, too," my mother told me when I was nine. "You can be best anything. What does Auntie Lindo know? Her daughter, she is only best tricky."

America was where all my mother's hopes lay. She had come here in 1949 after losing everything in China: her mother and father, her family home, her first husband, and two daughters, twin baby girls. But she never looked back with regret. There were so many ways for things to get better.

We didn't immediately pick the right kind of prodigy. At first my mother thought I could be a Chinese Shirley Temple. We'd watch Shirley's old movies on TV as though they were training films. My mother would poke my arm and say, *"Ni kan"*—You watch. And I would see Shirley tapping her feet, or singing a sailor song, or pursing her lips into a very round O while saying, "Oh my goodness."

"Ni kan," said my mother as Shirley's eyes flooded with tears. "You already know how. Don't need talent for crying!"

Soon after my mother got this idea about Shirley Temple, she took me to a beauty training school in the Mission district and put me in the hands of a student who could barely hold the scissors without shaking. Instead of getting big fat curls, I emerged with an uneven mass of crinkly black fuzz. My mother dragged me off to the bathroom and tried to wet down my hair.

"You look like Negro Chinese," she lamented, as if I had done this on purpose.

The instructor of the beauty training school had to lop off these soggy clumps to make my hair even again. "Peter Pan is very popular these days," the instructor assured my mother. I now had hair the length of a boy's, with straight-across bangs that hung at a slant two inches above my eyebrows. I liked the haircut and it made me actually look forward to my future fame.

In fact, in the beginning, I was just as excited as my mother, maybe even more so. I pictured this prodigy part of me as many different images, trying each one on for size. I was a dainty ballerina girl standing by the curtains, waiting to hear the right music that would send me floating on my tiptoes. I was like the Christ child lifted out of the straw manger, crying with holy indignity. I was Cinderella stepping from her pumpkin carriage with sparkly cartoon music filling the air.

In all of my imaginings, I was filled with a sense that I would soon become *perfect*. My mother and father would adore me. I would be beyond reproach. I would never feel the need to sulk for anything.

But sometimes the prodigy in me became impatient. "If you don't hurry up and get me out of here, I'm disappearing for good," it warned. "And then you'll always be nothing."

Every night after dinner, my mother and I would sit at the Formica kitchen table. She would present new tests, taking her examples from stories of amazing children she had read in *Ripley's Believe It or Not*, or *Good Housekeeping, Reader's Digest*, and a dozen other magazines she kept in a pile in our bathroom. My mother got these magazines from people whose houses she cleaned. And since she cleaned many houses each week, we had a great assortment. She would look through them all, searching for stories about remarkable children.

The first night she brought out a story about a three-year-old boy who knew the capitals of all the states and even most of the European countries. A teacher was quoted as saying the little boy could also pronounce the names of the foreign cities correctly.

"What's the capital of Finland?" my mother asked me, looking at the maga-zine story.

All I knew was the capital of California, because Sacramento was the name of the street we lived on in Chinatown. "Nairobi!" I guessed, saying the most foreign word I could think of. She checked to see if that was possibly one way to pronounce "Helsinki" before showing me the answer.

The tests got harder—multiplying numbers in my head, finding the queen of hearts in a deck of cards, trying to stand on my head without using my hands, predicting the daily temperatures in Los Angeles, New York, and London.

One night I had to look at a page from the Bible for three minutes and then report everything I could remember. "Now Jehoshaphat had riches and honor in abundance and . . . that's all I remember, Ma," I said.

And after seeing my mother's disappointed face once again, something in-side of me began to die. I hated the tests, the raised hopes and failed expecta-tions. Before going to bed that night, I looked in the mirror above the bathroom sink and when I saw only my face staring back—and that it would always be this ordinary face—I began to cry. Such a sad, ugly girl! I made high-pitched noises like a crazed animal, trying to scratch out the face in the mirror.

And then I saw what seemed to be the prodigy side of me—because I had never seen that face before. I looked at my reflection, blinking so I could see more clearly. The girl staring back at me was angry, powerful. This girl and I were the same. I had new thoughts, willful thoughts, or rather thoughts filled with lots of won'ts. I won't let her change me, I promised myself. I won't be what I'm not.

So now on nights when my mother presented her tests, I performed listlessly, my head propped on one arm. I pretended to be bored. And I was. I got so bored I started counting the bellows of the foghorns out on the bay while my mother drilled me in other areas. The sound was comforting and reminded me of the cow jumping over the moon. And the next day, I played a game with myself, seeing if my mother would give up on me before eight bellows. After a while I usually counted only one, maybe two bellows at most. At last she was beginning to give up hope.

Two or three months had gone by without any mention of my being a prodigy again. And then one day my mother was watching *The Ed Sullivan Show* on TV. The TV was old and the sound kept shorting out. Every time my mother got halfway up from the sofa to adjust the set, the sound would go back on and Ed would be talking. As soon as she sat down, Ed would go silent again. She got up, the TV broke into loud piano music. She sat down. Silence. Up and down, back and forth, quiet and loud. It was like a stiff embraceless dance between her and the TV set. Finally she stood by the set with her hand on the sound dial.

She seemed entranced by the music, a little frenzied piano piece with this mesmerizing quality, sort of quick passages and then teasing lilting ones before it returned to the quick playful parts.

"*Ni kan,*" my mother said, calling me over with hurried hand gestures. "Look here."

I could see why my mother was fascinated by the music. It was being pounded out by a little Chinese girl, about nine years old, with a Peter Pan haircut. The girl had the sauciness of a Shirley Temple. She was proudly modest like a proper Chinese child. And she also did this fancy sweep of a curtsy, so that the fluffy skirt of her white dress cascaded slowly to the floor like the petals of a large carnation.

In spite of these warning signs, I wasn't worried. Our family had no piano and we couldn't afford to buy one, let alone reams of sheet music and piano lessons. So I could be generous in my comments when my mother bad-mouthed the little girl on TV.

"Play note right, but doesn't sound good! No singing sound," complained my mother.

"What are you picking on her for?" I said carelessly. "She's pretty good. Maybe she's not the best, but she's trying hard." I knew almost immediately I would be sorry I said that.

"Just like you," she said. "Not the best. Because you not trying." She gave a little huff as she let go of the sound dial and sat down on the sofa.

The little Chinese girl sat down also to play an encore of "Anitra's Dance" by Grieg. I remember the song, because later on I had to learn how to play it.

Three days after watching *The Ed Sullivan Show*, my mother told me what my schedule would be for piano lessons and piano practice. She had talked to Mr. Chong, who lived on the first floor of our apartment building. Mr. Chong was a retired piano teacher and my mother had traded housecleaning services for weekly lessons and a piano for me to practice on every day, two hours a day, from four until six.

When my mother told me this, I felt as though I had been sent to hell. I whined and then kicked my foot a little when I couldn't stand it anymore.

"Why don't you like me the way I am? I'm *not* a genius! I can't play the piano. And even if I could, I wouldn't go on TV if you paid me a million dollars!" I cried.

My mother slapped me. "Who ask you be genius?" she shouted. "Only ask you be your best. For you sake. You think I want you be genius? Hnnh! What for! Who ask you!"

"So ungrateful," I heard her mutter in Chinese. "If she had as much talent as she has temper, she would be famous now."

Mr. Chong, whom I secretly nicknamed Old Chong, was very strange, always tapping his fingers to the silent music of an invisible orchestra. He looked ancient in my eyes. He had lost most of the hair on top of his head and he wore thick glasses and had eyes that always looked tired and sleepy. But he must have been younger than I thought, since he lived with his mother and was not yet married.

I met Old Lady Chong once and that was enough. She had this peculiar smell like a baby that had done something in its pants. And her fingers felt like a dead person's, like an old peach I once found in the back of the refrigerator; the skin just slid off the meat when I picked it up.

I soon found out why Old Chong had retired from teaching piano. He was deaf. "Like Beethoven!" he shouted to me. "We're both listening only in our head!" And he would start to conduct his frantic silent sonatas.

Our lessons went like this. He would open the book and point to different things, explaining their purpose: "Key! Treble! Bass! No sharps or flats! So this is C major! Listen now and play after me!"

And then he would play the C scale a few times, a simple chord, and then, as if inspired by an old, unreachable itch, he gradually added more notes and running trills and a pounding bass until the music was really something quite grand.

I would play after him, the simple scale, the simple chord, and then I just played some nonsense that sounded like a cat running up and down on top of garbage cans. Old Chong smiled and applauded and then said, "Very good! But now you must learn to keep time!"

So that's how I discovered that Old Chong's eyes were too slow to keep up with the wrong notes I was playing. He went through the motions in half-time. To help me keep rhythm, he stood behind me, pushing down on my right shoulder for every beat. He balanced pennies on top of my wrists so I would keep them still as I slowly played scales and arpeggios. He had me curve my hand around an apple and keep that shape when playing chords. He marched stiffly to show me how to make each finger dance up and down, staccato like an obedient little soldier.

He taught me all these things, and that was how I also learned I could be lazy and get away with mistakes, lots of mistakes. If I hit the wrong notes because I hadn't practiced enough, I never corrected myself. I just kept playing in rhythm. And Old Chong kept conducting his own private reverie.

So maybe I never really gave myself a fair chance. I did pick up the basics pretty quickly, and I might have become a good pianist at that young age. But I was so determined not to try, not to be anybody different that I learned to play only the most ear-splitting preludes, the most discordant hymns.

Over the next year, I practiced like this, dutifully in my own way. And then one day I heard my mother and her friend Lindo Jong both talking in a loud bragging tone of voice so others could hear. It was after church, and I was leaning against the brick wall wearing a dress with stiff white petticoats. Auntie

Lindo's daughter, Waverly, who was about my age, was standing farther down the wall about five feet away. We had grown up together and shared all the closeness of two sisters squabbling over crayons and dolls. In other words, for the most part, we hated each other. I thought she was snotty. Waverly Jong had gained a certain amount of fame as "Chinatown's Littlest Chinese Chess Champion."

"She bring home too many trophy," lamented Auntie Lindo that Sunday. "All day she play chess. All day I have no time do nothing but dust off her winnings." She threw a scolding look at Waverly, who pretended not to see her.

"You lucky you don't have this problem," said Auntie Lindo with a sigh to my mother.

And my mother squared her shoulders and bragged: "Our problem worser than yours. If we ask Jing-mei wash dish, she hear nothing but music. It's like you can't stop this natural talent."

And right then, I was determined to put a stop to her foolish pride.

A few weeks later, Old Chong and my mother conspired to have me play in a talent show which would be held in the church hall. By then, my parents had saved up enough to buy me a secondhand piano, a black Wurlitzer spinet with a scarred bench. It was the showpiece of our living room.

For the talent show, I was to play a piece called "Pleading Child" from Schumann's *Scenes from Childhood*. It was a simple, moody piece that sounded more difficult than it was. I was supposed to memorize the whole thing, playing the repeat parts twice to make the piece sound longer. But I dawdled over it, playing a few bars and then cheating, looking up to see what notes followed. I never really listened to what I was playing. I daydreamed about being somewhere else, about being someone else.

The part I liked to practice best was the fancy curtsy: right foot out, touch the rose on the carpet with a pointed foot, sweep to the side, left leg bends, look up and smile.

My parents invited all the couples from the Joy Luck Club to witness my debut. Auntie Lindo and Uncle Tin were there. Waverly and her two older brothers had also come. The first two rows were filled with children both younger and older than I was. The littlest ones got to go first. They recited simple nursery rhymes, squawked out tunes on miniature violins, twirled Hula Hoops, pranced in pink ballet tutus, and when they bowed or curtsied, the audience would sigh in unison, "Awww," and then clap enthusiastically.

When my turn came, I was very confident. I remember my childish excitement. It was as if I knew, without a doubt, that the prodigy side of me really did exist. I had no fear whatsoever, no nervousness. I remember thinking to myself, This is it! This is it! I looked out over the audience, at my mother's blank face, my father's yawn, Auntie Lindo's stiff-lipped smile, Waverly's sulky expression.

I had on a white dress layered with sheets of lace, and a pink bow in my Peter Pan haircut. As I sat down I envisioned people jumping to their feet and Ed Sullivan rushing up to introduce me to everyone on TV.

And I started to play. It was so beautiful. I was so caught up in how lovely I looked that at first I didn't worry how I would sound. So it was a surprise to me when I hit the first wrong note and I realized something didn't sound quite right. And then I hit another and another followed that. A chill started at the top of my head and began to trickle down. Yet I couldn't stop playing, as though my hands were bewitched. I kept thinking my fingers would adjust themselves back, like a train switching to the right track. I played this strange jumble through two repeats, the sour notes staying with me all the way to the end.

When I stood up, I discovered my legs were shaking. Maybe I had just been nervous and the audience, like Old Chong, had seen me go through the right motions and had not heard anything wrong at all. I swept my right foot out, went down on my knee, looked up and smiled. The room was quiet, except for Old Chong, who was beaming and shouting, "Bravo! Bravo! Well done!" But then I saw my mother's face, her stricken face. The audience clapped weakly, and as I walked back to my chair, with my whole face quivering as I tried not to cry, I heard a little boy whisper loudly to his mother, "That was awful," and the mother whispered back, "Well, she certainly tried."

And now I realized how many people were in the audience, the whole world it seemed. I was aware of eyes burning into my back. I felt the shame of my mother and father as they sat stiffly throughout the rest of the show.

We could have escaped during intermission. Pride and some strange sense of honor must have anchored my parents to their chairs. And so we watched it all: the eighteen-year-old boy with a fake mustache who did a magic show and juggled flaming hoops while riding a unicycle. The breasted girl with white makeup who sang from *Madama Butterfly* and got honorable mention. And the eleven-year-old boy who won first prize playing a tricky violin song that sounded like a busy bee.

After the show, the Hsus, the Jongs, and the St. Clairs from the Joy Luck Club came up to my mother and father.

"Lots of talented kids," Auntie Lindo said vaguely, smiling broadly.

"That was somethin' else," said my father, and I wondered if he was referring to me in a humorous way, or whether he even remembered what I had done.

Waverly looked at me and shrugged her shoulders. "You aren't a genius like me," she said matter-of-factly. And if I hadn't felt so bad, I would have pulled her braids and punched her stomach.

But my mother's expression was what devastated me: a quiet, blank look that said she had lost everything. I felt the same way, and it seemed as if everybody were now coming up, like gawkers at the scene of an accident, to see what parts were actually missing. When we got on the bus to go home, my father was humming the busy-bee tune and my mother was silent. I kept thinking she wanted to wait until we got home before shouting at me. But when my father unlocked the door to our apartment, my mother walked in and then went to the back, into the bedroom. No accusations. No blame. And in a way, I felt disappointed. I had been waiting for her to start shouting, so I could shout back and cry and blame her for all my misery.

I assumed my talent-show fiasco meant I never had to play the piano again. But two days later, after school, my mother came out of the kitchen and saw me watching TV.

"Four clock," she reminded me as if it were any other day. I was stunned, as though she were asking me to go through the talent-show torture again. I wedged myself more tightly in front of the TV.

"Turn off TV," she called from the kitchen five minutes later.

I didn't budge. And then I decided. I didn't have to do what my mother said anymore. I wasn't her slave. This wasn't China. I had listened to her before and look what happened. She was the stupid one.

She came out from the kitchen and stood in the arched entryway of the living room. "Four clock," she said once again, louder.

"I'm not going to play anymore," I said nonchalantly. "Why should I? I'm not a genius."

She walked over and stood in front of the TV. I saw her chest was heaving up and down in an angry way.

"No!" I said, and I now felt stronger, as if my true self had finally emerged. So this was what had been inside me all along.

"No! I won't!" I screamed.

She yanked me by the arm, pulled me off the floor, snapped off the TV. She was frighteningly strong, half pulling, half carrying me toward the piano as I kicked the throw rugs under my feet. She lifted me up and onto the hard bench. I was sobbing by now, looking at her bitterly. Her chest was heaving even more and her mouth was open, smiling crazily as if she were pleased I was crying.

"You want me to be someone that I'm not!" I sobbed. "I'll never be the kind of daughter you want me to be!"

"Only two kinds of daughters," she shouted in Chinese. "Those who are obedient and those who follow their own mind! Only one kind of daughter can live in this house. Obedient daughter!"

"Then I wish I wasn't your daughter. I wish you weren't my mother," I shouted. As I said these things I got scared. I felt like worms and toads and slimy things were crawling out of my chest, but it also felt good, as if this awful side of me had surfaced, at last.

"Too late change this," said my mother shrilly.

And I could sense her anger rising to its breaking point. I wanted to see it spill over. And that's when I remembered the babies she had lost in China, the ones we never talked about. "Then I wish I'd never been born!" I shouted. "I wish I were dead! Like them."

It was as if I had said the magic words, Alakazam!—and her face went blank, her mouth closed, her arms went slack, and she backed out of the room, stunned, as if she were blowing away like a small brown leaf, thin, brittle, lifeless.

It was not the only disappointment my mother felt in me. In the years that followed, I failed her so many times, each time asserting my own will, my right to fall short of expectations. I didn't get straight As. I didn't become class president. I didn't get into Stanford. I dropped out of college.

For unlike my mother, I did not believe I could be anything I wanted to be. I could only be me.

And for all those years, we never talked about the disaster at the recital or my terrible accusations afterward at the piano bench. All that remained unchecked, like a betrayal that was now unspeakable. So I never found a way to ask her why she had hoped for something so large that failure was inevitable.

And even worse, I never asked her what frightened me the most: Why had she given up hope?

For after our struggle at the piano, she never mentioned my playing again. The lessons stopped, the lid to the piano was closed, shutting out the dust, my misery, and her dreams.

So she surprised me. A few years ago, she offered to give me the piano, for my thirtieth birthday. I had not played in all those years. I saw the offer as a sign of forgiveness, a tremendous burden removed.

"Are you sure?" I asked shyly. "I mean, won't you and Dad miss it?"

"No, this your piano," she said firmly. "Always your piano. You only one can play."

"Well, I probably can't play anymore," I said. "It's been years."

"You pick up fast," said my mother, as if she knew this was certain. "You have natural talent. You could been genius if you want to."

"No I couldn't."

"You just not trying," said my mother. And she was neither angry nor sad. She said it as if to announce a fact that could never be disproved. "Take it," she said.

But I didn't at first. It was enough that she had offered it to me. And after that, every time I saw it in my parents' living room, standing in front of the bay windows, it made me feel proud, as if it were a shiny trophy I had won back.

Last week I sent a tuner over to my parents' apartment and had the piano reconditioned, for purely sentimental reasons. My mother had died a few months before and I had been getting things in order for my father, a little bit at a time.

I put the jewelry in special silk pouches. The sweaters she had knitted in yellow, pink, bright orange—all the colors I hated—I put those in moth-proof boxes. I found some old Chinese silk dresses, the kind with little slits up the sides. I rubbed the old silk against my skin, then wrapped them in tissue and decided to take them home with me.

After I had the piano tuned, I opened the lid and touched the keys. It sounded even richer than I remembered. Really, it was a very good piano. Inside the bench were the same exercise notes with handwritten scales, the same second-hand music books with their covers held together with yellow tape.

I opened up the Schumann book to the dark little piece I had played at the recital. It was on the left-hand side of the page, "Pleading Child." It looked more difficult than I remembered. I played a few bars, surprised at how easily the notes came back to me.

And for the first time, or so it seemed, I noticed the piece on the right-hand side. It was called "Perfectly Contented." I tried to play this one as well. It had a lighter melody but the same flowing rhythm and turned out to be quite easy. "Pleading Child" was shorter but slower; "Perfectly Contented" was longer but faster. And after I played them both a few times, I realized they were two halves of the same song.

Melanie Rae Thon

XMAS, JAMAICA PLAIN

MELANIE RAE THON's (1957–) most recent book is the novel *Sweet Hearts*. She is also the author of *Meteors in August* and *Iona Moon*, and the story collections *First, Body* and *Girls in the Grass*. She has just completed *Heavenly Creatures*, a collection of stories. Her work has been included in *Best American Short Stories* (1995, 1996), two *Pushcart Prize Anthologies* (2003, 2005), and *O. Henry Prize Stories* (2006). She is also a recipient of a Whiting Writer's Award, a fellowship from the National Endowment for the Arts, and a Writer's Residency from the Lannan Foundation. Originally from Montana, she now lives in migration between the Pacific Northwest, Arizona, and Salt Lake City, where she teaches at the University of Utah.

I'm your worst fear.

But not the worst thing that can happen.

I lived in your house half the night. I'm the broken window in your little boy's bedroom. I'm the flooded tiles in the bathroom where the water flowed and flowed.

I'm the tattoo in the hollow of Emile's pelvis, five butterflies spreading blue wings to rise out of his scar.

I'm dark hands slipping through all your pale woman underthings; dirty fingers fondling a strand of pearls, your throat, a white bird carved of stone. I'm the body you feel wearing your fox coat.

I think I had a sister once. She keeps talking in my head. She won't let go. My sister Clare said, *Take the jewelry; it's yours.*

My heart's in my hands: what I touch, I love; what I love, I own.

Snow that night and nobody seemed surprised, so I figured it must be winter. Later I remembered it was Christmas, or it had been, the day before. I was with Emile who wanted to be Emilia. We'd started downtown, Boston. Now it was Jamaica Plain, three miles south. *Home for the holidays,* Emile said, some private joke. He'd been working the block around the Greyhound Station all night, wearing nothing but a white scarf and black turtleneck, tight jeans. *Man wants to see before he buys*, Emile said. He meant the ones in long cars cruising, looking for fragile boys with female faces.

Emile was sixteen, he thought.

Getting old.

He'd made sixty-four dollars: three tricks with cash, plus some pills—a bonus for good work, blues and greens, he didn't know what. Nobody'd offered to take him home, which is all he wanted: a warm bed, some sleep, eggs in the morning, the smell of butter, hunks of bread torn off the loaf.

Crashing, both of us, ragged from days of speed and crack, no substitute for the smooth high of pure cocaine but all we could afford. Now, enough cash between us at last. I had another twenty-five from the man who said he was in the circus once, who called himself the Jungle Creep—on top of me he made that sound. Before he unlocked the door, he said, *Are you a real girl?* I looked at his plates—New Jersey; that's why he didn't know that the lines, didn't know that the boys as girls stay away from the Zone unless they want their faces crushed. He wanted me to prove it first. Some bad luck once, I guess. I said, *It's fucking freezing. I'm real. Open the frigging door or go.*

Now it was too late to score, too cold, nobody on the street but Emile and me, the wind, so we walked, we kept walking. I had a green parka, somebody else's empty wallet in the pocket—I couldn't remember who or where, the coat stolen weeks ago and still mine, a miracle out here. We shared, trading it off. I loved Emile. I mean, it hurt my skin to see his cold.

Emile had a plan. It had to be Jamaica Plain, *home*—enough hands as dark as mine, enough faces as brown as Emile's—not like Brookline, where we'd have to turn ourselves inside out. Jamaica Plain, where there were pretty painted houses next to shacks, where the sound of bursting glass wouldn't be that loud.

Listen, we needed to sleep, to eat, that's all. So thirsty even my veins felt dry, flattened out. Hungry somewhere in my head, but my stomach shrunken to a knot so small I thought it might be gone. I remembered the man, maybe last week, before the snow, leaning against the statue of starved horses, twisted metal at the edge of the Common. He had a knife, long enough for gutting fish. Dressed in camouflage but not hiding. He stared at his thumb, licked it clean, and cut deep to watch the bright blood bubble out. He stuck it in his mouth to drink, hungry, and I swore I'd never get that low. But nights later I dreamed him beside me. Raw and dizzy, I woke, offering my whole hand, begging him to cut it off.

We walked around your block three times. We were patient now. Numb. No car up your drive and your porch light blazing, left to burn all night, we thought. Your house glowed, yellow even in the dark, paint so shiny it looked wet, and Emile said he lived somewhere like this once, when he was still a boy all the time, hair cropped short, before lipstick and mascara, when his cheeks weren't blushed, before his mother caught him and his father locked him out.

In this house Emile found your red dress, your slippery stockings. He was happy, I swear.

So why did he end up on the floor?

I'm not going to tell you; I don't know.

First, the rock wrapped in Emile's scarf, glass splintering in the cold, and we climbed into the safe body of your house. Later we saw this was a child's room, your only one. We found the tiny cowboy boots in the closet, black like Emile's but small, so small. I tried the little bed. It was soft enough but too short. In every room your blue-eyed boy floated on the wall. Emile wanted to take him down. Emile said, *He scares me.* Emile said your little boy's too pretty, his blond curls too long. Emile said, *Some night the wrong person's going to take him home.*

Emile's not saying anything now, but if you touched his mouth you'd know. Like a blind person reading lips, you'd feel everything he needed to tell.

We stood in the cold light of the open refrigerator, drinking milk from the carton, eating pecan pie with our hands, squirting whipped cream into our mouths. You don't know how it hurt us to eat this way, our shriveled stomachs stretching; you don't know why we couldn't stop. We took the praline ice cream to your bed, one of those tiny containers, sweet and sickening, bits of candy frozen hard. We fell asleep and it melted, so we drank it, thick, with your brandy, watching bodies writhe on the TV, no sound: flames and ambulances all night; children leaping; a girl in mud under a car, eight men lifting; a skier crashing into a wall—we never knew who was saved and who was not. Talking heads spit the news again and again. There was no reason to listen—tomorrow exactly the same things would happen, and still everyone would forget.

There were other houses after yours, places where I went alone, but there were none before and none like this. When I want to feel love I remember the dark thrill of it, the bright sound of glass, the sudden size and weight of my own heart in my own chest, how I knew it now, how it was real to me in my body, separate from lungs and liver and ribs, how it made the color of my blood surge against the back of my eyes, how nothing mattered anymore because I believed in this, my own heart, its will to live.

No lights, no alarm. We waited outside. Fifteen seconds. Years collapsed. We were scared of you, who you might be inside, terrified lady with a gun, some fool with bad aim and dumb luck. The boost to the window, Emile lifting me, then I was there, in you, I swear, the smell that particular, that strong, almost a taste in your boy's room, his sweet milky breath under my tongue. Heat left low, but to us warm as a body, humid, hot.

My skin's cracked now, hands that cold, but I think of them plunged deep in your drawer, down in all your soft underbelly underclothes, slipping through all your jumbled silky woman things.

I pulled them out and out.

I'm your worst fear. I touched everything in your house: all the presents just unwrapped—cashmere sweater, rocking horse, velvet pouch. I lay on your bed, smoking cigarettes, wrapped in your fur coat. How many foxes? I tried to count.

But it was Emile who wore the red dress, who left it crumpled on the floor.

Thin as he is, he couldn't zip the back—he's a boy, after all—he has those shoulders, those soon-to-be-a-man bones. He swore trying to squash his boy feet into the matching heels; then he sobbed. I had to tell him he had lovely feet, and he did, elegant, long—those golden toes. I found him a pair of stockings, one size fits all.

I wore your husband's pinstriped jacket. I pretended all the gifts were mine to offer. I pulled the pearls from their violet pouch.

We danced.

We slid across the polished wooden floor of your living room, spun in the white lights of the twinkling tree. And again, I tell you, I swear I felt the exact size and shape of things inside me, heart and kidney, my sweet left lung. All the angels hanging from the branches opened their glass mouths, stunned.

He was more woman than you, his thick hair wound tight and pinned. *Watch this,* he said, *chignon.*

I'm not lying. He transformed himself in front of your mirror, gold eyeshadow, faint blush. He was beautiful. He could have fooled anyone. Your husband would have paid a hundred dollars to feel Emile's mouth kiss all the places you won't touch.

Later the red dress lay like a wet rag on the floor. Later the stockings snagged, the strand of pearls snapped and the beads rolled. Later Emile was all boy, naked on the bathroom floor.

I'm the one who got away, the one you don't know; I'm the long hairs you find under your pillow, nested in your drain, tangled in your brush. You think I might come back. You dream me dark always. I could be any dirty girl on the street, or the one on the bus, black lips, just-shaved head. You see her through mud-spattered glass, quick, blurred. You want me dead—it's come to this— killed, but not by your clean hands. You pray for accidents instead, me high and spacy, stepping off the curb, a car that comes too fast. You dream some twisted night road and me walking, some poor drunk weaving his way home. He won't even know what he's struck. In the morning he'll touch the headlight I smashed, the fender I splattered, dirt or blood. In the light he'll see my body rising, half remembered, snow that whirls to a shape then blows apart. Only you will know for sure, the morning news, another unidentified girl dead, hit and run, her killer never found.

I wonder if you'll rest then, or if every sound will be glass, every pair of hands mine, reaching for your sleeping son.

How can I explain?

We didn't come for him.

I'm your worst fear. Slivers of window embedded in carpet. Sharp and invisible. You can follow my muddy footprints through your house, but if you follow them backward they always lead here: to this room, to his bed.

If you could see my hands, not the ones you imagine but my real hands, they'd be reaching for Emile's body. If you looked at Emile's feet, if you touched them, you could feel us dancing.

This is all I want.

After we danced, we lay so close on your bed I dreamed we were twins, joined forever this way, two arms, three legs, two heads.

But I woke in my body alone.

Outside, snow fell like pieces of broken light.

I already knew what had happened. But I didn't want to know.

I heard him in the bathroom.

I mean, I heard the water flow and flow.

I told myself he was washing you away, your perfume, your lavender oil scent. Becoming himself. Tomorrow we'd go.

I tried to watch the TV, the silent man in front of the map, the endless night news. But there it was, my heart again, throbbing in my fingertips.

I couldn't stand it—the snow outside; the sound of water; your little boy's head propped on the dresser, drifting on the wall; the man in the corner of the room, trapped in the flickering box: his silent mouth wouldn't stop.

I pounded on the bathroom door. I said, *Goddamn it, Emile, you're clean enough.* I said I had a bad feeling about this place. I said I felt you coming home.

But Emile, he didn't say a word. There was only water, that one sound, and I saw it seeping under the door, leaking into the white carpet. Still I told lies to myself. I said, *Shit, Emile—what's going on?* I pushed the door. I had to shove hard, squeeze inside, because Emile was there, you know, exactly where you found him, facedown on the floor. I turned him over, saw the lips smeared red, felt the water flow.

I breathed into him, beat his chest. It was too late, God, I know, his face pressed to the floor all this time, his face in the water, Emile dead even before he drowned, your bottle of Valium empty in the sink, the foil of your cold capsules punched through, two dozen gone—this is what did it: your brandy, your Valium, your safe little pills bought in a store. After all the shit we've done—smack popped under the skin, speed laced with strychnine, monkey dust—it comes to this. After all the nights on the streets, all the knives, all the pissed-off johns, all the fag-hating bullies prowling the Fenway with their bats, luring boys like Emile into the bushes with promises of sex. After all that, this is where it ends: on your clean wet floor.

Above the thunder of the water, Clare said, *He doesn't want to live.*

Clare stayed very calm. She said, *Turn off the water; go.*

I kept breathing into him. I watched the butterflies between his bones. No flutter of wings and Clare said, *Look at him. He's dead.* Clare said she should know.

She told me what to take and where it was: sapphire ring, ivory elephant, snakeskin belt. She told me what to leave, what was too heavy: the carved bird, white stone. She reminded me, *Take off that ridiculous coat.*

I knew Clare was right; I thought, Yes, everyone is dead: the silent heads in the TV, the boy on the floor, my father who can't be known. I thought even you might be dead—your husband asleep at the wheel, your little boy asleep in the back, only you awake to see the car split the guardrail and soar.

I saw a snow-filled ravine, your car rolling toward the river of thin ice.

I thought, You never had a chance.

But I felt you.

I believed in you. Your family. I heard you going from room to room, saying, *Who's been sleeping in my bed?*

It took all my will.

I wanted to love you. I wanted you to come home. I wanted you to find me kneeling on your floor. I wanted the wings on Emile's hips to lift him through the skylight. I wanted him to scatter: ash, snow. I wanted the floor dry, the window whole.

I swear, you gave me hope.

Clare knew I was going to do something stupid. Try to clean this up. Call the police to come for Emile. Not get out. She had to tell me everything. She said again, *Turn the water off.*

In the living room the tree still twinkled, the angels still hung. I remember how amazed I was they hadn't thrown themselves to the floor.

I remember running, the immaculate cold, the air in me, my lungs hard.

I remember thinking, I'm alive, a miracle anyone was. I wondered who had chosen me.

I remember trying to list all the decent things I'd ever done.

I remember walking till it was light, knowing if I slept, I'd freeze. I never wanted so much not to die.

I made promises, I suppose.

In the morning I walked across a bridge, saw the river frozen along the edges, scrambled down. I glided out on it; I walked on water. The snowflakes kept getting bigger and bigger, butterflies that fell apart when they hit the ground, but the sky was mostly clear and there was sun.

Later, the cold again, wind and clouds. Snow shrank to ice. Small, hard. I saw a car idling, a child in the back, the driver standing on a porch, knocking at a door. Clare said, *It's open.* She meant the car. She said, *Think how fast you can go.* She told me I could ditch the baby down the road.

I didn't do it.

Later I stole lots of things, slashed sofas, pissed on floors.

But that day, I passed one thing by; I let one thing go.

When I think about this, the child safe and warm, the mother not wailing, not beating her head on the wall to make herself stop, when I think about the snow that day, wings in the bright sky, I forgive myself for everything else.

Alice Walker

NINETEEN FIFTY-FIVE

ALICE WALKER (1944–) is the author of the novels *The Third Life of Grange Copeland; Meridian; The Color Purple,* which won an American Book Award and the Pulitzer Prize; *The Temple of My Familiar; Possessing the Secret of Joy; By the Light of My Father's Smile;* and *Now Is the Time to Open Your Heart.* She is also the author of two short story collections, *In Love & Trouble* and *You Can't Keep a Good Woman Down;* six volumes of poetry: *Once; Revolutionary Petunias; Good Night, Willie Lee, I'll See You in the Morning; Horses Make a Landscape More Beautiful; Her Blue Body Everything We Know;* and *Absolute Trust in the Goodness of the Earth;* and five volumes of essays, *In Search of Our Mothers' Gardens, Living by the Word, Anything We Love Can Be Saved, The Same River Twice,* and *We Are the Ones We Have Been Waiting For: Light in a Time of Darkness.* She has edited a Zora Neale Hurston reader, and her short story "To Hell with Dying" has been published as an illustrated children's book. Born in Eatonton, Georgia, she now lives in northern California.

1955

The car is a brand-new red Thunderbird convertible, and it's passed the house more than once. It slows down real slow now, and stops at the curb. An older gentleman dressed like a Baptist deacon gets out on the side near the house, and a young fellow who looks about sixteen gets out on the driver's side. They are white, and I wonder what in the world they doing in this neighborhood.

Well, I say to J. T., put your shirt on, anyway, and let me clean these glasses offa the table.

We had been watching the ballgame on TV. I wasn't actually watching, I was sort of daydreaming, with my foots up in J. T.'s lap.

I seen 'em coming on up the walk, brisk, like they coming to sell something, and then they rung the bell, and J. T. declined to put on a shirt but instead disappeared into the bedroom where the other television is. I turned down the one in the living room; I figured I'd be rid of these two double quick and J. T. could come back out again.

Are you Gracie Mae Still? asked the old guy, when I opened the door and put my hand on the lock inside the screen.

And I don't need to buy a thing, said I.

What makes you think we're sellin'? he asks, in that hearty Southern way that makes my eyeballs ache.

Well, one way or another and they're inside the house and the first thing the young fellow does is raise the TV a couple of decibels. He's about five feet nine, sort of womanish looking, with real dark white skin and a red pouting mouth. His hair is black and curly and he looks like a Loosianna creole.

About one of your songs, says the deacon. He is maybe sixty, with white hair and beard, white silk shirt, black linen suit, black tie and black shoes. His cold gray eyes look like they're sweating.

One of my songs?

Traynor here just *loves* your songs. Don't you, Traynor? He nudges Traynor with his elbow. Traynor blinks, says something I can't catch in a pitch I don't register.

The boy learned to sing and dance livin' round you people out in the country. Practically cut his teeth on you.

Traynor looks up at me and bites his thumbnail.

I laugh.

Well, one way or another they leave with my agreement that they can record one of my songs. The deacon writes me a check for five hundred dollars, the boy grunts his awareness of the transaction, and I am laughing all over myself by the time I rejoin J. T.

Just as I am snuggling down beside him though I hear the front doorbell going off again.

Forgit his hat? asks J. T.

I hope not, I say.

The deacon stands there leaning on the door frame and once again I'm thinking of those sweaty-looking eyeballs of his. I wonder if sweat makes your eyeballs pink because his are sure pink. Pink and gray and it strikes me that nobody I'd care to know is behind them.

I forgot one little thing, he says pleasantly. I forgot to tell you Traynor and I would like to buy up all of those records you made of the song. I tell you we sure do love it.

Well, love it or not, I'm not so stupid as to let them do that without making 'em pay. So I says, Well, that's gonna cost you. Because, really, that song never did sell all that good, so I was glad they was going to buy it up. But on the other hand, them two listening to my song by themselves, and nobody else getting to hear me sing it, give me a pause.

Well, one way or another the deacon showed me where I would come out ahead on any deal he had proposed so far. Didn't I give you five hundred dollars? he asked. What white man—and don't even need to mention colored—would give you more? We buy up all your records of that particular song: first, you git royalties. Let me ask you, how much you sell that song for in the first place? Fifty dollars? A hundred, I say. And no royalties from it yet, right? Right. Well, when we buy up all of them records you gonna git royalties. And that's gonna make all them race record shops sit up and take notice of Gracie Mae Still. And they gonna push all them other records of yourn they got. And you no doubt will become one of the big name colored recording artists. And then we can offer you another five hundred dollars for letting us do all this for you. And by God you'll be sittin' pretty! You can go out and buy you the kind of outfit a star should have. Plenty sequins and yards of red satin.

I had done unlocked the screen when I saw I could get some more money out of him. Now I held it wide open while he squeezed through the opening between me and the door. He whipped out another piece of paper and I signed it.

He sort of trotted out to the car and slid in beside Traynor, whose head was back against the seat. They swung around in a U-turn in front of the house and then they was gone.

J. T. was putting his shirt on when I got back to the bedroom. Yankees beat the Orioles 10-6, he said. I believe I'll drive out to Paschal's pond and go fishing. Wanta go?

While I was putting on my pants J. T. was holding the two checks.

I'm real proud of a woman that can make cash money without leavin' home, he said. And I said *Umph*. Because we met on the road with me singing in first one little low-life jook after another, making ten dollars a night for myself if I was lucky, and sometimes bringin' home nothing but my life. And J. T. just loved them times. The way I was fast and flashy and always on the go from one town to another. He loved the way my singin' made the dirt farmers cry like babies and the womens shout Honey, hush! But that's mens. They loves any style to which you can get 'em accustomed.

1956

My little grandbaby called me one night on the phone: Little Mama, Little Mama, there's a white man on the television singing one of your songs! Turn on channel 5.

Lord, if it wasn't Traynor. Still looking half asleep from the neck up, but kind of awake in a nasty way from the waist down. He wasn't doing too bad with my song either, but it wasn't just the song the people in the audience was screeching and screaming over, it was that nasty little jerk he was doing from the waist down.

Well, Lord have mercy, I said, listening to him. If I'da closed my eyes, it could have been me. He had followed every turning of my voice, side streets, avenues, red lights, train crossings and all. It give me a chill.

Everywhere I went I heard Traynor singing my song, and all the little white girls just eating it up. I never had so many ponytails switched across my line of vision in my life. They was so *proud*. He was a *genius*.

Well, all that year I was trying to lose weight anyway and that and high blood pressure and sugar kept me pretty well occupied. Traynor had made a smash from a song of mine, I still had seven hundred dollars of the original one thousand dollars in the bank, and I felt if I could just bring my weight down, life would be sweet.

1957

I lost ten pounds in 1956. That's what I give myself for Christmas. And J. T. and me and the children and their friends and grandkids of all description had just finished dinner—over which I had put on nine and a half of my lost ten—when who should appear at the front door but Traynor. Little Mama, Little Mama! It's that white man who sings ⸺ ⸺ ⸺. The children didn't call it my song anymore. Nobody did. It was funny how that happened. Traynor and the deacon had bought up all my records, true, but on his record he had put "written by Gracie Mae Still." But that was just another name on the label, like "produced by Apex Records."

On the TV he was inclined to dress like the deacon told him. But now he looked presentable.

Merry Christmas, said he.

And same to you, Son.

I don't know why I called him Son. Well, one way or another they're all our sons. The only requirement is that they be younger than us. But then again, Traynor seemed to be aging by the minute.

You looks tired, I said. Come on in and have a glass of Christmas cheer.

J. T. ain't never in his life been able to act decent to a white man he wasn't working for, but he poured Traynor a glass of bourbon and water, then he took all the children and grandkids and friends and whatnot out to the den. After while I heard Traynor's voice singing the song, coming from the stereo console. It was just the kind of Christmas present my kids would consider cute.

I looked at Traynor, complicit. But he looked like it was the last thing in the world he wanted to hear. His head was pitched forward over his lap, his hands holding his glass and his elbows on his knees.

I done sung that song seem like a million times this year, he said. I sung it on the Grand Ole Opry, I sung it on the *Ed Sullivan Show*. I sung it on Mike Douglas, I sung it at the Cotton Bowl, the Orange Bowl. I sung it at Festivals. I sung it at Fairs. I sung it overseas in Rome, Italy, and once in a submarine *underseas*. I've sung it and sung it, and I'm making forty thousand dollars a day offa it, and you know what, I don't have the faintest notion what that song means.

Whatchumean, what do it mean? It mean what it says. All I could think was: These suckers is making forty thousand a *day* offa my song and now they gonna come back and try to swindle me out of the original thousand.

It's just a song, I said. Cagey. When you fool around with a lot of no count mens you sing a bunch of 'em. I shrugged.

Oh, he said. Well. He started brightening up. I just come by to tell you I think you are a great singer.

He didn't blush, saying that. Just said it straight out.

And I brought you a little Christmas present too. Now you take this little box and you hold it until I drive off. Then you take it outside under that first streetlight back up the street aways in front of that green house. Then you open the box and see . . . Well, just *see*.

What had come over this boy, I wondered, holding the box. I looked out the window in time to see another white man come up and get in the car with him and then two more cars full of white mens start out behind him. They was all in long black cars that looked like a funeral procession.

Little Mama, Little Mama, what it is? One of my grandkids come running up and started pulling at the box. It was wrapped in gay Christmas paper—the thick, rich kind that it's hard to picture folks making just to throw away.

J. T. and the rest of the crowd followed me out the house, up the street to the streetlight and in front of the green house. Nothing was there but somebody's gold-grilled white Cadillac. Brand-new and most distracting. We got to looking at it so till I almost forgot the little box in my hand. While the others were busy making 'miration I carefully took off the paper and ribbon and folded them up and put them in my pants pocket. What should I see but a pair of genuine solid gold Caddy keys.

Dangling the keys in front of everybody's nose, I unlocked the Caddy, motioned for J. T. to git in on the other side, and us didn't come back home for two days.

1960

Well, the boy was sure nuff famous by now. He was still a mite shy of twenty but already they was calling him the Emperor of Rock and Roll.

Then what should happen but the draft.

Well, says J. T. There goes all this Emperor of Rock and Roll business.

But even in the army the womens was on him like white on rice. We watched it on the News.

Dear Gracie Mae [he wrote from Germany],

How you? Fine I hope as this leaves me doing real well. Before I come in the army I was gaining a lot of weight and gitting jittery from making all them dumb movies. But now I exercise and eat right and get plenty of rest. I'm more awake than I been in ten years.

I wonder if you are writing any more songs?

Sincerely,
Traynor

I wrote him back:

Dear Son,

We is all fine in the Lord's good grace and hope this finds you the same. J. T. and me be out all times of the day and night in that car you give me—which you know you didn't have to do. Oh, and I do appreciate the mink and the new self-cleaning oven. But if you send anymore stuff to eat from Germany I'm going to have to open up a store in the neighborhood just to get rid of it. Really, we have more than enough of everything. The Lord is good to us and we don't know Want.

Glad to here you is well and gitting your right rest. There ain't nothing like exercising to help that along. J. T. and me work some part of every day that we don't go fishing in the garden.

Well, so long Soldier.

Sincerely,
Gracie Mae

He wrote:

Dear Gracie Mae,

I hope you and J. T. like that automatic power tiller I had one of the stores back home send you. I went through a mountain of catalogs looking for it—I wanted something that even a woman could use.

I've been thinking about writing some songs of my own but every time I finish one it don't seem to be about nothing I've actually lived myself. My agent keeps sending me other people's songs but they just sound mooney. I can hardly git through 'em without gagging.

Everybody still loves that song of yours. They ask me all the time what do I think it means, really. I mean, they want to know just what I want to know. Where out of your life did it come from?

Sincerely,
Traynor

1968

I didn't see the boy for seven years. No. Eight. Because just about everybody was dead when I saw him again. Malcolm X, King, the president and his brother, and even J. T. J. T. died of a head cold. It just settled in his head like a block of ice, he said, and nothing we did moved it until one day he just leaned out the bed and died.

His good friend Horace helped me put him away, and then about a year later Horace and me started going together. We was sitting out on the front porch swing one summer night, dusk-dark, and I saw this great procession of lights winding to a stop.

Holy Toledo! said Horace. (He's got a real sexy voice like Ray Charles.) Look *at* it. He meant the long line of flashy cars and the white men in white summer suits jumping out on the drivers' sides and standing at attention. With wings they could pass for angels, with hoods they could be the Klan.

Traynor comes waddling up the walk.

And suddenly I know what it is he could pass for. An Arab like the ones you see in storybooks. Plump and soft and with never a care about weight. Because with so much money, who cares? Traynor is almost dressed like someone from a storybook too. He has on, I swear, about ten necklaces. Two sets of bracelets on his arms, at least one ring on every finger, and some kind of shining buckles on his shoes, so that when he walks you get quite a few twinkling lights.

Gracie Mae, he says, coming up to give me a hug. J. T.

I explain that J. T. passed. That this is Horace.

Horace, he says, puzzled but polite, sort of rocking back on his heels, Horace.

That's it for Horace. He goes in the house and don't come back.

Looks like you and me is gained a few, I say.

He laughs. The first time I ever heard him laugh. It don't sound much like a laugh and I can't swear that it's better than no laugh a'tall.

He's gitting fat for sure, but he's still slim compared to me. I'll never see three hundred pounds again and I've just about said (excuse me) fuck it. I got to thinking about it one day an' I thought: aside from the fact that they say it's unhealthy, my fat ain't never been no trouble. Mens always have loved me. My kids ain't never complained. Plus they's fat. And fat like I is I looks distinguished. You see me coming and know somebody's *there.*

Gracie Mae, he says, I've come with a personal invitation to you to my house tomorrow for dinner. He laughed. What did it sound like? I couldn't place it. See them men out there? he asked me. I'm sick and tired of eating with them. They don't never have nothing to talk about. That's why I eat so much. But if you come to dinner tomorrow we can talk about the old days. You can tell me about that farm I bought you.

I sold it, I said.

You did?

Yeah, I said, I did. Just cause I said I liked to exercise by working in a garden didn't mean I wanted five hundred acres! Anyhow, I'm a city girl now. Raised in the country it's true. Dirt poor—the whole bit—but that's all behind me now.

Oh well, he said, I didn't mean to offend you.

We sat a few minutes listening to the crickets.

Then he said: You wrote that song while you was still on the farm, didn't you, or was it right after you left?

You had somebody spying on me? I asked.

You and Bessie Smith got into a fight over it once, he said.

You *is* been spying on me!

But I don't know what the fight was about, he said. Just like I don't know what happened to your second husband. Your first one died in the Texas electric chair. Did you know that? Your third one beat you up, stole your touring costumes and your car and retired with a chorine to Tuskegee. He laughed. He's still there.

I had been mad, but suddenly I calmed down. Traynor was talking very dreamily. It was dark but seems like I could tell his eyes weren't right. It was like some*thing* was sitting there talking to me but not necessarily with a person behind it.

You gave up on marrying and seem happier for it. He laughed again. I married but it never went like it was supposed to. I never could squeeze any of my own life either into it or out of it. It was like singing somebody else's record. I copied the way it was sposed to be *exactly* but I never had a clue what marriage meant.

I bought her a diamond ring big as your fist. I bought her clothes. I built her a mansion. But right away she didn't want the boys to stay there. Said they smoked up the bottom floor. Hell, there were *five* floors.

No need to grieve, I said. No need to. Plenty more where she come from.

He perked up. That's part of what that song means, ain't it? No need to grieve. Whatever it is, there's plenty more down the line.

I never really believed that way back when I wrote that song, I said. It was all bluffing then. The trick is to live long enough to put your young bluffs to use. Now if I was to sing that song today I'd tear it up. 'Cause I done lived long enough to know it's *true*. Them words could hold me up.

I ain't lived that long, he said.

Look like you on your way, I said. I don't know why, but the boy seemed to need some encouraging. And I don't know, seem like one way or another you talk to rich white folks and you end up reassuring *them*. But what the hell, by now I feel something for the boy. I wouldn't be in his bed all alone in the middle of the night for nothing. Couldn't be nothing worse than being famous the world over for something you don't even understand. That's what I tried to tell Bessie. She wanted that same song. Overheard me practicing it one day, said, with her hands on her hips: Gracie Mae, I'ma sing your song tonight. I *likes* it.

Your lips be too swole to sing, I said. She was mean and she was strong, but I trounced her.

Ain't you famous enough with your own stuff? I said. Leave mine alone. Later on, she thanked me. By then she was Miss Bessie Smith to the World, and I was still Miss Gracie Mae Nobody from Notasulga.

The next day all these limousines arrived to pick me up. Five cars and twelve bodyguards. Horace picked that morning to start painting the kitchen.

Don't paint the kitchen, fool, I said. The only reason that dumb boy of ours is going to show me his mansion is because he intends to present us with a new house.

What you gonna do with it? he asked me, standing there in his shirtsleeves stirring the paint.

Sell it. Give it to the children. Live in it on weekends. It don't matter what I do. He sure don't care.

Horace just stood there shaking his head. Mama you sure looks *good*, he says. Wake me up when you git back.

Fool, I say, and pat my wig in front of the mirror.

The boy's house is something else. First you come to this mountain, and then you commence to drive and drive up this road that's lined with magnolias. Do magnolias grow on mountains? I was wondering. And you come to lakes and you come to ponds and you come to deer and you come up on some sheep. And I figure these two is sposed to represent England and Wales. Or something out of Europe. And you just keep on coming to stuff. And it's all pretty. Only the man driving my car don't look at nothing but the road. Fool. And then *finally,* after all this time, you begin to go up the driveway. And there's more magnolias—only they're not in such good shape. It's sort of cool up this high and I don't think they're gonna make it. And then I see this building that looks like if it had a name it would be The Tara Hotel. Columns and steps and out-door chandeliers and rocking chairs. Rocking chairs? Well, and there's the boy on the steps dressed in a dark green satin jacket like you see folks wearing on TV late at night, and he looks sort of like a fat dracula with all that house rising behind him, and standing beside him there's this little white vision of loveliness that he introduces as his wife.

He's nervous when he introduces us and he says to her: This is Gracie Mae Still, I want you to know me. I mean ... and she gives him a look that would fry meat.

Won't you come in, Gracie Mae, she says, and that's the last I see of her.

He fishes around for something to say or do and decides to escort me to the kitchen. We go through the entry and the parlor and the breakfast room and the dining room and the servants' passage and finally get there. The first thing I notice is that, altogether, there are five stoves. He looks about to introduce me to one.

Wait a minute, I say. Kitchens don't do nothing for me. Let's go sit on the front porch.

Well, we hike back and we sit in the rocking chairs rocking until dinner.

Gracie Mae, he says down the table, taking a piece of fried chicken from the woman standing over him, I got a little surprise for you.

It's a house, ain't it? I ask, spearing a chitlin.

You're getting *spoiled*, he says. And the way he says *spoiled* sounds funny. He slurs it. It sounds like his tongue is too thick for his mouth. Just that quick he's finished the chicken and is now eating chitlins *and* a pork chop. *Me* spoiled, I'm thinking.

I already got a house. Horace is right this minute painting the kitchen. I bought that house. My kids feel comfortable in that house.

But this one I bought you is just like mine. Only a little smaller.

I still don't need no house. And anyway who would clean it?

He looks surprised.

Really, I think, some peoples advance *so* slowly.

I hadn't thought of that. But what the hell, I'll get you somebody to live in.

I don't want other folks living 'round me. Makes me nervous.

You *don't?* It *do?*

What I want to wake up and see folks I don't even know for?

He just sits there downtable staring at me. Some of that feeling is in the song, ain't it? Not the words, the *feeling*. What I want to wake up and see folks I don't even know for? But I see twenty folks a day I don't even know, including my wife.

This food wouldn't be bad to wake up to though, I said. The boy had found the genius of corn bread.

He looked at me real hard. He laughed. Short. They want what you got but they don't want you. They want what I got only it ain't mine. That's what makes 'em so hungry for me when I sing. They getting the flavor of something but they ain't getting the thing itself. They like a pack of hound dogs trying to gobble up a scent.

You talking 'bout your fans?

Right. Right. He says.

Don't worry 'bout your fans, I say. They don't know their asses from a hole in the ground. I doubt there's a honest one in the bunch.

That's the point. Dammit, that's the point! He hits the table with his fist. It's so solid it don't even quiver. You need a honest audience! You can't have folks that's just gonna lie right back to you.

Yeah, I say, it was small compared to yours, but I had one. It would have been worth my life to try to sing 'em somebody else's stuff that I didn't know nothing about.

He must have pressed a buzzer under the table. One of his flunkies zombies up.

Git Johnny Carson, he says.

On the phone? asks the zombie.

On the phone, says Traynor, what you think I mean, git him offa the front porch? Move your ass.

So two weeks later we's on the Johnny Carson show.

Traynor is all corseted down nice and looks a little bit fat but mostly good. And all the women that grew up on him and my song squeal and squeal. Traynor says: The lady who wrote my first hit record is here with us tonight, and she's agreed to sing it for all of us, just like she sung it forty-five years ago. Ladies and Gentlemen, the great Gracie Mae Still!

Well, I had tried to lose a couple of pounds my own self, but failing that I had me a very big dress made. So I sort of rolls over next to Traynor, who is dwarfted by me, so that when he puts his arm around back of me to try to hug me it looks funny to the audience and they laugh.

I can see this pisses him off. But I smile out there at 'em. Imagine squealing for twenty years and not knowing why you're squealing? No more sense of endings and beginnings than hogs.

It don't matter, Son, I say. Don't fret none over me.

I commence to sing. And I sound —— wonderful. Being able to sing good ain't all about having a good singing voice a'tall. A good singing voice helps. But when you come up in the Hard Shell Baptist church like I did you understand early that the fellow that sings is the singer. Them that waits for programs and arrangements and letters from home is just good voices occupying body space.

So there I am singing my own song, my own way. And I give it all I got and enjoy every minute of it. When I finish Traynor is standing up clapping and clapping and beaming at first me and then the audience like I'm his mama for true. The audience claps politely for about two seconds.

Traynor looks disgusted.

He comes over and tries to hug me again. The audience laughs.

Johnny Carson looks at us like we both weird.

Traynor is mad as hell. He's supposed to sing something called a love ballad. But instead he takes the mike, turns to me and says: Now see if my imitation still holds up. He goes into the same song, *our* song, I think, looking out at his flaky audience. And he sings it just the way he always did. My voice, my tone, my inflection, everything. But he forgets a couple of lines. Even before he's finished the matronly squeals begin.

He sits down next to me looking whipped.

It don't matter, Son, I say, patting his hand. You don't even know those people. Try to make the people you know happy.

Is that in the song? he asks.

Maybe, I say.

1977

For a few years I hear from him, then nothing. But trying to lose weight takes all the attention I got to spare. I finally faced up to the fact that my fat is the hurt I don't admit, not even to myself, and that I been trying to bury it from the day I was born. But also when you git real old, to tell the truth, it ain't as pleasant. It gits lumpy and slack. Yuck. So one day I said to Horace, I'ma git this shit offa me.

And he fell in with the program like he always try to do and Lord such a procession of salads and cottage cheese and fruit juice!

One night I dreamed Traynor had split up with his fifteenth wife. He said: *You meet 'em for no reason. You date 'em for no reason. You marry 'em for no reason. I do it all but I swear it's just like somebody else doing it. I feel like I can't remember Life.*

The boy's in trouble, I said to Horace.

You've always said that, he said.

I have?

Yeah. You always said he looked asleep. You can't sleep through life if you wants to live it.

You not such a fool after all, I said, pushing myself up with my cane and hobbling over to where he was. Let me sit down on your lap, I said, while this salad I ate takes effect.

In the morning we heard Traynor was dead. Some said fat, some said heart, some said alcohol, some said drugs. One of the children called from Detroit. Them dumb fans of his is on a crying rampage, she said. You just ought to turn on the TV.

But I didn't want to see 'em. They was crying and crying and didn't even know what they was crying for. One day this is going to be a pitiful country, I thought.

Steve Yarbrough

THE REST OF HER LIFE

STEVE YARBROUGH (1956–) is the author of seven books: *Family Men* (1990), *Mississippi History* (1994), *Veneer* (1998), *The Oxygen Man* (1999), *Visible Spirits* (2001), *Prisoners of War* (2004), and *The End of California* (2006). He is the James and Coke Hallowell Professor of Creative Writing at California State University, Fresno, where he is also the director of the MFA program.

The dog was a mixture of God knows how many breeds, but the vet had told them he was at least part German shepherd. You could see it in his shoulders, and you could hear it when he barked, which he was doing that night in 1977 when they pulled up at the gate and Chuckie cut the engine.

"Butch is out," Dee Ann said. "That's kind of strange."

Chuckie didn't say anything. He'd looked across the yard and seen her momma's car in the driveway, and he was disappointed. Dee Ann's momma had told her earlier that she was going to buy some garden supplies at Western Auto and then eat something at the Sonic, and she'd said if she got back home and unloaded her purchases in time, she might run over to Greenville with one of her friends from work and watch a movie. Dee Ann had relayed the news to Chuckie tonight when he picked her up from work. That had gotten his hopes up.

The last two Saturday nights her momma had gone to Greenville, and they'd made love on the couch. They'd done it before in the car, but Chuckie said it was a lot nicer when you did it in the house. As far as she was concerned, the major difference was that they stood a much greater chance of getting caught. If her momma had walked in on them, she would not have gone crazy and ordered Chuckie away, she would have stayed calm and sat down and warned them not to do something that could hurt them later on. "There're things y'all can do now," she would have said, "that can mess y'all's lives up bad."

Dee Ann leaned across the seat and kissed Chuckie. "You don't smell *too* much like a Budweiser brewery," she said. "Want to come in with me?"

"Sure."

Butch was waiting at the gate, whimpering, his front paws up on the railing. Dee Ann released the latch, and they went in and walked across the yard, the dog trotting along behind them.

The front door was locked—a fact that Chuckie corroborated the next day. She knocked, but even though both the living room and the kitchen were lit up, her momma didn't come. Dee Ann waited a few seconds, then rummaged through her purse and found the key. It didn't occur to her that somebody might have come home with her momma, that they might be back in the bedroom together, doing what she and Chuckie had done. Her momma still believed that if she could tough it out a few more months, Dee Ann's daddy would recover his senses and come back. Most of his belongings were still here.

Dee Ann unlocked the door and pushed it open. Crossing the threshold, she looked back over her shoulder at Chuckie. His eyes were shut. They didn't stay shut for long, he was probably just blinking, but that instant in which she saw them closed was enough to frighten her. She quickly looked into the living room. Everything was as it should be: the black leather couch stood against the far wall, the glass coffee table in front of it, two armchairs pulled up to the table at forty-five-degree angles. The paper lay on the mantelpiece, right where her momma always left it.

"Momma?" she called. "It's me and Chuckie."

As she waited for a reply, the dog rushed past her. He darted into the kitchen. Again they heard him whimper.

She made an effort to follow the dog, but Chuckie laid his hand on her shoulder. "Wait a minute," he said. Afterwards he could never explain to anyone's satisfaction, least of all his own, why he had restrained her.

Earlier that evening, as she stood behind the checkout counter at the grocery store where she was working that summer, she had seen her daddy. He was standing on the sidewalk, looking in through the thick plate-glass window, grinning at her.

It was late, and as always on Saturday evening, downtown Loring was virtually deserted. If people wanted to shop or go someplace to eat, they'd be out on the highway, at the Sonic or the new Pizza Hut. If they had enough money, they'd just head for Greenville. It had been a long time since anything much went on downtown after dark, which made her daddy's presence here that much more unusual. He waved, then walked over to the door.

The manager was in back, totaling the day's receipts. Except for him and Dee Ann and one stock boy who was over in the dairy aisle sweeping up, the store was empty.

Her daddy wore a pair of khaki pants and a short-sleeved pullover with an alligator on the pocket. He had on his funny-looking leather cap that reminded her of the ones policemen wore. He liked to wear that cap when he was out driving the MG.

"Hey, sweets," he said.

Even with the counter between them, she could smell whiskey on his breath. He had that strange light in his eyes.

"Hi, Daddy."

"When'd you start working nights?"

"A couple of weeks back."

"Don't get in the way of you and Buckie, does it?"

She started to correct him, tell him her boyfriend's name was Chuckie, but then she thought *Why bother?* He'd always been the kind of father who couldn't remember how old she was or what grade she was in. Sometimes he had trouble remembering she existed: years ago he'd brought her to this same grocery store, and after buying some food for his hunting dog, he'd forgotten about her and left her sitting on the floor in front of the magazine rack. The store manager had taken her home.

"Working nights is okay," she said. "My boyfriend'll be picking me up in a few minutes."

"Got a big night planned?"

"We'll probably just ride around a little bit and then head on home."

Her daddy reached into his pocket and pulled out his wallet. He extracted a twenty and handed it to her. "Here," he said. "You kids do something fun. On me. See a movie or get yourselves a six-pack of Dr Pepper."

He laughed, to show her he wasn't serious about the Dr Pepper, and then he stepped around the end of the counter and kissed her cheek. "You're still the greatest little girl in the world," he said, "even if you're not very little anymore."

He was holding her close. In addition to whiskey, she could smell aftershave and deodorant and something else—a faint trace of perfume. She hadn't seen the MG on the street, but it was probably parked in the lot outside, and she bet his girlfriend was in it. She was just three years older than Dee Ann, a junior up at Delta State, though people said she wasn't going to school anymore. She and Dee Ann's daddy were living together in an apartment near the flower shop he used to own and run. He'd sold the shop last fall, just before he left home.

He didn't work anymore, and Dee Ann's momma had said she didn't know how he aimed to live, once the money from his business was gone. The other thing she didn't know—because nobody had told her—was that folks said his girlfriend sold drugs. Folks said he might be involved in that too.

He pecked her on the cheek once more, told her to have a good time with her boyfriend and to tell her momma he said hello, and then he walked out the door. Just as he left, the manager hit the switch, and the aisle lights went off.

That last detail—the lights going off when he walked out of the store—must have been significant, because the next day, as Dee Ann sat on the couch at her grandmother's house, knee to knee with the Loring County sheriff, Jim Wheeler, it kept coming up.

"You're sure about that?" Wheeler said for the third or fourth time. "When your daddy left the grocery store, Mr. Lindsey was just turning out the lights?"

Her grandmother was in bed down the hall. The doctor and two women from the Methodist church were with her. She'd been having chest pains off and on all day.

The dining room table was covered with food people had brought: two hams, a roast, a fried chicken, dish upon dish of potato salad, coleslaw, baked beans, two or three pecan pies, a pound cake. By the time the sheriff came, Chuckie had been there twice already—once in the morning with his momma and again in the afternoon with his daddy—and both times he had eaten. While his mother sat on the couch with Dee Ann, sniffling and holding her hand, and his father admired the knickknacks on the mantelpiece, Chuckie had parked himself at the dining room table and begun devouring one slice of pie after another, occasionally glancing through the doorway at Dee Ann. The distance between where he was and where she was could not be measured by any known means. She knew it, and he did, but he apparently believed that if he kept his mouth full, they wouldn't have to acknowledge it yet.

"Yes, sir," she told the sheriff. "He'd just left when Mr. Lindsey turned off the lights."

A pocket-sized notebook lay open on Wheeler's knee. He held a ballpoint pen with his stubby fingers. He didn't know it yet, but he was going to get a lot of criticism for what he did in the next few days. Some people would say it cost him reelection. "And what time does Mr. Lindsey generally turn off the lights on a Saturday night?"

"Right around eight o'clock."

"And was that when he did it last night?"

"Yes, sir."

"You're sure about that?"

"Yes, sir."

"Well, that's what Mr. Lindsey says too," Wheeler said. He closed the notebook and put it in his shirt pocket. "Course, being as he was in the back of the store, he didn't actually see you talking with your daddy."

"No," she said. "You can't see the checkout counter from back there."

Wheeler stood, and she did, too. To her surprise, he pulled her close to him. He was a compact man, not much taller than she was.

She felt his warm breath on her cheek. "I sure am sorry about all of this, honey," he said. "But don't you worry. I guarantee you I'll get to the bottom of it. Even if it kills me."

Even if it kills me.

She remembers that phrase in those rare instances when she sees Jim Wheeler on the street downtown. He's an old man now, in his early sixties, white-haired and potbellied. For years he's worked at the catfish processing plant, though nobody seems to know what he does. Most people can tell you what he doesn't do. He's not responsible for security—he doesn't carry a gun. He's not front-office. He's not a foreman or a shift supervisor, and he has nothing to do with the live-haul trucks.

Chuckie works for Delta Electric, and once a month he goes to the plant to service the generators. He says Wheeler is always outside, wandering around, his head down, his feet scarcely rising off the pavement. Sometimes he talks to himself.

"I was out there last week," Chuckie told her not long ago, "and I'd just gone through the front gates, and there he was. He was off to my right, walking along the fence, carrying this bucket."

"What kind of bucket?"

"Looked like maybe it had some kind of caulking mix in it—there was this thick white stuff sticking to the sides. Anyway, he was shuffling along there, and he was talking to beat the band."

"What was he saying?"

They were at the breakfast table when they had this conversation. Their daughter Cynthia was finishing a bowl of cereal and staring into an algebra textbook. Chuckie glanced toward Cynthia, rolled his eyes at Dee Ann, then looked down at the table. He lifted his coffee cup, drained it, and left for work.

But that night, when he crawled into bed beside her and switched off the light, she brought it up again. "I want to know what Jim Wheeler was saying to himself," she said, "when you saw him last week."

They weren't touching—they always left plenty of space between them—but she could tell he'd gone rigid. He did his best to sound groggy. "Nothing much."

She was rigid now too, lying stiffly on her back, staring up into the dark. "Nothing much is not nothing. Nothing much is still something."

"Won't you ever let it go?"

"*You* brought his name up. You bring his name up, then you get this reaction from me, and then you're mad."

He rolled onto his side. He was looking at her, but she knew he couldn't make out her features. He wouldn't lay his palm on her cheek, wouldn't trace her jawbone like he used to. "Yeah, I brought his name up," he said. "I bring his name up, if you've noticed, about once a year. I bring his name up, and I bring up Lou Pierce's name, and I'd bring up Barry Lancaster's name, too, if he hadn't had the good fortune to move on to bigger things than being DA in a ten-cent Delta town. I keep hoping I'll bring one of their names up, and after I say it, it'll be like I just said John Doe or Cecil Poe or Theodore G. Bilbo. I keep hoping I'll say it and you'll just let it go."

The ceiling fan, which was turned off, had begun to take shape. It looked like a big dark bird, frozen in midswoop. Three or four times she had woken up near dawn and seen that shape there, and it was all she could do to keep from screaming. One time she stuck her fist in her mouth and bit her knuckle.

"What was he saying?"

"He was talking to a quarterback."

"What?"

"He was talking to a quarterback. He was saying some kind of crap like 'Hit Jimmy over the middle.' He probably walks around all day thinking about when he was a football player, playing games over in his mind."

He rolled away from her then, got as close to the edge of the bed as he could. "He's just like you," he said. "He's stuck back there too."

She had seen her daddy several times in between that Saturday night—when Chuckie walked into the kitchen murmuring "Mrs. Williams? Mrs. Williams?"—and the funeral, which was held at the Methodist church the following Wednesday morning. He had come to her grandmother's house Sunday evening, had gone into her grandmother's room and sat by the bed, holding her hand and sobbing. Dee Ann remained in the living room, and she heard their voices, heard her daddy saying, "Remember how she had those big rings under her eyes after Dee Ann was born? How we all said she looked like a pretty little raccoon?" Her grandmother, whose chest pains had finally stopped, said, "Oh, Allen, I raised her from the cradle, and I know her well. She never would've stopped loving you." Then her daddy started crying again, and her grandmother joined in.

When he came out and walked down the hall to the living room, he had stopped crying, but his eyes were red-rimmed and his face looked puffy. He sat down in the armchair, which was still standing right where the sheriff had left it that afternoon. For a long time he said nothing. Then he rested his elbows on his knees, propped his chin on his fists, and said, "Were you the one that found her?"

"Chuckie did."

"Did you go in there?"

She nodded.

"He's an asshole for letting you do that."

She didn't bother to tell him how she'd torn herself out of Chuckie's grasp and bolted into the kitchen, or what had happened when she got in there. She was already starting to think what she would later know for certain: in the kitchen she had died. When she saw the pool of blood on the linoleum, saw the streaks that shot like flames up the wall, a thousand-volt jolt hit her heart. She lost her breath, and the room went dark, and when it relit itself she was somebody else.

Her momma's body lay in a lump on the floor, over by the door that led to the back porch. The shotgun that had killed her, her daddy's Remington Wing-master, stood propped against the kitchen counter. Back in what had once been called the game room, the sheriff would find that somebody had pulled down all the guns—six rifles, the other shotgun, both of her daddy's .38s—and thrown them on the floor. He'd broken the lock on the metal cabinet that stood nearby, and he'd removed the box of shells and loaded the Remington.

It was hard to say what he'd been after, this man who for her was still a dark, faceless form. Her momma's purse had been ransacked, her wallet was missing, but there couldn't have been much money in it. She had some jewelry in the bedroom, but he hadn't messed with that. The most valuable things in the house were probably the guns themselves, but he hadn't taken them.

He'd come in through the back door—the lock was broken—and he'd left through the back door. Why Butch hadn't taken his leg off was anybody's guess. When the sheriff and his deputies showed up, it was all Chuckie could do to keep the dog from attacking.

"She wouldn't of wanted you to see her like that," her daddy said. "Nor me either." He spread his hands and looked at them, turning them over and scrutinizing his palms, as if he intended to read his own fortune. "I reckon I was lucky," he said, letting his gaze meet hers. "Anything you want to tell me about it?"

She shook her head no. The thought of telling him how she felt seemed somehow unreal. It had been years since she'd told him how she felt about any-thing that mattered.

"Life's too damn short," he said. "Our family's become one of those statistics you read about in the papers. You read those stories and you think it won't ever be you. Truth is, there's no way to insure against it."

At the time, the thing that struck her as odd was his use of the word *family*. They hadn't been a family for a long time, not as far as she was concerned.

She forgot about what he'd said until a few days later. What she remembered about that visit with him on Sunday night was that for the second time in twenty-four hours, he pulled her close and hugged her and gave her twenty dollars.

She saw him again Monday at the funeral home, and the day after that, and then the next day, at the funeral, she sat between him and her grandmother, and he held her hand while the preacher prayed. She had wondered if he would bring his girlfriend, but even he must have realized that would be inappro-priate.

He apparently did not think it inappropriate, though, or unwise either, to present himself at the offices of an insurance company in Jackson on Friday morning, bringing with him her mother's death certificate and a copy of the coroner's report.

• • •

When she thinks of the morning—a Saturday—on which Wheeler came to see her for the second time, she always imagines her own daughter sitting there on the couch at her grandmother's place instead of her. She sees Cynthia looking at the silver badge on Wheeler's shirt pocket, sees her glancing at the small notebook that lies open in his lap, at the pen gripped so tightly between his fingers that his knuckles have turned white.

"Now the other night," she hears Wheeler say, "your boyfriend picked you up at what time?"

"Right around eight o'clock." Her voice is weak, close to breaking. She just talked to her boyfriend an hour ago, and he was scared. His parents were pissed—pissed at Wheeler, pissed at him, but above all pissed at her. If she hadn't been dating their son, none of them would have been subjected to the awful experience they've just gone through this morning. They're devout Baptists, they don't drink or smoke, they've never seen the inside of a nightclub, their names have never before been associated with unseemly acts. Now the sheriff has entered their home and questioned their son as if he were a common criminal. It will cost the sheriff their votes come November. She's already lost their votes. She lost them when her daddy left her momma and started running around with a young girl.

"The reason I'm kind of stuck on this eight o'clock business," Wheeler says, "is you say that along about that time's when your daddy was there to see you."

"Yes, sir."

"Now your boyfriend claims he didn't see your daddy leaving the store. Says he didn't even notice the MG on the street."

"Daddy'd been gone a few minutes already. Plus, I think he parked around back."

"Parked around back," the sheriff says.

"Yes, sir."

"In that lot over by the bayou."

Even more weakly: "Yes, sir."

"Where the delivery trucks come in—ain't that where they usually park?"

"I believe so. Yes, sir."

Wheeler's pen pauses. He lays it on his knee. He turns his hands over, studying them as her daddy did his a few days before. He's looking at his hands when he asks the next question. "Any idea why your daddy'd park his car behind the grocery store—where there generally don't nothing but delivery trucks park—when Main Street was almost deserted and there was a whole row of empty spaces right in front of the store?"

The sheriff knows the answer as well as she does. When you're with a woman you're not married to, you don't park your car on Main Street on a Saturday night. Particularly if it's a little MG with no top on it, and your daughter's just a few feet away, with nothing but a pane of glass between her and a girl who's not much older than she is. That's how she explains it to herself anyway. At least for today.

"I think maybe he had his girlfriend with him."

"Well, I don't aim to hurt your feelings, honey," Wheeler says, looking at her now, "but there's not too many people that don't know about his girlfriend."

"Yes, sir."

"You reckon he might have parked out back for any other reason?"

She can't answer that question, so she doesn't even try.

"There's not any chance, is there," he says, "that your boyfriend could've been confused about when he picked you up?"

"No, sir."

"You're sure about that?"

She knows that Wheeler has asked Chuckie where he was between 7:15, when several people saw her mother eating a burger at the Sonic Drive-in, and 8:30, when the two of them found her body. Chuckie has told Wheeler he was at home watching TV between 7:15 and a few minutes till 8:00, when he got in the car and went to pick up Dee Ann. His parents were in Greenville eating supper at that time, so they can't confirm his story.

"Yes, sir," she says, "I'm sure about it."

"And you're certain your daddy was there just a few minutes before eight?"

"Yes, sir."

"Because your daddy," the sheriff says, "remembers things just a little bit different. The way your daddy remembers it, he came by the grocery store about 7:30 and hung around there talking with you for half an hour. Course, Mr. Lindsey was in the back, so he can't say yea or nay, and the stock boy don't seem to have the sense God give a betsy bug. Your daddy was over at the VFW drinking beer at eight o'clock—stayed there till almost ten, according to any number of people, and his girlfriend wasn't with him. Fact is, his girlfriend left the country last Thursday morning. Took a flight from New Orleans to Mexico City, and from there it looks like she went on to Argentina."

Dee Ann, imagining this scene in which her daughter reprises the role she once played, sees Cynthia's face go slack as the full force of the information strikes her. She's still sitting there like that—hands useless in her lap, face drained of blood—when Jim Wheeler tells her that six months ago, her daddy took out a life insurance policy on her momma that includes double indemnity in the event of accidental death.

"I hate to be the one telling you this, honey," he says, "because you're a girl who's had enough bad news to last the rest of her life. But your daddy stands to collect half a million dollars because of your momma's death, and there's a number of folks—and I reckon I might as well admit I happen to be among them—who are starting to think that ought not to occur."

• • •

Chuckie gets off work at Delta Electric at six o'clock. A year or so ago she became aware that he'd started coming home late. The first time it happened, he told her he'd gone out with his friend Tim to have a beer. She saw Tim the next day buying a case of motor oil at Wal-Mart, and she almost referred to his and Chuckie's night out just to see if he looked surprised. But if he'd looked surprised, it would have worried her, and if he hadn't, it would have worried her even more: she would have seen it as a sign that Chuckie had talked to him beforehand. So in the end she nodded at Tim and kept her mouth shut.

It began happening more and more often. Chuckie ran over to Greenville to buy some parts for his truck, he ran down to Yazoo City for a meeting with his regional supervisor. He ran up into the north part of the county because a fellow who lived there had placed an interesting ad in *National Rifleman*—he was selling a shotgun with fancy scrollwork on the stock.

On the evenings when Chuckie isn't home, she avoids latching onto Cynthia. She wants her daughter to have her own life, to be independent, even if independence, in a sixteen-year-old girl, manifests itself as distance from her mother. Cynthia is on the phone a lot, talking to girlfriends, to boyfriends too. Through the bedroom door Dee Ann hears her laughter.

On the evenings when Chuckie isn't home, she sits on the couch alone, watching TV, reading, or listening to music. If it's a Friday or Saturday night and Cynthia is out with her friends, Dee Ann goes out herself. She doesn't go to movies, where her presence might make Cynthia feel crowded if she happened to be in the theater too, and she doesn't go out and eat at any of the handful of restaurants in town. Instead she takes long walks. Sometimes they last until ten or eleven o'clock.

Every now and then, when she's on one of these walks, passing one house after another where families sit parked before the TV set, she allows herself to wish she had a dog to keep her company. What she won't allow herself to do— has never allowed herself to do as an adult—is actually own one.

The arrest of her father is preserved in a newspaper photo.

He has just gotten out of Sheriff Wheeler's car. The car stands parked in the alleyway between the courthouse and the fire station. Sheriff Wheeler is in the picture too, standing just to the left of her father, and so is one of his deputies. The deputy has his hand on her father's right forearm, and he is staring straight into the camera, as is Sheriff Wheeler. Her daddy is the only one who appears not to notice that his picture is being taken. He is looking off to the left, in the direction of Loring Street, which you can't see in the photo, though she knows it's there.

When she takes the photo out and examines it, something she does with increasing frequency these days, she wonders why her daddy is not looking at the camera. A reasonable conclusion, she knows, would be that since he's about to be arraigned on murder charges, he doesn't want his face in the paper. But she wonders if there isn't more to it. He doesn't look particularly worried. He's not exactly smiling, but there aren't a lot of lines around his mouth, like there would be if he felt especially tense. Were he not wearing handcuffs, were he not flanked on either side by officers of the law, you would probably have to say he looks relaxed.

Then there's the question of what he's looking at. Lou Pierce's office is on Loring Street, and Loring Street is what's off the page, out of the picture. Even if the photographer had wanted to capture it in this photo, he couldn't have, not as long as he was intent on capturing the images of these three men. By choosing to photograph them, he chose not to photograph something else, and sometimes what's outside the frame may be more important than what's actually in it.

After all, Loring Street is south of the alley. And so is Argentina.

"You think he'd do that?" Chuckie said. "You think he'd actually kill your momma?"

They were sitting in his pickup when he asked her that question. The pickup was parked on a turnrow in somebody's cotton patch on a Saturday afternoon in August. By then her daddy had been in jail for the better part of two weeks. The judge had denied him bail, apparently believing that he aimed to leave the country. The judge couldn't have known that her daddy had no intention of leaving the country without the insurance money, which had been placed in an escrow account and wouldn't be released until he'd been cleared of the murder charges.

The cotton patch they were parked in was way up close to Cleveland. Chuckie's parents had forbidden him to go out with Dee Ann again, so she'd hiked out to the highway, and he'd picked her up on the side of the road. In later years she'll often wonder whether or not she and Chuckie would have stayed together and gotten married if his parents hadn't placed her off-limits.

"I don't know," she said. "He sure did lie about coming to see me. And then there's Butch. If somebody broke in, he'd tear them to pieces. But he wouldn't hurt Daddy."

"I don't believe it," Chuckie said. A can of Bud stood clamped between his thighs. He lifted it and took a swig. "Your daddy may have acted a little wacky, running off like he did and taking up with that girl, but to shoot your momma and then come in the grocery store and grin at you and hug you? You really think *anybody* could do a thing like that?"

What Dee Ann was beginning to think was that almost everybody could do a thing like that. She didn't know why this was so, but she believed it had something to do with being an adult and having ties. Having ties meant you were bound to certain things—certain people, certain places, certain ways of living. Breaking a tie was a violent act—even if all you did was walk out door number one and enter door number two—and one act of violence could lead to another. You didn't have to spill blood to take a life. But after taking a life, you still might spill blood, if spilling blood would get you something else you wanted.

"I don't know what he might have done," she said.

"Every time I was ever around him," Chuckie said, "he was in a nice mood. I remember going in the flower shop with momma when I was just a kid. Your daddy was always polite and friendly. Used to give me lollipops."

"Yeah, well, he never gave me any lollipops. And besides, your momma used to be real pretty."

"What's that supposed to mean?"

"It's not supposed to mean anything. I'm just stating a fact."

"You saying she's not pretty now?"

His innocence startled her. If she handled him right, Dee Ann realized, she could make him do almost anything she wanted. For an instant she was tempted to put her hand inside his shirt, stroke his chest a couple of times, and tell him to climb out of the truck and stand on his head. She wouldn't always have such leverage, but she had it now, and a voice in her head urged her to exploit it.

"I'm not saying she's not pretty anymore," Dee Ann said. "I'm just saying that of course Daddy was nice to her. He was always nice to nice-looking women."

"Your momma was a nice-looking lady too."

"Yeah, but my momma was his wife."

Chuckie turned away and gazed out at the cotton patch for several seconds. When he looked back at her, he said, "You know what, Dee Ann? You're not making much sense." He took another sip of beer, then pitched the can out the window. "But with all you've been through," he said, starting the engine, "I don't wonder at it."

He laid his hand on her knee. It stayed there until twenty minutes later, when he let her out on the highway, right where he'd picked her up.

Sometimes in her mind she has trouble separating all the men. It's as if they're revolving around her, her daddy and Chuckie and Jim Wheeler and Lou Pierce and Barry Lancaster, as if she's sitting motionless in a hard chair, in a small room, and they're orbiting her so fast that their faces blur into a single image that seems suspended just inches away. She smells them too: smells aftershave and cologne, male sweat and whiskey.

Lou Pierce was a man she'd been seeing around town for as long as she could remember. He always wore a striped long-sleeved shirt and a wide tie that was usually loud-colored. You would see him crossing Loring Street, a coffee cup in one hand, his briefcase in the other. His office was directly across the street from the courthouse, where he spent much of his life—either visiting his clients in the jail, which was on the top floor, or defending those same clients downstairs in the courtroom itself.

Many years after he represented her father, Lou Pierce would find himself up on the top floor again, on the other side of the bars this time, accused of exposing himself to a twelve-year-old girl. After the story made the paper, several other women, most in their twenties or early thirties, would contact the local police and allege that he had also shown himself to them.

He showed himself to Dee Ann too, though not the same part of himself he showed to the twelve-year-old girl. He came to see her at her grandmother's on a weekday evening sometime after the beginning of the fall semester—she knows school was in session because she remembers that the morning after Lou Pierce visited her, she had to sit beside his son Raymond in senior English.

Lou sat in the same armchair that Jim Wheeler had pulled up near the coffee table. He didn't have his briefcase with him, but he was wearing another of those wide ties. This one, if she remembers correctly, had a pink background, with white fleurs-de-lis.

"How you making it, honey?" he says. "You been holding up all right?"

She shrugs. "Yes, sir. I guess so."

"Your daddy's awful worried about you." He picks up the cup of coffee her grandmother brought him before leaving them alone. "I don't know if you knew that or not," he says, taking a sip of the coffee. He sets the cup back down. "He mentioned you haven't been to see him."

He's gazing directly at her, and his big droopy eyelids give him a lost-doggy look.

"No, sir," she says, "I haven't gotten by there."

"You know what that makes folks think, don't you?"

She drops her head. "No, sir."

"Makes 'em think you believe your daddy did it."

That's the last thing he says for two or three minutes. He sits there sipping his coffee, looking around the room, almost as if he were a real estate agent sizing up the house. Just as she decides he's said all he intends to, his voice comes back at her.

"Daddies fail," he tells her. "Lordy, how we fail. You could ask Raymond. I doubt he'd tell the truth, though, because sons tend to be protective of their daddies, just like a good daughter protects her momma. But the truth, if you wanted to dig into it, is that I've failed that boy nearly every day he's been alive. You notice he's in the band? Hell, he can't kick a football or hit a baseball, and that's nobody's fault but mine. I remember when he was this tall—" he holds his hand, palm down, three feet from the floor "—he came to me dragging this little plastic bat and said, 'Daddy, teach me to hit a baseball.' And you know what I told him? I told him, 'Son, I'm defending a man that's facing life in prison, and I got to go before the judge tomorrow morning and plead his case. You can take that bat and you can hitch a kite to it and see if the contraption won't fly.'"

He reaches across the table then and lays his hand on her knee. She tries to remember who else has done that recently, but for the moment she can't recall.

When he speaks again, he keeps his voice low, as if he's afraid he'll be over-heard. "Dee Ann, what I'm telling you," he says, "is I know there are a lot of things about your daddy that make you feel conflicted. There's a lot of things he's done that he shouldn't have, and there's things he should have done that he didn't. There's a bunch of *shoulds* and *shouldn'ts* bumping around in your head, so it's no surprise to me that you'd get confused on this question of time."

She's heard people say that if they're ever guilty of a crime, they want Lou Pierce to defend them. Now she knows why.

But she's not guilty of a crime, and she says so: "I'm not confused about time. He came when I said he did."

As if she's a sworn witness, Lou Pierce begins, gently, regretfully, to ask her a series of questions. Does she really think her daddy is stupid enough to take out a life insurance policy on her mother and then kill her? If he aimed to leave the country with his girlfriend, would he send the girl first and then kill Dee Ann's momma and try to claim the money? Does she know that her daddy intended to put the money in a savings account for her?

Does she know that her daddy and his girlfriend had already broken up, that the girl left the country chasing some young South American who, her daddy has admitted, probably sold her drugs?

When he sees that she isn't going to answer any of the questions, Lou Pierce looks down at the floor. It's as if he already knows that one day he'll find himself in a predicament similar to her father's: sitting in a small dark cell, accused of something shameful. "Honey," he says softly, "did you ever ask yourself why your daddy left you and your momma?"

That's one question she's willing and able to answer. "He did it because he didn't love us."

When he looks at her again, his eyes are wet—and she hasn't yet learned that wet eyes tell the most effective lies. "He loved y'all," Lou Pierce says. "But your momma, who was a wonderful lady—angel, she wouldn't give your daddy a physical life. I guarantee you he wishes to God he hadn't needed one, but a man's not made that way . . . and even though it embarrasses me, I guess I ought to add that I'm speaking from personal experience."

Personal experience.

At the age of thirty-eight, Dee Ann has acquired a wealth of experience, but the phrase *personal experience* is one she almost never uses. She's noticed that men are a lot quicker to employ it than women are. Maybe it's because men think their experiences are somehow more personal than everybody else's. Or maybe it's because they take everything personally.

"My own personal experience," Chuckie told Cynthia the other day at the dinner table, after she'd finished ninth in the voting for one of eight positions on the cheerleading squad, "has been that getting elected cheerleader's nothing more than a popularity contest, and I wouldn't let not getting elected worry me for two seconds."

Dee Ann couldn't help it. "When in the world," she said, "did you have a *personal* experience with a cheerleader election?"

He laid his fork down. They stared at one another across a bowl of spaghetti. Cynthia, who can detect a developing storm front as well as any meteorologist, wiped her mouth on her napkin, stood up, and said, "Excuse me."

Chuckie kept his mouth shut until she'd left the room. "I *voted* in cheerleader elections."

"What was personal about that experience?"

"It was my own personal vote."

"Did you have any emotional investment in that vote?"

"You ran once. I voted for you. I was emotional about you then."

She didn't even question him about his use of the word *then*—she knew perfectly well why he used it. "And when I didn't win," she said, "you took it personally?"

"I felt bad for you."

"But not nearly as bad as you felt for yourself?"

"Why in the hell would I feel bad for myself?"

"Having a girlfriend who couldn't win a popularity contest—wasn't that hard on you? Didn't you take it personally?"

He didn't answer. He just sat there looking at her over the bowl of spaghetti, his eyes hard as sandstone and every bit as dry.

Cynthia walks home from school, and several times in the last couple of years, Dee Ann, driving through town on her way back from a shopping trip or a visit to the library, has come across her daughter. Cynthia hunches over as she walks, her canvas backpack slung over her right shoulder, her eyes studying the sidewalk as if she's trying to figure out the pavement's composition. She may be thinking about her boyfriend or some idle piece of gossip she heard that day at school, or she may be trying to remember if the fourth president was James Madison or James Monroe, but her posture and the concentrated way she gazes down suggest that she's a girl who believes she has a problem.

Whether or not this is so Dee Ann doesn't know, because if her daughter is worried about something she's never mentioned it. What Dee Ann does know is that whenever she's out driving and she sees Cynthia walking home, she always stops the car, rolls her window down, and says, "Want a ride?" Cynthia always looks up and smiles, not the least bit startled, and she always says yes. She's never once said no, like Dee Ann did to three different people that day twenty years ago, when, instead of walking to her grandmother's after school, she walked all the way from the highway to the Loring County courthouse and climbed the front steps and stood staring at the heavy oak door for several seconds before she pushed it open.

Her daddy has gained weight. His cheeks have grown round, the backs of his hands are plump. He's not getting any exercise to speak of. On Tuesday and Wednesday nights, he tells her, the prisoners who want to keep in shape are let out of their cells, one at a time, and allowed to jog up and down three flights of stairs for ten minutes each. He says an officer sits in a straight-backed chair down in the courthouse lobby with a rifle across his lap to make sure that the prisoners don't jog any farther.

Her daddy is sitting on the edge of his cot. He's wearing blue denim pants and a shirt to match, and a patch on the pocket of the shirt says *Loring County Jail*. The shoes he has on aren't really shoes. They look like bedroom slippers.

Downstairs, when she checked in with the jailer, Jim Wheeler heard her voice and came out of his office. While she waited for the jailer to get the right key, the sheriff asked her how she was doing.

"All right, I guess."

"You may think I'm lying, honey," he said, "but the day'll come when you'll look back on this time in your life and it won't seem like nothing but a real bad dream."

Sitting in a hard plastic chair, looking at her father, she already feels like she's in a bad dream. He's smiling at her, waiting for her to say something, but her tongue feels like it's stuck to the roof of her mouth.

The jail is air-conditioned, but it's hot in the cell, and the place smells bad. The toilet over in the corner has no lid on it. She wonders how in the name of God a person can eat in a place like this. And what kind of person could actually eat enough to gain weight?

As if he knows what she's thinking, her father says, "You're probably wondering how I can stand it."

She doesn't answer.

"I can stand it," he says, "because I know I deserved to be locked up."

He sits there a moment longer, then gets up off the cot and shuffles over to the window, which has three bars across it. He stands there looking out. "All my life," he finally says, "I've been going in and out of all those buildings down there and I never once asked myself what they looked like from above. Now I know. There's garbage on those roofs and bird shit. One day I saw a man sitting up there, drinking from a paper bag. Right on top of Delta Jewelers."

He turns around then and walks over and lays his hand on her shoulder.

"When I was down there," he says, "scurrying around like a chicken with its head cut off, I never gave myself enough time to think. That's one thing I've had plenty of in here. And I can tell you, I've seen some things I was too blind to see then."

He keeps his hand on her shoulder the whole time he's talking. "In the last few weeks," he says, "I've asked myself how you must have felt when I told you I was too busy to play with you, how you probably felt every time you had to go to the picture show by yourself and you saw all those other little girls waiting in line with their daddies and holding their hands." He says he's seen all the ways in which he failed them both, her and her mother, and he knows they both saw them a long time ago. He just wishes to God *he* had.

He takes his hand off her shoulder, goes back over to the cot, and sits down. She watches, captivated, as his eyes begin to glisten. She realizes that she's in the presence of a man capable of anything, and for the first time she knows the answer to a question that has always baffled her: why would her momma put up with so much for so long?

The answer is that her daddy is a natural performer, and her momma was his natural audience. Her momma lived for these routines, she watched till watching killed her.

With watery eyes, Dee Ann's daddy looks at her, here in a stinking room in the Loring County courthouse. "Sweetheart," he whispers, "you don't think I killed her, do you?"

When she speaks, her voice will be steady, it won't crack and break. She will display no more emotion than if she were responding to a question posed by her history teacher.

"No, sir," she tells her daddy. "I don't think you killed her. I *know* you did."

In that instant the weight of his life begins to crush her.

Ten-thirty on a Saturday night in 1997. She's standing alone in an alleyway outside the courthouse. It's the same alley where her father and Jim Wheeler and the deputy had their picture taken all those years ago. Loring is the same town it was then, except now there are gangs, and gunfire is something you hear all week long, not just on Saturday night. Now people kill folks they don't know.

Chuckie is supposedly at a deer camp with some men she's never met. He told her he knows them from a sporting goods store in Greenville. They all started talking about deer hunting, and one of the men told Chuckie he owned a cabin over behind the levee and suggested Chuckie go hunting with them this year.

Cynthia is out with her friends—she may be at a movie or she may be in somebody's backseat. Wherever she is, Dee Ann prays she's having fun. She prays that Cynthia's completely caught up in whatever she's doing and that she won't come along and find her momma here, standing alone in the alley beside the Loring County courthouse, gazing up through the darkness as though she hopes to read the stars.

The room reminds her of a Sunday-school classroom.

It's on the second floor of the courthouse, overlooking the alley. There's a long wooden table in the middle of the room, and she's sitting at one end of it in a straight-backed chair. Along both sides, in similar chairs, sit fifteen men and women who make up the Loring County grand jury. She knows several faces, three or four names. It looks as if every one of them is drinking coffee. They've all got Styrofoam cups.

Down at the far end of the table, with a big manila folder open in front of him, sits Barry Lancaster, the district attorney, a man whose name she's going to be seeing in newspaper articles a lot in the next twenty years. He's just turned thirty, and though it's still warm out, he's wearing a black suit, with a sparkling white shirt and a glossy black tie.

Barry Lancaster has the reputation of being tough on crime, and he's going to ride that reputation all the way to the state attorney general's office and then to a federal judgeship. When he came to see her a few days ago, it was his reputation that concerned him. After using a lot of phrases like "true bill" and "no bill" without bothering to explain precisely what they meant, he said, "My reputation's at stake here, Dee Ann. There's a whole lot riding on you."

She knows how much is riding on her, and it's a lot more than his reputation. She feels the great mass bearing down on her shoulders. Her neck is stiff and her legs are heavy. She didn't sleep last night. She never really sleeps anymore.

"Now Dee Ann," Barry Lancaster says, "we all know you've gone through a lot recently, but I need to ask you some questions today so that these ladies and gentlemen can hear your answers. Will that be okay?"

She wants to say that it's not okay, that it will never again be okay for anyone to ask her anything, but she just nods.

He asks her how old she is.

"Eighteen."

What grade she's in.

"I'm a senior."

Whether or not she has a boyfriend named Chuckie Nelms.

"Yes, sir."

Whether or not, on Saturday evening, August 2, she saw her boyfriend.

"Yes, sir."

Barry Lancaster looks up from the stack of papers and smiles at her. "If I was your boyfriend," he says, "I'd want to see you *every* night."

A few of the men on the grand jury grin, but the women keep straight faces. One of them, a small red-headed woman with lots of freckles, whose name she doesn't know and never will know, is going to wait on her in a convenience store over in Indianola many years later. After giving her change, the woman will touch Dee Ann's hand and say, "I hope the rest of your life's been easier, honey. It must have been awful, what you went through."

Barry Lancaster takes her through that Saturday evening, from the time Chuckie picked her up until the moment when she walked into the kitchen. Then he asks her, in a solemn voice, what she found there.

She keeps her eyes trained on his tie pin, a small amethyst, as she describes the scene in as much detail as she can muster. In a roundabout way, word will reach her that many of the people on the grand jury were shocked, and even appalled, at her lack of emotion. Chuckie will try to downplay their reaction, telling her that they're probably just saying that because of what happened later on. "It's probably not you they're reacting to," he'll say. "It's probably just them having hindsight."

Hindsight is something she lacks, as she sits here in a hard chair, in a small room, her hands lying before her on a badly scarred table. She can't make a bit of sense out of what's already happened. She knows what her daddy was and she knows what he wasn't, knows what he did and didn't do. What she doesn't know is the whys and the wherefores.

On the other hand, she can see into the future, she knows what's going to happen, and she also knows why. She knows, for instance, what question is coming, and she knows how she's going to answer it and why. She knows that shortly after she's given that answer, Barry Lancaster will excuse her, and she knows, because Lou Pierce has told her, that after she's been excused, Barry Lancaster will address the members of the grand jury.

He will tell them what they have and haven't heard. "Now she's a young girl," he'll say, "and she's been through a lot, and in the end this case has to rest on what she can tell us. And the truth, ladies and gentlemen, much as I might want it to be otherwise, is that the kid's gone shaky on us. She told the sheriff one version of what happened at the grocery store that Saturday night when her daddy came to see her, and she's sat here today and told y'all a different version. She's gotten all confused on this question of time. You can't blame her for that, she's young and her mind's troubled, but in all honesty a good defense attorney's apt to rip my case apart. Because when you lose this witness's testimony, all you've got left is that dog, and that dog, ladies and gentlemen, can't testify."

That dog can't testify.

Even as she sits here, waiting for Barry Lancaster to bring up that night in the grocery store—that night which, for her, will always be the present—she knows the statement about the dog will be used to sentence Jim Wheeler to November defeat. The voters of this county will drape that sentence around the sheriff's neck. If Jim Wheeler had done his job and found some real evidence, they will say, that man would be on his way to Parchman.

They will tell one another, the voters of this county, how someone saw her daddy at the Jackson airport, as he boarded a plane that would take him to Dallas, where he would board yet another plane for a destination farther south. They will say that her daddy was actually carrying a briefcase filled with money, with lots of crisp green hundreds, one of which he extracted to pay for a beer.

They will say that her daddy must have paid her to lie, that she didn't give a damn about her mother. They will wonder if Chuckie has a brain in his head, to go and marry somebody like her, and they will ask themselves how she can ever bear the shame of what she's done. They will not believe, not even for a moment, that she's performed some careful calculations in her mind. All that shame, she's decided, will still weigh a lot less than her daddy's life. It will be a while before she and Chuckie and a girl who isn't born yet learn how much her faulty math has cost.

Barry Lancaster makes a show of rifling through his papers. He pulls a sheet out and studies it, lets his face wrinkle up as if he's seeing something on the page that he never saw before. Then he lays the sheet back down. He closes the manila folder, pushes his chair away from the table a few inches, and leans forward. She's glad he's too far away to lay his hand on her knee.

"Now," he says, "let's go backwards in time."

PERMISSIONS